PATRICK

SON

OF

IRELAND

Patrick

SON

OF

IRELAND

A NOVEL

STEPHEN R. LAWHEAD

wm

WILLIAM MORROW
An Imprint of HarperCollins*Publishers*
ZONDERVAN™

HarperCollins books may be purchased for educational, business, or sales promotional use. For information please write: Special Markets Department, HarperCollins Publishers Inc., 10 East 53rd Street, New York, NY 10022.

FIRST EDITION

Designed by Jo Anne Metsch

Printed on acid-free paper

Library of Congress Cataloging-in-Publication Data

Lawhead, Steve.
Patrick : son of Ireland / Stephen R. Lawhead.—1st ed.
p. cm.
ISBN 0-06-001281-1
1. Patrick, Saint, 373?–463?—Fiction. 2. Ireland—History—To 1172—Fiction.
3. Christian saints—Fiction. I. Title.

PS3562.A865 P37 2003
813'54—dc21   2002031535

03 04 05 06 07 JTC/RRD 10 9 8 7 6 5 4 3 2 1

TO THE MEMORY OF

DAVE HASTINGS

Seven years your portion, under a stone, in a quagmire,

without food, without taste,

but the fire of Christ you ever torturing

the law of judges your lesson,

prayer your language;

And if you like to return

You will be, for a time, a Druid, perhaps.

—ANCIENT IRISH POEM

In a book belonging to Ultán, Bishop of Connor, I have
found four names for Patrick: Succat, when he was born;
Magonus, which means "Famous"; Patricius, when he was
ordained; and Corthirthiac, when he served in the House
of Four Druids.

—MUIRCHÚ, CA. A.D. 680

CONTENTS

LTÁN WATCHES ME with wary eyes. He is afraid. The others are no less fearful, but they are older, so hide it better. I do not berate them nor belittle their lack of faith. Their fear is well founded. High King Loegair has decreed that to strike a fire on this Beltaine night is certain death to him who strikes it. And here on the hill of Cathair Bán we are about to kindle a beacon that will be seen from one end of this dark island to the other.

I do what I can to calm them. "Brothers," I say, "I pose a question. Answer if you can. Which is greater, a salmon or a whelk?"

"The salmon, king of fish, is obviously greater," answers the trusting Forgall.

"Beyond all doubt?"

"Beyond any doubt whatever," he replies; the others nod and murmur in agreement.

"Then tell me this: Which is greater, a salmon or a man?"

"Not difficult, that," replies Forgall. "A man is certainly greater."

"And is God then greater than a man?"

"Infinitely so, lord."

"Then why do we stand here with long faces?" I say. "Kindle the flame and light the bonfire. King Loegair—for all his warriors and weapons, horses, chariots, and strongholds—is but a whelk upon a rock that is about to be overturned by the hand of God."

They laugh uneasily at this.

To demonstrate the power I proclaim, I make a motion in the air with my staff and speak the quickening words. The damp air shimmers, and a sudden warmth streams around us. Raising the staff, I touch the topmost branch on the heap we have labored all day to raise. A red spear of flame leaps from staff tip to sodden branch. "Great of Light," I cry, "honor your servant with a sign of your approval!"

The dull red flame flickers, clinging to life. High in the unseen sky above, there is a rush of wind, and brightness falls from heaven; fingers of light trickle downward through the thick tangle of wet wood we have erected. Down, down it seeps. The sodden branches sizzle and crack.

The red flame fades and appears to die. The men hold their breath.

As darkness closes around us, I shout, "Behold! The rising sun has come to us from heaven to shine on those living in the darkness and in the shadow of death, to guide our feet along the paths of peace!" I stretch out my hand to my companions. "Brothers, you are all Sons of the Light. You do not belong to the night. Therefore darkness can have no dominion over you."

A flash of fire strikes up through the heart of the pyre. Blue sparks rush into the air in a fountain of dazzling light. The good brothers fall back as tongues of flame seize the rain-damp fuel. Instantly the great heap kindles to blazing warmth, scattering the shadows and illuminating the hilltop.

The brothers fall on their faces in reverent awe, but in my mind is kindled the memory of another night, long ago. And another fire.

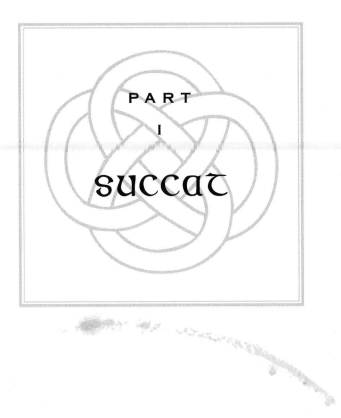

PART

I

SUCCAT

1

ONCESSA LAVINIA LIVED in fear of thieves carrying off her spoons. They were fine spoons. Each teardrop-shaped bowl was a masterpiece of smithery balanced on a long, elegant handle capped by a tiny Corinthian finial: eight in all, and older than Elijah. Our silver—the spoons and matching plate, an enormous bowl, and two large ewers—was old and costly; it had come from Rome sometime in the dusty past, handed mother to daughter longer than anyone could remember.

My mother's treasured silver held pride of place on the black walnut table in the banqueting hall: a large, handsome room with a vaulted ceiling and a floor that featured a mosaic depicting Bellerophon riding the winged horse Pegasus and killing the Chimera with a flaming spear. This scene occupied the center of the room and was surrounded by a circular braidwork border picked out in red, black, white, and brown tesserae and, in each corner of the room, a likeness of one of the Four Seasons.

On frigid winter evenings I would lie on my stomach on that wonderful mosaic and feel the delicious warmth seeping up from the hypocaust beneath. The floor above the hall was given to sleeping rooms for ourselves and those few servants my mother would suffer to abide in the house.

Our villa was called Favere Mundi, an apt name for one of the most pleasant places in the whole of our island realm. It was built in the traditional manner: a low, hollow square with a red-tiled roof surrounding a central courtyard that contained a pear tree, a fountain, and a statue of Jupiter in repose. As a child I thought the statue bore the likeness of my grandfather. Scarcely a day went by that I did not run to greet the image. "Hail, Potitus!" I would cry and smack the carved marble limbs with my hands to make him take note of me. But the frozen, sightless gaze remained fixed on higher things, perpetually beyond heed of the merely mortal and mundane.

Two long wings on either side of the enclosed square contained the work-rooms: one each for wood, leather, and cloth and one where our candles, lamps, and rushlights were made. Between the wings rose the main section of the house, comprising two floors; the lower floor was given almost en-tirely to the great hall, and the upper opened onto a roofed gallery which overlooked the court.

Like my father before me, I was born in my grandfather's house. We were wealthy people, noble Britons, and our villa near Bannavem Taburniae lacked for nothing. Sixty families lived on our estate and worked our lands. We grew grain to sell in the markets of Maridunum, Corinium, and Lon-dinium; we raised cattle and sold to the northern garrisons—Eboracum and beyond; we bred horses for the *ala*, the mounted auxiliary of the legions. Harvests were bountiful; the land prospered; our labor was rewarded a hundredfold.

Wine from Aquitania, woven cloth from Thracia, Neapolitan glass, Macedonian olives, pepper, oil—all these things and very much more were ours. We lived well. No senator born in sight of the Palatine Hill lived bet-ter. It is but one of the many follies of luxury which lead men to believe that plenty now is abundance always and fortune is everlasting. Pure folly.

My grandfather was still alive when I was born. I remember white-haired Potitus, tall and straight, towering in his dark robes, striding with a face like thunder down the oak-lined avenue leading from our gate. He was a pres-byter, a priest of the church—not well liked, it must be said, for his stern demeanor frightened far more than it comforted, and he was not above smiting obstinate members of his flock with his silver-topped staff.

That aside, he was not overstrict in his observances, and no one ever complained about the length of his services. Unlike the tedious priests of Mithras and Minerva—so careful, so exact, so smug in the enactment of their obscure rituals—old Potitus saw no need to weary heaven with cease-less ceremony or meaningless repetition. "God knows the cry of our hearts," he would say, "before it ever reaches our lips. So speak it out and have done with it. Then get about your business."

My father, Calpurnius, did just that. He got on with business. In this he displayed the remarkable good sense of his British mother and refused to follow his father into the priesthood. Industrious, ambitious, aggressive, and determined—a man of little tolerance and less patience—hard-charging Calpurnius would have made a miserable cleric. Instead he married a high-born woman named Concessa Lavinia and enlarged our holdings exceedingly. Owing to his diligence and tireless labor, the increase in our family fortunes year by year was little short of miraculous. With wealth came responsibility, as he never ceased reminding me. He became a decurion, one of the chief councilmen for our little town—a position which only served to increase his fortunes all the more, and this despite the taxes which rose higher and ever higher.

Invariably, after depositing his taxes in the town treasury, he would come home complaining. "Do we need so many servants?" he would say. "They eat more than I am worth. What do they do all day?"

"Certainly we need them, you silly man," my mother would childe. "Since you insist on spending dawn to dusk with your blessed council, who else does any work around here?"

There were perhaps only a dozen servants in all, but it was my mother's entire occupation to protect them from the sin of idleness. In this she excelled. Lavinia had all the natural gifts of a military commander, save gender alone. Had she been born a man, she might have conquered Africa.

Her sole weakness was myself. No doubt because I was the third of three infants and the only one to survive beyond the first year, she found it impossible to deny me anything. With her, to ask was to have. And I never tired of asking. I beseeched her day and night for one favor, one trinket, one pleasure after another. My days as a child were a veritable shower of indulgence. It never ceased.

Of course, Calpurnius did not approve. As I grew older, he insisted I should apply myself to books and such in order to improve my mind and build a steady character. But inasmuch as my father was ever only seen through a blurred haze of busyness, it fell to my doting mother to arrange for my education.

Here, if only here, little Bannavem showed its provincial meanness. The mild green hills, fertile fields, and sweet-flowing rivers of my homeland might have been blessed with nine separate aspects of paradise, but a decent school was not one of them. The nearest of any repute was at Guentonia Urbs, and it was a pitiful thing—full of horny-handed farmers' sons and mewling merchant boys united in the singular misfortune of being taught by witless drudges too indolent to secure better employment elsewhere.

Be that as it may, the fault lay not in Guentonia's deficiency but in my own. I was never destined to wear a scholar's cope. Difficult to say in those early years just *what* my destiny might be. Nor, as I came of age, did the augury improve. Old Potitus ceaselessly assured me I was going straight to hell by the swiftest means available. My father despaired of making his spendthrift son a prudent man of business. My own dear mother could only cluck and shake her head and gaze at me with her large, doleful eyes. "Succat, there is more to life than revel and games," she would say, sighing. "One day you will wish you had made some account of your lessons."

"Fair Lavinia," I would reply, taking her hands and spinning her around, "the sun is high, the breeze is warm, and the birds sing sweetly in the trees. Who but a dullard would spend such a day scratching chicken tracks in wax when there are cups to be drunk, girls to be kissed, and silver to be wagered?"

With a carefree peck of her matronly cheek, I would be off to the village, where I would meet Julian, Rufus, and Scipio. Together we would ride to Lycanum, a market town and the nearest proper *civitas* with a garrison. Wherever there were troops, there was gambling and drinking and whoring aplenty.

My friends, like myself, were sons of noblemen. Julian's father was a magistrate, and Scipio's family owned the tax-gathering warrant for the town and outlying region. It was, of course, a source of deep embarrassment to my grandfather the priest that I should be openly consorting with tax collectors.

But what could he say? "One of our blessed Lord Jesu's best friends was a tax collector," I would tell him, "and *he* became an apostle. Who knows? Maybe I shall become an apostle, too!" Then off I would go to some fresh excess, some greater, more debauched dissipation, as fast as my feet could carry me.

Usually we would hie to the Old Black Wolf, a public house serving indifferent meals and rude lodging to unwary travelers, but also beer to the local population of sots and soldiers—marvelous beer which they cellared in oaken casks in underground vaults so it became cool and dark and frothy and vastly superior to the thin, tepid brew made at home. Like the town and the garrison it served, the poor decrepit Wolf was now much reduced from its former glory. It was ill thatched and filthy with smoke from the half-collapsed chimney, and the floorboards sagged and creaked; the perpetually muddy yard stank of stale beer and urine, and the presence of soldiers meant it was always hot and crowded, reeking of sweat and garlic, and deafeningly loud.

To us it was a palace.

Many a night we plumbed the depths of youthful bacchanalia—nights of roister and revel which will forever live in my memory. It was there I lost my virginity—the same night I lost my purse in my first game of dice. It was there I discovered the ways of the world and men in the talk around the Wolf's bare boards. It was a haven, a sanctuary. We were there on the night I was taken, and even now I cannot help but wonder what might have happened if I had stayed.

AIL, SUCCAT!" CALLED Rufus as I came into sight. He and Scipio were waiting for me in the shadow of the column beside the well in the center of the village square. Rufus was sitting on the edge of the well, kicking his heels against the moss-covered stone; Scipio was leaning against the column, flicking the reins of their horses back and forth against the side of his leg.

The two were near enough in appearance to be brothers—both slim, dark, and fine-featured; Rufus was slightly older and taller, more gregarious and daring, while Scipio cultivated that air of wry detachment much admired by the aristocratic and intellectual elite. Their clothes, like mine— long, loose linen tunics over short *bracae*, or riding trousers, good leather belts and high riding boots—resembled those favored by the legionaries in appearance but were of the finest cloth bought from merchants who traded in Gaul, where the best quality was to be obtained. In fact, we all prided ourselves on our exquisite taste in clothing. No one ever saw more preening, self-congratulatory peacocks.

It was past midday in high summer; the sun was beginning its long, slow, sinking decline into the west, and Bannavem's little square was empty save for the mangy, half-blind dog that lived in a hole behind Hywel the butcher's stall.

"Does your father know you've taken his best horse?" inquired Scipio, regarding the fine black with languid envy.

"Calpurnius, as we all know, is generous to a fault," I replied, reining up before the well. "When he learned we were to go a-roistering, why, the man insisted I take Boreas here. I tried my best to talk him out of it. 'No, father,' I said, 'I will not hear of it. Just let me take old, lame Hecuba and I shall be perfectly happy.' And do you know what the man said?"

"No," sniffed Scipio, feigning disinterest. "What did he say?"

"He said, 'No son of mine will be seen riding a broken-down plow pony. It is Boreas for you, my boy, or I shall never be able to hold my head up in the council again.'" I reached down and patted the proud black's shapely neck. "So, here we are. But where"—I glanced around—"is Julian?"

"He should be here," agreed Rufus. "We have waited long enough. I say we go."

"Leave without him?" said Scipio. "We can't do that. Besides, we'll need his luck if we are to win back our losses from last time."

"It is *because* of his inscrutable luck that we lost so much *last time*," answered Rufus. Snatching the reins from Scipio, he made to mount his horse.

"Here!" shouted a voice from across the square. "You there!"

I turned to see Hywel the butcher charging out into the square. He was a squat, bull-necked Briton, as wide as he was tall. "Greetings, my good man," I called, adopting my father's tone of breezy condescension, "I trust that the gods of commerce have blessed your tireless industry with the wealth you deserve."

He glared at me dismissively and shook his fist at us. "You know you cannot bring horses into the square! Clear out!"

Little Bannavem Taburniae entertained ideas far above its humble station. It seemed someone had heard that a few of the great market towns had, for purposes of cleanliness and decorum, banned horses from their squares and marketplaces, and so the practice was instituted for our village, too. We, of course, happily ignored the prohibition.

"Just look at that!" shouted Hywel, pointing at the pile of fresh dung Scipio's brown mare had dropped onto the dusty flagstones. "Just look!"

"What, have you never seen horse shit before?" inquired Scipio idly.

"You are going to clean that up!" cried the butcher, growing red in the face. "We keep an orderly square in this town. You are going to clean it up now."

"Since you put it that way . . ." said Rufus. He glanced at me, and I recognized the wicked glint in his eye. Stooping to the green clods of manure, he took a soft, ripe ball into each hand, then straightened, and, with a quick flick of his wrist, lobbed one right for the butcher's head.

"Here, now!" squawked Hywel, ducking as the first missile sailed past his ear. The second struck him on the chest just beneath his chin. "Here!"

"Stand still, rogue," said Rufus, stooping for more dung. He sent two more handfalls whizzing straight to their target. Each left a satisfying green splat on the butcher's round chest.

Hywel back-stepped quickly, hands waving before him. "Here! Stop that, you!"

Scipio quickly joined in. The dung flew, and the little butcher could not elude the stinking clods swiftly enough. He dodged one missile, only to have another strike him full on the face. "Now! Now!" he spluttered, wiping muck from his cheek. "I warn you, I am telling the council about this!"

"My father is the council," I replied. "Tell him whatever you like. I am certain you will find a sympathetic ear for your complaint despite a distinct lack of witnesses."

Another clod splatted onto his mantle. Realizing he was beaten, the butcher beat a graceless retreat under a heavy hail of horse manure. He disappeared into his stall, cursing us and shouting for someone—anyone—to witness the outrage against his honest and upright person.

"Let's leave," said Scipio, glancing guiltily around the square.

"You can go around smelling like a stable hand if you like," replied Rufus coolly. "I am going to wash." He pulled up the leather bucket from the well and proceeded to wash his hands in it. When he finished, he dumped the water into the street, then mounted his horse and, with a snap of the reins, cried, "Last one to Lycanum buys the beer!"

"Wait!" shouted Scipio. Caught flat-footed with the leather bucket halfway down the well, he dropped the rope, vaulted into the saddle, and pounded after us. Rufus reached the archway first and galloped through. I followed, emerging from the square and onto the track just as Julian came ambling up on his brown mare. "After us!" I shouted. "We're for Lycanum. Scipio's buying the beer!"

Julian slapped life into his mount and fell in behind me, ignoring Scipio's cries to wait and allow him to catch up. We struck the single track leading out from the village and flew toward the high bluff on the edge of the town where it joined the coast road. Upon gaining the top of the hill, we came in sight of the sea, gleaming like beaten brass beneath the clear, cloudless sky.

The day was warm, and it was good to let the horses run and feel the wind on our faces. Rufus led a spirited race all the way to Lycanum, stopping only when he reached the town gates. Unaccountably, one of the doors was closed, and there were soldiers from the garrison standing in front of the other.

"What goes here?" called Rufus to one of the legionaries.

"There is report of a raid last night near Guentonia," replied the soldier.

"Guentonia?" wondered Rufus. "That is miles away."

The soldier shrugged. "The magistrate has warned everyone to be on guard."

"Well, we saw nothing on the way just now," put in Julian. "Guentonia is full of old women."

"Just so," replied the soldier, waving us through.

"Come to the Wolf later," called Rufus, moving on. "We will give you a chance to win back your losses."

The soldier laughed. "If your purse is that heavy, friend, you can count on me to help lighten the load, never fear."

We clattered through the gate and into the town. Because it was market day, the streets were thronged with buyers, sellers, and their various wares. We moved through a herd of sheep being led by an old man and a ragged boy. Oblivious to what was going on around him, the toothless yokel stepped right into the path of Julian's horse and was knocked down. He rolled on his backside and came up shouting unintelligibly and waving his stick.

"Imbecile," scoffed Julian. He wheeled his horse and scattered the sheep, which sent the old rustic into a paroxysm of rage. His boy darted after the panicked beasts, and we rode on deaf to the shepherd's ranting.

The market square swarmed with cattle and pigs making a foul stench in the hot sun, so we did not linger but went straight to the Old Black Wolf for the first of many good pots of beer that day. The revered institution was owned by a Briton named Owain, a jovial fellow who knew neither stranger nor enemy in all the world. Possessed of a naturally tolerant and magnanimous nature, his fat, round face beamed with good pleasure on all that passed beneath his serene, slightly nearsighted gaze. Fond of barking half-hearted orders and threats to his hirelings, he governed his tumbledown empire with all the bluff and bite of a hound grown comfortable and complacent in its warm place by the hearth.

His wife, a sturdy matron of indeterminate years, wielded the real power behind the throne. She clumped around the Old Wolf in wooden shoes, her long gray hair bound in a dirty white cloth, deploying her sloven brigade of gap-toothed handmaids. With a word or a wink, cups and bowls were swiftly filled and loose order maintained within the rowdy precinct of the inn. Her name might have been Bucia, or perhaps Becca—I never knew which—and though she had a face like a ripe prune, she also brewed the incomparable black beer, which made her a goddess in our eyes.

We arrived, as was our custom, clamoring for drink and sausages. "Good lads!" cried Owain, wiping his hands on the damp, greasy scrap of apron hanging from his broad belt. "Splendid to see you again. There is beer aplenty, of course, but sausages we have none."

"No sausages?" wondered Rufus in feigned anguish. "Man, what are you saying? We have ridden all the way from Bannavem on the mere promise of one of your incomparable sausages. What are we to do?"

"What am *I* to do?" countered Owain genially. "They come from Guentonia, you know. And there has been no sign of a delivery today."

"But it is market day," offered Julian, as if trying to help the misguided fellow see the error of his ways.

"My point exactly, sir," replied the innkeeper. For some reason, even though we were all of an age together, Owain always regarded Julian as the elder and more sensible of the four. In truth, he was neither. This disguise of respectability masked a dissident spirit; it was one of Julian's best deceits. Nevertheless, Julian was "sir" while the rest of us were "lads."

"They come from Guentonia, as you—"

"As *you* never tire of telling us," said Rufus.

"Right you are! They are saying the fortress there was attacked last night," continued Owain.

"We saw no sign of any trouble along the way," Scipio informed him. "No doubt the gatemen saw their own shadows and pissed themselves with fright."

"No doubt you are right." The innkeeper sighed. "As for the sausages . . . well, the little darlings were to have been here this morning, and I am still waiting."

"A sorry state of affairs," agreed Rufus.

"There will be chops later, if you like," said Owain, moving to the back of the inn. "But now I will send the beer."

He disappeared into the fuggy darkness of the kitchen, and we heard him calling for someone to come and serve his thirsty guests. A few moments later a round-hipped young woman appeared with a pottery jug and a stack of wooden cups. She dropped the jug onto the board with a thump and clacked down the cups, eyeing Julian with a peculiar warmth in her cowlike gaze.

"Why, hello, Magrid," Julian said. "And how is my buxom, broadbeamed beauty?"

She smiled with dumb modesty. "Hello, Julian," she said, pouring a cup and pushing it toward him. "I've missed you these past days."

"For me the absence has been torture beyond enduring. But pine no more, my dainty flower, for the love of your life is here."

His flattery was as thick as it was insincere. Nevertheless her smile broadened, and the light came up in her eyes. She glanced around furtively and bent nearer; her bosom threatened to spill from the top of her dress. "Will you come to me later?"

Julian reached out and took the top of her low-cut bodice and pulled her toward him; one overample breast bobbed free for all to see. "Not even wild animals could keep me away, heart of my heart," said Julian, cupping the wayward breast.

She slapped at his hand and straightened, rearranging her clothing. "Wait until tonight." She gave him a seductive smile and moved off.

"Would you bed that blowzy cow?" wondered Scipio incredulously.

"Life is short and youth shorter still. Take your pleasures where you find them," replied Julian with a superior shrug.

"The trouble with Scipio is he finds no pleasure in anything but his own company," said Rufus. "Not so, my virgin son?" He ruffled Scipio's hair.

"Better a crust in humble solitude than a banquet with barbarians," muttered Scipio. Reaching for the jar, he filled his cup and one other, which he shoved across to me. "Succat understands, if you do not."

"Of course," I said, raising the overflowing cup. "I have been known to utter the same sentiment myself from time to time. But tonight, my friends, it looks like a banquet with barbarians. So fill the jars, I say! And let the doxies beware!"

Rufus laughed and raised his cup to mine, adding, "Let chaos reign!"

"To chaos!" shouted Scipio.

"Chaos and rebellion!" cried Julian, lofting his cup.

We drank until the beer flowed down our chins, and smacked the empty cups on the board with a solid thump. Then we filled the cups and drank again. After a fair time Owain returned with a pile of chops on a wooden plate. We sent Magrid for two more jars and set about working our way through the chops, tossing the bones to the dogs as we went along.

We were just finishing when the first of the legionaries came into the place. There were three of them: Darius, a tall, rangy fellow with short curly hair and a scar that puckered the side of his face; Fillipio, a squat, square-headed, bluntly good-natured trooper; and Audager, a large brooding lump of a man, a Saecsen and member of one of the many auxiliary cohorts which now supplied the British legions.

We had seen them before and diced with them on occasion. "Hail, Legioni Augusti!" called Rufus when he caught sight of Darius stooping under the lintel. "Come! Bring your cups and sit with us."

We made room at the table, and the soldiers joined us. "So," said Fillipio when he had settled himself on the bench, "the ala of Bannavem honors us with its exalted presence." He looked at each us in turn. "What are you doing here?"

"Where else should we be?" answered Rufus. Of the four of us, he most imagined himself a legionary—a general perhaps, or the commander of an elite cavalry troop. "A fast ride in the hot sun raises a thirst which nothing but the Black Wolf's best will slake."

"You heard about the trouble at Guentonia."

"We heard," said Rufus. "What of it?"

"Two cohorts departed as soon as word reached the garrison," Fillipio said. "They have not returned."

"Sleeping off their wine beside the road, I should think," offered Scipio.

"Guentonia is a fascinating place, of course," Julian said. "Perhaps they decided to stay and take in the cultural amenities."

The soldiers grunted and dashed down the contents of their cups. I took up the jar to pour them each another drink, but Fillipio stood. "No more. We are back on patrol soon."

"Well, then," I said, still holding out the jar, "just a small one to keep your tongues wet."

Audager took the jar from my hand and placed it firmly on the table. "You should go home." His words were thick in his mouth, but the warning was clear.

"When we feel like it," Rufus replied, rising to the implied threat, "and not before."

The big Saecsen looked at him, then turned on his heel and walked away.

"Audager is right," Darius told us. "You should not be on the road after dark."

"Go home, lads," said Fillipio, moving away. "If you leave now, you can be back in Bannavem before nightfall. We will drink and dice another day."

We watched the three soldiers out the door, and then Rufus said, "Afraid of their own shadows."

"Obviously," replied Julian. His agreement lacked force, I noticed, and Scipio did not voice an opinion at all.

"Are we going to let them spoil a good night's roister?" I said, pouring more beer.

In the end, however, the revel was spoiled. Although we waited long, few people came to the inn: just some merchants and a heavy-footed rustic or two stopping for a drink before heading home from the market. There were no more soldiers and, to my particular disappointment, none of the local girls of easy favor whose company we often purchased for the night. Even the promise of Magrid's bountiful charms failed to ignite our damp spirits.

As dusk fell, so, too, did a pall. The effort of forcing mirth and merriment into the increasingly dull proceedings grew too much at last. Julian disappeared after a while, and the rest of us sat clutching our cups in the gathering gloom as a dank uneasiness seeped into our souls. Finally, I grew weary of the squalid drear and rose. "Friends," I said, "let us bury the corpse of this stillborn night." I drained my cup and tossed it aside. "Misery and woe I can get at home for nothing."

I called for our horses and bade farewell to Owain, who said, "The rumors have everyone frightened, is all. Come again another night, and you will find us jolly enough."

"Don't worry," replied Scipio, "we'll return another day to redeem this misspent night."

"Until then," said Rufus, "farewell."

We went out into the yard and waited for our horses to appear. "Where has Julian got to?" wondered Scipio. "Why are we always waiting for that laggard."

"I'll fetch him," I said, and walked around to the back of the house, where I found him and Magrid leaning against one of the outbuildings. Magrid had her mantle up around her hips, and Julian was pumping away, his face buried in her mounded bosom.

I gave a little cough to announce my presence, and Magrid pushed Julian's face around. "What now?" demanded Julian, his voice thick with lust.

"We are leaving," I said.

"In a moment," he replied.

"Now." I turned on my heel and walked away. "Good night to you, Magrid."

I returned to the yard, where the stable hand brought our horses, and Julian joined us soon after. We gave the boy a denarius for his trouble and then rode out; the guards at the gate were not for allowing us on the road, but Rufus told them they were behaving like fretful maidens, and they grudgingly opened the gate and let us go.

The dying embers of a fiery sunset still glowed in the western sky, gleaming dull red and gold in the dark clouds sailing in from the sea. We turned onto the coast road and urged our horses to speed. Evening deepened around us as we rode; stars kindled and began to shine through gaps in the clouds. After a while we slackened our pace and continued in silence. The road was well known to us, the hills were quiet, the air warm and calm; it was a fine and peaceful night to be out in the world beneath the stars.

Then, as we crested the last hill and turned inland toward Bannavem, I halted.

"What is it?" said Scipio, reining up beside me.

"Can't you smell it?"

"Smell what?"

"Smoke."

"There!" said Rufus, joining us. I looked where he was pointing. A faint ruddy glow stained what appeared to be a dirty fog hanging just above the hilltops.

"Christ in heaven . . ." I murmured; then, with a slash of the reins, I lashed Boreas to speed.

Julian, last to join us, called after me. "Succat, what are you doing?"

"Bannavem is burning!"

3

REACHED THE TOP of the last hill and paused to look down upon the town below. Gashes of flame streaked the filthy sky. Along with the stench of smoke came a thin, almost ethereal wail, snaking along the trail to reach us as a cry of terror that chilled the warm marrow in our bones.

Behind me I heard Scipio suggest, "Someone has been careless with a lamp."

I turned on him. "Fool!" I cried. "Bannavem is attacked!"

I started down the slope, but the others hesitated.

"Follow me!" I shouted.

Still they hung back.

I wheeled my horse and urged them to follow. "Hurry! The town is attacked!"

The three looked uneasily at one another. None made a move to join me.

"What can we do?" said Rufus.

"We have no weapons," added Julian.

"It won't help anyone if we get ourselves killed down there," Scipio pointed out.

Their stubborn refusal angered me. "Cowards!" I shouted, and left them behind.

"It is too late for them," Julian called after me. "We can only help ourselves."

"The devil take you!" I shouted. "The devil take you all!"

Heedless of the danger, I rode for the town, fearing only that I would come too late to help save our lands, and that my mother would be worried about me. As I came nearer, I could hear shouting and the sporadic clash of weapons. In the darkness I could make out the walls and what appeared to be a knot of men on the road: raiders. I glimpsed flames through the broken gates and knew that the town was lost. I turned Boreas off the trail and raced for Favere Mundi.

The countryside between the town and our estate was quiet; so far as I could see, none of the smallholdings outside the town had been attacked. I arrived at the entrance to find the gate securely barred and locked. My shouts failed to raise anyone, so I left the trail and continued along the boundary hedge to a particular place I knew—I had long ago discovered how to enter and leave the estate when the gates were shut after dark—and, pausing to listen one last time, urged Boreas through the hawthorn gap and into the grain field behind the house.

Sliding from the saddle, I ran for the open archway leading into the courtyard, where, to my great relief, my mother stood calmly ordering the packing of the family treasure. "Mother!" I shouted, running to her.

"There you are, Succat," she said, turning from a wagon which was being loaded with various objects from the house. "You came back." A frantic servant tossed a carved box into the wagon and hurried away again.

"Bannavem is attacked. They will come here next."

"Yes, of course, my darling boy. As you can see, I have grasped that much."

"We must flee."

"All in good time."

"No, Mother. Now. We must go now, while there is still time to get away."

"I will not have my precious things dumped into a hole like so much rubbish."

"There is no time," I said. An elder servant, a man named Horace, hurried past carrying one of my mother's fine glass bowls. I grabbed him by the arm and took the bowl from his hands. "Saddle the horses, Horace," I ordered. "Run!"

I placed the bowl on the ground, took my mother by the elbow, and pulled her away from the wagon. "We are leaving. Where is Father?"

"He rode to town to help the militia."

"You let him go?" I cried.

"He is leader of the council," she replied. "It was his duty." She picked up the bowl and turned to place it carefully in the wagon.

"He will be killed," I said. For the first time a quiver of fear passed through me. "The town is overrun." Snatching the bowl from her hands, I threw it against the trunk of the nearby pear tree. The bowl smashed, scattering pieces everywhere.

"Succat!" shouted my mother, aghast at my action. "Can you even imagine the value of that bowl?"

"Leave it," I told her, pulling her away again. "Leave it all."

"I will *not* have you shouting at me like this."

"Go to the stable, Mother, and get on a horse. I know a place nearby where we will be safe until the invaders have gone. I'll look after this." I pushed her away from the wagon. "Hurry!"

She seemed to understand at last and moved off toward the stable. Frantic now, I turned and ran into the house in search of a weapon. My father and the men of the estate had taken all the swords and javelins, of course, and the shields, leaving only a few light hunting spears behind. I took two of these and ran through the house shouting for everyone to abandon the place.

Then, with the help of one of the servants, I pulled the wagon to the end of the courtyard and pushed it out into the field, where, at the near end, lay a pile of straw. "There!" I said, indicating the straw. We pushed the wagon to the pile and then heaped straw over it until the wagon and its cargo of valuables could no longer be seen.

Returning to the courtyard once more, I found my mother holding yet another of her large glass bowls. I was about to shout at her to drop the damned thing and get back to the stable when I heard a sound which seemed to come from the front of the villa. I darted inside and ran to the entrance hall, opened the door, and looked out to see a dozen or more men on the path leading to the house. My heart leapt to my throat.

I fled at once to the courtyard, took my mother by the arm, and led her away. "I thought we were to take the horses," she complained.

"No time." At the archway I stopped and shouted a last time for everyone to flee. Horace reappeared, and several of the younger women servants ran from the house. "This way!" I shouted, desperate to get everyone clear of the house. "Follow me, everyone. Horace, see to my mother. I will lead the way."

At the end of the field stood a small grove of beechnut trees; they grew low to the ground, their branches forming a screening breastwork of dark leaves. In the full leaf of summer, no one would know we were there—a fact I often put to good use in trysts with one of my mother's handmaids. Inside the hollow of their protecting branches was an old disused well that still held water. This would be useful if we were forced to stay any length of time. The ground sloped sharply down behind the grove where a small brook ran to the woods from which our fields had been cut. If worse came to worst, I thought, we could make an unseen escape along the shallow waterway and into the woods.

We reached the grove and settled down to wait. I crept to the low-sheltering edge of the branches and lay down on my stomach, staring at the house and straining for any sound. The small ticks and chirps of the night creatures and insects seemed to fill the entire valley. The servants grew restive, and the sound of their scratching and twitching distracted me. "Quiet!" I hissed. "Keep still."

As I spoke, I heard a door slam. Instantly everyone froze. A long moment passed, and then I heard someone shouting from the courtyard.

". . . Succat! . . . Concessa! . . . Succat!"

"It's Calpurnius," I said.

"There. You see, dear?" replied my mother. "We are saved."

"Perhaps."

"We can go back now." She started to her feet.

"Wait," I said, taking hold of her arm. "I'll go and look. Stay here until I come for you."

Leaving the spears with the servants, I darted out from the grove and ran back through the field to the villa. I paused at the archway and heard my father call again, whereupon I entered the courtyard and ran to him. "Here! Here I am!" I shouted.

"Thank God you are safe." His face was smudged black with soot, and he was bleeding from a cut to the side of his neck, but he appeared unharmed otherwise. He looked behind me. "Where is your mother?"

"At the old well," I told him. His smoke-grimed face wrinkled with incomprehension, so I added, "In the beech grove. Remember?"

"Ah," he said, "good thinking."

"Shall I go get them?"

"No," he said, turning away. "Leave them. They are safer there."

"Father, wait," I called, hurrying after him as he dashed to the house. He turned to me abruptly. "Where were you tonight?"

"In Lycanum," I answered, "with the others."

"Was it attacked?"

"There was no trouble when we left."

"Good. We still may have a chance." He placed a hand on my shoulder. "I want you to go to Lycanum and bring the soldiers—bring as many as you can."

"But I could never reach—"

"I sent two riders to Guentonia," he said, hurrying on, "but they will not reach the garrison in time."

"Father, listen, I—"

"Go, Succat. We do not have much time."

Still I hesitated. "What should I tell them?"

"Bannavem is lost," he said. "But there is still time to save the outlying settlements if they hurry. Tell them that."

There came a sound from inside the house. "Come with me," I said, and made to pull him away. "They are here already."

"It is the militia," he said, removing my hands. "I brought them here. We will hold the villa until you return with troops to aid us." He saw my indecision and put his hand to my shoulder once more. "You can do nothing here," he said. "Ride to Lycanum and bring soldiers. These Irish thieves will not stand against legionaries. Go. *Quickly.*"

"Very well," I said, accepting his judgment at last. I turned and rushed away.

"Take Boreas!" he called after me. "And God speed you, my son."

I paused at the bottom of the courtyard and called farewell, then hastened through the arch once more. Boreas was still in the field where I had left him. He would be tired from the evening's ride, but he was young and his strength green; I reckoned that, even fatigued, Boreas was still the fastest mount we had.

Snatching up the reins, I leapt to the saddle and streaked across the field to the break in the hedge wall, passed through, and raced out across the open countryside to the place where the path from our villa joined the coast road. I flew along the gently rippling road: dark hills on my right hand, the wide, moon-speckled sea on my left, and the high, bright, star-dusted sky above. My heart pounded in my chest, thudding with every beat of brave Boreas' hooves.

I drove that good horse hard and reached Lycanum far more swiftly than I imagined possible. Because of the rumored trouble, there was a watch before the gates: six legionaries standing around a fire, leaning on their javelins. They started from their gossip as I clattered up, and three of them ran to meet me with weapons ready.

"Help!" I cried. "Bannavem is attacked! We need soldiers!"

"Is that Succat?" said one of the men.

I looked down and recognized Darius. "Hurry! The town is overrun. My father sent me. We need soldiers."

"How many?"

I stared at the man. "All you have!" I shouted.

"I mean," replied Darius evenly, "how many raiders? How big is the attack force?"

"I cannot say. Hundreds. Maybe more."

"Ships?"

"I did not see any."

"Did you look?"

"Of course I looked."

Darius regarded me with a stern, searching expression. "Do not lie to me, boy. Did you look?"

"No, but—"

One of the soldiers spat a curse of exasperation. Darius remained unmoved. "How many militiamen do you have?"

"A dozen, I think, maybe a score."

"Bannavem is lost, boy," said one of the soldiers, turning away.

"Sorry, Succat," said Darius.

"You will not help us?"

"We cannot, lad," replied the legionary. "Most of the troops were sent to Guentonia. There are only two cohorts left behind to protect the town."

"Then bring them, for God's sake!" I snarled. "There is still time to save the settlements. Hurry!"

"Know you, if it was my decision, I would," answered Darius. "But we cannot leave Lycanum unprotected."

"Besides," added the other legionary, "with those odds it would make no difference."

"You mean to do nothing?" I said, my voice growing tight with disbelief. Tears of frustration welled in my eyes.

"I am sorry."

"Not as sorry as the dead of Bannavem." Wheeling my horse, I made to gallop away before the soldiers could see I was crying.

"Stay, Succat," called Darius. "We can protect you here. You will be safe."

"Damn you to hell!" I cried, my voice shaking with rage as I blindly lashed Boreas for home.

Back we raced, over the empty, night-dark road. Boreas—lathered, sweating, his sides heaving—gamely answered my command. Foam from his muzzle spattered my leg; I looked down and saw the white flecks streaked with blood. Still I did not relent. I would not leave my family to face the marauders alone. Help was not coming; it was time to abandon the villa and save ourselves.

On and on we went, at length reaching the slope rising to the last hill above our estate. Boreas labored up the long incline, gained the top, and galloped headlong into a swarm of Irish raiders.

Before I could dodge or turn, I was in among them. With a cry of surprise, the dark heathens scattered, leaping in all directions.

I put my head down and lashed Boreas hard so as to drive through them.

Two great half-naked hulks appeared directly in my path, running, screaming, the blades of their spears glinting in the moonlight.

I threw the reins to the right; Boreas, frightened now, tried to swerve, but his strength was gone. His legs tangled; he stumbled and fell. I slid from the saddle as he went down, rolling free of his flailing hooves. Still holding the reins, I scrambled to my feet and tried to pull him up. "Hie! Boreas! Up!" I shouted, pulling with all my might.

The poor exhausted beast made one last effort, and then his heart gave out and he collapsed. His head struck the road, a shudder passed through his body, and he lay still.

A strong arm encircled my waist, and I felt myself lifted from the ground. I kicked the heels of my boots—aiming for his knee or groin. Instead, I caught his thigh. He gave out a roar and threw me down on the ground. I hit hard; for a moment I could not breathe.

Gasping, gagging, I squirmed onto my knees and tried to gain my feet. I heard a whiffling sound behind my ear and felt a jolt that seemed to take off the back of my head. I was lifted up and hurled facefirst into the dust. Flaming black stars burst before my dazzled eyes. My head was filled with the sound of a thousand angry hornets.

Hands grasped me by the hair and arms. I was yanked upright and half dragged, half carried away down the hill. When my vision cleared somewhat, I saw that I was being lugged toward the shore. I tried to wriggle free and received a sharp cuff across the side of my face.

As we descended to the coast, I twisted my throbbing head around and saw, over my shoulder, a dirty red-orange glow in the sky. Our villa was aflame. I cried out at the sight and struggled once more to free myself. "Mother!" I screamed. "Father!"

My shouts were silenced by a crack on my skull which rattled my teeth like dice in a cup and knocked all sense from me. My stomach, bladder, and bowels emptied themselves at once, and all strength fled. The raiders bore me up between them and dragged me down to the sea.

I LAY ON THE strand with a mouth full of sand and the roar of the sea in my ears. Knowing I should get up and run away while it was still dark, I lacked both strength and will, and instead writhed on the beach, panting and groaning, my eyes squeezed shut against the pain. The darkness was filled with rushing and shouting and cries of terror, but I paid no heed to any of it. Gradually, the frenzy and noise receded, and I sank into a dark, empty silence.

Sometime later I opened my eyes on a dawn raw as an open wound, to find that I was lying on a heap of rotting seaweed with no memory of how I came to be there.

My horse threw me, I thought. Boreas had thrown me and bolted. I must have crawled down to the strand from the road. Or maybe I had fallen and rolled down. We were at the inn—my friends and I. But where were they now? And why had they deserted me when I needed them?

These thoughts, fragments only, circled lazily in and out of my hazy memory. There was something else . . . the sound of breaking glass . . . a cry for help . . . someone whimpering . . . the moon glowing red through a dark pall of smoke.

Smoke . . .

With the word came the scent in my nostrils—and with that, the awful memory of what had happened: the attack . . . the villa ablaze . . . my home destroyed.

I raised my head, which started a cascade of pain. When it passed, my vision cleared and I looked around. In the dim dawn light I could make out the huddled forms of others nearby. I heard the sound of sobbing and carefully turned my head to the left, where a young girl was sitting—knees to chin, arms wrapped around her legs, hugging herself, rocking back and forth, whimpering in her misery. Her eyes were closed, and tears glistened on her thin, dirty face.

"Who are you?" I croaked. The voice which issued from my mouth was as dry and feeble as an old man's, but the girl opened her eyes and gazed at me.

"I thought you dead," she said after a moment.

"Not yet," I gasped.

She regarded me with an expression that said she was far from persuaded.

"Where are we?"

"They killed my mother," the girl replied, her lips quivering. She sniffed back the tears. "They came for us at night. I don't know what happened to my father."

"Where are we?" I asked again, raising my voice slightly. Even that sent spasms of pain spinning though my head. I closed my eyes and gritted my teeth.

"Are you injured?" asked the girl.

"My head hurts," I replied between breaths. When the pain subsided, I opened my eyes and said, "What is your name?"

"Drusilla,"

"Do you know where we are?"

She shook her head slowly. The entire side of her face was a mass of purple-black bruises; her hair was matted with dried blood, her slender arms streaked with soot and dirt.

I looked beyond her to some of the other survivors farther along the beach. I made to call to them, but the pain in my head began as soon as I raised my voice, so I desisted until I could make myself heard without setting the waves of agony thundering through my poor battered skull.

Carefully, I turned and looked back up the rising slope to the top of the cliff, then along the strand to the right and left. The coast seemed vaguely familiar. I guessed we were no great distance from Bannavem. The enemy seemed to have gone, and I thought that if I could get to my feet and gain the clifftop, I might yet reach home.

"Drusilla," I said, "I'm going to climb up to the road. I need you to help me."

She looked at me sadly and shook her head again. The resignation in her expression angered me.

"Why not?" I demanded. "We have to try at least."

Without a word she stretched out one leg to reveal an iron shackle tight around her skinny ankle. Glancing quickly down at my own feet, I saw that I was shackled, too. Cold, hard drops of sweat stood out on my throbbing temples as I beheld the iron rings and chain.

I grabbed at the chain with my hand and loosed a strangled cry of rage and frustration. Captive! The word beat in the pulse of my broken head. Captive! I had been taken prisoner. My vision dissolved in tears of helplessness, humiliation, and defeat.

After a moment I swallowed my distress, drew a deep breath, and turned to the young girl once more. "Listen," I said, "we can do this if we help each other." I rolled onto my knees and held out my hand. "Here. Take hold of me."

She crawled to where I was kneeling, took my hand, and allowed me to help her to her feet, whereupon she took my elbow and held me up while I tried to stand. The movement brought a rush of nausea, and my stomach heaved, but there was nothing to vomit save the bile which burned my throat. I stood bent double until the rippling ceased, then wiped my mouth with my sleeve, put my arm around Drusilla's bony shoulder, and we started forth one painful step at a time—like blind beggars hobbling uncertainly over alien ground.

I coaxed Drusilla along much as I would a skittery colt: soothing her with reassurances, telling her she was doing well and that we would soon be free once more. Together we crept to the foot of the cliff; here the ground was covered with shattered slate, fallen from the rocky cliffs above to form mounded heaps. The flat rock tilted and slipped beneath our feet like smashed tiles, and we fell; I struck my knee on a sharp edge, and the impact set the pain beating in my head like a drum. I knelt there gasping for breath until the pain receded.

When I was ready to go on, Drusilla helped me to my feet and we continued.

The cliffside rippled with many eroded ravines and shallow furrows filled with brush and small shrubs. Although these little valleys were steep, I thought we might at least have branches and suchlike to hold on to as we climbed. We made our way to the nearest defile. "I'll go first," I said. "Follow me, and do what I do."

On elbows and knees I pulled myself up, grasping stones and sticks and clumps of sea grass, wriggling like an eel through the undergrowth. It might have worked, too; we might have succeeded but for the dogs.

We had just begun our ascent when there came a shout from the beach, and then I heard barking. Glancing back over my shoulder, I saw two huge brown hounds bounding toward us, growling as they came. Behind them ran three raiders carrying spears; two others stood on the strand watching.

The dogs were on us in an instant. Drusilla screamed. One of the beasts snatched at my leg as I kicked out. It seized me by the cloth of my trousers and began pulling. I slid down the defile and lay curled on the broken slate with my arms before my face to protect my head and throat until the handlers came and pulled the hounds away.

No doubt they would have punished us more severely for trying to escape, but their hands were full—what with the dogs and spears—so they cuffed me halfheartedly about the shoulders a few times and hauled us back to the beach where, with a whack on the arm with the butt of a spear, they shoved me back down on the sand. Drusilla began sobbing again, and my head pounded with such ferocity I could not see. I lay on my back with my eyes sqeezed shut, moaning, bereft in my misery.

In a little while the sun rose full and with it the tide. When I stirred myself again, I saw there were more raiders on the beach now—fifty, maybe sixty or more—standing in a clump, many leaning on their spears in postures of fatigue. They seemed to be waiting for something. . . . With this thought I turned my eyes to the sea as the first sails came into view: three brown-and-red squares billowing in the light morning breeze, gliding around the far headland and into the bay. These were soon joined by five more, and then seven.

Fifteen ships! Even if most were not fully manned, it still meant five or six hundred warriors. I reckoned that Guentonia boasted but two centuries, Lycanum only one, and Bannavem none at all—fewer than three hundred soldiers for the defense of three towns. While it is true that a trained legionary is worth five or more barbarians, even legionaries cannot be three places at once. Bannavem was lost before the battle ever began, just as Darius had said.

The first of the ships came close to shore, and one bedraggled knot of captives after another was led out into the surf: men, women, and children—whole families ripped from their beds in the dead of night and marched to the coast. I looked for any familiar faces among the first unhappy passengers but saw no one I knew.

And then it was my turn. Two raiders came, and without a word I was pulled to my feet and dragged out to a nearby ship. The cold waves washed around my legs, and then I was roughly hauled over the side like a fish. Drusilla tumbled in after me, and we huddled together in the bottom of the boat. When the shallow hold was full, the warriors turned the ship and pushed it out into the bay. I heard the hull grind against the sand and hoped for a moment that we would be grounded and unable to sail. Then a wave lifted the ship, the sail puffed out, and we slid away.

I pulled myself up the side and looked out over the rail at the slowly receding coast. Black plumes of smoke rising into the clear morning sky marked the ruins of Bannavem; around the countryside smaller gray-white columns indicated other burning villas—of which Favere Mundi was but one of many. I wondered if my parents had escaped or whether my bull-headed father had stayed to fight to the death. I wondered what my friends would say when they learned I had been taken. I wondered if I would ever see my homeland again.

Leaving the bay, the ship bounded out into deeper water, and more of the coastline came into view. Away to the south, in the direction of Lycanum, a great, heavy dark cloud of smoke hung like a continuous storm above the gentle hills; and to the north more ships—and still more, strung out all along the coast. I stared in disbelief at the low knifelike hulls, and the full extent of the attack broke over me: it was not a raid, it was an invasion.

Sadness such as I have never known descended over me as I watched the land of my birth slowly shrink and shrink, growing ever smaller until at last the green headlands disappeared beneath the clear horizon. My heart felt as if it would crack in two; I wanted to cry, but, stunned by grief, I could only stare in dry-eyed wonder.

Out on the open sea, the breeze stiffened, the sail snapped taut, and the sharp prow bit deep into the waves. I settled back in my place and turned my attention to our captors. There were eight of them aboard ship: big men all, well muscled, and dressed in coarse handwoven, voluminous trousers dyed red, orange, or brown. Most were bare to the waist, with long hair that they wore in one or more braids down their naked backs. Their beards were shaved except for mustaches, which they wore untrimmed. Two had smeared pitch on their faces, chests, and arms in rippled stripes; three had armbands of gold, and all wore torcs around their necks: one of silver, the rest of bronze or iron. They were filthy brutes, one and all.

My fellow captives sat slumped against the sides of the boat or curled on the narrow central deck. Sunk in despair, they did not lift their heads. Young and old wore the same witless, dead expressions. Most were, so it appeared to me, farmhands and servants. I knew none of them. They stared with dull eyes at the far horizon, mute in resignation, patient as cattle awaiting the slaughter.

The pilot of the boat was an older man with a blackened stump on the end of his right arm where his hand should have been. He worked the steering oar keeping one eye on the sail and one on the sea. Three other ships traveled in our wake, and the waves, running smooth and calm, seemed to fly beneath the prow. We sailed through the morning, and while our captors talked among themselves and drank from wineskins and the water stoup from time to time, none of them spoke so much as a word to any of us nor offered us anything to drink.

After a time, the tedium of the voyage began to tell. I dozed, awakening once to find that Drusilla had fallen asleep with her head against my chest. My first instinct was to push her aside, but I restrained myself. Her troubles, like mine, were just beginning, and I did not care to add to her distress by even such a trivial act. I was thirsty, but there was no relief, so to prevent myself from thinking about it, I went back to sleep.

I woke again later with a burning thirst and decided to do something about it. Gently shifting Drusilla aside, I rose unsteadily and made my way to the water stoup. One of the guards saw me as I dipped the ladle; he challenged me, but, ignoring him, I drank my fill and then turned and offered the ladle to the captive beside me. The guard, angry now, came to where I stood and snatched the water away from the man. He shouted something at me and pushed me aside, but the pilot called something to him. An argument ensued, which ended with the truculent guard being forced to fill the ladle and pass it along to the captives until everyone had been given a drink.

I crawled back to my place and dozed again until sunset, when I awoke and saw, against the crimson and purple sky, the low humps of an island far off in the west. I thought this our destination, but when the island had drawn close enough, the pilot turned the ship, and we proceeded on a northerly course. The sky held the light long, and the sea remained calm. I lay back in my place and listened to the ceaseless swish and surge of the waves against the hull. It was a tranquil sound, and the light of the rising moon turned the sea to liquid silver. Stars in wild abundance filled the sky bowl with glittering light.

How, I wondered, could heaven look down upon such a great calamity as if nothing had happened? Was not the desecration perpetrated on my homeland worthy of God's consideration?

Yet, the moon rose in perfect serenity in a calm, untroubled sky; the peaceful stars turned in their slow, steady arcs; the sea spread out like a friendly meadow—and all as if the catastrophe of the day were of such small consequence as to be unworthy of heavenly regard.

The more I thought about this, the more absurd it seemed and the angrier I became. That the distress of so many innocent people should fail to provoke even so much as an angry retort from the Ruler of Heaven and Earth was an outrage.

It was then I learned one of life's fundamental lessons: the lord of this world is a coldhearted king, unmoved by the suffering of his subjects, demanding complete homage, unstinting love, and total, unthinking obedience of all who pass beneath his stony gaze, yet lifts nary a finger to lessen the severity of their travails.

If this was the way of things, then I would look to myself for the preserving and sustaining of my life. There was despair in this conclusion, true, but there was freedom, too. For I reasoned I could go my own way and never trouble myself with another thought about God, his church, or any of his insufferable mob of simpering damp-eyed priests, ever again.

And yet . . . my grandfather's hold on me was stronger than I imagined. His stern, disapproving voice seemed to call to me across the years. *Blasphemy and sacrilege! I could hear him rumble. What do you know of things, boy? What do you know of the world? What do you know of anything?*

The thought chastised me sufficiently to amend my harsh appraisal somewhat. I decided to put the Good Lord to the test. I would propose a simple bargain.

God of my fathers, heed me now, I said within my heart. *Aid me in my escape, and I will worship you with all my soul. Aid me not, and I will turn my back on you forever. Hear me: Succat of Morgannwg makes this vow.*

That done, I closed my eyes and slept again for a while, awakening when I heard shouting. I opened my eyes. It was near dawn, and one of the other ships had drawn up beside us; the guards were calling to one another. I looked across the narrow distance between the hulls as the warriors from the other boat hauled a man onto his feet. Gray-faced, his hair matted with sweat, he seemed to be pleading, begging, his voice shaking.

Two brawny barbarians picked him up like a sack of meal and made him stand atop the rail. He balanced there, clinging to one of the mast ropes while they removed his shackles. Even from a distance I could see that the poor wretch's arm was broken; the limb flopped uselessly, and the hand was blue.

As soon as the leg chains were removed, one of the guards raised a spear and prodded the man in the back to make him jump. The fellow refused. He began weeping in anguish, howling like a beaten dog. The coward with the spear prodded him again, harder, poking him in the shoulder.

Still the man refused to jump. There came a cry from the boat, and a woman thrust herself forward. She wrapped her arms around the man's legs and held on to him, crying for the thugs to let him back in the boat.

This went on for a time, drawing great snorts of laughter from the barbarians in both boats. Then, tiring of the game, the warrior with the spear slashed the man in the back of the leg, severing the cords behind his knee. Unable to stand, the wretch toppled into the sea. He came up spluttering and coughing, flailing in the water with his good arm. The woman screamed and held out her hands to him, receiving a blow in the teeth with the shaft of the spear. Even then she did not desist. She wailed the louder through her bloody lips and stretched out her arms, trying to reach him. When that failed, she leaned out over the rail and would have joined him in his fate—indeed, she was half in the water before the thug noticed; he snagged her by the edge of her mantle and dragged her back into the ship. I saw the butt of the spear rise and fall sharply, and her cries ceased.

I looked back in the water and saw the man's hand flutter above the surface of the waves, fingers reaching for a last, hopeless, fleeting grasp of life. And then he sank from view.

When I saw he would not rise again, I turned my eyes away, my face burning with pent rage at the way he had been treated. When my anger subsided, I saw that the land was now much nearer than before. Soon we were passing through the low scattering of islets and rocks of the darkly wooded coast of my new home.

5

HE BAY WAS wide and deep, stone-lined and sheltered by a high, craggy promontory on either side. On
the rocks stood a rude settlement of mud huts, inhabited, so far as I could see, by barking dogs and barefoot,
snotty-nosed brats. There were already four ships in the bay when we arrived, delivering their human cargo to the shore.

I counted the captives as they went ashore; there were more than sixty in
the first three ships alone. Then it was our turn. The raiders manned the
oars, and the pilot maneuvered the boat to the loading place—a crude
wharf where men with ropes and poles held the vessel in place while the
boards were extended, one to either end of the boat. With shouting and gestures our captors indicated that we were to disembark. Because of the shackles, most of the captives had difficulty getting onto the narrow timbers;
when prodding with spears did not help, the brutes would heave the struggling wretch onto the plank and push him along. More than one captive
fell into the water, to the amusement of the ruffians on shore, who made
great sport of it before hauling out the half-drowned victim.

I, too, almost fell, but refused to give the thugs any delight in my misfortune, so went down on my knees instead and, gripping the edges of the
board with both hands, made my way onto the rocks, where I joined the
others. There were almost eighty of us now, by my reckoning. We were
made to stand in the sun while the other ships unloaded their unwilling
passengers. One ship after another entered the bay, and when I thought that
must be the end of it, more arrived.

In a little while we were marched a short distance into a clearing in the wood, where we were given water from the hewn-stone basin of a cattle trough. Drinking from such a vessel was humiliating, certainly, but I was thirsty, and the water was clean and reviving. I gulped down as much as I could before I was jabbed with the butt of a spear and forcibly moved on. We were then herded together into the center of the clearing, where we squatted on our haunches beneath the wary gaze of the guards, who cuffed anyone who spoke or moved. The surrounding trees provided a little relief from the sun, but we were given no food, and by this time more than a few were growing faint.

All day long the ships came, and all day long we waited, our numbers swelling with each arrival. For a while, I occupied myself with trying to search out anyone I knew, but it was no use. Few town dwellers appeared among the captives—a dozen or so itinerant merchants, as it seemed to me—and no members of the nobility at all. I wondered about this. Had the noble families simply been slaughtered outright? Or had they been singularly successful in fending off the attack?

Neither possibility seemed likely. Even given the enormity of the attack, some few noblemen must have escaped slaughter, and these would have been rounded up for slaves just like all the rest. Then again, the invaders had overwhelmed the entire countryside, so how was it that only the nobility escaped? I puzzled over this a considerable time as, boatload by boatload, the number of captives grew.

Then it came to me: the poor folk, the rustics, the *pagani*, those without recourse to ransom had been brought to Éire, where they would become slaves. But the noble families, the wealthy aristocracy, the landowners, had not joined us because they were being kept in Britain, where they could be ransomed for ready gold.

Darkest dread spread its numbing tendrils through me, but before it could take root, another thought sprang up: a grave mistake had been made. I was neither a rustic nor a pagan. I was a Christian from a noble family. I could easily raise the ransom price. A slender shaft of hope, like a beam of light striking to the bottom of a well, suffused my soul. I set the matter squarely before me and marveled at the simplicity. All I had to do was make myself known, and the error would be rectified. I would be taken back to Britain, where my father, the wealthy decurion, would gladly and handsomely pay for my release. Thus encouraged, I settled down to bide my time until I found someone in authority to whom I could explain the blunder.

Toward evening the last ship arrived, and its captives were brought to our now-sizable conclave. I added their number to the rest: seven hundred and eighty-five. It was, I felt certain, the largest raid ever known in Britain.

Yet for all our numbers, there was no outcry or struggling; a thick silence of misery prevailed. Men and women stood or sat, silent, faces impassive, sight turned inward. They seemed to me like houses in which the roofs had collapsed; the walls were still intact, but the interior—indeed, everything that made it a house—was gone.

A hump-shouldered man standing nearby saw me counting on my fingers and seemed anxious to know what I was doing. Despite the guards, I made bold to tell him the tally as I made it. The ignorant lout merely gawped at me like a deaf dog. I explained again, and still he stared, shaking his head slowly and muttering under his breath. I realized then that he did not speak Latin. "Cretin," I muttered, dismissing him with a sneer.

Little wonder they were such easy pickings for Irish raiders. *Unschooled, backward boors,* I thought. *However do they keep themselves alive?* Nevertheless the insight bolstered my hope, for it served to heighten the difference between myself and the others. No one could fail to see the mistake for the gross error that it was, and I would soon be returning home, where ransom would be arranged and I would be set free.

The guards were now joined by a host of warriors—more than a hundred of them, big brutes in full battle regalia—who stood watch while their comrades came among us and removed the chains of any who, like myself, were still shackled. They then divided the throng into two companies, one somewhat larger than the other. The larger of the two was led apart, leaving the smaller one behind. Some families were divided by this exercise. I saw many women distraught and weeping to have their husbands torn from them. I would gladly have stayed behind to allow two to remain together, but heaven decreed that I was among those chosen to depart, and we marched off into the wood. During this confusion, I lost sight of Drusilla; I determined to watch out for her, but I did not see her in the crowd.

A path led up through the wood into the low hills beyond the coast, and we were pushed onto this path and commenced walking, singly or two together, with the setting sun on our right hand. As I walked along, I listened to the woodland sounds—birdcalls, small rustlings in the dry leaf matter along the path. For all our numbers we passed as silently as fog through the trees—silently, silently, as if we ourselves might disappear in silence.

All the while a blue dusk deepened around us, and still we did not stop. By the time the moon rose, I reckoned we were going to walk all night. With darkness, the way became uneven underfoot. The guards grew more watchful, lest anyone try to escape into the night. Whenever anyone stumbled, the guards ran to thump him with the butts of their spears by way of punishment for his clumsiness, then yanked the unfortunate to his feet and pushed him back onto the path.

The moon was high overhead when we finally stopped to rest. The wood ended, and we came out into a wide clearing on the top of a hill, where in the starlight I saw the rings and ditches of an old *ráth*, or ring fort. The palisade walls were gone and the ditches filled with briars and nettles, but a large, reed-thatched house still stood in the center of the ring, and beside it a small enclosure for sheep and cattle.

We sat down in the long grass to rest while the guards shared out their drink among themselves from the skins they carried. The captives, however, were given nothing. For many of us it had been a long day without food, and our hunger was growing onerous. Some began chewing grass and so received some small comfort that way. Grazing like a dumb animal was beneath me, and I refused.

Even so, I did, I confess, pluck a few leaves on which the dew was beginning to form, and drew these through my lips. It did little more than wet my tongue and stoke the fire in my throat all the more, so I desisted. I lay back and rested for a time, and when the moon had all but set, we were awakened once more. I sat up and looked out at the captives scattered here and there across the hillside like the corpses of a defeated army after a great and terrible battle. The guards moved among them like grim survivors, prodding the bodies with their spears as if trying to rouse the dead. Stirred to life, the dead arose, stood on their feet, and walked.

The trail took us further inland and into heavier wood—larger trees surmounting a thick undergrowth of brambles: hawthorn, blackberry, and elder. The thorny vines of the blackberry snatched at the unwary, scratching flesh and snagging clothing—a trifling obstacle in the daylight but a very danger at night. I walked with my hands before my face and caught more than one swinging branch before it reached my eyes.

After a time the path began to descend, the slope growing gradually sharper until it became clear we were coming into a valley. Soon there arose a cry from far ahead on the trail, and the captives began to shuffle more quickly. And then, passed back along the line, came the word: water!

The mob surged forward in a rush. Like horses with the scent in their nostrils, they put their heads down and charged blindly for the stream that was yet a short distance ahead. Pushing and jostling one another, they ran, heedless of the brush and branches of the undergrowth. Some of the less agile became tangled in vines or tripped up on roots and went down; these were shamefully trampled by those behind.

Just ahead of me I saw a woman fall on the path; two more fell atop her, and all three were overrun. They screamed and kicked, but failed to slow the onslaught. As I came near, I looked down and saw that one of them was

Drusilla. The girl shrieked and reached out to me, her fingers clutching like claws.

"Here!" I cried. "Take my hand."

She lurched toward me, and I snagged hold of one thin wrist. The mob, desperate for water, plunged over and around us. Tumbled along like a pebble in a swift-rushing stream, I tried with all my strength to haul the young girl upright. I succeeded only in dragging her a few paces down the path before my grip failed.

Jostled, pummeled, knocked sideways by the swarm, I could not fight my way back to her. I watched in horror as the life was crushed from her slender body by the feet of those charging blindly to the stream.

Using the shafts of their spears, several guards forced their way to the place, but arrived too late to save her. Battered and injured, the other two women were at least able to rise. Poor Drusilla, however, was left were she had fallen. Anger and sorrow surged up inside me, and I cursed the senseless waste of that small, insignificant life.

But there was nothing to be done. Driven by their thrist, the crowd raced on, and I was carried along with it. I was well back in the pack, so by the time I reached the ford, it had become a mud bath. In their inhuman haste the fools had churned the small, clear-running stream into a pig wallow. Men and women were flopped facedown in the muck, eagerly sucking up the stuff. Some had drunk too much too fast and were choking and puking on it, fouling the water for the rest; others knelt in the middle of the stream, laving the gunk over themselves. The mire ran in filthy rivulets down their faces and beards and from their gaping mouths.

I tried to go upstream to get at cleaner water, but the guards refused to allow anyone to move even a few paces apart, so I had to make do with a few mouthfuls of muddy slop sucked from the hollow of my hand. And then, with much shouting, shoving, and threatening, we were moved on once more.

We walked until dawn and emerged from the forest and onto a well-traveled track that passed between two sown fields. The grain was green and high, the fields clean and well tended. In the distance rose a large, conical hill, and it was to this prominence we were led. As we came nearer, I observed that the top of this hill had been leveled; ramparts and ditches formed rings around the upper elevations, and the top was crowned by a high palisade wall of timber lined with sharpened stakes at its base. A great wooden gate, surmounted by a walkway on which warriors strutted and gestured as we drew nearer, formed the entrance.

It was not for us to enter this settlement; we were taken instead to a stone-

and-timber cattle enclosure at the base of the hill, where we were watered from a wooden trough and penned up like so much livestock. The enclosure was mean, and we were packed in until there was no room to move about. We stood in mounting misery as the sun rose higher through the clear morning sky, beating down on our sorry heads.

At midday the fortress began to stir. From where I stood I could see through a chink in the enclosure onto part of the road. People were arriving in groups, large and small: most on foot, but some on horseback, and one—I tell the truth!—in a chariot pulled by two fine gray horses. I caught the glint of gold at this fellow's throat and perceived that he styled himself a prince of some account. He was accompanied by six riders bearing spears and large square shields which were painted black and embellished with symbols copied from Roman insignia. The ignorant savages did not know what the symbols meant, I could tell, for the images were all mixed and mingled together: the jagged lightning bolt of II Augusta and the winged *pilum* of XX Valeria Victrix, the proud eagle of the legions along with the double-ended trident and the triple running foot of the infantry, and others which were not emblems at all but merely letters jumbled up anyhow.

They rode up to the fortress and through the open gate. The others on the path moved aside to let them pass. They were followed by at least seven wagons pulled by heavy horses; these wagons were stacked high to overflowing with the treasure pillaged from towns they had ransacked, and it made my heart sick to see it. More people followed after that, some with lengthy retinues in their wake, but most without. All day long we stood in the cattle pen: thirsty, tired, the hot summer sun striking down through an empty sky. Many captives, weak from lack of food, could not endure this abuse and fainted. There was no place for them to lie, so they remained propped between those on either side, or held upright by members of their family. If that were not bad enough, others who could no longer hold their bladders and bowels relieved themselves where they stood, and the bare earth soon grew wet and rank.

As evening approached, there came the blast of a horn from the fortress above. This was followed by a mighty cry and then silence. After a while we could see smoke rising in a thick column from behind the high palisade, and wood ash drifted down upon us like warm gray snow. As night descended, the glow from the fire lit the sky above the fortress; sparks ascended into the night, forming a glittering ladder to heaven. The revel continued through the night, and shortly after dawn the cattle pen was opened and we were led out onto the plain at the base of the hill.

There slaves passed among us with buckets and stoups of fresh water, while bags of broken bones and fragments of food were brought out and dumped upon the ground—the leavings of the previous night's feasting collected for us to eat. Most disgraced themselves by rooting through this garbage like rats, but I would not demean my family name with such a low spectacle. Instead, I contented myself by drinking my fill of the water and held myself aloof from the waste pickers.

Some of the guards passed among us then, and we were separated men from women, youths from adults—although younger children, of which there were a few, were allowed to remain with their mothers. We were formed into groups of five, six, or more. I watched this haphazard process and decided that we were being sorted according to the strength and fitness of those making up the group.

This went on for some time, with much discussion and arguing on the part of the guards. Once established in a group, we were allowed to sit down. Meanwhile, the population of the hill fort emerged from the gates and assembled on the plain. A large table was erected, beside which a chair was placed. When all was ready, we were made to stand for the inspection of the barbarian dignitaries who walked among us, stroking their mustaches, examining the various groups, and discussing the captives between themselves.

When this ritual had been observed, the prince—the one I had seen in the chariot the day before—sat in the chair and, with the aid of several advisors who stood around him with lengths of rawhide rope in their hands, began receiving the petitions of those present. One barbarian approached, stretched himself prostrate in front of the chair, and caressed his lord's bare foot. When he was given leave to rise, he turned and pointed to the group he had chosen. There followed a brief negotiation, whereupon the buyer produced a bag of coins. The price was counted out and placed on the table, and the transaction recorded by a servant who tied a knot in the length of rawhide he held in his hand.

The subject honored the prince once more and then quickly departed, leading his newly acquired slaves. I saw then how the thing would go and determined I would make myself known to the prince and present my case for ransom. The bargaining and slave selling continued apace. Those who went quietly walked away of their own accord; those who shouted and struggled were beaten, bound, and dragged off. I waited patiently for my turn, and as the sun mounted higher, so, too, did my hopes, for the prince seemed more interested in the money he was receiving than in the homage from his subjects.

My chance finally came when my group—a thin young man a few years older than myself, a farmer and his boy, a toothless old woman, and two young girls—came to the attention of one of the buyers. As he examined us, I looked him in the eye and said, "*Salvete! Colloqui cum una tu et ego!*"

He looked at me as if I had fouled myself. Clearly, he did not understand Latin. Nevertheless I repeated my wish to speak to him, and he turned to the nearest guard; the two held a brief discussion, whereupon the man nodded and turned to walk away. I saw my chance fading, so I reached out and took the fellow by the arm. He shook off my hand and kept walking.

I darted after him but ran only a few steps before I was tripped up; I fell, sprawling on the ground. The guards hauled me to my feet and dragged me back. "I must speak to the prince!" I shouted. "There has been a mistake!"

This brought no response save that the guards produced a rope and began tying my hands together. I did not struggle but shouted the louder. They began leading me away. "Ransom!" I cried. "I demand to be ransomed!"

At this the prince stood up and called an order. To my immediate relief he gestured to the guards, and I was brought before him. They forced me to my knees and pushed my head to the ground. Still I did not struggle, but allowed myself to remain in this posture until the prince spoke to me.

I lifted my head and saw him looking at me with dark, inquisitive eyes. He was a young man—younger than I had first imagined—strong, well formed, and proud in his strength. A great torc of twisted gold bands—an archaic ornament indicating nobility—encircled his throat, gold bracelets and arm rings adorned both arms, and a belt of silver rings sewn onto soft black leather girdled his waist. He wore a short red-and-yellow checked cloth that reached to his knees. His feet were bare, but there were thick gold bands on each ankle. His mustache was long and trimmed to a fine point at either end; his long dark hair was brushed back on his head to fall over his shoulders like the mane of a lion. On the right pectoral of his well-muscled chest was a woad-stained scar in the shape of a hand, made up of a spiral pattern with slender protrusions where fingers and thumb would be. He was, I thought, as imposing as any Roman emperor and, in his rude way, just as majestic.

He spoke a word, which I did not understand. When I did not reply, he motioned one of his advisors to attend him. He spoke again, and the advisor turned to me and said something which I could almost grasp. Although the sounds and rhythms were faintly familiar, I could not make out the words. Thinking it might be a dialect of British, I tried the speech of our estate farmers, saying, "Please, hear me. A grave mistake has been made. I should not be here."

The advisor repeated his statement, and I repeated mine, whereupon he shrugged and turned away.

"I am a nobleman!" I shouted, my Latin falling on deaf ears. "I was brought here in error. I demand to be taken back to Britain and ransomed."

The advisor stepped before the prince and shook his head. The prince made a motion with his hand, and the guards began hauling me off.

"My father is decurion of Bannavem Taburniae!" I shouted desperately. "He will pay my ransom. Whatever you ask, he will pay it! Listen to me!"

My pleas went unheard and unheeded. I was led away. The man who had purchased me took leave of his lord, gathered his retinue of warriors and women, and departed. Angry, frustrated beyond words, bereft, heartbroken, and sick to my soul, I was dragged along with the others. Thus began my life as a slave.

6

ING MILIUCC MOCU Bóin, Lord of Sliabh Mis
and the Vale of Braghad, was ruler of a wilderness
realm of mountain, stream, and forest; of rocks, barren
heath, and steep, sun-shy valleys. The land was poorly
suited to farming, so he and his people lived by breeding cattle and sheep,
fattening the beasts on the lush grass of the hillsides and high mountain
meadows. He possessed more sheep than subjects, did my lord Miliucc.

In my first days and weeks, I learned all I could from what I observed
around me. I saw that he and his *tuath*, his tribe, lived in either of two principal settlements, one high, one low: the former a sizable ráth on a broad
hump of rock overlooking the valley, the latter a circle of stick-and-mud
huts near the banks of the small, fresh-running river where the only fields
could be sown and crops grown and tended. There were other smallholdings as well—fishing camps on a nearby bay—but these were occupied only
in summer. Within sight of the western coast in the north of Éire, the region was cool and wet during the summer, cold and wet in the winter, and
damp and chill all the rest of the time.

The fortress itself was made of wood, as were the low, thatched houses inside. The ráth was reached by a long, narrow trackway which passed
through two sets of high timber gates separated by a deep ditch into which
the tribe threw their refuse. The entire hillside reeked of excrement and the
rotting entrails of butchered animals. A cacophony of carrion birds circled
the fortress, filling the air with their cries.

Miliucc's people were a dirty, stinking rabble. How else? They all lived like animals. Lacking any civilizing amenities and possessing only the most basic of human necessities, they wallowed in their own filth morning to night, their crude existence little better than that of the beasts to which they owed their rough survival.

Unlettered, unlearned, untroubled by any obligations of intellect, they went about their temporal activities gabbling like chickens and displaying the childlike love of ostentation and extravagance of appearance shared by barbarians the world over. If any possessed a trinket or bauble, it was worn with inordinate pride, be it merely a painted shell or a carved bone. Gold rings adorned filthy fingers, and silver necklaces ringed throats begrimed with sweat and soot, delicate bronze bands gleamed on dirty arms.

Their clothes, although grease-stained and muddy, were nevertheless woven of the brightest colors: gaudy orange and green stripes; red and blue checks; white-, black-, and yellow-patterned plaids—the more garish the better. The men wore loose, outsize trousers that they called *briste*, wrapped knee to foot with long leather straps attached to their soft boots. Women wore shapeless, ankle-length mantles bound at the waist by wide, extravagantly woven girdles and fastened at the shoulder with brooches of wood, bone, bronze, or other stuff. Men and women alike wore a kind of simple cloak which they called a *fallaing*, made of the same heavy wool as the rest of their cloth and, again, striped or woven into closely worked checked patterns in audacious colors.

Judging from the inordinate number of naked infants and dogs scurrying around the ráth, they seemed overly indulgent of children and animals, neither of which they bothered to discipline or husband in any way. And all, young and old alike, loved nothing more than listening to their hideous, screechy music—played by men given the task and made listenable only after numerous bowls of sour, heady beer, which they brewed in vast quantities in great wooden tubs and then drank until inebriation either put them to sleep or stirred their blood and made them contentious and brawly. Should the latter condition arise, as it usually did, they would fall out fighting. They would be singing and laughing and, but a moment later, bashing one another with fearsome blows—only to collapse in one another's arms with pledges of eternal friendship and loyalty when the beating brought them to their soggy senses. A more tempestuous and belligerent people I truly never saw.

Oh, they were barbarians through and through, vile savages in thought, word, and deed.

On our arrival at Miliucc's fortress, the other slaves and myself were fitted with collars; mine was a simple torc of twisted iron, much like those some of the servants and younger people wore, save that it had an iron ring at the back by which I could be tethered when the need arose. At the king's command I was held tight in the grasp of two hulking brutes while a third bent the ring of still-hot iron around my neck. The heated metal blistered my skin, and though it hurt with a fury, I refused to cry out. As soon as the ends were closed, the torc was doused with water and I was led away to be fed: a thin gruel of fish and barley. Despite my hunger, the stuff was foul and I refused to swallow more than a few bites. The next day I was established in a shepherd's bothy on the side of a mountain overlooking the Vale of Braghad and this because, of all the slaves, I was deemed most fit, and therefore most suitable to watch their precious sheep.

A hut of timber and mud was to be my home. It was small, even for a hovel, measuring only a few paces on each side, with a roof so low a man could not stand upright. Even so, it was sturdy. The walls and roof were split logs, the chinks and gaps between them stuffed with moss mixed with mud. There was room inside to lie down fully stretched, but for little else. Nor did I have this bucolic villa to myself, for I was apprentice shepherd to an ancient, grizzled, half-wild pagan named Madog.

Old Madog was, or had once been, a Briton. He had lived the life of a slave so long he could not remember whence he came to Éire. He could still speak a few words of the British tongue and some of the Irish, but could no longer tell the difference between them—a fact which, however frustrating, at least made our discussions blessedly brief. Not that he ever had much to say. His life was his flock: leading them out by day, gathering them in by night, and watching over them all the time in between—the only variation provided by the occasional sick cow brought up from the herd for special treatment.

Gray, thin, tough as boiled leather, Madog roamed the mountain trackways barefoot, bounding like a ram over the rills and rocks, arms flapping in his sleeveless mantle of rags, his toothless whistle resounding from the crooks and crannies, his inane cackle echoing through the empty heights. Bare-headed in every weather, he stood out with his flock, his brain teeming with half-mad thoughts and queer observations that kept him chuckling to himself for days on end.

He had a crook, which he had fashioned from a bound hazel sapling, a flint knife that he had also made, and a small iron caldron. His only other possession was a flint-and-steel striker tied to a leather loop, hung on a knot inside the door of the bothy and used only in the rarest circumstance to light the fire when the embers had gone out and could not be coaxed to life once more. Because the meadow was surrounded on all sides by thick forest, we enjoyed a ready supply of firewood and kept the fire going day and night—as much for warmth and something to do as to keep any preying animals away from the nearby sheepfold.

Every so often someone would come up from the settlement and bring us bread—hard black loaves that we hacked to pieces with Madog's flint knife and soaked in warm water to make edible—and other bits of food: a turnip or two, a few leeks or onions, some beer. This we added to our usual fare, which was, without fail, mutton. Madog knew his sheep well, and he knew which ewes were past bearing and which would not make it through the next cold season. These he culled from the flock, supplying the ráth and giving us a fair store of meat, some of which was boiled or roasted and eaten with sea salt and mountain thyme, and the rest salted and dried in the sun.

Over the first few days he showed me what was expected of a shepherd in the keep of Lord Miliucc. I applied myself to the work and found it not overtaxing, but the pleasures of sitting on a damp rock watching sheep all day soon palled, and I began to yearn for other ways to occupy myself. Thus I swiftly turned my attention to planning my escape.

Miliucc's realm lay, as I say, in the northwestern part of Éire, no great distance from the coast. From the upper heights of our mountain perch I could glimpse the flat, iron-colored northern sea. Once or twice I even saw ships—small, coast-crawling vessels, but ships nonetheless—and reckoned that there must be a port or fishing settlement somewhere within reach. I need only locate the port, and I would find a ship to take me home.

All that remained was to choose the right time. It would have to be soon, I considered, before the winds of autumn brought an end to sea travel. I had no wish to spend a cold winter on the mountainside in the company of Madog and his sheep.

While I waited, I readied myself as best I could. Obtaining a food ration proved no difficulty; I merely helped myself from Madog's store of dried mutton and hid it where I could quickly recover it again. Water was more of a problem. I would need enough for two or three days, I reckoned, but had nothing in which to carry it. I set about devising a container from wood. I made a hand axe out of a piece of flint recovered from a streambed and tried hollowing out a chunk of half-rotten log, but gave up after several inept attempts.

As it happened, Madog saw what I was doing and misunderstood my purpose. One evening as we were sitting outside the hut by the fire, he rose and went in, returning a moment later with a thin, white, misshapen leathery bag, which he gave to me, indicating with winks and pointing that I should hang it around my neck.

I did so, and he cackled happily. "Da, da!" he said. "Da!" This outburst signified his approval. Then, winking and pointing, he began jigging around the water stoup—a large stone basin filled by the tiny trickle from a spring that welled up from an outcropping of rock beside the bothy. I could not make out what the old idiot intended until at last he pulled me up and, taking the bag, plunged it into the water. Then I understood: It was a waterskin. Made from the bladder of a sheep, it would hold, I imagined, three or four days' scant ration of water.

I filled the thing and was pleased to discover that it did indeed hold water admirably well. Grinning to signify my pleasure, I thanked Madog with a bow, which set the old addlepate chuckling and gurgling in delight all the rest of the night.

The next day dawned clear and bright, and I decided that the time had come. As soon as Madog had gone to take the sheep to the meadow, I gathered my provisions and set off walking toward the coast, keeping to the sheep trails until I was out of sight of the valley, then made my way down to the river and followed it to the coast, reaching the shore a little after midday.

Now came the difficult part of my plan, for I had no clear idea which way to go. I had hoped on reaching the coast to be able to see the port or some other settlement, but this was not to be. I looked long in either direction and saw only the rough, rocky shoreline and the towering headlands beyond, and no port in sight. So, lacking any better guide, I decided to take my chances and head north.

Following the craggy coast, I walked quickly and steadily, pausing every now and then to look back in case I should be followed and laughing at the ignorance of my barbarian captors. That escape should be so easy showed how utterly unthinking they were.

The day passed without my meeting anyone or encountering any settlements. With the gathering twilight, clouds sailed in on a keen northerly wind, and it seemed best to find shelter for the night. I chose a hollow in an outcropping of rock at the base of a cliff a short distance up from the shore. From my shallow cave I could see a fair distance down the beach in both directions and would have plenty of time to hide if anyone should come along.

As darkness fell, so did the rain; in great, gushing torrents it fell. My hollow in the rocks kept out most of the water but none of the wind, which scoured the cave the whole night long. Sleep was all but impossible, and I did not wait for the dawn before setting off again as soon as the storm had ceased. I walked until sunrise, and then stopped and ate a bit of dried mutton and drank fresh rainwater from a pool in a rock.

A great deal of seaweed had been heaved ashore on the waves during the night, making the rocky shingle slippery. Skirting the worst stretches and proceeding with care over the rest, I at last reached a sheer rock wall that had its foundations deep in the sea. The strand on which I had been walking came to an abrupt end. I had no choice but to cross over the top of the headland. Although it cost me considerable time, I retraced my steps until I found a place to climb up without too much difficulty, and so began the ascent.

My effort was crowned with success; from the high ground the shoreline stretched out below and, a short distance to the east, settlement. A small place, little more than a handful of huts set above the high-tide mark on the edge of a wood, it seemed a very haven to me. What is more, there were three boats on the beach. I hunkered down to watch the dwellings for a while, to see what might be learned.

When no one appeared, I moved down the hill for a closer look. After a time a woman came out of one of the huts accompanied by a child. They walked to the edge of the water, where the child splashed in the shallow sea while the mother gathered seaweed. When she had collected enough, she called the little one to her, and they disappeared into the hut again. No one else appeared after that. So, taking my fate in my hands, I went down.

Warily I approached the settlement, passing the first huts without rousing any attention. When I came even with the hut in which the woman and child dwelled, I paused and called out in a loud voice, "Pax vobiscum!"

I shouted twice more before I saw the woman's thin face peering out from the low doorway. As I had no weapons and was obviously a stranger, she eventually came out, advancing hesitantly and looking around to see if I might be accompanied by anyone. I smiled and talked gently to reassure her and, pointing to the boats, made gestures to indicate my wish to be taken up the coast to the nearest port.

She frowned mightily, shook her head, and jabbered at me in her incomprehensible tongue, then flung her hands at me as if to drive away a bothersome dog. I persisted in trying to make myself understood, but to no avail. Finally she pointed out toward the sea, where a boat was just then making for shore. There were three men in the boat, and the foremost of these leaped out and waded to meet us as soon as the keel touched the shingle.

A tall, gaunt, weather-beaten son of the sea, he greeted me, presumably—it was difficult to tell from his rough speech—and I repeated my greeting and indicated the boats. Thus, by means of pointing and gestures, I conveyed my wish to be taken to the nearest port. To my immense satisfaction, the ignorant fellow agreed. He called to the others, who were pulling the boat onto the shingle; they stopped at once, and the fisherman beckoned me to follow. They held the boat while I climbed in, then pushed off once more.

Taking up the oars, the two others applied themselves to rowing while the third man steered, and I sat on the small bench in the center of the craft with my waterskin on my knees. They rowed with solid strokes, proceeding up the coast as soon as we gained deeper water.

The sea was still somewhat high after the storm of the night before, but they stood to their work, and we soon rounded the headland to the north of the settlement. There in the distance, beneath the sheltering brow of a high promontory, lay the port.

With each strong pull of the oars, our destination came nearer. I sat on my bench exulting in my shrewdness and mastery. With the first fair wind, I would be on my way home once more.

The little seaport was an untidy aggregation of hovels and houses large and small, all of which seemed to encircle the standing stone that marked the center of the town. Despite its diminutive size, the holding boasted a sturdy timber wharf for larger boats and ships; as we came nearer, I was pleased to see that there were two of these tied up there. Many other smaller vessels lined the pebbled shingle, and we soon joined them.

As the boat touched the shore, the foremost fisherman called out to a group of men standing on the wharf. These, I reckoned, belonged to one of the ships, and as they took an interest in me, I addressed them politely and asked if anyone spoke Latin. "*Latinum loquamini?*" I asked several times. They made no reply, so I pointed out to sea. "*Britannia,*" I said, repeating the word until the light of understanding dawned on them.

They regarded me closely, talking among themselves the while. They seemed to come to a favorable conclusion, and two of the men ran off toward one of the larger houses, where, at their summons, a white-haired man emerged. He looked out to where we were standing and beckoned us to attend him.

That this old rogue was head man of the town I had no doubt. He looked at me, nodding with satisfaction at what he saw. "Pax vobiscum," I said, offering him a bow of deference. "I give you good greeting."

He grunted and, lifting a hand, pointed out to sea. "*Prytani?*" he said.

I smiled and nodded. "Yes, Brittania. My home. I wish to go there."

He smiled and nodded in return. "Prytani." He spoke to the fisherman and the others, who replied, and, dismissing them, beckoned me to join him in his house. I supposed it was to observe some formality of hospitality, so I agreed, hoping we would soon come to terms regarding my passage.

The house stank of dogs and rotting fish, but I followed him in; a table and chair stood next to an open hearth in the center of the single room. He bade me sit in the chair and poured out a drink of sour beer. He drank and passed the wooden bowl to me. Not wishing to offend him, I held my breath and took a drink, quickly relinquishing the bowl when I had finished. He pointed to my waterskin, so I unslung the strap from around my shoulder and offered it to him. He examined it approvingly and tried a drink, grinning as he returned it.

An old woman came in, and he sent her scurrying away; she returned a short time later with a small round loaf of bread, which she put on the table, and hurried off again. The man indicated that I should eat, which I reluctantly did, for although I did not like to make myself beholden to these barbarians, I was hungry and I could not risk offending them in any way.

I ate, tearing off pieces of bread, chewing slowly, smiling, and drinking from the beer bowl. Meanwhile, the old man busied himself at the hearth and soon had a fire kindled. The old woman reappeared with a dish containing three cleaned and gutted fish. With practiced efficiency the old man spitted them and set them to cook over the fire. Fearing to interrupt their meal—and not wishing to stay in any event—I stood, thanked my host, and started for the door. The old man jumped up and, with smiles and nods of reassurance, led me back to my place at the table.

He sat me down, pointed to the bread, and made eating motions. He poured more beer and placed the bowl in my hands. I drank, and he went back to tending the fish on the fire. In a little while the food was cooked, and he brought the plate to the table. He selected a fish and offered one to me. We sat down together then—he on a stone by the hearth, I in his chair—and ate our simple meal.

The fish was a change from mutton; it tasted good and, with the bread and beer, made a passable meal. Indeed, I would have welcomed another morsel or two but for a commotion that commenced outside just then. There came a shout and then the sound of voices and people running. The next thing I knew, there appeared in the doorway a huge, black-haired warrior with a sword in his hand.

Two strides carried him into the room, where he stood over me looking down impassively. Before I could think what to do, he took hold of the ring at the back of my torc and pulled me to my feet. The old man looked on with a self-satisfied grin. "You scabby old toad," I spat.

He cackled in reply—which I did not, of course, understand—and, lifting a hand, lay a filthy finger on my slave torc and laughed. Until that moment, I had not given the iron collar a thought.

The warrior marched me outside, where the entire population of the fishing village had gathered. Two more warriors stood waiting to receive us and, as we emerged from the house, the foremost of these stepped forward and honored the old man with a curious salute, touching the back of his hand to his forehead. Then, reaching into a leather bag at his belt, he withdrew two small sticks of gold. He broke both of these in half and gave half of one to the old man; the others he gave to the fishermen who had brought me to the village in their boat.

While the villagers and fisherfolk rejoiced, the warriors returned to their horses, dragging me with them. They mounted, and I was slung like a sack of grain across the front of the big warrior's horse and hauled in disgrace back to Miliucc's ráth.

7

THE DISCOMFORT OF my return was nothing to the humiliation I felt in being captured again so easily, for just beyond the sea bluffs behind the fishing settlement, the Vale of Braghad opened, and at the far end of it lay King Miliucc's ráth. I had traveled many times the distance around the coast, only to bring myself to a harbor I could have reached on an easy walk the morning of my escape.

My cheeks burned with shame at the recognition of my own witlessness—made all the worse for the realization that my slave collar had given me away. How could I have been so stupid?

Then again, was it stupidity or arrogance which had led me to believe escape would be so effortlessly accomplished?

Both, I concluded: stupidity and arrogance in equal, ample measure. Here was the clever and resourceful Succat, so proud, so assured, full of scorn at the brute ignorance of the barbarians, now returned in disgrace. The warriors had not even broken a sweat to retrieve me. I could have wept at my foolishness, except I did not wish to show any such emotion before my captors.

We soon reached the hill fort, and I was presented to my lord, who, without so much as a cursory glance in my direction, called a command to his men, who seized me by the arms and set about beating me with their fists. I took a blow to the stomach that doubled me over; allowing me to collapse, they proceeded to kick me. I lay on the ground, trying to protect my head with my arms as blow after blow rained down upon me. There was no anger in it, merely skilled, dispassionate efficiency as they aimed and placed their kicks at the muscled areas of my body. When this had gone on for a time, Miliucc called another command, and the kicking ceased.

I thought they would release me then, but they took hold of my legs and stripped off my boots, and while two warriors held me by the ankles, the third began striking me on the soles of my feet with a stout willow wand. I had never felt such pain before. With each blow new and amazing sensations of agony shocked through me. Tears streamed from my eyes, and though I tried not to cry out, the pain tore scream after ragged scream from my throat.

When they finally stopped, I lay limp and sobbing on the ground. The king came and stood over me, spoke a few harsh words, and gestured for the warriors to take me away. I was put back on the horse and ridden up the mountain, where I was dumped outside the shepherd's bothy. They rode off, and I lay on the ground, whimpering, throbbing, unable to even drag myself inside.

Madog returned at dusk and found me still curled on the ground. He made clucking noises while he examined my feet, then dipped out some water for me from the stone basin and set about building up the fire. When he had the blaze going, he brought out the caldron, filled it with water, and put it on a stone at the fire's edge. Too sore and miserable to move, I lay on my side and watched as he took his flint knife and cut one of his precious onions into pieces, which he put into the pot along with a few handfuls of dried mutton, some barley, and a sprinkling of leafy herbs and salt.

He settled himself on a large round stone beside the fire ring to stir the pot. Every now and then he would look at me and shake his head. I could see he felt sorry for me, and I was grateful for this sympathy; mute though it was, it comforted me somewhat. I rolled onto my back and lay there listening to the crackling fire and watching the stars kindle in the cloudless sky. In a little while the caldron began to steam and boil, filling our rude courtyard with the scent of mutton stew. When it was finished, Madog dipped out the stew into two wooden bowls. He broke pieces of black bread into the bowls and brought me one.

I had no appetite for supper, but he placed the bowl beside my head and indicated that I should take some. As I did not wish to spurn his kindness, I raised myself up on my elbows and, taking the bowl in both hands, lifted it to my mouth. The stew quickly disappeared, and I found my spirits considerably improved.

Sufficiently strengthened, I dragged myself into the bothy and went to sleep, waking the next morning at dawn. Madog had already gone with the sheep to the meadow. I lay for a while, taking stock of my bruises. Sitting up brought tears to my eyes, and it was some time before I dared move again. Eventually, I got myself outside. The embers were still hot, so I tossed some twigs onto the coals and soon had the fire going once more. A little stew remained in the pot, so I pulled it close to the fire to let it warm.

Meanwhile, I tried to examine my feet. Bending my stiff, aching limbs was difficult; even the slightest movement sent pain racing through me. Eventually, I got one leg crossed over the other and turned my foot so I could see the underside. What I saw made me gasp: the sole was a mass of purple welts and puffed up so much it was almost round. In one or two places the swollen skin had broken, and a thin watery pus wept from the wound. I touched the broken flesh lightly as tears came to my eyes, and I cried for my poor ruined feet.

As I cradled my foot and sobbed softly, the full import of my condition came crashing down. The death and destruction unleashed on my homeland that dire and dreadful night—brutal, swift, and terrible, easily overwhelming the inadequate British defenses—the burning, the killing, the rampaging destruction of whole cities defied belief. Whether my parents were alive or dead, I knew not—nor did they know my fate. If they lived, they might well think me dead. The thought would hasten my softhearted mother to her grave if she was not there already.

My friends—Rufus, Scipio, Julian—had they escaped? Most likely they had been caught and held for ransom in Britain. Or, perhaps like me, sold into slavery to some Irish king. No doubt they were facing the same tribulation I faced now.

All this and more settled like a mountain upon my bruised and aching shoulders, bending me low to the ground. I eased myself down and lay with my arm across my face, feeling the immense weight of a limitless grief crushing the spirit within me into a hard, stonelike kernel.

I was utterly alone. I knew that now. Many were dead, but I was alive, and while I was alive, I would hold my life in my own two hands, trusting no one but myself. Friends deserted, kinsmen failed, God ever turned his hard face away, and in the end each man must look to himself for his own survival.

The rising sun warmed me where I lay, and after a while I felt well enough to raise myself up and sit straight-legged on the ground. Pulling the caldron close, I ate some of the leftover stew and looked around. The day was bright, the sky clean and wide and filled with high, white clouds. Birds darted among the branches of the trees behind the bothy, spilling liquid song into the soft summer air. The quiet of our mountain retreat was a balm to my battered heart, and I embraced it, willing it to do its healing work.

Thirsty upon finishing the stew, I decided to try to stand. Carefully, achingly, I drew my legs beneath me and touched the soles of my feet to the ground. Pain, as fierce and angry as ever before, stole the breath from my lungs. I lay back gasping and panting until the agony subsided, then rolled onto my stomach and, on hands and knees, crawled to the water stoup, pulled myself up, slid the cover aside, and drank, laving water into my mouth with one hand while bracing myself on the side of the basin with the other.

When I finished, I washed my face and then eased myself down to sit in the sun with my back against the bothy wall. Two things were now clear in my mind: I would have to learn to speak a little of the confounded Irish tongue—enough to express simple needs at least—and I would have to find a way to remove my slave collar or disguise it in some way. Then, and only then, could I contemplate another attempt at escape.

I spent the rest of the day deep in thought, and when Madog returned at dusk, I set to work.

He was pleased to see me sitting up. He squatted to look at my feet, frowned, and shook his head sadly. As he sat back on his heels, I placed my hand squarely on my chest and said, "Succat," repeating this a few times until he said it for himself.

I pointed to him. With childlike glee he patted himself on his chest and said, "Madog." He repeated this many times for me, although I was pronouncing it correctly the second time he said it.

I pointed to the fire. "*Ignis.*" Then, since he did not understand Latin, I added, "*Tán*" thinking he might remember the British word.

"*Tine,*" he replied, repeating it happily.

The similarity of the words instantly buoyed my hopes. If the two languages were so close, the Irish tongue would be easily mastered, for I possessed a great store of British words, since it was what most of the servants and farmers spoke on our estate. Pointing to the hut behind us, I said, "*Tugurium.*" Madog frowned, so I abandoned Latin altogether and said, "*Bwth.*"

Delight lit the old shepherd's wrinkled face. "*Bothán!*" he cried, almost hugging himself with excitement.

I smiled, too, elated at the easy similarity between the two tongues. Next I pointed to the water basin. "*Cerwyn.*" Madog frowned, so I tried another word: "*Cawg.*"

He repeated the word and then paused. Pointing, his mouth working, he rolled his eyes and tapped his head, but the word would not come. At last the effort proved too much, and he threw his hands into the air and grunted in defeat. That was the end of our exercise.

Next day, however, he returned to the bothy with a wide grin of triumph on his ruddy, weather-creased face. *"Dabhach!"* he exclaimed, pointing to the water stoup. *"Dabhach . . . dabhach!"* Plunging his hands into the basin, he scooped up water and let it dribble through his fingers saying, *"Uisce!"*

"Uisce," I repeated, then tried the British word: *"Dwfr?"*

"Da! Uisce, da!" he said triumphantly.

My heart fell. Neither word was remotely similar. In truth, the Irish tongue might not be so easily learned as I had allowed myself to imagine. But there was nothing for it. Casting discouragement aside, I repeated the words until I could say them to Madog's satisfaction.

This proved a durable game for him. Over the next days he pillaged his raddled memory for more words he could teach me. When he ran dry, I suggested some, pointing to the sky, the sheep, the forest, a stick, a rock— anything near to hand. Often his face would squeeze itself into a fist of thought in his strain to remember, and sometimes the word would pop out. Other times, he would go stumping off to the sheepfold, head down, shoulders bent by the weight of cogitation, returning sometime later with the word he had dredged up from the murky depths of remembrance.

In my idle times, of which there were many, I recited the words to myself, repeating them until my tongue grew numb in my mouth. As the days and weeks went by, I gradually built up a knowledge of the barbarian speech, adding more and more words as Madog was able to supply them. I knew that to speak properly I would one day have to find another to teach me; until then, I worked the old shepherd mercilessly. I made him tell me numbers, colors; the names of animals, plants, and parts of the body; the words for simple actions, for smells, for emotions, for anything and everything I could think to ask.

For his part, Madog warmed to the chore and surprised both of us by his increasing abilities to remember. The more we worked, the greater grew his capacities; words came back to him—often in a rush, as if a disused spring suddenly gushed forth with long-pent waters. On these occasions he danced around the fire ring flapping his arms with infantile delight.

One day I tried my speech on one of the women of the ráth; she had brought us some bread and turnips, for which I thanked her. She looked a little astonished but smiled pleasantly and said something which I did not follow. But I took the bread and said, *"Arán."*

Still smiling, she replied, *"Is ea siúd."*

"It is that," I repeated.

Next she took up a turnip and held it between her hands. *"Tornapa rúta."*

I dutifully repeated the word and thanked her, saying, *"Go raibh maith agat do na tornapa rúta."*

She laughed and took her leave, calling something over her shoulder as she went. I did not know what she said, but considered my accomplishment a triumph and added the new words to my growing store.

The day finally came when I was able to walk comfortably again, and I accompanied Madog to the hillside to watch the sheep. We spent the day practicing our speech together; on the way back to the bothy, he turned to me and said in the Irish tongue, "This is good."

"It is that," I agreed.

"I am here many *samhradh*," he said.

"Many . . . *samhradh*? What is *samhradh*?"

"Now," replied Madog. "This." He waved an arm to indicate the world around, his gesture taking in the forest, sky, and meadow.

The meaning came to me: "Summer," I said. "How many summers?"

He was silent for a time, and I could see him working it out in his mind. But the calculation eluded him, and at last he gave it up, shaking his head slowly. Our elemental conversation cast him into a pensive mood. He ate little that night and went to sleep without speaking again; next morning I heard the sheep bleating before dawn and woke to see that Madog had gone. I rose later to a light rain and went out to the grazing land, where I found him hunched on a rock in the rain, his crook across his lap.

He was working with something, and as I drew nearer, I saw that he had his flint knife and was carving notches on the shaft of his crook. I greeted him and watched as he carefully carved a new notch beside the last, brushed the chipping aside, and rubbed it with his fingers. Then, starting with the first notch, he moved his thumbnail along the row of notches to the end.

Absorbed in this task, he paid no attention to me, so I walked out to where the sheep were grazing, picking up a stick along the way. Around midday the rain stopped and the sun came out. I returned to the rock, where Madog still sat.

The flint knife lay on the ground, having slipped from his hand, and he sat gripping the crook, staring at the notches he had made.

"Finished?" I asked.

He raised his head, and I saw the tears running down his face. "*Triocha is ocht.*"

It took me a moment to work out what he meant. "Thirty-eight?" I asked. And then it came to me. I knelt down before him and ran my finger along the neat row of notches: the years of his captivity. He had been a slave for thirty-eight years.

"A long time," I told him. He nodded but said nothing.

I left him to himself and returned to the sheep. Every now and then I glanced over to the rock where he sat, wrapped in misery for the waste of his life.

I vowed I would escape—or die trying. I would choose death a thousand times before I allowed myself to become like Madog.

I labored at my words and speech with a diligence born of insatiable ambition, practicing night and day, plundering Madog's memory tirelessly, amassing a trove of words like a jealous miser. Summer was moving on; the days were growing shorter, the nights cooler. If I was to make another attempt at escape, it would have to be soon—or wait until next spring, and I could not abide the thought of spending the winter on a freezing mountainside watching a flock of poxy sheep.

At last I judged my knowledge of the Irish tongue sufficient; I felt I would be able to make myself understood wherever I went. I knew, too, which direction to avoid. All that remained was to find a way to disguise my slave torc.

I had tried from time to time to remove the collar, but I was not strong enough to bend the cold iron. I pondered this problem while I busied myself weaving a bag out of the tough grass which grew down along the riverbank in the valley where we sometimes took the sheep to drink. I had often watched the servants at home weave such bags, and though I had never done it myself, after several attempts I soon mastered the skill. When the bag was ready, I set about gathering the food I would need, tucking away bits and pieces, taking scraps when Madog was not looking. I saved a fair quantity of dried meat, hard bread, nuts, and such and was soon ready—save for the problem of the torc.

In the end I could do no better than to cover it. This I did by pulling up my tunic and tying it at the neck with a strip of cloth ripped from the hem. The twisted metal ends protruded at the front, and the ring stuck out at the back, but at least it was out of sight. I thought that if chance allowed, I might get a cloak somehow and, by pulling it up around my head, hide the thing better that way.

The next day dawned wet and cool. I made up the fire and heated some gruel in the caldron. Madog and I sat in the rain, dipping bread into the soup and watching the clouds. It looked like clearing by midday, so when Madog left to take the sheep to the meadow, I made a pretense of building up the fire and cleaning the caldron. As soon as he had gone, I picked up my bag of provisions and made my escape.

8

WALKED TO THE sea, following the same track as before, keeping well out of sight from the valley below until it passed from view. On the mountainside the wind blew stiff from the west, bearing the taste of sea salt on the heavy, damp air. Upon reaching the coastal headland, I climbed down onto the strand and this time, instead of turning to the right, I turned left.

Again the coast was rocky and wild, with great black humps of tortured stone tumbling into the foamy green water as far as the eye could see. The wind whipped hard off the sea, driving a light, misty rain into my eyes. I was soon wet to the skin and so decided to stop for a while. I found a crevice in the rocks which offered some protection from the wind and rain, and climbed in to wait until the weather cleared. I curled up, wrapping my arms around my chest to keep warm, and fell asleep.

I woke to bright sunlight pouring down through a hole in the clouds as they churned across the sky. The wind still blew, flinging flecks of sea-foam across the pebbled shore. I rose and began walking, searching the way ahead for any sign of habitation, but the shore was barren, and it was all my own. I walked until the sun began to drift toward the sea, and then sat down to eat a little. I drank rainwater from a hollow in a rock before moving on.

I had gone only a few dozen paces when I heard a dog bark behind me. I turned to see three riders in the distance. Led by the dog, they were cantering along the sea strand.

Turning, I scanned the cliffs above. They were steep and high, but I reckoned I could climb them—or at least hide in one of the many deeply seamed crevices until the riders had passed by. Wasting not an instant, I scrambled up the nearest rill and reached an eroded pocket, where I stopped and tucked myself inside.

The riders followed my footprints to the cliffside. I could hear the hound barking below and the voices of the men as they discussed the matter, but I did not risk a look to see what they were doing. The barking quickly ceased, and all was silent once more. I waited. And then, hearing no more, I leaned out for a quick glance below; a single rider remained: judging by his clothing and weapons, a warrior, most likely from Miliucc's war band. His two companions and the dog had gone; I could not see them but assumed they had continued on down the beach.

Quietly, and with the utmost stealth, I edged my way higher up the crevice. I had gained a fair distance when my hand closed on a loose rock that came away in my grasp. The rock fell, alerting the rider on the ground. He looked up, saw me, and raced back to the cliff face, dismounted, and began climbing.

He was the bigger man, but I was quicker. Hand over hand I pulled myself up the ragged face of the cliff, scrambling as fast as I could, letting the rocks fall to hinder my pursuer as they would.

Sweating and out of breath, I reached the top and, with a last great effort, dragged myself up over the edge and into the long grass. Gathering my legs beneath me, I raced straight across the grassy plain for the line of trees a short distance ahead. I was halfway there when out from the wood charged the two missing riders. The hound uttered a long, baying cry. I turned and raced back toward the seacliff, hoping to descend another way before the riders could cut off my retreat.

Just as I reached the edge, the pursuing warrior appeared. He clambered up the rest of the way, and I dived for the slope a few paces to his right. My descent abruptly halted when I felt myself caught by the tunic. Thinking that a root had snagged me, I tried to jerk free and was instead hauled back up and over the rim of the cliff and flung like a bag of fish onto the grass.

The warrior stood over me, scowling, breathing hard from his exertion.

The hooves of the horses drummed on the thick turf. The warrior looked up as the others galloped in. His attention momentarily diverted, I lashed out with my foot and caught him behind the knee; he toppled backward. I rolled onto my stomach and, squirming, diving, scrambled for the edge of the cliff once more—only to be caught by the leg and dragged back.

The one who had caught me raised his arm to hit me, but I shouted. "I am King Miliucc's man!"

At these words the foremost rider called an order to his comrade. The warrior let his fist fall, aiming for my head. I threw my hands up, and he struck my arm. I shouted again, and the rider called, "Cernach! Stop!"

My captor hesitated, still glaring murderously at me. He made a reply I could not understand.

"He is King Miliucc's man," the rider said.

"The king's *daor*," sneered the warrior, meaning "slave."

"Then it is for the king to punish him. It will be dark soon." With that the rider wheeled his horse and began riding away.

Cernach gave a growl of frustration, reached down, and yanked me roughly to my feet, shaking me once or twice for spite. He dragged me to the second rider, who passed him down a length of braided leather rope with which he tied my hands. Thus secured, I was led away, and Cernach disappeared over the cliffside to retrieve his horse on the strand below.

It was dark before we reached the ráth. Even so, I was taken to stand in the yard outside the king's hall. Larger than all the others, it housed his queen and children and some of the more intimate members of his retinue, which I estimated to be twelve or fifteen men, mostly warriors. Upon our arrival they all came spilling out of the hall to gather behind the king, who stood in the flickering torchlight, gazing impassively at me.

After a moment he said, "My slaves do not escape." Just that, nothing more. But I understood. He lifted his hand, and four great brutes of warriors advanced bearing stout branches pulled from the fire.

The foremost approached and swung at my head with the flaming brand. I ducked as the flame whiffled through the air. He swung again, and I dodged to the side, but my hands were still tied and the warrior on the other end of the rope pulled tight so I could not move as freely as I might. A second man approached from the side, swinging at me. I darted away, and he missed, but the first warrior caught me a glancing blow on the shoulder. The searing heat made me cry out.

Sparks flew from the end of the firebrand, and this delighted the crowd, which now consisted of the entire population of the ráth. A third warrior, taking up a position behind me, thrust his torch at my legs. The fourth joined the others to form a loose circle around me, and they began taking it in turn to swipe at me with their burning torches.

I moved to the side and kept moving, dodging and feinting as the fiery cudgels whirled around me. The circle tightened, and the strikes came faster.

A blow caught me on the arm and another on the hip. The crowd roared its approval. I kept moving, circling. The firebrands riffled and fluttered in the air. I could feel the heat on my skin when they passed near. More and more often they found their mark—one struck my hand, another found my shin, my back, my side. Each strike left a burn mark on my ragged clothing or skin. The rope prevented me from evading all the blows, but I stayed on my feet and kept moving—eluding one brand only to have another catch me. One of the warriors struck me hard on the shoulder, and another landed a solid thump to my chest. The flames licked my throat.

The circle tightened further. I could no longer avoid the swift-flying branches, and the warriors began striking at will. I covered my face with my arms and tried to keep moving, but my feet soon tangled, and I fell. I climbed to my knees. The rope jerked taut, dragging me forward.

The strokes were coming thick and fast now. One after another. Crack! Crack! Crack! Again and again. They stood over me, raining fiery blows. I curled into a ball and rolled in the dirt to keep from getting my clothes and hair set alight.

The beating proceeded with rhythmic precision—as if they were chopping wood, hoeing weeds, or thrashing grain. Even when, one by one, the firebrands went out, the men beat me with the smoldering ends. They were not glancing blows now but solid, hurtful thumps and knocks. I ground my teeth to keep from crying out and endured the pain as best I could.

Just when I thought I could take no more, the king spoke a word, and the frenzied thumping stopped. They lifted me to my feet, but I could not stand, so they dragged me to one of the nearby horses and threw me across the back of the beast. As before, I was carried up the mountainside and dropped outside the shepherd's bothy.

Madog emerged from the hut as soon as the warriors had gone; he stood for a time clucking his tongue and shaking his head. Then he built up the fire and fetched some water from the stoup. I drank and eased my battered body into a more comfortable position. Madog sat with me for a little while, but as there was nothing he could do, he gave soon up and went back to bed.

I lay by the fire and felt the fierce ache spread through my body—one weal melding with another until I was a single great palpitating bruise. I closed my eyes and tried to sleep but could not for the pain.

Thus I lay awake all night, unable to move, watching the fire and wishing I had that arrogant king and his cowardly warriors trussed up and spitted to turn slowly over the flames. I would listen to their screams, exulting in their agony as I tossed more sticks onto the fire.

Morning found me still awake but incoherent with pain. My limbs had grown stiff, and I could not move. The fire had burned to embers, and I was cold, but it hurt too much to try to reach more fuel, so I stared at the cooling ashes until Madog awoke and came out. He built up the fire again, gave me another drink, and then left to take the sheep out to the grazing land. Before he departed, he paused to stand over me one last time.

"You should not run away," he said, then turned on his heel and moved off, leaving me to my torment.

He did not speak to me that night when he returned, nor the next morning either. This, I concluded, was my punishment for leaving him. During the day the shadow of the high trees drew across me as I lay there on the ground, and it was to me the shadow of a powerful guilt: not for trying to escape my slavery—I would do that again in an instant—no, I felt guilty for deserting Madog, for running away without a word of farewell.

My coming had been the saving of him, in a way. Under my urging he had recovered more and more of himself—his speech, his memories, his life. My companionship—contemptible, selfish thing that it was—had nevertheless allowed him to regain some small, sacred shred of his former humanity. Running away again as I did had shown him just how little I cared about him. He liked me, he honored me, and I esteemed him not at all. He knew that now, and it cut him deep.

I dozed through the day, my conscience squirming with shame, and awoke as the sun passed behind the western ridge of the mountains. Although it hurt to do so, I roused myself and sat up, nearly swooning from the pain. I dragged myself to the water stoup, drank and washed my face, and then crawled to the woodpile and pulled out some loose sticks and branches to feed the fire.

Each of these simple chores required a rest until the pain subsided and I could breathe again. I pulled up my tunic and looked at myself. Chest, ribs, and stomach were a lumpy mass of bluish-black bruises; likewise my thighs, shins, and arms. My once-handsome clothes were blackened from soot and singed through in a dozen places. The warriors had been most thorough in their beating; there was scarcely a place on my whole body where I could put a finger without touching discolored flesh. And when I could not put it off any longer, I got up to pass water; it hurt so much I could hardly unbuckle my belt, and when I was at last able to relieve myself, I was alarmed to see that my piss ran red with blood.

I sat down and cried. When the tears ceased, I crawled back to my place by the fire and dragged more fuel to the flames. By the time Madog returned with the sheep, I had a fine fire going once more. A small thing, but it pleased the old shepherd to see that, battered as I was, I had at least made an effort to help with the daily chores.

He brought with him a lamb that had fallen from the rocks earlier in the day and broken its back. He had put the poor creature out of its misery, skinned and cleaned it with his flint knife, and brought the carcass back to the bothy for us to eat. I watched as he quartered it and put two meaty haunches on spits.

We sat opposite one another across the fire ring as the sky grew dark, watching the meat sizzle, turning the spit from time to time, smelling the oily smoke, and listening to the rooks croak and call as they flocked to their treetop roosts. As the meat cooked, we pulled juicy bits from the spitted haunches and ate.

"Where did you go?" asked Madog at last. The smoke swirled up from the roasting meat, rising silvery blue in the evening air.

I looked up to see him watching me across the flames. "To the sea."

He shook his head gently. "They will always catch you there."

I accepted this in silence, and we sat for a while longer. The first stars came out, and the moon peeped through the high, thin clouds. "Did you ever try to escape?" I asked.

"No," he said. "But if I did, I would not go to the sea. They will always catch you there."

"Where would *you* go?"

He looked down and busied himself with the spit.

"Please, Madog," I said, "tell me. If you wanted to escape, where would you go?"

He thought for a moment. "I would go that way," he said, indicating with a jerk of his head the unseen mountains rising behind us.

"Into the forest?"

He nodded.

"But that would be very . . . ah . . . ," I faltered, searching for the word.

"*Baolach*," Madog suggested.

"Dangerous? For fear of wolves and such?"

"Aye."

"Then is not escape through the forest a very dangerous thing?"

"It is that," he agreed. "But you can hide. There are many good places, and they will not hunt more than a day or two."

We spent the whole of the night talking and eating, and in this way made peace with one another again. As dawn edged into a low, gray eastern sky, Madog yawned and rose. "I am glad they did not kill you," he said.

The simple, heartfelt sentiment moved me deeply. I thanked him and meant it. He merely nodded and picked up his crook and went down to the sheepfold, lowered the top two timber poles, and led the sheep up the track toward the high meadow. I slept then and did not awake until late in the day. I rose and went to the basin, hobbled and shuffling like an old man, and bent stiffly to remove the cover. I drank and washed and then went into the nearer trees to relieve myself. I was pleased to see that my piss ran clear once more. I knew then that my bruises would heal and I would live to escape another day.

But that day would have to wait until next summer, I concluded. Already the nights were drawing in; soon the gales of autumn would arrive, and none but a fool would trust a boat to the unchancey seas of Mare Hiberniae when the wild wind blows. I would have to spend the winter on the mountain with Madog and his sheep.

The thought produced a melancholy that laid my spirit low. I remembered all that had been taken from me: my home, my family, my friends, the easy life I had known. Down and down I sank, into an unfathomable sadness—a sorrow as full and deep as the sea separating me from my homeland. Away in Britain, I imagined, life had resumed much as before the raid, and I was all but forgotten. Julian, Scipio, and Rufus were riding the coastal road and plaguing the girls at the Old Black Wolf, laughing and drinking, their old friend Succat nothing but a distant, swiftly fading memory.

For two days I lay beside the fire and wallowed in this sick bereavement for my former life, wishing I could by some miraculous power simply rise from my bed and fly across the sea and that all I had lost would be returned to me. I vowed I would escape again as soon as I was well enough to walk. Ah, but no, there was nothing for it. By the time I was hale once more, the ships would be securely anchored in snug harbors awaiting the gentler tides of spring.

I resigned myself to enduring this hardship as best I could, and decided that my time was best spent learning as much as possible about the mountains and forest surrounding our bothy. Thus, when I was well enough to resume my wood-gathering chores, I took to walking farther and farther into the forest, searching out unexplored paths and following them as far as the short days allowed. In this way I gathered a fair knowledge of the place Madog called the Wood of Focluit—a great forest that covered, so far as I could tell, the whole of the northern part of Éire.

All through the bleak, cold days and endless nights of winter, I consoled myself with the thought that by the time the sun reclaimed the heavens for its own, I would be ready.

9

ONE MORNING I awoke to a fine white powdering of frost on the ground and a crisp, cutting edge to the air. Shivering, we rose and built up the fire, and as we went about our chores the dark clouds came in a long line, concealing the tops of the mountains. The air took on a tingling of ice, and I knew that snow would not be long in coming.

I had no cloak, but Madog had saved the fleece of the injured lamb, and, using brine and oak bark, I had tanned this after a fashion; at least it did not stink too badly. Draping this skin over my shoulders and fastening it with a string of plaited rawhide, I busied myself fetching wood, building up our stack, which already towered above the bothy. On my second trip into the forest, I saw a wolf.

Now, I had seen wolves before, once or twice when hunting with Rufus and the others—always at a distance, however, and always running away. This one was young and hungry and unafraid.

I caught sight of its lean, ghostly shape gliding silently among the dark boles of the trees, and I froze, the small hairs prickling on the back of my neck. It is never a good idea to try to outrun a wolf. Huntsmen say it is best to stand your ground and hope for the best.

After circling me several times, the animal disappeared. I dropped the armload of wood I had collected, save for one stout stick which I kept to use as a club. I waited, gripping my weapon and peering into the mist-filled shadows. When the beast did not show itself again, I quickly gathered the wood and made a hasty retreat to the bothy.

As soon as Madog returned, I told him what I had seen.

"Are you certain?"

"I am that," I replied.

He gripped his head with his hands. "This is very bad."

"It was only one," I said, "and a very young one."

"There is never only one," he said, the whites of his eyes showing in the gloom. "They smell the sheep, and they will come for them."

"What should we do?"

"We will build up the fire here and light another down at the entrance to the sheepfold. Then you must go to the ráth and tell the king."

While Madog and I spoke easily enough to one another on most things, there was still much I did not know, and I had little confidence that I could address the king in his own tongue. Also, there was the fact that I was possibly the last person the king wished to see; he had nearly killed me last time we met, and I had no wish to confront him again so soon—even if I could somehow make myself understood. Madog, on the other hand, had become almost garrulous; indeed, he had recovered the greater portion of his speech during our time together.

"Maybe it would be better if *you* went to tell the king," I suggested. "I do not speak well."

Madog dismissed this idea at once. "If the wolves came while I was gone, you would not know what to do."

We carried a double load of logs and branches down to the sheep enclosure and built a large heap before the opening. The walls of the pen were made of stone and topped by a rough timber palisade to keep the sheep from jumping out and predators from climbing in. Once the fire was burning strong, I departed for the ráth, taking a blazing brand for a torch to light my way.

The path down the mountainside to the settlement is well traveled, and even in the dark I had no difficulty. On the way I tried to think of all the words I might possibly need and repeated them to myself over and over again until arriving at the ráth. The gate was closed for the night, and so I had to stand out on the rampart shouting until someone came to see what I wanted. "*Faolchúnna!*" I cried at the first head to peer over the top of the palisade. "Wolves!"

The fellow disappeared, and a few moments later the gate opened and a skinny youth emerged with sword in hand. He looked at me and sneered. "Why are you making this unseemly noise?"

To my relief I understood him clearly enough. "Wolves," I repeated. "Madog says to send warriors."

"The king's warband is at meat," he informed me. "I will not disturb them."

The superior smirk on his face sent a sheet flame of anger flashing through me. I wanted nothing more than to shove my burning torch into his smug barbarian face. Instead I said, "Then I will tell them. I am not afraid."

He made to stop me, but I pushed past and strode directly to the hall, my face hot as the torch in my hand. The door was wooden and covered by an ox hide to better keep out the wind. Throwing aside the skin, I pulled open the door and stepped within.

The air was thick with smoke from a large fire in the center of the hall. A long board lined one wall, with benches on one side, and these were filled with men, their shields and weapons hung on the wall behind them. Young women of the ráth knelt at the edge of the hearth with long flesh forks in their hands, roasting meat, which they brought to the warriors at the board. Other members of the king's retinue reclined on piles of rushes covered with hides and fleeces to form large beds in nooks along the wall opposite the board.

King Miliucc sat at the center of it all surrounded by his warriors. He balanced a drinking bowl in his hand and held it high for the serving boy who stood behind his seat. No one seemed to take the least notice of me, so I moved boldly into the room. The youth from the gate entered behind me and stood sniggering behind his hand as I walked to the board and stopped opposite the king.

"Mo tiarna!" I said in a loud voice. "My lord."

He looked up to see me standing before him and rose to his feet, instantly angry. He slammed down the bowl, splattering its contents. The hall fell silent. I could feel the eyes of everyone on me, but what did I care for that?

"Slaves are not allowed in my house!" he shouted.

I stood to his wrath. "And are wolves allowed in your sheep pen?"

He regarded me with a frown as my meaning broke upon him. "The sheep have been attacked?"

"Madog says to send warriors." Having delivered my message, I turned and walked from the hall; the youth tried to bar my way. I stopped a pace before him and regarded him with searing righteousness.

Slightly taller than myself, he was thinner; his long dark hair hung in a thick braid from the side of his head, and he had a slim gold bracelet high on his right arm next to his elbow. "You smell like a pig," he told me.

I stared back at him, trying to work out what he had said.

"I said," he repeated, enjoying himself extravagantly, "you smell like a pig."

"Better the pig," I replied, "than the pig's turd."

He drew back his hand to strike. I still held the torch and would have hit him with it, but the warriors, having taken up their weapons, came clattering to the door just then. "Lead the way, slave!" roared the foremost warrior, pushing me through the door and into the yard outside.

We hastened up the mountain track to the sheepfold, where Madog stood guard over the flock with his crook in one hand and a firebrand in the other. The warriors looked around and, seeing no wolves, began laughing at him and calling him a cowardly old woman. One of them picked up a stone. "Here, shepherd! I found a wolf!" He tossed the stone. "There, it's gone. I chased it away." The others, half drunk, laughed all the more.

"These wolves of yours, Madog, where are they?" demanded the foremost warrior. He was, I realized, the same man who had prevented Cernach from throttling me when I was captured the second time.

"They are coming, Forgall, never fear," answered the old shepherd, speaking with a fluency that surprised the war chief. "The snow brings them."

As if in answer to this assertion, a long, wavering cry came snaking down from the forest, plaintive as the wail of a lost soul. The warriors fell silent, the laughter dying in their mouths. In a moment the cry was repeated, and another, more distant voice, made a long, ululating reply, echoing out across the valley before drifting off on a falling note of feral loneliness.

"Only a dog that has lost its mate," scoffed Forgall. But I noticed he raised his eyes to the darkling forest and held his breath when the cry came again, slightly closer. "And there is no snow."

"The wolves are coming," insisted Madog. "And so is the snow."

"Perhaps," allowed Forgall, "it would be no bad thing to wait a little."

The howls from the forest grew in frequency and number as they came closer and ever closer; I counted no fewer than eight animals giving voice from just beyond the circle of light thrown out by our fire. The sheep heard the sound and careened around the pen, bleating piteously and leaping over one another, desperate to escape the terrifying sound.

The howling seemed to swirl around us in a weird, unseen dance. We watched and waited and listened but saw not so much as a sliver of firelight reflected in a yellow eye or the glimmer of a curved fang. Still, we waited.

And then there came a snarling growl from behind the sheepfold. Forgall called for two men to follow him; they took up torches and ran around to the back of the pen, shouting and waving their firebrands.

Glimpsing a dark shape moving just out of the circle of the firelight, I yelled and pointed to the place. One of the warriors cried out, "There!" as two more dark forms glided by, drifting into the light. I saw their gray-black shapes slide out of the darkness and melt away again. Another warrior shouted, and suddenly the wolves seemed to be everywhere.

They ran at darting, glancing angles to the fire. Every time one of the phantom creatures appeared out of the darkness, a warrior would charge at it with torch and spear, and the wolf would snarl and disappear. When the sly beasts understood that they could not get us to give chase one at a time, they came at us by twos.

Defense became more difficult then, for the warriors had also to charge at them in twos, which drew strength from the numbers standing guard at the fire. And while we were occupied with guarding the entrance, the wolves turned their attack to the unprotected sides of the sheepfold.

Time and again they came at the pen and were chased away. I saw a large black wolf leap up onto the stone wall and try to climb over the top. I shouted the warning, and one of the younger warriors dashed forward as the animal clawed at the timbers to pull itself up and over. The warrior took aim with his spear and let fly.

I thought it a good throw, but Forgall rounded on his kinsman. "Hold!" he cried as the spear sliced the air just above the wolf's shoulder. The animal jumped down from the wall and bounded away. "You do not throw at a wolf."

"Why?" demanded the youth angrily. "I could have hit him."

"But you did not," replied Forgall. Raising his hand, he pointed into the wolf-ridden darkness. "Now, tell me, who is going to go out there and recover your spear? You, Echu?"

The warrior looked to his swordbrothers for help.

"Well?" demanded Forgall.

Echu shook his head.

"No?" said the big barbarian. "Stupid you may be, Echu, but not a fool. Get away with you. Find a torch and stand over there," he pushed him toward the fire.

So it went, all through the night. Never once did the wolves make an outright attack. They ran here and there, sometimes showing themselves, most often remaining out of sight. And they wailed as if to wake the moon, but we would not be moved.

Finally, as a raw, freezing dawn leaked into the eastern sky, the howling ceased.

When it grew light enough to see the ground, we went to inspect the tracks. Taking flaming branches from the fire, we walked around the perimeter of the sheep pen and up to the bothy and wood beyond, finding no end of tracks—so many that it was impossible to say how large the pack had been.

"Here is the leader!" called Forgall, squatting over a paw print in the mud. Others gathered around as he held his torch near and spread his hand over it. The print was almost as big as his hand.

"It is too big for a wolf," said the warrior called Echu. "It must be a *sídhe.*"

The others laughed at this; although I did not know what Echu meant, it seemed to me the word was spoken only half in jest.

"It will take more than a few changeling sídhe to keep me from my bed," declared Forgall. He rose and turned to Madog, who was leaning exhausted on his crook. "It was good for you to call us when you did," he said. He looked at me and chuckled to himself. "You are a bold one," he declared. "Coming into the king's hall like that . . ." He shook his head as if it were a wonder he could not fathom, and I felt an unaccountable flush of pride warm me head to heel. It was instantly followed by a pang of disgust that I should exult, however trivially, in the praise of a brute barbarian.

Some of the warriors meanwhile had gone to retrieve Echu's errant spear; Forgall called to say that he was ready to leave, and as they started through the trees, he turned to Madog and said, "Perhaps you should bring the sheep down to the ráth tonight."

Madog frowned. "I will think about it."

The warriors departed then; Madog and I watched them descend the mountain track until they were lost in the morning mist. When they had gone, I said, "This word they used—what does it mean?"

The old shepherd lifted his eyes to the forest that was rising like a black, bristly cloud behind us. "Some words it is not wise to speak aloud."

"Echu said it. I only want to know what it means."

"Sídhe," Madog replied, his voice falling to a respectful whisper. "It is the name of a great and terrible race of . . ." He faltered, struggling for the words. "Of folk who delight in destruction and harm. They are full of spells and evil magic to befuddle men."

I rolled my eyes in exasperation. "Madog, these were *wolves*, not magical beings."

"Aye," he agreed uncertainly. "That may be."

He would say no more about it, so we set ourselves to putting out the fire at the entrance to the sheepfold—scattering the branches and throwing dirt on the embers until only a mound of smoldering earth remained. Madog pulled aside the timber poles to open the gate and walked into the pen. The sheep knew him and came to him; they gathered around the lanky old man to have their curly heads rubbed while he soothed them with soft words.

I went back up to the bothy and rekindled the campfire, for it would be a damp, cold day. The snow arrived shortly after sunrise, and soon a fair, even spread of white covered the grass of the high meadow. The near trees looked as if they were wearing woolen mantles, and the upper slopes became spectral, disappearing in a snow-laden mist.

Snow had come early to Sliabh Mis, and already the wolves were gathering. It would be a long winter.

ROUND MIDDAY I trudged up to the high meadow and found Madog half asleep on a snow-covered rock. He started as I drew near. "Hail, Madog Wolf-Fighter," I said, and this made him smile.

I settled beside him on his rock and looked out at the sheep, scraping the snow off the grass with their small hooves. "Maybe we should do as Forgall says," I suggested, "and move down to the ráth tonight."

"I do not like the ráth."

"Nor do I. But at least we can sleep, and the sheep will be safe."

"They will be safe here."

"We could ask the king to send his warriors out to hunt the wolves," I offered. "We could come back when they have been driven off."

"Perhaps." The way he said it gave me to know he had no intention of leaving his sheepfold and bothy for the safety of the ráth.

We watched the sheep for a while. Low clouds flowed over the sides of the mountains like silvery hair, and wind gusted out of the north in cold fits, making me shiver beneath my single small fleece. "What is wrong with the ráth," I asked, "that you should fear going there?"

"I am not afraid," sniffed Madog, wearing his petulance like a cloak.

"Then why?"

"There are too many people and dogs. It bothers the sheep."

"Wolves bother them more."

He was silent for a moment; I could see him struggling with it. His wrinkled mouth worked over the words a few times before he said, "They laugh at me."

"The bastards."

He liked this. "The bastards," he repeated happily.

"Let them laugh, I say. What do we care? We are noble Britons, you and I, and we fight wolves with our bare hands!"

He laughed again. After a time he said, "Well, we can sleep in the ráth tonight."

The sun began to fade, drawing a freezing mist from the cold heights. We herded our sheep together and led them down the mountain trail to the settlement. As we were leaving, a thin, wailing howl arose from the forest above the bothy—as if our lean and long-legged brothers wished to let us know we would be missed that night.

Upon reaching the fortress, Madog and I busied ourselves with penning up the sheep for the night, using a number of wattle-woven hurdles that we found behind a storehouse. We tied the hurdles together to form a crude enclosure to keep the sheep from wandering around and then set about finding a place for ourselves to sleep—not an easy thing, for, as Madog had intimated, the old slave was such an object of scorn and ridicule that no one would suffer us even to sit under the low eaves of a house.

"We must sleep with the sheep, I think," Madog concluded gloomily.

"The king has horses, not so?" I said.

"He does," Madog affirmed. "Fine horses."

"Then he also has a stable full of hay, and that is where we shall sleep."

He hesitated, unable to hope for such a luxury, but I took him by the arm. "Come, Madog, show me this stable, and tonight you shall sleep in the king's chariot."

The king's grooms gave us an uncertain reception. They would have driven us out, and Madog would have let them, but I stood behind him and made him stand his ground. "Tell them it is because of the wolves," I urged, preventing the old shepherd from fleeing the confrontation.

"You tell them," he countered.

"You are the chief shepherd, Madog," I countered quickly, "so you must tell them. They will listen to you."

"What should I say?"

"Tell them if they let us stay here for the night, we will watch the horses and they can go drink beer."

The old shepherd hesitated, his face rigid in refusal. "Go on, tell them," I said, prodding him in the back.

He drew a breath and blurted out what I had told him to say. The nearest stableman turned his face toward us, interest flickering across his bland features. He called something to his elder companion, who dropped the hank of rope he was carrying and came to stand before us.

"So!" he challenged. "You are shepherds and know nothing of horses. What makes you think you can govern the king's stable?"

Madog stared back at him, his mouth open, unable to think of a reply. I whispered, "Tell him we do not presume to take his place. We only mean to watch them for one night." Madog looked at me in dismay. "He is listening," I insisted. "Just tell him."

Turning once more to the chief groom, Madog plucked up his sagging courage and repeated what I had told him to say, his voice trembling. The stableman regarded us narrowly, stroking his mustache in thought. His fellow groom had come near, and the two discussed the matter for a moment. I heard the younger one say, "It is for one night only. What harm can come in one night?"

"That is true," I put in. "One night only—and the horses are asleep anyway."

The chief groom hesitated; his companion looked at him hopefully, as did we all. Finally he made up his mind. "Let it be as you say." He raised a stern finger. "One night. And if there is any trouble, you come for me, yes?"

"There will be no trouble," Madog said.

"But if something should happen"—he walked to the door and pointed to a low-roofed hut, one of four or five dwellings adjacent to the king's hall—"I will be in that house. You come tell me, yes?"

"At once."

Delivering himself of this command, he turned and indicated a pile of cut hay that half filled an empty stall. "You can sleep there," he told us. "Come, Ruarhdri," he said, but his fellow groom was already out the door.

They hurried away, leaving us alone in the stable. It was a large, dry building, big as a house, its walls lined with stalls for eight horses; only six were occupied. The room was warm and pungent with the smell of horse-flesh. I walked around and looked in each of the stalls, one of which contained the king's chariot. "Here is where you will sleep tonight," I told Madog. He fussed and fluttered and said he would never dare so much, but he eyed the graceful, curving yoke and gleaming wheels all the same.

"The beasts have been fed and watered," I said. "Now it is for us to find something to eat."

Madog pursed his lips doubtfully.

Seeing it was up to me, I said, "You guard the horses. I will go and see what I can find."

Leaving a very anxious shepherd at the door, I walked out into a damp twilight and moved down the narrow, winding lane formed by a double row of storage buildings and small wattled huts. The lane was well trodden and muddy, with puddles of standing water in the footprints of men and animals. Smoke rose through the hole high up in the thatch of some of the huts, and I smelled meat and savory herbs roasting. I slowed as I came to the first of the huts and paused outside the door, thinking how best to ask for what I wanted. The thought of scavenging like a contemptible beggar rankled, but I considered that as a slave of the king I had as much right to a little food as anyone else.

As I was standing there, I heard voices inside the house: a man's voice, flaring, angry, and a woman's shrill reply. Interrupting an argument would not likely produce the desired result, I reckoned, so I continued along. From the next house came the cries of a squalling infant. I moved on.

The last house was quiet inside, and as I stood there listening and working out what I would say, the door opened and a young woman stepped out. She was, I think, about the same age as myself, hazel-eyed and slender, with a sharp nose and small chin that gave her a curious, birdlike appearance. Two small gold combs held an abundance of long black hair, wayward strands of which blew across the rounded oval of her face. Her cloak was deep green, the color of winter ivy, and although the night was cold, she wore it folded so that it exposed a bare shoulder and arm. She pulled the door shut behind her and turned. Her eyes widened in surprise.

"Och!" she said. "You have given me a *scaoll!*"

I did not know the word but said, "Please, I mean no harm."

She smiled—a slightly crooked thing, as if she did not trust herself to share her amusement with the world—and I saw the light leap up in her large, luminous eyes. She lifted a hand and flicked her fingers at the air. "It is nothing." She edged past me.

I caught the scent of balsam as she passed, and I let my eye trail down along the rounded curves of her shoulder, waist, and hip. I felt a familiar stirring and hastened after her. "I am the king's shepherd," I said, falling into step beside her.

"You are that," she said. "I know."

This assertion puzzled me. "Just so?"

My expression must have amused her, for she laughed and said, "Just so." She regarded me out of the corner of her eye, her crooked smile deepening as she explained. "I was in the king's house serving the *fianna* last night."

"Just so?" I countered, grimacing at my own rank ineptitude.

But she laughed again and repeated, "Just so."

"Because of the wolves," I said, stumbling on, "we have come to the ráth."

Ignoring my presence, she continued walking.

"But we have nothing to eat."

She stopped and looked me up and down, her glance quick and dismissive. At once, I was acutely and painfully aware of my dirty face, my uncombed hair, and the fetid smell emanating from my filthy, unbecoming clothes. "And is it for me to feed you now?"

"I only—"

She thumbed her nose at me. "Be off with you, beggar boy."

With that she was gone, leaving only the hint of balsam on the cold night air. Stung by her remark, I stood and stared, feeling very small and stupid.

She flitted away, light as a bird darting through the gloom, skipping over the puddles as she went. The wind gusted, and I felt cold mist on my face as I turned and hurried back to the stable. Madog was sitting in the hay waiting for me. "What did you get?" he asked, starting up as I entered.

I told him I did not get anything but that I met a girl, and I asked, "What does *fianna* mean?"

Madog tapped his head with his finger for a moment and then said, "Ah, it is the warriors, you know?" He made a circular, inclusive motion with his hands.

"The warband?" I suggested.

"Yes," he agreed. "The fianna is the king's warband."

"This girl serves the fianna."

"But she did not give us anything?"

"No," I replied.

With no hope of getting anything to eat, we decided to settle down to sleep. I bade Madog a good night and crawled into an empty stall—but not before establishing the old shepherd in the king's chariot as I had promised. He protested but allowed himself to be led to the chariot and covered with a fleece which I found rolled on the small bench inside the vehicle.

The gloom of the stable deepened around us. I lay in the sweet-smelling hay listening to the soft snuffling of the horses as they slept; now and then a hoof would chafe the wooden floor or a board would creak, but all remained peaceful.

Dawn came long before I was ready to wake. Madog, eager to return to his flock, pulled me from my warm bed, and we walked out into a morning white with frost to lead the sheep from the ráth. Since the upper meadow was mostly under snow, we stayed in the valley that day and allowed the sheep to share the water mead with the cows and pigs. They drank from the clear-running stream and grazed the high grass along the steeper banks where the cattle did not go. I watched them through the day and wished I could appease my own hunger so easily.

The short day was filled with wind and clouds but no rain, and we did not have far to go to return to the ráth that evening. Madog grouched and grumbled about his empty stomach and kept reminding me that we had food at the bothy. "We do," I agreed, "if the wolves have not eaten it."

"We should not be here."

"I will get us something, never fear. We will not go hungry again tonight."

Our welcome at the stable was less than cordial. "You again," the chief groom said. "Away with you now. One night only—that is what you said."

I saw the face of the younger man fall and knew we had an ally. "One night to prove ourselves worthy," I whispered to Madog. "Tell him."

Madog did as I said, but the stableman remained unmoved. "Go on with you now." He put his hand to the door and began to pull it shut. "You are not needed here."

"But, Temuir," the younger man protested, his voice tight with urgency, "they kept a good watch. Aoife has caught a duck and said she would make me a meal."

The elder man hesitated, pulling on the end of his mustache. I could see him weakening.

"Was not the beer sweet in your mouth?" I asked. "Was not the hearth warm on your back as you slept? Why stay in the stable when you have somewhere better to go"—I paused, appealing to the younger man, and added—"and something better to do?"

The chief groom's resolve collapsed. "Do tonight as you did last night, and you can stay," he said, and then he told us once more where he could be found if anything should happen that might require his attention. The younger man was out the door and gone before his elder had finished. With a firm warning about what we could expect if any ill befell the horses in his absence, Temuir left, and we had the stable to ourselves once more.

"Wait here," I said, "while I go find us something to eat."

Moving along the narrow lanes, I strode boldly to the door of the first house I came to. I smacked the door with the flat of my hand, and it was opened by an older woman. When she saw me, her face creased into a scowl of distaste. "Shoo! Shoo!" she said, as if I were an odious pest.

"Please," I said, putting my foot against the bottom of the door, "we are starving. Can you give us anything?"

"No," she said, trying to close the door on me. She saw my foot in the gap and tried to push me away. "Get on with you now!"

"We have had nothing to eat for two days," I said, holding my ground. "We are hungry."

"Why tell me?" she snapped. "Go tell the king."

She pushed me back and closed the door. I stood for a moment and saw that she was right. Madog and I were Miliucc's slaves; it was his duty to feed us.

Thus determined, I marched directly to the big house, where my con-

viction wavered slightly. I paused in the yard outside to observe what passed
and to work out what to say. As I was lingering there, trying to decide how
best to make myself understood, I heard voices and turned to see a group of
young women approaching. One of them was the girl I had spoken to the
night before.

I watched as they entered the yard, heads together, deep in conversation.
My presence was beneath their regard, so I waited until they had reached
the door and then moved to join them. "You!" said one of the young
women, turning on me abruptly, "You are not allowed here. Go away."

"Please," I said. "I only want—"

"You stink!" sneered another. "Get away from me!"

A warrior appeared in the doorway just then. "Here now," he began,
stepping into the yard.

"Send him away," said the first serving maid, thrusting her finger at me.
"He is trying to get into the king's house."

"He is dirty and he stinks," added the second.

The warrior's eyes shifted to me. "You! Get away from here! Leave these
women alone!"

"Please, I must speak to the king."

The warrior moved nearer. "Slaves are not allowed here. Go back to your
dung heap."

"I demand to speak to the king."

"You demand!" snarled the warrior. "Demand?" Placing his hands on my
chest, he gave me a shove which sent me sprawling to the ground. He stood
over me, glowering down. "Here is what your demand is worth." His crude
gesture made it clear my request ranked very low in his estimation.

To emphasize his point he drew back his foot and kicked me in the side.
I squirmed away from the blow, and my scrabbling on the ground made the
serving maids laugh. Angry now, I glared at them. "Even slaves must eat!" I
shouted. "We have no food, and I am hungry. I will not leave until I speak
to the king."

"Go on," said the warrior, stooping to pick up a rock. "Move!"

He drew back his hand to let the rock fly, but the young woman I had encountered the night before stepped in quickly. "Conla, wait." She put her
hands on his arm. "He is one of the king's herdsmen. They have had nothing to eat for two days."

The warrior hesitated, hefting the rock. "Let them beg scraps somewhere
else."

"There *is* nowhere else," I told him.

"Well, you cannot stay here," Conla insisted. "Get you gone now before
I—" Minded to throw the rock, he raised his arm and let fly. I twisted

around, allowing the missile to strike me on the back of the shoulder. It stung, and I cursed him between my teeth.

"Stand still, beggar!" muttered the warrior, bending down for another stone.

"No, Conla," said the dark-haired serving maid, tugging on his arm. "Leave him be. Go back inside." She pushed him toward the door. "All of you, go in."

The warrior flung the rock halfheartedly, and I dodged easily out of the way.

"Go now, Conla. A warrior of your rank should not be seen tussling with a slave. Leave him to me. I will send him on his way."

"Very well," replied the warrior. With a last glare at me, he opened the door for the young women. "But if he gives you any trouble—"

"Go now. I will join you soon."

The other serving maids entered the king's house behind Conla, favoring their companion with scornful looks as they passed. To her credit she ignored them. "The king will not see you," she told me when they had gone. "And you'll only heap more trouble on your head if you stay. They'll beat you again."

"What do you care?" I spat bitterly. "It is not for you to feed us—as you so rightly pointed out yesterday."

Her reply surprised me. "I am sorry I said that."

I shrugged.

"Just stay here." She went into the house, and I waited awhile, watching the sky grow dark. When she finally reappeared, her hands were empty.

"I could not get anything just now," she told me. "Conla and Ercol are coming out. If they see you, there will be trouble."

"You are no better than the others," I replied, my voice thick with scorn. Turning on my heel, I started away.

She took two quick steps after me. I felt her hand on my arm. "Where do you sleep?"

I stopped at her touch. "The stable. We sleep in the stable."

She nodded. "I must go now, but I will bring you something."

"When?"

"Tonight. I must go in; the fianna are waiting."

I walked slowly back to the stable. Madog was less than pleased to see me return empty-handed. "The serving maid," I told him, "the one I met before. She promised to bring us something."

"Huh!" he sniffed, and crawled into the king's chariot to sleep.

I settled myself in the stall, pulled my fleece over my chest, and dozed, waking from time to time to look out to see if she was coming. On one such occasion I rose and went to the door. As I reached for the leather strap, the door swung open and the young woman stepped quietly in, almost colliding with me. "Och!" she gasped in surprise. "And are you always lurking in doorways, then?"

"I am that," I said.

Pale light spilled in through the open doorway; the sky had cleared in the night, and now the moon and stars were shining. The girl brought out a cloth-wrapped bundle from beneath her cloak. "Here," she said, placing it in my hands, "I brought you this."

"I thank you, *banrion*," I said, using a word that I thought meant "noble-woman."

I saw her crooked smile. "I am not the king's wife," she replied lightly. "I just serve the fianna." She turned and stepped quickly outside.

"What is your name?"

She hesitated, looking back at me in the darkness of the stable. "And is that any business of yours?"

"Please," I said, following her out, "tell me your name."

She walked a few more paces and, glancing back over her shoulder, disappeared between the houses in the lane.

I roused Madog, and we sat down to eat our meal in the dark. Unwrapping the bundle, I laid it on the floor between us. Instantly the aroma of roast pork pervaded the air. I reached down into a mound of meat still warm from the king's hearth. There were also round objects that turned out to be small loaves of rye bread.

I divided the loaves and meat between us, and we fell to. The pork was firm and succulent, and seasoned with salt and spices I did not know but which left a pleasant, warm sensation in my mouth. I savored each bite. Had we a little beer, I reflected, lifting a juicy piece of meat to my mouth, we would have dined like kings—or at least as well as Lord Miliucc had dined that night.

In our hunger we made short work of the meat and bread. Alas, it vanished all too soon. I licked the last crumbs from my hands, then bade good night to Madog and crawled back into the stall to dream of lovely maidens serving me choice morsels from long silver flesh forks while I reclined on a soft featherbed in fine robes with a torc of gold around my neck and a band of loyal warriors alert to my every command.

HE KING AND warriors rode out the next morning to hunt the wolves. Madog and I were still asleep when the grooms came clumping into the stable; they pulled us from our warm slumbers and pushed us out into a raw, miserable dawn. Along with half the population of the ráth, we stood stiff-legged in the thin light and watched the king and his fianna depart. Spears high, gleaming shields upon their backs, their many-colored cloaks trailing as they galloped through the gate—I confess I found it a stirring sight.

I looked for the young woman who had fed us the night before but did not see her in the close-gathered crowd. When the hunters had gone, Madog and I gathered our sheep and led them out to graze in the valley. The day began blustery and wet and slowly sank into a grim, bone-gnawing cold. I huddled behind a tree beside the river, my hands tucked into my armpits to keep warm, and waited for the short day to end so we could return to the ráth.

As dusk gathered over the valley, we heard the sound of hooves and peered into the gloom to see the king and his warriors approaching; the carcasses of five or six wolves were slung over the backs of the horses.

"Well," said Madog, "the wolves will trouble us no more. Now we can return to the bothy."

"Perhaps we should wait another day or two," I suggested, "just to be certain they are truly gone."

"They are gone," he said, and began leading the sheep toward the mountain trail.

I pointed out that it was already growing late and that we would not reach the bothy until after dark; I complained that it would be cold and we had little to eat up there; I told him that the grass was better for the sheep in the valley—but nothing I said persuaded him to change his mind. Madog would not stay in the stable another night, and that was the end of it. I had no choice but to go with him.

Although it was small, the bothy was snug, and the fire burning outside warmed it well enough. We ate a hearty supper of boiled mutton and turnips, and went to bed. I lay awake listening, expecting the wolves to start howling at any moment, but the night remained quiet, nor did we hear them the next night or any night thereafter.

Winter deepened. From time to time people would come up from the ráth to bring us provisions; occasionally they would take back a sheep to slaughter, but we did not go down into the valley again until the festival of midwinter which is called Alban Arthuan. It came about like this:

One evening, I found Madog standing before the entrance to the sheep-fold gazing intently at the flock. I imagined he was counting them and had discovered one missing. But when I asked, he said, "No, it is for the fobairt. I must choose the one which is to be given."

"fobairt?"

"It is . . . ," he squinted one eye and stuck out his lip with the effort of his thought—"when a thing is burned for the good of the ráth."

"A sacrifice," I suggested. "The sheep is killed for the people."

He nodded. "It is that," he said, and went on to describe the event as a very great feast in which the entire tribe came together to observe the rite and celebrate.

"Celebrate what?"

Madog thought for a moment, then shook his head. He could not say.

He chose a young male from the flock and around its neck tied a length of braided rope, the other end of which he tied to a post in one corner of the enclosure. The next morning he led the sacrificial sheep out from the others, fed and watered it, and then we descended the trail to the valley, leading the young sheep by a bit of rope, with the rest of the flock follow-ing as they would.

It had snowed a day or so before, making the narrow track slippery in places. The Vale of Braghad stretched out below: a wide expanse of glis-tening white extending all the way to the sea. By the time we reached the valley floor, the sun had broken through the clouds; the sky cleared, re-vealing patches of astonishing blue which grew larger as the day progressed.

Tribesmen from the other settlement joined us on the trail leading to the ráth; among the usual barbarians were men I had never seen before. In appearance they were wholly unlike any of the others. There were six of them, walking in pairs, a young man together with an elder. The younger men wore gray robes and cloaks of the same color, the older men cloaks and robes of various colors: one green, one blue, one yellow. They kept to themselves, neither talking to nor joining in with the others on the trail. The elder men carried long staffs or rods; the younger held branches cut from yew trees.

"Who are they?" I asked when they had passed.

"They are," Madog answered, his voice dropping to a whisper, ". . . the *filidh*."

I could make little of the word—and Madog could tell me nothing more—so I waited to see what I could learn.

Upon reaching the ráth the others on the road stepped aside to allow these men to enter first, and then the rest of us followed. The six went directly to the king's house, where they entered at once. Madog and I took the sheep to the far side of the settlement, where a special enclosure had been set up; in it were a young bull and a red pig. One of the valley herdsmen was keeping watch over the animals, so we left the sheep in his care.

"What happens now?" I asked.

"There will be food," Madog replied. He looked away and added, "But they do not let me have any."

"Why not?"

He shrugged.

If they were going to deny me a portion of the feast, I would need a better reason than that. "Show me where it is."

He led me to a place behind the king's hall where a pit had been dug in the ground and filled with burning embers. Over the pit, timber beams supported an enormous spit on which an entire ox was roasting. A long iron trough lay across the coals to catch the melting fat, and the aroma of that roasting meat filled the wintry air.

Across from the cooking fire a large wooden vat rested on a tripod of tree stumps. People thronged the vat as cups and bowls of beer were poured and distributed. Nearby, another fire was burning beneath an iron tripod from which was suspended a great black caldron in which a thick stew of beans, salt pork, and turnips was cooking.

"Stay there by the fire," I told Madog, indicating the pit where the ox was roasting. "I will soon return," I said, and waded into the crowd around the beer vat. Intent on their own cups, no one paid any attention to me; I stuck out my hands and soon came away with two big wooden bowls of foaming beer.

I returned to where Madog was waiting, gave him a bowl, and said, "*Salve, frater!*"

The first bowl went down quickly, so I fetched a second, and we stood drinking and warming ourselves by the fire, watching the men turn the ox on the spit. The beer was cold and good, and the fire pleasantly hot on my face and hands. I was enjoying the sensation when I felt something sharp jab me in the back, high up between my shoulder blades.

I turned and saw a young warrior standing behind me, a short spear in his hand. It was, I recognized, the one who had accosted me at the gate the night I entered the king's house.

"The *fleá* is not for slaves," he said. Despite the cold he wore neither cloak nor tunic but went about bare-chested. His face was red, and I guessed he had been standing too near the vat for some time.

"If the king sends me away, I will go," I told him. "Until then I will stay."

"I say you will go now." He advanced on me and, holding the spear cross-wise, shoved me with it. I lost my balance and fell, sending the cup and contents flying. He stood over me laughing.

As it happened, this deed did not go unnoticed. I heard a voice call out and looked around to see Forgall and two other warriors approaching. They said something to the young warrior, who pointed to me and made a slurred reply; the words 'filthy Briton' were the only ones I understood.

I rolled onto my feet and stood to face him. Forgall called the youth, beckoning him away. "It seems you are the one who is to go," I told him.

I turned from him and walked to retrieve my cup. I bent to pick it up, and as I straightened, felt another sharp jab in my back, harder this time. I let out a cry and whirled around. He leveled the spear, ready to plunge the blade into my stomach.

Forgall shouted. "Ercol, stop!"

The youth hesitated. I saw his eyes slide away. Seizing my chance, I took hold of the shaft of the spear and yanked it forward and down. Ercol's grip was strong; he did not release the weapon but followed it. His face met the wooden bowl in my hand as he went down. He fell on hands and knees, blood streaming from his nose. I picked up the spear and stood over him.

"Enough," said Forgall, putting out his hand. "It is an offense to fret this day with bloodshed. Ercol was wrong. He has been punished. That is the end of it."

"Let it be as you say," I replied. Taking the spear, I turned and tossed it into the flaming pit beneath the ox.

There came a growl from behind and Ercol threw himself at me. His arms went around my legs, and before I knew it, I was on the ground and he was on top of me. He grabbed a handful of my hair and began banging my head against the dirt. I swung out with my fist and caught him on the neck, but he did not let go. I swung again and again—to no avail. I could not loosen his hold.

Ercol gave my head a last hard slam and released me. I rolled onto my knees, and he was there before me with a knife in his hand and a wicked grin on his bloody face.

I climbed slowly to my feet. He took a cautious step forward, and I edged back—only to find myself hard up against the cooking pit. Heat from the flaming coals lashed my legs and back.

I made to move aside and away from the pit, but he lunged and closed off my retreat. I could tell from the sickly look on his face that he meant to either gut me or shove me into the fiery coals. I glanced to the warriors for help, but they stood looking on, content to let the fight take its course. Others had gathered, too; they ringed the pit, jeering, and shouting advice to one or the other of us. I could not see Madog; he must have fled when the trouble started.

Ercol swung out with the knife. I dodged. My foot caught the edge of the pit and went in. I fell forward onto my hands, dragging my foot up out of the hot coals. Ercol saw his chance and swung again. I hurled myself to the side and felt the blade slice through the sleeve of my shirt.

A thin, cold sting nipped the flesh of my upper arm. I tried to roll away before he could strike again, but he was there, standing before me, the knife making lazy circles in front of my face. The next thrust would cut deep, and there was nothing I could do about it.

I saw his face tense. His arm drew back. I braced myself to take the blow, clinging to the desperate hope that I might yet evade it somehow.

He drew a breath, and I saw his hand start forward.

In the same instant I heard a shout: very loud, very clear, and with a force that seemed to shake the earth. The cry was a single word, which I did not know, but which halted the headstrong warrior's hand in midstroke.

In the uncanny silence that followed the shout, I stared at the knife, expecting it to slash forward at any moment as Ercol's hate overcame the shouted command. One moment passed and then another, and still the knife hung before my face. And then it began to quiver—as if all Ercol's strength were bent on pushing that slender blade forward but he could not. I looked up and saw that indeed his face was pinched in pain with the effort, but something restrained him. Although he struggled against it, some greater strength stayed his hand. The point of the knife began to shake and then to dip toward the earth. Still Ercol resisted. I stared in amazement at the strange sight of a man striving with all his strength against an invisible opponent.

This astounding contest lasted only a moment longer. Ercol, the veins bulging from his forehead and neck, gave out a strangled cry and then collapsed; the knife went spinning to the ground, and he fell back, panting like a beaten dog, exhausted.

I tried to stand, but my legs were unsteady, and I fell forward onto my hands and knees. I became aware that someone was there with me, kneeling beside me. I turned my head to see a young man dressed all in blue—one of those I had seen entering the king's house.

I tried to get up again, but he said, "Rest a little. Catch your breath."

I gulped down some air, and my head cleared. The man bending over me was but a few years older than myself. His clothes were plain but well made; his belt was cloth and of the same stuff as his robe and cloak. He wore neither brooch nor pin, bands nor rings, his only ornament the thick silver torc around his neck. Although no taller than myself, he was stout-bodied, with big hands and a large, square, close-shorn head of thick dark hair, giving the appearance of a much larger man.

"You are a bold one," he said amiably, "taking on a warrior like that."

"I am not feeling so bold now," I said.

"Perhaps it was a mistake to throw Ercol's spear into the fire."

"No doubt you are right." I made to stand and felt a strong hand take me under the arm and lift me to my feet.

He plucked at the cut in my sleeve and looked at the gash on my arm. "No great harm done," he concluded. "Wash the wound and keep it clean."

With that he inclined his head and walked away.

"I thank you—whoever you may be," I called after him.

"I am Cormac Miach," he replied, looking back over his shoulder. "Farewell, slave boy."

Forgall directed the warriors to haul Ercol away. They picked him up, set him on his feet, and led him off toward the beer vat. Madog came puffing up, shaking with excitement. "He did it. He saved you," he said, brushing ineffectually at my clothes. "I knew he would."

"I suppose he did," I allowed. "But what did he do?"

"He used the *briamon*. Did you not hear it?"

"I heard. What is it?"

"The druid folk have many powers. They can do wonders."

I stared at him. "Druids?"

Madog paused. "They are druids, yes. That is what they are called in Prydain."

"I know that," I told him bluntly. "I thought you said they were called filidh."

"Filidh . . . druid—it is the same."

Before I could question him further, there came a blaring sound like the bellow of a bull elk. "Hurry!" said Madog, pulling me away. We joined the crowd as it assembled outside the king's house, where a large stone had been set up in the center of the yard. The throng formed a wide circle around the stone. It was crowded, but Madog and I found places in the front rank, so that my view was unobstructed and I could see all that took place.

When the gathering was complete, the carynx—a large, circular horn of worked bronze—sounded again, and the filidh emerged from the king's house, led by the young men in gray, each of whom held a yew branch. Their elder brethren followed, each with a different implement or instrument: One carried a strange curved knife with a golden blade, another a small harp, and the last a flat silver pan. They proceeded to the stone and took their places beside it. King Miliucc, his brown-haired lady Queen Grania and several members of his house came to stand a little apart while the warrior with the carynx moved slowly around the outer rim of the circle, pausing at each of the four points—north, east, south, west—to sound the long, low, belly-shivering note.

As that note faded into silence, the fellow in the green robe wielding the curved knife stepped forward. "That is the ollamh," Madog informed me. "He is their chieftain."

The ollamh gestured to the one with the harp, who came forth and took his place before the standing stone. This stone was buff-colored, almost as tall as a man, domed at the top, and shaped along its length so that it was nearly round. He stood a few paces from the stone, facing it and cradling the harp against his chest. At his behest the three gray-robed druids approached and, using their yew branches, began to brush the stone all over from top to bottom, slowly revolving around the stone as they brushed. Then, still circling slowly, they swept the ground around the stone.

Striking a chord with his hand on the strings of the harp, the druid sang out in a loud, chanting voice, "*Dearc!*" he cried, "Behold! Kinsmen, brothers, sisters, behold: the Lia Óráid!"

I puzzled over this for a moment before the meaning came clear. Lia Óráid . . . Stone of Speech.

"Alban Arthuan is at hand! Behold, the tomb of every hope!"

At this, the gray druids carefully placed the yew branches to form a triangle at the base of the yellow stone, whereupon they retired to the perimeter to watch as one by one the animals were led to the sacrifice.

The ritual slaughter itself was quickly and skillfully performed. The first to come forward was a young bull; the beast was led to the stone and placed so to stand over one of the yew branches. Then, after moving three times around the stone while the ollamh strummed the harp, the two remaining druids proceeded to where it stood. While one held the silver pan beneath its neck, the other stepped close, spoke softly into the animal's ear and, with a swift motion, drew the golden knife beneath its neck. The blood spurted hot and red, and in a moment the bull collapsed.

There was no terror, no struggle; the beast simply relaxed into death. The blood of the animal was collected in the silver pan and poured onto the stone. The sheep and the red pig were likewise dispatched, and their blood mingled with that of the bull.

I had heard of such barbarities—many times, to be sure. My grandfather had fulminated against them at every opportunity. He used to condemn druids and their pagan practices, which he called vile superstition of the most insidious kind. "They eat children, Succat," he once told me, "and worship demons. The light of the Lord's salvation shines not for them."

But as I stood there, a member of Miliucc's tribe, the curious ritual did not produce in me the revulsion I should have felt. Instead I found myself strangely moved by the well-meaning seriousness of the druids and the quiet respect afforded the sacrifice by the people themselves. There was nothing lurid or obscene about it, however misguided.

As the last animal died and its blood was poured onto the stone, the ol-lamh began playing the harp and singing. I could not understand much of the song—a few words here and there, but not enough to produce any meaning for me. When he finished, he cried, "Behold!" again, and pointed to the eastern sky, where the moon was just rising over the hills to pour a pale light into the Vale of Braghad. "Alban Arthuan," he called, "the tomb of every hope, my people, for death is the gateway of all hope. Hear and re-member!"

It was, I had to admit, very well done. The sacrifices were completed and the new season marked at the precise moment at which the sun set in the west and the moon rose in the east—a most auspicious time, Madog in-formed me with a knowing wink.

There was more singing then, and the sacrificial animals were taken away to be cleaned and cooked; their flesh would be shared out among the people of the tribe the next day. Ceremony completed, the feast resumed. There was singing and piping—odd, bag-shaped bladders with shrill, screechy pipes attached: an instrument to wake the dead—and a curious sort of jerky dancing. But with coming of night, the meat and ale made men belligerent. Both Madog and myself grew increasingly wary and fearful as it soon became apparent our presence was not warmly embraced by one and all. So after a little more to eat and drink, we crept away to a quiet cor-ner to sleep beneath the eaves of one of the houses while the revel wore on.

At dawn, when the celebration was just ending, we gathered the flock and departed the ráth to make our slow way up the mountain. It would be many days before I saw either sun or moon again, but the quaint ritual of Alban Arthuan did somehow rekindle my hopes.

And if it is true that death is the gateway, old Madog's foot was already on the threshold.

1 2

ESPITE THE SACRIFICE and celebration, winter, the old tyrant, remained firmly enthroned. Day succeeded day, bringing fog and freezing mist, rain and sleet, and nights of cold, raging wind. One morning I awakened to the sound of Madog coughing. We rose and went about our duties, and decided to take the sheep to graze. Madog reckoned that the snow had melted enough on the more distant south-facing slopes to make it worthwhile taking the sheep all that way. As the day seemed good, we packed some victuals and set off.

By the time we reached the grazing land, however, a fierce, biting wind had blown up out of the west. We had not thought to bring the flint and steel, and could not make a fire. It was too far back to the bothy to fetch it, so we huddled down behind some rocks, and I spent the day shivering and listening to the old shepherd snuffling and sniveling until, at last, he rose and declared it time to gather the flock.

Madog's cough worsened that night, and the next morning I asked him, "Are you feeling well, Madog?" His face was as gray as gruel, his eyes red-rimmed and rheumy.

"Well enough," he replied, rubbing his watery eyes. "I will make some stout broth, and that will put me right."

He tried to stand, and I saw how he shook and shivered. "No," I told him, jumping up quickly, "you sit by the fire. I will make the broth."

"You should go. The sheep are waiting," he complained, struggling up once more.

"Let them," I said, easing him down. "We spend whole days waiting for them. They can wait for us a little while."

He seemed satisfied with this and hunkered down beside the fire while I filled the caldron and gathered a few ingredients. He fell asleep again while waiting for the broth to boil—something I had never seen him do before. I roused him when it was ready, and we ate. He told me it was the best broth he had ever tasted, and then climbed shakily to his feet. "Well, we have kept the sheep waiting long enough," he said, which brought on a fit of coughing that doubled him over.

"You are sick, Madog," I told him. "Stay here by the fire and keep warm. I will watch the sheep today."

But he would not. "The broth will see me right." He picked up his crook and stumped off. We did not go to the south slope; the wind was still gusty and cold, the clouds thick and low, the day unsettled. Once it started pelting down sleet on our wet heads, and I went to Madog, "Look, even the sheep are miserable. Let us go back to the bothy and get warm."

Shivering, shaking, sick as he was, he refused; so we stood out in the icy sleet and waited for dusk. Only when the dark mist had begun to claim the lowlands did the stubborn old shepherd allow me to lead the sheep back to the fold. On our return, I built up the fire hot and high and cooked some of the salted mutton into a thick stew, using our last turnip, most of the barley, and two onions—which Madog said was a sorry waste. "I will go down to the ráth and get more tomorrow," I told him, throwing in the rest of the barley and another onion for good measure.

He sat watching me cook, hugging his knees and dabbing at his nose while the snot streamed over his blue, quivering lips. Despite the heat of the flames, he did not begin to warm until he had some of the hot stew inside him.

"The bothy will be cold," I said when we finished eating. "Why not let me make up our beds beside the fire. I will tend the flames and keep us warm all night."

He rebuffed the suggestion at first, but I saw that he lacked the strength and will for an argument, so I coaxed him along, saying, "The sleet has stopped, and the stars are coming out. The moon will be bright—a good night to sleep by the fire."

"Let it be as you say," he muttered, sinking deeper into himself.

I made him a bed as near the fire as I dared and fetched enough wood to keep the flames high until morning, then settled back to doze, rousing myself from time to time to add more fuel to the flames. Madog slept fitfully; his cough had become a ragged, brutal thing that shook him with increasing violence. When he slept, he slept with his mouth lolling open and his breath shallow.

We passed a fretful night, and as soon as it was light enough to see the trail, I rose and made ready to depart. "Listen, Magod," I said, bending low to his ear, "I am going down to the ráth to get some more food. Understand?"

He turned his rheumy eyes toward me and nodded.

"Good. Now, I have put some wood close to hand so you can feed the fire until I return. There is stew in the pot when you get hungry. I will go and hurry back as quickly as I can, but you stay here and keep warm."

"The sheep . . ." he protested weakly.

"Do not worry about the sheep. One day in the fold will not harm them, I will feed and water them when I get back. Rest now, and stay close to the fire."

He muttered something and lay down. He was asleep again as I took up his crook and departed.

The morning was misty and cold; a freezing fog lay over the valley. Lit by the rising sun, it looked like a sea of pearly water, and the ráth on its hump of rock an island surrounded by the milky waves washing around its lonely shores. I gazed upon this sight as I picked my way down the mountain trail, and it produced in me a most powerful yearning, for it seemed to me that I was that fortress, lost in a cold and obscure sea.

By the time I reached the valley, the sun had burned off much of the fog. I crossed the river at the ford and hurried up to the ráth, pausing before the king's house to think how best to say what I wanted. As I was standing there, another thought came to me. I turned and ran to the hut of the serving maid instead. She had helped me once, I thought; she might help me again.

Not knowing what else to do, I pounded on the lintel of the door with the flat of my hand. When nothing happened, I pounded again and was about to turn away when I heard a movement inside. "Is anyone there?" I called.

The door opened, and a man thrust out his head. He had been asleep, and I had awakened him. He stared blearily at me, and his stare hardened into a glare. "You," he grunted.

I recognized him then. It was Cernach, the warrior who had climbed the cliff to cut off my escape. I took a step backward, unable to think what to say. A hand snaked out, snagged me by the arm, and held me. "What do you want here?" he said, jerking me toward him.

I gaped at him, trying to make the words, but in my dismay my mouth and tongue would not obey.

A quick left hand caught me on the side of the face. The resounding smack stung like the lash of a whip and made my eyes water. He moved to strike again. I found my voice. "Please, no. I mean no harm. I am sorry. . . ."

His hand flicked out. I ducked the blow, and he hit the back of my head. I tried to pull away. He seized me with both hands and held on. "Please!" I cried, "I mean no harm."

A voice called out from inside the hut. "Cernach, what is it?"

In the doorway behind the big warrior's shoulder, a pale, round face appeared. It was the young servingwoman. She stepped lightly around him. "Stay back," he warned.

"Cernach, stop." She put her hands on his and tried to remove them from my arm. "You are hurting him."

"Please," I said, "I need help."

"Here is help for you, boy," Cernach sneered, drawing back his hand.

"Let him go!" the serving maid shouted.

"Sionan, get back!" he growled. "Do as I say!" He tried to move her aside with a nudge of his elbow, but she lost her balance and fell. His eyes turned to where she lay sprawled on the muddy ground. Cernach's lips curled in a gloating sneer and a sheet-flame of anger flashed through me.

The instant his eyes slid away, I swung my fist and struck him with all my strength. I aimed for his neck, but missed and hit him on his thick-muscled shoulder instead. "Leave her alone!" I shouted.

The big brute turned his gaze on me once more. "I do what I please," he snarled. With that he kicked out at the sprawling girl. She tried to roll aside, but his foot caught her in the stomach.

"No!" I cried and swung on him again. "I said to leave her alone!"

Cernach easily fended off my punch; he snatched me by the arm and yanked me close. "It's none of your business, slave," he said, his foul breath hot in my face. He hit me hard with the flat of his hand; my head snapped back, and I tasted blood in my mouth.

"Cernach!" shouted the young woman, climbing to her feet once more. She flew at him, and began striking him with her fists. "Let him go." When this appeal failed to produce the desired result, she added, "I will tell Cormac about this."

A greasy smile appeared on the warrior's face. "I am not afraid of Cormac."

"I *will* tell him this time," she said sternly. "And he will denounce you before the king. Now let him go."

The warrior regarded me, his mouth writhing with disgust and rage. "Save your breath, woman," he muttered. "The filth is not worth it."

With that he gave me a shove that sent me flying backwards. I landed on my side in the mud. "Don't ever come here again," he told me, then disappeared back into the hut.

The young woman was beside me the instant he had gone. "You defended me," she said, her voice soft with awe.

"He should not have hit you." I replied, working my jaw from side to side.

"I thank you, but it was a foolish thing to do. He might have killed you."

"Sionan—is that your name?"

"You cannot come here anymore," she said, helping me to my feet. "I am married now."

"I meant no harm," I told her. "But Madog is sick. He needs help. I didn't know what to do. I thought you could tell me."

She frowned. "You must go."

"But, Madog—"

"Hush," she said, dropping her voice to a whisper. "Go to the king's house and wait. I will come there as soon as I can. Now go."

I did as she told me and moved off to the king's house. The ráth was stirring now as people began going about their various chores and duties. None of them paid any attention to me as I took up my place outside the door of the king's hall. From time to time a warrior or two would come out, and several of them carried weapons. I watched as they proceeded to practice among themselves, perfecting their skill at arms.

I was immersed in the clack and clatter of the warriors' games when I saw Sionan darting across the yard. She glanced at me as she came near, and I started toward her, but she warned me off with a stern glance that gave me to know I was not to speak to her. I stepped aside, and she entered the hall. A few moments later a man emerged. "You there," he said, "shepherd."

I stood and turned as he addressed me.

"I am told the old one has fallen sick."

"In truth," I said. "Can someone come and help?"

He pursed his lips. "Is it bad, then?"

"It is that," I told him, "or I would not have come."

He nodded. "Return to the flock. I will send for the filidh."

This made no sense to me. "What can they do?"

"You may go." He turned and opened the door.

"We need food, too," I said. He paused. "We have had nothing from the ráth since the fleá."

He cast a dismissive glance over his shoulder.

"Please," I said, "we are hungry."

"Wait here," he commanded, and went back inside the king's hall. In a little while the door opened again, and a young boy came out lugging a leather bag.

"This is for you," the boy said, laying the bag at my feet.

When he had gone, I stooped to the bag and opened it. There were loaves of bread, a haunch of pork, a stoppered jar of beer, and some other fragments left over from last night's supper. Closing the bag, I slung it over my shoulder and proceeded to make my way up the mountain to the bothy. Before leaving the ráth, I paused to look back, hoping Sionan might appear. When she did not, I shifted the bag onto my other shoulder and departed.

Madog was still asleep when I reached the bothy. The fire had burned down, allowing the chill air to settle on him. I built it back up and set about making a meal for us from the food in the bag.

The smell of roasting pork wakened the old shepherd. "Geriandol?" he said, sitting up. "What is this?"

He looked around our little camp, his expression at once frightened and confused.

"All is well," I told him. "It is only myself, Succat—returned from the ráth."

"Succat?" he said, shaking his head. Recognition came over him, and his fright turned to disappointment.

"Look, I brought good meat, bread, and beer from the king's house. We shall eat like kings today."

He peered at the haunch warming near the flames and licked his lips. I broke a small loaf of bread and offered him half. "Here," I said, "try this. It is still fresh."

He accepted the loaf but sat there holding it loosely in his hand. "You should eat something," I coaxed. "You might feel better."

The old man gazed at the loaf for a moment, and then, as if remembering what it was, he pinched off a bit and put it in his mouth. When that was gone, he tried another, eating slowly, forcing himself to make the proper motions to bite, chew, and swallow.

"Geriandol," I said. "Who is that?"

At my use of the name, his gaze quickened. "Where did you hear that?"

"You said it to me when you woke just now. Was it someone you knew?"

His head fell. "She was my wife," he murmured.

"You never told me you were married."

"She was to be my wife," he amended.

I did not know what to say to this, so I held my tongue lest I trespass on a tender memory. I ate my bread in silence, then fetched the bowls and poured some beer. As Madog lifted the bowl to his lips, a shudder passed through him which set him coughing—a deep, rattling, hack that amazed and worried me with its severity. When it finished, I offered him the beer again and then tried to get him to eat a little of the meat. He pulled off a morsel and chewed slackly.

"The king's man said he would send the filidh," I told him. "Perhaps they will know how to help you."

Madog looked at me; a strange expression came into his eyes, and I thought he had not heard what I said, so I repeated it. "I know," he snapped. "I have ears."

He threw down the scrap of bread and stood. He looked around as if searching for something he had lost, and then started walking toward the bothy. I thought he meant to get a fleece from his bed, but when he passed the hut and started on the trail leading into the forest, I jumped up. "Madog," I called, "where are you going?"

Removing the meat from the fire and stowing the rest of the food in the bag, I took up his crook and hurried after him. He heard me on the trail behind him and turned on me. "Stay away!"

He started off again, so I followed. "Madog, what is wrong?"

The old man mumbled something, lowered his head, and walked faster.

The forest trail was wet; there was snow in the shadows where the sun did not reach, but the track was clear enough. I did not try to engage him again but contented myself to follow a short way behind—as much to prevent him from coming to harm as to see where he would go. We were a fair distance into the forest when he turned off the trail and started up the slope into the deep wood.

The climb grew steep, and Madog had to stop to catch his breath—a thing I had never seen him do before. I came upon him bent low, leaning against a tree, lost in a spasm of coughing. "What are you doing, Madog? It is cold up here. Come back to the bothy and warm yourself by the fire."

"Go back yourself," he said, and charged off again. "Get away from me."

I could make nothing of this behavior—only that the illness had affected his mind. Nevertheless, he seemed to know where he was going and made no further attempt to discourage me, and we soon came to a rocky place on the mountainside: an outcropping of huge old stones, some of them larger than the bothy and covered with moss and lichen.

Madog slowed as he approached the rocks; he circled the heap, and I followed. As I came nearer, a strange sensation drew over me—a dread anticipation, wanting to see but fearing what I was about to find. The flesh on my arms and the nape of my neck tingled with expectation. I drew nearer and saw that it was not, as I thought, a natural outcropping. It was a dolmen.

We had them in Britain, too, of course. The countryfolk maintained that they were the burial houses of the Old Ones, the people—or giants, as some would have it—that had held the island long ago, even before the Celts. But where the dolmens I had seen were made of three or four upright stones capped by a large table stone, on the whole no larger than the height of a man, this dolmen was easily twice the height of a man. The rear portion was covered with earth and built into the slope so that the ancient structure seemed to be the entrance to the mountain itself.

Madog stopped outside the cavelike opening and stood staring into the gaping black hole, shivering and shaking as he gazed into that dark gate. I crept up close beside him, saying nothing, merely standing with him. In a moment, he seemed to apprehend my presence. "Crom's house," he said. "And I shall be Crom's servant."

"What do you mean, Madog?"

"All who enter Crom's house become his servants."

He seemed disposed to talk about it, so I said, "Who is this Crom?"

"The Dark Lord of the Underworld," replied the old shepherd, "and Crom Cruach is his name. He feeds on the souls of those who serve him. Once you enter his service, you are his forever. There is no escape. You are his slave forever."

He moved closer to the entrance, and I followed. "That," he said, pointing to a crude symbol cut into the side of one of the great slabs of stone "—that is his sign."

The carving was so old and so badly eroded that I could make nothing of it myself—a blotch with a few lines—but Madog appeared to set great store by it. "He is in there," he said, and began to shiver again. "He is waiting for me." As he spoke, his expression grew so anguished that my heart went out to him.

"See here," I said, stepping boldly into the entrance of the dolmen. "The chamber is empty, Madog. There is no one waiting for you."

Moving farther back into the chamber, I followed the thin corridor of light that proceeded dimly from the entrance. A few paces inside, a great pillar of rock stood in the center of the chamber; on it was carved a half circle above a rough bowl shape made of three curved lines. At the base of the standing stone sat an immense rock which had been crudely shaped— chiefly, the top had been carved out to form a shallow basin. It was empty, but the center of the basin bore the same circle and bowl carving with the addition of two small triangles also enclosed by circles.

"There is nothing here, Madog," I called, my voice booming with a hollow sound.

I moved deeper into the dolmen. Behind the center stone the chamber divided; one side formed a stall-like box and the other a long, low passage with short slab stones projecting out from the sides. I could see nothing in the darkness at the end of the passage, but I smelled the musty, damp, metallic scent of old wet stone and earth. In the larger stall was a niche in the wall and in the niche a small round stone. I stepped into the stall and took up the stone; holding it in the thin light from the entrance, I could see that it was incised with two slits for eyes and a slit mouth. That was all: just three lines, but the shape of the stone and the slant of the eyes combined to produce in me a sensation of dread—or perhaps it was the force of Madog's words working in me, for I looked at the complacent arrogance etched on the face of the stone head and my apprehension increased.

I returned the stone to its place and backed away from the niche, retreating from the curious encounter. But even as I prepared to flee, I saw myself running from the chamber in disgrace. That I, a noble Briton, should become squeamish and fearful before such a vulgar image disgusted me. Instantly my trepidation left me. I felt an inexplicable urge to smash the thing

I reached into the niche and took up the stone head once more. "Crom Cruach," I said, "you have eaten your last soul."

With that I hurled the head into the corner of the stall, where it collided with the wall. The impact broke a chip from the stone head, and this emboldened me. I picked up the head and returned to where Madog was waiting.

"See here, Madog," I said, "I have conquered Crom Cruach." I held up the stone head for him to see and then heaved it against the massive slab which formed part of the entrance to the dolmen. There was a loud crack, and the stone head split in half. I retrieved the two halves. "Look, it is just a bit of stone after all," I told him, holding half in each hand. "There is nothing to fear."

The old shepherd regarded the broken rock dubiously. He reached a tentative finger to the clean-cracked stone and felt the rough edge. "He is gone?"

"Crom is gone," I confirmed, tossing the two halves aside. "Come, let us go back to the bothy now and get warm."

Madog allowed himself to be led away; he was quiet on the walk through the forest. Upon our return, I built up the fire and set about warming the food once more to give him a fine supper. He ate little, however, and soon lay down to sleep, exhausted by the exertion of the day. While he slept, I fed and watered the sheep and then sat to watch the day slowly fade. A blue-gray mist rose in the valley as the sun bled to a pale, ghostly white: the color of dead men's bones.

13

ADOG DID NOT rise the next morning but lay the whole day by the fire, shivering despite the heat of the flames. I gave him some bread and the rest of the beer at midday, and he sat up for a while. He did not seem to remember what had happened the previous day, so I told him about visiting the dolmen. He liked the story and lay like a child gazing at the flames while I spoke.

When I finished, he made to get to his feet, but the effort started him coughing. I was alarmed to hear the deep, liquid gurgling sound as he struggled to catch his breath. I went to ease him down again, but he pushed my hands away. "The sheep . . ." he gasped between spasms. ". . . the sheep . . ."

"I have already seen to the sheep," I said. "We must stay here and wait for the filidh to come."

I coaxed him back to his place by the fire, and he soon fell asleep again. He passed a restless, fever-fraught night. His breathing grew labored, and the coughing, when it came, was deeper in his chest. Once he awoke and sat up, saying he was going to take the sheep out to graze.

"It is night, Madog," I told him. "It will be morning soon enough. We will take them then. Go back to sleep."

He lay down, and the trembling started soon after. He shuddered and shook so much I thought he would break the few teeth he had left in his mouth. I built up the fire and put his fleece over him, but there was little more I could do.

Later, as the sun rose, he woke, saying he was going to take the flock to the south meadow. "Good," I told him. "Just rest a little and get your strength before you go."

He protested that he felt better, so I suggested that we eat something before we departed. While I readied the meal, he fell into a fit of coughing that squeezed him hard and left him weak and breathless. After that he sank into a deep sleep and did not wake again until evening. He ate and drank and then asked for his crook so that he could get up to relieve himself. I had to help him with this, and then he said he wanted to see the sheep, so I helped him down to the enclosure, where he stood for a while, leaning on his crook. He soon grew cold, however, and began coughing.

We went back to the fire, where he lay down, utterly spent. He slept then, resting more easily, it seemed to me; he woke only once, looked at me, and chuckled. "Crom Cruach," he said, repeating that portion of the story I had told him, "you have eaten your last soul."

He liked that, and he made me tell him again how we had walked into the forest and he showed me the dolmen, and how I had gone inside and found the round stone head and . . . he was asleep again before I finished.

I dozed off and on through the night and rose just before dawn, when I heard Madog call out in his sleep. I waited, but he said no more, so I got up and went to the water stoup and dipped out a bowl; I drank some myself and then took a bowl to Madog.

Though I shook him and snapped his ears with my fingers, I could not rouse him. The old shepherd's breathing was light and shallow, with a deeper gurgling sound that reminded me of the swish and surge of the sea. I poured a little water on his mouth to wet his lips and went to fetch wood from the pile. There was frost on the ground and on the trees; my feet crunched lightly as I walked.

I built up the fire and sat down to wait. At last Madog woke. He looked at me and said something, but his voice was so soft I could not make it out. "What is it, Madog?" I said, bending near.

He swallowed and drew a shaky breath. "Take care of the sheep," he said in a voice thin as spider thread. Then, closing his eyes, he gulped a little air, exhaled, and died.

It took me a moment to realize that Madog was dead. He seemed simply to drift away between one faint breath and the next.

I was still sitting there, wondering what to do next, when I heard a voice on the mountain trail. I rose and went to look and saw a man coming up from the valley. I hailed him and watched as he toiled up the last steep portion of the track.

"They told me the old shepherd was ill," he announced. Over his plain gray robes the druid wore a dark cloak ornamented with tufts of white fur, which gave him a curious speckled appearance. He carried a long staff made from a rowan sapling and a large leather bag on a strap across his chest.

"Madog is dead," I told him. "He died this morning. You came too late."

He nodded, his expression placid. "Show me."

"There by the fire," I said.

He walked to where the body lay curled by the edge of the fire ring. He knelt down and put his hand on the old man's neck, rested it there for a moment, and then turned to me. "In truth, his spirit has gone. He is dead."

"He is that," I agreed snidely. "And he has you to thank."

He looked at me curiously. "I know you," he said. "You roused Ercol to fury at the fleá."

I stared at him as a hazy recognition came to me. "Is it Cormac?"

His smile was wide and welcoming. "None other." Indicating Madog's body, he said, "I am sorry."

"Why sorry?" I said. "He was nothing to you." My peevish tone irritated even me. I do not know why I took on so. I suppose I wanted to rebuke him for taking so long to come to Madog's aid.

"You are right to feel grief for your friend," he said. "But he is beyond hardship, beyond care, beyond the pains of this world. Even now his feet are treading wondrous paths in the Otherworld, and his joy is richer than any he has ever known. You can believe this. It is so."

That a heathen druid, not much older than myself, should lecture me so with words my old grandfather might have used rankled me. "So you say."

He regarded me once more with a mild, almost pitying look and then said, "There is a dolmen near here. We can take the body there—unless you have any objection."

"It makes no difference to me."

The young druid made quick work of straightening the body and arranging the lifeless limbs. He uncurled the crooked hands and folded them over Madog's chest, then took a bone-carved comb from his bag and proceeded to smooth the old man's hair. Cormac's care surprised and even moved me, but I was still too irritated with him to credit the kindness.

When he finished, he indicated that I should take hold of Madog's feet, while he took the head and shoulders. Together we lifted the dead weight between us and started off. "Wait," said Cormac, stopping suddenly. "I forgot."

We lowered the corpse to the ground once more. Cormac stretched out his staff and, walking slowly around the body, spoke in a low, chanting voice. On the completion of his third circuit, he lowered his staff and bal-

anced it lengthwise on Madog's body. Then, taking his place at the head
once more, he indicated that I should grasp the feet. We raised the corpse
again, but this time it weighed nothing at all.

We resumed our walk, but it was as if I did not so much carry the body
as simply guide it along the path. Thus, holding to the old shepherd's ankles, I led the way into the forest and to the dolmen. Upon our arrival Cormac directed me to enter the burial chamber. We placed Madog's corpse
in the long, low passage; I bade him farewell and retreated from that damp
tomb.

The druid lingered, performing some heathen rites I heard him singing,
but the words were strange and unnatural. I considered leaving him there,
but waited nonetheless—more out of respect for poor dead Madog than for
any wish for companionship from the druid.

"He brought me here yesterday," I told Cormac when he joined me outside once more. "I think he knew he was about to die."

"That is sometimes the way of it," he replied.

"He was afraid of Crom Cruach."

I watched the druid closely to see what his reaction would be, but he
merely nodded.

"I told him Crom Cruach held no power over his soul."

I said this last part somewhat defiantly. I wanted to challenge the druid
to see what he would say in defense of his pagan beliefs. I did not, however,
tell him I had smashed the idol's carved head.

To my surprise, Cormac's gaze quickened with undisguised interest.
"Did he find some comfort in what you said?"

"It seemed to ease his mind."

"Then you did well," he replied. "The time for such fear is long past. The
world has changed, and men must change, too."

My attempts to rebuke the druid or raise his ire had failed. Perhaps my
efforts in the Irish tongue lacked the necessary cut and thrust, but he
seemed disposed to benevolence; no matter what I said or did, he received
it with benign—and aggravating—tolerance.

Even so, on the way back to the bothy, I could not help being drawn to
the pagan magician. "With Madog just now," I asked, "what did you do?"

He glanced at me, his expression earnest and thoughtful, but he made
no reply.

"And at the feast—Ercol was but a blink away from gutting me like a fish,
yet you prevented him with a word. How was that done?"

He nodded, considering the question carefully. At last he said, "The filidh have their ways. It is not for everyone to know how we do what we do.
It is enough that *we* know, is it not?"

"Perhaps." His refusal to answer irritated me anew. "I was always taught that druids consorted with, ah . . . *deamhana*, yes?—with demons."

Cormac pursed his lips in contemplation and nodded again to himself. Finally he said, "Now you have seen for yourself. Is that what you believe?"

"I have seen nothing," I retorted. "Nothing to alter my belief."

"Then ask yourself this question: Would a demon have rescued you from Ercol?"

The question was stupid, and I did not deign to answer it, lest I become entangled in a disputation I could not win. Everyone knows that Satan is a liar, the Father of Lies, who can plait words into pretty snares for the unwary, so I ignored him the rest of the way back to bothy. On our return he said, "Have you enough food here?"

"When someone remembers to bring us something," I said, and then realized there was no "us" anymore; there was only me.

"I will see that they remember." He looked around the area of my tiny settlement with the bothy, the fire ring, the sheepfold below and the forest above. "You will be lonely here," he said.

"I am a slave," I told him. "Slaves do not get lonely."

He smiled. "I will remember that." He wished me farewell then, but I gave no response.

I watched him until the slope of the mountain took him from view, then went to tend the sheep. It was not until I brought the flock back to the fold that night and set about making a meal from the remains of the food in the leather bag that I first missed Madog's presence.

As the days passed, his absence became an ache which grew stronger every day. I had not realized how much I had come to depend on the old shepherd. Now that he was gone, not only had I to do everything myself, but I had to do it alone. I missed his quirky companionship. I also missed talking to him. From Madog I had learned all I knew of the Irish tongue. Moreover, I had seen how my presence had forced him to recover his failing powers of speech. Without someone to talk to, I realized that, like poor old Madog, I might soon lose all I had gained.

Day after day I sat out in the rain and wind watching the sheep, gazing into the mist at the dumb creatures wandering around on the mountainside. And though my body was shivering in the bone-aching cold, my mind and heart were very far away. As the days passed, I could feel myself beginning to slide into loneliness and despair. How long, I wondered, before my sanity began to suffer? How long before I became as Madog had been when I first saw him?

I talked to the sheep, yelled at them; I hated them and vented my anger and frustration on their dull, witless heads. When one of them wandered off, I did not look for it. When one of them died, I did not care. I simply hauled the carcass back to the bothy, took the pelt, and gorged on the meat until I grew sick.

My clothes, little more than flapping rags, failed to cover me, but I did not care. By day I sat on the mountainside, picking lice from my filth-matted hair and beard. At night I dined on putrid meat, picking maggots from gobbets of flesh before searing them in the flames. My fingernails grew long and hard like claws, my skin tough as leather. Some days I roamed the mountainside roaring with rage like a caged beast; other days I lay by the fire, whimpering and whining like a beaten dog.

In my misery I imagined I could feel madness circling me like a wolf: wary yet, but soon, very soon, to attack.

Then, as winter began to ease its icy grip and the weather softened toward spring, I heard about the *boru*—the annual tribute levied by High King Niall.

I returned with the sheep one day to find two men waiting at the bothy. They had brought me some provisions and said they wanted to count the sheep. "There are the sheep," I replied. "Count them how you will."

One of the men drew out a length of rawhide rope and, while the other told out the number, tied a series of knots and double knots in the rope. The first fellow took out a second rope, already knotted, and held it up next to the first. Both men studied the ropes in silence, then looked from one to the other with expressions of such desolation that I could not help asking what catastrophe they saw in the knots.

"There are fewer sheep than last year," the man replied. "There will not be enough for the boru."

I did not know what he meant, so I asked, and the second man replied. "King Niall is king of all kings in Éire," he said, "Niall is Aird Righ, yes? And King Miliucc, his subject lord, must pay him many cattle each year."

"Yes," added the second man, his mouth squirming as he spat out the words, "and every year greedy Niall wants more."

"Tribute," I said. *'Teyrnged.'*

The man gaped in ignorance, but his companion said, "The high king's demand is too great. There will not be enough left for us, and we will grow hungry."

"Some of the sheep are near to lambing," I suggested.

"We will send someone to help you," said the first man. "To lose even one lamb would be a shame."

As he spoke, an idea formed in my head. "When must the payment be made?" I asked.

"Just after Beltaine," he replied. "It is always the same."

"And where do you take the cattle?"

"We take them to the high king's ráth at Tara."

The two left me then, and I sat down to think; for I saw in this the shape of my salvation. When Miliucc departed to take his cattle tribute to Niall, I would be among the herders. And once we were far away from this accursed mountain, I would make good my escape at last.

14

 BECAME DILIGENT. MY neglected sheep were my sole obsession. I led them out early and brought them home late, taking them to the best pastures, moving them from place to place so that the land did not become overgrazed. I watered them, pampered them, guarded them day and night; I even talked to them, praising their excellence and sagacity.

When the day came to deliver the boru tribute to High King Niall, I wanted to be among those making the journey, and my unstinting care of the sheep would create this singular opportunity.

As Miliucc's man had promised, I received some help during lambing time. Three herders came up; one of them was a slave and a fellow Briton—Aud, by name, the thin young farmer who had been taken in the same raid as myself. Ordinarily he worked in the valley with the pigs, so I had not seen him since coming to Sliabh Mis.

"How do they treat you?" I asked. We were sitting out on the windy slope a little apart from the others.

"I have a bed in the shelter behind the swine hut," he said. "It is not so bad."

"Sleeping with pigs?" I said. "You think that is not so bad?"

He pressed his mouth into a firm line and held his silence.

"No doubt pigs are better company than sheep," I allowed generously. "For myself, I would chose horses."

He nodded knowingly. "The king would never suffer a slave to tend his horses."

"No, I suppose not."

"I would rather tend sheep," he said. "At least they do not smell so bad."

"That is true."

He was quiet for a time, and then said, "Did it hurt very much when they beat you with the firebrands?"

"Of course."

"You must be very brave."

"I do not like being a slave," I replied. "Do you? Would you never try to escape?"

"I never would," said Aud. "I have nowhere to go."

"You could go home," I suggested. "Back to Britain."

He shrugged. "It is not so bad here."

I regarded him narrowly. Upon my life, I could not believe what I was hearing. "You *like* it here?"

"It is not—"

"I know," I interrupted, "it is not so bad. So you say."

He grew petulant. "At least," he muttered darkly, "it is no worse for me here."

A great surge of shame drew over me like a cloud passing before the sun. Embarrassment brought the color to my cheeks; my face grew hot with the knowledge that, for Aud, the fate of a slave to barbarians in Éire was not much different from his lot among kinsmen in Britain.

"I am sorry, Aud," I told him.

He turned to regard me, ignorant suspicion sharpening his gaze. "Why?"

"It must have been a hard life."

He shrugged again and looked out across the valley. "Was it better for you in Britain?"

Better? It was a thousand times better for me in Britain, I thought. Instead, I merely nodded and said, "Better, yes."

"Then you were lucky."

"I suppose."

The herders stayed with me through the lambing season, and seven more lambs were added to the flock. All lived, which made the herders happy. When they left to return to the valley, they said they would tell the king the good news. This made *me* happy. I wanted Lord Miliucc to hear good things about my care of his flock.

Winter departed in a spate of howling gales, and then, suddenly, it was spring. Small flowers appeared on the high meadows, and the winds and rain softened. My sheep and I roamed about the mountainside searching out lush grazing places; besides those Madog had showed me, I discovered others just as good. I groomed the sheep, too—pulling the burrs and matted dung from their wool to improve their normal bedraggled appearance. I also tried to groom myself: tying back my long, uncut hair and mending my tattered clothing. I bided my time, preparing myself as best I could, and at last the day came.

I sat up on the mountain before the sheepfold and watched the king's Beltaine fire in the valley below. I did not go down to the celebration, though I wanted to, lest some unfortunate incident befall me—Ercol, perhaps, might take it into his dull head to sharpen his knife on me again. Wounded, I would be unable to accompany the cattle tribute to Tara.

The Beltaine observances lasted all night. From time to time, the sounds of the revel reached me as a raucous commotion, more akin to a battle than a festivity. It ended at dawn, and I roused myself, retrieved my grass-cloth bag and water bladder, took up my crook, and, without waiting for them to come to me, I pulled the timber poles from the entrance to the fold and led out all but twelve of the sheep.

We arrived in the valley well before any of the others were ready, but I set the flock to graze on the soft new grass beside the river and waited. After a time the gates of the ráth opened, and some men emerged. I watched as they busied themselves at the cattle enclosure below the settlement mound; presently one of the men came to me. "You are ready," he said, and I sensed approval in his tone. "When the cattle have been gathered, we will leave."

Not wishing to give any hint of the excitement I felt, I merely nodded with what I hoped was dull indifference. As soon as he had gone, I complimented myself on my cunning and forethought. I watched as the cows and pigs were led out, and before anyone could tell me otherwise, I joined the train, keeping my flock a short distance apart—as if to allow them to snatch at the grass along the way.

As we prepared to set off, I heard someone shout, and I turned. Two men came running, calling me to halt. "What are you doing?" demanded the first to reach me.

"I am leading the sheep for the boru tribute."

"Go back to your bothy," he said, swelling with importance. "We do not need you. Slaves have no part in this."

"Very well," I replied. "*You* lead the sheep." I shoved Madog's crook into his hand.

I saw the two glance at the quickly scattering flock as I turned and stumped away. I could hear the two men arguing, and I had not gone far when the second man called me back. "Do not heed Ladra," he said, returning the crook to me. "You have care of the sheep. See you keep them out of the way."

We moved through the valley toward the hills to the east in a slow mi-

gration—twenty-five or so men with three wagons full of provisions and
more than a hundred head of cattle, pigs, and sheep. As we gained the slope
of the first hill, there came a rattle and clatter behind us as Lord Miliucc
and a dozen members of his warband and retinue galloped past. They
would go ahead of us and prepare the place where we would camp for the
night. With cattle it was a seven-day journey to Tara, and the king wanted
to secure all the best places along the way for his livestock to graze and
water.

One hill and valley, one wood and rill, gave way to another—through
sun mostly, but also fits of rain, and the long day ended in a meadow beside
a sweet-running stream. The next six days were as the first. As twilight descended over the land on the seventh day, we crested the last hill and saw
the immense Magh Fál, the Plain of Fál, spread out like a table. Many another tribute party had reached the plain before us, for the great flat expanse
glittered with the winking light from dozens of campfires.

Looming over all stood the brooding black mound of the Hill of Tara,
royal residence of the Éireann kings, with its triple ring of ditches surrounding not one but two great ráths, strong behind stout timber. From this
hill the Aird Righ ruled the petty kings of the north and kept a tight grip on
the reluctant, contentious subject lords of the south—many of whom had
come to bestow their tribute also.

It was dark by the time we found our place among the camps and settled
the livestock for the night. As had become my custom, I took my food and
ate apart from the others, then lay down to sleep near the sheep. Next morning we joined the great gathering.

King Niall of the Nine Hostages, High King of Éire, had established a
pavilion on the plain below the royal ráth. Beneath a canopy of red cloth
stretched between a half circle of yellow-painted pine poles was his throne.
Here he received the boru tribute of his subject kings, of which our Lord
Miliucc was but one of many—far more now than the nine that had won
Niall his name.

The whole first day was given to ceremony, most of which I observed
from a short distance. Many filidh were in attendance, dressed in their col-
orful robes. The leader of the druids was an old man whose cloak was made
from the feathers of birds, mostly crows and ravens, as it seemed to me, but
others also—red, blue, green, and white—so that when he moved about in
the sunlight, he glistened and gleamed like a giant speckled bird himself.

The druid chief held forth with a long, obscure recitation. It was difficult
for me to follow, because the druid used many words I did not understand;
but the declamation seemed to consist mainly of an exhaustive list of
names—kings and more than a few queens—and the salient qualities of

their various reigns. It went something like this: Brocmal Leather Cloak, King of Má Turand, peace and plenty blessed his nine years and two. . . . Scoriath Long Jaw, King of Fir Morcha, increased his realm through toil and battle; short his rule, cut down in the sixth year of his reign. . . . Conn of the Hundred Battles, wise and generous host, father of six kings; two tens and two his reign . . . and so on and on.

Our shadows stretched long on the ground before the recitation ended, only for another to begin: a song this time, in exaltation of King Niall's life and reign, sung by a filidh accompanied by another with a harp. The song was easier for me to follow, for although it was extremely elaborate in its lengthy, looping, intricate melodies and continuously repeated refrains, the story was that of a prince born into the noble house of King Eochaid, who took to wife a British-born slave girl named Carthann and made her queen. By another wife Eochaid had four more sons. This wife, the daughter of an Irish king, a bitter, ambitious, and conniving woman named Mongfhinn, soon grew jealous of her rival and plotted to make certain one of her sons succeeded the old king as Aird Righ.

But Niall, owing to his bright and winsome nature, won his father's heart while still a child. Seeing this, the jealous queen did not rest until she had soured the king's good opinion and made outcasts of Queen Carthann and her son. Through treachery, subtlety, and lies, Mongfhinn turned the king's heart against his British beauty, and she became a menial in the king's court; day and night she was made to serve the Irish queen, who made her water carrier for the royal house.

One day, Niall was discovered at play with some of the boys of the tuath by Torna, the king's ollamh and chief advisor. The old druid observed the remarkable qualities of the boy, took pity on him, and rescued him; he took young Niall into fosterage and educated him in kingcraft. When Niall came of age, Torna brought him back to court and restored him to his rightful place. The first thing the young prince did was liberate his mother from the drudgery of her slavery and install her in a house with servants of her own.

The old king was overjoyed to have his son restored, and he devised a test by which he might choose from among his five sons which was best suited to be king after him. So old Eochaid sent the princes to the blacksmith's forge in the middle of the ráth to choose weapons for themselves from among those the smith was making. While they were about this task, the smithy caught fire and the youths, seeking to rescue what they could from the flames, rushed from the forge with the items they reckoned of most value.

The eldest, Brian, saved a newly finished chariot, pulling it from the flames by hand; next Ailill rushed through the door carrying the sword and shield he had been examining; Fiachra followed, bearing the smith's good water trough on his broad shoulders; Fergus came close behind, carrying the king's fine harness for his favorite horse and an iron war cap. And then they waited. When waiting availed nothing, they shouted, "Niall!" They cried, "Out with you now! The flames are upon you!"

Niall emerged from the smoke-filled doorway bearing in his arms the anvil, hammer, bellows, and tongs. Torna, standing in watchful observance beside the king, raised his hands and called out, "See here! I call upon everyone to witness: Alone among his brothers Niall has rescued the soul of the forge and saved the smithy from ruin."

At this, King Eochaid leapt to his feet and declared, "By virtue of his quick wit and good judgment, it is Niall who shall succeed me to the throne!"

When the hardhearted Mongfhinn heard about this, she tore her hair and raged so hotly that no one dared approach her for two days. Even so, the vengeful queen buried her spite deep and set dark schemes in motion, so that when the aged king died soon after, she took the sovereignty to herself and bestowed it upon her brother Crimthann, who agreed to hold it until young Brian came into his manhood.

The plan succeeded wonderfully well; Crimthann took the crown, and Niall fled with his mother that same night to a remote and lonely place. But Mongfhinn, at first satisfied with her handiwork, grew increasingly worried as her brother developed a taste for the kingship. As Aird Righ, Crimthann gathered his power and made successful raids in the south of Éire, and against the Britons, capturing many slaves and winning a mountain of plunder—which he shared out to his warriors and noblemen, so they continued to uphold and acclaim him.

As Crimthann's fame increased, so, too, did his sister's wrath. When her anger and bitterness reached the boiling point, she plotted his downfall. In secret she concocted a strong poison, which she introduced to his cup one night when he sat at meat with his retinue. The Aird Righ drank from the cup and died screaming in the night; he was laid to rest, and Brian, the bitter queen's favorite, was at last proclaimed king. As the young man stood in the assembly of noblemen and was about to take the kingship into his hands, who should appear but Niall, with three fifties of warriors at his back.

In the hearing of all, Niall reminded the noblemen that his father, Eochaid, had decreed that he should be king after him; he praised the dead Crimthann for keeping the kingship so well and thanked Brian for his willingness to step into the breach and occupy the throne in the absence of the rightful ruler. "But I am here now," said Niall, "so your services, and those of your mother, are no longer needed. Stay with me if you like, or go. The choice is yours."

Brian eyed the massed warriors thoughtfully and, to his mother's horror, chose to stay and uphold Niall in his kingship. The old woman was so outraged by this twist of events that her flintlike heart swelled with anger and burst; she gave out a scream of rage and fell down dead. Niall wasted no time but gathered a fleet of ships and set out to put the Picti and the Albanach Irish beneath his reign. With his warrior host he sailed to Alba and was warmly received by the Dal Riada tribes, who welcomed him as savior from the ever-encroaching predations of the cruel Picti.

In Alba, Niall rallied the Irish tribes of the Scotti and harried the Picti over the moors; Niall chased the troublesome Picti back to their mountain strongholds, where he fought them and defeated them and claimed a hostage from each of the three largest tribes. Then the young Aird Righ turned his attention to the south, waged war on the Saecsen settlements along the northeast coast, and made them acknowledge his rule—again taking royal hostages in order to bind the belligerent tribes to observe peace with him. He raided in Britain and in Armorica, carrying all before him by the might of his warhost. When the battle season ended, he had established himself as king of Éire and Alba and overlord of nine subject tribes.

Thus, with this reminder of the high king's authority and power fresh in our heads, did the ritual of the boru tribute commence.

As with most ceremonies of the Irish, it began with a feast. Thirty oxen had been roasting since early that morning and, after another recitation by the ollamh, the great king invited his lords to eat and drink with him. Since no one told me otherwise, I joined in the feast, too. Indeed, there were so many noblemen and servants of noblemen that no one paid any attention to me. I took some meat as it was carried through the throng by servants bearing enormous wooden troughlike vessels on poles. Beer circulated in wooden buckets, brass bowls, and large clay jars. There was other food, too: salmon, venison, boiled eggs, and three kinds of bread.

I helped myself liberally to all that came my way, and what I did not eat I secretly tucked away in the bag I wore beneath my shirt. I did very well, and soon the bag was bulging, so I found a place where I could retrieve it later and stashed it there for safekeeping.

Then I sharpened my eye for the best opportunity to make my escape.

The chance came the next day when, having eaten and drunk their fill, the subject kings were summoned to council and, as their names were called, stepped forward to declare the size and composition of the tribute they had brought. I stood with Miliucc and his men and sensed their growing unease as one by one the lords, upon delivering the tally of their live-stock, were informed by the Aird Righ that their tribute was not enough.

"This is very bad," I heard one of Miliucc's men mutter. "If Gulban's trib-ute falls short, ours will not fare better."

"We shall have to raid this summer to make up the difference," another grumbled. "And that, too, is costly."

When the audiences ended for the day, there was more eating and drink-ing. This time, however, the mood was ugly. The first noblemen were angry and agitated by the failure of the high king to accept the payment of their tribute, and the rest were anxious that theirs, too, would fall short. As is ever the way of things, they took out their frustration on one another.

At first it assumed the form of boasting and raucous humor at one an-other's expense—the sort of thing I had seen often enough in the Black Wolf when the legionaries were displeased with their commander. As drink took hold, the humor turned cruel and tempers began to simmer, flaring now and then as when fat hits the fire.

I did not wait for the fights to start. As night drew in on the increasingly brawly festivities, I left the flock, collected my bag of provisions, ran for the shelter of the nearest wood, and disappeared into the all-concealing shadows.

15

 HE PLAIN OF Fál stretches far to the west and south, but to the east there are thickly wooded hills and streams. This is the direction I chose, and I reached the edge of the wood before night was half gone—pausing briefly to climb an oak tree to see if I had been followed. Pulling myself up into the upper branches, I looked out over the moonlit plain. There was no sign of pursuit, so I quickly clambered down and hastened into the wood, following an old and well-used hunting run.

All night long I walked, without rest, stopping only at dawn when I came to a divide. On one hand the run continued in a wide, lazy arc around the base of the hill; on the other it narrowed to a track which rose into the heart of the hills. One way seemed as good as the other to me, so I chose the second way and hoped for the best.

All the next day, I followed the track into the wood—stopping to eat when hungry and drinking from the fresh-running streams whenever one could be found. I kept my waterskin filled and refilled it often so the water would not grow stale. Midday on the second day, the wood ended; standing in the shelter of the trees, I looked out upon a hillside field which had been plowed and sown. There seemed to be no habitation nearby, so I continued, keeping to the wood and skirting the field until I could see who tended it.

As I came around the breast of the hill, two men leading an ox and wagon appeared. They saw me, too, and, fearing that if I ran into the wood a chase might ensue, I decided to brazen it out. Plucking up my courage, I resumed my pace and hailed them as they drew near. "Good day to you," I called.

They made no answer but regarded me warily.

"I've come from the boru tribute," I said, telling them the truth. Touching my slave collar, I continued, "As you see, I am a slave."

"What do you want here?" demanded the driver, swinging the ox goad in his hand.

"My lord has sent me to fetch him word of the nearest settlement," I replied, departing from the truth altogether.

"The nearest settlement," repeated the driver suspiciously.

"Yes," I affirmed. "Is your lord and master nearby?"

They looked at one another, and the second said, "Our lord maintains his ráth at Lios Beag; that is the nearest settlement, and it is not far from here."

"But you will not find him there," said the first. "He and his men have gone to the boru tribute."

"Of course," I agreed. "Even so, if it is agreeable to you, I might go there."

"Is there any reason we should object, friend?" asked the farmer.

"None that I can think of," I replied.

"The ráth is that way," the farmer informed me. "We have just come from there, and you are welcome to try your luck at the gate."

I thanked the men and continued on my way, making as if I would go to the ráth. Once around the hill, I saw the timber palisade rising up across the way, and I saw also what I hoped to find: a road.

Hurrying by the small, mean-looking fortress, I headed off along the path instead and was soon passing through a more settled and prosperous-looking farming country of large fields and grazing lands. In some of these, men and women were working; I greeted them as I passed and likewise greeted anyone I happened to meet on the road. Once I met an old man carrying a young child in his arms.

The child—boy or girl, I could not say—had a swollen eye running with pus and matter. I knew the complaint, for I had seen it once or twice among the children of our estate back home, and knew my mother's remedy. I stopped to greet the old fellow and asked how far the road continued and what lay ahead.

"This *búthar*?" He looked at me as if I were a fool for asking. "Why, it runs to the sea, and some say it goes all the way to Britain and back again."

"To the sea, you say." I nodded respectfully, taking this in. "And is it far?"

"Far for some," he said, eyeing my slave collar. "Less far for others."

"I see." I thanked him for his inestimable help and said, "I see the child is afflicted with a stye." Indicating the swollen eye, I offered, "A warm cloth with—" Here I faltered; I knew the remedy, but not the Irish names for the plants. "Wait," I said and, darting into the wood beside the road, I quickly gathered a handful dock leaves and a few twigs of green willow. "Here," I said, giving them to the old man. "Mash the leaves and scrape the bark from the branches into a bowl of hot water. Soak a cloth and press it gently to the infant's eye. Leave it for as long as you can, changing it now and then. This will draw out the venom."

The old man stared at me in wonder. "Truly?" he asked. "And are you slave to a Brehon?"

"I have seen it work before," I replied, and continued on my way.

The old fellow stood in the road and watched me until I was out of sight. I waved to him once or twice until I could see him no more.

Dusk found me on a hillside looking toward the east, where the road descended into a valley to run along the bank of a river. On a rise overlooking the lowland was a large hill fort, and there were a number of huts and barns ranged along the valley floor between the river and the ráth. A trio of herdsmen was leading a small herd up from the river. As it was soon dark, I decided to wait and make my way past the fortress under the cover of night, so I found a hidden place off the road and settled down to sleep until it was time to move on.

I lay in my secluded hollow listening to the ravens as they flocked to their roosts high in the surrounding trees. They filled the wood with such a cacophony of creaks and croaks that I despaired of getting any rest. I dug into my bag of provisions, brought out some bread and meat, and ate a little while I waited for the sky to grow dark.

Owing to the commotion raised by the birds, I did not hear the horses on the road until they were well upon me. Probably they would never have found me if not for the hounds. The first I knew of them, they were already bounding into the wood, barking as they came. I threw aside my meal and leapt to my feet. There was no place to hide, and the trees were too tall to climb; I could not outrun them, and even if I could, such a race would only alert the riders that they had found something worth pursuing.

My only hope, I decided, was to brazen it out with them as I had with the others I had met; it had worked for me before, and the small successes elevated my confidence. So, adopting the air of a weary traveler, I put my food away, hung the bag on my shoulder, took up my staff, and waited for the dogs to arrive.

Within moments they came plunging into my little glade—three of them, great black, slat-sided beasts; they tumbled in one after another, saw me, and halted at the perimeter, where they stood stiff-legged, baying as if at a prize stag.

Right behind them came two warriors on foot with spears at the ready. I suppose they thought they had a wild boar or a badger, but the sight of a lone youth standing calmly in the center of the hollow brought them up short. While one of the warriors called off the dogs, the other approached, his spear leveled.

"Who are you?" he asked.

I greeted him politely and said, "I am as you find me — a traveler seeking a little rest beside the road."

"This is King Eoghan mac Fionn's land," he informed me stiffly.

"I am glad to know it," I answered. "Please give my respects to your lord when next you see him."

He looked at me, unable to decide what to make of me. His friend, having leashed the dogs, called something over his shoulder as he led the pack away. "You can pay him your respects yourself. He is waiting on the road."

He gestured with the spear, indicating that I was to go before him. We walked the short distance to the road, where eight riders were waiting. The warrior presented me to a white-haired man with a red cloak over his shoulders, saying, "We found him lurking in the wood. He says he is a traveler."

I raised my hand in greeting. "*Mo tiarna,*" I said. "My lord, I am a stranger to these lands. It was not my intention to trouble you or your people in any way."

"Why are you hiding in the wood?"

"I am about an errand on behalf of my master," I replied. "I hid because I was afraid of the dogs."

The nobleman nodded. "Who is your master?"

"Lord Miliucc of Sliabh Mis and the Vale of Braghad."

"Your collar," said the sharp-eyed king, "declares you a slave."

"And so I am," I replied calmly. "I serve at my master's pleasure."

A frown appeared on the lord's wide, good-natured face. My free admission of slavery and my forthright answers to his questions perplexed him. He scratched his jaw, then gestured to the man who had fetched me from the wood. "Bring him," he said, lifting the reins, and he and his retinue rode on.

I fell in behind the dog handlers who, once they saw I meant to do as I was bade, ignored me. It was no use trying to run away in any case. I could hear them talking as they walked along but could judge little from their voices, save that the tone was strained and peevish.

The ominous mood continued after we reached the fortress. The tuath came out to welcome home their king and the menfolk, but after the greeting the crowd departed in a somber humor. The boru tribute had gone badly for everyone, I suppose, and now that it was over, tribes were having to come to terms with how to deal with the shortfall penalty imposed upon them by the Aird Righ.

I was taken to Eoghan's hall, which was similar to Miliucc's except that it was larger and the houses which surrounded it more numerous and in better repair. I was brought to stand before the king, who sat in his big chair beside the hearth, while his queen and sons greeted him and his handmaids prepared his bowl.

The white-haired lord was served, drank deep, and set the bowl aside. Only then did he deign to notice me. He slapped his knee with his hand and said, "A slave you are, a slave you shall remain."

"My lord," I objected, "I am Miliucc's man."

"Miliucc's loss is my gain."

"Certainly I am not worth the trouble which will come of this. I think it would be best for all that I should be allowed to continue my journey."

Ignoring my implied threat, he said, "Your loyalty to your previous lord is laudable. What service did you perform for Miliucc?"

I saw the way the thing was going and swallowed my disappointment; to resist would only make matters worse, so I tried to improve my position as best I could. "I was chief of my lord's stables," I told him.

His white eyebrows arched in surprise. "Indeed?"

"My lord keeps but six horses," I added. It helps to mix in as much of the truth as possible in these situations. "Most of his wealth is in sheep and pigs."

Eoghan rubbed his whiskered chin and slowly made up his mind. "Then you shall serve me likewise." He gestured to one of the men standing ready beside the door. "Take this one to the stable."

The man took me by the arm and pulled me away. As I reached the door, the king called out, "What is your name, slave?"

"I am called Succat."

"You will find me a fair and generous master. Serve me well, Succat, and you will be well treated."

I did not know what to say, so I thanked him and followed the king's man to the stable, where I was put under the command of the chief stabler, a grunting, humpbacked fellow with a potbelly and a squint.

"Eoghan sends you to me, does he?"

"He does," I replied.

"You a Briton?"

"I am that."

"You smell like one."

"Thank you."

That brought a smile to the stabler's lips. "I like you, British."

"My name is Succat."

"I am Gamal. I keep fifteen horses, but only five in the ráth at any time. I will show you the others tomorrow. You sleep over there." He pointed to an empty stall. "Hungry?"

"Of course."

"We eat after the king eats. They bring us our food here. You look a strong lad. Mind what I say, and we will get on."

"Fifteen horses are a good many for one man," I said. "Do you care for them all by yourself?"

"I had two servants to help me," Gamal answered. "One was kicked in the head by a horse and died. The other allowed a mare to founder; she died with loss of the colt besides."

I shook my head as if in dismay at this regrettable news.

"Aye," said Gamal. "It cost him a hand, and he is now herding pigs." He nodded, satisfied with this punishment. "Lord Eoghan is a fair-minded king."

What little I knew of horses I had gained on our own estate. In truth, I knew far more about riding than stabling, but I reckoned it would not be difficult to learn—and to disguise my ignorance in the meantime. In any event, I did not plan to stay in Eoghan's employ any longer than necessary. As soon as the next opportunity presented itself, I would be gone.

Eoghan proved better than his word. He was indeed a generous lord, and on the whole I did not mind my work. It was not demanding, and it gave me a chance to gain the measure of the tuath and search out the ways by which I might make my escape.

The aftermath of the boru tribute continued to exercise Eoghan and his people mightily. The tuath was so unsettled that even I, a stranger, could tell that they were not only displeased but near to despairing. The dark undercurrent of fretfulness and unease bubbled away like a caldron on the boil. I was not surprised when, a few days after my arrival at the ráth, the announcement came that, in consequence of failing to meet the demand of the boru, the king had no choice but to raise his warband and go raiding.

I thought this meant they would sail across to Britain, and I saw my chance. When those boats set sail, I wanted to be on board. Once I set foot on shore, they would not see me again. Of that, I was more than confident.

I schemed how best to get myself included in the raiding party but could come to no firm decision on how to bring this about, and after two days I was no closer to finding a solution.

"Oh, a raid is a very fearsome thing," Gamal informed me when I asked when it would likely take place. "It's the horses that pay the heaviest cost."

"I do not doubt it," I replied, remembering poor Boreas' last ride.

"We have not raided in more than fifteen years," he said. "I used to go."

"Truly?"

"Oh, aye," he said, "I may not look like much now, but there was a time I could fight with the best of them." He patted his potbelly. "I am too old now, of course."

Before I could respond, he said, "Maybe you should go."

"Me?"

"Aye, there is no need to look so surprised. The king often takes a man along to mind the horses. You would not have to fight."

"Well," I allowed, "if you think I might lend a helpful hand, I have no objection."

The next day I was called before King Eoghan. "Gamal thinks you would be helpful on the raid, and I agree."

"My lord," I said in all humility, "I know nothing about boats, but if you think—"

"Boats?" replied Eoghan, his face creasing in bewilderment before I could finish. "I have neither boats nor need of them."

"How then shall we reach Britain?"

"Ah!" answered the king. "We are not going to raid in Britain. We are going to Tir Brefni of the Connachta."

I had no idea where this might be but reckoned that if I was not to be taken to Britain, at least I would get a horse. With a horse many things are possible. "Forgive your servant's stupidity, my lord. I await your command."

Thus, when the warband departed three days later, I rode with them.

16

THE PEOPLE OF the Connachta are as harsh and wild as their wind-ravaged, crag-riven land. If the people I had lived among until now were barbarians, these were feral savages. Little liked or respected—even by their own kind—they were forever warring with one another and with everyone else. The tuatha of Connacht were a race without: without learning, without culture, without virtue, without hope.

Thus, whenever any of the other tribes decided to raid in Ireland, it was to Connacht that they went. Raiding in that untamed realm was chancy and it was perilous, but it brought no worrisome backlash of condemnation or retaliation from other tribes, for everyone did it, and the Connachta were so fractious they could never unite under one war leader to mount a serious raid beyond their own borders.

King Eoghan kept but a dozen warriors. My private qualms about such a small warband were quickly dispelled, however; by the end of the first day's journey, we had been joined by two more lords and their retinues. On the third day our number had effectively quadrupled, and by the fifth day the warhost had swelled to ten times the size it was when we first set out, and more joined the nearer we came to our destination.

The evening before we crossed over into the realm of the Connachta, there was a celebration of sorts: a riotous revel of the kind common to gatherings of warriors—useful, I suppose, for exciting courage and hardihood in men who must fight the next day. As one of the many slaves and servants who did not take part, I stayed near the horses and watched as the warriors engaged one another in trials of mock combat. As the sun faded in the west, the vigorous boasting and foolhardy demonstrations of skill took on an increasingly threatening aspect. I was more than content to remain a safe distance apart.

As I had the care of the king's horses, it was my normal chore to water them at sunset before settling them for the night. I was leading two of the beasts down to the stream when I met a group of late-arriving warriors hurrying to the celebration. As they passed me, I glanced over at one of them, and my heart seized in my chest. It was Forgall, Lord Miliucc's chief of battle.

I quickly turned my face away, fell back a step to hide behind one of the horses I was leading, and hurried on.

While the horses drank, I stood at the water's edge quivering in frantic distraction, trying desperately to think what to do. There was no telling where or when I might encounter my former master or one of his men. Next time they would recognize me.

I decided that the only course open to me was flight—as soon and as swiftly as possible. I would leave at once. Now.

Pulling the horses' heads from the water, I led them back to the picket. Stealing a horse was a serious offense, and I was of two minds: while it represented my best hope of getting away fast, if I were to be caught with a stolen horse, I would certainly lose a hand—or worse.

Tempted though I was, I came to the conclusion that it was a risk too great. I would go on foot. With the raid to occupy them, I could be well away before anyone thought to look for me. So as night descended over the camp, I set about collecting a few provisions to take with me.

One of the lords had brought a small, two-wheeled wagon that was loaded with food—hard bread, salt pork, and the like. It was to this wagon I went, hoping to filch a few loaves and some meat. As expected, there was no one near the wagon when I arrived, so I took what I could carry, stuffing it into the grass bag beneath my tunic. I turned to hurry away, making for the perimeter of the camp, where I thought to pause and wait until darkness was complete and I could slink off unseen.

I darted around the side of the wagon and ran headlong into three warriors. I humbly excused myself and begged their indulgence, turned and started away again—only to be yanked backward by a strong hand on my arm.

"I know you," said a too-familiar voice in my ear. I froze. My captor spun me around to face him. Disaster clasped me to its thorny breast—in the form of my old adversary Cernach. "All that time looking for you, and now here you are."

"I can explain, Cernach," I said.

"Good," the beefy warrior said, his voice thick with menace, "Lord Miliucc will be glad to hear it."

"Let me go." I appealed to the other two warriors, who stood looking on with puzzled expressions on their faces. "He is making a mistake."

"You are the one who has made a mistake, my slippery friend." The deeply malicious grin widened on his face. "And now you are going to pay." He turned to the two with him and said, "He's a runaway slave." The two nodded knowingly, quickly losing interest in the affair.

In that instant Cernach's grip loosened slightly. I took the chance and pulled my arm free, ducked around him, and raced off toward the center of the gathering, hoping to lose him in the general confusion of the massed warhost. I reached the near edge of the assembly and dived into a clump of warriors standing on the periphery. I wormed through them and out the other side, sliding deeper into the knotted clusters of men standing around the fire ring, where the flames were just being kindled.

I heard shouting behind me, but I ran on, flitting around the circumference of the ring. I reached a fair-size group and pushed in among them as they stood watching a wrestling contest. I could hear Cernach and his two friends shouting as they worked their way through the crowd. As they came nearer, I squatted so as not to be seen.

My intentions were mistaken, however, and one of the warriors looked down and, seeing me, cried, "Here! What are you doing?"

Laying his hand to my slave torc, he jerked me to my feet and shoved me out from among them. I fell to the ground, and before I could gather my feet under me, Cernach pounced. He clasped a heavy hand to my slave collar and hauled me upright.

He held me with one hand and punched me in the stomach with the other. The first blow forced the air from my lungs; the second brought bile to my mouth. I swallowed it down and, gasping, cried for someone to help me—thinking that if any of Eoghan's men were near, they might come to my aid. But if they heard me, they did not heed my cries.

"Cernach, please!" I screamed. "You have caught me. Enough!"

"No, boy, *I* say when it is enough. We are just getting started." With that he drew back his fist and smacked me on the side of the face, splitting my lip and loosening the teeth in my jaw.

"Cernach, please! I surrender!" I spluttered, spitting blood.

The sight of blood seemed to satisfy the two who were with him. "Leave off," said one of them. "You might kill him."

"Save your strength for tomorrow, brother," the other advised.

Cernach gave me a last, halfhearted punch and then pulled me roughly away. "Come, you," he said. "We will see what Miliucc will do with you."

King Miliucc, although surprised to see me, hid his astonishment behind a frown of regal rebuke at my disloyalty. He was standing with two other lords, one of a number of noblemen, and clearly did not wish to deal with me then and there, however much he might have preferred it. He glanced at me indifferently and said, "Chain him."

Cernach, exulting in his authority over me, imagined it was his superior cunning which had allowed him to capture me. He dragged me to the place where Miliucc had established his camp and, with a mouthful of boasts and curses, passed one end of a chain through the ring on my slave toru and proceeded to tether me to a tree. And there, with a kick in the ribs for good measure, he left me.

When he had gone, I tried to find how he had fixed the chain, but it was not long enough. I could kneel down but not sit, and I could not reach around the tree to find the end of the chain, nor could I move it one way or the other. I was well and truly caught.

Disappointment sharp as the burning ache in my side surged through me, and tears came flooding to my eyes. No criminal destined for the chopping block ever felt worse than I did then. I knelt whimpering in shame and misery, cursing my luck and wishing I had taken the horse after all. If I had followed my first instinct, I would have been far away from the camp and out of reach of the bloody-minded Cernach. I cursed him, too, and damned him to hell for his infernal interference.

All through the night, the warriors stoked their courage. I remained by my tree—sometimes standing, sometimes kneeling, as the chain permitted—and listened to the sounds of the warriors as they lashed themselves to fighting frenzy. The cries echoed into the surrounding wood and resounded in the empty hills 'round about: loud, bellowing, bloodlusting cries.

They left at dawn—close to two hundred mounted warriors riding out in ranks and waves—and an uncanny silence descended over the camp. The few of us left behind settled back to await the warhost's return. I tried to get one or another of the servants to release me. Every time someone would pass, I would plead and whine to be let go, but no one heeded me. A chained slave is a forlorn and fearful sight, and few will make bold to free him, lest they suffer a similar fate.

I languished through the day, forsaken and alone.

As the sun began to slide down behind the rim of rocky hills, the lords and their warbands returned—fewer in number than when they rode out, to be sure, and far less zealous. Some of the dead were brought to camp; the majority were not. I suppose they had fallen in the most hotly disputed places, and retrieving their bodies was not possible.

Despite the losses, the raids seemed to have produced the desired effect, for the victors came leading sheep and cattle, and carrying bags of treasure: objects and ornaments of gold, silver, and bronze which they had plundered, along with weapons they had taken from the dead on the battlefield.

Immediately upon their return the warhost set about preparing to leave. I suppose that, having made a most successful sortie, they did not wish to linger any longer than necessary in case the Connachta tribes regrouped and came looking to reclaim their stolen goods. The warriors washed in the stream and bound their wounds, some of which were fearsome indeed: One man I saw had a long, ragged gash in his side that oozed blood with every movement; another had lost three fingers on his left hand, and the rags he wore were stained bright crimson.

I stood watching as the warriors went about their business, and I wondered whether Lord Miliucc would return and what would happen if he did not. For a brief moment I entertained the hope that I might yet evade the king's wrath—but that was folly, and it swiftly vanished at the appearance of Miliucc and his warband with the last of the raiders. Like the others before them, the tired warriors bathed in the stream and hastened to break camp.

The entire gathering moved out, and I with them. Whatever words passed between my former master and my new one, I never learned; from the moment Cernach caught me, I did not see Eoghan again. I was unchained from the tree by one of Miliucc's warriors and led away behind a horse, and that was that.

Exhausted by the day's fighting, the warhost did not travel far—just far enough to put some small distance between them and any retaliation the Connachta tribes might attempt. The night passed quietly—but not without event for some; morning found three dead among the warriors. They had expired in the night. The kings would not countenance their burial so far beyond the borders of their own realms, so the dead were rolled in their cloaks and tied to the backs of their horses.

We broke camp once more and started off. I was tethered to the warrior who held the end of my chain. As the day passed, the various warbands dispersed one by one, going their separate ways, and taking with them the cattle and plunder each had won. Just after midday, Lord Miliucc bade farewell to his brother lords and turned his face to the north. The clouds closed in soon after that, and it began to rain.

Thus we made our way back to the Vale of Braghad. When the wide green valley opened before us, my spirits were as low as my chain dragging in the mud. I had tried not to think what would happen to me when we reached the ráth, but now that it was in sight, a deep and sickening dread came upon me. Images of the beating I was to receive pushed their way into my thoughts; as fast as I could quench one, another would spring up to take its place.

Oh, but as violent as was my imagining, the ordeal, when it came, was far worse.

We rode up to the fortress to be welcomed by the entire tuath. The king announced that the raid had been successful and that though they had lost four good warriors, they had acquired enough plunder to meet the boru tribute. He then dismounted and embraced his queen, who had the welcome cup ready. She placed it in his hands, and he drank. The people cheered their lord's success with shouts of praise and acclamation for him and the warband.

Then, turning to the warrior who held my chain, he said, "I will deal with the slave now. Bring him to me."

I was dragged to where the king waited. They forced me to my knees before him, and he stood gazing down at me, his expression calm but determined. "Three times you have run away, and three times you have been caught. What I do now, I do for the last time. If you should ever defy me and escape again, I will catch you. And when you are caught, you will be killed. Do you understand?"

I nodded.

"Hear me," he continued. "You are my shepherd, but you abandoned your flock. A good shepherd never leaves his sheep. He watches over them through all things. Do you understand?"

Again I nodded. Abject and wretched, I nodded.

Then, with a gesture, he summoned four warriors. "Spare nothing but his life."

The first blow took my breath away—the shaft of a spear brought down hard on the top of my shoulder. I screamed in spite of myself and struggled to my feet, only to receive a sharp jab in the gut from the same spear shaft. The second warrior joined in. Taking up the end of my chain, he pulled with all his might, yanking me backward off my feet. I tried to rise, but he kept pulling the chain, dragging me by the ring attached to the iron collar around my neck. I had to hold on to the torc to keep from being choked.

Meanwhile the other warriors began kicking me and thrashing me with spear shafts. I rolled on the ground, trying to avoid the blows, but to evade one was to open myself to another. No part of my body was safe. One of them landed a kick to my face; my jaw clacked, my head snapped back. Blood filled my mouth. Another kick caught me full in the ribs; I heard a dull, meaty pop and felt something give way deep inside.

Curling on my side, I tried to make myself as small an object for their abuse as possible. Each time I gained a modicum of protection, however, the chain was pulled to strangle and straighten me.

I gathered my strength and made one last attempt to climb to my feet. Confused, my vision blurred, I struggled upright and too late saw the butt of a spear swinging toward my head. The fire-hardened ash struck the back of my head with a crack that opened a rift in my skull and set my stomach churning. I vomited over myself, and my sight dimmed. My ears filled with a loud, juddering roar, and I was once more back on the beach in Britain on the night I was taken. I smelled the rank seaweed and heard gulls shrieking overhead as bloodred stars streaked to earth.

"I surrender," I gasped as my last conscious thought sped from me.

17

T HE OCEAN'S CEASELESS soughing filled my ears through the night. I woke with the sun in my eyes and blood on my tongue. My lips were gashed and puffed. My legs were numb, but my side ached with a fiery fury—as if a live coal had burned its way through my skin to lodge beneath my ribs. My hair was stiff with sweat and blood, and I lay on cold damp ground. I tried to sit up, and the movement brought a dazzling torrent of pain. I cried out, and this started my lips bleeding again.

From somewhere below me I heard the bleating of sheep, and knew that I was outside the shepherd's bothy on Sliabh Mis. They had returned me to my place and left me to live or die as I would.

I chose to die.

Indeed, I was as good as dead already. My breath was but a shallow thready wheeze that rattled in my chest; any attempt to draw air more deeply made the ache in my side flare with an agony that brought tears to my eyes. My left arm tingled oddly; it felt as if mice were nibbling at a place just below the elbow. But most worrisome was the feeling in my head—as if a fog of wool enfolded every wispy thought, blunting it, stifling it. I drifted in and out of a waking sleep, aware but distant, drifting, dreaming. Everything seemed remote and insubstantial, as if the world were as thin as the surface of water and the slightest movement would shatter it into millions of tiny reflections.

Sleeping or waking brought no comfort. My side burned, my head boomed with a hollow noise that was at once a gnawing ache and a soporific balm; the crack in my skull had grown a lump the size of a swan's egg. My mouth tasted foul from the sick-sweet blood I had swallowed; I longed for a sip of water to wet my tongue. The acrid stink of vomit was rank in my nostrils. My clothes were clammy with sweat and bile and blood.

My bladder, unrelieved since the day before, stretched uncomfortably taut, but I could not move. Instead I drifted into a reverie in which I strolled beside a clear stream winding its way through a peaceful valley in the full blush of summer; I came to an apple tree and stopped to smell the fragrance of the delicate white blossoms. When I woke, I found that I had pissed myself.

Unable to move, I lay wet and cold beside the dead ashes of the fire ring, whimpering like the beaten dog that I was. I do not know how long I remained there—a single moment stretched to fill whole days of agony—but once I felt a shadow move across my face as a cloud passed before the sun. The momentary cessation of heat caused me to open my eyes. I looked up to see a disembodied face gazing down at me. A fiery corona of living light blazed all around the angel's head.

"So you are still alive." The voice seemed to come streaming from an immense distance. Even so, it hurt my ears.

"Are you an angel?" I asked, my voice little more than the creak of a dry reed.

"I was worried about you," replied my visitor, and I felt a cool, feathery touch on my forehead.

"Have you come for me?"

"Yes."

There was a swift movement, which I tried to follow with my eyes, but the angel was gone. I drifted back to the weird, sleepful waking which extended an eternity; a thousand suns burned through the sky path, spinning like firebrands thrown through the empty heavens. Suddenly I was being lifted up and held close. A bowl was pressed to my lips.

"Drink," commanded a voice. I opened my eyes to see that the angel had returned with a bowl of water.

I obeyed the command and opened my mouth to let the cool water slide down my throat.

"Again."

Once more I dutifully obeyed. I drank down the clean water, and the sick-sour taste in my mouth was washed away. I looked up into the face of the angel to see that her large brown eyes held an expression of motherly concern. What is more, there was something about the face of this angel that made me feel I had seen it before, but I could not think where, or when.

"I am going now," she said; her voice, though gentle, pierced me to the marrow, and I cringed from it.

"Take me with you," I whispered.

I felt myself lowered back to the damp earth that was my bed, and Madog's old fleece was placed over me. "There is water in the bowl beside your head."

"Please," I gasped, "I want to go with you."

"Rest now. I will come back soon."

The angel vanished, and I sank into an unquiet, pain-filled sleep in which I dreamed strange, portentous things: ferocious, pelt-covered men battling with clubs and spears against steel-clad Romans . . . morning sun striking through a cloudless sky, filling a silent dolmen with light . . . a great beacon flame burning on a high, windy hill in the dead of night . . . an enormous basilica of red brick without a roof, its walls slowly crumbling, sinuous tree roots lifting its colored mosaics. . . .

I woke in darkness to the sound of crackling flames. The forest seemed to be on fire; the heat of the flames scorched me, but I could muster neither strength nor will to move out of its path. I closed my eyes instead and consigned myself to the inferno.

Sometime during the night the fire ceased. I dreamed of warriors bathing in a stream, washing the blood from their battle-weary limbs, and I awoke once more to the touch of a cool, wet cloth on my forehead. I opened my eyes to see that the angel had returned, and she had brought another angel with her. He was large, with wide shoulders and strong hands; his face, too, was curiously familiar, but I could not place it. They hovered in the air above me, the light of the morning sun filling their eyes, their countenances grim and disapproving.

"Forgive me," I croaked.

"Has he eaten anything?" asked the larger angel, drifting from my sight.

"No," answered the other, vanishing on the word.

"Soak some bread in sheep's milk," he advised. "See if he can eat that." His darkly angelic face moved into view again. "Can you hear me?"

"Yes."

"Do you want to live, Succat?"

"I want to go with you," I said. "Please, don't leave me here alone."

"If you want me to stay, I will," he said. "You must eat and drink something."

Suddenly the bowl was at my lips. I opened my mouth, and water gushed in—too much; I choked on it and coughed. The cough awakened the pain in my side. It felt as if a spear point lodged between my ribs was being twisted in the hands of an enemy. I screamed aloud. The bile rose in my throat; my stomach heaved, but it was empty, so nothing came up. I gasped for breath, but the pain was excruciating. Cold mist descended over me, and I passed from consciousness.

Sometime later I revived. I opened my eyes on a brilliant golden sunset and the smell of meat roasting on the fire. I moaned as I opened my eyes to find the large, dark angel hovering over me. He held a bowl to my mouth and dipped out a morsel of milk-soaked bread, which he pressed to my lips. I opened my mouth and allowed him to put the soggy tidbit on my tongue. The milk and bread were warm. My jaw was stiff and aching, but I chewed and swallowed, and the procedure was repeated—once more and again—until I could eat no more.

"That is better," said the angel.

"Am I dead?"

"Almost," he replied, then smiled. "Almost, but not yet."

The mice which had from time to time been nibbling on my arm returned and began gnawing with a vengeance. "My arm tingles," I said.

"Let me have a look." He pulled away the fleece covering me and lifted the arm. I could see it from the corner of my eye, and I no longer recognized it as my own: The limb was swollen, discolored, and misshapen, with an odd, bulging knot in the middle. He laid the palm of his hand on the knot, and instantly the tingling sharpened to a throbbing ache that made me cry out.

"Move your fingers," he commanded.

I obeyed, but nothing happened.

"Again."

I worked them again, but they moved only very slightly.

"It is as I thought," he said. "The bone is broken."

I understood the words but could not think what they meant. "The bone is broken," I repeated.

"Yes," the angel replied, "and two or three of your ribs." He lowered the all-but-lifeless limb gently to my side and replaced the fleece. "The arm is more worrisome, but I can help it to heal," he said. "The pain will be unbearable."

I looked up at him, wondering why he appeared so pleased with my wounds. "Where is the other angel?" I asked.

"Sionan?" he said, and laughed. "She has gone to get supplies." He produced the bowl again and said, "I want you to eat some more. We must strengthen you for the trial ahead."

Sionan, I thought, is my angel—she who came to me, she who brought help and healing to me.

"And is it Cormac?" I asked.

"Cormac and none other," the dark angel replied. He gave me another milksop, and I swallowed it down.

"Why are you doing this?"

"Are you not one of the Good God's creatures?" he asked, pushing another gob of milk bread into my mouth. "How else should I behave?"

I chewed and swallowed. "You could just let me die."

"No," he said, his smile quick and light, "that would be a sin."

This small exchange exhausted me, and I lapsed into a deep and dreamless sleep, waking once in the night to see Cormac, wrapped in his cloak, gazing up at the stars, his face illuminated by the fire. His lips were moving, and a soft droning sound issued from his lips—a gently undulating tone that rose and fell like the ocean's swell; if there were words, I could not make them out. The sound was pleasing, however, and I quickly fell asleep again.

Sometime later I was shocked by a shattering pain which brought me screaming from my sleep. I woke to find Cormac crouched at my side with my broken arm in his hands. Sionan knelt at my head, holding my shoulders firmly to the ground while Cormac straightened the arm, grasping it tightly above the wrist. Ignoring my cries, he reared back with a mighty heave, pulling on the injured arm with all his strength.

I felt a grating, grinding sensation in my forearm and heard a dull snap—like the sighing crack of a damp twig—and a pain unlike any I had ever known stole the breath from my mouth. I screamed, but no sound emerged. The agony seemed to last forever, but in a moment the fiery torture had dulled to an angry, livid, throbbing ache, and I lay on my back on the ground and wept. Meanwhile Cormac busied himself over me, deftly binding my arm to a slightly flattened rod with short strips of cloth he had prepared.

"There, now," Sionan said gently, cradling my head in her hands. "The worst is over." She raised my head a little and pressed a bowl to my mouth. "Here, drink this. It will help dull the pain."

I drank, and the thick sweetness of honey mead filled my mouth; I tasted also the dark tang of another substance mixed into the mead, but I was past caring. I emptied the bowl; Sionan set it aside and laid my head in her lap. Then she began to sing, very softly, very gently—and stroked my head until I fell asleep a short time later.

More herbs and elixirs followed, and slowly, achingly slowly, my body began restoring itself. In my waking times, which were few and brief, either Sionan or Cormac attended me, hovering like the ministering angels they were. I ate and drank what was given me and, having eaten and drunk, I eventually had to get up to relieve myself. As it happened, only Sionan was there with me, and though I put it off as long as possible, the time came when I could hold it off no longer.

"When will Cormac return?" I asked.

"Tonight," she said, adding, "perhaps. He had duties with his master."

"I see."

"Are you disappointed?"

"No, it is just that—"

"If you are uncomfortable, Cormac said I could give you some more of the potion."

"I have to relieve myself," I told her.

"Oh." She looked at me for a moment. "Well, we will get you up, then. Here"—she bent near and took me beneath the arms to raise me—"let me be your strength."

With a deft movement she lifted me into a sitting position, where, despite the ferocious ache in my side, I remained panting to catch my breath.

"Are you certain you want to do this?" she asked, the corners of her mouth bending down in sympathy. "I could bring you a bowl."

"I will not pee into a cup like a child. I want to stand."

It was a tedious procedure, fraught with pain and not a few curses, but in the end I was on my feet—dizzy, swaying, half faint with exhaustion. Every bone and sinew in my body hurt, every muscle ached. My bruised skin stretched tight on swollen limbs. The splint held my broken arm at an unnatural and uncomfortable angle, but I was on my feet.

Resting my weight on Sionan's shoulders, I hobbled a few steps beyond the edge of the fire ring, then stood in humiliation to pass water while she bore me up. That finished, she helped me pull up my trousers and stagger back to my place.

"Would you rather lie in the bothy?" she asked.

"No, I like it better by the fire. It is warmer."

"Wait a little," she said on our return to the fire ring. "Stand here and do not move."

Sionan darted away, retrieving Madog's shepherd's staff, which she put into my hand. "Lean on this while I prepare you a proper bed."

I stood gripping the staff with my good hand while she rushed around making up a bed for me from stuff she had gathered. Upon a bed of fresh pine boughs she placed several armloads of dry reeds, which she covered with the pelt of a red deer and some fleeces from the bothy. Then the excruciating act of lying down commenced. By the time I was settled again, I was shaking and sweating, and one or two of the wounds had reopened, but I felt as if I had conquered an entire army. I knew then that I would live and not die.

The bed of pelts and pine boughs was more comfortable by far than the damp bare ground. "Thank you, Sionan," I said. "If not for you, I would be dead long since."

She smiled sadly. "I could not believe they would beat you so and then leave you up on the mountain by yourself." She shook her head. "Stupid, stupid men."

"What will your husban—" Somehow I could not say the word. "I mean, what does Cernach think about you spending all your time up here tending me?"

"Cernach was killed in the raid against the Connachta." She said this as if describing yesterday's weather. There was neither sadness nor regret in her tone, and she did not seem the least sorry for the death of her new husband.

I thought back to the day of the raid. I had, of course, seen Cernach before the raid—if not for him, I would have made good my escape—but I had not seen him after. And when the warriors returned, I had worries enough of my own. "Oh, I am sorry, Sionan."

"Why should you be sorry?" she asked simply. "Cernach was no friend to you."

"That is true," I agreed. "But I thought you might be sad."

"Well, I am not," she replied, the fire flaring up in her eyes. "I was given to Cernach by the king. Our marriage pleased one person and one person only, and that was never me."

"I see."

"Cernach was a dull and ill-tempered man. He cared little for anything save fighting and drinking. He raised his hand to me more than once, and I vowed he would die—or I would—before the year was out. The Connachta saved us all a lot of trouble."

Sionan's bitter outpouring surprised me, and I could think of nothing to say.

"You condemn me for my hardness of heart," she said, gazing at me defiantly.

"Not at all," I replied. "Who am I to condemn anyone?"

"I don't care what you think. I did not like Cernach, and I never loved him. That is the truth of it." She frowned, lowering her dark eyes. "Still, I tried to be a good wife to him . . ." she paused, shaking her head, "but he should never have beat me."

She raised her head and looked away. I saw tears glimmering in her eyes. "I'm sorry, Sionan."

She rubbed away the tears with the heels of her hands, and an awkward silence stretched between us. "What about the sheep?" I asked at last.

"The sheep?" she tilted her head to one side. "Oh, they have been moved down to the valley. One of the pig lads is looking after them for now, never worry."

"When will Cormac come back?"

Her lips bent into a slow, teasing smile. "What, are you tired of me already?"

"By no means," I said quickly. "I only wondered."

She regarded me with benign concern for a moment. "You should rest now. When you awake, Cormac will be here, no doubt."

"Thank you, Sionan," I said, overcome by a sudden outpouring of gratitude. "Thank you for saving me."

"You said that already," she answered lightly. "Now, go to sleep."

She sat with me a long time, watching over me while I slowly sank into a deep, exhausted sleep. The next morning when I awoke, she was gone.

18

I T WAS LATE morning when Cormac returned to the bothy. The young druid stayed with me for the next three days, and we had many wide-ranging talks. His knowledge of his island realm seemed inexhaustible. I, however, was too easily exhausted. Try as I might, I could not keep up with him. Our mild encounters left me bemused, bewildered, and slightly disconcerted by the things he said.

For example: One day, as I was lying on my bed looking up at the dark clouds swirling overhead, he sat down cross-legged beside me and said, "Do you believe there are objects of such potency that the sick are healed simply by touching them?"

"I suppose." Certainly the rustics and pagan Britons held similar beliefs.

"It is true," he affirmed with a sharp nod. "There are other objects which protect their bearers from all harm and still others that cause no end of harm and mischief to anyone unfortunate enough to encounter them."

"That seems reasonable."

"Likewise there are seers able to view the past simply by holding an object."

"Have you ever witnessed this?"

"Oh, aye."

"How do you know what they say is true?" I asked, drawn into the discussion somewhat despite myself. The pagan practices of the godforsaken heathen were beneath the regard of civilized men. Yet, Cormac was my physician and friend, and I had no wish to insult him. He seemed intent on talking, so I listened.

"Ah! You are a quick one, Succat. You cut to the heart of the matter there."

"Well? How do you know?"

"Alas." He sighed. "It is hopeless. You see, no matter how persuasively they speak to earn their meat and meal, it is impossible for anyone to tell how much of what they say is true and how much is merely dream, how much speculation, and how much invention. Not even they themselves always know." He leaned slightly forward. "To this I can testify," he said confidently, "for I myself have the same gift."

"Truly?"

He nodded. "Even so, I can tell you that something is retained in objects that have been used and loved by their owners over time, or which are associated with great good or powerful evil." He picked up a twig and began scratching in the dirt. "A certain subtle power remains that can be felt and interpreted. But it is vague and dreamlike and fully as illusory as it is true."

"That is interesting," I told him. "Is there any more of the mead left?"

"And did you know," he said, warming to the subject, "there are sacred places so potent with holiness that they can be recognized by anyone who sets foot within the charmed circle of their grace—although no altar, no votive stones, no carved images mark the site?"

Before I could reply, he continued.

"Usually these are places where tremendous good has triumphed over evil," he said, rocking back and forth slightly, "or where unimaginable calamity has claimed a victory over the forces of light and reason. To step within the radiant sphere is to join the human spirit to the spirit of the place, for good or for ill."

I thought of the dolmen Madog had shown me and where we had laid the old shepherd to rest when he died. "It does not surprise me."

"All this I know." Cormac regarded me with a wise and judicious look. "All this I have observed."

We talked then of his druid training, and he told me many things. All the time we talked, he seemed to be assessing me, trying me—though for what purpose I could not guess. Perhaps my receptiveness to the ideas he expounded interested him. In my own way I was agreeable—at least I did not wish to offend him. I owed him a great debt of gratitude for my healing.

Whatever he saw in me, he seemed determined to delve deep and bring it out; thus our discussions grew by turns more earnest, solemn, and weighty.

"All men yearn for certainty," he proclaimed one night. This is how our discussions usually began; Cormac would announce the topic, and off we would go. Sionan had been with us earlier in the day but had gone down to the ráth, leaving Cormac and me to talk long into the night. "Do you believe this?"

"I do. It would be a great boon to know where we stand in this world, what is, what has been, what will be. And to know it absolutely."

"Indeed." He seemed well satisfied with my answer. "All men pray for assurance that time cannot corrupt nor doubt corrode. Thus the soothsayers compare the liver of a slaughtered sheep with the clay model in their hands and declare sureties which can never exist. Divine inspiration is lacking, therefore they are fallible."

"My grandfather said such men were wicked for deceiving those who trusted, and it was a sin even to speak to them."

"Nor is that all. There are priests who have learned the secrets of discerning the future from flights of birds." At my questioning glance he said, "Truly. But when they are confronted with signs they do not recognize, they become confused and utter their predictions blindly. Likewise, there are some who seek answers in the smoke and flames of sacrificial fires and others who claim to read destiny in the issue of blood and bile of dying men."

"How is this accomplished?" I asked.

Cormac frowned. "No, I will not speak of them. Nor will I stoop to mention the interpreters of lightning who ascend the hilltops before the storm in order to rank the thunderbolts according to their color and position in the vault of heaven, which they have divided into sixteen celestial regions, each ruled by a separate deity."

"Tell me, Cormac," I insisted.

But he would not. "I will not speak of such things, for thus it has ever been and thus it shall ever be. Nothing is more lamentable than dead and ossified knowledge: fallible human understanding instead of divine perception. A man can learn much, but learning is not knowledge. The only true source of infallible certainty is divine illumination."

"Now you sound like my grandfather," I told him.

"So you say. Tell me about him."

"Potitus? There is little enough to tell. I was still very young when he died. He was the presbyter of Bannavem. He performed the observances of the Holy Church for our town and the surrounding countryside."

"He was a Christian."

"Yes."

"And you?"

"I was," I replied, "but no longer."

"Why not?"

"Do you need to ask?" I said, my voice growing tight with irritation.

"Look at me, Cormac. I am a slave. I prayed for deliverance—with all my heart I prayed—and *this* is how God answered me."

"Then why not accept his answer?"

"Bah!" I sneered, exasperation getting the better of me. "Now you *do* sound like my grandfather."

"Is that so strange?"

"Strange? It is uncanny," I retorted. "I mean no disrespect, Cormac, but I find it more than strange that you, a heathen, should hold the same views as my grandfather."

"Where is the difficulty?" he asked. "Is it that your grandfather and I should agree, or that a heathen should know something of God?"

I stared at him. "What do you know of the Christian God?"

"I know what is to be known," he answered. The druid-kind, I was learning, rarely answered a thing straight when they could evade it somehow.

Before I could protest that this was no answer at all, he said, "Iosa the Mighty, son of the Goodly Wise, has long been known to us."

It was such rank nonsense I could think of no apt reply, so I said, "Who is this 'us' you speak of? You and your fellow idol worshippers?"

My nasty remark cut him; he did not expect it, and it stung. He winced, and fire came up in his eyes, but he held his tongue. In a moment, his expression softened. "You should not mock what lies beyond your grasp."

He stood.

"I am sorry, Cormac. You are right. It was a stupid thing to say. Please, forget I said it."

"Three things cannot be called back: the arrow when it speeds from the bow, the milk when the churn is upturned, the word when it leaps from the tongue."

The color crept to my cheeks, and my ears burned under his gentle rebuke. "I am sorry, Cormac."

He drew himself up. "Words are worth little when the heart refuses to hear. Therefore, judge us by our works."

The offended druid turned and stumped away. I tried to call him back, to no avail. I was left alone with my regretful thoughts for the night.

Sionan arrived late the next day with supplies. "Never fear," she said when I told her what had happened. "He cannot remain angry for long. Cormac is the mildest of men; when next you see him, he will have forgotten all about it."

"You seem to know him very well."

"How not?" she asked. "He is my brother."

"Then I'm even more sorry than before. You and Cormac have been nothing but kindness itself. I had no right to speak to him as I did."

"And I tell you he has already forgiven you." She regarded me with an expression I could not read, then said, "But if you wish to make amends—"

"I do."

"Then take off your filthy clothes and let me wash them."

"But I—"

"Tch!" she said, raising a smooth eyebrow. "You should be happy someone is offering."

"Sionan, I cannot move as it is," I complained, "and anyway, I have nothing else to wear."

"All you have to do is lie there beneath the fleeces until they're dry." She lowered the bag of provisions to the ground and stepped nearer. "Here, now, I will help you get them off."

"Sionan, please, can we not let it wait?"

"I think it has waited too long already," she said crisply. "Off with them, now."

I began removing my tunic, every movement a trial of stiffness and pain. I got it raised to my shoulders and could go no further. Sionan had to help me get it over my head, but as she tried to draw it over my splinted arm, I heard a rip as the well-worn fabric gave way.

"Not to worry," she said, tossing my tunic aside. "Now your bríste."

This was more difficult; I could do little more than lie back as, having loosened my trousers, she slid them down over my unbending legs. I pulled the fleeces over me once again, and looked at my once-fine clothes—now merely filth-crusted rags. "I fear they will not survive the washing," I told her.

"Well," she said doubtfully, holding up the threadbare trousers, "I will see what can be done." Then she cast a critical eye over me. "And how long since you were bathed and washed?"

"I bathe," I replied.

"When?"

"You cannot expect me to wash like this." I held up my splinted arm.

"When?" she demanded.

"Not since the last beating."

"And not before either," she said.

"We have no soap," I offered by way of explanation. "No one ever brings us any."

"Well, I have soap," she said. "I was going to use it for washing your clothes. You can have that." She looked around. "Now, then . . ." She saw the stone basin outside the bothy. "There!"

"Sionan, have a heart," I pleaded. "I cannot bathe in that. I am too big. Besides, what would we drink?"

"Come." She moved quickly to me. "Get up on your feet. I will put some water aside for drinking, and then you can stand in the stoup."

"Even if I could move, I would not do it," I told her vehemently.

But she was no longer listening. She filled the bowls and waterskin and, taking some heated rocks from the fire, put them in the stoup to warm the water. And then, with no thought or care for my dignity, she pulled away the fleece and began pulling and prodding me to my feet. I shuffled on her arm to the basin and carefully stepped in, holding to the side of the bothy with my good hand. Even with the heated stones, the water was still icy cold, and I had to cling to the rough timber of the bothy to remain standing as Sionan doused me until I was drenched, and then she began to wash me.

The soap was hard and strong, and she was vigorous and unrelenting in her scouring of my poor, battered hide. Aching, shaking, humiliated, I stood to her ministrations. She talked while she worked, but I paid no attention; every movement brought a wince or a twinge of pain, and it took all my strength and concentration to keep from crying out.

Finally the ordeal was over. She emptied a few more bowls of water to rinse away the soap and then pronounced her victim clean. "Here, take my fallaing," she said, draping her cloak over my shoulders. "There," she cooed, "is that not better now?"

"It is," I lied.

She helped to dry me and then stood a little apart, her head held to one side. "Human again," she declared at last, and, with a quick, calculating glance at my long, unkempt hair, added, "nearly."

She led me to Madog's stone beside the fire ring and made me sit down. She fetched from the bag a bone comb and a pair of shears, small and finely made. "What is this?" I asked.

"Every sheep needs a good shearing now and then," she replied, "and likewise every shepherd. Not so?"

With some difficulty she began dragging the comb through the wet, massed tangles of my hair, clucking her tongue at the wretched condition I had allowed myself to get into. There was still a large bump on my head where the spear shaft had cracked me, and I cried out whenever she passed over it. "Be quiet," she ordered. "You could be making it easier, you know."

"You could just let the warriors have at me again," I whined. "I am certain they'd happily finish the job."

"No one is ever going to beat you again," she told me, her voice taking on an edge.

The quiet confidence of that bald declaration astonished me. I wanted to ask her how this miracle would come about, but dared not, for fear of proving her false. I held my tongue, and let the assertion go unchallenged.

Sionan worked over my bruised head and with quick, skillful snips reduced the untidy crop of hair to a more acceptable length. When she finished, she ran her fingers lightly over the short stubble of my lumpy pate and admired her handiwork.

"Better?" I asked.

"Not so bad. Next time will be better still." She stepped before me and frowned. "When I come up next time, I will bring a razor."

I rubbed my palm over my fuzzy jaw. "Do you not like a man with a beard?"

"Only savages wear beards," she informed me blithely. Once more she regarded me with that look I still could not decipher.

"Savages," I muttered, thinking it was *because* of the savages that I looked the way I did.

"Savages, aye, and men who have no women to keep them shorn."

"And the clothes—you'll find me some clothes, yes? I cannot be wearing your fallaing forever."

"No?" She smiled wickedly. "Well, I like it. Maybe I will keep you in it."

"Sionan, please. It is cold."

She relented. "Very well. I will see what I can find and bring them next time I come."

She helped me back to my bed, then busied herself with making up the fire. I lay there and felt a warming peace come over me. In truth, I felt better without my rags, but it was more than that. For the first time since coming to Sliabh Mis, I was content. Despite my infirmity I was happy.

I lay on my bed of pine branches and watched a golden dusk descend upon the mountains. As the shadows deepened in the valley, turning the river at its bottom into a gilt thread winding its way toward the distant silver sea, Sionan set about making a supper for us of salt pork and beans.

I watched her going about her chores, deft in her movements, her features composed and radiant in the firelight. My heart moved toward her with such strength that I was glad she was not paying the slightest attention to me.

When she finished and sat down to wait for the stew to cook, she looked out across the blue-misted valley and sighed. "I like it up here."

"It is not so bad," I replied. I would have agreed to anything just then.

"Are you lonely?" She did not look at me but gazed out across the wide vale toward the sea.

"Sometimes," I said. "But at least it is not so noisy as the ráth. All those dogs—how does anyone sleep?"

"*I* would not be lonely."

The way she said it—a soft, almost reverent defiance—made me think she was making a vow, or a wish.

"There are the sheep," I said. "They are always to be watched."

"Better sheep," she said, "than warriors."

I ate well that night, slept soundly, and awakened feeling better than I had for many days. Around midday Cormac returned with his staff and bag. He strode to where I lay, took one look at me, and said, "Well, now, there is a man I would not mind getting to know."

"*Salve*, Cormac," I replied, "come and sit. Tell me the news of the wide world."

"*Salve?*" he wondered.

"It is Latin," I explained, "a greeting of respect and welcome."

"Ah, now, that is a fine thing." He stood beaming down on me, and it was as Sionan had said: he had forgotten all about my poor behavior. "How are you, Succat?"

"I may live yet," I said.

"I am pleased to hear it," he said, his smile spreading across his wide, good-natured face, "for there is something I want to ask you."

"Ask and consider it answered." I glanced at Sionan, standing beside him. "I have no secrets anymore."

"When you are on your feet and able again, how would you like to come and serve in the druid house?"

The question caught me unawares. I gaped at him, unable to credit what I had heard. Sionan held her head to one side, studying me for my reaction.

"Of course," he continued, "if you would rather tend sheep . . ."

"No! Not at all. The sheep can tend themselves for all I care. But tell me, how will this come about? Lord Miliucc will never agree."

"I tell you the king has agreed already."

I still could not believe my good fortune. "Are you certain?"

"As certain as sunrise," he said. "No king would dare refuse a druid anything he asked, so long as it was in his power to provide."

"You asked for me?"

"I did, yes."

"Why?"

"Because you are far too intelligent to be wasted on the sheep," he replied lightly. "And unless something is done about it very soon, I fear you will die here alone on this mountain."

"Help me up." I raised my good arm to him. "I want to thank you properly." The big druid reached down and pulled me to my feet with a single strong tug. "Thank you, Cormac," I said, gripping his arm tightly, "for befriending me and helping me."

Turning to Sionan, I took her hand and raised it to my lips as I had seen visiting dignitaries do with my mother. "And thank you, Sionan, for saving me." I kissed her hand.

"You have thanked me already," she replied, but her eyes shone with delight all the same.

"And I will go on thanking you both for as long as I live," I said. "Truly, I owe you nothing less than my life."

"Then it is settled," Cormac concluded. "You will stay here and rest until you are well enough to take up your new duties."

"I am ready *now*," I boasted. In my exuberance I stretched too far, causing my broken ribs to shift; a sharp pain pierced my chest, and I winced. My eyes teared up, and I swayed on my feet so that Cormac and Sionan had to help me back to my bed.

"Well, perhaps another day or two would do no harm," I allowed. Cormac lowered me back to my place, and we talked the day away, discussing my new position in the druid house and what would be expected of me there. As the sun began to set, he and Sionan prepared a celebratory meal of smoked fish stewed with black bread, fresh greens, and the last of the old year's crop of turnips. Cormac had brought more mead with him, so while waiting for the food to cook, we drank and watched the day end and a fine twilight begin.

That night, as the stars spun slowly through the wide heavens, Cormac sang. The wonder of his song is with me still, for it was the first time I glimpsed something of the power of a True Bard.

PART

II

CORThIRThIAC

19

NOW COMMENCED THE slow torture of waiting. I writhed in an agony of anticipation, impatience, and fear: anticipation for the glorious day when I could leave the sheepfold behind forever, impatience for that day's arrival, and fear that I would yet be denied. I itched and groaned for leaving. However, the healing of my body would not be hurried. My head and ribs remained sore and tender to the touch, my broken arm still throbbed when I moved it, and the splint was heavy and made my shoulder ache.

Sionan continued her daily visits and insisted she could tell I was getting better, though I was far from certain. True, I no longer needed help to walk, but I grew breathless if I went too far or too fast. Sometimes, when I tried to do too much, my head began to ache and dark spots swam before my eyes so that I had to lie down and rest until they went away.

Each night I went to sleep thinking that the next day my healing would be complete, only to awaken the next morning to find that nothing had changed. Summer was passing, and I felt a sense of rank futility growing in me—as if the good thing promised would never come to be or that it would be withdrawn before I reached it.

"Why worry so?" Sionan asked one day. "The word of a filidh is stronger than a forest oak. Cormac will not forsake you."

"But if I can't carry out my duties, he will find someone else," I complained. Raising my useless arm, I said, "Look! It's hopeless. It refuses to heal, and I grow weary carrying it around like a dead stump."

"There was a time," she reminded me, "and not too long ago, when you could not raise that arm at all. See? Rest and take your ease. The day will come soon enough when you will wish you had lingered here a little longer."

"Why?" I asked, suspicion quickening. "You know something. What is it?"

"I only meant—"

"If you know something, you must tell me, Sionan. What is it?"

"Succat, hush. I meant only that those who go to the druid house are kept very busy all the time. From what Cormac tells me, there is no end of work needing done."

This, of course, only increased my worries. What if they found I was not suitable for their purposes? What, in fact, *were* their purposes? What if they changed their minds about me? How long would they wait? I desperately wanted a chance to prove myself. Not because I cared a fart for druids. No. I had instead conceived a new plan for escape. This time, however, I would not run away. Lord Miliucc threatened to kill me if I ran away again, and I had no doubt he would do it. Never again would I allow myself to be caught and beaten like that.

When I left Ireland, it would be as a free man. Cormac had given me the inspiration. *No king would dare refuse a druid anything he asked*, he had said. They had asked for me, and their request had been granted. Very well, I would so ingratiate myself to the druids that one day they would ask the king to grant me my freedom, and, like it or not, Miliucc would obey.

Oh, it was freedom I was after, make no mistake—but I would bide my time; I would wait as long as it took. All the same, if I could not escape Éire tomorrow, then I would at least leave Sliabh Mis and the daily drudgery of the flock. The thought—nay, the *fear*—that something might yet prevent me filled my every waking moment and not a few of my dreams as well.

Thus I waited, fizzing with fidgety anticipation—until one day . . .

"See here, Succat," Cormac said as he finished his latest examination, "the day after tomorrow is Danu Feis—the Feast of Danu. The filidh will be leading the observance at the ráth. Come down and attend. When the celebration is finished, we will return to the druid house, and you can come with us."

I rose slowly, and looked him in the eye. "Thank you, Cormac." I embraced him, which sent a sting of pain through my arm and side. "I thought this day would never come."

Sionan stood a little apart, her brow creased in contemplation. She said nothing.

The big druid accepted my thanks and we talked of the feast, whereupon he took his leave, saying he had many things to do in preparation for the festival. "I will look for you tomorrow," he said as he departed.

I stood at the top of the trail and watched until I could see him no more, and then I returned to the fire ring to find Sionan with her chin in her hand, her face drawn and weary.

"Ah, tomorrow!" I said. "This is wonderful, is it not?"

To my astonishment she did not appear as delighted with the prospect as I might have thought. She smiled wanly and said it was a fine thing and that she was happy for me.

"Yet you wear disappointment like a crown, Sionan," I told her. "See here. After weeks of waiting, the day has finally come when I can leave this miserable mountain forever. You of all people should be glad, because you won't have to lug food and supplies up here every other day in the rain and mud."

She looked at me glumly, then turned her face away. "I thought you welcomed this as much as I did," I said, "but here you sit looking like you just swallowed a putrid egg. Why is this?"

She did not look at me, but kept her eyes on the smoldering ashes of the fire ring. "You have what you want. Why should anything be wrong?"

"I thought you would be glad for me."

"And have I not already said that I am?" she snapped. Angry now; her glance grew sharp, her voice tight. "It is good for me, too. As you say, I will not have to climb this mountain anymore or sleep beside this filthy fire one night and another." She stood up and, fists on hips, glared at me with defiance. "Best of all, I will not have to listen to *you* moaning and groaning about how miserable you are! I can go back to the ráth and . . ." Here she faltered, her anger giving way to anguish. "Anyway, what do you care? Go on with you."

"You are annoyed because I am leaving," I said, trying to tease it out of her.

She sniffed and turned away.

"Yes, you are," I challenged. "You are annoyed because I am leaving and going to the druid house, and you think you won't see me anymore."

She turned on me with a vengeance. "Why would I want to see you anymore? I do not care where you go or what you do."

"Yes, you do," I told her. "You like me."

"No, I do not like you at all."

"Yes, you do." I stepped closer. "That's it isn't it? You like me, and you are afraid now that I'm better, I won't need you anymore."

She regarded me from beneath lowered brows, her frown pushing out her lower lip. On impulse I leaned forward and kissed her. Sionan reared back as if struck. She glared at me and then, stepping close, took my head between her hands and returned my kiss with an eagerness that was both gratifying and breathtaking. I felt a rising hunger in the pit of my stomach and heard the sound of the sea rushing in my ears.

We stood and clung to one another for a moment and, still entangled in a tight embrace, lowered ourselves onto my bed of pine branches and fleeces. I caressed her with my good hand. Beneath the coarse-woven stuff of her mantle, her skin was soft and cool against my fingertips. I let my hand glide up her leg to the rounded smoothness of her hip and then down to the silky warmth of her thigh.

Sionan's hands were not idle. She slid her palm down my chest and stomach and then lower, until I stirred beneath her hand, thrilling to her touch. There was nothing but Sionan and then—nothing at all in the world. I pulled her over on top of me.

We made love fiercely, two young and hungry animals feeding a physical appetite, each taking pleasure from the other, once and again. I was, alas, too easily exhausted, but Sionan appeared well satisfied as she gave out a shuddering sigh and collapsed upon my chest.

We rested in the warm sunlight, our bodies joined in a wanton embrace. "I will come and see you every day," I told her.

"They will keep you very busy," she said.

"Then I will come to the ráth whenever I can," I told her. "I will sneak away if I have to."

"You must not," she told me. Turning in my arms to face me, she warned me solemnly, "You must not break faith with the filidh. If you leave the druid house, you will not be taken back again."

"Then you will have to come and see me."

"Why would I ever come to see you?" she asked.

"What, and have you forgotten so soon?" I heaved a heavy sigh. "Very well, I will just have to show you again, so you remember."

Enfolding her in my arms, I nuzzled the hollow of her neck and kissed her. Our passions roused, we made love again, slowly this time, each motion deliberate and unhurried. She matched my passion with her own, and we moved as one beneath the sun-bright sky.

That day was surely the best of my life. I found in Sionan more than a lover; she was also a friend I knew I could trust. Something changed in me that day, and though it would be a long time before I could put a name to it, I felt the change.

Sionan and I luxuriated in our pleasure, and when twilight came, we lay before the fire—dozing, dreaming, wrapped in one another's arms. The next morning we descended the mountain to join in the Feast of Danu, the celebration marking midsummer.

The journey was taxing to me. Perhaps I was not so strong as I imagined, or perhaps the lovemaking the day before had taken its toll. In any event I found I could not move quickly, nor without frequent stops to rest. The fleá had already begun by the time we arrived. We passed through the gates and made our way to the yard outside Lord Miliucc's hall, where the tuath had gathered to watch the first of many observances held throughout the day—this one a recitation by the ollamh. So far as I could tell, it was all about a pact made by the god Aengus with the Tuatha DeDanaan, which ended a drought and blessed the rain in perpetuity to the people of Éire so long as they honored him on that day.

After this there were songs and dancing. As at Beltaine an ox and several pigs had been killed to provide food for the feast and the vat of beer set up to wet throats dry from singing. Sionan went to help with the cooking, and I drifted here and there, watchful and wary, uncertain what reaction my presence might provoke. I could have been a phantom for all anyone noticed. I did manage to raise a sneer from Ercol when I encountered him at the drinking vat, but even that lacked conviction.

Just when I thought the day would end without the slightest mischance, I ran into the king. He was more than a little drunk, but he had not forgotten our last encounter. "So!" he said, drawing himself up as if offended by the sight of me. "You are to go to the druid house, and I must find another shepherd."

I did not know what to say to this, so I merely nodded.

"I do not know what the druids want with you," he proclaimed loudly, his words slurring gently in his mouth. "I suppose that is their business."

"Yes, lord."

"Well, they are welcome to you," he told me, "but try to escape again and nothing will prevent me from making good my vow." He paused, glaring at me. "Understood?"

"I understand, lord." I bowed low, and the king moved off without another word.

"Here, Succat! I have been looking for you."

I turned to see Cormac striding toward me. "Hail, Cormac Miach," I called. "I am glad to see you."

"How are you feeling?"

"Never better," I lied. "What is more, I am eager to begin my new duties."

"All in good time," said Cormac. "The ceremonies will end at dusk," he told me, "and although the fleá will continue until dawn, we must return to the druid house."

"I will be ready."

In all it was a fine celebration, and it put me in mind of the harvest festivals my father hosted for the families and laborers on our estate at Favere Mundi. The Irish were noisier by far and more contentious, to be sure, but their childlike exuberance put the British to shame. When they danced, their bodies were seized and taken up by the fleeting joy of the dance—as if the moment would never come again and they must wring the utmost from it. Although I could but sit and watch, it was exhilarating just to see them.

The weather remained dry and warm; the food was good, the drink plentiful. Very few fights broke out, and there was hardly any bloodshed. I ate and drank with the rest of them, and the beer eased the dull ache of my wounds until I could almost forget I had been injured at all. Every now and then I caught a glimpse of Sionan; once she smiled when she saw me watching her. I was just on the point of suggesting we sneak away somewhere to be alone when Cormac appeared to tell me it was time to leave.

"So soon?" I said, looking quickly around. Sionan had disappeared once more.

"Was there something?" the druid asked.

"I wanted to bid Sionan farewell."

"Oh? Well, she must have gone to the king's hall." He turned abruptly. "You will see her again one of these days. But now it is time to go."

Still I hesitated. I hated leaving without telling her good-bye. Frantically I searched the crowd, but she was nowhere to be seen.

Cormac stopped and turned back. "Changed your mind already?"

"No," I said, hurrying to join him.

At the gate of the ráth, I paused to take a lingering look behind me, hoping for one last glimpse of Sionan, but no one appeared at the gate. So, swallowing my disappointment, I fell into step behind Cormac and went to begin my new life in the druid house.

20

HE DRUID HOUSE occupied the center of a wood atop a hill on the other side of the valley from the king's ráth. The house was a large, round structure of ancient design; whole tree trunks had been embedded in the ground and their tops joined with stout beams. Slats of unfinished timber were attached to the upright posts, which also supported a steep, conical roof thatched with reeds. The floor was clay, smooth as polished stone, packed hard, and overlain with mats woven of dry river grass. There was but one door and no windows.

Inside, the single great room was divided into two levels, the lower of which was further divided by screens of stretched skin. The upper level was a circular platform with sleeping places that overlooked the round fire pit in the center of the room. Save for certain occasions, the fire was never allowed to go out, and the smoke rose through a large open hole high up in the roof.

"Welcome, to Cnoc an Dair," said Cormac.

"Mound of the Oak," I said. The huge round house, with its high sloping roof, *did* look like a hill made of solid oak.

"Come." He beckoned me in. "I will show you our house."

The other filidh had gone before us, and I thought to meet them, but the house was empty. When I asked where they were, Cormac explained, "Tonight is the summer solstice—a good night for watching the stars. We observe their movements and mark their courses. Here, now"—he led me to a wooden stairway and up to the circular platform—"our sleeping places are here."

Although there was room for perhaps twenty or more people to rest comfortably on the platform, there were only four places prepared, each equally distant from the others. "As you can see," said Cormac, "there are only four filidh in residence now."

"Now?" I wondered.

"There were more. When I came, there were seven, but now there are only four of us." The way he said it made me think that something lamentable had happened to reduce the population to an undesirably low number.

"Will I sleep here, too?" I asked.

"No," he replied, "your bed is below."

My sleeping place was a square reed mat on the floor beside the hearth. The mat was covered with a pile of rushes topped by a double fleece, which in turn was covered by a thick woolen batting—like a cloak in size, but much thicker and woven of undyed wool. I would sleep near the hearth so that I could tend the fire and keep it burning. "This fire," Cormac told me, indicating the glowing flame, "is the need fire for King Miliucc and his people. It must never go out."

Beside the bed place were a pottery jar and a small oil lamp in a stone bowl. I picked up the jar, removed the stopper, and looked inside. "Water?" I asked, thinking it must be used in some odd ritual connected with my duties.

"Do you never get thirsty in the night?" wondered Cormac.

He then led me around the ground floor and showed me how the large, circular expanse was divided for the principal activities of the filidh—most of which had to do with study and learning. Some of these were screened off from one another, but mostly the great room was open, save for a single large area hived off behind thick timber walls.

"This is the storeroom," said Cormac, pushing open the door, "and here, as you can see, are our provisions." The room was filled with bags, casks, bundles, and baskets containing all kinds of supplies: grain and ground flour; oil; dried peas and beans; dried, salted, and smoked meats; ropes of onions; chains of garlic and leeks; whole honeycombs; and even huge jars of wine. The storeroom was almost as well-supplied as my mother's kitchen at Favere Mundi. There was also a caldron, two smaller pots, and an assortment of vessels of various sizes made of pottery, stone, and wood. There were spoons, flesh hooks and toasting forks, and several good sharp knives.

"This will be your realm, Succat. You will prepare and cook our food," the druid told me, "and maintain the stocks of provisions."

"With pleasure." I saw one sumptuous meal after another stretching into the future. There would be no more hungry days for me and no more miserable nights trying to sleep with a gnawing emptiness in the belly because someone could not be bothered to bring provisions to the shepherds.

"You will also fetch water, fill the lamps, cut wood for the fire, and tend the garden and midden heap—all the things which make for the proper and efficient function of this house."

"I will do my best, Cormac."

Cnoc an Dair occupied the top of a sacred hill, site of an ancient spring which fed a pool and holy well. The pool, although considered holy, too, was where the druids bathed at least once a week. After showing me the house, Cormac led me out to the well and pool, provided me with a hunk of soap, and told me to bathe. The water was cold, and I made short work of the exercise. While I washed, Cormac took away my old clothes and brought me a new tunic, mantle, and fallaing.

Unlike most of their countrymen, the filidh did not wear trousers; they robed themselves instead in the finest tight-spun cloth. The tunic was a close-fitting garment with long sleeves, covering the body from wrists to ankles; the mantle was shorter, fuller, and had wide, slightly shorter sleeves. Both garments were woven of pale, wheat-colored linen; the cloak, for summer, was linen, too, and a fine light green.

The druids loved good leather; their shoes, belts, and satchels were the best of their kind anywhere. I was glad to get new shoes—my old ones had long since worn through—and the belt, although plain, was as thick and broad and easily as fine as any I had ever worn.

When I was dressed, Cormac pronounced me fit to begin my new duties. That night, while the filidh watched the stars, I made myself comfortable in my new bed and went to sleep full of determination to make a good beginning.

The next morning, however, I rose too late. My masters came to the table ready to break their fast, and I was still asleep. How was I to know druids rose before dawn and went out to greet the new day with a song of welcome?

I leapt from bed and set about making up the fire and preparing the first meal of the day. The filidh were accustomed to two meals: one in the morning and one in the early evening. They most often fasted from sundown to sunrise the next morning and broke fast before sitting down to their work for the day—which, I soon discovered, consisted mainly of learning.

That first day I made a simple porridge of cracked oats with a little milk and salted fish, which I served with bread and butter. After they had eaten, Cormac and Datho, master of the house, came to me. "That was well begun," the ollamh said. "Continue likewise and you will be happy here."

I thanked him and said, "You must tell me what food you like, and I will do my best to make it."

"As to that," said Datho, "I am very fond of honey bread. Do you know it?"

I confessed that I did not know how to make honey bread, nor any other kind, whereupon Cormac said, "Perhaps my sister can show you." Turning to Datho, he said, "With your permission, Ollamh, I will ask Sionan to come here one day soon and show Succat how to make the honey bread."

"Of course, yes. You have my permission," said the chief druid. He turned and started away, "Come, Cormac, let us return to our labors."

They left me then to get on with my duties, and I spent the afternoon in the pleasant knowledge that I would see Sionan again very soon. Although my injuries still pained me and the splint made movement fatiguing and awkward, I did my best to get on with my chores. I emptied the jars and re-filled them with fresh water and topped up the lamps with oil; I brought in wood for the hearth, scrubbed the pot, and carried water from the well to the cistern inside the house. When I had finished all this, it was time for me to begin preparing the main meal of the day, which was taken early in the evening.

For Madog and myself it was simply a matter of boiling up or roasting whatever came to hand. For the druids, however, meals were more elabo-rate; also, they were more particular in their preferences, especially where seasonings were concerned. Thus my cooking responsibilities took a great deal of thought and effort, and I had little time for anything else. I marveled at how quickly the days sped past.

On the mountain I would sit on a rock or laze in the meadow with the sheep whole days at a time—swooning from the blinding tedium. In the druid house I worked as fast as I could all day and still failed to get every-thing done as required. The cooking, cleaning, washing, sweeping, chop-ping, carrying, and all the rest kept me occupied from dawn's first gleam until I collapsed into bed at night, my injured limbs throbbing from the ex-ertion.

I quickly came to know my masters. Foremost among them was Datho, the ollamh, or Chief Bard: he of the high-domed head, and beaklike nose. Tall and thin, possessed of an intense and penetrating gaze, he reminded me of a great heron. Like many of his rank, he shaved the hair from the front of his head, passing the razor in a line from ear to ear. This gave him a fiercely stern, almost frightening aspect—an expression belied by the glinting kindliness of his dark eyes. Forbidding in aspect, exacting in his de-mands, he was nevertheless a tenderhearted, thoughtful man, and I liked him.

Slightly below him in rank was Iollan, eldest of the druids in the house, with sparse gray hair—also shaved from the front of his head—and a long nose above a small, even mouth. Quiet, he rarely spoke, his thoughts so deep and impenetrable he was apt to forget where he was or what he was doing. At supper one night he reached for bread, but his hand paused halfway to his mouth and stayed there, its motion suspended until sometime later when the inner turmoil had been resolved and he could continue his meal. On another occasion I found him standing outside the house, immobile, lost in thought, oblivious to the rain pelting down on his uncovered head. I led him back inside to stand by the hearth until he dried out.

Then there was Cormac, a big man, as I say. He and Sionan, I learned, were offspring of the former king's champion; Cormac's father had placed him in the care of the Learned Brotherhood when he was still an infant. Having never known another way of life, he was a druid heart and soul.

Buinne, last and least among the filidh, had no discernible virtues. He was a dark-haired, dough-faced youth with a lumpy chin and small, close-set, suspicious eyes set in a narrow, disapproving face, which gave him the appearance of an aggrieved weasel. He had the temperament to match. Indeed, in petulance and rancor he reminded me of the departed Cernach, lacking only the dead warrior's endearing strength of character. How Buinne ever came to be among the high-minded druids was a mystery I never solved.

In those first days and weeks, my work occupied me entirely. As I became better acquainted with my chores and more proficient at performing them, I began to find little snatches of time here and there for myself. When I had a moment to spare, I would usually go listen to the others as they engaged in learned discussion with Datho. Creeping near, I settled quietly to hear what they said.

"Consider the Wheel of the Winds," Datho declared one day, "all-encompassing, perpetually turning, forever assailing, its manifold constituents producing both benefits and calamities." To Buinne he said, "Tell me, brother, what is the name of the principal wind and its qualities?"

"Hear me, my brother, and judge my reply," Buinne answered, bowing slightly from the waist as he sat cross-legged on his reed mat. "The Chief of Winds is named Solan, Champion of a Thousand Battles: salutary to all fruiting things, yet plague-fermenting."

"Continue," said Datho with a nod.

"Next in rank is Saron, Benefactor of Rich Harvests and also fish of wondrous size." The ollamh gestured with his hand for the young druid to continue. "Just below Saron is Favon: Destroyer of Corn when heavy and cold, Sifter of Blossoms when light and warm."

"Good," said Datho. "Now tell me, if you can, what Favon signifies when it departs its true path and roars out of the west."

"It signifies the death of a king when it comes out of the west, my brother."

"Well said," affirmed Datho with satisfaction. Turning to Cormac, sitting at his left hand, he said, "Recite the lineage of true poetry, if you please."

"With pleasure, brother," replied Cormac. Placing the palms of his hands together, he tilted back his head and, in a voice imbued with the rhythm of song, replied,

> True poetry is born of scrutiny,
> Scrutiny, the son of meditation,
> Meditation, the son of lore,
> Lore, the son of inquiry,
> Inquiry, the son of investigation,
> Investigation, the son of knowledge,
> Knowledge, the son of understanding,
> Understanding, the son of wisdom,
> Wisdom, the son of Surrender to the Divine Will.

The chief bard nodded serenely and pronounced, "Well said, brother, and worthy to be remembered."

In this way they proceeded throughout the day, and I gradually began to learn the order of their existence. Sometimes Datho held forth on subjects the others required to make their learning more complete. At other times he set them a question or a challenging task which they were to explore or undertake; they would go away to perform their explorations or undertakings, returning later to discuss what had happened and what was learned. Sometimes the filidh would question the ollamh, who would answer them by means of riddles they would have to solve in order to discover the answer.

Iollan pursued his learned activities on his own; he neither consulted much with Datho nor engaged those beneath him in the same way as the ollamh. His method—his purpose, perhaps—was to ask awkward questions. Indeed, he often posed questions so difficult that either discussion ceased or disputes broke out which could only be settled by lengthy study and investigation.

I listened to everything they said, spending as much time with them as my never-ending duties allowed. One night, as they sat at their supper, I stood a little apart and listened to them discuss one of the many uses for a druid's staff. "This is why," Cormac said, "the staff must be chosen very carefully."

"It is the power of the filidh that works through the staff, is it not?" said Buinne.

"Of course," granted Cormac.

"If that is so," continued Buinne, "then any tree or indeed any object fashioned of wood may serve for a staff, since one length of timber is much like any other."

"So it would seem," agreed Iollan. He smiled wanly, paused, and then drew a weary breath. "But have you considered what is told of the *clidh*?"

Cormac and Buinne glanced at one another and winced. Datho only smiled, nodding to himself.

"The clidh, like the filidh, partakes of the nature of his staff, which is strong and straight. It elevates and is elevated; it protects and is protected. Thus it is with the poet himself: His art is powerful, protecting, elevating, and his judgment straight and strong. The staff of a True Bard must be likewise."

Cormac accepted the assertion with a bow of deference to the elder's wisdom, but Buinne pounced. "Forgive me, brother," he said. "It seems to me you speak of mere similitude only. Certainly a slight rhetorical semblance cannot imbue power or potency."

Iollan nodded in acceptance of this view, and Buinne in triumph looked to his brothers for approval of his mastery.

But Iollan was not finished. "And yet," he said, "I recall what the great Oengus said in this regard: 'To what shall the filidh be compared if not to the staff by which they are known? For they shall be exalted in their resemblance to the Sacred Tree.' "

"Well said, brother," Datho replied.

Buinne was not willing to acknowledge defeat so easily. "Again I must ask your indulgence, for I do not understand. In what way do the filidh find their exaltation in the likeness of a tree?"

"What else can it mean," said Datho, "but that the filidh and the Sacred Tree are united by the likeness of their common attributes? As it is said: Under the oak shall the poet acquire his art."

This was not the first I had heard of the Sacred Tree. Grandfather Potitus used to fulminate against the heathens who bowed the knee in secret groves, as he said, and worshipped forest shrubs rather than Almighty God. What he might have said had he known that his grandson would be serving tree worshippers at that very moment, I could scarcely imagine.

Still, for all their interest in trees, they did not appear to worship them but merely to hold them in high regard. When the discussion ended and the others prepared to go their separate ways, I approached Datho and said, "Forgive my presumption, Ollamh, but I am curious. Of all the things which inhabit the earth, why should trees be held sacred?"

He regarded me for a moment, and then said, "Why do you ask?"

"Because it seems to me that trees live, grow, and die like any other living thing. Also, a tree can be cut down and burned, and it is no more. Would it not be better to worship a thing which cannot be so easily destroyed?"

Datho gazed at me for a long moment, and I thought I had earned the chief bard's reproach for my impertinent observation, but suddenly his tight-lipped mouth opened in a wide grin. Extending his right hand over my head, he cried aloud,

> Behold! A bard who has not chanted yet.
> Soon he will sing,
> And by the end of his song
> All the people will cry, "Amen! Amen!"

This unnerved me more than if he had slapped my face for impudence. He lowered his hand onto the top of my head and let it rest there for a moment while he gazed into my eyes, as if to confirm his unlikely prophecy.

I grew even more uncomfortable under such close scrutiny, but I stood to the examination. After a time he removed his hand and said, "Your question is well considered. If you would know the answer, hear then. This is the way of it: Trees live out of themselves; they neither kill to eat—like the creatures of land and sea—nor do they toil for their food, but the All-Wise nourishes them in season, and their span outlasts all other living things in creation. Their wisdom runs deep as their roots in the earth, even as their branches reach toward heaven in exaltation of their Creator.

"Yes, they may be cut down, and when they fall, they die. But whether they are burned in the fire or used for building, their lives are given for those they serve—either for warmth in the cold or to support the roof above"—he lifted a hand to the stout roof beams over our heads—"so that even in death these giants of the land serve those who depend upon them. In this they are the emblem of the druid-kind, who seek to emulate these noble qualities in all our ways.

"Although trees such as the oak and hazel are much revered by the filidh, we no longer worship them as of old. Worship of the creature is blind folly, but worship of the living Creator is the beginning of wisdom."

I thanked the ollamh for his thoughtful reply. His answer raised many more questions, but I resisted asking and let him go his way. As he walked off, I heard a sound behind me and turned to see Buinne disappearing into the shadows. He had seen and heard what had passed between us, and I wondered what he made of it. Nor did I have long to wonder, for later, as I was smooring the hearth fire for the night, Buinne approached the hearth and stood watching me.

I finished with the embers and ashes and made to greet him. He moved quickly to my side, his face hard as the glint in his eyes. "I know what you are doing, slave boy," he sneered, "and you will not succeed. I warn you, I will not suffer an upstart to usurp my place."

"Usurp your place?" I said. "But I could never—"

Raising a cautionary finger, he leaned close, his breath hot in my face. "You have been warned."

21

FEW DAYS LATER, Sionan came to Cnoc an Dair. It was fair day in high summer, warm and dry, the sky flecked with pale clouds. Looking out from the hilltop, I could easily imagine it was Morgannwg shining green and lush beneath the summer sun. Longing flooded over me, and I wished I were home again in Britain. On such a day my mother would be fussing about the heat, and my father would be complaining about his taxes, and I would be guzzling down beer at the Old Black Wolf with Julian, Scipio, and Rufus. No doubt they would all be doing those very things right now—but doing them without me . . . *if,* that is, they had survived the raid.

In truth I did not know whether my friends and family walked among the living still or were long dead in their graves—and that thought made it even worse somehow, as it was not for myself alone that I felt sorry, but for those whose fate I could not guess.

These thoughts plunged me into a forlorn melancholy which left me as bleak and bereft as any new orphan. I spent the morning adrift on a sea of sorrow for my misfortunes, real and imagined.

Then Sionan appeared. Cormac had gone to the ráth the evening before and returned with his sister. As soon as I saw them on the path, I shook myself from my mirthless meditations and walked down to meet them. Even from a distance, I could see she had come dressed in her best clothes.

Sionan smiled as I drew near. Her black hair glistened in the sun beneath the glint of golden combs; her eyes, shaded by long lashes, reminded me of the light on the high meadow when the deep green glows with warmth. Desire flashed through me. In that moment I wanted nothing more than to take her away to some secluded place and make love to her, but I contented myself with a modest kiss on the cheek instead. "Hello, Sionan."

"You are much improved since last I saw you." She brushed her fingers along my chest, feeling the fine cloth of my new robe. She let her hand linger.

"They treat me well," I replied.

"I am glad to hear it," she said. Her smile grew sly. "Do you not miss your sheep, then?" she asked. "Not even a little?"

"There is only one thing I miss about the mountain," I told her, "and it isn't the sheep."

Cormac, standing nearby with a bemused look on his face, stirred himself then and said, "Here now, the day flies before us. Sionan has come to teach you to bake bread, and bread you shall bake."

Once in the kitchen she became purposeful and efficient. I listened to all she said and followed her every move: mixing, kneeding, setting, baking—everything just as she instructed. Nevertheless it was all my soul was worth to keep my mind on the task before me. I kept stealing glances at her and thinking how good it would be to lie with her once more.

The chance came when, as the bread was baking, we went out to the well to wash the flour and bits of drying dough from our hands. As she bent to retrieve the leather bucket, I stepped behind her and pressed myself against her. She straightened at once and turned; I put my arms around her and pulled her to me. "I've missed you," I said.

"I can tell," she said, sliding her hand down between my legs.

I stole a kiss; her lips were warm and tasted of the honey she had used in making the bread. "Come with me," I said. "I know a place we can be alone."

"Mmmm," she said, pulling away. "I would like nothing better, but the bread will be done soon."

"Leave it." I pulled her close and kissed her again. "We can always make more."

"Succat," she said, pushing me away, "you've made a good start. It would be a shame to ruin it now."

"Then after. As soon as the bread is finished."

"When it is finished, I have to go."

"So soon? I thought you would spend the night at least." She shook her head. "Stay," I insisted, "and we can be together."

"Another time," she said firmly, then smiled. "But it is good to see you have not forgotten me."

"Sionan, how could I ever forget you?"

We went back into the house and waited until the bread was finished. At Sionan's direction I removed the loaves from the small hearthside oven, and we each pulled off a little. Sionan chewed for a moment and pronounced the loaf edible. "You've done well," she said, "for the first time. Just remember all I've told you and you can't go far wrong. And now," she concluded briskly, "I must go."

She put a hand to my cheek. "But we will see each other again."

"When?"

"Soon."

I walked with her down the hill and across the valley as far as the stream, then bade her farewell and returned to Cnoc na Daire scheming how I might contrive a visit to the ráth. Seeing Sionan again roused a potent craving, and I felt slightly ill treated that she had not stayed just a little longer.

The shadows lay deep in the wood by the time I slipped back into the house. I hastened to the storeroom and began selecting items with which to make supper. I carried them to the hearth and set about building up the fire so it would be ready when the time came to cook. I was about this task when I heard a soft step behind me and turned to see Buinne watching me. "I saw what you did," he said thickly.

I could not think what he meant. "Have I done something, Buinne?"

"Do not try to lie your way out of it. I saw, and I will tell Datho. Now he will send you back to the sheep where you belong."

"What did I do?"

"You know." He took a menacing step forward. "I saw you—you and that girl."

"It is nothing to do with you," I said stiffly. "Anyway, 'that girl' is Cormac's sister, and her name is Sionan."

"Sionan," he hissed, his eyes narrowed with lewd spite. "She is a slut— as everyone knows."

I felt the heat of anger rising in me. Without a flicker of hesitation, I reached into the hearth, snatched a piece of wood from the flames, and swung out at the weasel-faced sneak. He loosed a startled cry and stumbled back—but too slowly. The flaming brand struck him on the side of the head. Had he not been so inept, he would have taken the blow harmlessly on the shoulder; as it was, the fire seared the side of his face and set his hair alight. He screamed and danced, batting at the flames with his hands, scattering sparks, and filling the room with the acrid stink of burning hair.

I caught him by the sleeve, reached down, and pulled the back of his robe up over his head, smothering the flames in an instant. He fell to the floor and lay there cringing and whimpering, the left side of his face an angry red and the stubble of hair above his ear still smoldering.

I took up the water jug and poured the contents over him. He spluttered and whined, glaring at me like a beaten dog but saying nothing. I let him cower before me for a moment, then tossed the burning brand back onto the hearth and, in a voice hard and sharp as struck flint, said, "For Sionan's sake, no less than for your own, I will not tell Cormac what you said."

Reaching down, I took him by the arm and pulled him upright. "Get up on your feet," I told him. "Go see to yourself. And if you ever so much as breathe Sionan's name again, a few burned hairs will be the least of your worries."

He shook himself free of my grasp and retreated a few steps. Into his dull, hateful glance stole a small quiver of doubt. "You cannot frighten me. I know the ways of the Dark Speech. I could—"

I moved toward him, narrowing the distance between us by half. "You keep talking when you should be leaving. Why is that?"

He sucked air as if he would spit me from his mouth. Whatever was in his mind, he thought better of it, however, for he turned on his heel and started away. When he reached the safety of the shadows, I heard him snarl, "You will pay for this, slave boy. And it will cost you dear."

The next day Buinne appeared with his head completely shaved. He gave out that he had been bothered by lice. About the puffy red splotch on the side of his face he said nothing, and no one, to my knowledge, asked what had happened. He did not so much as look in my direction the whole day, and I made a point to stay away from him. I considered the incident resolved, but in this I was more than mistaken.

After the evening meal Cormac informed me that we were to attend the Comoradh as Filidh—the Gathering of Druids—and I would accompany them as cook and fire keeper. Gatherings of one sort or another were common enough, but this one was particularly important. "Every third year after Lughnasadh," he said, "the filidh gather to hold trials of skill and feats of recitation. It lasts seven days, and druids from every part of Éire take part."

"Lughnasadh?"

"It is the Festival of First Fruits," he explained. "Have you never heard of it?"

"Never." I told him that my father and grandfather would rather have had their tongues torn out than be seen creeping off to the forest to offer sacrifices to a heathen idol.

"Well, you need have no fear for your tongue. There will be no pagan sacrifices at the gathering."

"I makes no difference to me," I replied. "I am done with all that mumbling in the dark."

He gave me that look of his he used whenever I said something he considered outlandish—a peculiar blend of interested yet abashed astonishment. "Would it surprise you to learn that there are but few pagans among the Learned Brotherhood?"

"Perhaps," I replied, unimpressed by this revelation. "Truly, Cormac, I could not care less."

"Keep your eyes open, Succat. You will see wonders to charm and amaze you."

The next days were given to preparations for Lughnasadh, which the filidh would celebrate at the ráth with King Miliucc. As this did not involve me greatly, my chores continued much as before. I practiced making bread so that I would not forget all that Sionan had taught me. I enjoyed baking, because I thought of her while I worked the dough and tried thinking of ways by which I might sneak away with her.

"Prepare whatever provisions you think we will need," instructed Datho. "It is a fair distance, remember, and we will require supplies for seven days once we arrive."

"Of course, Ollamh," I said. "But if I take that much, how are we to carry it?"

"The king will give us a horse or two if I ask."

This echoed what Cormac had told me, but I wanted to be certain. "Ollamh," I asked, "is it true that a king is bound to grant a druid's request?"

"True?" he mused. "In what way do you mean?"

Trust a druid to turn a simple question into a philosophical inquisition. "Cormac told me that no king would refuse a druid anything he asked, so long as it was in the king's power to grant. Is this the way of it, or have I misunderstood?"

"Kings receive their sovereignty through the authority of the filidh," Datho explained. "Thus, for a king to refuse the request of a druid would be to renounce his own kingship. No king could do that and remain king; it would be an offense against nature. The realm and the tuatha would bear great suffering."

As with much of what the filidh said, I did not understand the close-pared logic of his assertion. I accepted that it was so, however, and thanked him for enlightening me on this matter. Confirmed in my plan, I renewed my resolve to increase the druids' indebtedness to me, so that when I asked Datho to request my freedom from the king, the chief druid would be more than happy to comply.

That night I made a fine supper for them, and the next day I helped

Cormac and Iollan prepare for the Lughnasadh festival, which was, I learned, only the first of the two-part harvest observance. The second part took place at the conclusion of the harvest season and was called Alban Elved.

Of the two, Lughnasadh was much the more elaborate. There were sacred fires to be kindled, cattle to be blessed, ceremonies of earth and sky to be enacted; there was also dancing, feasting, drinking, and games of strength, cunning, and endurance. For many it was the most keenly anticipated festival of the year. For many, I say, but not for all.

"It is of course an important *feis*," Cormac confided. He wrapped the special fire-making utensils in a piece of soft deerskin. "But there are those among the Learned who have come to despise the festival and think it should be abandoned."

The way he said it made me ask, "Are *you* one of them?"

He considered his reply for a moment. "No," he answered at last, "I do not despise it." He tied a strap of thin leather around the bundle he had made. "But I think our people abuse a very ancient and holy rite and in their ignorance pervert what is good."

My grandfather, never one to suppress his disapproval of the more popular pagan rites, might easily have said exactly the same thing. "If you think it perverse," I suggested, "why not change it?"

Cormac frowned and straightened. "This is what some of the Brotherhood have been saying—that the rites have grown into a mockery and should be changed. I agree, but it is not so easy."

"How not?" I asked. "You are the ones who control the festival."

"No." He shook his head. "We have no such authority. As always, the power of these rites derives from the belief of the people. If the filidh wish to change even the smallest feature of the observance, we must first change the hearts and minds of the people to accept a new way."

"Then do that," I said. The thing was perfectly simple after all.

Cormac shook his head again and chuckled. "And do you not think that is the very thing we are doing?"

"Well?"

"Only the most shallow-rooted weeds grow up overnight, Succat. You must know that. We are not about planting a weed which is here today and gone tomorrow. We are about growing a mighty yew under whose spreading limbs the land will shelter for all time."

I heard in his voice something I had never heard before. Pride was there, certainly, and defiance, too—but also a quality I could not readily identify. For, despite hints and insinuations, great and small, which he had dropped from the very moment I first met him, he had never put a name to this mysterious group to which he obviously belonged. I sensed he was very close to doing this now, so I said, "You make it sound like the work of many hands, Cormac. Is anyone to help you with this great tree-planting work?"

"I am not alone, if that is what you mean."

"No," I told him, "that is not what I meant. But if you do not wish to tell me, I will understand."

"But will you understand if I tell you?" He regarded me intently, his dark eyes weighing me against the worth of his secret.

"I can but try."

"Within the ranks of the filidh," he answered, "there are many who believe as I do, and our numbers are growing. We are the Ceile De," he said, savoring the name with evident pride, "and one day soon our influence will stretch across Éire from one end of this island to the other."

I accepted his assurance. "Ceile De," I mused. "A good name. What does it mean?"

"I have said enough," replied Cormac, tapping me on the chest with his finger. "The rest you must discover for yourself."

THE FESTIVAL OF Lughnasadh is one of the more enjoyable of the many interminable and inexplicable celebrations the Irish perpetrate. There is food and drink and music, as at every celebration, combined with some extremely peculiar rites, the purpose of which I could not grasp: Queen Grania sprinkling beer over two young boys who were holding mice while the smiling king looked on, for example. In another, a harvest cart drawn by an ox and festooned with pine branches was paraded three times around the well, whereupon a great loaf of bread shaped like a maiden was pulled from the well and laid in the wagon bed; Cormac said that the maiden loaf would be kept in the king's hall wrapped in one of the queen's robes until the harvest was complete, and then it would be broken into pieces and distributed to each family.

The concluding ritual came when the ollamh produced a small golden knife shaped like a scythe and cut the first sheaf of grain. This was bundled, tied with a specially braided rope made of hair from the heads of all the women of the tuath, and carried in triumph to the ráth, where it was hung on a silver hook above the door to the king's hall. Then the feasting commenced, along with its attendant revel. Clothed like a druid, I passed among the people without incident or comment and found myself warming to the raucous proceedings immensely.

But all else paled in comparison to Sionan, for when the revel began in earnest, we crept away to the stables and a deserted stall. There, in the dry, sweet-smelling straw, we indulged ourselves in our own private celebration.

I lost myself in her warm, delicious flesh and exulted in the way her body moved with mine. Sionan made love with zeal and an abandon which delighted even as it astonished; she provoked a passion in me to match her own and left me sweating and exhausted in her wake.

Spent with pleasure, we crept from the stable. No sooner had we rejoined the feast, however, than Cormac informed me that it was time for us to go. "So soon?" inquired Sionan, giving me a sideways glance.

"Might we stay just a little longer?" I asked.

"We leave for the council in the morning," he replied, "and it is a long way to travel. Make your farewells and come along. The king has given us the use of a horse. Go to the stable and see that it is ready."

With a last furtive kiss, I took my leave of Sionan and hurried off. The grooms, as I knew, were enjoying the feast like everyone else, and since there was no one about to tell me otherwise, I selected the finest-looking animal from among the three in the stable, slipped a simple halter around his neck, and led him out.

Cormac was waiting for me at the gate; the others had gone ahead. He nodded with satisfaction when he saw me, and then he turned and led the way out across the moonlit valley. We went back to the druid house for a too-brief sleep, and when sunrise was yet a distant rumor in the east, I rose and loaded our provisions onto the horse. We departed shortly after, walking through the still-dark forest—Iollan, Buinne, Cormac and myself with the horse, and Datho leading the way along paths I could not see: druid roads, Cormac called them, and he explained how these unseen pathways stretched through the land in an invisible web, connecting each of the five sacred realms of Éire: the northernmost lands of the Ulaidh, Mumhain in the south, western Connacht, Laighin in the east, and, in the center, little Mídhe, formed, it was said, of portions taken from all the others.

Mídhe, he told me, was our destination. By the time the sun was up, we were already well on our way.

As we went along, I observed what a fine and splendid land was Ireland, blessed with lush, low hills; wide, inviting meadows watered by gentle streams; and, everywhere, mature forests of oak and ash, beech and elm filled with wild pigs and deer. The clouds sailed through a clean, wind-scoured sky, and the fertile ground was warm beneath our feet.

"Tara," Cormac continued, "is where the high king reigns." Druids, as I say, cannot resist teaching anyone they suspect might be ignorant of one thing or another. They love nothing more than teasing the least triviality into a daylong lesson. "The Hill of Tara is the omphalos—the sacred center of the island."

"Are we going to Tara, then?"

"No," the big druid answered. "A small distance away from Tara is Cathair Bán, a temple of ancient origin, and that is where the gathering of bards takes place."

"And will there be Ceile De at the gathering?"

Cormac's lips twitched into a fleeting smile at my clumsy attempt to draw him out. "You shall see."

We walked on, and he told me about the various orders of druids I might encounter in the days ahead. All filidh, he said, were students of history, medicine, law, and the hidden order of the natural world; in short, nothing passed beneath the gaze of a druid that did not in some way concern him. Kingship and its privileges and obligations, farming methods, trade between tribes and nations, the lineages of noble houses, philosophy, the movements of heavenly bodies, religious rites and observances—in all these things and more, they were masters.

Even so, not all filidh were equal. Within what they called the bardic orders were particular, sometimes subtle, distinctions. "Foremost among all druids are the *fáidh*," Cormac told me; they were the most learned and accomplished of all, possessing great powers of mind—including the ability to control the natural elements and discern, through various means, the shape of forthcoming events. Next came the bards, those well skilled in recitation, song, and the power of the spoken word. These were followed by the druids themselves, who excelled in healing the ills and wounds of the body, whether in man or beast, and the ability to converse with the myriad inhabitants of this world and the Otherworld.

All filidh were bards, he said, but not all bards were fáidh. Nor was this all, for within the ranks were further divisions, mostly pertaining to the interests of the individual filidh. Some, for example, made it their habit to inquire into the mysteries of wind and rain and fog, while others delved into the properties, uses, and creation of fire, water, air, and light. Yet others charted the heavenly realm and everything in it, much as sailors chart the seas of the world, and still others gleaned the lore of plants and trees and animals and all living things.

In their perpetual quest for knowledge, the druids were indefatigable, searching everywhere for wisdom and sparing neither expense nor hardship in its acquisition. As a result, no obscure or hidden thing remained obscure or hidden from them very long, for they would pry and pry until they forced the object of their attention to yield up its secrets.

"Any king worthy of the name keeps at least one druid," Cormac said. "The high king maintains nine. It would be a poor king indeed who had no bard to be his advisor." The druid kind, he said, were held to be faithful and trustworthy beyond reckoning, and so were often called upon to act as judges in legal disputes and matters of justice. "The word of a filidh is to be trusted in all things concerning the kingdom and the protection of the tuath."

This assertion put Cormac in a contemplative mood, and we gradually lapsed into a companionable silence. As for the others, Iollan held his own council, and Buinne ignored me with a stiff and ugly silence, for which I was grateful; I had no use for the rancorous lump and would sooner address a poison-spitting viper as talk to him. Thus, as the day progressed, I followed along, letting my thoughts flit where they would. Mostly I thought about Sionan, and experienced a delicious ache in the pit of my stomach whenever I brought her to mind.

The next day was much the same as the first. The pace was not demanding. Much to my relief, my strength held good—although I welcomed every stop and rested whenever I could. On the third day we passed Mhag Fál, and I saw Tara in the distance, the mounded hill crowned by its double-ringed timber palisade. We moved on, meeting a road that we followed for a time. "There are four roads in Éire," Datho told me, "one to each of the four realms, joining at the Hill of Tara. They are sacred highways by which the king maintains the order of the land."

We ascended a ridge of low hills and crossed over into a long, shallow valley through which a deep river pushed its sluggish way. "Behold!" said Datho. "The Boínn, Mother of Waters, nourisher of the land. And there"— he pointed to a low, rounded hill which seemed to rise from the river—"is Cathair Bán."

Looking where he indicated, I saw only what appeared to be a smooth hump rising from the roundness of the hill. As we came closer, however, this unassuming hump slowly took on a more commanding aspect. We walked along the path beside the river, losing sight of our destination for a time, so that when at last we turned away from the river and started our ascent, I was surprised that the hill seemed to have grown inexplicably and that what had first appeared to be a lowly hump was in fact an enormous earthen mound. Two other, smaller earthworks stood a few hundred paces behind the first and, just below it on the right side, a tall, slender standing stone.

The sun-facing side of the mound was flattened and lined with course after course of spherical white stones rising to double the height of a man; black stone balls were set in among the white to form a loosely curved, rising pattern. In the center of this white expanse was a low, dark door, blocked by an enormous oval-shaped stone carved with curious swirls and spiral designs and laid sideways before the entrance.

"Where is the temple?" I asked, looking around.

"This," said Cormac, indicating the hill and mound and standing stone altogether, "is the temple. As I say, it is very old."

It looked like no holy edifice I had ever seen—with neither roof nor walls, open to the wind and sky. "Who built it?"

"The Tuatha DeDanaan," explained Cormac as we slowly mounted the hill, where there were perhaps sixty or more filidh gathered in groups around the hilltop and standing stone. Ollamh Datho gave out a shout of greeting and hastened to join his friends.

The top of the hill was flattened and, on the ground a short distance in front of the entrance to the mound, a fire pit had been dug, and several pigs were roasting on spits over the flames. A number of women in green robes stood nearby talking among themselves while watching the men who were cooking the meat.

There were a fair number of younger children—boys and girls of no more than six or seven summers—running here and there, playing about the perimeter of the circular mound; others climbed to the top, where they shouted and pushed one another at the summit, filling the air with exuberant shrieks. Clearly they were enjoying the fine summer day; nevertheless their presence seemed incongruous to me, so I asked, "Why are there women and children here?"

"Women and children?" Puzzled, Cormac looked around, trying to determine what I meant. "Those women?" He lifted a respectful hand to them and said, "They are filidh. The children you see are filidh-to-be." At my expression of disbelief, he chuckled. "Did you think only men could be druids, Succat? As for the young ones, there is much to learn before one can become a bard, so it is best to begin early, when the mind can be properly trained."

The rest of the day was taken up with preparing a suitable camp for my filidh masters. Many of the druids had established their camps at the foot of the hill; I chose a place among these, unloaded the supplies, and led the horse to the river to drink. There were other servants watering their pack animals or fetching water for their masters, and I noticed that, unlike myself, they were not slaves. Indeed, there was not a slave collar to be seen anywhere.

When the horse finished, I led him along the riverbank to a place where he could graze. In a little while another servant came along leading a horse. "A fine animal, that," I told him as he passed.

"I have not seen you before," the youth said, stopping nearby.

"This is my first gathering," I said.

"Who is your ollamh?"

"Datho," I replied. "Do you know him?"

He shook his head. We talked a little more, and I asked him how he came to be a servant to the filidh. "I am going to be a bard myself one day," he told me. I did not know what to say to this, so I merely nodded amiably. "Are you?" he asked.

"No," I answered. "I am just a slave. But I thought the filidh must begin their schooling very young." He bristled slightly at this, so I quickly continued, "I mean no offense. This is what I was told. I have not been long in the druid house."

"Of course," he agreed reluctantly, "most begin the training as soon as they are chosen. Some of us have not such good luck."

"I know *I* have never been very lucky," I replied, "and that is the naked truth."

"For us older ones," he continued, "the only way is to become a servant to the filidh." He went on to describe how by working in the druid house he learned much about the filidh and their ways, so that one day, having demonstrated his suitability, he could, despite his age, enter the formal training.

"Is this the way of all the servants?" I asked, the plan already forming in my mind.

"Most," he granted, "if not all."

I thanked him for enlightening me on this matter and returned to the camping place below the hill, where I set about making supper, thinking of how best to use what I had learned. In the end I decided that there was no harm in asking Datho if I could become a bard. If he said no, I was no worse off than before. But if he said yes, then I was a great deal closer to perfecting my escape.

It was past dark when the others returned to camp. I served them their meal, whereafter they went to sleep. I sat by the fire for a long time, thinking of what I would say, trying to guess how the ollamh might respond, and how to counter any objections he might make. I went to sleep that night determined to seek this boon at first opportunity.

I decided to ask Cormac what he thought. "Could *I* become a filidh, do you think?"

His expression took on a curiosity bordering on suspicion. "Why do you ask?"

I told him then what Datho had said about me: a bard who had not chanted yet. Cormac considered this for a moment, "Well, then, it must be that our wise ollamh has seen something in you which has called forth this prophecy. In any case it is not for me to say one way or the other. We must ask Datho."

The ollamh was occupied with discussions far into the night, so it was the next day before the opportunity arose for us to seek Datho's opinion on whether I might be allowed to become a bard. Cormac asked the question, while I stood waiting patiently to one side. The ollamh pursed his lips and looked at the sky and then at me. He looked at the sky again and finally said, "Well, why not?" He smiled. "If that is what he wants, why not?"

"Succat is well past the age when one must begin the training," Cormac pointed out.

The chief druid shrugged. "What of that? The desire of a true heart can overcome much." Turning to me, he said, "Tell me, Succat, is it in your heart to join the Learned Brotherhood?"

"It is that, ollamh," I replied. Then, having bent the truth as far as it would go, I added, "I waited all night to ask you, and while I waited, the desire grew in me. Indeed, I feel a burning in my heart which I have never known before." I did not tell him, of course, that this burning was for freedom; it was not wisdom I so desperately wanted, but escape. "You said that I was a bard who had not chanted yet," I reminded him. "How will I become a bard unless I am allowed the chance to learn?"

"How indeed?" He motioned me to him and placed his hands on my shoulders. "You have shown yourself a willing and able servant. Your curiosity is genuine, and your mind is quick. Therefore let us strike a bargain, you and I: Serve us well for the next year, prove yourself worthy, and let the desire ripen in your heart—do this, and when we come again to the council, I will oversee your initiation." He gazed at me solemnly. "This is the bargain I propose."

"We are here now, ollamh," I pointed out. "Could I not begin at once? As Cormac has said, I am already older than the others. To wait another year . . ."

The chief druid shook his head. "This is my decision."

I glanced at Cormac but received no encouragement there. To begin by arguing with my benefactor did not augur well for any future progress, so I swallowed my disappointment. "No doubt it is for the best," I conceded. "I accept your gracious offer, ollamh, and I will abide."

"Good," replied Datho, nodding with satisfaction. "I understand your impatience, but the year will pass quickly. There is much to be done." He turned to Cormac, who regarded me dubiously. "Cormac will aid you in this. From today he is responsible for your preparation."

"If you think it best, ollamh," replied Cormac. Although he tacitly agreed, his disapproval was obvious.

"I have spoken."

Cormac accepted his superior's judgment with a low bow. When Datho had gone, I asked Cormac why he doubted my suitability. "Is it because you find me unacceptable in some way?" I said.

"I do," he admitted. "You possess a most formidable will, Succat. That is your strength and your great weakness. In the days, to come you must relinquish your will a thousand times over. Can you do that?"

"I can do that."

"I wonder."

"Would you prevent me, Cormac?"

"The ollamh has spoken, and I will obey." He paused. "Whether you succeed or fail, however, will be determined by your own abilities."

"I ask nothing more than that."

The thought of having to wait another year chafed me sorely, and Cormac's distinct lack of enthusiasm irritated me more than I would have imagined. That night, as I set about making supper for my druids, I thought about what Datho and Cormac had said. When we left Cathair Bán two days later, I was determined to make the best of my year's preparation.

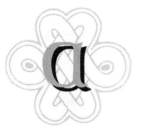A s DATHO PREDICTED, the year passed swiftly for me. I performed every duty with utmost care and attention. All they asked of me, and more, I did. Never so much as a sigh of complaint passed my lips — even when Buinne ordered me about on silly errands. Oh, he had not forgotten the beating I had given him; if anything, his spite had only grown — not that I paid much attention to him one way or another — but, needless to say, he relished every opportunity to demean me. I took his routine humiliation in my stride — as much for Sionan's sake as for my own — refusing to dignify his continual threats and insinuations so that I would not betray her love. My meek acceptance merely infuriated him all the more, however. He began to fulminate against me whenever we were alone, and when I did not answer his threats and slanders, he crowed like a cock in triumph over a bloodied rival.

I saved up his abuse, reckoning every slur and embarrassment I endured, and one night at dinner I gave him a bowl of stewed venison which contained a powerful purgative derived from the dried root of a marsh plant I had been keeping. That night he did not go to his bed but remained outside in the woods with his loose bowels.

Sionan and I continued to see one another whenever we could. Widowed and no longer a virgin, she could not serve in the king's house, but Queen Grania had taken pity on her and given her a place among her own servingwomen. On rare occasions Sionan would contrive some excuse to come to the druid house on an errand for the queen; more often I went to the ráth. Once, during the winter, I was caught in a snowstorm and forced to stay in the ráth for two days. For two days and nights Sionan and I ate and slept and made love in a bed heaped with fleeces before the fire-bright hearth of her little house.

Thus I occupied myself while I waited. I bore my captivity with as good grace as I could, and tried not to think of Britain or of the time passing. The year slowly turned, and the time came to test whether I was well prepared for the ordeal of initiation. A few days before we were to depart for the druid gathering, Datho called me before him. He took a long time examining me—posing questions, weighing my replies. Finally he declared himself satisfied with my readiness. "Tell me, Succat, do you still wish to join the Learned Brotherhood?"

"I do, Ollamh Datho," I replied, "more than ever."

"That is well. Providing you successfully complete the initiation, I will undertake your instruction. In time you shall become a bard."

As before, we celebrated Lughnasadh at the ráth, where I shared my good news with Sionan. "Tell me," I said, "which you would rather be: the wife of a druid or the wife of a shepherd?"

"Wife now, is it?" She gave me a silky smile. "Well, if you are as poor a druid as you were a shepherd, I would not be wife to you for anything."

"I was a wise and skillful shepherd."

"You were a sorry shepherd."

"But I was sincere at least."

"Not even that."

"Well, then," I said, pulling her close, "I can hardly be a worse druid."

"True," she agreed, kissing me lightly, "but it is the chief bard for me or no one at all."

"If that is the way of it," I said, pulling her down onto the soft bed of fleeces, "then I shall become the best chief bard that anyone this side of Sliabh Mis has ever seen."

"Do that," she replied, settling herself on top of me, "and I shall marry you after all."

We enjoyed a sweetly satisfying night together, and the next morning I departed with the filidh to attend the Comoradh at Cathair Bán.

Anticipation grew with every step, so that by the time we reached the hill with its temple mounds, I could hardly walk. Truly, I had to keep reminding myself that I was only using the initiation as a means to gain my freedom. That, only that, and nothing more. This proved no easy task, however, for I had long since fallen under the thrall of the druids. I had seen and heard things in my year of preparation that gave me to know that the filidh were both wise and powerful and that their knowledge was far above the blather and nonsense so prized by the ignorant priests of Mithras, who still plied their disreputable trade around the garrisons of southern Britain.

The filidh, for the most part, possessed genuine skills which they employed for the good of the people. The thought that I was to join them, albeit deceitfully, filled me with an awe verging on alarm.

Upon arrival the others went up the hill to the temple mound, leaving me to make camp. A little later Datho returned to say that he had spoken with the other druid chieftains, who agreed with his recommendation to allow me to be added to the number of new initiates. "Tonight you will sleep on the hill," he told me. "You will be given a special meal of meat and broth, and at dawn the initiation will begin."

Accordingly, dawn found me standing with two other skinny, anxious boys—both much younger than myself—naked save for a loincloth; we were each given a fresh-cut yew branch, which we held in our hands while an ollamh examined us.

"Let the initiation begin," said the ollamh upon completing his examination.

Three druids approached and, each holding a torch, came to stand before the trembling initiates. Datho took his place before me. "All who would join the Learned Brotherhood must die to their former lives so that they may be born anew into the life of the filidh," he said. "If this is your desire, follow me."

The other druids spoke likewise to their candidates, who were then led off to the turf-covered mounds a short distance away. I was taken to the great mound. Stepping over the oblong stone blocking the entrance, Datho approached the doorway, indicating that I was to stay close behind him. Crouching low, he led me into the darkness of a long, narrow corridor, the walls and roof of which were enormous slabs of stone. The floor was uneven, rising slightly the further in we went; the walls pressed tight and then, suddenly, opened into a large, roughly circular room which, revealed in the fluttering light of Datho's torch, held several smaller chambers, or niches.

Two of the smaller chambers contained great shallow stone bowls. One of these held a haunch of rotting meat and the other, rank and stagnant water. The stench made my eyes water, and I gagged. In the third chamber a thick mat of rushes covered the floor, which was itself covered by a bearskin. A rolled-up deer hide lay to one side.

Indicating the bearskin, Datho said, "Lie down, Succat."

I did as I was told, and the chief druid, placing the torch in a crevice in the rock, stooped and folded my arms over my naked chest. Taking the yew branch from my hand, he laid it across my chest. "The yew is ever green and everlasting," he said, "like your soul. Let your mind dwell on this."

Taking up the deerskin, he unrolled it and drew it over my body. Then, stretching out his hands over me, he closed his eyes and chanted in a tongue I did not recognize. I listened to the rhythmic rise and fall of his voice and felt myself growing sleepy. After a time his voice seemed to fade into silence. I waited and opened my eyes in utter darkness. Datho was gone, and I was alone.

I did not know what was to come or how long I would remain in the chamber. I simply lay on the bearskin, waiting for whatever would happen next.

The air inside the niche was lifeless, neither warm nor cold; there was not the slightest breath of movement in it. Even so, it filled my nostrils with the smell of earth and stone and the faint stink of rotting meat and rank water emanating from the niches in the chamber beyond.

The silence of the chamber was complete. I could hear nothing of the world outside the great womb of earth. I imagined that the sun had risen and men in the wider world were going about their various activities—all without me. At first this produced a curious disquiet—as if, forced to endure silence and darkness, I were being made to bear a burden others did not share. Oddly, as time passed, this feeling hardened into a sense of oppression. Deprived of light and movement, I was made to suffer while those outside went blithely about their affairs without regard to my plight. I resented them for their careless freedom. I despised them for their thoughtlessness. As my discomfort increased, it was all I could do to keep from leaping up and rushing out of the mound and castigating them for their coldhearted indifference.

At length I realized that this thinking was only making me morose and angry, so I tried to think of something less irksome. At once my mind turned to Sionan, and I wondered what she might be doing. I imagined her making bread, as we had done, and instantly the musty niche seemed to fill with the sweet, warm, floury scent of her baking. I saw her face, features knit in a frown of concentration, a slight sheen of sweat on her forehead, her hands dusted with flour as she kneaded the pale dough. I beheld her willowy form as she swayed to her work, and my heart swelled with love for her. Yes! Sionan—my wife in all but name, she was dearer to me than my life.

I held my beloved's image in my mind's eye and sent good wishes winging her way, and I suddenly found myself surrounded by a solid yet gentle presence which folded all my anxiety into itself, giving back only reassurance as fathomless as the sea. I was buoyed up and carried along, a leaf swirled upon on the broad, heaving breast of the ocean by unseen currents.

In the dark and silence of my chambered tomb, my spirit took flight. Into my mind came the image of countryside, and I saw, as if spread out far below me, the rumpled green cloak of Ireland with its hills and forests, streams and lakes, shining silver in the sun. I saw the narrow sea and, away to the east, the mainland of Britain. I saw the coast, with waves dashed white against the tumbled line of rock cliffs, towering headlands, and high promontories. I saw the fields and woods of my homeland—farmers with teams of oxen, plowing, sowing, chopping wood to clear the land. I saw soldiers on foot, marching along fine, straight roads; they moved eastward, where, looming up before them, rose great black clouds of smoke and storm.

Bodiless and unencumbered, I streaked swift as thought across the empty sky, watching the rippling land and glittering sea below me. I saw the coast of Morgannwg where I was taken and, up beyond the protecting hills, our estate, Favere Mundi, deathly still beneath the glowing sun, its courtyard empty. I had feared it destroyed, but there it was. And while I looked, I saw my mother come out into the yard with a jar in her hand; she went to the pear tree and poured out the water around the old tree's roots.

Beyond the villa I saw the road leading to little Bannavem and then the town itself set in among the fields and meadow pastures. I saw the town square and the busy market—only now it was not so busy; there were fewer people in the square, and the normally raucous mood was sharply subdued. I was taking this in when who should come striding into the square but my friend Rufus, and Scipio with him. They walked together to the well in the center of the square and perched on the stone breastwork to talk in the drowsy summer sun. I wanted to shout to them, to let them know somehow that I saw them and that I was alive and well. But I clutched my yew branch instead, and the world rushed on beneath me.

I saw the edge of approaching night, sweeping like a shadow line across the land. It came so swiftly. The luscious golden sunshine faded; the bright, flame-tinted sky relinquished its light; and the evening stars began to shine. As night gathered strength, the land sank away beneath a weight of darkness. Here and there the quick glint of open fires burned holes in night's black robe, but for the most part the land was invisible beneath the occluding veil.

I turned my eyes to look above and saw heaven's vast canopy aglow with stars—a wide and glittering band of spangled silver, a spray of gleam, illuminating the darksome nether realms no man had ever seen. The moon shone like a great glowing wheel as it rolled up and over the sky's curved vault. I felt myself to be as small and trifling as an empty shell upon the world's enormous strand. The universe spread before me, forever, without end.

Out beyond the shining rim of stars, I saw the dark, inscrutable heart of the deep, impenetrable and unknowable. Here lay the mystery of all existence, wrapped in infinite layers of time yet unwound. Though I could not see it, I could feel the long, slow stirring of its elemental pulse in the pit of my soul. I felt the steady, rhythmic beat as an ineluctable tide force, rising and falling, drawing and sending, moving in arcing ripples through the ordered ranks of creation, setting here an entire world in motion, there a tiny heart.

I saw these things—I know not how—and felt myself lifted high and exhilarated by the vision. It seemed as if I had dipped myself in a bottomless sea of wisdom; a knowledge older than the rivers of the world, older still than the rocks beneath the mountains, as old as the ever-circling heavens above the earth, flowed all around me . . . divine knowledge.

The unformed presence in my cavelike chamber took on the aspect of a living being. What is more, this living presence, closer than my own breath, bound me to itself, enfolded me within its all-encompassing strength. It had ever been with me, and it would remain with me henceforth and forever in whatever realms I might wander. Though I live or die, it would be with me still, enfolding me, upholding me, encircling me.

Lying there in the silent darkness of my chambered tomb, I allowed this knowledge to seep into me, into my hair and mouth and nostrils, into the pores of my skin and beneath my skin; I let it soak into my bones, into the pith and marrow of my frame—until I became saturated with it. This knowledge trickled in, filling all the hidden, hollow places within, suffusing body and soul with the invincible awareness that I need never be lost or alone again. And more, that my life had been given for a purpose yet to be fulfilled.

I lay on the fleece-covered bearskin luxuriating in this knowledge, exulting in it, rejoicing in the very great gift which had been given me.

How long I remained like this, I cannot say. It seemed at once a lifetime and only moment. Indeed, time seemed no more than a trick of the senses, the flicker of a candle flame in a bowl, the shifting of a water shadow in a stream. Presently I became aware of my surroundings once more. I drew a deep breath and threw aside the deerskin covering. In the darkness of the burial niche, I rose and started crawling on hands and knees into the main chamber and from there down the long, low passage leading to the light.

Upon emerging I stumbled from the entrance to stand blinking in the early-evening sun. It took a moment for my eyes to accept the light. I heard a voice. There was a rush of movement toward me, and I was gathered in strong arms and all but carried from the mound.

They bore me away and sat me down in the shade of a cloth canopy which had been erected on the grass a little distance down the hill from the mound. "Are you well, boy?" asked a voice. I turned to see Datho's anxious face looming over me, dark eyes keen and searching.

I tried to speak but found I could not move my tongue.

"Here," said another voice, "take this."

I looked around as Cormac pressed the cool rim of a brass bowl to my lips. "Drink," instructed Datho. "It will revive you."

I drank and tasted water mixed with honey. I squeezed my eyes shut and opened them again. "How long?" I asked. "How long was I in there?"

"Three days," replied Cormac.

This seemed impossible to me. "Truly?"

Datho nodded solemnly. "Three days have passed since you entered the mound." He smiled. "We were beginning to worry about you."

"Did you see anything?" asked Cormac excitedly.

"I saw . . ." I closed my eyes; the images cascaded through my mind. "Amazing things."

"Tell us quickly," urged Cormac, "before you forget."

Datho intervened. "Hush, Cormac. He has been gone three days. Give him a moment to come back."

I turned to Cormac, who was eagerly bending over me. "I will *never* forget what I saw."

24

RESTED FOR A time, sipping the honey water while Datho rubbed my hands and feet. Gradually my limbs warmed as the blood started flowing again and, under Datho's gentle probing, I began to tell them what I had seen. As I talked, Cormac crept away, returning quickly with three other druid chieftains. They settled themselves beneath the canopy to listen; occasionally one or another would ask a question, which I would answer without thought or hesitation as the words simply sprang to my tongue.

When I finished, they rose and withdrew a few paces apart to deliberate. Cormac offered me another drink of honey water, which I gratefully accepted. "What are they doing?" I asked in a low voice.

"Thinking," said Cormac. "Are you hungry?"

I nodded. Now that I was once more in the land of the living, my appetite was swiftly returning. Although it still seemed to me that less than half a day had passed, I was suddenly hungry enough to believe I had endured three days without food or water.

"Rest here," Cormac said. "I will bring you something to eat." He rose just as the filidh chieftains returned from their contemplations. "Stand up," commanded Datho. Cormac helped me to my feet; I rose too fast and became dizzy. The big druid put out a hand to steady me. Datho, steeped in vast authority, drew himself up and addressed me while his brothers stood looking on.

"Fortunate are you among men," he said. "It is a rare gift you have been given. Few who undergo the ritual death emerge with a vision of such power. That this has happened to you is a great and wondrous sign and a cause for rejoicing."

The three chieftains with him stroked their beards and muttered their agreement. Datho continued, "Therefore, we respectfully request that you allow us to honor this sign with a rite of consecration."

I did not know what to say to this, so I replied, "If it pleases you, Ollamh." The druids murmured their approval.

"The ceremony will take place tonight," Datho informed me, then bade Cormac to get me something to eat and allow me to rest. He and the others moved away, heads together in fervent conversation.

"You have stirred the pot, my friend," said Cormac, easing me down gently.

"What did he mean, 'wondrous sign'?"

"Visions are given for a reason," he replied. "Yours—if it was a genuine vision—was one of great power, and so the purpose for which it was given is likewise very great."

"Do you doubt me, Cormac?" It rankled me to be disbelieved—especially on those rare occasions when I was telling the truth.

He regarded me with a dubious expression and shrugged. "We will see if anything comes of it."

Leaving me with the bowl of honey water, Cormac went off to fetch some food. I lay down beneath the canopy and felt the warmth of the lowering sun on my skin, realizing for the first time since emerging from the mound that, save for the loincloth, I was naked. I closed my eyes and dozed, waking when Cormac returned with some cooked fish and a bowl of blackberries.

"Do you think I could have my clothes back now?" I asked, accepting the fish on a skewer. He said that he did not see any reason why this should be prevented, and went in search of my missing garments. I ate the fish slowly and then started in on the berries, listening all the while to the sounds around me as the day faded.

The filidh and their disciples dotted the hillside in small clumps of three, four, or more. Wherever I looked, I saw heads bent in earnest discussion. The murmur of their voices filled the air like the drone of bees. I saw them, saw the hillside and the valley beyond with its dark, snaking river. It all seemed to me less substantial now—as if the fabric of the natural world had worn thin. It seemed to me that if I concentrated very hard, I might see right through it and into the world beyond—but the effort required was too great, or I was too listless and lazy to try.

After a time Datho returned, now in the company of an old woman dressed in a long white robe. Her hands were gnarled and curved like claws; her eyes glittered like polished pebbles set deep in the orbits of her skull. "Here he is, Meabh," he said. They stood over me, gazing down as if at a curiosity of nature.

"Come here, boy," said the old woman, indicating that I should rise. Her voice, though rough, held a firm note of authority.

I rose and stood. Her elderly face was a puckered web of creases and crinkles, her hair a wispy nimbus through which I could see her balding pate. She squinted one dark eye and leaned close. "Handsome," she said, and I smelled the scent of onions on her breath. "They tell me you have had a vision. Well? I would hear it."

I began to recite what I had seen. Meabh lifted her head and gazed skyward while she listened to my somewhat disjointed account. When I finished, she nodded. "It is good." To Datho she said, "You are right."

Then, turning to me she said, "The healing dream is as powerful as it is rare. You have been blessed."

"Thank you . . . Banfilidh," I replied, uncertain how to address the hag. It was a word I had heard once or twice, one she accepted without comment.

"Datho has asked to be your ollamh," she said, her gaze sharp and shrewd as a weasel's. "Are you content?"

"I am that, Banfilidh."

"Very well, I consign you to Datho's able care. Heed him closely, that you may grow into your prominence."

I accepted her judgment with a bow, whereupon Cormac returned with my clothes. "Ah, Cormac Miach! How well you look. I am pleased to see you." She held out her thin arms to him, and he embraced her warmly. "Datho tells me you have completed your twelfth year. He tells me also that you have made good progress."

"Thank you, Ollamh," he replied. "No one could ask for a more able and resourceful teacher. His patience and wisdom are inexhaustible—I should know, I have tried both often enough."

Datho protested this assessment. "It is the ability of the student, in this case, who makes a master of his teacher."

Embarrassed by this odd gush of emotion between the two, I took my clothes and quickly dressed, turning away so they would not see the sour expression on my face while they carried on in this peculiar, deferential way. When I turned back, old Meabh was eagerly gripping Cormac by the arm. "I think the time has come for you to sit at my feet for a season, Cormac. Would that please you?"

"Beyond measure," he said. Glancing at Datho, he added, "If my ollamh would allow it, I would be happy to serve you in any way I can."

"Go, my son, and with my blessing," said Datho, a slight resignation creeping into his tone. "You will profit mightily from Meabh's tutelage. But know, too, that you will always have a place with me when you are finished."

"Then I am honored to accept your offer, ollamh," Cormac said, scarcely able to hide his jubilation.

"Come to me after the Comoradh," she told him, and then, taking Datho's arm, she led him away down the hillside.

"Who was she?" I asked Cormac when they had gone.

"Meabh is the oldest ollamh in Éire — or Britain either, so far as I can tell. Her knowledge of the masters is beyond that of any living filidh. She is very particular about those she accepts for instruction. It is a very great honor to be chosen."

"Then you will be leaving," I said, suddenly aware of how much I had come to depend on the big druid. "I will miss you, Cormac. I will."

"Oh, we can still see one another from time to time," he replied lightly. "But you will be so busy from now on you will not have time to miss *anyone* — not me, perhaps not even Sionan." Resting a heavy arm on my shoulders, he drew me close to whisper in my ear. "I know that you and Sionan sleep together," he told me. "I said nothing because it was what she wanted. But from now on you must think of her welfare." His voice was firm and his glance direct. "Understood?"

"I understand."

"Good." He gripped my shoulder hard. "Disappoint her and, brother bard or not, you will soon wish you had never been born."

He released me then with a hearty smack on the back. "I am glad we are agreed."

When I made no reply, he slapped me on the back again and said, "Cheer up, Succat, I do not begrudge you. In fact, when the time comes, I will happily perform your marriage rite myself."

Later, as the moon was rising in the east, the filidh gathered on the hillside. Along with two others I was led by Cormac up a long, torchlit path to stand before the heel stone. Datho, who was to be my teacher, received me, spreading wide his hands in welcome. He raised his voice to the throng, saying, "Brothers of the Oak! You will have heard that one among us has received a healing dream. Here" — he indicated me with a wave of his hand — "he stands before you now. I bid you welcome him."

To my surprise a loud shout of acclaim suddenly erupted from the Learned Brothers looking on. I glanced around for Cormac and saw him standing in the front rank of the crowd and, behind him, Buinne, staring at me, his pallid face twisted into an expression of such intense and malignant hostility that I almost did not recognize him. The sight took me aback, and I looked away again.

"My son," said Datho when the crowd had silenced once more, "this is a sacred moment—neither day nor night, when all creation hangs between light and darkness. It is a time when decisions undertaken can bring manifold blessings. Therefore I urge you with the strong entreaty of a father to a beloved son to hallow this holy moment with the vow I shall give you."

Ollamh Datho took a step back from me. Holding his druid staff in his left hand, he raised his right hand and, in a resounding voice, began to chant. "Three kinds of light obtain: that of the sun and, hence, fire; that of the knowledge obtained from the instruction of wise teachers; and that which is possessed in the understanding of God, which illuminates the heart and is the true light of the soul.

"Therefore, my son, seek the True Light in all your ways; search diligently and with tireless perseverance. Take the Light as your law, your love, and your guide, now and henceforth, forever. If you would do this, answer now upon your life."

He paused, and nodded to me, indicating that I should answer. I had not reckoned on having to make such a profession, but the vision was still strong in me and the answer came readily to my lips. "Upon my life, I make this vow," I said, and in that moment—if only for that most fleeting moment—I meant it with all my heart.

Oh, but the heart is desperately wicked above all things. For, my first thought was not of how I might become a dutiful student, but how I might use this chance to aid my longed-for escape. This, and the vow was still fresh in my mouth.

"Then I commend you to the path you have chosen. May the blessings of the Living Light speed you on your journey so that you may remain in the Land of the Living all your days."

Datho turned and addressed the gathered crowd, saying, "Do you accept this man as a brother, and will you look to his welfare as you look to your own, aiding him in every way as he begins his journey?" He paused, turning to scan the druid throng. "How say you?"

The assembly answered with one voice. "We accept him and welcome him as a brother."

He stepped before me once more and said, "Kneel and receive your sacred name."

I did as he commanded and knelt in the grass on the hillside. Then, in the light of the rising moon, the wise ollamh placed his hand upon my head. He struck the ground three times with his staff and cried, "Succat you were, but Succat is no more. From this day you are Corthirthiac: strong bulwark against the gale of contention. May your strength endure to the end which the Mighty Maker has ordained for you.

"Rise, Corthirthiac," he said, "and take your place among your brothers."

I rose and, seeing Cormac standing nearby, went to stand beside him. I crossed the short distance between us and saw Buinne staring at me. Our eyes met, only for the briefest instant, for as he realized I saw him, his features changed; the unvoiced snarl of hatred vanished, and his expression became coolly impassive. As I took my place beside Cormac, Buinne edged back into the crowd and disappeared.

The ceremony continued. The two young boys who had also undergone initiation were added to the brotherhood; these, like myself, were given to Datho to begin their training. This ritual completed, it was then the turn of all who had completed one level of training to be recognized and advanced to higher ranks. There were many of these—including Cormac and, to my surprise, Buinne as well.

The next day the druids held council to discuss matters of importance which had arisen during the interval since the last gathering. "Watch and learn," Cormac whispered as the proceedings began. "Your questions will be answered."

Because Datho was one of the high-ranking bards empowered to speak in council, we were allowed to stand behind him and so had good places from which to see all that would take place. The council began with a long recitation in a tongue I did not understand, and then the filidh—an old man with a hump on his back—declared that the council was begun.

"That is Gwyn Gryggyn," Cormac told me, "called the Far-Seeing. He is Chief Bard of Mídhe."

"Gwyn?" I wondered. "That is a British name."

"And so he is."

"But—"

"Listen."

The old man looked all around him and smiled at those he knew up front, including Datho, nodding and mouthing greetings to his acquaintances while waiting for the crowd to settle.

When all was quiet, he said, "A year has passed, brothers, since it was decided to defer the question of the Ceile De. In the passing of the year, I trust we have all given the matter its due consideration. The time has come to determine how we will answer the charge that has been laid before us concerning the institution of the *Cadair Glân*."

The name was in my native tongue. Cadair Glân—it meant "Holy Chair."

At this there came a fretful murmuring from many of those looking on.

Old Gwyn turned his kindly face this way and that, until the grumblers had finished. "So now, brothers," he continued, "I put the question to you: Shall the Holy Chair be established among us for the dignity and elevation of the Ceile De?"

He had scarcely got the question out when there arose shouts and cries of both affirmation and dissension. Again he waited until the commotion had subsided and then said, "I observe that the Brotherhood is divided on the issue. Therefore we will proceed by the telling of stones." He gestured to one of the nearby filidh, who brought forth a large leather bag and took his place beside the old druid. Gwyn raised his hand, and I saw he held a small white pebble. "White for affirmation of the question," he said, "and black"—he now showed a dark pebble—"for rejection." Indicating the bag, he said, "Come, brothers, render your judgment."

There was a general surge toward the center, where the druid stood with the bag, but the jostling soon resolved itself into an orderly line of filidh who passed, briefly dipping their hands into the bag and moving on. Not everyone cast a stone into the bag; it seemed to me the privilege of the higher-ranking filidh. When the last stone had been cast, the bag was closed and, in the sight of all, handed to Ollamh Gwyn, who raised it in his hands. He carried it to Datho and declared, "I say that the cast was done properly in the sight of all present. How say you?"

"I am satisfied," replied Datho.

Moving on, the old druid carried the bag to several other high-ranking filidh and asked them the same question. Upon receiving a positive answer from each ollamh, he returned to the center of the ring and summoned another bard, who approached holding a large wooden bowl. Gwyn once more raised the bag, untied it, and poured the contents into the bowl.

"Who will count the stones?" he asked.

From among the several volunteers, he chose Meabh. The old woman stepped forth and gazed into the bowl. "More light!" she said, and torches were brought near. She reached into the bowl and picked out a black stone, held it up, for all to see, and said, "One!"

Returning her bent hand to the bowl, she brought out four more dark pebbles in quick succession. "Two, three, four, five," she said, and then, reaching into the bowl, declared, "That is all. The rest are white." So saying, she picked up a handful of white pebbles and let them fall back into the bowl.

At this the dissident bards loosed a low growl of disapproval. But the matter did not end there. As soon as the gathering had quieted once more, wise old Gwyn chose one from among the dissenters and called him forth. "Brother Senach," he said, "I would have you count the stones."

Frowning, the filidh proceeded to sort through the stones in the bowl. The tally was brief, and Senach declared, "I also make it five opposing and twenty sustaining." He turned and stepped back to his place.

"Hear and know," cried old Gwyn, "by the telling of the stones, the Cadair Glân is established!" These last words were swallowed in the shouts of approval which greeted his pronouncement. "This night the will of the Brotherhood of the Oak is declared. The Holy Chair of the Ceile De is herewith created. Those who wish to make application to this chair may do so now."

There ensued a lengthy disputation—much of which I did not follow, but during the discussion the dissenters and their followers gathered in a group and, crying defiance on the proceedings, quit the gathering. There was much shouting on both sides, and attempts were made to persuade the rebels to stay, but they would not. They departed the Comoradh then and there.

When they had gone, I asked one of the lower-ranking brothers why the dissenters were so angry. "Oh, they resent the influence of the Christians."

"The Christians?" I wondered. "What Christians?"

"The Ceile De," he told me. "Do you not know this?"

"I have not been among the filidh very long," I replied. "Many things are still new to me."

"The Ceile De are followers of the Christian god, Esu," he told me. "They revere him with the same esteem as An Rúnda."

"An Rúnda," I repeated. "The Mysterious."

"Indeed," he agreed. "The Ceile De have grown in number among the Learned, and their presence is seen as a threat to those who think that the brotherhood should remain forever unchanged."

"What do the Ceile De think?"

"Ah," he said, "they think this Esu is the completion of everything the filidh believe. Truth against the world—you have heard of this, yes?"

Unwilling to confess further ignorance, I said, "I may have heard it once or twice."

"Well, this Esu," he confided, "*is* the truth by which all others must be reckoned. At least," he added with a diffident shrug, "that is what the Ceile De believe."

"And you?" I asked. "Do you also believe this?"

"I do," he confided, then glanced around quickly as if afraid someone might overhear. He caught himself and smiled. "What is more, from tonight there is no longer any fear or shame in discussing these things. Now that the Cadair Glân is established among us, we can all speak freely."

That very night the new chief of the Holy Chair was chosen from among the applicants, and it was none other than Datho. Cormac, standing beside me, was elated. He sprang forward and wrapped his teacher in a jubilant embrace, lifting him off his feet. The dignified ollamh protested weakly, patting his former pupil about the head and shoulders, while the other fil-idh acclaimed the choice with shouts and cheers.

Several other matters were decided then, and it was after midnight when the formal gathering concluded. We stayed on two more days, however, to allow Datho to hold council with his fellow Ceile De. I think they talked about how best to establish and organize the Cadair Glân, but as I was not included in the talks, I found time to fish in the river, pick berries, and laze in the sun with Datho's two younger pupils. I stayed out of Buinne's way for the most part, seeing him only at mealtimes; where he went and how he oc-cupied himself the rest of the time, I could not say and did not care so long as it was far away from me.

Finally the day of leaving dawned, and it was a sad day, for it meant that Cormac was going with Meabh and I would see him no more. "Of course we will see each other," he told me. "There will be gatherings, and I will come to the ráth if I can. Anyway, the time will pass quickly."

"You have been better than a brother to me, Cormac," I told him. "If not for you, I would not be alive to stand before you and thank you now."

"I did only what anyone would do."

"Buinne would not have done it," I replied. "He bears me ill, I know."

"You may be right," Cormac conceded. "But you need have no further concern for him. He will be leaving Datho soon."

"Not soon enough for me."

He smiled and gripped me by the shoulder. "Farewell, my friend. Work hard at your learning, and the time will pass swiftly enough. I will come and see you as soon as I can." He paused, "Oh, yes—and tell Sionan I have ad-vanced in rank and now sit at the feet of Meabh herself. Tell her that, will you?"

"I will."

Still smiling, he stood before me, reluctant to leave. From the riverbank one of Meabh's servants called him away. He embraced me one last time and departed. "Farewell, Cormac!" I called after him. "Until we meet again!"

Alas, could even Gwyn the Far-Seeing have guessed how long that would be?

25

LIFE IN THE druid house resumed. I was no longer strictly a servant, although I retained some of my former duties and still wore the iron collar of a slave. The two younger boys, Heber and Tadhg, took on the more menial daily chores; I began lessons with Datho and Iollan, and the house quickly settled into a new rhythm—one that, much to my relief, did not include Buinne. In view of his advancement in rank, he was sent to house somewhere on the other side of the mountains to learn the making of elixirs, potions, unguents, and suchlike for healing. I did miss Cormac at first, but it was as he said: With the demands of learning, I soon had little time for missing anyone.

I waited a few weeks and then asked Datho if my slave collar might be removed. He regarded me with an expression of benign curiosity. "Why?"

Of all the questions I had imagined as I practiced the discussion over and over in my mind, this was one I had not anticipated. Without thought I blurted, "Because it is hateful to me!"

"Ah," he said, accepting my evaluation, "I see." He fingered his beard thoughtfully for a moment and then said, "You have shown yourself a trustworthy servant and a ready student. If it would please you to remove this token of your bondage, then I see no harm."

His decision was more than gratifying. I thanked him and then respectfully inquired when he thought the deed could be accomplished.

"It must be done with the king's permission, of course," he said. "I will ask him when next I go to the ráth."

Sensing that I had found an opportune time, I decided to risk the greater prize. Plucking up my courage, I asked, "And do you think we might also ask Lord Miliucc to grant my freedom?"

The wise old bard considered this for a moment. He looked into the air, his lips pursed. I did not press him but waited, trying to quell the uneasy feeling in my stomach.

Finally he said, "Insofar as a king is bound to honor the request of his druid, it is best to make only the most judicious entreaties."

"I understand," I told him. "Perhaps it might not seem a thing of much account to some, but to one noble born it chafes me worse than this iron collar ever did." I gave the twisted iron ring a hard yank for emphasis.

"Lord Miliucc will no doubt ask a boon in return," said Datho. "Do you have anything to offer him?"

I had not thought of this. "I have but myself," I answered. "Perhaps the king would look favorably on a pledge of future service as a filidh. Certainly a willing bard would be more valuable to him than an unwilling shepherd."

"Well said," concluded Datho. "If you are content to offer yourself as a bard in the service of the king—should he require a boon to help persuade him—then I will ask him to grant your freedom."

"Thank you, Ollamh, you have made me very happy."

Happy? It was all I could do to keep from leaping about the room and yelping with glee. I thanked Datho again and then, lest I betray my true intentions somehow, retreated with my victory. Soon, soon, and very soon, I would be free! In light of this joyous event, my vision and vow were all too swiftly forgotten.

In the meantime, having secured Datho's promise, I renewed my ardor for my duties. I did not wish to give the chief bard even the least cause for concern or suspicion. I threw myself into the work of the druid house, adopting the air and attitude of the perfect servant.

Datho was an exacting but not unreasonable master. His knowledge was veritably oceanic in breadth and his learning encompassed the universe, both seen and unseen, and this deep and boundless erudition he undertook to pour into my own pitiful bowl of a brain. On good days we walked out in the wood or meadow or up to the mountain. On rainy days we sat together in the druid house, where I would listen to him expound on the movements of the stars; on the lineages of kings and their kingdoms; on the various shrubs, herbs, and vegetables and their useful properties; on the habits of forest animals, the migrations of races and nations, or the correct way of healing certain diseases.

Mostly, however, I spent my time writing. Datho would recite whole movements of various songs—"The Protection of the Honey Isle," "Finn and the Phantoms," "The Four Pillars of Song," "The Contention of Bards," "Mabon and the Mysteries," and many others—while I, struggling to keep pace, repeated the lines and wrote them on the ever-present wax tablet all bards-in-training used for their lessons. When the tablet was filled, front and back, he would send me away to commit the section to memory. When I could recite the tale perfectly without looking at the tablet, then I would melt and smooth the wax and we would begin again, adding the next section, building on what I had learned.

In his first year a fledgling filidh is expected to learn no fewer than twenty songs, or tales, and to be able to recite them beginning to end whenever asked. In addition to this, because I was not a native Irish speaker—and even my knowledge of the British tongue was not extensive—Datho instructed me in the use and meaning of words, which he said I would need if I were ever to acquire the briamon, the word of power or, as it was often called by normal folk, the "Dark Tongue," by which the druid-kind performed many wonders.

Thus my days were filled morning to night with work and study. Curiously, the learning appealed to me. I enjoyed mastering the obscure lore—especially the songs and stories—and delving deep into the peculiar wisdom of the Learned Brotherhood. Be that as it may, what little time I could steal from study or chores I spent at the ráth with Sionan. Sometimes she would walk back with me as far as the stream, where we would sit on the bank and talk, or, if it was evening, we might lie in the grass together.

More and more she was in my thoughts—along with Cormac's stern warning not to disappoint her. Sionan herself breathed no word of either frustration or hope; she seemed to accept the way things were between us and did not seek to alter them one way or another. Still I thought about her and about what she would think when, one day soon, I left.

That day seemed as far away as ever, for, despite the ollamh's promise, the days went by and Datho made no mention of going to the ráth. I began to fear he had forgotten or that he had thought better of his decision and changed his mind. All the same, I dared not ask him again in case my impatience provoked or angered him. I bore my apprehension in silence, pretending to be the dutiful student and then racing off to take my frustrations out on Sionan.

One warm day, upon approaching the ráth, I saw her, alone, by the stream; she was washing a garment in the water. I sneaked up and surprised her with a kiss and then led her down along the stream where some willow trees grew. There we stripped off our clothes, swam in the stream, and then made love in the long grass. Afterward we lay together and talked while the sun dried us.

"I asked Datho to seek my release from the king," I told her. "He said he would do it."

She rolled over on her stomach and looked at me with her dark eyes. "What will you do then?"

The question caught me off my guard. "What do you mean?"

"You know what I mean," she said pointedly, and I thought she had somehow guessed my secret. But she continued, saying, "Once you have your freedom, what will you do?"

"I will keep studying," I told her firmly, "until I become a bard." She regarded me silently, and I could not tell what she was thinking, so I added, "Datho thinks I may have to offer the king a few years' service as a filidh in exchange for my slave collar."

"Well," she said, "then at least you can stay in the ráth. We can be together whenever we like. We can even be married."

That was all she said, but it cut at my heart like a knife. For despite my exuberant—and ill-advised—words on the subject, I knew I must soon forsake her.

"Of course, my love," I told her, Cormac's stern warning echoing in my thoughts. Not caring to discuss the matter further, I reached out and pulled her to me. I kissed her mouth, and throat, and breasts, and then rolled her on top of me.

The first stars were showing through gaps in the clouds when at last I took my final lingering kiss and started back to the druid house. Sionan stood on the bank and watched until I was out of sight.

On the way I was assailed by guilt and shame for deceiving Sionan. I hated myself for doing it. Moreover, I thought she was beginning to suspect I was not telling her the truth. The only solution, I could see, was to try to move the matter along somehow. I resolved to speak to Datho again at the first good opportunity.

That night, I lay on my pallet and thought how best to do this, and quickly arrived at several appeals he could not possibly gainsay—and just as quickly discarded each as unsatisfactory in one way or another. The next morning, when it came time for my lesson, Datho took me out to one of the oaks where, in good weather, he liked to do his teaching. Heber and Tadhg were with Iollan, who was letting them practice scratching ogham lines on a scrag of rock behind the house.

Before I could ask about my slave collar, the druid said, "Cormac told me your grandfather was a presbyter in the church of the Holy Esu."

"He was that," I replied, somewhat surprised that he should raise the subject.

Datho nodded and lowered himself onto a small three-legged stool he kept under the oak. He put out his hand and indicated that I should sit on the ground before him. "As chief of the Ceile De of Éire, I have decided that it shall be my work to build a bridge to Britain. What do you think of that?"

"I think it most ambitious, Ollamh," I answered. "Perhaps a boat would be a better choice."

He laughed, his voice resounding through the little wood like the peal of a bell. "The bridge I shall build, Corthirthiac, is made not of stone or timber but of faith and goodwill."

When we were together as master and pupil, he always called me by my filidh name; the rest of the time I was still Succat. "Not the most durable of materials, Ollamh," I replied.

"Perhaps not," he allowed. "But the ties between the druid-kind of Éire and Britain are ancient and many. Those ties will be strengthened, but it is the church of your grandfather that I wish to reach with my bridge."

Unable to think of any possible value which might be derived from this attempt, I could only stare and ask, "Why?"

"Truth against the world," he replied in the elliptical fashion much beloved of bards.

It was the same thing the young bard had told me at the gathering. I still had no idea what he was talking about, but I held my tongue.

"This," he continued after a moment, "is the soul of our teaching: *Truth against the world*. So it has always been, so shall it ever be."

I was about to ask what this odd saying meant, but Datho held up his hand. "Only listen," he said. Closing his eyes, he began nodding his head, and in a moment he started to sing. He sang:

> In every person there is a soul,
> In every soul there is intelligence,
> In every intelligence there is thought,
> In every thought there is either good or evil,
> In every evil there is death,
> In every good there is life,
> In every life there is God.

He repeated the little verse once more. "Now you sing it with me," he instructed, and I sang it with him several more times until I had it. "This the filidh believe," he told me, "and it is the beginning of wisdom. So tell me: Do you think your grandfather would have agreed?"

"Without a doubt," I replied.

"Even so," he said. "This we have believed from the beginning. But many people—especially the Roman priests of Britain—have forgotten this. They look upon the Ceile De and see enemies where they should see brothers. Everywhere they go, they strive to uproot our traditions and plant their foreign observances instead. Yet we have been in the land far longer than they. Our traditions were not passed on to us by men but were given to us by the All-Wise himself."

I suppose I could not disguise my skepticism any longer. Datho read the disbelief on my face and said, "I see you are the child of your grandfather."

"How should I be otherwise?" I asked.

Datho did not reply at once. He laced his fingers beneath his chin and looked down his nose at me for a long moment. "You have never heard 'The Tale of the Strong Upholder'?"

"No, Ollamh, you have not told me."

"Then this," he said, his eyes lighting with pleasure, "is a most auspicious day. Listen, and I shall tell you how it is that True Belief came to DeDanaan's children."

Closing his eyes, he tilted his head back and, drawing a deep breath, made a sound halfway between a moan and a sigh. Rather than trailing off into silence, however, the utterance grew until it seemed to fill the wood with a low, droning, sonorous tone. When it finished, silence reigned in the wood—as the calm and serenity that follows a storm.

"In the days before the present age," the wise ollamh began, "when Aedh Slane was high king and Fintan mac Dara was chief bard of Éire, word went out that the high king had determined to build a great hall at Tara. This he decreed, and this he did. Gathering the best builders and finest crasftmen in all the island, he assembled them on the plain below the hill and set forth his plan, which he had drawn in gall upon a deerskin.

"One glimpse of the king's plan and the workers fell back in amazement. 'To be sure,' said Oscar, the Master Builder of Éire, 'this hall is the most prodigious ever seen in all this land. A whole forest will be required for the timber, and a lake of gold for its fittings. Though we labor fifty years, it will require fifty years more before it is finished.'

"Hearing this, the king puffed up his chest with pride and said, 'Then why do you yet stand gaping? There is the plan and yonder the forest. Go to work!'

"So the king commanded, and so they did. The workmen had not felled many trees, however, when the lords and princes of Éire who had been deprived of builders and laborers began grumbling about the high king's new hall. They found fault with its size, which was larger than any of their own, and with its cost, which, like a flood running downhill, would eventually find its way to them.

"Now: Tuan mac Carell, filidh of vast renown, was alive in those days, abiding in the wood by himself. He heard the axes of the workmen cutting the great oaks, and he heard the grumbling of the small kings and lords. Up he gets, and off he goes. He summons the small kings and lords and addresses them, saying, 'Why do you stand there moaning and making mouths at the high king? If you have a grievance, why not go to him, speak out your complaint, and demand satisfaction?'

"The small kings looked at each other in dismay. One of them, Lord Goiben, plucked up his quivering courage and said, 'If we fail to heed the wisdom of your urging, the reason, you will find, is this. King Aodh is the greatest king ever seen in this island. He will not suffer anyone to gainsay his decrees, and anyone who tries is instantly set upon by the king's warhost. That unfortunate fellow is flayed alive, and his skin is sent to his widow for a keepsake.'

"Old Tuan mac Carell blew out his cheeks. 'Is it a man who speaks thus or an insect? Hear me then. Though he may not listen to one of you, yet he might listen to two. And though he may not listen to two of you, yet he will surely listen to three. And though he may not listen to three of you, yet I believe he will listen to four. And though he may not listen to four of you, yet I insist he will listen to five. And though he—'

"The small kings threw their hands in the air. 'Enough!' they cried. 'We understand. We will all go together to the high king at Tara, and he will not fail to hear our complaint.'

"The small kings and kinglets went home and gathered their bards, their wise counselors, and their learned advisors, and they all marched to Tara to confront the high king over the extravagance of his great hall. Early one day, as dawn lit the morning sky, the great company assembled on the Plain of Tara, which is below the sacred hill, and called to the king to attend them.

"High King Aedh, making a circuit of the royal ráth in the morning, looked out and saw all the lords and lordlings gathered with their bards and advisors and wise counselors, and he called Fintan to him and said, 'Chief Bard, look out upon Magh Fál and tell me what you see.'

"Fintan, wise and good, looked down from the sacred hill. 'O, Mighty King,' he said, 'I see a great assembly of nobles and bards.'

" 'And what, from this, do you foretell?' inquired the king.

" 'From the frowns on their faces, I foretell contention and disputation, controversy and argument. In a word: trouble.'

" 'Can it be eluded?' wondered the king.

" 'Great King, the time for evading this contention is long past.'

" 'Well, if it cannot be avoided,' replied the king, 'then we will go down and see what remedy they seek.'

"The high king gathered his counselors, advisors, musicians, and not a few of his finest warriors; he mounted his noble chariot with the silver wheels and, with the carynx blaring and drums booming, he drove down to the plain with this great company to see what had stirred the small kings from their nests.

"Driving his chariot into their midst, High King Aedh warmly greeted his lords and lordlings and all their retainers and retinues, and asked, 'What event of great moment has brought you here today, my friends? Can it be you have come to pay the tribute yet owing?'

"Lord Goiben, who had been chosen to speak for them all, dismounted from his horse and approached the chariot; he stretched forth his hand to touch the king's foot. 'Wise King,' he said, 'Champion of Justice, Friend of the Oppressed, Generous Giver, we come to you today because we cannot rest for the torment of a question only you can answer.'

"High King Aedh looked at the great assembly and shook his head sadly. 'Well,' he sighed, 'since I am not to have the tribute, the least you can do is tell me the question that is causing you such torment.'

" 'The question, Great King, is this: If the king is servant of his people, is it right that he should have the greatest portion?'

" 'Now, that,' said Aedh, 'is an excellent question. Allow me to confer with my wise counselor, and I will soon provide the answer you require.'

"The high king turned to his druid Fintan and said, 'Evil is this day! Some cunning is behind this, believe me. For if I say the king's portion must be smaller, then they will say I cannot build the great hall. If I say the king's portion must be larger, then they will say that I am neither just nor righteous, and they will take the kingship away from me. What wicked person put them up to this? Tell me, and I will have his skull for a drinking cup.'

"Fintan, loyal as he was wise, replied, 'If you would keep your hall, then you must pose them another question. If they cannot answer you, then you need not answer them.'

" 'An excellent plan!' cried the high king. Then, considering all the fil-idh, bards, and ollamhs, he despaired, and added, 'But what question can I possibly ask that they cannot answer?'

"Fintan leaned close; putting his lips to the king's ear, he said, 'The question you must ask is this: Why and wherefore is Éire, most favored of islands, divided as it is?'

"High King Aedh embraced his faithful counselor and, removing a gold band from his arm, gave it to Fintan, saying, 'Now I know you are the wisest of the wise! Who else could have thought of such a question? Tell me, what is the answer?'

"At this Fintan merely shook his head and said, 'I do not know.'

"The high king glowered. 'If you do not know, let us hope no one else does either. Come what may, I will ask them.' Turning to the great assembly, he raised his voice and said, 'I will gladly answer your question. Indeed, I am anxious to do so. But first you must answer the question I shall pose.' And he asked them the question Fintan had given him.

"When the members of the assembly heard this, they quickly came together to discuss how best to answer. All the kings and their wise advisors and counselors pondered long. One after another cast, but failed to strike the answer. Finally Lord Goiben called Tuan mac Cairell to him and said, 'You have heard the question. You are the wisest and most learned among us. What is the answer?'

"Wise Tuan shook his head. 'That there is an answer cannot be denied. But I have never heard it—and I am the oldest human being who ever lived. Therefore I think you must accept your defeat as gracefully as you can.'

" 'Though we do many another thing,' replied Goiben, 'that is the one thing we will not do. Back to the forest with you!'

"The kings and kinglets fell to arguing then about what should be done if no answer could be found. They were still writhing in disputation when the sun soared high overhead. Suddenly ugly black clouds boiled up to cover the sky and the sound of a mighty wind filled all the world. And though it was bright midday, the heavens grew dark as twilight after the sun has set. Not the slightest breath of wind could be felt, yet the roaring of the unseen wind grew louder. There was thunder but no lightning, and the hair stood up on the necks of men and beasts alike. Clots of hail fell out of the sky and lay in the grass smoldering as if on fire.

"All at once they heard a voice crying out to them. They turned and saw, approaching out of the west in the direction of the setting sun, a mighty champion, fair and tall—taller than any three of the tallest warriors among them and more wonderful to look upon than the most handsome man they had ever seen. His eyes were the color of the windswept sky, and his teeth were straight and white. His chin was smooth-shaven, and his brow was high and fine.

"For a cloak the magnificent stranger wore a shining veil as radiant and rainbow-hued as crystal, and for sandals, hammered bands of purest gold. His hair was pale as flax and uncut, falling in curls to the middle of his back. This mighty champion carried two stone tablets in his left hand and a silver branch with three fruits in his right, and these were the fruits which were on the branch: apples, hazelnuts, and acorns. Around his waist he wore a girdle of bronze plates, and each plate could have served as a platter for four kings. In his girdle he carried a knife with a blade made of glass that was sharper than the sharpest steel.

"Around the stranger's neck was a golden torc as thick as a baby's arm, and on the ends were jewels: a ruby on the right and a sapphire on the left. His hands were broad and strong, and when he spoke, his voice sounded like the waves upon the shore or like the rushing of many waters.

"He came to stand before the assembled kings of Éire, and he said, 'Greetings, friends—if friends you be.'

"The princes and princelings quailed before him, but High King Aedh drove his chariot to where the stranger stood. He raised his hand in kingly greeting and said, 'I am king here, and this is my realm. I welcome you, champion—if champion you be. What has brought you here?'

" 'I have come from the setting of the sun, and I am going to the rising. My name is Trefuilngid Treochair,' answered the stranger.

" 'A strange name,' replied the king. 'And why has that name been given you?'

" 'Easy to say,' replied Trefuilngid, 'because it is myself, and no one else, who upholds the sun, causing it to rise in the east and set in the west.'

"The high king regarded the towering stranger with curiosity. 'Forgive me, friend, for asking,' he said, 'but why are you here at the setting of the sun when it is at the rising you must be?'

" 'Easy to say,' answered the marvelous stranger, 'but not so easy to hear, I think. For, in a land far away from here, a man was tortured today—and for that reason I am on my way to the east.'

" 'This tortured man,' inquired the king, 'of what account was he that one such as yourself should take notice?'

" 'You cut to the heart of the matter, to be sure," replied the stranger, 'for the man of whom I speak was born to be the ruler of the world. He was called the Prince of Peace, Righteous Lord, and King of Kings.'

"At these words Lord Aedh and his noblemen groaned. 'Certainly this is a grave injustice, and deeply to be lamented,' observed the king, 'yet such things are known to happen from time to time. Even so, it does not explain why you have come among us like this.'

" 'The man I speak of was crucified and killed by the men who tortured him,' Trefuilngid explained. 'His name was Esu, and he was the rightful High King of Heaven, Son of the Strong Upholder, Lord of Life and Light. When he died, the sun stepped aside, and darkness has covered the face of the earth. I came forth to find out what ailed the sun, learned of this outrage, and now I am telling you.'

"The king drew himself up and said, 'I thank you for telling us, friend. But tell us, one thing more: Where can we find the vile cowards who perpetrated this injustice? Only say the word, and rest assured we will not cease until we have punished them with the death they undoubtedly deserve.'

" 'Your wrath is noble and worthy, friend,' replied the magnificent stranger, 'but it is misplaced. For in three days' time the same man who was crucified will break the bonds of death and rise again to walk the world of the living. Through him death itself will be conquered forever.'

"When they heard this good news, the king and all the noblemen and bards of Éire wept for joy. They demanded to know how this had come about, and the glittering stranger told them, 'It has been ordained from the foundation of the world. But it has been revealed to you now so that you may prepare your people for the age to come.' "

Here Datho finished his recitation. Silence stretched between us as I contemplated the tale. "Now you know," he said after a moment, "how knowledge of the Truth came to Éire and why it is that I wish to build my bridge."

26

OR ALL DATHO'S good intentions, I was no nearer to gaining my freedom. Discouraged and dissatisfied, I determined to seize the very next opportunity to advance the matter—come what may. Events overtook me, however; like a storm at sea that hurls the poor sailor and his boat wherever it will, my plans and I were blown far off course.

It came about this way: The next day a rider appeared at Cnoc an Dair with a summons from the king. It seems a party of traders working the western coast had put in at the fishing settlement on the shore. They were Gauls with a ship full of goods obtained in Baetica, Lusitania, Aquitania, and elsewhere: glass cups, bowls, beads, steel knives, fine cloth, leather, olives, and suchlike. A few of the traders approached the ráth to invite the nobles down to the ship where they could see the goods for themselves.

The traders' dexterity with the elusive Irish tongue was crude and clumsy. Still, while they were trying to entice their prospective buyers to come and view their wares Sionan overheard one of the men speaking Latin to his fellow. She told Queen Grania that I knew this speech, and so the king sent Forgall to fetch me. "The king has need of his slave," the warrior said, and explained his errand to Datho. "He is to come with me at once. I will return him to you when he is finished."

"Perhaps you might accompany us as well, Ollamh," I suggested, hoping that while we were at the ráth, I could get him to speak to the king about my release.

Datho declined, but was more than happy to send me off, so I rode to the seaside settlement with Forgall, whereupon I performed the task of translating between the Irish and the Gauls.

It was easily done. The traders were little better than thieves, and when they saw that I was not to be taken in by their extravagant boasts over the qualities of their merchandise, they assumed a businesslike demeanor and their prices became more reasonable.

In the end I made good bargains for Lord Miliucc, acquiring for him a large jug of red wine and a length of fine blue cloth for his lady at prices my own mother would not have been ashamed to accept at home. I also gained a valuable boon for myself, as the queen was mightily impressed with my ability to haggle with the traders and asked if I might teach her some of this useful speech. I suppose she thought that next time traders came, she might bargain for herself.

With Datho's permission I agreed, of course; if nothing else, it meant I could see Sionan more often. On certain days I would go to the ráth to teach rudimentary Latin to Queen Grania and some of her ladies. She preferred meeting with me late in the day, and it was almost always dark by the time we finished and therefore too late to return to the druid house. So naturally I stayed with Sionan in the hut the queen had given her. Sionan told me the gossip of Miliucc's court, and I told her what I was learning from Datho. We held each other through the night, and though I ached to leave the warmth of her bed, dawn found me flitting across the valley and toiling up the hill to the druid house.

This arrangement, agreeable though it was, lasted a few weeks and then began to sour. Despite my repeated offers, Datho never accompanied me to the ráth as I hoped he would; therefore the subject of my freedom still had not been put before the king. Sionan, for her part, began to speak as if our arrangements should be formalized. Mindful of Cormac's warning, I resisted such a notion—but it did not take a druid to see that, should we continue, Sionan's cruel disappointment loomed like a storm-troubled mountain before us.

And then Cormac suddenly appeared one day to say that he was leaving Éire. I happened to be in the ráth when he arrived, and I went to with Sionan to greet him. "Meabh is taking me to Britain to learn from an ollamh there named Cethrwm," he told us. "It is a very great honor."

"Where will you go?" asked Sionan.

"It is a druid house in the north," he said, "not far from Cend Rigmonaid on the eastern coast. Do you know it?"

"No," I said. The name meant nothing to me.

"How long will you be away?" asked Sionan.

"Oh, a season or two," replied Cormac lightly. "A year at the most."

"A whole year?"

"What of that? Before you remember I've gone, I'll be back. And when I return, I will be an ollamh."

I complimented him on his swift advancement and wished him well. Although Sionan declared herself delighted with her brother's good fortune, it was all she could do to force a wistful smile.

"Now," he said, "I must go and beg the king's leave, but I will return with beer and bread, and we will drink a celebration to my safe journey and swift return."

When he had gone, I turned to Sionan. "Why so sad? We've seen him little enough this summer. A season or two more will make no difference."

She frowned and turned away. "It's not that."

"What then?"

"If he goes, he will never return."

"Of course he will return," I insisted.

Reaching out, I touched her shoulder; I could feel her trembling.

"Sionan, what is wrong?" She made no answer. "Tell me."

She turned her face to mine. Tears filled her eyes. "No one who goes to Britain ever returns."

"They do!" I assured her.

"No." She shook her head firmly. "They do not."

"Of course, they do!" I insisted. I forced a chuckle at the absurdity of her claim, all the while cringing inside with the knowledge that I, too, would hie away to Britain as soon as I could and never return. "It is only a day's sailing from here, after all."

She grew petulant. "Now you are mocking me," she said, pulling away.

"Listen," I reasoned, "people come and go to Britain all the time—as I should know. Cormac will go and study for a while, and when he is finished, he will come back. You'll see."

Though Sionan said no more about it, I could see she was far from convinced. I wondered what had put such a notion into her head; I might have pursued it further, but Cormac appeared with the food and beer, and we all sat down to eat and drink in celebration of his good fortune.

We walked back to the druid house that night so Cormac might bid farewell to Datho and Iollan, and we arrived to find that while we were at the ráth, Buinne had also returned.

In all the time he had been away, I had not held a single thought about the contemptible bard. I had forgotten precisely how unpleasant he could be. Before the night was through, however, he more than reminded me.

"You have wasted no time, I see," he said the first moment he got me alone.

"Good to see you, too, Buinne. What happened? Did they grow weary of your creeping around and throw you out?"

"Busy, busy." His smile was thin and icy. "But your schemes will come to nothing. I will see to that."

I glared at him with dull loathing. "Let us make a pact, you and I. Stay away from me, and I promise I will stay far away from you."

"And let you cloud Datho's good judgment with your tricks and lies?" He shook his head slowly. "No. That I will not do."

"Then it will be on your head."

He ignored me, his lips writhed with distaste. "You vile, insignificant worm. You sicken me."

"I warn you, Buinne, stay away from me."

I could feel the cold flame of his hatred on my back as I turned and walked off.

I did my best to avoid him over the next few days. I sensed he was watching me, waiting for me to make some gross mistake he could use as a wedge to drive between Datho and myself. I remained on my best behavior, determined not to allow Buinne the slightest opportunity to attack me for any reason. After all, summer was going, and I still wore my slave collar.

I worked hard at my studies, acquiring not only knowledge but a little judgment along the way. I delved into the many secrets of the earth and its subtle energies as Datho introduced me to the manipulation of elements, which simple folk consider magic. I even gained my first staff: the druid's rod of power, without which the filidh can do but little. It was merely a willow wand, but I prized it nonetheless.

"It appears you may surpass even my lofty hopes for you, Corthirthiac," wise Datho told me when presenting me with this token of my achievement.

"I trust you will never have cause to regret your decision, Ollamh."

"What decision, my son?"

"To allow me to become a bard. You saved my life."

He raised his hands in gentle reproof. "You honor me too highly. The All-Wise has gifted you with everything you require to thrive. If I have done anything, it was merely to open the way to you."

"More than that, Ollamh, far more." The time had come, I decided, and I plunged ahead. "It is because of your unstinting generosity that I hesitate to ask anything more of you."

"Ask me anything. If it is in my power, I will grant it gladly."

"If I hesitate," I began, "it is only for fear of offending you—and that I would never wish to do."

"I am your ollamh," Datho replied with benign patience. "How can any-thing you ask offend me?"

"It is just that . . . well, some months ago you said you would ask the king to grant my freedom." I touched the cold iron at my throat. "Yet the collar remains, and I am still a slave."

"Is that all?" he said, his voice ringing with good humor. "You have no cause for concern, my son. Lughnasadh is soon upon us. This is a most propitious time for making such requests. It has long been in my mind to ask the king then. I thought I told you."

"I never heard it."

"Well, it makes no difference. You have worked hard and achieved much. I am proud of you, my son." Placing his hands on my shoulders, he raised his eyes to the leafy canopy of oak branches above. "A wonderful destiny stretches before you. I have seen it. I have seen you standing among the brightest stars of the heavenly firmament commanding a mighty army. You will be a prince among bards, and men yet unborn will bless your name."

I knew the proper response for a blessing of this magnitude, and I was happy to perform it. Taking his hands into my own, I kissed them, where-upon he embraced me like a son.

Datho must have mentioned it to the others, for a short while later Iollan complimented me on my impending freedom. "Losing your slave collar," he said. "Well and good—and not before time."

"Thank you, brother," I said. He went away smiling and nodding, soon lost in the inexplicable thoughts that filled his days.

This, I think, is how Buinne also came to hear of it—or, more probably, he overheard us talking and decided to make his move.

"So here sits the smug slave," he hissed, sidling up to me as I sat beneath the oak. I was writing an epigram in the ogham Datho had set for me that day, and I had stopped for a moment to think, resting my head against the tree trunk. "Exhausted from all your scheming?"

"Did I hear a rat vomit in the wood?" I opened my eyes. "No, it is only Buinne."

"You have overreached yourself, slave boy."

"I warned you to stay away from me."

"Something will have to be done."

He stood over me with such malevolent mirth that I wanted nothing more than to strike the odious smirk from his impudent face. Tossing aside the wax tablet, I took up my willow wand and rose, ready for whatever he had in mind. "Do your worst, Buinne. Go to it—I am not afraid."

"You *will* be, slave boy," he said, backing away, his grin widening to a deathlike grimace. "You will be."

I said nothing of this to anyone, of course, and returned to my lessons as if nothing had happened. But the world changed that day, and I was too blind with conceit and arrogance to see it.

27

HE PAST IS seen with a clarity wholly lacking in the present. Memory is an illusion formed of equal parts recognition and regret. Nothing is ever what it seems.

Of all men alive beneath wide heaven's ever-circling sun, I know this to be true. For, wrapped in false security, I continued as if nothing had happened. Yet already the world and my place in it were tumbling like a fragile greenwood bower in the first fierce gale of winter.

I saw nothing of this. Blissful in my ignorance, I strode boldly forth, believing the path stretching before me into the future was solid under foot. Poor, blind idiot that I was—there *was* no path, no destination, no future. I was sinking in a morass and did not know it.

The days remained fair and full, the cattle grew fat and sleek, the crops stood tall in the fields, and the tuath enjoyed an uncommon prosperity. I saw Sionan whenever I could; we talked of my freedom, and I continued deceiving her with easy words about how it would be when we were free to marry. In truth I intended escape, and the entanglements of marriage were the last thing I wanted.

I eagerly counted the days until Lughnasadh and the Festival of First Fruits. Datho and Iollan occupied themselves with plans for the Comoradh, the gathering of bards; Buinne was nearly always away collecting various herbs and plants to make his concoctions, and so it fell to me to prepare for the festival. I examined the cattle and chose those acceptable for

the sacrifice, and I saw that the wagon, maiden loaf, and scythe were prepared to Datho's exacting instructions.

The first hint that anything was amiss came the day before the celebration. I returned from the ráth, where I had made the final inspection to see
that all was ready, and went to make my report to Datho. I could not find
him, and there was no response to my call. I made a quick search, however,
and eventually found him in the nearby wood. He was sitting on a rock in
a clearing; the sun was on his head, but he was fast asleep.

"Ollamh?" I said, creeping near.

At the sound of my voice, he started. His eyes flickered open, and he
started up, his expression wild and fearful. The look passed in an instant.
He saw me and came to himself at once. "Oh! You startled me, Succat. I
grew tired. . . ."

I noticed he did not use my bardic name. "I have been looking for you,
Ollamh."

"Well, here I am." He rose and quickly turned to glance behind him, as
if expecting to catch someone—lurking in the shadows. "Where have you
been?"

"You sent me to the ráth—for Lughnasadh. I was to make the arrangements, remember?"

"Ah, yes. Then come, tell me, is everything in order?"

He started off toward the druid house and then turned again. "My staff!"

"Here it is, Ollamh," I said, stooping to retrieve his good oak staff from
beside the rock where it lay.

We walked back to the house—he striding ahead, myself behind with a
puzzled frown over his curious behavior. But the lapse was soon forgotten
as we busied ourselves with making ready for the Comoradh. That night we
ate a simple meal; Heber and Tadhg cooked and served it and, while we
ate, recited their day's lesson for us. Quiet, well-mannered boys, they stood
straight and tall and chanted a portion of "Fionn and the Salmon of Wisdom," a splendid tale, one of the first learned by young bards.

". . . then Fionn lay down on the grassy banks of the stream," the boys
chanted, their high, reedy voices ringing clear, "and he began to sing.
While he sang, he let his hand fall gently into the water, dangling his fingers in the clear, glassy pool, where he knew the ancient salmon was to be
found. . . ."

We all sat listening: Iollan, eyes half closed, tapping his fingers lightly on
the table as the boys recited the age-old song; Buinne, staring beneath
hooded eyes, brooding and bored; Datho distractedly fingering his mustache and glancing around anxiously.

"There in the cool, shadowed depths of the pool, the wise old salmon heard Fionn's fine, melodious voice and awoke. He said to himself, 'What manner of man is it who sings so sweetly and so well?' So saying, the venerable fish bestirred himself to swim up and—"

Suddenly Datho leaped to his feet. "Enough!" His voice was tight, his eyes wild, as he rushed from the table.

"Ollamh!" I started after him but had run only a few paces when he turned on me.

"Stay back!"

"Have you seen something, Ollamh?"

He stared at me, and recognition came flooding back to him; his eyes lost their wild appearance, and he flushed with embarrassment. "Oh, Succat . . ." He looked back at the others, who were now gazing at him with concern.

"Are you well, Ollamh?" I moved to help him.

"Go back," he said. "Go back to the table." A sickly smile appeared on his face. "Let them finish the tale." He turned and strode from the house. "I am sorry . . . I cannot . . . stay. . . ."

Later that night I was lying on my pallet, awake, and heard Datho come up the stairs to the sleeping room. He lay down with a groan and was soon heavily asleep. I slept, too, and woke early the next morning. I gathered my things and went outside to wash and then dressed in my new gray robe, for I was to take part in the Lughnasadh ceremony.

One by one the others rose and began making themselves ready. I quickly finished my preparations and then, eager to be off to the ráth, where Sionan waited, went to help the young ones. "Where is Datho?" I asked Heber as he tied the thin corded belt around his slender waist.

"He has not come down, master." He glanced over to Tadhg, who shrugged. "Do you want me to rouse him?"

"No," I replied, "I will do it. Finish dressing. We will leave as soon as Datho is ready."

I went up to find the ollamh lying on his pallet, sound asleep. Kneeling beside him, I touched his shoulder and said his name. This brought no response, so I shook him gently. "Ollamh," I said, "all is ready. It is time to rise." I shook him again. "Datho?"

It was then I noticed the pale foam on his lips and at the corners of his mouth.

I shook him harder this time and called his name aloud, my heart sinking into the pit of my stomach. When he did not respond, I ran to the stairs and called Iollan to come help me. "Hurry!" I shouted. "I cannot waken Datho!"

As Iollan hurried up the stairs, I returned to the pallet and lightly placed my hand to the druid's neck, but felt no surge of life there, and his flesh was cold to the touch.

"Here!" said Iollan, joining me. "Datho! Datho! Wake up!" The filidh took his old friend by the shoulder and began shaking him violently.

"No, brother," I said, pulling his hands away. "He is not sleeping. He is dead."

The old druid regarded me with a pale, bewildered expression. "Dead, you say? Ah, no, no . . . dead?"

"He must have died in his sleep."

Iollan turned his eyes to the body and at last comprehended my meaning. He sat back on his heels, resting his hands on his thighs. "Ah, poor Datho," he sighed; his hands began to tremble.

Buinne came running up the stairs. "What's happened? What have you done?"

"Poor Datho," said Iollan again. Raising sorrowful eyes, he said, "He is dead, Buinne. Our ollamh and master is dead."

Buinne stared at the body for a moment. He drew a deep breath, as if trying to calm himself. "How?"

"I cannot say," I answered. "I came just now to rouse him and found him as you see him."

"We must send to the king; he must be told at once," said Iollan.

"What about the Lughnasadh celebration?" I asked.

"Oh, we cannot possibly lead the rites now," Iollan said. "We must make preparations for his burial."

Buinne frowned. "No, the celebration will take place as planned."

"It is not possible," Iollan objected. "When an ollamh dies, there is much to be done—ceremonies to perform, services to render. The Learned Brotherhood must be informed. We must begin at once to—"

"And I say it can wait!" snapped Buinne with a ferocity that rocked doddering Iollan back on his haunches. The young druid started away. "Leave him. We will go to the ráth now."

"But we cannot just leave him," protested Iollan weakly.

Buinne rounded on the elder bard. "Get moving!" He snatched Iollan by the arm and yanked him to his feet. "We are going to lead the Lughnasadh ceremonies," he said, his voice a snarl of pent rage. "And then we will attend the gathering." He put his face close to the old man's, his eyes hard and unfeeling. "Everything will take place as planned."

There was a purpose at work in Buinne's determination, and I knew better than to disagree. What he suggested was, after all, for the best; the celebration would have to go ahead as planned. In any case a clash with him would avail nothing, so I decided to bide my time and stood looking on without a word. Buinne whipped his head around to glare at me. "Understood?" he shouted.

"Perfectly," I answered softly.

I turned to leave but instead watched as Buinne drew Datho's cloak over the dead man's face. It may have been my imagination, but it seemed to me that he took inordinate satisfaction in performing that simple service. He had never been able to disguise his thoughts—whatever he was thinking appeared on his face for all to see—and in that instant I saw a man who exulted in his elder's death: an untimely death about which I suspected even then that Buinne knew more than he was saying.

We gathered our things and proceeded to the ráth, where the people had assembled. The mood was high and bright as the sky that day and, if not for Datho's demise, it would have been a splendid celebration.

Soon after our arrival Buinne, Iollan, and myself sought out the king and informed him of our ollamh's death. "Datho dead?" said Miliucc, taken aback by the news.

"Lord and King," replied Iollan, "we are confounded and bereft. It has overtaken us without sign or warning."

"How did it happen?" asked Queen Grania gently.

"Who can say, my Queen?" said Iollan. "Corthirthiac went to wake him and found him dead."

"He died peacefully," I offered. "His end was serene and quiet. We knew nothing of it."

"Indeed," confirmed Iollan sadly, "we knew nothing at all."

"It is unfortunate," said Miliucc. Turning to Iollan, he said, "Datho was a loyal and faithful friend. I will miss his wise counsel and shrewd judgment."

"Of course," said Buinne, deftly interposing himself, "you will not lack the counsel and wisdom of a druid so long as I am here."

The king regarded him dully.

"You are quick to dismiss your master and friend," the queen observed. "But Datho's place will not be so easily or readily filled, I think." She regarded the young druid with a look of unconcealed rancor.

Buinne, realizing his mistake, quickly became solicitous. "Naturally we are all mindful of our loss. With your permission, lord, we will depart for the Comoradh as soon as the celebration is completed, and we will take the body with us. There are rites to be performed."

"You have my permission," said Miliucc. "Do as you think best."

"Thank you, my King. I will obey." The snake—he made it sound as if it were all the king's idea and he but the dutiful servant carrying out his lord's command.

The festivities were conducted. Owing to my having to take a larger part in the observances, it was past midday before I found a chance to speak to Sionan alone. I waited until our absence would not be noted and pulled her into the stable with me. "I have missed you," she said, enfolding me in a passionate embrace. She kissed me hard and, taking my hands, pulled me down into the hay in one of the empty stalls.

I returned her kiss, but she sensed my lack of ardor. "Well! Have you grown tired of me already?"

"Never say it," I answered. "I have something to tell you."

"Tell me, then," she said, kissing my neck. "And when you finish, make love to me."

"Sionan, listen," I said, taking her hands and holding them still. "Something dreadful has happened. Datho is dead."

She stopped kissing me. "When?"

"During the night, I think, or early this morning. I found him in his bed."

"Oh, *mo croí*, I am sorry." She put her hand to my cheek. "He was a good friend to you and Cormac."

"That is not all. I think Buinne might have had something to do with it."

"You think Buinne killed him?"

"Yes—I mean, I think so. It is merely a suspicion, but I think he poisoned Datho."

"Have you told anyone?"

"Not yet."

"But you must tell the king."

"Not until I can be certain."

"What will happen now?"

"We will take the body to the Comoradh. The other filidh will help with the—"

"No," she interrupted, "I mean, what will happen to *us*?"

"Us?" I could not think what she was saying.

"Datho was going to ask the king for your freedom."

The shock of Datho's death had completely driven that fact from my mind. A great surge of dismay rolled over me, and I went down beneath it. I stared at Sionan, unable to speak.

"Succat, did you not think of that?"

I fell back in the hay and lay there as despair clasped me to its cold heart and claimed me for its own. "No," I groaned, "I did not think of that."

"What are we to do now?" she asked, her voice taking on a shade of the woe I felt.

I heard the question but was so dismayed I could make no reply.

"Succat?"

"Well," I said at last, "I suppose it will have to wait until I can find someone else."

"What about Iollan?"

I considered this possibility. "I could talk him into it, I suppose. In any
case he is my last hope."

"What about Buinne?"

"Buinne hates me," I told her. "He would know I put Iollan up to asking
the king for my freedom, and he would find some way to prevent it. He
would, I know it."

"Well, we can worry about that some other time," she said. Putting her
hand behind my head, she drew my lips to hers. "One way or another all
will be well, I know."

She meant to cheer me, of course, but her vague assurance only made it
worse. The prospect of having to worry about what Buinne might do cast
me into a dismal, hopeless state which not even Sionan's ardent lovemaking could banish.

28

HE JOURNEY TO Cathair Bán was markedly unpleasant. It rained most of each day, slowing our labored progress all the more. The weather suited my
mood, for we were carrying my best hope for freedom
to an untimely grave. Lord Miliucc had given us an oxcart for the purpose
of conveying the ollamh's body from the druid house to the Cormoradh,
where Datho would be accorded all the dignities of his rank. Now, wrapped
in his feathered cloak, oaken staff firmly grasped in his cold, unfeeling
hands, he rode for the last time through the land he so loved.

I remembered how Cormac and I had carried Madog's body with the aid
of a simple rune of power, and I wondered why we had not done so now.
When I ventured to suggest that such transport would be preferable to con-
tending with an ox and cart all the way to Cathair Bán, I received merely a
growl of disdain from Buinne and a shrug from Iollan, which suggested that
neither of them possessed this particular skill. Thus we were forced to lum-
ber along in a monotonous parade, wet to the skin and miserable. Heber
and Tadhg took it in turns to help, one riding in the cart while the other led
the ox, so I had little to do but endure the long, slow march and keep out
of Buinne's way.

I still had my suspicions that he had somehow abetted Datho's demise,
and I watched for any sign that might betray him, but Buinne gave away
nothing, and so my misgivings settled into a nebulous haze of doubt, suspicion, and sour distrust.

Forlorn, dispirited, and increasingly wary, I very soon began to contemplate running away. I might simply slip off in the night, I thought, and would be long gone before anyone thought to search for me. With every step the impulse grew—until I could think of nothing else.

All that prevented me was the certain knowledge that if I was caught, I would be killed. Without help or aid of any kind, I *would* eventually be caught, and, fledgling bard or not, I reckoned that Lord Miliucc would have no qualms about carrying out his promised retribution. So I grimly slogged on, heartsick with self-pity and writhing in a torment of frustration.

The gathering received the news of Datho's death with profound sorrow. Owing to the inevitable fact of decomposition—we had been more than a few days on the trail, after all—within moments of our arrival, the necessary ceremonies were begun. The whole of the first day was taken up with rituals of passage devised to ease the transition of the newly deceased to another form of life. The filidh believed that the human soul not only survived death but continued its existence in the Otherworld with all faculties intact. Sometimes, however—as when the attachment to this life was unusually strong for one reason or another—the soul had difficulty in passing.

An ollamh, it was thought—owing to the very nature of his deep knowledge and appreciation of life—often experienced this difficulty acutely. Thus the Learned Brotherhood had created a series of rites to alleviate any suffering on the part of a deceased brother and ease his passage into the world beyond.

The first sequence of rituals was conducted around the oxcart—declarations of lamentation mostly, along with staff waving, bowing, and recitations of a highly symbolic nature that I could not follow at all. When these were finished, Datho's body was taken up and carried to the nearer of the two small mounds adjacent to the great mound; it was laid at the entrance to the mound, and the eldest ollamh present sat with the corpse while the rest of us stood off a short distance and chanted a simple refrain of farewell. Spreading his cloak so that it covered both his head and that of the deceased, the ancient ollamh remained in this morbid communion despite the ripening stink of death.

After a time the old druid emerged to announce that the soul of Ollamh Datho had made its way safely and without undue trauma to the Otherworld. This declaration was met with cheers from the filidh, and the next series of rites commenced; in contrast to those already performed, these were to celebrate the life and achievements of the departed brother and lasted until dusk, when the body was taken up and carried three times very slowly around the mound in solemn torchlight procession while the filidh sang a song of triumph for a life journey well completed. At the conclusion of the third circuit, the body was borne into the mound, where it would rest until the bones could be gathered and removed for secret burial elsewhere.

Upon leaving the mound the principal filidh and all the rest of us looking on placed our burning torches in a heap at the mound's entrance, whereupon the officiating ollamh invoked a powerful rune of protection for the guarding of our dear friend's corpse. The rest of the night was spent in silence as we meditated on life's brevity.

Next morning the main business of the gathering resumed. During the course of the day, several of the filidh came to express their sorrow over Datho's passing. They made it a point to inquire how I was bearing up under the loss of my master. I told them in all honesty that my grief was more for myself and those left behind than for Datho, since while he had a new world to delight in, the rest of us were deprived of the presence and company of our good friend. Beyond that I could not mourn for him. In truth, this was how I felt.

This frank sentiment produced a fair reaction among the Learned, who took it as a sign of profound faith; perhaps it was. I could not say one way or another. Nevertheless they commended me to my studies. One of the druids, a high-ranking ollamh named Calbha, came to pay his respects; we talked for a while, and then he said, "As you know, our departed brother considered you a filidh marked for greatness."

"I know he was encouraging to me in every way," I replied.

He nodded and pulled on his mustache. "Have you given any thought to where you might go now?"

"Indeed," I answered truthfully, "I have thought of little else since Datho's death."

"Be assured," the wise ollamh said, "this very question has occupied our thoughts as well. It has been decided that you will come and join my house." He peered at me with hopeful intent. "Is that agreeable to you?"

"To be sure, I would like nothing better," I lied, "but my lord Miliucc may have other ideas about the best use for his slave. I expect he will put me to herding sheep again."

Calbha's brow furrowed slightly. "I assumed Datho had made it clear to your lord that you were now to become a filidh."

"Datho was going to request my freedom from the king." I raised a hand to my slave collar. "But as you see, I am still Miliucc's slave. And now that Datho is dead . . ." I let my voice trail off into uncertainty.

"The king's wishes will not be allowed to interfere with our purposes," Calbha declared. "After all, anyone can herd sheep, but a filidh of promise is more difficult to find." He nodded sharply, deciding the matter then and there. "Let him find another shepherd, I say."

"Will you intercede for me, Ollamh?"

"It is as good as done," Calbha answered. "I will come to Cnoc an Dair in the autumn to celebrate Samhain. I will ask the king to release you then."

I thanked the ollamh and asked what I should do until Samhain. Calbha replied, "What I have told you will be formally announced before the end of the gathering. Your questions will be answered then."

Pleased as I might have been to receive the ollamh's assurance, the prospect of having to wait until Samhain to gain my freedom only increased my despair. As the day drew to an end, the clouds covered the hill and the rain set in, reflecting my dismal state.

I waited for word the next day, but none came. It was not until the following day, just before the Comoradh broke up and the druids began their journeys home, that Calbha summoned me. He was standing with another, and he introduced me to his companion. "This is Ollamh Tirlandaio, great among the Learned of Éire. He will deliver the judgment of the Brotherhood."

I greeted him and took my place before him. "Your bardic name, son," he said in a deep voice, "tell me."

"Corthirthiac," I replied, "given to me by Ollamh Datho."

He nodded. "Your situation is unfortunate, Corthirthiac," he told me, "but not unknown. Our deceased brother considered you a young man possessed of enormous potential. He had high hopes that with the proper training you would become a great and powerful bard." He regarded me thoughtfully. "Did you know that?"

"I know he was pleased to allow me to serve in his house," I replied.

This brought a smile to Calbha's lips. "Modesty sits uneasily on your shoulders, Corthirthiac—as it does on the shoulders of all who are born for renown." He glanced at Calbha and smiled. "You can speak freely to us, as we will to you."

"Since the two of you have already reached an understanding between one another, I will make this short," said Tirlandaio. "We have decided that Ollamh Calbha is to be your master." He paused, perhaps noting my lack of enthusiasm. "Is that agreeable to you?"

"In every way, master."

"You have no objection?"

"What objection could I have?" I said. "Only perhaps that I must wait so long to sit at the feet of my new master."

"I understand your eagerness," said Calbha, "and I commend it. Unfortunately, I cannot begin this undertaking until after Samhain. I must see my present filidh through to the completion of their fourth year. When they have moved on, I will be free to take on a new and promising pupil."

They dismissed me then, and I walked back to our little camp, where I learned, much to my dismay, that Buinne had not been idle. Owing to Iollan's reluctance to assume Datho's position, Buinne had requested the honor of becoming the master of Cnoc an Dair, and—beyond all reason—his request had been granted. Buinne had assumed authority over the druid house.

My heart sank as I heard the news. Afterward I sought out Iollan to ask how this could have come about. "You should take Datho's place in our house," I told him, "not Buinne."

"That is so," he allowed. "But I asked to be excused."

"Why?" I said, far more sharply than I intended. "How could you do that?"

"The rule of a house is too much for me," he said, his voice breaking with sorrow. "Until they can find a new ollamh to replace Datho, Buinne will be our master."

"But he is not ready for such responsibility," I objected. "He cannot possibly be master."

"It is only for a short time," Iollan said, pleading to be released from my remorseless inquisition. I turned and stumped away. "It is only until Datho's successor can be found," he called after me.

Dreary as our outward journey had been, it was a festival in comparison to our return. I walked through the rain leading the ox and cart, which was empty save for the times Heber and Tadhg rode in it. The two youngsters, mindful of the black mood of their elders, talked quietly with one another and did their best to stay out of the way. From time to time I diverted myself by questioning them about their lessons or asking them to recite portions of the stories they had learned—but nothing lifted our spirits for very long, and we traveled mostly in an unrelievedly grim silence.

Upon our return to the druid house, Buinne let us all know that he would be a very different master from Datho. He lorded it over us with offensive and insulting impunity, swaggering about, calling commands as if he were an emperor and we his laggard minions. Meanwhile I swallowed the indignity and schemed for a way to get to the ráth to see Sionan and share the bad news with her.

Just when I was thinking I would have to risk sneaking out at night, a warrior appeared with a saddled mount and a message for me from the king. "Lord Miliucc says you are to come at once."

"Gladly," I replied. "Am I to know the reason for my lord's request?"

"The traders have returned. He wants you to speak to them."

"Of course." I bade him wait for a moment and went to inform Buinne that I would be away a few days helping the king.

He did not like it. He glowered at me and fumed and went out to see for himself if what I said was true. But as the king's man was there waiting with a horse for me, there was nothing Buinne could do save let me go. Thus I spent the remainder of the day greasing the axles of commerce for my lord. That night, instead of returning to Cnoc an Dair, I accompanied the king and queen back to the ráth where, upon leaving my mount at the stable, I hurried to the queen's house in search of Sionan.

"Succat!" She came into my arms in a rush and greeted me with a kiss. "How long can you stay?"

"Tonight at least—perhaps tomorrow as well. I am helping the lord and lady with the traders. We have just come from the ship."

"The queen has returned?" She pushed me away. "Then you must go."

"In good time." I felt the tingling rush in the pit of my stomach and pulled her to me.

"The queen will be here any moment! You must not let anyone see you."

"Let them see me," I said carelessly.

"No!" She spun from my arms and shoved me toward the door. "Go to my house and wait for me. I will come to you as soon as I can."

I slipped out the door and entered the narrow path between the royal houses. I walked around to the courtyard in front of the king's hall and then ambled here and there about the ráth, allowing myself to be seen in various places. I spoke to some of the farmers as they returned from the fields and to a few of the warriors, too.

In a little while I made my way to Sionan's house and, when I was certain I was not observed, went in to wait. It grew dark, and I fell asleep, awakening when she arrived. "I brought us some food," she said; kneeling beside me, she ran her hand along my arm. "Are you hungry?"

"Famished," I replied.

"Then light the fire and we will eat."

I set about kindling a fire in the hearth, and we were soon sitting before a tidy blaze, drinking the king's beer and holding flesh forks to roast choice bits of pork. "The queen is very pleased with her new silver combs and bracelet," Sionan told me. "She thinks you a shrewd trader."

"I wish I had been able to get combs for you." I lifted my hand to stroke her hair. "One day perhaps."

She caught the wistful undercurrent in my tone. No doubt I had already decided in my heart what I would do, and now I was beginning to realize what my leaving would mean. It must have come out in my speech, for she turned and observed me with concern. "What is wrong?"

"At the gathering," I said, "things did not go so well." I told her then about being given a new ollamh. "And if that were not bad enough," I concluded, "Buinne has been made master of our house. He is making life a misery for everyone, and he hates me most of all."

"Then it will be good for you to have a new ollamh," Sionan observed, misunderstanding the situation completely. Nor did I have the heart to correct her.

I spent that night with Sionan and the next as well. Then the traders moved on, and I had to return to the druid house. I left the ráth reluctantly, dreading my arrival and the inevitable confrontation with Buinne. Indeed, I had but reached the mound when the disagreeable druid pounced, "I know where you go and what you do," he hissed, stepping out to meet me on the path.

"Do you, Buinne?" I said.

"How long did you and your whore think you could hide it from me?"

I had long ago decided to deny everything; whatever Buinne knew or suspected would not be confirmed by me. "What are you talking about, Buinne?"

He took a step closer, his mouth twitching with hatred. "I mean to put a stop to it."

I regarded him cooly and made no reply.

"Nothing to say?"

"When a man's anus does the talking, I try as much as possible to ignore the stench."

His eyes flared with anger, and his jaw bulged. "You hold yourself so superior," he growled, shaking with rage. "This is what I have always hated about you. You should have remained a slave. You have no business here."

"Datho disagreed."

"Datho was a fool; his liberality made him weak and easily deceived." He took a menacing step toward me. "But *I* am master now, and you will not deceive *me*." His lip curled back in a savage, gloating sneer. "You will never become a bard. I will see to that. I am going to have you sent back to your sheep on the mountain."

I let him stew in his vile juices for a moment, then asked, "Tell me, Buinne, have you finally gone mad at last?"

"Mock me if you will, slave boy," he growled, "but I swear on my life you will never be free."

He grinned maliciously and tilted back his head. I wanted to smash him in the face for his insolence and spite. Instead I waited until he turned and started away, then called after him, "Was it poison, Buinne? Was that how you murdered Datho?"

He halted in midstep and turned. "What?" he said, the blood draining from his face.

He gaped at me, sucking air like a winded animal; and I realized that until that instant the arrogant, duplicitous Buinne had never imagined anyone might have suspected him of bringing about Datho's death. Consequently he had not thought to create a denial, plausible or otherwise. Or perhaps the accusation surprised him so that he forgot the lie he meant to tell.

He lurched clumsily toward me, demanding, "What did you say?"

"Your secret is safe with me, Buinne," I told him, plunging ahead recklessly. "I am not going to tell anyone—unless, that is, you keep poking your rat nose into my affairs. I warn you, Buinne, leave me alone."

White-faced, stunned into silence, the treacherous bard gazed at me with dull horror. I decided to leave him before he recovered his wits. I did not see him the rest of the night. He did not come to the table and did not sleep in the druid house—nor did I.

Instead, I spent a wretched night, restless and wakeful, tormented by the awful expression on Buinne's face when I guessed his guilty secret correctly. The dread realization pulsed with every beat of my heart, producing an anguish that drove all thoughts of sleep from my head. Again and again, like a circling bird, my mind returned to the terrible question: *How long before he poisons me?*

29

 HURRIED TO SIONAN'S house, pulled the strap to lift the latch, and let myself in. She was still asleep in bed, so I went and lay down next to her. I kissed her forehead and stroked her hair to wake her. She smiled as she opened her eyes. "Succat, you've come to me very early."

I kissed her again and said, "I could not sleep. I had to see you as soon as I could."

"Come here," she said, and pulled me into her embrace.

We lay for a time simply holding one another until I worked up the courage to say, "I have something to tell you." Before she could speak, I blurted, "I must leave Sliabh Mis."

The smile faded from her lips.

"Now. Today. I have to go."

She looked at me in disbelief. "Why?" she asked after a moment.

I had already decided on the lie; I had planned out my story as I hastened to the ráth. "It is Buinne. I know he killed Datho, and now he has tried to kill me." Oh, the lie came easily to my lips. Indeed, I half believed it myself.

"Succat!" Sionan gasped, sitting upright in bed. "How?"

"Yesterday, when I left here, he was waiting for me. He said he knew about us and that he was going to make trouble." That part was true enough. "Then last night at supper I tasted something in my food. I pretended to eat but did not swallow. I waited until he was asleep and came here as quickly as I could."

"You must tell the king."

"Buinne would just deny it, and then it would be a slave's word against that of a filidh. Buinne might even say *I* killed Datho, and Miliucc might believe him."

She searched my face with her eyes. "What will you do?"

"This is what I have been thinking," I said, taking her hands in mine. "I must go and find Cormac—find him and bring him back. He will know how to deal with Buinne."

"Succat, no—"

"Now, listen," I told her. "The traders who were here, they have moved down the coast a little, but I can find them. I will go to them and beg passage to Britain."

"If you escape again, the king's warriors will catch you," Sionan told me gravely, "and this time they will kill you."

"That is why I need your help. You must make certain no one knows I've gone."

"What if the king wants to see you?" she countered. "What if he sends someone to fetch you?"

"If he asks for me, just tell him that I have been sent to collect plants for a potion. Tell him I will return in two days." I squeezed her hands to make her understand. "Two days are all I need. By then I'll be aboard ship, and no one will be able to stop me."

She bit her lip but said nothing.

"Two days, Sionan," I repeated. "That is all I ask."

She looked at me for a long moment and then wrapped her arms around me and laid her head against my chest. In a moment I could feel warm tears seeping through the fabric of my robe.

"Ah, Sionan, my love." I sighed. "Don't cry."

She did not raise her head but continued to sob. "If you go away to Britain, I know I will never see you again."

"Of course you will. That I promise." I lied boldly, trusting her to believe me; my life lay in her slender hands.

"No. It is true. Once you see your homeland again, you will forget all about me."

"Sionan, listen to me." Taking her by the shoulders, I pushed her back gently. "The only reason I am going is to find Cormac. When I have found him, I will bring him back to deal with Buinne. But if I don't go, Buinne will kill me. Cormac is the only one who can help me now. Understand?"

"Then take me with you," she said. "We will go together. I can help you."

I had thought of this—indeed, I had often entertained the notion that she and I might make a life in Britain. But, blind as I was, I could never see her there. I told myself I feared she would not be accepted by my country-men and would forever remain an outcast no matter what I might do to help her. In truth I think the thought of returning with a barbarian Irish-woman for a wife embarrassed me. My embarrassment shamed me, yes, but I was weak and could not help it.

"You know I would take you with me if I could," I told her. "But if you go with me, the king will catch us both before the day is out. If you want to help me, then you must stay here. I need you here to delay the search as long as possible so I can escape them."

Sionan had turned her face away and gazed into the darkened corner of the room.

"Now, look at me and tell me you understand." I peered at her intently, willing her to accept what I said as the truth.

Instead her eyes teared up once more, and she bent her head, letting the teardrops fall onto her breast.

"Oh, Sionan." I gathered her in my arms once more. "I *will* come back, I promise." After so much deception what was one more empty vow?

She refused to be consoled. "Then go! Be off with you."

"Sionan," I pleaded, "believe me, if there was any other way, I would take it."

She stared at me a long moment, making up her mind. "You are right. This is the best way. You must go." She rose abruptly, strode to the door, and looked out. "There is no one waiting for you. Go now while you have the chance."

I stepped to the door. There I lingered, knowing that this was the last time I would ever see Sionan. It was she who had saved me, and she had been my strong and sheltering rock ever since. My debt to her was incal-culable. I owed her my life.

The terrible weight of my deception settled full upon me then, threat-ening to crush me into the ground. My stomach squirmed with the awful knowledge of what my leaving would mean to her—no less than what Cormac would do when he learned I had broken faith with him and shat-tered his sister's loving heart. But the yearning, the insatiable desire to be free once more, was eating me alive. Despite all the good things that had happened to me since coming to the druid house, I still could not accept my lot. Since my feet had touched the soil of Ireland, my one aspiration had been to regain my freedom. I had the chance now as never before, and I could not let it pass me by. Somehow—God alone knows how—I bore up under the fearful strain and even managed a smile of farewell.

Sionan drew me into a last embrace. I put my hand to her face and ca-ressed her cheek. "I love you, Sionan." I had never said those words to anyone in my life. I said them now, and even though I was abandoning the one I spoke them to, they were no less true. "I do love you."

She smiled sadly and lowered her head. "You will have your two days," she said, and then turned from me. "Now, go."

I could not bring myself to lie to her further, so bade her farewell and forced myself to step through the doorway. I stood for a moment on the path—hesitating even then, wanting to return to her—but I heard the sound of someone coming and, turning away, stole quickly from the ráth lest anyone see me.

With tears in my eyes, I made for the coast. Retrieving the water gourd and bag of provisions I had hidden beside the stream on my way to the ráth, I hastened along the valley toward the sea, pausing every now and then to look behind to see if anyone was following and then moving on again. The whole of the first day I followed the coastline; that night I slept in a hollow in the rocks, rising again at first light. I ate a little from the bag, and drank some water, and pushed on. When I finally came in sight of the ship later in the day, relief washed over me in waves, and my heart pounded so hard I became light-headed and had to sit down to catch my breath.

The settlement was little more than a fishing camp, and I knew that the traders would not wait there long, so I hurried to summon one of the fishermen to take me out to the ship in his boat, which he reluctantly agreed to do—seeing that to deny a filidh such a simple request was certain to bring bad luck, for even a novice druid might satirize the witless drudge who refused or chant a rune to drive the fish from the nets of the villagers, thereby causing needless misfortune. Thus was I soon sitting on the slippery bench of a small boat while the fisherman rowed through the waves out to where the ship lay at anchor in the bay.

Upon drawing near the ship, I called a greeting to those on board, and several men hailed me from the rail. I answered them and asked to speak to the ship's master, who duly appeared. I made a respectful greeting and begged permission to accompany them to their next destination. The master—a large, beefy, bull-necked, rough-handed man, smooth-shaven but with dark hair that he wore long and braided like a barbarian's—returned my greeting pleasantly and, recognizing me as the one who had helped him with Miliucc, said he would be happy to allow me to come aboard to discuss the matter.

"Wait for me," I told the fisherman, "until I give you leave to go."

"We have good wine and fine cloth," the master told me when I had come to stand before him. He spoke the simple Latin of the market, which most traders understood readily enough. "We have also fine pottery, glass, worked gold, and many other things, of course. Very valuable items, worth much, as you know."

"Yes," I replied, "you showed it all to the king and queen yesterday."

"Ah! So I did." He laughed. "But tell me, why are you running away?" Indicating my iron collar, he said, "Will not the king miss his slave? Perhaps he would reward me to take you back instead."

"Take me back," I countered with casual indifference, "and Miliucc may give you a few bits of silver for your trouble. Let me stay, however, and I will prove myself ten times over with the wealth I will bring you."

"Ah," replied the master, his dark eyes glinting shrewdly, "but you are a canny bargainer. This I have seen. You know the value of things and make good deals. We are trading in the south next," he said. "Help me in the same way that you have helped Lord Miliucc and I will take you where you wish to go."

"Britain is where I wish to go," I told him outright. "Can you take me there?"

He laughed. "As it happens, yes. After we finish in the south, we go to the Dal Riada—do you know it?"

"No," I confessed, "I do not."

"No matter. Help me and I will see you safely ashore among friendly people. I am Heracles, and that is my vow to you."

"I accept," I told him.

"Now, then," he said, "let us seal the bargain we have made."

With that he pulled open his tunic and exposed his hairy chest. "In my homeland," he said, "it is customary to honor a pledge in this way." He offered me the fleshy part of his chest. "Come, suck at my breast."

"That I will not do," I told him. "For in my homeland such customs place one man under the authority of another, and I will not be bound."

Truly, that is the way of it. If I had sucked his nipple, I would become his bondsman and that was the last thing I desired.

"I am master here," Heracles declared. "No one comes to my ship unless they swear loyalty to me."

I thought for a moment and then raised a hand to my slave collar. "Remove this iron ring from my neck, and I will gladly do as you ask."

"That I cannot do," he said. "It is death to him who frees another man's slave."

Heracles frowned and pursed his lips. "What is so important in Britain that you must get there so fast?"

I had decided on the story I would tell to disguise my true intentions; I would tell enough of the truth to satisfy the curious, without giving away my actual purpose. "My friend and master has gone to Britain," I answered forthrightly. "I am going to find him and bring him back to help settle a matter that has arisen in our village."

"I see." The ship's master regarded me with narrowed eyes. "It must be a very important matter for you to go to so much trouble."

"It is that," I replied. "Nothing less than life and death."

Heracles accepted this with a nod. "Then let me propse another bargain—serve me well and wisely, and the day we leave Irish waters, I will remove your slave collar and see you safely on your way." Although the smile remained perfectly in place, his voice now took on a threatening tone. "But if I catch you cheating or stealing from me, then I will sell you back to the Irish the next time we drop anchor."

He let the warning hang between us for a moment, then spat on the deck of the ship. "Agreed?"

With no other choice before me, I followed his example and spat on the deck. "Agreed."

Heracles' laugh was a sudden, violent burst; he put his hand on my shoulder. "You are a stubborn bargainer, my friend. And that is why I will take you—even though you refuse to swear fealty to me. Make me rich and we will be good friends, never fear."

I thanked him, whereupon he gave orders for his men to up anchor and make ready to sail. They set about the task with reassuring alacrity, and we were under way before the fisherman reached the shore. Once we were out of the bay, the master turned the prow, and we sailed up around the northern tip of Éire. Just before midday, we turned again and then proceeded down along the eastern coast. Although I stood at the rail and searched for the place where I and my fellow captives made landfall years before, I did not see it. Or, if I did, I no longer recognized it.

I cannot say whether it was the coast that had changed or myself. There is no denying that I saw the land now with different eyes than I saw it then. Only when the last headland rose between me and Miliucc's realm did I turn away from the rail.

At last, I thought, sweet relief surging through me like a wind-hurled wave, *I am on my way home. Home!* The word filled me with a delicious ache. Home . . . I was going home at last. Only this time there would be no chase, no capture, and no beating on my return. Before my master Lord Miliucc knew I was gone, I would be over the sea and far beyond his reach.

30

D ESPITE MASTER HERACLES' oft-repeated as-
surances of a swift journey home, three months later I
was still aboard the ship with him. The summer was
fading into autumn golds and browns, and still we
plied the coasts, trading in every seaside settlement we came upon and
many inland, too, each stop taking a day, or two, or more—days that chafed
me raw with frustration. Reasoning, pleading, complaining availed nothing;
Heracles blithely refused to hear my complaints. God knows I made so
many my teeth hurt. All my efforts met with the same knowing smile and
the words: "Soon my friend, very, very soon. Like the wind, we go."

I slowly came to realize that I had wildly underestimated the value of
my services to the ship's master. It was not just my knowledge of the Irish
language—a perpetual battle for the Latin speakers—but that I understood the Irish people. I knew how to present the trade goods in the best
possible way to attract ready buyers. For example, the lords liked wine—
or they did as soon as they tried it—but most considered it much too expensive for a mere drink. But when I told them I knew in truth that the
high king of Rome drank only wine and drank it every day, they were
amazed and duly impressed. Eager to show themselves the equals to any
Roman king, they had to drink it, too, and cheerfully bought whatever we
could carry.

Another time Heracles labored mightily against steady and stubborn resistance from a tight-fisted pack of southern noblemen. He showed his best
wares—the bright-patterned cloth, the sweet wine, the gleaming steel

knives, and all the rest—to little interest and no sales whatsoever. "It is hopeless," he said, wiping his hands on his shirt. "They are not for buying today."

He bade me wish the Irish lords farewell and tell them we would come again next year when, perhaps, we might have something they desired. But as the crewmen began packing up the goods, I noticed one of the Irishmen eyeing the basket containing a number of small glass jars of the kind useful for storing unguents and aromatic oils. We sold a few of them now and then, but mostly Heracles used them to sweeten a bargain, throwing in a handful to help persuade a waverer.

I moved to the man's side and, taking up one of the little jars, told him, "These are made in Rome. I will make you a good price. A fine gift for your wife or daughter. How many would you like?"

He took the jar and held it between his thumb and finger, turning it this way and that in the light, and then dropped it to the ground and stepped on it. The glass surrendered with a brittle crunch, and he removed his foot to reveal a pile of shiny fragments. The fellow laughed, thinking, I suppose, that anything so fragile could not be of significant value.

He made to turn away but hesitated, looking once more at the heap of glass jars. I followed his gaze and realized it was not the jars he desired, it was the basket: a large pottery bowl topped by a wicker ring onto which was sewn a coarse-woven cloth band. Very useful aboard a ship, these were, as they could be securely fastened by way of a drawstring to keep the contents intact even on the roughest seas.

"Ah!" I said, seizing the vessel at once. "You like the basket."

He nodded. "How much?"

"It saddens me to tell you," I replied with a sigh, "but this basket is not for sale. It is too valuable on the ship, you see. I cannot sell it."

He nodded and pointed again to the container. "How much?"

"It is impossible," I replied, clutching the basket and half turning my back to him. "We have only so many of these to carry our wares, and when they are gone, we cannot get any more until we return to Rome."

Tell an Irishman that he cannot have a thing and that is the very thing he craves more than all the world.

"How much?" he said, unmoved.

"My master would have my head nailed to the mast if I sold his baskets," I pleaded. "I could never do it. Where would we keep the jars?"

Adamant now, the chieftain folded his arms across his chest. "Come, let us bargain," he said. "Name a price."

Taking a glass jar from the heap, I held it up and declared, "These are worth nothing compared to the basket." Throwing the jar to the ground, I smashed it beneath my heel. "See?" I made to turn away again, saying, "Maybe if the basket were empty . . . but no."

"I will buy them," he declared, taking my hint. "Then you will give me the basket, too."

I frowned, as if deeply troubled by this suggestion. "I would have to ask my master," I said at last.

"Ask him now."

I turned to Heracles, who was by this time watching the transaction with interest. "What does he want?" he asked me in Latin.

"The basket."

"Give it to him," sighed Heracles, "and let's be gone from this miserly tribe."

Returning to the chieftain, I announced, "My master says that if you bought all the jars, he would give you the basket to carry them home."

"Then I will buy them all," proclaimed the nobleman proudly.

We quickly fixed a price, and it was done. I took his gold and carefully tied up the strings at the top, whereupon the chieftain snatched the basket from my hands and bore it away like a trophy of war—much to Heracles' amusement and gratification.

Such was my service to my master in payment for my passage and, his collusion in my escape. And while I strove to be fair to one and all—I had no heart to cheat the local lords—the amount of gold and goods that changed hands with my assistance increased steadily from the moment I climbed over the rail.

The ship itself was built for trade—spacious rather than fast—and Master Heracles was a cautious sailor. He picked his way along the coast with care, never in a hurry and always with one eye on the weather. At first hint of a storm, he made for the nearest cove to wait until it was safe to move on. "This is my ship," he told me once, "and my ship is my life. I cannot afford to lose it, for I will never get another one."

The reason for this, I learned eventually, was that although the ship belonged to Heracles, the cargo did not. The trade stuffs had been purchased with money given to him by merchants in the south of Gaul. These merchant traders were awaiting his return and expecting a fair increase in their investment.

Day after day we sailed unmolested along the coast while the cargo dwindled and the sea chests filled to overflowing—and still we did not turn and sail for Britain.

I suffered Heracles' cheerful lies and even found their unvarying repetition somewhat reassuring, but I woke one day as the sun tinted the sky with a low autumn light and knew that Heracles had no intention of letting me

go until the gales of winter brought the trading season to a close—and even
then he might contrive to keep me with him somehow. This knowledge
produced such a heavy despondency in me that I did not bother getting out
of bed but lay there in my dark misery mourning, yet again, my stupidity
and lack of wisdom.

When I did not appear on deck, the master sent one of the crewmen to
see if I had taken ill. "The master is asking for you, Irish."

"Tell the good master that he can go merrily to hell."

"Are you sick, Irish?"

"No," I replied. "I am finished."

He did not know what to say to that, so he stood there for a moment,
thinking. "Do you want something to eat?" he said at last.

When I made no reply, he left—only to return a short while later with a
bowl of pea soup and some brown bread. He approached quietly, and laid the
wooden bowl on my stomach. "It will make you feel better to eat something."

"Thank you," I replied. "But I told you, I am not sick." Lifting the bowl
in my hand, I flung it across the hold, splattering porridge everywhere.
"Now, go away and leave me in peace."

He went without a word, and I had just closed my eyes when the master
himself appeared. "Are you sick, my friend?"

"I am not sick, and I am not your friend."

"Of course you are my friend." He laughed, trying to cheer me out of my
gloom. He came and sat down on a box nearby, smoothing the front of his
mantle with his hands. "Do you think I am staying in business this long
without knowing who is my friend and who is my enemy? Come, get up,
let us go and make some money."

"No," I told him. "I am finished."

"What is this 'finished'?" he said, chuckling to himself. "You are my very
good luck indeed."

"Good luck for you," I agreed, "bad luck for myself. Since I am never to
see Britain again, I might as well stay here."

"Is *this* what is troubling you?" he cried happily. "You will see Britain
again. I declare it. Very, very soon now we are crossing the narrow sea. I will
see you safely among people who will help you find your friend."

"So you say. But it never happens. Always there is one more stop to make,
one more settlement to visit, more goods to trade. It will go on and on without end, I know that. But it will go on without me. I am finished."

"Ptah!" he scolded amiably. "You expect me to turn away when we are
making such excellent trade? This is madness." He clucked his tongue as if
he had caught me uttering an obvious falsehood. "Listen, I tell you what I
will do—"

"That is the very trouble, Heracles: You tell me anything that comes into your head, knowing full well you will never do it."

He pretended umbrage at my harsh estimate of his integrity. "I am a man of honor, my friend, as you very well know. I have given you my word."

"Your word, like your honor, is worth whatever you can get for it in the marketplace," I told him. "You sell it every day to anyone fool enough to buy. You know it, and I know it. Why pretend otherwise?"

He looked at me sadly for a moment. "Will you not come up and help me?"

"No, I am finished. Next time we make landfall, I will say farewell."

"But you will never get to Britain if you leave the ship," he pointed out.

I turned my face and looked him in the eye. "I will never get to Britain so long as I remain with *you*," I answered. "In truth I could have swum there and back six times by now."

"You cannot leave," he said, growing mildly irritated. "We made a bargain, you and I."

"And I have honored my half of the bargain—more than half! Yet you refuse to honor yours. So be it. I am done with you."

He sighed loudly. "Well, then."

I said no more, and after a while he left. Next day we made landfall at a small settlement on the southern coast. The master sent some men to fetch me, as I knew he would. This time they did not ask me to come with them; they simply picked me up and carried me onto the deck.

"Ah, there you are," Heracles said, smiling broadly.

"Tell them to put me down."

He nodded to his men, and they set me on my feet.

"I am a man of honor—" he began.

"So you say."

"Now I will show you." With that, he produced a small, flat object and held it before my face.

"A file?" I said, recognizing the tool at last. "But it is much too small."

"It is the only one we have," Heracles replied. "Yet, it will serve." He made a spinning motion with his hand. "Turn around."

I did as he commanded, and he took hold of the back of my slave collar. He drew the edge of the file over the hard iron a few times and then proclaimed, "There! It is begun."

He took my shoulders and spun me around to face him once more. "Hear me, my friend, and believe me when I tell you that each day I will cut away a little more until the day comes to depart. When we finish we will raise the sail and make for Britain, and on that day, I will remove your collar." He smiled his oily, ingratiating smile. "One week more, my friend, is all I ask."

"Very well," I agreed, feeling foolish and abused. "One week more."

"Maybe two."

"Heracles, no," I groaned.

"If the trade is good, we would be fools to leave before we finish. Not so?"

Against all experience and better judgment, I gave in and let him have his way. For two more weeks I oversaw the exchange of goods and gold in the weedy wilderness settlements in the far south of the island. And every day, true to his word, Heracles would take out his tiny file and scrape a little more off the deepening notch at the back of my collar—a symbolic act only, I considered, but it showed that he had not forgotten.

At the end of the second week, with the clouds lowering in the west, dark with rain, Heracles hoisted himself over the rail and, with the wind in his beard, declared, "My friends! We have done well this year. But it is time to go home." Grinning wide, he turned to me. "With the permission of my Irish friend, we will set sail at once."

And we did set sail. But not for Britain.

Without the bulk of the trade goods for ballast, the vessel rode too high in the water and was easy prey for unpredictable autumn blasts and blows. We sailed along the coast until we came to a rocky bay where we could take on stones to fill the hold and help lend some stability to the craft. We spent a whole day hefting rocks into the hold, secured them well, and prepared to depart the next morning.

The wind gusted smartly out of the north as we set off. Heracles chose an easterly course, hoping to bring us shortly to the western coast of Britain. The wind rose steadily, however, and, try as he might, the master could not hold the ship on course. We were pushed farther and farther south, and for two days were out of sight of land. When we finally glimpsed the coast again, it was the southwestern peninsula of Dumnonia, a wilderness of ragged hills and dense, low brush.

Far south of our intended destination, Heracles offered me a choice. "My friend, it is for you to decide. As you see, the weather has turned against us. I cannot be blamed for that. You know I would prefer it otherwise." He stretched out a hand toward the dark, rough hills before us. "There is Britain. If you like, I will make landfall and you can go your way. But hear me, Irish—and I hope you heed me well—if you wish, I will take you to Gaul with me. You can winter in my house and return with us in the spring when we come again to trade." He grinned expansively. "Well, what do you say? Come with me and live like a king all winter, or go now and face peril and danger and wild animals."

"Heracles, my wily friend," I said, "you make the choice difficult, to be sure. But, fearful as it may be, I must test my fate against the wild animals."

The master frowned. "I hoped you would choose the other way. I am a man of my word, as you well know. So I will tell you what I am going to do. Spend the winter with me and I will take you to Dal Riada in the spring. Surely that is where your friend is to be found, and you could not reach him any more swiftly even if you ran all the way."

"No doubt," I conceded. "But after so late a start, I am determined to make up the time I have lost. So," touching my collar, I said, "if you will finish what you have begun, I will thank you and take my leave."

After a few more attempts to sway me, Heracles gave up and while we sailed along the coast in search of a suitable cove, he worried away at the iron collar with his tiny file. When he tired, another of the ship's crew took over, and then another, until at last we came to a deep, rock-lined bay where the ship put in.

"Here now," said Heracles. He motioned the sailor with the file to step aside and took his place before me. "It is time to redeem my vow." So saying, he took the ends of the iron torc in either fist and, using his considerable strength, began to bend the weakened metal. I felt the collar loosen and then give way. There came a dull snap and suddenly I was free.

It felt as if an anvil had been removed from around my neck. I raised my hands and rubbed the place where it had sat for so long. Tears came to my eyes, and I thanked Heracles for honoring his word. Then, taking the two halves of the torc, I walked to the rail and threw them as far as I could into the sea. I watched the splash as the hateful thing disappeared, and then I turned away. It was done, and I was free once more.

Heracles handed me a bag of provisions and ordered one of the crewmen to row me to shore in the small boat he kept as a tender. The boat was quickly readied, and as I was climbing over the side, the master called to me. "Wait! I have something for you."

He disappeared belowdecks, returning a few moments later with a small leather pouch. "You will need this, I think," he said, tossing me the sack.

I caught it, opened it, and peered inside. It was full of the little sticks of gold that the Irish used in trade. I thanked Heracles, praised his generosity, and, feeling much better about my parting, swung my leg over the rail.

"Wait!" cried Heracles, rushing forward. "Here," he said, putting his hand to his belt. He brought out his excellent knife and offered it to me. "You will be needing this, too, I think. For the wild animals."

"Again I thank you," I said, and, tucking the knife into my belt, lowered myself into the waiting rowboat.

Heracles and the crewmen stood at the rail and watched me as the small boat pushed away. "Farewell, Irish!" called Heracles. "Perhaps if you do not find your friend, you will come again with us next year, eh? Look for me in Dal Riada in the spring!"

I waved a final farewell and, upon reaching the shore walked inland a short distance and climbed the sloping dune to watch as they put out from the bay. As soon as the wind caught the sails, they were gone.

I struck off in good spirits, knowing that if I kept to the coast with the sea on my left, I would eventually reach the great estuary called Mare Habrinum by the Latin speakers and Mor Hafren by everyone else — a wide tidal basin that split the lower portion of Britain like a spearpoint jutting inland. Following little sheep trails over the deserted moorland cliff tops, I walked along with eager steps.

Oh, but it was a forsaken, empty land. I met neither man nor beast in all that wild region. I ate and slept as I would and moved ever eastward over the barren hills and headlands. Any people living thereabouts, though there could not have been many, no doubt lived inland, away from the constant buffeting of the wind off the sea. I did not attempt to seek them out, however, because I wanted to get home as quickly as possible and did not care to let the estuary out of my sight for long.

On the third day I glimpsed land across the tide basin, and four days later, I reached a small fishing settlement tucked in to a dell where a stream emptied into the estuary. I called out a greeting but received no reply. Nothing more than a couple of huts and a few sheds, the place was lately abandoned; the fisherfolk had moved elsewhere to avoid the cold winds and high water of winter. All the same it was my good fortune to find a hide boat in one of the sheds — a little coracle that had been left behind. It was damaged, of course, but not so badly that it could not be repaired.

This I set out to do at once. Using bits of cast-off netting which I unraveled to make stout thread and a fishhook for a needle, I sewed up the dogleg tear in the underside of the boat, then bound up the broken rib. In my search for something to use as a paddle, I chanced to find some oakum, coiled for use and stuck up over the lintel. This I used to pack the tear in the bottom of the coracle. I broke off a section of flat-planed wood from the door of the shed, and that became my oar.

It was almost dark by the time I finished, and so I waited until low tide the next day. Meanwhile I gathered blackberries and currants to add to my ration of food and drank water from the stream. Although I had nothing to make a fire, the larger of the two huts was dry and kept the wind off.

Next morning dawned cool and bright. I rose and sat for a while watching the tide flow, trying to determine how the currents moved. The water was dense and dirty; its long, lazy swirls and eddies constantly shifted and changed. For all my study I remained none the wiser. I did, however, determine the best place to launch my unsteady vessel, so that when I saw that the tide had reached the lowest ebb, I began to drag the coracle down to the water's edge, which, as it happened, could now be reached only by crossing a great, flat expanse of mud.

I started off well, but the farther out from the bank I went, the deeper became the mud. I quickly sank in over the tops of my shoes before I thought to take them off. Then, standing in mire up to my knees, I decided to strip off the rest of my clothes, too, before taking up the rope and proceeding on.

By the time I reached the water, I was covered in muck to my naked thighs. I tried washing off some of it before clambering into the boat, but it was useless. I scraped off as much as I could and then got in.

Launching myself on the mudflat while sitting in the boat proved far more difficult than I could have imagined. Using the paddle, I humped and nudged my way forward and was heartily glad no one was there to witness this ridiculous spectacle. I was just about to get out and push some more when I felt the rounded keel slide a little more easily. Two more nudges and a few strokes of the paddle and I slid off into deeper water.

Then it was simply a matter of making for the opposite shore. I paddled with strong, steady strokes for a goodly while but did not seem to make any headway. What is more, the still-outflowing current in the main channel was far stronger than I had calculated, and the opposite shore was moving past at a worrying rate—such that I appeared in danger of being swept down the channel and out to sea! Fool that I was, I had chosen the wrong tide. If I had waited for the incoming tide, it would have carried me closer to my destination, not farther away.

Cursing my stupidity, I put my head down and redoubled my efforts with the paddle. Another arduous stint produced no better results; I succeeded only in raising blisters on my hands and getting myself caught in a giant eddy that spun the little coracle around and around. After a while the eddy dissipated somewhat, allowing me to break out of the current.

About this time the boat began to leak. I suppose the oakum did not hold, or the thread stretched, or whatever; in any event I suddenly found myself sitting in water. There was nothing to be done but paddle all the harder. I rowed like a galley slave and eventually reached what I imagined to be the middle of the estuary, where I noticed that the shoreline had slowed its relentless race. The water in the boat was much deeper, however. I moved my bundle of clothing higher, ceased paddling long enough to bail out some of the water with my hands, and then resumed.

In a little while the tide flow all but ceased. In the still water I began making the first good progress since starting out. Indeed, I entertained the hope that I would yet reach the bank before disaster overtook me. In this I showed myself no seaman, for the instant the thought was born in my head, I heard a popping sound, and water began trickling into the boat.

I rowed for all I was worth. My hands were raw and bleeding by this time, but I had no other choice than to ignore the pain and drive my increasingly waterlogged vessel forward. Paddling like a madman, I was rewarded by the sight of the bank drawing slowly closer.

Too slowly, to be sure. Long before I reached the shore, the stitches I had made in the hide parted, and the rip in the bottom of the boat expanded. Water gushed through the rent. I had time but to grab my shoes and clothes and abandon the coracle. With the shoelaces in my mouth and the bundle of clothes on my head, I departed my leaking craft—rather, I allowed it to sink beneath me and began swimming.

I made but a few strokes, and the soft ooze of the riverbed met my toes. A few more strokes brought me to a depth at which I could stand. With my feet under me at last, I strode for the bank, wading through water to my waist. I reached the broad mudflat, floundered across, and dragged myself up the bank onto dry ground, where I collapsed into the long river grass, sweating and panting, filthy with muck, but happy to have made a successful crossing.

The sun felt good on my skin, and I lay dozing, gathering my strength, until dark clouds moved in and took the sun away. Loath to rise, I nevertheless gathered my things and made for the higher bank of the estuary. The mud had dried on my skin, and I was disinclined to put on my shoes and robe until I could wash properly; so, tucking my shoes and bundle under my arm, I set off naked, climbing the rest of the way up the steep bank and setting off along the trail.

At every turn I expected to come to some holding or settlement, but the day ended before I reached any habitation—although I did find a clear-running brook where I could wash off the caked mud and bathe my raw hands. When I finished, I drank my fill of the sweet, clear water and then found a hollow beside the stream filled with dry leaves, where I settled down to sleep. Thus ended my eighth day in Britain, and still I had seen no other human being.

 N A HOLLOW near a river grew a little stand of ash saplings. I cut one to act as a staff and to carry my provision bag. Anyone I happened to encounter would take me for a bard, I reckoned, and would not have been far wrong. Yet I met no one.

Day by day I walked. Often in the rain and wind, but what of that? In my time on Sliabh Mis, I had spent whole winters outside in every weather under heaven. The chill damp of my homeland did not daunt me. I walked along, in fog and mist, content in my own company, secure in the knowledge that if I continued in an easterly direction along the banks of Mor Hafren, I would eventually reach Morgannwg and my home. Before that, however, I would come to any number of smallholdings and settlements along the coast, and inland there were scores of villas and larger estates where I might get help.

On the fourth day after crossing the estuary, I came upon the old post road that linked the towns of the coast. The sight of it snaking off over the low hills sent an unexpected pang of longing through my heart. Who could have imagined that the mere sight of anything so mundane as that scruffy, overgrown scrape of a track could have moved me so? It came to me then, as I put my feet on the long-familiar path, that I was indeed home at last.

Oh, but it was a home I no longer knew.

The first settlement I encountered proved this beyond any doubt. Through the rain I saw a clutch of dark rooftops cramped into the fold of a valley. There was no smoke coming from any of the houses, and all was silent. No barking dogs greeted me as I came into the midst of the holding—and I soon discovered why: the place had been sacked and put to the torch. I looked in some of the burned-out houses, but aside from a broken chair, a cracked pot, and a worn-out broom, I found nothing of value. Everything worth taking away had been removed—although I did find some leeks growing in a disordered patch beside one of the houses. I pulled a few to take with me, put them in my bag, and moved on.

This was not the last abandoned settlement I passed. Would that it were! I put several more derelict holdings behind me before I came to a villa— an estate, very like my father's in size and extent—and at first sight it, too, appeared deserted and forsaken. Some of the buildings had lost their roofs, and most bore the signs of fire. Even so, there were people living in the ruined southern wing.

Thinking me a druid, they hailed me as I drew near and all but pulled me into the filthy yard. Needless to say, my hosts were not the original owners of the villa. Far from it. Tenant farmers, they had been driven out when their villa fell to a barbarian raid.

"How long have you been here?" I asked, first in Latin and then, when that brought no response, in Briton.

"Four years," replied the head man of the group after a moment's calculation.

"What happened to the owners here?"

He shrugged. "Killed or run off. Either way they're gone."

I asked them how far it was to Lycanum, but, having come from somewhere farther north, none of them seemed to know the place. They asked me to stay the night with them then, and as much as I would like to have moved on, I thought it unwise to refuse the invitation. "Nothing would delight me more," I lied. "I am hungry and could use a good meal."

That night they all gathered to feed the bard and hear him sing: this being the price of my food. I did not begrudge them their song, mind. Indeed, adapting freely from the Irish, I sang a lengthy portion of "The Battle of the Birds" and "Math ap Mathonwy" in payment for my meal and lodging. I did my best to make a good tale of it, and they went away well satisfied.

They would have had me stay longer, but I told them I was expected elsewhere. I promised I would come back one day soon and see them again, and then took my leave. Wretched as they were, they would not have it but that I should take some onions and turnips with me. I intoned an elaborate declamation over them, which prophesied coming abundance and prosperity for the settlement, and then went on my way.

More ruined settlements and half-populated holdings followed; every-where it was the same story: Those who could leave had gone; those who remained eked out a niggling subsistence in the wake of their much more prosperous predecessors.

Whether sleeping in ditches or welcomed as a bard, I held firm to my purpose, moving on early each morning. In this way I at last reached Ly-canum in Morgannwg, where I found the first of my true countrymen—fif-teen days after coming ashore.

Sadly, Lycanum, like the rest of the southern region, so far as I could see, had changed. The walls of the town were higher and thicker now, encir-cling the little market town in a tight embrace, broken only by the stout double gate through which I entered. The streets were empty of the bustling activity I remembered. Many of the houses were deserted, and most of those that were still inhabited stood in urgent need of restoration and repair. The market was gone, and in its place stood a small field planted with grain. I walked around, looking at the once-thriving town, recognizing it, to be sure, but not knowing it anymore.

Hungry, footsore, thirsty, and disappointed beyond words, I remembered the Old Black Wolf and, surprised that I had not thought of it sooner, made my way to the inn without further delay. On the way I wandered past the garrison. The big iron-clad gate was open. I could tell at a glance that the legionaries were gone. The parade ground had become a midden heap for the people living in the barracks, stores, and outbuildings. Three forlorn-looking cows stood in a too-small enclosure beside the wall, and a skinny, swaybacked horse was tethered to a chain; chickens strutted in and out of the houses as they would, and goats stood watching from the rooftops.

How, I wondered, *could they allow it to come to this?*

I continued, meeting the same disheveled, desolated appearance at every turn. And then, all at once, I found myself running along a narrow street where I had so often come with my friends. I turned the corner, and there it was: the Old Black Wolf. The building was still there, but it was no longer a tavern. Dark smoke rolled up out of the chimney, wheels and rims leaned against the walls, bits of harness, broken plowshares, mended scythes, and such lay about the yard. A trough stood on the stump where the tree had been. The sight astonished even as it appalled.

From somewhere inside came the ring of a hammer and the breathy whoosh and wheeze of a bellows. The place had been taken over by a blacksmith, and I could but stand and shake my head. Overcome by the un-relenting strangeness of the town, I shuffled to the trough, sat down on its edge, and dipped out some water to drink, thinking only to rest a little be-fore continuing on. While I was sitting there, a woman came out of the house, saw me, and fled back inside. A few moments later, a man in a leather apron emerged carrying a hammer.

I stood to greet him. "Pax vobiscum," I said, the Latin feeling clumsy in my mouth after such long neglect. "I grew up near here; I have been away and have only just returned." He eyed me suspiciously. Putting out my hand, I indicated the building behind him. "I knew this place when it was the Black Wolf."

He looked me up and down before answering. "It's no inn anymore," he concluded. "If your looking to buy something, I'm selling—otherwise, I've work to do."

"What happened to the garrison?" I asked. "Where are the soliders?"

"I don't know nothing about it, do I? You got questions—go ask the magistrate." When I made no move to leave, he said, "Now clear off. I'm busy." He hefted the hammer for good measure.

I thanked him for his trouble, turned on my heel, left the yard and walked back along the near-deserted streets to the center of town. I asked an old woman where I might find the magistrate, and she pointed to the house that had once belonged to the garrision commander.

I went to the house and presented myself to the sallow, pockmarked youth who answered the door. "I want to see the magistrate. Tell him I have traveled a long way to speak to him."

The young fellow took one look at me sniffed. "Wait here."

After a time the youth returned, and I was led to an inner chamber where two men sat in chairs beside a table. One was bald and thick-waisted, dressed in a long tunic, and the other a tonsured priest in drab brown robe and hooded cloak.

The sullen young man ushered me into the room without ceremony and brought me to stand before the magistrate, who glanced up angrily at the interruption, sighed and said, "I suppose this cannot wait." He cast a hasty eye over me. "Do you speak Latin? Hmm? Can you understand me?"

"I understand you perfectly," I answered, drawing myself upright.

"Well, what do you want?" he said. Before I could reply, he said, "Speak up. Where are you from?"

"I was born and raised in Morgannwy."

His eyes widened. "The devil you say!"

"My family owned an estate near Bannavem. My father was a decurion there; his name was Calpurnius—perhaps you knew him?"

The magistrate stared at me. "Yes, yes, I knew him."

"Great God in heaven!" said the magistrate's visitor, starting up suddenly.

I turned to him. "The name means something to you?"

The man, agape with wonder gazed at me. "Succat? Can it be . . . ?"

"That was once my name," I replied.

"Do you know me, Succat?" he said.

I stared at the man; full of face and form, a young man still, but his body running to fat, he seemed somehow familiar. Through the fleshy features of the man before me, I glimpsed the ghost of the youth he had once been. A name came to my lips. . . .

"Julian?"

OR THE LOVE of Mary and Joseph!" cried the priest, leaping from his chair. "It *is* Succat!" He seized me by the arms, gazing rapturously into my face. "It is me—Julian! Of course you remember. How could you forget?"

In truth I did not know him. Gone was the instigator of so many fine adventures, the cheerful fornicator, the heathen-hearted anarchist and scofflaw. Gone was the blithe and feckless scapegrace leader of our rebellious tribe of four: Rufus, Scipio, Julian, and myself. In his place stood a substantial, solemn, shaven-pated priest. Here was a wonder: wanton, worldly, profligate Julian—a priest of the church! Julian—quite possibly the last person under God's blue heaven I might have imagined would take the tonsure.

"Julian, I—"

He squeezed me in an enthusiastic embrace. Relief and amazement flooded through me. Tears came to my eyes, slid down my cheeks, and into my mustache. I clutched at him and felt all certainty and self-assurance melt away.

"Succat, my old friend," he said, thrusting me back from him again, "let me look at you. I would never have known you."

"Nor I you," I confessed, my mind numbed by the strange fortuity of our meeting. Recovering myself quickly, I asked, "My family—what happened to my father and mother? Are they alive?"

"Alas, no," said Julian with a sharp shake of his head. "Your father was killed in the fire that took your house." He paused, allowing me to absorb this unfortunate news. "Your mother lived on but succumbed a few months later. She lost the will to live, I think, and simply wasting away."

The thought of my toweringly capable mother wasting away through grief knocked me back a pace. Although I had prepared myself somewhat for the fact that, in all probability, my parents were long dead, the very suggestion that she, who bent all wills to her own, could merely surrender her life to the grave like some faithful old hound pining for a departed master was impossible to credit. I could but stand in blinking amazement that anyone could propose such an incredible, preposterous idea.

Mistaking my silence, Julian said, "I am sorry, Succat. There was nothing to be done. So many families were devastated that night. . . . We thought you dead, too." He looked to the somewhat perplexed magistrate. "Did we not, Father? We all thought him killed."

"We did," said the magistrate, shaking his head slowly. "Calpurnius' son . . . who could believe it?"

"This is your father?" I said. "You were magistrate of Bannavem."

"Bannavem is no more," he informed me. "Much has changed—and not for the better."

This I had seen in my journey through the region, but his blunt assessment cast a pall of sadness over me, confirming as it did what I understood in my heart: The place I knew had vanished and would never return.

"Here, sit down," said Julian, pushing me into one of the chairs. "I will get you something to drink."

I sat for a moment—numb and slightly dazed while Julian poured out a cup from a jar on a nearby table. "Drink this," he instructed, pressing the cup into my hand.

The wine was thin and sour, but it brought me to myself once more. I drained the cup and passed it back to Julian. "A priest now. How did this come about?" Before he could answer, I said, "What of Rufus and Scipio? What has become of them? Did they survive?"

"Indeed, they did!" He touched the cloth of my gray robe, feeling the weight and heft of the fabric. "But what about you? Tell me, how did you get here?" He shook his head as if to clear it. "Come to that, where have you been these many years?"

I did not know where to begin to answer him.

Julian put up his hand. "Wait! There is wine at the priest house. We will drink. Are you hungry? Of course you are—you look half starved. We will eat together, and you will tell me all that has happened to you since we last saw one another." He gathered me under his arm and led me from the yard. "How many years has it been? Six? Eight?"

"Six at least. I think. Seven maybe."

"It matters not a whit. The important thing is that you are back—risen from the dead, as it were." He shook his head in merry bewilderment. "Who could have dreamed it?"

A short while later, as we sat over our cups in the big house next to the tiny Lycanum church, he was still shaking his head. "Succat, back from the dead. It is a very miracle." He paused, then added, "But, believe me, I always knew that if anyone could perform such a miracle, it would be you. I knew we would see you again. I never gave up hope."

It was a lie, of course, a small one, spoken in the exuberance of the moment—a nothing, a whim voiced without a thought. But it rankled me nonetheless. In truth he thought no such thing. I could tell. Until he saw me standing before him, he had not given my plight a moment's thought. Ever.

"Well," I replied, brushing aside the unfortunate comment, "there were times I never thought I'd see any of you again either."

"Here!" He raised his cup to me. "Let us drink to your return."

We drank then, and I asked him to tell me of Scipio and Rufus, where they were, what they were doing—everything.

"It is easily told," he replied. "After the legions left, Scipio and his family moved to Rome—can you believe it?"

"No," I replied, smiling amiably.

"They have a villa outside the city. I hope to see it one day. He used to write to me from time to time, but not for a few years now. The letters do not get through anymore, you see." He shrugged. "So much has changed."

"And Rufus? What has happened to him?"

"Dear old Rufus is now a soldier, a very good one by all accounts—a centurion."

"Is he stationed nearby? Can we see him?"

"There are no garrisons in Britain anymore. The troops were called away and have not come back. The governor says now they may never return."

He dropped this extraordinary fact so casually it took me a moment to assess the grave enormity of what he was saying. "No troops at all?" I said. "Anywhere?"

"All were called to Gaul to man the northern borders." Seeing my astonished expression, he added, "I wouldn't worry about it. We are far from defenseless. We have the militia, of course, and—"

"What? A handful of fainthearted farmers with rakes and spades?"

Julian favored me with a smile such as one would give to a slow-witted child. "Still the same old Succat—in a lather over nothing." He drank from his cup and filled them both again. "Now, then, as I was saying, Rufus is in

Gaul. As it happens, I am due to leave for Gaul in a few days. My bishop is attending a council in Turonum, and I am going with him."

"Then it is lucky I found you when I did."

"Not at all. It is God's own providence." He looked at me hopefully. "I want you to come, too."

"Julian, I—"

"We'll have to get you some new clothes, of course. Why are you dressed in that ridiculous robe anyway? People will think you're a druid."

"But I am," I told him, "I mean, I was." A curious feeling of pride surfaced inexplicably, and I suddenly found I could not bring myself to renounce my training. "That is," I added, "I was a filidh under instruction."

Julian threw back his head and laughed out loud. "That is possibly the worst jest I've ever heard."

My ears reddened and burned with embarrassment, but I determined to stand my ground. "It is no jest."

"Do you expect me to believe this?" hooted Julian. "You—Succat the Druid?"

Rank resentment hardened in me. Although I imagined I could put it on and take it off as easily as the robe I wore, instead I found that I felt profoundly protective of my bardic association, and I did not want anyone belittling it. "I am in earnest."

Julian, now the disapproving priest, favored me with a superior frown, his mouth turned down in distaste. "Come now, it is a guise, certainly. Tell me the truth."

"What I am telling you *is* the truth," I insisted, and began relating what had happened since the night I had been captured and taken as a slave to Ireland. Julian, to his credit, listened without comment and let me speak as I would. I did not tell him everything, of course, but enough for him to know how I had fared in Éire. "When the chance came to serve in the druid house, I took it," I concluded. "I joined the bardic order and have been studying to become a filidh ever since."

"Well," he said, sitting back in his chair, "that is a tale and a half. I never would have thought you would become a tree-worshipping barbarian."

"But they are not barbarians, Julian—that is to say, not all of them. They are different from us, true, but there are some among them as wise and good as any Briton you care to name, or any Roman either."

"Hoo!" he snorted. "Listen to that! Next you will be telling me you took one of the sluts to wife."

Seeing how he had taken my first admission, I decided in that instant to keep any mention of Sionan from him. I did not want him demeaning her memory with his insolent and ignorant mockery.

But I was not quick enough. Julian saw my hesitation and pounced on it. "You did! You married a barbarian bitch."

His accusation stung. I denied the charge. "No," I said.

"Yes you did. I can see it on your face."

"No," I smiled, fighting to keep my voice even. "I never did." Although the words were true, my heart knew I spoke a lie. Sionan was as much wife to me as any woman who ever loved a man.

"You can tell me, Succat, I am a priest. Your secret is safe with me."

I smiled and shook my head. "There is nothing to tell."

He gazed at me with fierce intent. I returned his scrutiny with calm defiance, and he blinked first. "Hmph!" he snorted. "Well, it is of no importance. You have returned to your kin and countrymen, and that is all that matters. Now, then, as I said, I must leave very shortly. You, my friend, must come with me. I insist. Indeed, I command it."

"Julian, please understand. I cannot. I have been traveling for—for I don't know how long. Months at least. The last thing I want is another journey. I have just returned home, and I mean to stay."

"And what will you do now you're here? Hmm?"

"Why, I'll—I mean, I have to . . ." Here I faltered. I had not yet worked out what I wanted to do.

"You see?" Julian said. "There is nothing." He smiled pityingly. "You are home, but your home is no more. It grieves me to say it, but there it is. You and I both know there is nothing here for you now." He leaned forward. "Come with me to Gaul."

I gazed at him. Sadly, he was right: There was nothing to hold me here anymore. "I will think about it," I replied reluctantly.

Julian was no longer listening. "Now, then, first we must do something about your clothes as I say. Fortunately, I know someone who can help. Come, we will begin at once."

"Thank you, Julian, but I don't—"

He held up his hands. "No need to thank me. I am placing myself at your service. It is the least I can do for a friend of my youth." He rose and started off at once, bidding me to follow.

I remained seated. "There is no need," I declared. "I am happy as I am."

"Nonsense," he scoffed. "We must get you looking like a true-born British nobleman—which is what you are." He pulled me to my feet and hustled me out the door.

"Julian," I protested, "I appreciate your concern. I do. But believe me when I tell you there is no need. My clothes are agreeable to me. I am not ashamed—nor, I think, should you be embarrassed for me."

"Oh, I do not blame you, Succat," he said without slackening his pace.

"I can see they have turned your head—indeed, it would be unnatural, I suppose, if they had not. But that will pass. Trust me. It will go. A few days back among your people and you will begin to forget all about the unpleasantness of the last few years."

Before I could say anything, he dashed on. "You survived, Succat. I knew you would. You are free once more, and you have a chance few people ever get: You can begin again." He placed his hand on my shoulder; it was a fatherly gesture, and I resented it.

"You do not understand, Julian."

"No, I suppose you are right. I do not understand. Probably no one ever will. But that will matter less and less in the days to come. You'll see. In the meantime you must begin again, and you will, Succat. You will. Never fear, I will see to that."

Thus I was carried along in the strong current of his determination to make me, as he saw it, a suitable human being once more. Although it does me no credit to say it, I confess that I began to soften under his benevolent bullying. After so long a time living by my own wits, so often alone, so often confused and overwhelmed by forces beyond my control, I might be forgiven for allowing someone else to take an interest in my affairs.

The rest of the day was spent, as Julian put it, organizing my restoration and return to civilization. He found me a place to stay—a small room in the priest's house—and purchased new clothes for me. This last I was less pleased about, but inasmuch as I insisted on keeping my druid robes also, it did not make much difference.

"We are leaving in two days, Succat," Julian said. It was late; we had shared dinner with his superior, Bishop Cornelius, and had quit the dining room at last. "I expect you to come with us."

"I thank you for all you have done for me, Julian. Do not think me ungrateful, but I have no wish to go to Gaul," I told him—not for the first time.

"I know, I know," he said impatiently. "But allow me to propose something."

"Please, Julian, it is no use tr— "

He raised an imperious palm to stop me. "You do not know what I am going to say."

"Very well." I sighed. "What is it this time?"

"Although it saddens me to say this, it must be said."

"Say it, then."

He regarded me with a sober, fatherly expression. "Your lands are gone."

"How can that be? The villa may be ruined, yes, and the barns and fields. But the land could be reclaimed."

"And it will," he said, "by someone else."

"Who?"

"Does it matter?"

"Certainly it matters!" I snarled angrily.

"No," he said, shaking his head firmly. "It does not matter in the least, because, you see, all abandoned lands have been claimed by the state and sold. It was by decree of the governor. You have to remember, after the raid there were many abandoned farms and estates. Something had to be done."

"But our lands are *not* abandoned. I have returned. I will reclaim them."

"Yes, but you have come too late, my friend. It was decreed that after five years any unclaimed properties would be sold. Who knew you were ever coming back?"

I stared at him, unable to speak.

"What is done is done, Succat. Look instead to the future. Come with us to Gaul. Begin again."

"I want to see the estate," I muttered grimly.

"Very well, I will take you tomorrow," he agreed. "We can ride out there in the morning, and you will see what I mean."

3 3

**S** SOON AS it was light enough to see the road beneath us, Julian and I lit out for Favere Mundi. I had long ago determined what I would find, and now I steeled myself for it. Oh, but the reality was far worse than anything I could have dreamed.

From a distance it was almost possible to think that nothing had changed. The fields were overgrown with weeds, yes, and the trees were untended, but I could see the ruddy glint of the roof tiles over the grand entrance and imagined for a moment that all was well, that inside my mother shrilled at her lazy servants while my father growled and grumbled over his ever-rising taxes.

Closer, however, I could see that the entrance was all that was left of the central portion of the villa. It towered above a ruin so complete I could but wonder at the wreckage. It came to me as I stood looking that it was not simple destruction that had reduced the hall and wings to rubble; no, it was the plundering of stone by our onetime neighbors. No doubt they had carted off good building material by the wagonload.

Leaving my mount with Julian, I hurried through the entrance, scrambled over lumpy, weed-grown mounds of debris, and walked into the empty space where the great hall had been. All that was left was a low rim of broken stone that formed a ragged perimeter. In what had once been my favorite room in all the world, I knelt and scraped away the dried crust of dirt and scum to reveal the remains of that beautiful mosaic—a shattered expanse of tesserae scattered and loose like teeth in a broken mouth. I picked up a few of the little marble cubes and held them in my hand.

Then, as I knelt in the debris, the grief I had so long held at bay broke over me. I bent my head and wept for the loss of my home, for my dead parents, the ruined estate, and the cruel waste of it all. I let my tears fall freely in the dust.

After a time I wiped my eyes, got to my feet, and picked my way out through the uneven clumps of wreckage to what had been the courtyard. The pear tree was still there, a few dry leaves yet clinging to mostly bare branches. The fountain was smashed; a large blackthorn bush grew up through a crack in the empty basin. The pedestal where the statue had stood was overturned, but the statue was still there; half buried in the long grass lay Jupiter, serene in defeat, his face blackened by mildew. "Hail, Potitus," I murmured.

Looking out through the razed wings of the villa into what had once been tidy and productive fields, I saw a stack of hay and remembered what I had hidden there on the night I was taken. I went out and began pulling the ancient matter, rank with decay, from the stack and was soon rewarded by the sight of the wagon. My heart beat a little quicker as the wagon box came into view. The silver, the precious objects—could it all still be there?

Alas, no. I threw off the last of the rotten hay and saw that the wagon box was empty. No doubt some of the servants had remembered the wagon and come back for the treasure. Or perhaps the looters had found it and carried it off with the stone, timber, and tiles. I turned and started back to the house.

My father's estate—land that had been owned by my family for three or more generations—had been taken by the state and sold to usurpers. What of that? Even if it was somehow possible to obtain the return of the lands, I had nothing with which to work them—no tools, no implements, no animals, no servants. The families that had lived on the estate were gone; there was no one to help me. With the little money I possessed, I might hire someone, but I had no money to buy livestock or seed and no funds to rebuild the villa, granaries, and storehouses.

Nor could I work the land alone and survive for very long. Even if the work did not kill me, a lone farmer was prey to every hazard from mice to marauders. With nothing set by in store, a single season of bad weather could destroy years of work, and what did I know about planting and tilling anyway? No, trying to reclaim the estate would be death through slow starvation, backbreaking labor—or both.

I gazed mournfully around at the ruined villa and neglected fields and shuddered inwardly as the utter hopelessness of my circumstances came clear. What Julian said was true: There was nothing for me here. Moreover, if I were so stubborn as to remain, I would find in Britain not a home but a grave. I was, I concluded bitterly, better off in Ireland.

The thought produced an unexpected lift of the heart. Perhaps if I had not been standing knee deep in the rubble of my former life, the thought would never have occurred to me. Then again, perhaps desperation would have eventually driven me to the same conclusion. In any event the idea carried the force of undeniable recognition. I *was* better off in Ireland.

At least, that is, if I could remain in the druid house. On this point my fledgling euphoria plunged sharply. Buinne was there, and so long as he was master of the house, my life would be at hazard. And if Buinne didn't kill me, Lord Miliucc surely would the moment I entered the ráth. In any event Ollamh Calbha, I knew, would not suffer my return—why should he? I had broken faith with the Learned Brotherhood; I had run away like the disloyal and deceitful slave that I was. Worse yet, worst of all, I had betrayed Sionan, the kindest, gentlest woman I'd ever known, whose only fault lay in the fact that she loved me.

Oh, the bitter irony was not lost on me: Fool that I was, I had spent years and suffered savage beatings in the hope of returning to Britain and reclaiming my future—only to discover that any hope of a future lay in Ireland, where I could not hope to return.

I found Julian standing amid the destruction. "I thought we might eat something before going back," he said, holding out a small bag. Inside were bread and cheese and a few apples. I accepted my portion of food, and there, in the desolation of my father's house, I sat down and ate a meal in the once-grand hall, where some of the most festive dinners in our little corner of Britain had been served. I ate slowly and deliberately, as if observing a cheerless sacrament, remembering my mother and father and the happy times we had shared in that place.

Truly, there was nothing for me here, I decided bleakly. It was time to move on. But where?

Once more the vapors of gloom closed around me. I finished eating and returned to my horse, mounted to the saddle, and gazed one last time upon the devastation of my childhood home. I then turned my back on it forever.

We were halfway back to Lycanum when the solution to my difficulty struck me, and then it was so obvious and self-evident I could not imagine why I had not thought of it at once: Cormac. He was in Britain after all; find him and any worries I might have about Buinne, or anything else, would wonderfully disappear. With Cormac by my side, I could then return to Ireland without fear. I could resume my life in the druid house. I could return to Sionan; indeed, I could marry her.

How strange life is sometimes, I reflected. The lie I told to assist my escape was now my only hope of return. To gain Sionan's trust and ease her fears, I had told her I went to Britain only to find Cormac and bring him back. Well, now that I had no better choice, that is exactly what I would do. What is more, I could redeem my promise to Sionan. In fact, I could redeem myself before she even knew I had deceived her.

The more I thought about this, the more the idea appealed to me—especially since the alternative was poverty, privation, and the tacit slavery of a bondsman or hired laborer. There was nothing to hold me in Morgannwg anymore and no help for me in Lycanum if I stayed. By the time I reached the town, the idea had hardened to resolve: I would find Cormac, secure his aid, and return to Ireland, the druid house, and Sionan.

I wasted no time informing Julian of my plan. He listened with a doubtful expression on his smooth face. "Do you know where this Cormac person is to be found?"

"I know he is in the north," I replied, "near a place called Cend Rigmonaid. He said it was on the eastern coast. It cannot be too difficult to find."

"And you propose just to go charging off in search of this fellow in the belief that he will help you?"

"I *know* he will help me," I replied. "All I need is a horse and a few provisions. I was hoping I could borrow them from you."

Julian placed his palms together and peered at me over the top of his fingertips. "And if you do not find your friend, what then? What will you do? Where will you go?"

I had not thought that far and was forced to confess ignorance. "Well, I will be no worse off than I am now."

He paused to consider this and then declared, "You are fortunate indeed, for I see the hand of God at work here. The bishop has decided to postpone the trip to Turonum until the spring."

"I thought you were leaving tomorrow."

"We are—" he said, saw the objection forming on my tongue, and quickly added, "and if you would be quiet long enough for me to finish, all will be revealed."

"Go on."

"The bishop will go to Turonum in the spring. Until then he plans to sojourn at Candida Casa. 'What is that?' I hear you asking. Permit me to tell you."

"Yes, yes. Get on with it."

"It is a priest house in the north." He nodded knowingly at my reaction. "I thought that would interest you."

"Where in the north?"

"The west coast somewhere, I believe."

"And I could go with you?" I said. "I mean, you would let me travel with you?"

"My son," he said, his natural condescension breaking forth, "you would have a horse and traveling companions, and a place to stay while you looked for this Cormac person." He nodded again. "There, what do you say to that?"

"Well, Julian, this is wonderful. I accept. I only wish I—"

He held up a hand. "There is, of course, one condition."

"And that would be?"

"Simply this: that if you do not find friend Cormac, you would look kindly on the prospect of accompanying us to Gaul when we leave in the spring."

"Well, I cannot s—"

"Do not dismiss this. Think about it, Succat. The bishop is being very generous in making this offer. You would be a fool to reject it outright."

"I mean no disrespect to the bishop," I replied, "but why is he so anxious for *me* to accompany him to Gaul? Before the other night he had never even seen me."

"To tell you the truth," Julian replied, "Bishop Cornelius does not care if you go to Gaul, or Ireland or stay here and grow a beard of moss. But *I* care. You are my friend, and I want to help you if I can. In Gaul a young man can still make something of himself. There is opportunity to be found; you can start anew."

The offer of a horse and a place to stay was not to be sneered at; I would travel swiftly and safely, and that was of utmost importance to me just then. So, with no better prospects of my own, I agreed—if only to further my plan to find Cormac.

We departed Lycanum the next day, eleven of us in all. Besides Julian, myself, and the bishop, there were three novice priests, four members of the local militia, and a cook. I will not call the militiamen soldiers; they were little more than brigands—men who only a few years before would have been outlaws, hunted by the very legionaries they now impersonated. Nevertheless they gave our company something of an imposing presence which might have deterred bandits not unlike themselves.

The novices drove oxcarts heaped high with supplies and provisions. The road north was good for the most part, wet or dry—and as autumn drew on, there was much wet and wind; we followed Silurum Street, which led through the rounded hills of Morgannwg to Deva and beyond to Mamucium and, eventually, Luguvallium. Once past the Wall we would head west along the peninsular coast to our destination.

Oh, but the going was damnably slow. Oxen are not the swiftest creatures afoot, and we stopped early each day so that the bishop might have a proper evening meal. If that were not enough, we also stopped at every little town, settlement, and holding along the way. Wherever a crowd, however reluctant, could be herded together, the churchmen performed a service—more for their own diversion, I suspected, than for any good it might have done the poor souls dragged along to endure the bishop's tirade in scholarly Latin.

Cornelius did not preach so much as berate and belittle. However amiable and friendly he might have been in the saddle, as soon as he mounted his pulpit—be it only a stump beside a pig wallow—he became an orator of dour and frightful mien. Compassion, encouragement, comfort, consolation—these virtues became distant strangers to him the moment he opened his mouth in formal address to a congregation. I could not help but compare him with good Datho, whose tireless kindliness shone through in every word.

Clearly Bishop Cornelius enjoyed traveling in this manner; as a senior churchman he luxuriated in his holy office. When I came to know him better, I saw a man who styled himself an enlightened potentate, magnanimous yet thoroughly mindful of the impression he wished to make on those who saw him. In short, he was a vainglorious, pretentious priest who wore his love of pomp as he wore his fur-trimmed bishop's robe. He never supped, he dined; never prayed but rather communed with the Almighty on high; never conversed but rather engaged in private discourse with his fellows; never laughed but rather yielded to jocularity. In fact, so far as I know, he never peed beside the road but rather paused briefly for micturation. He was a round-faced, nearsighted prig with bad breath, hanging dewlaps, and a sour stomach from too much rich food.

Yet for all his airs and affectations, he was intelligent and decisive. He knew his mind and was not a man to be dissuaded from a course, however difficult or unpleasant it might prove. And once he said a thing, he owned it regardless of the consequences. Thus he was a man whose word could be trusted.

"Julian told me of your slavery in Ireland," he said as we rode along one cool, drizzly day. "And that you had been undertaking instruction in Druidism."

"I was studying to become a filidh, yes," I replied.

"Your grandfather was a priest, I believe."

"Potitus, yes. Presbyter of Bannavem. Did you know him?"

Cornelius shook his head. "I grew up in the north—near where we are going, as it happens. I was appointed to establish a bishopric at Lycanum only four years ago."

"And before that?"

"Londinium—but I was not a bishop then." He paused, glancing back along our train for a moment, then turned to me and said, "We must do what we can to wean you away from this ill-considered Druidism."

"With all respect, Bishop," I replied as mildly as I could, "I do not regard it as a condition to be eradicated. It is not a disease, after all."

"Oh, but that is where you are wrong. It is very much a condition which must be extirpated and exterminated wherever it rears its ugly head."

His blinkered appraisal was provocative, but I did not care to be drawn into an argument with him, so I said, "Have you ever known any druids?"

"Thank God Almighty, no. I saw one once, as a boy. Nasty creature—all gnarled and twisted like one of the monstrous oak trees they worship."

I accepted his opinion equably. "If I told you that the filidh did not worship trees, would that make any difference at all?"

The bishop thought for a moment. "Perhaps," he allowed, "although I shudder to think what they worship instead."

"The deity they hold in highest reverence is called by many names," I explained. "One such is the High King of Heaven, but there are others— Maith Dé or, as we would say, the Good God. Also Tabharfaidh Bronntóir, which means Gifting Giver. But the name most often preferred is An Rúndiamhair, or simply An Rúnda, the Mysterious."

"Typical pagan affinity for endowing their brutish gods with wondrous attributes, I should imagine," mused the bishop. "Still, the more gods, the better, I suppose—if you are forever trying to appease the fearful elements." He tut-tutted disapprovingly. "Poor benighted wretches."

"So anyone might think," I agreed. "Yet on closer inspection the god addressed by many names is one and the same."

"All the same god?" wondered Cornelius.

"One and the same—and, what is more, he is the very same god *you* worship one Sabbath to the next."

"Blasphemer!" exclaimed the bishop in mock alarm. "Tempt me with no more with your lies."

"It is nothing less than the simple truth," I replied evenly. "They hold their god to be the creator of heaven and earth and of all things seen and unseen. He rules the cosmos and everything in it with benevolence for his creatures. In fact, they even know about Jesu, his son, whom they also hold in highest honor. They call him Iosa or, Esu."

"You mean to tell me that the entire Irish race expounds these religious tenets?"

"Not everyone, no. Not by any means. They have their pagans much as we have ours," I conceded. "But many of the filidh, the druid-folk, believe and teach these things."

"Ho!" he cried suddenly. "There it is! These druids of yours are beginning to sound suspiciously like the Culdee of ours."

"You know the Ceile De?"

"Root and branch. The north is full of the vermin. The Culdee are a very bane and a curse. If I had my way, they would all have millstones hung around their roguish necks and be heaved bodily into the nearest sea."

"Is this," I inquired, "a conviction you have reached through long and careful investigation? Or could it be simply a prejudice formed in ignorance and bolstered by pride?"

He huffed and puffed at my presumption. But, to his credit, Bishop Cornelius contemplated the question seriously. "I must confess to the latter," he said at last. "Although nothing I have ever seen leads me to doubt the veracity of my conviction in the least."

"Then we must do what we can to wean you away from this ill-considered intolerance, Bishop."

"Ho, ho!" he laughed. "Not likely, I think." Chuckling to himself, he slapped the reins across his mount's shoulders and rode on.

We were to have several of these discussions over the course of the journey. But it was not until a few days after we reached our destination that I learned the reason for our visit and discovered that the pompous bishop had been less than forthright with me.

34

T WAS AN estate on the wet and windblown western coast of Britain that received us. I use the word "estate," for Candida Casa—the White House, as it was known for the pale-colored stone of its walls—was of far greater extent than anything so simple as a house or church. It was more on the order of a grand villa with residences, storehouses, a church and oratory, a refectory, and various other workshops and outbuildings set amid its own plowed and tended fields. Surrounded by forest and yet near to the sea, it enjoyed a far milder winter than its northern position warranted.

It was, I happily concede, a fine place. For me, however, the difficulty was not with the estate itself but with the inhabitants—priests of a peculiarly proud and haughty stripe who seemed to think their doctrines should be taken as holy writ by all lesser mortals—that is, the mass of humanity which did not reside within the high, protecting walls of their order. The imperious monks of Candida Casa seemed to think it their duty to harangue any hapless creature unlucky enough to wander within spitting distance; the air grew brown and turgid with their endless sermonizing. I could not endure it, so went on my way as quickly as possible, taking as many provisions as I could weasel from the kitchen monks. I also took my filidh robe and my good sharp knife.

Julian came to see me off. "You will return in a few days, I presume?"

"That depends on what I find," I replied.

"Go, then," he said, embracing me, "and may God speed you."

"Farewell, Julian." I climbed into the saddle, took up the reins, and sat looking down at him.

"Farewell," he said. "I will have the monks pray every day for your safe return."

I thanked him for all he had done on my behalf. I might have thanked him for the horse, too, for once I found Cormac, I had no intention of returning to Candida Casa, but instead head for Ireland and my waiting Sionan. My guilt for this omission lasted only until I was out of sight of the place.

My brown horse was a fine and spirited young animal, and we understood one another well. I made certain to find him adequate grazing and water each day, which was not difficult in the wild northern hills, and we made good speed in our search for druid strongholds. Directed by local knowledge gathered along the way, I arrived at Bras Rhaidd, a very monastery of a druid house—a rival, in its own way, to Candida Casa. I came dressed in my filidh robe, carrying a new hazel staff I had cut three days before, and, to my great relief and delight, I was greeted warmly by my bardic brothers: seven Britons and an Irishman from Dal Riada, who recognized me and received me as one of their own.

I wasted not a moment, inquiring after Cormac as soon as the first of many rituals of welcome had been observed. "My name is Corthirthiac," I told them in Irish, "and I have come in search of a dear and close friend of mine—a filidh by the name of Cormac Miach. He is in the company of a wise and powerful ollamh named Meabh."

"Then you have done well to direct your search here," replied the chief bard, a short, dark-haired man named Sadwrn. "They were here. Indeed, they sojourned with us for several months." He regarded me hopefully and added, "We were greatly blessed by their presence."

Taking his hint, I said, "Is this a Ceile De house?"

"It is that," he said with a smile. "If you call yourself friend to Cormac, then you are no less our friend."

I thanked him and said, "You said they have been here. Where have they gone; can you tell me?"

"Oh, yes," replied Sadwrn. "They were on their way to Tuaim Bán to see the chief bard, Cethrwm."

"Yes," I said eagerly, "the very bard he mentioned."

"It must be three months at least since they left here."

"I see. Is it far, this Tuaim Bán?"

"It is a fair distance, yes, for it lies some way northeast of here on the coast near Muir n'Guidan."

Cormac had said it was on the coast. "Is it near a place called Cend Rigmonaid?" I asked.

"Oh, aye, it is that. But I would not advise you to make the journey just now. Much of the way is through mountain and forest, and the trails can be treacherous this time of year."

"I have a horse," I pointed out. "I can travel quickly. Indeed, if you would direct me to the place, I will set off at once."

Sadwrn would not hear of it. "You have traveled far already, I think. Stay here and rest a little—a day or two will not matter. Then, if you are still determined, you may go."

"There is nothing I would like better than sitting by your warm fire," I said. "Very well, I accept. But one day only. I must find my friend."

"Of course." Indicating the gathering gloom, Sadwrn said, "Come inside. Let us discuss the way over supper."

This I did, and spent an enjoyable night in their company. They sang for my benefit a song I had never heard: "Pwyll and Rhiannon," and we traded news of our respective gatherings. Next day, after I had seen my horse fed and watered, Sadwrn told me the best way to Tuaim Bán. It was all I could do to force myself into the saddle once more. As I was taking my leave of the bards, one of them, a fellow named Tarian presented me with a chart he had made. "I know it will be of little use to you," he said apologetically, "but winter comes quickly to the north, and even well-marked trails can become difficult to find." He handed me the little scrap of lambskin he had prepared. "If that should happen, this might help."

"I thank you, brother," I told him. "I hope we meet again one day in Ireland, and I can return your kindness." I bade them all farewell and was genuinely sorry to leave them so soon. Their "God speed you, brother!" was still resounding in my ears as I snapped the reins and moved on.

The land to the north grew more extreme in every way. If the south had forests, in those of the north the trees were taller, the wood denser, darker, and more forbidding; if the south had hills, the north had mountains of jagged rock surrounding steep-sided valleys almost always filled with cold, black, deep water lakes. And if the south had wind and rain? Well, the north had raging tempests which drove stinging sleet through the warmest cloak and drenched a body to the bone.

The few hardy souls who lived in the region clung precariously to the sides of the hills, hunting in the forests and fishing in the lakes for their food. Mostly, however, the high, wild, craggy hills were empty, desolate, and forsaken by all save red deer and eagles.

Despite the dangers of the wood—wolves, bears, and the large spotted wildcats—I much preferred the quiet of the forest pathways to the barren hills; at least the sheltering trees kept the worst of the wind and rain and snow off me. My horse proved good company. A confident mount, he showed no fear of the dark wood, and even when we heard the occasional howl of a wolf, he did not shy but trotted on regardless. I named him Boreas in memory of another stout-hearted beast, and took care to dry his coat with grass or leaves whenever we stopped.

But the days were short and growing shorter. Though we made use of every last moment of light we were granted, we did not advance so rapidly as I hoped; the rough trails and increasingly bad weather conspired to keep us moving at a crawl. Once, during a storm, Tarian's chart proved invaluable as snow wiped out the trail and I was forced to reckon by the landmarks he had painstakingly indicated.

In summer the journey might have taken eight or ten days. Instead it took all of seventeen—the last two into the teeth of a ferocious northern gale. It took all my strength of will just to keep moving. I buoyed my resolve with the thought that I would soon be with Cormac again and the world would right itself once more. This thought alone kept me going.

No one was ever so glad as I was when, gazing across a frozen stream, I saw the dark, lumpy mass Sadwrn had described—a great black rock of a hill rising across the valley—and hoped against hope that we had arrived at last. "This has to be the place," I said, relief quickly mounting to elation. "It must be."

I let Boreas pick his way carefully across the stream and then gave him a slap of the reins. "Hie! Hie, up!" I shouted, and we galloped the rest of the way as fast as he could run, reaching the base of the black hill breathless and exhilarated. I worked my way around the lower slopes until I found the trail leading up to the top. Twilight was upon me by the time I reached the large timber house. I called a greeting and slid from the saddle, hurrying at once to the door.

In my elation at having found the place and arrived safely, I failed to notice that no smoke issued from the smoke hole in the roof. The house and yard were quiet. I called again, lifted the latch, and pushed open the door.

The druid house was empty. One glance at the dark, cold interior showed that no one had been there for a long time. I walked to the hearth and put my hand to the ashes, hoping, I suppose, to find them still warm— even though I could see that the embers were long since dead.

As my fingers touched the lifeless ash, the heart went out of me. I closed my eyes against the tears already welling there and bent my head as a sob tore from my throat. I wanted to die. Disappointed, frustrated, exhausted, hungry, and cold, I rolled onto my side and lay there wishing I might just rest my head on the stones of the hearth and never have to rise again.

The gloom of the house was all but complete when at last I forced myself to my feet and made a desultory search of the place to see what I might discover. I found some dry goods in the storeroom: a measure of fine-milled flour in a stoneware jar and oats and barley in leather bags. There was also water in the stoup, but it was stale. I discovered a wedge of cheese—hard as rock—and a few dry white beans. There was no meat or bread, but there was some lard and a lump of salt.

I went back outside and tended to Boreas. I dried him with some pine needles and put him in one of the two small outbuildings behind the big house. There was a wooden tub, which I filled with water, and I found some dry fodder hanging in a bale from one of the roof beams. I pulled down a fair portion of the hay and left him to rest for the night.

Returning to the house in the fast-falling darkness, I brought in wood from the stack beside the door and set about building a fire in the hearth. As soon as I had a blaze going, I busied myself making supper and, exhausted from the journey, went to sleep before the fire. Sometime during the night a storm moved in, and I woke the next morning to a fresh covering of snow.

I decided to stay at Tuiam Bán for a few days to rest and think what to do next. It was possible, I told myself, that the filidh might return to the house and find me waiting. I did not hold out much hope that this would happen, however; it seemed to me that they had gone elsewhere for the winter.

I occupied myself with small chores throughout the day: fetched clean water from the well for the horse and myself, piled rush mats and fleeces beside the hearth for a bed, set a handful of beans to soak for supper, and made a batch of dry, crumbly bread. I carved the lump of salt in half and took one half out into the woods, cleared a space for it beside the trail, and left it there. Returning to the house, I cut a piece of leather strap and bound my knife to the end of a slender length of ash, then went back out to sit behind a tree within sight of the salt.

I waited long, but as the sun began to fade, my patience was rewarded by the appearance of a large, fat hare. Readying my makeshift spear while the animal tasted the salt lick, I took aim and let fly. It was not the cleanest kill; the wounded animal darted into the bush, but I quickly caught and dispatched it. I took the plump little carcass back to the house to clean and dress it, pleased to add roast hare to my meal of bean soup and bread.

There was no beer, of course, but I had filled the stoup with fresh water, and while the hare was cooking, I went to fill a bowl, taking up one from among those beside the basin. However, upon my leaning forward to dip the wooden vessel into the basin, a strange sensation came upon me—as if someone had called my name. There was no sound. I heard nothing. Even so, the sensation that I had been addressed by someone—or something—was unmistakable.

I paused, the bowl halfway to the water. "Yes?" I said aloud. The sound of my voice resounded in the empty house.

There came no answer, so I resumed my task and dipped the bowl, filled it with water, and brought it to my lips. In that instant I felt Cormac beside me: inexplicably but unequivocally Cormac. Indeed, the impression was so strong I turned my head, knowing there was no one there yet unable to stop myself from doing it anyway.

The uncanny sensation so surprised me that the bowl slipped from my fingers and fell into the stoup with a splash. The sense of his presence ceased immediately, and I was alone once more. I waited for a moment to see if the ghostly presence would return, but when it did not, I drew the bowl from the water and filled it again. The sense of Cormac's closeness returned as soon as I touched the bowl.

This, it came to me, was the *imbas forosnái*: the knowledge of enlightening—a bardic skill which Ollamh Datho had spoken of many times and had encouraged me to investigate. That it should come to me now, in this way, surprised and disconcerted me a little. *Why now?* I wondered.

Straightaway I grasped the bowl and brought its edge to my forehead, closed my eyes, cleared my mind of thought, and tried to see if I might learn anything more from the object. Alas, aside from a very strong, almost corporeal sensation of my friend's presence, nothing else came through. Nevertheless I welcomed the knowledge as confirmation that Cormac had indeed spent time in the house.

I carried the bowl back to my place at the hearth, where I ate my solitary meal beside a fine warm fire and considered what to do next. I might, with difficulty, spend the winter at Tuaim Bán—but spring was still very far off, and the thought of staying in the house all alone through the bleak season did not sit well with me. I decided to chance the long ride back to Bras Rhaidd, where I might spend a more comfortable winter with Sadwrn and the others and resume my search for Cormac with their help in the spring.

Next day I made all the flour into bread and packed the remaining supplies to take with me, then watered and fed Boreas with more of the dry fodder. Thus prepared, I spent a last warm night beside the fire and departed the druid house at dawn. The sun rose bright in a clear blue sky, and though my breath hung in clouds before my face, the sun was soon warm on my back—a good sign, I thought, that I had chosen well.

Ah, but signs can be deceiving. The world is impossibly vicious and contrary, delighting always in the destruction of men and their dreams. This I know.

35

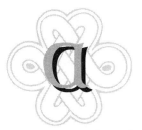A T DUSK, ELEVEN days after leaving Tuaim Bán, disaster overtook me. As the short-lived sun faded, clouds had come in on a sharp northern wind and it began to snow. I came to a break in the wood where a stream ran through the forest and decided to halt for the night in a stand of tall pines just across the river; their branches, wide and low, seemed to offer a dry spot to sleep. The water, though fast, was not deep, so I urged Boreas into the frigid flow.

I was halfway across when the horse stumbled on an icy rock. But it was nothing serious; horses stumble all the time. It was a warning nonetheless—a warning which went unheeded. I should have dismounted then and there and led the exhausted animal the rest of the way across. But the water was freezing cold, and I was tired; I did not care to spend the night in wet clothes. So I kept my saddle and coaxed Boreas to finish the crossing and climb the opposite bank. Unfortunately, the bank was steeper than I realized. Snow and ice on the rocks made the footing treacherous; the horse stumbled twice, and I was just sliding from the saddle when the animal slipped again.

Unbalanced, I was thrown down onto the rocks, and Boreas, unable to find his footing, stepped on me, his hoof striking me on my left side. I heard a soft crunch and felt something give way in my chest. I let out a scream of pain, and the horse, frightened now, reared. I saw his forelegs pawing the air as his hind legs struggled, hooves skittering on the ice-covered rocks. The poor beast went over backward and landed on his side in the stream.

Gulping air against the pain, I jumped up and plunged into the water to grab the reins, lest the frightened animal take it into his head to charge off into the wood without me. I snagged the reins and tried to calm Boreas and get him on his feet again.

The horse neighed and thrashed about, but try as he might, he could not rise; he had broken his right hind leg in the fall. There was blood in the water, and he brayed with pain every time he tried to get up.

There was nothing to be done. I could not leave him in the middle of the freezing stream all night, and I could not move him out myself—and even if I might have accomplished that somehow, I could not have bound and healed the broken leg overnight.

Taking my makeshift spear, I unstrapped the knife from the ash branch, and then, kneeling in the water, I got Boreas' head around and, speaking soothing words into his ear, calmed him, telling him how he had been my bold, good champion, my strong, brave steed, and how sorry I was that he had been injured through my willful negligence. I asked him to forgive me for what I was about to do and then, with a quick, biting stroke, drew the knife blade across the soft skin of his throat beneath the jaw.

Distracted by the pain of his broken limb, I do not think he felt the blade at all. I continued to hold his head and stroke him, filling his ear with kindly words as his life flowed from him. In a little while he slumped down; a quiver passed through his body, and he lay still. "Farewell, Boreas, good friend," I said and, my heart aching with regret, I dragged myself from the ice-rimmed stream.

My own pain, held in abeyance until now, set in with a fierce, fiery throb. I lay on the frozen bank panting like a winded dog, until I realized the light was going. I had no choice but to return to my dead mount to get the supplies he carried behind the saddle. Wheezing like a broken bellows, my side throbbing with every step, I slogged my way into the water and to poor dead Boreas once more. Working quickly, I loosened the knots and dragged the leather bag back onto the bank, then collapsed beside it in the snow, tears streaming from my eyes.

After a while I marshaled my strength and rolled myself under the low pine branches. It was dry there, and the pine needles were deep. I scooped out a hollow and, taking the flint and iron from the bag, soon had a tiny flame fluttering in the dry needles. I fed small twigs into the fire until it took hold, then lay down beside it and heaped masses of pine needles over me.

The snow continued through the night. I lay in agony, biting the insides of my cheeks to keep from crying out, listening to the thin wail of the wind sifting through the trees, and waiting for daylight, when I crawled from my crude nest to survey the damage. Slowly, carefully, I opened my robe, pulled up my tunic, and looked down at my side. The sight which greeted me brought the gorge to my throat. From hip to chest the entire left half of my body was a virulent, deep-colored bruise. That was bad enough, but the sight that alarmed me most was a crescent-shaped bulge of dull, angry red just below my last rib.

With trembling fingers I brushed the hoof-shaped bulge lightly with my fingers and felt that it was hot to the touch. Picking up a handful of wet snow, I pressed it gently to my side. The intense cold made my flesh writhe, but it gradually leached away some of the pain.

Closing my robe, I got to my feet and edged my way down the slippery bank to the stream; I cupped freezing water to my mouth, swallowing as much as I could hold. Then, with a last farewell to my dead horse, I hefted the leather bag and, taking up the ash pole for a staff, resumed my journey on foot.

By my closest reckoning I was at least seven days' ride from Bras Rhaidd—on foot, eleven or more. Allowing for the weather, I would be fortunate to reach the druid house in twice the time. Indeed, injured as I was, I would be lucky to reach Bras Rhaidd at all.

My best hope, I decided, was to find a nearer settlement. True, I had passed very few on the journey north, and thus the chance of finding one now seemed particularly remote. Even so, Tarian's rudimentary map identified a road to the south—one of those serving the garrisons north of the Wall. If I could reach that road, I might soon find a settlement along the way. In the bag was food enough for another three or four days—after that I would grow hungry. But I was used to hunger. And cold, too. Neither of those hardships worried me. I had endured them often enough on Sliabh Mis, and I could do so again.

Thus, with confidence banked high in my heart, I set off in the certainty that I would soon reach a settlement where I could get help and wait out the worst of winter.

For two days I walked south and east, following Tarian's chart as well as I could. The way was rough and wild and made more difficult by snow and ice. I stumped along through the wind and cold, half frozen, dragging the leather bag of rapidly dwindling provisions behind me. At night I slept in the driest places I could find—usually under low-lying pine boughs, huddled beside a small sputtering fire. Often I heard wolves, sometimes close, and once I even saw one; but as it was early winter and he was not so hungry yet, he was content to leave me alone.

At the end of the third day, I finished the last of the food. Taking the empty bag, I split it down one side and along the bottom to open it up. This I tied around my head and shoulders to give me better protection from the wind, rain, and snow. I could do nothing for my injured rib, however; the perpetual pain deepened to a fiery ache that throbbed with every step. I wheezed when I drew breath now, and there was an ugly gurgling sound deep down in my left lung which I did my best to ignore.

For the next two days I stumbled on, head down, suffering with every step. My hands and feet felt like lumps of ice on the dead ends of my limbs, and my chest burned with a low, angry fire. I could no longer walk upright but held myself crooked to one side to appease the pain. My steps grew slower, my rests more frequent. I drank from icy pools and ate snow to ease the pangs of hunger, but as the unrelenting cold sank into my bones, I could feel my strength dwindling.

I dragged myself up the side of one hill and down the other so many times I lost count, and then, toward the end of the fifth day since losing the horse, as the last lights failed in the west, I glimpsed a thin, dark line snaking through a nameless valley below: the road.

In a crevice between two rocks, I spent the night and at sunrise climbed back onto unfeeling feet, took up my staff, and moved on, keeping the undulating line of the road in my sight for fear that if I looked away, I would lose it—and that would be the end. Step by step I willed the road to come closer, and as the sun made an all-too-brief appearance at midday, I finally reached the flat, stone-paved track. I paused to rest while the sun shone, and I read the last milestone, which indicated that the nearest garrison was Banna, sixteen miles away. When the sun disappeared once more behind the dark clouds, I stood and shuffled on.

The road rose up and over a ridge and descended into a treeless moor, and though it was flat and easy underfoot, the wind whipped sharply out of the north, slicing through my perpetually damp cloak to freeze my already numb flesh to the bone. The bite of the wind caused tears to well up in my eyes, yet I struggled on, half blind, wheezing and gasping like an old man, dragging one foot in front of the other, and vowing with every step that if I reached help alive, I would never stir beyond sight of the hearth again.

Soon the day ended. As twilight gathered, I saw ahead the edge of a wood where I might find shelter for the night. Dark spots floated in my vision; my head felt as if it were stuffed with wool. Though I gulped greedily, I could not seem to get enough air. Still I hauled myself forward toward the wood as if it were my salvation. Over and over the words screamed in my brain: *sixteen miles!*

I would never make it.

Step by aching step, the edge of the wood drew closer. The light was going, the day leaving me straggling far behind. Holding the promise of rest and shelter before me, I stumbled on toward the wood and had almost reached it when I saw, emerging from the trees, a great, misshapen beast. The animal had a low head and high humped back, and it heaved itself slowly onto the road with six or more short, stout legs.

I stopped and stared, unable to believe the thing that passed before my eyes. The old pagans told of strange creatures inhabiting the ancient forests, but I had always accounted it rank superstition of the most ignorant kind. Yet here was one of those tales come to lumbering life.

As I stood looking on, the beast turned and proceeded down the road away from me. It was then, in the last glimmer of daylight, that I saw the wheels and realized that what I was seeing was not a monster but a high-sided cart pulled by an ox with a farmer walking beside it.

I tried to call out to him, but it hurt me so to draw breath that I could make no sound above a whisper. I started after him, hurrying as fast as I could: not fast enough, however, for it was soon clear that I was falling behind. My side hurt; my legs were numb and unsteady. I could hardly breathe, let alone run, and the farmer with his slow ox and cart were leaving me behind. I stopped to think what to do.

It came to me to try the briamon, the word of power. Standing there in the middle of the road, I closed my eyes, raised my staff, and stretched forth my left hand. I drew a breath deep as I could and held in my mind the word I meant to speak.

"Unite word and will together," Datho had taught. "Let your command gather volition and power before sending it out into the world. Above all, believe that what you say has been ordained from the foundation of the world and that all creation stands ready to uphold your bidding."

Concentrating the entire force of my will into the word, I did as Datho had taught me to do, drawing heart and mind together into a single weapon—as if mind were the bow and heart the string. I bent both to my will and held the word taut.

Then, when I could contain it no longer, I released it and let it fly.

To my astonishment the shout resounded in the wood and echoed from the surrounding hills. The farmer stopped. I saw him turn. He saw me. I waved my staff at him and started forth on unfeeling legs. I took but half a dozen paces, and the last of my strength gave out. I stumbled on the uneven stone and fell headlong onto the road. The fall awakened the fury in my side; I squeezed my eyes shut, gritted my teeth, and held on to consciousness until the farmer could reach me.

Presently I heard the clomp of his wooden-soled shoes on the paving stones and raised my head. A heavy man, wrapped in rags and fur against the wind and cold, stood looking down at me with mild brown eyes.

"Help, me," I gasped. "I am hurt."

He made a reply in speech I could not understand and then bent to pick me up. I felt his hands under my arms, and he lifted me up like so much grain in a bag. The movement brought a cry from my lips, but the farmer seemed not to notice. He did, however, observe my robe.

"*Derwyddi?*" he said.

"Yes," I told him. "Filidh."

"Ahhh . . . ," he said, as if this answered a long-suspected but never-revealed secret. "Filidh."

"*Cymorth,*" I said, my tongue tripping over the British words. "Help. I need help."

"Ah," he said again, and gathered me under his arm. Without another word he all but carried me back to where his wagon and ox were waiting. The wagon, open at the back, was filled with bits and scraps of dead wood he had collected that day. A long-handled ax lay safely tucked against the side. He shoved some of the wood to the front of the box to create a space and then picked me up and set me in the back.

He returned to his place at the head of his ox, and a moment later the wagon juddered on, the heavy wooden wheels rumbling over the stone road. Each lurch and bump brought agony to my side, but I no longer cared. Whatever came would come. All other concerns fell away, and I clung only to one last thought: *At least I will not die alone on the road.*

36

Y RESCUER WAS a member of a small farming clan that scratched out a slender living in a nearby valley. Sheltering in the wind shadow of a massive rocky crag, the holding occupied a narrow strip of land between the lower stone-covered slopes of the towering hill and a clear-water lake. In this settlement, home to twenty or more hardy souls, the farmers grew rye and oats, fished the lakes, and made hunting forays into the forest, where, as it happened, they also scavenged wood for the hearth when stocks ran low.

Four high-peaked, half-sunken houses served the clan, which was made up of two principal families. The houses were built of sturdy timber with beaten-earth floors; wattle partitions offered a modicum of privacy in the large single room—half of which the oxen shared; sleeping places on raised platforms ran along either side of the house. A large central hearth served for cooking and warmth, and it was here they gathered during the long winter nights.

My arrival threw the clan into commotion. They saw from my robe that I was a druid, and though they deemed my presence a rare honor, they were more than a little frightened of my supposed powers.

Nevertheless they welcomed me with simple sincerity. With slightly frantic ceremony I was lifted up and carried into the largest house in the cluster of buildings which made up the settlement.

Two women were tending a large iron caldron when the company of four strong men bore me in. They jumped up and, shouting instructions to a gaggle of children, quickly prepared a place for me by the hearth using rushes, pelts, and fleeces which the children quickly fetched. Amid much gabbling discussion, I was placed on this bed while one of the men ran to inform the rest of the clan of my arrival.

I guess this is what happened, for the house was soon filled with people—all of them roughly similar in appearance: broad and stocky with short, muscular limbs, thick waists, and heavy shoulders. All the men had long dark hair and beards; the women's hair, likewise long and dark, was worn loose. Their clothing was made of sheepskin and coarse-woven wool. None of them wore any ornament or bauble that I could see, although several had a dark blue mark on their cheeks and upper arms—a curved line in the shape of a fish.

While they assembled to look at me, I slumped beside the hearth, too weak to move, my face to the shimmering flames as the delicious, lifesaving warmth seeped into my frozen bones. Truly, never was a man more grateful for fire than I was that night.

The children, stiff-legged with excitement, gawked at this odd-looking stranger and whispered loudly to one another. Presently an old man emerged from the hushed consultation just inside the doorway. Nodding, smiling, he approached, the very image of aged humility, as he settled himself beside me on the bare dirt floor. "Welcome, Father," I said, trying Latin first, and I thanked him for taking me in. When that produced no result, I tried Irish and British, too.

He regarded me with a puzzled look and at last made a reply in a tongue I did not recognize. Certainly it was no language I had ever heard before.

"I am sorry," I said. "I do not understand you—and I can see you do not understand me either."

Still smiling, he rose and called to one of the men. The two held close conversation for a moment, and the younger man left the house, returning a moment later with an old, white-haired woman. Although she seemed the most venerable of all present, they did not appear to hold her in any great regard but shoved her roughly forward to inspect me.

"Filidh? Filidh?" she asked, her toothless mouth slurring the words.

"Yes, filidh," I confirmed.

She nodded and began patting me here and there. She brushed my side, which brought a wince from me, whereupon she tugged on my clothes. I surmised she wanted to see my injury. Moving carefully, I slowly, painfully, opened my robe and lifted my tunic so she could see my side, which was now an inflamed and puffy mass of discolored flesh.

Frowning, she gazed a moment at the livid wound, the breath whistling over her gums. She muttered to herself, then addressed me; when I made no reply, she bent her white head over me, sniffing the wound and fingering it gently with cool fingertips.

After a moment she replaced my robe and stood. She said something to the two women standing at the caldron, and both hurried away, returning quickly—one with a small iron pot and the other with a small leather drinking bag and a wooden bowl. The old woman took the pot and set it in the embers beside the fire; the bowl she filled from the leather bag and brought to me. She put it to my lips, indicating that I should drink. I raised my head and took some of the liquid into my mouth; it was sweet and warming and slid down my throat easily. I tasted honey and heather on my tongue, and other herbs—but it left a bitter aftertaste in my mouth. Mead, I decided, but with something added.

The liquid was wonderfully reviving, however, and as I sipped, I felt a delicious numbness spreading through my injured body. I drank some more of the painkilling concoction and lay back, offering her a smile for her efforts. She nodded and continued with her ministrations. A bowl of hot broth followed, and then dry bread that had been soaked in milk and meat drippings. The old woman patiently spooned the food into my mouth, waiting between each spoonful for me to swallow until the bowl was empty.

Meanwhile the contents of the iron pot had begun to steam, infusing a sour scent into the air. When I finished, the old woman set the bowl aside and turned to the pot. Taking a stick, she fished a rag from the steaming liquid, felt it with her hand, and then, drawing aside my robe, placed the rag directly upon the wound on my side. The pungent stuff burned, but I, full of the drugged liquid, no longer cared about the pain. The old woman kept the hot rag on my side, returning it from time to time to the pot before replacing it on the wound.

The clan members gradually lost interest in the procedure and went about their business. They sat down for their supper and were served from the caldron, men first, then the women and children together. They ate noisily, talking incessantly in their thick speech; I listened but could make nothing of it.

Warmed by the food and fire and exhausted by the ordeal of the last many days, I closed my eyes and quickly sank into a deep and dreamless slumber. I slept through most of the next day, waking when the old woman roused me to drink a concoction she had made of bitter herbs, milk, and the bark of certain trees. I drank the stuff and felt better for it, as much as for my long sleep.

When I tried to rise, I found that I lacked the strength; the pain in my side was greater now, although the swelling had gone down somewhat—owing, no doubt, to the old woman's steaming poultice. My head ached, and the entire left side of my torso throbbed and burned. She fed me some broth-soaked bread, but even the effort to eat proved too much for me, and I could not take more than a few mouthfuls.

I lay drifting and dozing until the men returned from their various chores and gathered for their evening meal. The clan chief came and squatted down before me; he offered me a word of greeting and then spoke to the old woman, who, frowning, shook her head, indicating, I supposed, that I was no better.

Nor was I better the next day. In fact, I could feel myself slipping. Despite the rest and food, my strength was diminishing and the pain in my side increasing in its pointed persistence and spreading down into my groin and leg.

When the old woman came to tend me, I looked her in the eye and said, "Bras Rhaidd."

She frowned and shook her head, then turned to tend the iron pot on the coals. I reached out and took her arm, gripping it hard, so she would stop what she was doing and listen to me. "Bras Rhaidd," I repeated, speaking as distinctly as I could, so she might catch the words and my meaning behind them. "Take me to Bras Rhaidd."

She paused this time and regarded me shrewdly, but the words meant nothing to her. Still, she caught something of the importance of what I was trying to tell her. I repeated the words twice more, whereupon she rose and left the house. I had just closed my eyes again to sleep when she returned, this time with the old man and another, younger man. The old woman nodded to me, prompting me to say the words again.

"Bras Rhaidd," I said. "Take me to Bras Rhaidd."

The three of them looked at one another. The old man said something to me, and I repeated the words again. They talked among themselves then, but nothing came of it. In despair of making them understand, I blurted the next name I knew. "Candida Casa," I said. "Do you know Candida Casa?"

The old man shook his head. No, he did not know what I was talking about. He said something to the old woman, who shook her head. As they were talking, the younger fellow leaned forward. "Casa?" he said hesitantly.

"Yes, Casa," I repeated. "Candida Casa—do you know it?"

His eyes grew wide with excitement. "Candida Casa," he said. The old man turned to the youth, who stretched out his hand as if pointing out a direction. "*Gebort hurdanka*, Candida Casa," he said insistently.

Understanding dawned on the old man then; he nodded enthusiastically, repeating the name to me. Lifting my hand, I tapped my chest and said the name, then pointed in the direction the young man had indicated, saying the name again.

Their reaction was gratifying. The young man, unable to sit still, jumped up. "Candida Casa, *ya! Ya!*" he cried over and over again.

The old man sat back on his heels and rubbed his forehead thoughtfully. The old woman called a command to the younger fellow, who fled the house on the run.

It was decided just like that, and before midday had passed, all was ready. The men came in, gathered me up, bed and all, and carried me out to a waiting wagon which had been hastily provisioned. The old woman followed with another drink of the pain-numbing liquor, and I was taken up and laid on a mound of straw to soften the jolting of the wagon; pelts were heaped upon me to keep me warm, and, with a shout from the driver to the ox, the wagon lurched off. The entire settlement came to watch my departure. I raised my hand in farewell and determined that if I should reach Candida Casa alive, I would see these people well rewarded for their help.

Two men attended me — the young man and the one who had found me on the road. They set off at a stately pace and walked without stopping until dusk; they made a camp on the trail and moved on before dawn the next morning. I slept most of the time, never stirring from the wagon save once, when we paused at a stream to allow the ox to drink and I rose and, with the aid of my young helper, stood long enough to relieve myself before crawling back to my warm nest.

I remember little enough of the next days. We journeyed west in the cold and snow, coming at last to the windblown coast. The farmers followed the coastline until reaching the monastery at dusk on the fifth day. The stopping of the wagon wakened me, and I raised my head to see three robed priests hurrying from the nearest house. "Julian . . . ," I said to the first who reached me. He peered into my face and bit his lip. "Bring Julian."

"Get him inside," someone called. "Thomas, run get Fychan! Hurry!"

The monks scattered, and others arriving just then pulled me from the wagon and began carrying me across the yard to the priest house. The farmers were forgotten in the uproar of my arrival. I saw them standing beside the wagon as I was hauled away. "Please," I said, "bring them in, too."

One of the monks called for the farmers to be conducted to the refectory, and I was borne away to a cell in the priest house where I was placed on a clean bed of rushes. The monk called Fychan soon appeared — a short, round man who fairly bounced into the room on his stubby legs. He took one look at me and cried, "*Deus Mei!*" Whirling to an unseen brother behind him, he shouted, "Bring hot water, Marcus! And dry cloths."

He came to my bed and knelt to examine me. "It is my side," I told him, my voice a low, dry croak in my throat.

"There, now," he said. "Rest easy. Let me have a look." With deft and gentle hands, he untied my belt, drew aside my robe and tunic, and began probing the wound. "Horse?" he said after a moment.

"Stepped on me," I whispered.

"I thought so," he replied. "You carry the mark of the hoof in your flesh." He put his hand on the swollen lump below my ribs. "Broken ribs," he said. "There has been bleeding inside. Did you vomit any blood?" I shook my head in reply. "That is good at least."

"Is it bad, then?"

"Bad enough. You were right to have them bring you here. Another few days and . . ." He left the thought unfinished, concluding, "God is merciful, however; he has provided the best physician in all of Albion. He is even now at your service, and he will see you mended."

"With God's helping hand to guide him," amended the brother just entering the room with a steaming bowl between his hands.

"Ah, Marcus, there you are. What kept you? Bring me the bowl and then go fetch my instruments."

"Of course, brother," replied Marcus, handing over the bowl.

"I cannot tell," offered Fychan when his helper had gone, "whether he is an especially adept student or whether I am merely the most brilliant of teachers." He sighed. "Perhaps we shall never know."

Together they worked on me, the brilliant physician and his able student, and I relaxed into their care. The last thing I remember, before succumbing to the tincture Fychan gave me to dull the pain, was asking after the two farmers. "Where are they?"

"They are enjoying a hearty supper, I should think," replied Fychan.

"Tell Julian to reward them well. They saved my life. Whatever he gives them, I will gladly repay—anything."

"I will tell him," said Marcus. "You are fortunate," he continued. "Most Picti would have killed you for your cloak."

"They are not Picti, surely," said Fychan.

"Well, they are not Romans," answered Marcus. "And they are not Scoti either."

"Pagans in any event," concluded Fychan.

Heavy-headed with the drug, I closed my eyes and slept, waking two days later with a sore head and an even more painful side. "That is to be expected," Marcus informed me. "Fychan incised the wound, bled it, and has bound the broken ribs. The pain will remain for some little time to come."

"It does not matter," I told him. "What of the farmers?"

"I know nothing of any farmers."

"Then where are my clothes?" I said. "I want to get up."

"We burned your druid garb," Marcus answered. "It was filthy with blood and whatnot, and unbecoming any decent christian."

"I want to get up," I insisted.

"Julian is nearby," said Marcus. "I will get him for you."

He stepped from the room, returning a few moments later with Julian, who smiled when he saw me. "Come back to us at last, I see," said Julian cheerfully. "The prayers of these good brothers have effected a wonderful cure."

Even as he spoke, I thought it more likely that the native kindliness of the farmers and Fychan's skill as a physician had far more to do with my rescue, than did the belated mumblings of the monks, however sincere.

"He is most anxious about these barbarians of his," said Marcus. "As you dealt with them, I thought you could best tell the result."

Julian agreed and said, "They departed yesterday with a wagon piled high with supplies: seed barley from the granary mostly, and also oats, rye, eggs, and cured pork." He smiled. "You got off lightly — the cost of your salvation was trifling, so to speak."

"No gold?" I asked. "Did you offer them gold?"

"Your concern for them is laudable, Succat," he answered. "But you need not worry. I offered gold, of course, but it is of no use to them. Trust me, the seed is far more valuable to barbarians."

"They saved my life," I told him.

"Fychan saved your life," Julian corrected blithely. "Another day or two with those pagani and the only service we could have afforded you was a funeral."

He gave me a superior smile and patted my hand as it rested on my chest. "Be not anxious," he said. "You are in God's hands now. We will not suffer you to fall again."

He and Marcus exchanged a few words regarding my care, whereupon he departed, saying, "I will inform Bishop Cornelius of your splendid progress. He has been most solicitous of your recovery."

"Thank him for me," I said, sinking back. Although it had been brief, I was already exhausted by Julian's visit.

My progress, as I saw it, was far from splendid. My side both ached and burned at the same time; the tight-wound bandage constricted my chest and made breathing an ordeal. I felt wan and ragged and weak as a newborn infant. It was all I could do to lie in one place and swallow the warm concoctions Marcus spooned into my mouth from time to time.

"I understand that you were captured by Irish raiders and sold as a slave," Marcus said one day.

"That is true."

He nodded. "And was it the barbarians who made you a druid?"

"They made me a shepherd," I answered. "Becoming a bard was my own idea."

"I see," he said, his mouth squirming in a way that gave me to know he did not understand at all.

"Among the Irish," I explained, "the filidh are held in highest esteem. They are the noblest of the noble. Even kings submit to them. All of creation is their occupation and concern; their lives are given to the study of whatsoever pleases them."

"The dark arts please them most, I presume."

"Then your presumption is wrong," I replied—with far less vehemence than I felt; I lacked the strength for a heated argument. "The object of their scrutiny is to learn the truth of all things. Among the filidh truth is said to lead to justice, and justice to harmony, and harmony to love."

"Well said," granted Marcus.

"So that learning and truth may increase," I continued, "they are free to travel where they will—to Britain, Gaul, and beyond."

"Ah," said Marcus, breaking in, "you became a druid in order to escape. I understand now."

His presumption, accurate though it was, irked me. I resented these smug priests and their arrogant ways, holding all beneath them. "I became a druid," I replied, "so that I might be a better man."

It was, alas, far from the truth. I said it merely to rub the self-righteous smirk off his face. Instead it had very much the opposite effect. "*That* is what the Ceile De always say," he sniffed, regarding me with a haughty expression. "They may call themselves Christians—but they are *heretics* of the most insidious kind."

His reply might have stung me far more than it did, I suppose, had I known what the word "heretic" meant.

Lacking the strength for more strenuous debate, I swallowed my ignorance along with his insult. "You might think differently," I told him, "if you had ever known one as I have."

37

VER THE NEXT many days, as I began to heal and regain my strength, I shuffled around the grounds of the monastery and observed all that was taking place. I noticed the presence of three or four bishops, which I thought to be a considerable number—even for such a place as the White House.

When I asked Julian about this, he said, "Of course they don't reside here. They are attending the council. Naturally you would not know about this since you were gone when they arrived. Nynia and Cornelius, prudent churchmen that they are, thought it best to convene a council to draw up letters of condemnation to take to the conference in Turonum."

Julian, Marcus, and I were walking in the walled courtyard of the monastic villa. "I see," I said. "And what are they condemning?"

"The Pelagian heresy," Julian answered. "And not only that, but Pelagius and all his followers as well."

"What have they done?" I asked. "Put a pig in priest's robes?"

"*Deus veniam habeat!*" exclaimed Julian, rousing himself to regard me in indolent amazement. "You have no idea who Pelagius is, do you?"

"I freely confess that I do not." I returned his gaze coolly. "Nor do I care. But it all seems like tedious nonsense to me."

"You stand in danger of heresy yourself, brother," Marcus warned.

"Do not mind Succat," Julian said, adopting the air of a long-suffering schoolmaster separating two rowdy pupils. "The Irish have befuddled him."

"Through their persistent and enthusiastic propagation of error, these

Pelagians weaken the body of Christ," Marcus insisted. "They are a canker that must be cut out if the body is to retain health and vigor."

Now, I had never heard of these Pelagians he mentioned, nor their leader. But the toplofty certainty with which these condescending clerics held their obtuse doctrines rankled and irritated me.

I am contrary that way.

Yet that I, who had thrown over the last weak dregs of Christian belief long ago, should care what a passel of pretentious, self-important priests thought or how they occupied their idle days seemed a peculiar absurdity, even to me.

Perhaps my natural tolerance for pomposity was wearing thin. Or perhaps Ollamh Datho's high regard for truth and justice and his insistence that the forthright exercise of these virtues—like the tireless search for knowledge—must be conducted in simple humility had taken root in my soul. However it was, I found myself sharply disapproving of the bishops' council before I knew even the smallest part of what it was about or what these heretics believed that was so damning to them.

Beside, if they were anything like the Ceile De, whom Marcus had likewise condemned out of hand, and who I knew to be unjustly accused, then these Pelagians had my entire sympathy.

The council of bishops commenced. As they were called away on other duties, I saw little of Marcus and less of Julian. I had whole days to myself with nothing to do. When the weather was fair, I walked down to the coast and prowled the shore, gazing out across the Irish Sea, hoping to catch a glimpse of the green Éireann hills, which, I was told, could be seen as a pale blue blur on the horizon when the days were bright and clear.

I never saw them.

Eventually this kindled in my mind the notion that I never would see Ireland again. Even as I stood on the strand with the waves lapping at my feet, searching the cloud-bound horizon, yearning for a glimpse of Éire, the notion was hardening into certainty. The world was turning and turning again. The tide of my affairs had already begun to change.

One night, as I lay on the pallet in my cell, I listened to the brother walk the grounds ringing his bell to call his brother monks to prayer. My heart squirmed within me, and I heard a voice saying, *"Rise and go. You should not be here."*

But where should I go? And how?

As these thoughts turned in my mind, the voice came again: *"Rise and go! Do not remain in this nest of vipers!"*

And I did rise. I walked to the door of my cell and peered out into the darkened yard. "Where should I go?" I demanded, speaking aloud. "Where, in God's holy name, should I go?"

There came no answer. The silence resounded through my heart and my soul. In that silence the hateful truth resounded: I belonged nowhere and had nowhere to go.

I spent a sleepless night and emerged the next morning with a sour taste in my mouth. I moved through the day and the days to follow like a sullen and dejected phantom, lost in pity and reeking of despair. Having done all I could to secure a future for myself, I had failed.

Wretched and ashamed, I took to my bed and did not rise from one day to the next. I lay in misery, berating myself for all my shortcomings, which had so richly contributed to my failure. From the beginning I had lied to friend and foe alike. I had stolen and cheated, seizing any advantage I could grasp, thinking of myself alone. I had deceived and betrayed almost everyone I met, but most of all Sionan, possibly the only person alive under heaven who loved me. Did she love me still? I wondered. No. She would have guessed the truth long since and would despise me now and evermore.

Rancorous, malicious, judgmental, and intolerant, I was swiftly becoming an object of loathing and disgust in my own eyes. My many failings weighed so heavily on me that I could no longer rise above them. Unable to alter the past or see any hope for the future, I sank lower and lower into an oppressive, desperate melancholy, mordant as grief and desolate as mourning.

When help did come at last, it was selfish and disloyal—but a drowning man will hung to any wreckage if it will delay the final dissolution. I grasped what was offered, and I hung on tight. It was all I could do.

Julian appeared in my cell one day. "Marcus tells me you have not been eating."

When I made no reply, he moved to my bedside.

"What is wrong with you?"

"Nothing," I said.

He sighed. "It is no use denying it, Succat. Plainly something is festering in you. Now, I ask you again: What is wrong with you that you hole up here like a wounded badger in his den, moaning and moping day and night?"

"You would not understand if I told you," I answered, and that was true. How could anyone have understood?

"Succat," he said, coming to stand over me, "the time has come to break clean with the past. It is no good yearning for something that can never be. You tried to find your friend Cormac—"

"Tried and failed," I said bitterly.

"Then why not simply accept that it was not to be?"

"Easy to say," I replied. "You have never known a fall, Julian. You cannot know how it hurts."

"You may have failed, as you say, but must you wallow in failure forever? Get up, gird your loins, seek the salve of absolution for your sins. Tomorrow we leave for Turonum. Let that be your genesis."

"You may be leaving for Turonum," I replied, "but I am not."

"No? I urge you to reconsider."

"Why? It won't change anything. You see before you a man who has lost everything: lands, home, family. The one person who might have helped me, I failed to find. In fact, everything I ever put my hand to has failed."

"Listen to me now," said Julian quietly. He sat down beside me. "You have had a great disappointment—"

"Great disaster, you mean."

"No one blames you for feeling the way you do," he said sympathetically. "It is only natural. But dwelling on the past and its hurts and harms will avail you nothing. The past is over and done. Let it go. Tomorrow you will begin again."

"Easy to say."

"In Gaul you will find yourself, Succat. I know it. There is opportunity for young men willing to work. You will have a fresh start. Think of it: You can begin again in a place where no one knows you and the past no longer matters. Your future is ahead of you, Succat, not behind. You must look to Gaul."

He left me then, but his words achieved their desired effect. A short while later, I got up from my bed and walked for a last time down to the shore. The day was far gone, the sun low on the water. I looked out and saw what I thought was a smudge of pale blue cloud close to the horizon. It was, I imagined, the distant hills of Ireland.

I stood for a long time, trying to make myself feel something for Éire and its people—for Cormac and Sionan at least. I felt nothing. The affection I had allowed myself to imagine was dead. No doubt it had died in the ice and cold of the Celyddon Wood or out on the old Roman road. Perhaps the agony and fever of injury and disappointment had burned it out of me. Perhaps it had never really existed.

Now, as I stood gazing out across the water, I felt nothing. Not remorse, not grief, nor even relief. Nothing. Nothing at all. So far as I could tell, I was dead inside. My heart had become a cold, hard cinder—a once-bright ember taken from the hearth and laid on the dull flagstone to cool and cool until the last spark died.

I stood and watched the sun plunge in fiery haze into the dark blue sea, and then I turned my face away and walked from the water's edge without looking back. When Bishop Cornelius and his entourage departed Candida Casa the next morning, I rode with them to begin my new life in Gaul.

PART III

magonus

AUL, ON FIRST sight, seemed very like Britain in most ways—save that the cities were more numerous and the garrisons were manned. Prosperity sat on the countryside like a matron grown plump with age. It was a broad land, with many woodlands, good streams, and few mountains. It seemed that perhaps Julian was right; this could well be a place where a man could thrive if he was willing to work hard.

Yes, and the more I saw of it, the more certain I became that hard work would be needed—and also luck. "Times being what they are," Bishop Cornelius said, "there are bandits, brigands, and barbarians aplenty. They rove at will through the settlements and towns."

Apparently this was only too true—especially in the north. This was why, he said, the garrisons had been removed from Britain. "The emperor has decided that the security of the northern frontier is the salvation of the empire," continued Cornelius. "Everything now depends on its protection."

So many legions had been amassed in the north that it left the great soft belly of Gaul open to the bandits and brigands, and these thought nothing of making swooping raids on the villas, farms, and settlements the soldiers could no longer defend.

From the moment we made landfall at Namnétes, we began hearing about all the atrocities perpetrated by the barbarians in their intolerable raids.

As Cornelius and Julian set about procuring provisions and hiring wagons, I strolled the lumpy streets of Namnétes, a fair-size market city on the banks of a wide river estuary to the south of the Armorican peninsula. I looked and listened and talked to the merchants in marketplace Latin. These bandits, they said, were rapacious, vicious, a scourge and a plague. No one was safe. The garrisons were inadequate; more soldiers were needed. The generals worried too much about the barbarians outside the borders and allowed murderous thieves free reign inside.

Such was the fear of the local population that I, too, began to grow concerned and was mightily relieved when Bishop Cornelius engaged five mercenaries to accompany us to Turonum, eight days' journey upriver. Although it was early spring, the weather was already fine, with high, blue, sun-warmed skies filled with towering clouds; even the rain, when it came, was soft and gentle. Everywhere men and oxen were hard at work in the fields of the villas and settlements we passed along the way.

The clerics—no fewer than five in our party—occupied themselves morning to night with discussions of theology which wearied me to the bone. I often overheard their disputatious questions: Which were more pernicious—the professions of Manichaeanism, or those of the Gnostics? Was Pelagianism a new form of Gnosticism, or was it merely Arianism in disguise? Was the Son of the same substance as the Father, or was there a material difference between them? Were individual souls created by God as need required, or were they made up from raw material supplied by the parents at the time of conception? Was the Logos preexistent with the Father, or did it come into being as a result of Divine Will and was therefore contingent upon it to be the agent of creation?

Of course I had even less interest in these questions than in the material difference between the farts of a bishop and those of a pope. The long and painstakingly detailed discussions seemed to me nothing more than the incessant nattering of toads in a water-filled ditch—and of no greater consequence.

I found the company of the soldiers more convivial, and I spent most of my time walking with them. They were rough men, illiterate, crude in thought and deed, and scornful of anyone or anything they judged weaker than themselves. They cared for nothing except fighting and drinking; the former they considered a chore to be dispensed with as simply and efficiently as possible so that more time could be lavished on the latter.

They prided themselves on two things: their skill at arms, which did not amount to much so far as I could tell, and their undying loyalty—not to the state, the landowners, or traveling dignitaries like us: these were merely their employers. No, their loyalty was to one another. Brothers in arms, they called themselves, and their disdain for any who stood outside the tight circle of their comradeship knew no bounds.

Yet I found their earthy practicality refreshing. They demanded nothing of the world but that it provide them with the means to earn their daily pay. With the legions in disarray, the opportunities for plying their needful trade abounded in luxurious profusion.

The leader of the five with us was a veteran named Quintus—a blunt, square-headed man with short curly hair, clear gray eyes, and a nose that crumpled at the bridge where the bone had been smashed by a Dacian club. "A grievous blow, that," he told me as we stumped along one day. "The battle was near over for us—just a few sulky brutes unwilling to lie down and die were left. Most of the boys were already stripping armor, and the general ordered a cohort to go and finish off the dregs, you know.

"Well, a bunch of us hopped up and hurried over there. The Daci are a fearsome tribe, true enough—screech like demons and fight like the furies. But, as with most barbarians I've ever seen, you get their chieftain down and they lose heart. Once your brute's lost heart, he grows meek as a lamb, and you can put him down without much fuss."

"Is that so?" I wondered. "I never knew that."

"It is a fact, son," answered Quintus. "Ask anyone who's been on the field and they'll tell you the same. Anyway, I put my sword into the first one I come to. He falls, and I look down and see this great gold ring on his arm, you know. I'll have this, I think, and I bend down to pull it off him.

"So there I am, tugging away on this gold ring, and the next thing I know I'm sitting on my butt end with my nose in my hands and blood gushing down my tunic. Up jumps the brute, swinging his club and yelling to crack the sky. He takes a swipe at my head, and I dip down, you know, but it's close—so close I can feel the splinters graze my bristles, and my hair was shorter then.

"He gives me another swipe or two before I can get my sword up and put it in his neck. He falls, and I give him a chop on the head just to make sure this time. My friend Flavius sees me bloody and comes over to see. 'Here now,' he says, 'you're wounded. Lie down.' And I look at him and say, 'If you think I'm going to lie down and let you steal this ring, then you're a bigger fool than I am, Flavius.' " The veteran chuckled to himself at the memory.

"Did you get the ring?" I asked.

"I did," replied Quintus. "We hacked off the brute's arm to get it, you know, and I sold it in the market at first chance. Got a fair price, too. That ring kept me in beef and beer the better part of a year entire. And that's the very truth."

I told him that all in all a smashed nose did not seem like such a bad trade for a year's worth of meat and drink. He laughed and said, "No, I suppose not. But it never would have happened in the old days. Then we did not get to keep the booty we took. It belonged to Mother Rome, you know."

"But now?"

"Now Mother can't pay her soldiers, so nine times out of ten the booty you take on the field is the only pay you'll see. Get no plunder, you get no pay." He paused, sucking his teeth philosophically. "Still, on a good day you can take more in a bauble or two than you could get in whole campaign in the old days. Save it up, make it last, boy, and you don't have to sweat too much, you know."

The more I talked to Quintus, the more I saw a way opening before me. On the day we came in sight of the walls of Turonum, I asked him, "What will you do now?"

"Well," he said, "after we wet our wicks in the town, we'll head north. The garrisons up on the border always need soldiers. The booty is good, too. We'll stay the summer up there and go down south for the winter. You don't want to be up on the northern border when the snow flies, and Massilia is as good a place as any to lay by and soak up the wine."

"Would they take me, too, do you think?"

He cast a seasoned eye over me. "You're tall enough and strong enough; you're certainly young enough. Can you fight?"

"I can fight," I told him. At least, I reflected, I knew one end of a sword from the other and was not afraid to swing it.

"Then they'll take you—so long as they don't have to pay you nothing."

We agreed then and there that if I found no better prospect by the time they were ready to leave the town, I would join them.

At Turonum the clerics took lodging at a monastery, where they joined other priests from Gaul. More arrived the next day and some the day after. Clearly this council was to be a sizable gathering, but since it concerned me not at all, I made myself familiar with the town instead.

A venerable Roman market town, Turonum housed a garrison which was manned—albeit to only a third of its capacity. I remembered what Julian had said about Rufus' serving as a soldier in Gaul, and I saw no harm in trying to establish his whereabouts. On my first circuit of the market square, I found myself standing at the garrison gate asking to speak to the commander. Thinking he might be addressing a new recruit, the commander agreed to see me straightaway.

"I am General Honorius Grabus," he said. "You wished to see me."

The man before me was a bluff, unsmiling soldier with quick, attentive eyes. I greeted him politely, thanked him for meeting me, and said, "I am searching for a friend of mine. He is a soldier in Gaul."

"There are many soldiers in Gaul," the commander informed me, his disappointment palpable. "It is doubtful I know your friend." He moved as if to dismiss me.

"I was hoping to enlist," I added quickly—just to keep the conversation alive. "I am told he is a centurion, and if I knew where he was stationed, I could perhaps join—"

"Your friend has a name?"

"Rufus," I said. "Licinius Severus Rufus—have you heard of him?"

General Grabus nodded. "Your gods are with you, friend. I do know this man. He served under my command at Trajectum and Agrippina."

"Excellent!" I replied. "Do you happen to know where I can find him?"

"He is serving at Augusta Treverorum. I know because I promoted him through the ranks. A good soldier, your friend."

"I am glad to hear it. Do you think I might obtain a posting under him?"

"It could be done," allowed the general. "I will write to the commander and request a sympathetic hearing."

"Thank you, General Grabus. I am in your debt."

His keen eyes searched me head to toe. "Are you a patrician?"

"My father was a nobleman."

"Do you have a horse?"

"I was riding before I could walk," I answered; this, at least, was little short of the truth. "Why do you ask?"

"The *ala* is our most useful weapon on the northern border. If you had a horse, your posting would be assured." He shrugged. "They will take you anyway, no doubt. We turn away no one these days. Wait here while I write that letter."

He strode from the room, and shortly a servant appeared with a scrap of rolled parchment in his hand. "I am to give you this," he said, handing over the scroll, "with the general's compliments."

"My thanks to the general. Tell him I hope we meet again."

Clutching my parchment, I returned to the monastery. Julian and the others were occupied with the arrangements for the council, so next day I made an inspection of the quarter behind the garrison where Turonum's less reputable inns shared a narrow street. I found Quintus and his comrades in a low tavern called The Cock. The only patrons, they were well in their cups and inordinately happy to see me.

"Hail and welcome!" cried Quintus when he saw me. "Here is Succat, swift to pry us from the clutches of Bacchus. Come, friend," he said, sweeping empty bowls and platters onto the floor to make room for me, "drink with us!"

"I will drink with you," I said, joining them at the wine-sodden table, "if you will allow me to accompany you on your journey north."

"Said and done!" replied Quintus, pouring a cup for me. He hurled away the jar and called for more wine, which appeared with ingratiating haste. "Let us drink to Mother Rome," he said, raising his cup.

"And the emperor's fat ass!" added one of his companions, who quickly dissolved in a fit of laughter.

We drank to seal our bargain and arranged to meet again in two days' time. Pleading an uneasy stomach, I made my excuses and left them to their sour wine. I found a moneychanger in the marketplace and exchanged two of my gold sticks for coins. Next I visited the town barber and had my hair cut as short as a fresh recruit's. He was an agreeable fellow, so I had him shave me, too, and I learned a great deal to my benefit of how matters stood in the northern territories of Gaul.

Upon returning to the monastery later that day, I heard that the council had begun and was already well on its way to drawing up articles of condemnation against Pelagius, his followers, and his teachings, which would then be sent to the pope in Rome. When they broke from this heady work to observe vespers and eat their supper, I sought out Julian to bid him farewell.

"What happened to your hair?" he wondered as I slid onto the bench across from him.

"I have found Rufus," I replied.

"Here? In Turonum?"

"No, he is at Augusta Treverorum, a garrison in the north. I am going to see him."

"Are you indeed? And how do you propose to do that?"

"The soldiers who accompanied us here, remember?"

"Certainly I remember."

"They are traveling north, and I am going with them."

"I see." He appeared to weigh the implications in his mind. "Well, if you are determined, then all that remains is for me to wish you a safe and uneventful journey. Give Rufus my warmest greetings when you see him."

I caught an undercurrent of relief in his tone and wondered why this should be. "We leave tomorrow," I said.

"How long do you plan to be gone?"

"I cannot say. All summer at least. Perhaps longer."

"Then do not fail to bid Bishop Cornelius farewell. We are returning to Britain before autumn. We may not see you again before we leave."

And that was that.

I do not know what I expected, but I left feeling vaguely disappointed that he had not made more of an effort to talk me out of my decision. He would not have succeeded, mind, but I would like to have seen him try all the same—if only to reveal some hint of the real reason for having talked me into coming to Gaul in the first place. He had said it was for my own good, and perhaps it was. Still, I could not help thinking that some deeper purpose lay behind his insistence. But nothing more was said, and we concluded our farewells shortly after that. Although I spoke briefly to Bishop Cornelius, I did not see Julian again, and the next morning I joined the soldiers to begin the long walk north.

ON A GOLDEN, sun-washed morning, eight merce-
naries left Turonum—the original five, myself, and two
others returning to the borders after wintering in the
south. At Senonum five more joined us. By the time we
reached Augusta Treverorum, our ranks had swelled to over thirty—nearly
all veterans and survivors of numerous conflicts, most of whom had served
in one Gaulish garrison or another, some in Britain as well. Several were
fresh recruits, young men like myself, burning to fight barbarians and eager
to begin amassing wealth through spoils on the battlefield.

I did not care about the wealth. Well, not so much. My own reasons for
going were less straightforward—or perhaps merely more desperate. If anyone had asked me why I wanted to become a soldier, I would have answered with a simple question: *What else?*

I had no skills, no trade, nothing with which to make my way in the
world. I still had a little gold in my bag, but, frugal as I was, it would not
last beyond the summer. My prospects were decidedly bleak. In truth all I
was fit for was to hire myself out as a day laborer—or worse still a shepherd!—and that, I knew only too well, would be to exchange one form of
slavery for another.

Thus I had no other choice but to seek refuge in the only place likely to
welcome me at all: the Roman army. I fixed my hope on the Legio XX Valeria Victrix—my last best hope for a future.

After a lengthy march through pine-covered hills, we descended to a
broad valley divided by a wide, slow river. There, on a high mound above

the riverbank stood a garrison unlike any I had ever seen. By that I mean it was fully manned and bristling with military might.

A plain carved out from the surrounding forest formed a boundary many hectares wide around the perimeter of thick outer walls. Although the expanse had been cleared of every last tree and plowed for cornfields, gardens, and pastureland, there were no estates, no villas, no farming settlements. Nor was there a town, save for a mean assortment of dwellings, granaries, and cattle enclosures huddled in the shadow of the walls.

The walls themselves were timber raised up on a foundation of uncut stone ten courses high, and they enclosed a space large enough to contain a parade field. The compound consisted of twenty *castra*, or barracks, for two hundred cohorts; an armory, forge, and tannery; six or eight granaries and a dozen kitchens, each with ten or more ovens; a *balneum*, or bathhouse; four bakeries and a mill; stables for three hundred horses; nine barns, a pottery, a lime kiln, and a score of workshops and storehouses. There was a grand *domus* for the legionary legate and a slightly smaller one for the garrison commander.

We approached on the southern road, marching in a long, straggling, knotted line through freshly tilled fields. "Most of the dwellings you see belong to soldiers and their families," Quintus told me as we neared the large double gate. To call them dwellings was, it seemed to me, extremely generous on his part; they had more in common with cow byres than with houses. "There is also a tavern."

"The Gladius," offered Pallio, a tall, fair-haired soldier who had joined us a few days earlier. "Watery beer, bad wine, and food you wouldn't give a pig." He grinned cheerfully. "I have heard there is also a brothel."

"You have *heard* this?" His companion, a swarthy Roman named Varro, laughed. I had yet to see either one outside the other's company. "Pallio, my friend, without your custom the owner would have starved and his rumored brothel become a kennel long ago."

The garrison was, as I say, manned to full fighting strength. Soldiers drawn from all over Gaul and Britain had been posted to the hostile borderland in anticipation of the summer raiding campaigns of the barbarians. Swelling the ranks of legionaries were many hundreds of mercenaries, mostly veterans, willing to sell their services for a chance at battlefield wealth. Nor was our group of veterans the only mercenary band to choose Treverorum; there were already a number of such groups encamped on the flats of the riverbank below the garrison.

Quintus took us directly to the commander's office to enlist us in one of the many auxiliary *numera*, or small divisions of irregular soldiers. We passed through the wide double gate beneath the watchful eyes of the guards in the towers and crossed the parade yard that was teeming full of soldiers, like ourselves, waiting to enlist. We joined the end of a long line stretching around the block-square building and passed the time talking to the others.

There is good pay for anyone joining the ala this year, they said. Fifty denarii a day in camp, eighty in the field. . . . Two raids already across the river this spring. . . . We are certain to see action before the month is out. . . . A shipment of new weapons arrived three days ago—good steel from Hispania. . . . If you get twenty men, they'll let you have a numerus of your own. . . . General Septimus is hard but fair. . . . General Septimus needs a great victory to grease his way into the senate. . . . General Septimus cares only for his ambitions and nothing for his men. . . . And so on and on. Rumor, speculation, and gossip were the staff of legionary life, I quickly learned.

I listened to all that was said and tried to sift the few good grains from the mountains of chaff. The day moved on, and then it was our turn to stand in the commander's office and swear the oath of allegiance to the emperor, administered by a harried camp prefect to a roomful of men at a time. We dutifully repeated the set phrases, promising to defend the honor, dignity, and person of the emperor and the citizens of the empire wheresoever the need arose, to the last breath of our bodies. We were then summoned one by one to sign the *notitia*, the legion roster. When my turn came, I took the reed pen, dipped it in the inkpot, and added my name to a list that already stretched to more than four hundred soldiers. I was then given a small wooden tile to take to the armory and exchange for my weapons.

Again we waited in a long line of men, until at last we gained the wide bar where the armorer, a sturdy old veteran with short white hair and a belly lopping over his wide belt, took the wooden tile from my hand and asked, "*Pedes aut ala?*"

"*Ala*," I replied.

The armorer regarded me with a dubious expression. Behind me Quintus said, "*Pedes*, tell him. We are infantrymen."

"But I can ride."

He shook his head. "Until you get yourself a horse, you are a foot soldier."

"Which is it?" demanded the armorer impatiently. "Speak up!"

"*Pedes*," I said. The answer was relayed to the back of the long building with a shout that brought two young boys running. One boy carried a *spatha*—a long sword—and a round, slightly curved iron-banded leather shield, called a *parma*. The other boy brought a bundle of cloth upon which rested a new pair of boots.

We were then dismissed to the yard, where no fewer than ten barbers were busily shearing the new flock of recruits. Once more we were made to endure another lengthy wait before submitting to the razor. My own hair was not long, but no exceptions were made, and, newly shorn, we gathered our armor and bundle of clothes and followed Quintus to the bathhouse outside the walls. "There are baths within the garrison, to be sure," he explained, "but this one is better."

We traipsed dutifully through the bare-earth streets to a large, rough-hewn building of timber and stone, where we piled our belongings on the ground. Quintus gave a serving boy half a denarius to watch over them while we were inside. Then we went in, stripped off our filthy clothes, and proceeded directly to the *tepidarium*, where we plunged ourselves into the cool, clean, running water and washed away the dirt of the trail. Because the pool flowed with fresh water diverted from the river, we were allowed to use soap to clean ourselves. I scoured myself with the rough, grainy stuff until I fairly gleamed, then continued to the *caldarium* to immerse in the hot-water pool.

Oh, it was splendid. I lolled in steaming water to my chin and tried to remember the last time I had sat in a genuine balneum. The place was crowded, of course, but it was paradise nonetheless, and I made full use of the various hot and cold rooms until my skin glowed pink as a new rose.

I strode from the bathhouse a better man, for now I was soldier in the Roman army—albeit a lowly mercenary foot soldier. Nevertheless I belonged.

My clothing bundle consisted of a *paenula*—a rough, red-dyed woolen cloak with a hood large enough to cover a helmet; a linen loincloth; a wide leather belt with a hanger strap for a sword; and thick-soled, high-laced, hobnail boots. I wound the loincloth around me and pulled on my tunic; since no one else wore trousers, I did not bother with them, but I buckled the belt around my waist, laced up my shoes, and followed Quintus and the others to the barracks.

"No room," said the *tabularius*, the man in charge of the barracks, a fat Iberian with one hand. "Camp in the field."

"Do you know who we are?" demanded Varro.

"No," replied the barracker. "But I know a barbarian when I see one."

"Barbarian!" cried Varro. "We have served this army for seven years, you blind dog!"

"The barracks are for legionaries," the Iberian countered. "If you want a bed, join the legion."

Varro was just drawing himself up to challenge the tabularium's courage and parentage when Pallio pulled him away. "Come, Varro, my friend, it is mercy itself this fellow is dispensing. Only a lunatic would sleep in his flea-infested beds anyway."

Quintus agreed. "This way, men. I know a place beside the river we can make camp."

Thus began my life as a soldier.

The first few weeks were spent in weapons practice. Each day I joined the raw recruits in their training; I worked until my bones ached, mastering the moves I was taught. When I had learned all I could from the instructors, I extracted more from Quintus and other veterans who knew how to stay alive.

"I miss the old sword, I do," Quintus told me one day. "But the spatha is better in many ways. See here, Succat"—he slashed the weapon through the air—"the blade is longer, narrower—better for striking at a distance."

"With the gladius," offered Varro, "you have to be right up face-to-face with the brute to thrust in sharp. You have his foul breath in your face and his greasy blood on your hands. Give me a spatha any day."

"Now what we have to do is keep our eyes open for a good mail shirt and helmet," said Quintus.

"Without them you'll be dead before the summer is run," added Varro.

"Too true," said Quintus. "A mail shirt will save your life; likewise a sturdy helmet."

"Where do we get those?" I asked.

"From the barbari!" hooted Pallio. "Where else?"

At my disbelieving frown, Quintus explained, "Brutes they may be, but they make good mail shirts, and their helmets are almost as good as the legion's, which the numera can't get anyway."

"You take it from them on the field," I said, guessing his meaning. "You strip the dead."

"How else?" said Quintus.

"The live ones won't let you have 'em," Varro said.

"You've done this before," I said.

"Many times," replied Pallio.

"Then where are your mail shirts and helmets now?" I wondered.

"We sold them in Massilia," replied Varro.

"They kept us in wine and women all winter long," added Pallio.

"The wine of south Gaul is like no other," affirmed Quintus sagely. "A good mail shirt and helmet can fetch a handsome price in the right place."

I accepted that they were right and redoubled my efforts to find Rufus. I had tried from the first, of course, but none of the other soldiers seemed to know him. As the weeks passed, however, I found opportunity to ask most of the officers in the garrison as well. Again no one seemed to have heard of him. In the end I was forced to assume that my information was wrong. Probably he was stationed at some other garrison by now.

As soon as training finished, patrols commenced. Every other day or so, another company of men would leave the garrison to go out to walk the frontier boundary. The auxiliaries joined the regulars in this as our lot was drawn. Most often we completed our circuit and returned to the garrison having encountered nothing more ferocious than a wild pig or a deer. Twice, however, we surprised barbarian tribesmen skulking through the forest on our side of the river. Both times we engaged them at once and drove them back without undue difficulty. I fought in both skirmishes and acquitted myself well enough to begin thinking that my future as a soldier was assured.

Then, one fine warm day in the middle of summer, the army assembled on the parade ground to be addressed by the commanding officer: General Sentius Papinius Septimus, a twenty-year veteran and hero of countless conflicts. He had led the Valerians into battle successfully for more than ten years, the last three of which had been spent patrolling the northern borders of Gaul and Germania, quelling barbarian incursions in brief, fierce encounters.

He was a short, stocky man with a thoughtful, almost melancholy aspect—until he mounted a horse or stepped before his troops. Then the true stature of the man became apparent. His troops revered him as a god.

At the long, piercing blast of the *bucina*, we all hastened to the parade ground and formed ourselves into rough ranks according to our cohorts—the legionaries first and the auxiliares after. We waited, standing easy, as a small delegation emerged from the commander's house. Before them went the *vexillium*, the revered golden-boar standard of the Valeria Victrix.

Foremost of this group, and shorter than the others, was General Septimus. He took his time, reviewing his soldiers, stopping here and there to speak to someone he recognized. One of those he knew was Quintus; I was standing close enough to hear.

"Well, what have we here?" said the general, pausing before the old veteran. "Are you back again, Quintus? I thought we'd seen the last of you."

"Hail, Commander Septimus, it is good to see you, too," replied Quintus affably.

"You told me you were going to retire, did you not?"

"Yes, well, let us say Massilia was not entirely to my liking."

General Septimus laughed. He placed a hand on the soldier's neck. "We will see some fighting this year, my friend. I will do what I can to keep your hide undamaged."

"I ask for no special favors, Commander."

"No," said the general, "of course not." Turning to regard the men clustered around Quintus, he said, "Is this your numerus?"

Quintus grinned. "They seem to have followed me, General."

Commander Septimus nodded to himself and then, looking along the ranks at us, said, "When the battle grows hot, you men stay close to Quintus. He will see you through the worst of it."

The old veteran smiled. I could tell he was moved by the general's oblique praise. "Thank you, General, I will do what I can."

Septimus moved on then and, when he finished his informal inspection, strode to his place before the standard, engaged our gaze, and spoke to us in a low, clear voice, his words both simple and direct. Listening to him, I imagined, was like listening to the ancient spirit of the empire itself.

"Soldiers of Rome!" he began abruptly, "I summon you today not to demand your allegiance but to demand your lives."

He scanned the ragged ranks before him with a stern, unapologetic gaze, an expression hardened by conflict into a flintlike determination.

"Even now our enemies are gathering in the forests to the north. Our scouts have encountered raiding parties larger than any seen in twenty years. When they believe themselves strong enough to overwhelm us, they will attack."

He walked a few paces along the front rank and then stopped to face his soldiers again. "They will attack, and they will succeed. Yes, this time they *will* succeed. . . ." He paused once more, letting us chew on that for a moment. "They will win, my friends—my brave *limitanes*—unless you give me your lives.

"What does this mean?" He stared with grim determination upon the wondering ranks. "It means: Deliver your fate into my hands. It means: Trust not to your gods, but place your trust in me. It means: Do not think about what you will do tomorrow—give all your tomorrows to me.

"Give *everything* to me: your hearts, your minds, your bodies. For unless you give me everything, the barbarians will take it from you, and you will lose it all."

His voice resounded in the silence of the yard. "Every time a man marches out onto the battleground, he has a choice to make: whether to hold fast to his life or let it go for the good of the legion. I do not ask you to give your lives to the legion, or to your comrades, or to the glory of the empire, but to *me*." He struck himself on the chest with his fist.

"Why do I ask this?" he said, gazing out over the assembled ranks. "Because, my friends, if you give *me* your lives, when this season of war is over, I will give them back. This is my pledge to you."

He raised his hands high and repeated his pledge, and it was greeted with a great outpouring of acclaim. Men roared their approval, shouting the general's name over and over again. I had never seen anything like it before, and I could not help being stirred.

When the shouts and cheers subsided, General Septimus continued, "I do not intend to allow the enemy time to build his strength. Therefore, tomorrow we take the offensive in the first of a series of raids on barbarian camps that our scouts have marked. Tomorrow, my friends, the battle begins."

More cheering greeted this declaration, but in fact it was ten days before any barbarians were sighted. Having marched north for nine days into the dark, tangled heart of Germania, we camped on the banks of the broad, gray waterway called Rhenus. Along the way I learned how a proper military force was organized, how troops in the field were provisioned, how to march all day under a heavy pack and then make camp, dig a barrier ditch, fetch water, cook food for a cohort, and clean up afterward without becoming too fatigued to move on come the following dawn.

Thus, after a nine-day march, I stood on the banks of the Rhenus and gazed across the mildly swirling water into the deep-shadowed denseness of the pine forest on the other side. The rolling expanse of water marked the farthest limit of the empire. Beyond the bank on which I stood lay a land untouched by the civilizing hand of Rome. Some of the younger men quailed to see it, but I looked on unafraid. I had lived in a barbarian land before. It held no terror for me.

We established camp in a meadow a short distance from the river. The first task was to dig a deep ditch around the entire perimeter of the camp, heaping the dirt along the inner rim to form an earthwork bank through which there was but one entrance. The sides and top of this rampart were lined with sharpened greenwood stakes cut from the surrounding forest.

This done, the soldiers carried water from the river to fill the large cisterns which had been dug and lined with great leather integuments brought especially for the purpose.

Each cohort and numerus hollowed out a place at the base of the earthen rampart near their lodgings to use for a hearth to cook their meals. For lodgings the legionaries had tents, but the auxiliaries either slept under the sky or erected makeshift shelters using their cloaks and javelins, or pikes. This is what those of us in Quintus' numerus did, and it was not so bad once I got used to it.

While we were making the field camp, the scouts were ranging north across the river to ascertain the enemy positions. They returned the second day with a report that a large number of Goth and Hun warriors were moving south toward a fording place on the Rhenus a day's march to the west of us.

Early the next morning, under a low, gray sky, we took up our weapons and marched out to meet the enemy at the ford.

HEY CAME AT us out of the forest without warning. One moment we were sitting in the shade of the trees at the edge of the ford, waiting for our scouts to return with word of the enemy's advance . . . the next moment we were fighting for our lives. The barbarians rushed in eager swarms, splashing across the shallow water and racing headlong toward our camp.

The trumpeter had time to sound but a single warning blast before the first wave closed on us. The legionaries scrambled to form the battle line— triple ranks of cohorts—to take the brunt of the attack while the auxiliaries flew into the forest on either side of the meadow to guard the flanks and prevent the enemy from getting behind the line or, in the final stages of the conflict, to prevent their escape into the wood.

At the trumpet call we took up our arms and ran to our positions. "Stay by me," shouted Quintus. I struggled to force my hand through the straps of the shield and hurried after him. "Do what I tell you."

General Septimus had placed us in sparse cover along the western side of the battlefield. We filled the gaps between trees and waited for the signal to close in.

"Remember what I told you," Quintus said. "Let your shield do the work and strike up under it. Aim for the belly. Short thrusts. Make it quick. Trade blows with them and you're dead."

Just then the first Goth raiders came into view, rushing up over the riverbank. They were big men, with long fair hair, huge muscled chests, and arms they had smeared with red and black designs. Some of the leaders wore the mailed shirt and war helm, while others wore leather tunics covered with iron disks or rings. Most, however, wore neither shirt nor head covering of any kind and, I noticed, ran into battle barefoot. For weapons many wielded swords and a few had axes, but the rest had spears of various kinds, mostly short and easily thrown or used in close fighting.

Upon sighting the cohorts ranged for battle, the barbarians sent up a tremendous cry: a sound to rattle the bowels and raise fear in the boldest heart. My hand trembled on the sword hilt.

"Steady," muttered Quintus. "Let it wash over you."

I did not know what he meant: the fear, the sound, the tremendous surge of energy? I let it *all* wash over me, drew a deep breath, and tried to stop my hand from shaking as I watched Goth warriors stream over the earthen rampart and across the meadow, closing with breathtaking speed.

The legionaries waited motionless, a rock headland about to take the battering of a wild and angry sea. Facing such a terrible assault, how could they stand so still?

Three heartbeats later the collision came with an ear-splitting crash. Shield met shield, and blade met blade. The swift advance shuddered, halted, and staggered backward upon itself. The solid Roman wall took the full onslaught and did not buckle or break, but stood firm. A shout of acclamation rose from the watching auxiliaries. I cheered, too, much emboldened by such a handsome display of disciplined courage.

The barbarians, stunned by the obvious and utter failure of their principal tactic, fell back a pace or two. Those still rushing up from behind were thrown into stumbling confusion as they collided with their own men.

Seizing the momentary disorder, General Septimus commanded the cohorts to advance; the ranks moved forward a few paces, shortening the distance the barbarians had to maneuver. Pinned between the unbending Roman line and the crush of their own numbers from behind, the Gothi in the first ranks gave out a roar of anguished frustration and began hacking at the shield wall before them.

The clatter of blade on rim and boss reached us as the sound of hail on a tile roof. The legionaries, safe behind interlocked shields, forced the enemy back step by unforgiving step. The Gothi fell beneath the slow, controlled onslaught like so much stubble sliding under the threshing sledge.

Unable to break the advancing line and desperate to get out of the way, the barbarians turned and made for the woods on either side of the battlefield.

"Now," said Quintus, his voice a growl, "here is where we earn our pay."

Tightening my grip on the sword, I hunkered down behind my curved shield, peering around the edge at the onrushing enemy. They ran blind, heedless of the danger awaiting them in the wood.

"Get ready. . . ."

The barbarians raced swiftly toward us, howling like wolves, their screams loud in our ears. They spread out as they came, making for the gaps in the trees. Only as they came in range of our spears did they realize that their escape was blocked. Some checked when they saw us, searching for another way out. Others drove in regardless, screaming with rage.

Three huge brutes broke from the main body of the enemy and made for the place where Quintus and I waited. I had time but to brace myself for the collision.

"Stand!" shouted Quintus, and my shield was struck by a blow that almost knocked me off my feet. My arm was thrown against my body and I fell back a pace. "Stand!"

I thrust my shield before me and resumed my place. The next blow nearly shattered my arm. I felt the impact as a jolt through every bone in my body, sending a sharp pang through the still-tender wound in my side. I gasped for breath but somehow remained unmoved.

"Strike!" cried Quintus.

A third blow rattled my shield, knocking it sideways. I saw the face of my attacker—a dark, bearded, bare-chested giant with a sword. Seeing his chance, he lunged at me again, swinging hard to knock the shield away. I let my arm fall. The brute's blade missed the top of the shield and carried on, opening him out wide.

I thrust out blindly in the same instant—striking low and straight, as Quintus instructed. The blade met but slight resistance, sliding in and up.

The barbarian gave out a scream, clutched his belly, and collapsed.

"Again!" shouted Quintus. "Again!"

But I could not move. I stood and stared at my fallen adversary as he rolled in agony on the ground.

Quintus stepped forward and delivered a quick jab in the center of the chest under the ribs. The brute ceased thrashing and lay still. The sight of my first dead barbarian produced a strange and unsettling sensation. In appearance he was very like the Irish warrior Forgall, Lord Miliucc's chief of battle. And while I no longer considered Forgall and his band rank barbarians, there was no clear difference between Miliucc's crew and those swarming around me now. Could I have so blithely and unthinkingly engaged Forgall and seen him slain?

I had no time to dwell on this question, however, as new foemen swarmed fresh to the fight.

"Eyes up," commanded Quintus. "Be ready!"

I raised my eyes from the dead barbarian as two more drove in toward us with spears at the level. The shafts of their spears were short, and they carried them low. I dropped my shield to better protect my legs and drew back my sword arm to await the assault.

Wild in their fury, the enemy fell on us. The blades of their spears struck the curved surface of the shield and slid away. Ignoring the growing pain in my side, I pushed forward, throwing the shield before me and into the nearest barbarian's face, knocking him back. As before, I gave a short, sharp thrust, catching him in the side. Blood gushed from the wound.

Unlike the first Goth, however, he did not fall. Heedless of the slash in his side, he came at me again. I saw the cold defiance in his dark eyes as, lips curled back over his teeth in a snarl of rage, he stabbed with the spear— once and again. Each time I countered his jab with my shield, and the spear point clattered away harmlessly.

His third assault surprised me. He jabbed with his spear as before, but when I knocked it aside, he swung his shield into mine, hooking the edge and pulling it away. For one brief instant I stood unprotected.

I saw the long spear blade start toward my chest, and I swung the sword with all my might. My blade caught the spear just below the shank, neatly shearing the spearhead from the shaft in a stroke.

The barbarian threw the useless shaft at me and reached for the knife at his belt. He loosed a furious cry and charged behind his shield, trying to knock me off my feet. I saw the knife in his fist as he drove into me and, without thinking, slashed at his wrist.

I watched in amazement as the both hand and knife spun to the ground in a crimson flash of blood. He screamed and raised the streaming stump as he fell to his knees.

Again Quintus was there to give the killing stroke. The barbarian slumped to his side with a grunt.

"Do not trade blows with them!" he shouted, pulling me back into position beside him.

He looked down the line and called to Pallio, Varro, and the others. "Shields up!"

I straightened my shield and renewed my grip on the sword hilt. But the attack was over. The Gothi were already running away, fleeing back across the river the way they had come.

Out on the battlefield the legionaries still advanced, but slowly. They were not giving chase, merely killing the wounded left behind.

"We have them on the run!" I cried.

"Stand easy," advised Quintus.

I stared in disbelief at the fleeing enemy. Pursue them and we could finish it here and now. "But we could wipe them out."

"It is over. The commander will not be drawn into a foolhardy chase through the trees."

"You mean that is all?"

"No, they'll be back." The veteran turned to the dead barbarians before us. "Here, let's see what we can get."

We all searched the bodies of those we had killed, but there was little enough booty to be had. I took the knife and shield from my second attacker and the sword from the first. Varro got a spear and sword, and Quintus got a war helm—a conical cap with disks of bone fastened to a hardened leather surface. "It will do," he said, "until I find something better."

Pallio did not get anything, so I let him have the shield.

After we had divided up the plunder, Quintus took me aside and said, "You were lucky just now, but you might not be so lucky next time."

I thanked him for helping me and said I would try to do better.

"You have the heart of a fighter, Succat," he told me, and then he smiled. "I pissed myself the first time, and it was only some miserable, weedy Daciani. Nothing at all compared with Gothi."

I accepted his praise. "You said they would come back."

"Yes, but not today. I suspect it was only a feint to test our strength. The real battle is yet to come." He gave my shoulder a fatherly pat. "Still, you did well. Two kills, and you won your first spoils."

In all, more than fifty enemy were killed outright or wounded—the injured were executed, too, as a matter of routine. General Septimus suffered the loss of only three—one dead and two wounded, although one of the wounded later died.

That night I lay awake thinking about the barbarians I had engaged. Were they, I wondered, so very different from the Irish I had come to know? Once I would have said that all barbarians were the same under the skin. Now, however, I was not so sure. Or maybe they were after all, and it was myself who had begun making fine distinctions. Certainly there was once a time when I saw the Irish in exactly the same way that I now saw the raging Gothi. And while I had no real difficulty defending myself against howling savages intent on slaughtering me, I could see how, having been mistaken about the Irish, I might now be just as mistaken about these northern tribes.

These thoughts occupied me far into the night. Sleep came long before I reached a satisfactory conclusion. In the end I simply decided to do my duty—which, as I saw it, was to stay alive by any means possible. Beyond that, all other considerations dwindled to insignificance.

As Quintus had suggested, the raid was a trial skirmish, a test of strength and will, nothing more. Our scouts returned at dusk with word that the main barbarian force remained encamped in the forest. It was estimated to be in excess of thirty thousand Goth and Hun, and also Angle, Saecsen, and Jute warriors in ten or twelve separate camps.

I heard this, and my heart sank. I could not see how we could stand up to, let alone defeat, such a force. The numbers alone would overwhelm us.

Nor was I alone in such thinking. As night drew in upon the meadow, talk around the cooking fires grew hushed and broken. Men sank into themselves, contemplating the brevity of life and the certain horrors the morning would bring.

It was then that Commander Septimus showed his wisdom. He summoned his troops and had all of us form a tight circle around him. "Some of you may be thinking the enemy has us overpowered and outwitted," he began. "This is what the barbarians think, too. But they do not know what I am about to tell you: Tomorrow, when they return in force, we will be joined by the legions and auxiliaries of Noviomagus, Moguntiacum, and Banna.

"Tomorrow, when the enemy returns, they will face a force four times that which drove them back today. But tomorrow they will not be allowed to retreat. For as soon as the battle is joined, the cunes and alae of Legio XIV Gemina from Noviomagus will cross the river and close in behind them. Legio XXII Pia Fidelis from Moguntiacum and Banna will close in from the west and east, sealing off any possible retreat." He paused, nodding to himself, as if satisfied with these arrangements. "There will be no escape, and the season's campaign will be finished in one day.

"Victory is certain, my friends," the general declared, standing by the fireside, the flames casting a golden glow upon his spotless tunic and his breastplate of bronze. "That is why we have been blessed by the arrival of the imperial vicarius, Aulus Columella, who has come to witness our glorious victory."

He turned to the group of men clustered behind him, and a tall man with a boyish face stepped forward. Dressed in a simple tunic and belt, with high boots of red leather, he smiled affably as he gazed around at the ranks of soldiers ringing him. His hair, long and swept back over a domed forehead, was almost the same shade as his boots. Aside from the expensive footwear, the only sign of his towering rank was the silver-edged pattern on the hem of his tunic and the slim silver circlet at his throat.

"Hail, valiant warriors!" he called in a voice made sonorous through, I supposed, many years in the senate. "I come bearing the emperor's greetings and his good wishes for a speedy and successful end to this campaign. He sends me with instructions to bring word back to him of your accomplishment.

"The campaign, I am informed, is well begun. I can tell you that nothing will please me more than to behold the rout of the enemy which has so long troubled this border." He struck the pose of a beneficent god dispensing favors: right arm extended, hand open, palm upward. "I can also tell you that I am charged by the emperor himself with the power to confer on each and every soldier who distinguishes himself on the battlefield tomorrow an advance in rank."

This brought an immediate clamor. "What about pay?" demanded a voice from the ranks. The question was instantly taken up by others, and soon everyone wanted to know: "What about our pay?"

Vicarius Columella raised his hands, smiling as if he were a merchant whose price has just been battered down by hard bargaining. "Your pay," he announced, "will be increased according to rank—" Jeers and catcalls interrupted him here; he waited patiently a few moments before he could make himself heard. "*With* appropriate bonuses, of course, and the increase will commence from this campaign."

This impromptu and judicious amendment was greeted with cheers all around, and Imperial Vicarius Columella smiled as graciously as if he had intended offering the increase from the first. The vicarius and the general retired to the commander's tent then, and we all went back to our camps to prepare for tomorrow's assault.

My side, though tender, ceased throbbing after a while, and I determined to fight more skillfully and protect myself better the next day. Beyond that I did not dare to contemplate.

Like the others in our numerus, I slept with my weapons ready at hand. Our camps were along the outer perimeter, and we would have little warning if the enemy tried to surprise us in the night. All remained quiet, however, and nothing disturbed our dreams of the money and advancement we would surely gain by battle's end. Not a man among us allowed his rest to be troubled by thoughts of death. Why should we? With four entire legions and a massive auxiliary force, what was there to fear?

 WAS AWAKE AND ready long before the trumpet sounded. The veterans always eat a little bread and watered wine before battle to settle the stomach and steady the spirit. As we sat and passed the cup, we were visited by one of the centurions moving from camp to camp to give the auxiliaries their marching orders. I listened carefully as the stern, scar-faced officer detailed our part in the day's activities. It came to this: The main body of the legionary force was to cross the Rhenus and move into the forest toward the barbarian encampment as if perpetrating a surprise raid. Meanwhile the numera were to follow in two divisions, one on either flank, maintaining our silence and keeping out of sight as much as possible.

The Gothi, defending their camp, would be expected to mount an immediate counterattack. The legion would then fall back to the river as if overpowered. Upon seeing the legion forced to the riverbank with deep-flowing water at its back, the barbarians would press their advantage and commit themselves to an all-out destruction of the army. Once they were fully engaged, the trap would snap shut.

For what the enemy did not know was that during the night the legions of Moguntiacum, Banna, and Noviomagus had been painstakingly working their way through the forest beyond the enemy encampment. As soon as the battle commenced in earnest, they would fall upon the barbarians from behind.

Those of us in General Septimus' command had merely to draw the enemy into a fight and hold them until the other legions swept in to obliterate them. We would be overpowered and outnumbered for a short time, true, but this risk was more than balanced by the fact that those first in the fight also had first chance at the plunder. If all went well, we would be sitting on a mound of wealth by the day's end.

Aglow with this hope, we ate a hasty meal, armed ourselves, and marched across the river at the ford. As predicted, the enemy was not expecting an attack. They were still in camp as we took up a position no more than a few spear casts away. We even had time to assemble three *catapultae*—spear-hurling machines of great might, if not accuracy.

Then the commander gave the order, and all three catapultae spat flaming spears into the dim, dawn-shy forest. Within moments a second strike followed. From our hiding place to the side and slightly behind the main body of our troops, I traced the fiery trajectory as the spears flew up through the trees. Their fall was answered by shouts and cries of rage.

Covered with branches and leaves, we hunkered down and waited, listening to the clamor of the enemy as they hastily armed themselves and rose to meet the supposed attack. The catapultae continued flinging spears, lighting the gloom with their passing. Soon the scent of smoke came sifting back on the breeze and, following right behind, the first hapless ranks of barbarians.

They ran in clumps and knots, scattered here and there among the tall trees, flying down the gentle slope leading to the ford only to plunge headlong into the waiting legion already formed for battle. The first Goth warriors into the fray paused in their onrushing attack to send up a warning cry to those following, then raced on.

The clash sounded as a sporadic stuttering clatter along the line, first one cohort and then another meeting the charge. The soldiers easily held their ground and even advanced a few hundred paces to make better use of the slope. More and more barbarians were joining the fight now. I could see groups of them coursing through the trees, screaming as they ran. Oh, they were eager to spill the blood of the hated Romans.

General Septimus maintained his position with rocklike tenacity. Even when it became apparent that the legionaries were outnumbered, Septimus did not move, giving our legionary comrades as much time as possible to get into striking position. Thinking that the signal to attack must come at any moment, we of the auxiliary numera prepared ourselves to join the combat.

We waited. The enemy numbers continued to grow.

Still the signal did not come.

"Behind!" shouted a voice from the flank.

We turned to see a host of Goth warriors descending upon us. With loud whoops and terrible screams they came, slashing through the underbrush in their frenzy. Quintus called us to form the line, but we had time only to turn and get our shields up before they were on us. Soldiers on either side of me squared off to meet the foe, and suddenly we were all immersed in private skirmishes.

I saw a spear go spinning past my head and heard the sharp chunk as it struck the trunk of a tree. A bare-chested barbarian rushed in behind the thrown missile. Raising my shield, I put one foot back and bent my legs to take the blow, which, when it came an instant later, rattled my teeth.

Jolted and dazed, I fell to my knees. My arm, suddenly heavy, drooped down slightly. I saw a livid, fleshy, hate-filled face scowling at me, and I strained to raise my shield, which seemed to have become caught on something.

I gave a hard jerk, up and back. To my surprise the attacking Goth came with it. His fingers closed on the upper rim of my shield, and he pulled with all his might to wrest it from my grasp. I flicked the blade of my sword along the edge, catching his fingers. He gave out a yelp, released his grip, and jumped back—only to lunge at me again.

All at once my shield began wobbling from side to side. I could not stop it; I could feel my hand beginning to slip on the strap. Desperate, I hurled myself into the attacking barbarian, knocking him backward. My charge carried me over him. Arms flailing, fingers clawing, he tried to grab my legs. I gave a downward slash with the sword, striking him a glancing blow on the arm. He made to roll away. I saw his side exposed and thrust in the sword as deep as it would go. He gave out a cry and succumbed.

It was then I saw that my shield was split, just below the boss protecting my hand. Protruding from the crack was the vicious blade of a Saescsen war ax, stuck fast in the wood. With his first blow my enemy had disarmed himself and sealed his fate. I tried to pull out the ax, but could not dislodge it.

Before I could find a way to loosen the ax, another barbarian was on me. This one, bigger than the last, leapt over the body of his comrade, swinging a great wooden hammer around his head. I stood firm as he rushed in, the hammer a dark blur above him. As he aimed his first blow, I pulled back half a step. The hammer glanced off the top of my shield and flew wide. I saw his arm swing out and away. In that instant I threw my shield before me and thrust blindly straight ahead with the sword. The blade met a yielding resistance.

The barbarian screamed and crashed to his knees. I peered warily around the edge of the shield to see him writhing on the ground with a wide gash in his naked thigh. He clutched at the wound with one hand while trying to fend me off with the other. My next thrust found the base of his neck. The blade went in, and he stiffened, hissing like a broken bellows as his breath rushed out through the gash in his throat.

"Succat! Here!"

Quintus darted past, calling me on as he ran. I turned and followed. The legion was moving back toward the river, beginning the feint that would spring the trap. Soldiers were retreating through the trees, pursued by enemy warriors roaring in triumph. How soon would those same voices be raised in shrieks of fury at the cunning of the Roman commanders?

We reached the banks of the river. The sight of water sent the barbarians into a murderous frenzy. They threw themselves at the solid line of cohorts, trying to batter down the stout shield wall with spears and hand axes. General Septimus drew the legions tight, shoulder to shoulder, and dug in. The auxiliaries on the flanks drew in close, too, lest we become separated from the main force.

I saw a shaft of sunlight striking through the leaf canopy above to illuminate the golden boar on its high pole. There is where General Septimus would be, biding his time until the surprise counterattack commenced.

But where were the other legions?

"They should have come by now," I suggested to Quintus, wiping my hands on my tunic. The enemy attack had moved away from us for a moment as the barbarians concentrated their efforts on the legion.

"They will be here," he said. With a swift upward motion, he slammed the hilt of his sword against the handle of the ax stuck in my shield boss— once, then again. The ax came loose on the third try, and he pulled it free. "There," he said, handing the weapon to me, "a keepsake of the battle. Now, get your sword up and look sharp."

It was a fearsome yet strangely fine-looking thing—curved and deadly, sharp as a razor, the sides chased with an intricate knotwork pattern. I tucked the ax into my belt, and we settled down to wait, watching wave after wave of enemy warriors beat against the Roman shield wall, break apart, lapse, re-form, and surge again. For the first time I began to appreciate the ebb and flow of battle. What before seemed to me irrational, incoherent chaos became the rhythmic surge and swirl of opposing energies, both dynamic, both defined and constrained by their own natures.

It occurred to me that anyone who realized this and could read the emerging patterns might move through the commotion at will, perhaps even master it. No doubt General Septimus possessed this ability, as any good commander would—probably Quintus as well and, for all I knew, most seasoned soldiers of the line. Perhaps it was only myself who, until now, had been ignorant of this commonplace revelation.

But as I watched the valiant legion meet wave after wave of attacking barbarians, I marveled at the obvious predictability of the apparently random action. It seemed to me that I could read the current as a sailor might read the drift of the sea tide.

"They should have been here by now," I said again.

Quintus agreed this time. "You may be right." He scanned the dark forest to the north, behind the attacking enemy, for a sign of the tardy legions. There was nothing. "Not good," he concluded ominously. "Not good at all."

A short time later a runner came from the commander. "Quintus!" he called. "Is there someone called Quintus among you?"

"Here!" answered the veteran. "Over here!"

"A message from General Septimus," said the soldier as he joined us. "Which one of you is called Quintus?"

"I am Quintus. What does the general want?"

"A scouting party is required to go alert the Gemina."

"We'll go," volunteered Quintus. "What is the message?"

"The general says to tell Commander Paulus that the trap is baited and ready, and if he does not strike quickly, the vermin may escape."

"I'll tell him."

The messenger darted off again, and Quintus called his numerus together. "General Septimus has chosen us for scouting duty. Who's coming with me?"

Since no one cared to be left behind, we all volunteered to accompany him.

"If that's your pleasure," said Quintus with evident satisfaction, "follow me—and stay low."

Off we went, twenty men in two long files, darting through the trees, working our way north in the direction of the barbarian encampment. I expected to be challenged at any moment, but our progress was both swift and unhindered. We reached the enemy camp and circled around it, giving it a wide berth and continuing north, deeper into the forest, whereupon Quintus stopped.

"See something?" asked Varro, stumbling up behind him.

"Listen!" Quintus hissed, breathing hard from his run.

We trained our ears to the trail ahead and heard the clatter of weapons. "It is just the battle," said Varro.

Quintus shook his head. "Not *the* battle," corrected the veteran. "*Another* battle." He turned his face toward the sound. "Our comrades are under attack. This way."

The sound of the clash grew with our every step until we reached the rising bank of a dry stream; in the deep-shadowed woods beyond, we could see the glint of weapons and the confused rush of motion. The air shivered with the shouts of men fighting for their lives. "That'll be the Gemina," muttered Quintus.

"Your message may have to wait," observed Pallio.

"What now?" wondered one of the men with us.

"We go back and tell Septimus."

"What of Legio Fidelis?" I asked. "Could we reach them, do you think?"

Quintus shook his head and turned to begin hurrying back the way we had come.

"Staying here alone?" wondered Varro as he passed.

I quickly fell in behind him, and we swiftly returned to the riverbank, where the battle still raged. "Stay here and guard our backs," said Quintus. "Varro, Pallio, and you two"—he pointed to the men—"come with me."

We resumed our positions and watched Quintus and his little band snake around behind the fighting and come up to where General Septimus was dug in, waiting to be rescued. Whatever passed between them was brief, for no sooner had they reached the legion than Quintus and the others were hurrying back.

"What did he say?" asked one of the men.

"The general says we are to cut through this sea of shrieking Saecseni and join up with the no-luck Gemina," said Quintus. "We move out at the trumpet. And then its keep up or be left behind. Any questions?"

"They'll come in on our tail," warned one of the men, "and cut off our retreat."

"True," Quintus agreed. "But if we stay here, we'll all be pissing in the Styx before sundown." He spat on the ground. "All the same, Janus, you do what you want. Me—I'm going with the general."

We had time but to tighten our shoelaces when the trumpet sounded. The legion advanced, and we ran to join them, falling in close behind the last ranks so that we would not become separated in the fray.

The legion gained ground with slow, methodical efficiency—a line of reapers cutting a swath through a ripe and ready field. The barbarians closed in behind us, as we knew they would, and harried the rearmost ranks.

It is difficult to fight and walk backward at the same time, as I discovered. Fortunately, I did not have to perform this feat too often, nor for too long, before we reached the enemy camp. There were women and children residing in the camp, and this caused General Septimus to halt the advance.

"Why are we stopping?" someone asked. "Let us push through."

"Patience," replied Quintus. "Let the mothers and their brats get free."

"It'd be short work," insisted another. "Give the filthy shriekers something to think about besides."

"It's beneath us," sneered Quintus, "and serves no useful purpose—except to make the bastards more angry than they are already. And that's angry enough for me."

"I thought the idea was to kill as many as possible," muttered a glowering man with a bloody sweat-soaked rag about his neck.

"Then you best leave the thinking to someone better accustomed to the chore," Quintus told him.

The women and children fled the encampment in a flurry of screams, and the legion resumed its slow forward march, torching the camp with brands pulled from the cooking fires as we went. The men complained about the sad lack of plunder to be found in the wreckage, and we moved on.

We soon came to the banks of the dry stream beyond which Legio Gemina was encircled by a barbarian force equal to the one that was now mostly behind us. It took a few moments for the Gemina to realize they had been joined by the Valeria Victrix, but when they did, a tremendous shout of relief and welcome went up.

Septimus wasted not a moment; he plunged into the thick of the battle, forcing a way through the Goth ranks to unite the two legions. The Gemina, though much battered and weakened by the ferocity of the assault, still possessed our best chance of turning the barbarian attack. The joining of the two legions renewed all our hopes for a swift and successful conclusion to the fighting.

"Stay where I can find you," Quintus told us, hastening away.

"Where you going?" one of the men called after him.

"To give the general the benefit of my superior wisdom," came the reply as the veteran disappeared into the tight-packed mass of soldiers.

It could be argued that our position had not vastly improved. Quite possibly it was now far worse. At least with the river at our backs, the barbarians could not surround us completely; now they did. Also, any gain in troop strength we might have made by uniting the two legions was more than offset by the increase in barbarian numbers as the two attacking enemy forces united as well.

So it seemed to me, but I was inexperienced and did not reckon on General Septimus' flinty determination to cut through any adversary he happened to meet, no matter the size of the force arrayed against him.

We stood behind our shields, waiting to be thrown into the fight, watching the battle swell and flow around us. Presently Quintus returned. "Neither Banna nor Moguntiacum's shown so much as a pimple," he reported grimly. "Gemina was ambushed here and failed to get the message to Fidelis."

"They'll know by now anyway," suggested Varro. "They'll be mounting a rescue."

"Unless they've been ambushed as well." Quintus shook his head grimly. "We're on our own."

"And I say they'll come," someone insisted. "You'll see."

"If they were coming," shouted Quintus, suddenly angry, "they'd have been here by now!"

"Not coming?" wondered a soldier from the rear of the group that was pressed close about the veteran. "Is that what you say?"

"I say nothing," Quintus growled. "Now, get your swords up, girls, and look smart."

Thus the day passed; the barbarians continued to hurl themselves against the Roman shield wall, availing little and wasting much. The combined legions took every opportunity to move west in the direction of the missing Pia Fidelis and in this way maintained a steady pressure on the attacking Gothi. Each time the assault waned, General Septimus ordered the cohorts to move out, and the enemy—desperate to keep the legions surrounded and immobile—leapt once more to a futile attack.

We fought in turn, rotating from the center to the front ranks and then withdrawing once more to the protected center; this allowed us to rest and maintain our strength through the long day. As dusk drew in upon the forest, the battleground was heaped with barbarian dead, whereas the legions had lost only a few dozen.

As light began to fade, so, too, did the enemy appetite for a swift victory. The waves of assault slowed, and as twilight began stealing through the trees, the onslaught gradually ceased.

This is what the commander had been anticipating. As soon as the last wave withdrew, word began circulating through the troops. "We move as soon as it is dark," they said. "Wait for the signal."

Water, oat rusks, and dried meat were shared out of the legionaries' pack provisions and canteens. Then we rested behind our shields and waited for darkness. The forest grew quiet—save for the distant commotion raised by the barbarians as they set about rebuilding their camp. As twilight gathered in the forest, filling the spaces between the trees and spilling shadows across the open ground, we watched and waited. When at last the gloom became impenetrable, we moved out—as quickly and as stealthily as possible for upwards of six thousand heavily armed men.

We met no resistance. With darkness the barbarian resolve seemed to have dissipated. No doubt, seeing that all efforts to force a breach in the

Roman shield wall had come to naught, they had decided to withdraw and regroup for the next day. Content to consign us to the forest and the night, they went back to their camps to rest and renew their strength for tomorrow's assault.

Once free of enemy resistance, we moved quickly, falling easily into long files of soldiers, marching in silent lockstep along the night-dark trails. We marched through the night, expecting at any moment to come upon the missing legion.

This we did, but not until dawn had begun to lighten the sky in the east. And by then we required no explanation why Legio Ha Fidelis had never arrived.

42

STOOD FLAT-FOOTED in the pale light of a threatening sky and stared at the shattered remains of Legio Pia Fidelis. Dead men strew the ground—wherever I looked, whichever way I turned . . . corpses and more corpses, bodies like so many broken statues, toppled and smashed. They had been ambushed on the trail and slaughtered as they ran.

Many had been stripped naked, their bodies mutilated: weapons and armor taken, heads and hands removed. I wondered at this, but as we moved on, we passed a tall pine tree along the trail, and I discovered the reason: Nailed to the trunk was the severed head of a Roman soldier.

Further along the trail more heads appeared—at first just here and there among the trees. And then, as we came closer to the center of the battle, every trunk of *every* tree was adorned with the bloody head of a legionary spiked through the skull.

Sometimes the hands were there, too, bloodstained and pierced through the palms or simply stuffed in the mouth; more often it was just the head—eyes wide, mouth agape. They were everywhere. Scores . . . hundreds . . . an entire legion, massacred, decapitated, and nailed up for display.

We came to a clearing in the wood where, it appeared, the legion had been surprised. Here the fighting had been most fierce, and the dead were most numerous. Yet if there had been any barbarians killed, we did not see any evidence of them. Their bodies had been removed, so all that remained were Roman dead.

Horses of the ala had been killed in the fighting, too, but far fewer than

I would have imagined; I counted only twenty-three. The rest, no doubt, had been taken for use by the enemy.

Any equipment deemed of little use had been piled in heaps and put to the torch. Corpses had been thrown onto these pyres as well, left to burn as they would. The heaps still smoldered, sending pale tendrils of smoke drifting through the surrounding forest and filling the dark air with a rancid taste.

We passed through the clearing, pressing on. Thunder grumbled in the distance. Quintus, a few paces behind me, cursed. A few more paces and he growled, "They should be properly buried."

"Stop if you want to," suggested someone farther back. "You'll join them if you do," added another.

"There was a time . . . ," snarled Quintus with barely controlled rage.

The words were still in his mouth when I heard a sizzling in the air. It seemed to pass over and behind me, followed by a curious sucking sound. I half turned to look behind me and saw Quintus standing in the trail, his jaws still working, a black-feathered arrow through his throat.

"Ambush!" cried a nearby centurion.

I hurried back to catch Quintus as he fell. Blood gushed from the wound as I lowered him to the ground. All around me men scrambled for cover as the air whizzed and whistled with arrows. I put my shield over both of us and squatted beside him on the trail.

He looked at me, his eyes imploring me to do something for him. I took hold of the arrow, broke off the end and, with an effort, pulled it through. This made the blood run more freely. Quintus mouthed a word I read as "Thanks."

"Leave him!" shouted Pallio, running past.

Arrows fizzed through the air, striking the ground around me. I hunkered down beneath the shield and hoped for the best. Quintus gurgled and gasped, struggling for air.

"Succat! Get up!"

I was plucked from the path and bundled into the brush beside the trail as more arrows streaked down through the trees and thudded to earth.

I looked to my savior. It was Varro. "Filthy vermin," he snarled. "Hiding in the trees."

"Quintus is hurt," I said, pointing back to where he lay on the trail.

"Quintus is dead," Varro answered, scanning the treetops. "Or soon will be."

"He's our friend."

"Let him go. He would do the same." Varro peered cautiously around the edge of his shield. "Where are they?"

As if in answer to his question, the surrounding forest erupted to sudden life. Barbarians, mounted on Roman horses, appeared out of the morning mist and swooped to the attack.

Soldiers dived for cover as they rode over us, killing as they went. Anyone unlucky enough to be caught on the trail was either hacked down or trampled under the horses' hooves. Varro, two others, and myself hid in the brush, watching as the enemy wheeled and wheeled again, slicing the legion to bloody pieces.

In the midst of this carnage, the trumpet sounded. "There!" cried Varro, leaping to his feet.

I looked where he was pointing and saw the golden-boar standard planted in the center of the clearing where the previous day's massacre had taken place. General Septimus had succeeded in rallying a few cohorts to the vexillium, and was quickly forming a *testudo*. Everywhere men were running to the protection of this close-locked covering of shields.

"Now!" Varro shouted. "This way!"

I leapt after him, running for my life. Arrows whined through the air, glancing off trees and rocks, but I reached the testudo unscathed. Two others of our numerus were not so fortunate. One of them took an arrow in the leg and the other in the back. Both made it to the shield wall, but neither was able to fight.

The mounted barbarians continued to harass the stragglers; many of those caught beyond easy reach of the shield wall were killed outright as they fled into the wood. We heard their screams as the riders caught them and cut them down. This went on for some time, and at last the attack ceased and the wood grew quiet.

General Septimus moved at once to form the legion into cohorts. The auxiliaries were included along with the regular soldiers, and men rushed everywhere as centurions called their divisions to order. This was swiftly accomplished, and the command was given to march. The trumpet sounded, and we all moved out, heading toward the river. I glanced once more to the place where Quintus lay and bade him a silent farewell, then turned my eyes to the path ahead.

We marched into the forest and were soon hacking our way through thick brush. This reduced our progress to a crawl, and we had gone less than a mile when the column stopped. Three big trees blocked the trail.

Scouts were sent to search out the way ahead, and we were ordered to remain vigilant. We stood shoulder to shoulder, shields up, weapons ready, looking this way and that into the shadowed forest. A long time passed, and the scouts returned. The legion was commanded off the trail and into the wood.

We moved a few hundred paces into the forest, and the trees began to creak and moan. Branches began to twist and shake, trunks tilted, limbs plunged earthward. Hidden ropes snapped taut, and all around us the great trees began to topple, spinning slowly as they fell, crashing into smaller trees and bringing them down, too, heaving dense clouds of dust into the air. Order collapsed as men scattered to avoid being crushed by the falling timbers. Many were caught, and the screams of the dying echoed back from the wood.

As the last trunk plummeted to the ground, the enemy charged—horsemen first, breaking through the brush, followed by more and still more warriors on foot, many, I saw now, wielding Roman swords. They swarmed in from every direction; there was no retreat.

The trumpet shrilled two short blasts. In the fuggy gloom I caught the faint glimmer of the golden boar, and I started for the place. "Varro!" I shouted. "Pallio! Over here!" They saw where I was running, and followed.

Upon reaching the vexillium, we took our places in the quickly forming triangle of locked shields. Enraged by the swiftness of the Roman response, the barbarians hurled themselves at us, beating on the shield wall with axes, spears, and war hammers. Every now and then one of them would strike a lucky blow, and a legionary would fall. Mostly, however, it was the barbarians who paid for their rashness with heavy casualties.

When at last they saw that they could not crack the hard shell of the testudo, they backed off and assailed us with arrows once more. We drew in further, overlapping our shields so that no arrow could probe even the smallest chink or crack.

The day ended in deadlock. The enemy could not breach the legion's stubborn defenses, and we, surrounded and outnumbered, could not break through the barbarian mass to escape.

As daylight faded, the dark skies opened and the rain began. Down it poured, cascading straight through the windless air like a waterfall, drenching everything in moments. The barbarians withdrew to the perimeter of the forest to watch through the night and wait.

"They will not attack again until daylight," Varro suggested.

"You know so much about barbarians," Pallio replied, "maybe you should be the commander, and then you can lead us out of this grave we have dug for ourselves."

"General Septimus is welcome to consult me anytime he pleases," answered Varro. "My advice is offered freely to one and all."

"Too freely, if you ask me," grumbled a nearby soldier.

"Shut your mouths!" hissed another irritably.

Nevertheless it was as Varro suggested. The enemy did not attack again.

All through the night we waited, watching their surrounding campfires for any sign that they might try to come at us by stealth; but, other than a few arrows loosed to keep us awake and on our guard, the barbarians maintained their distance.

The rain did not slacken. By morning the battlefield was a quagmire; the chewed-up earth dissolved into mud, and every depression became a puddle. Grim daylight found us shivering, hungry, and exhausted. The moment the rain did let up, the enemy came boiling out of the forest once more, resuming the attack with renewed ferocity.

Wave after wave broke itself upon the shield wall, and when that proved no more effective than before, the horses charged again. General Septimus was ready for this, however. During the night he had men secretly stripping the fallen trees of long, stout branches, the ends of which were sharpened and hidden behind the front ranks.

When the horses reached the shield wall, the soldiers stepped back, the sharpened poles appeared, and the horses were skewered. All along the line, animals and men rolled and thrashed in the mire, tripping up other attackers hurtling in behind them. Instantly the assault degenerated into confusion, as horses stumbled and fell, pitching their riders to the ground.

Seeing the first break in days, General Septimus ordered the attack. The trumpet sent a long, shrill blast, and the legion charged into the gap, leaping over the bodies of the floundering, dying horses and men.

For a time it looked as if the legion would yet fight clear of the ambushing enemy. But when the phalanx broke, more barbarians appeared. Perhaps the Goth host, eluded during the long march the night before, had caught up with us at last. Perhaps word of the legion's predicament had reached the nearby tribes, who now swooped down to be in for the kill. Or perhaps the scouts, so certain of victory, had underestimated the barbarian numbers from the first.

However it was, no sooner did we break formation than the enemy war horns sounded and barbarians without number flowed like floodwater into a trough. The legion was swiftly engulfed. With no chance to regroup and re-form the testudo, we were left to fight for our lives hand to hand.

The soldiers fought handsomely. One after another screaming barbarian went down before the disciplined Roman sword; but for every enemy warrior cut down, three more took his place. Gradually the legionaries succumbed. All around me men raised their voices to Apollo, to Mithras and Mars, to save them in their extremity; they vowed eternal allegiance, honor, and sacrifice if salvation could be delivered and life preserved. I knew well the worth of such vows. Needless to say, our numbers shrank before the onslaught, and still the Gothi kept coming.

I strove to keep up with the more seasoned soldiers, but despite my best efforts I fell steadily behind. I was neither quick enough with the blade, nor evasive enough to make any significant headway. Eventually I was separated from the remaining members of my numerus. I lost sight of Varro and Pallio . . . and then I was alone.

This, I decided, was how I would die: hacked to death by a barbarian war ax, my limbs severed, my skull nailed to a tree, the carrion crows pecking out my sightless eyes. That I, a noble Briton, last of my family line, should die this way angered me far more than it grieved me. Very well, so be it. I determined that I would set the highest possible price on my life and take as many with me as I could. Accordingly I stopped trying to find a way out of my dilemma and began trying to kill enemy warriors instead.

My sword had grown blunt and ragged with use, so I threw it away and drew the Goth war ax from my belt. I swung it a few times around my head to get the heft of it and then charged straight for the first foeman I saw: a huge, fair-haired barbarian with short hanks of wheat-colored braids jutting from beneath his iron war cap. He met my assault with a practiced feint and rounded on me with his spear.

I clipped the spear shaft with the edge of the ax, sending splinters flying. He swung his heavy wooden shield at me, trying to knock me off balance and open me up for a jab in the chest or side. At first I met the pressure, resisting with all my strength. Then, as he bore down harder and harder still, I yielded and jumped back. He fell forward, and I swung the ax, nicking him behind the knee as he passed.

Unbalanced, the brute growled and swung his spear at me—a clumsy blow, which I countered easily and caught him a glancing blow on the arm. He roared with pain, spun, and swung at me again. I ducked under the blow, came around his shield, and chopped into his side. The ax blade struck one of the many iron rings sewn onto his leather tunic, driving them into the wound.

He shouted and sprang back. Before he could raise the spear, I charged again, throwing both shield and ax into his face. His arm flew up, and the ax blade caught him just below the wrist, severing the cords of his muscles. He cried out in fury as the spear shaft spun from his grasp.

I raised the ax again, but my wounded adversary stumbled backward, fleeing the assault. So, replacing the ax in my belt, I picked up his spear instead and, well warmed to the fight, fell upon my next opponent.

Oh, I fought with sublime abandon. The next foemen to encounter me received a surprise when, out from behind the cover of my shield, jutted a long-bladed barbarian spear. I sliced one in the groin, and the other I pierced through the gut; another risked his life on a foolhardy throw of his ax, which bounced off my shield boss. I laid open his leg below the knee and, as he turned to run, thrust the blade deep into his back.

So it was I soon found myself looking at a space of open ground. Across from where I stood, nestled in a protecting bulwark formed by the massive trunks of two fallen trees, battled the last remnant of Legio Valeria Victrix, staunch beneath the much-battered golden boar. I put my head down and ran to join them.

Halfway across the gap a rider swooped into my path. His sword glimmered through the air, slicing toward my head. I tried to dodge. My feet slipped in the churned-up muck and flew out from under me.

The horse wheeled and reared. I squirmed in the mud, struggling to rise. My shield and spear, heavy and unwieldy in the mire, suddenly became awkward impediments to be cast off. Releasing my hold on the shield, I rolled away just as the horse's hooves came down.

I scrambled to pick up my spear but slipped again. The rider loosed a cry of triumph and raised the long blade above his head to dispense the killing stroke. Looking up into his eyes, a word came to my lips. *"Dachnaruhna!"* I shouted, using the briamon as Datho had taught me.

Now, I do not know if it worked or if, in my alarm, I even said it properly. But the word struck my attacker with the force of a command. A bewildered expression came into his eyes. The blade faltered slightly in his hand. I lunged for his mount's bridle. My fingers snagged the leather strap, and I pulled with all my might.

The horse's head came down. Its forelegs slipped on the soggy ground, and it stumbled, pitching the rider headlong over its neck. He landed in the mud on top of his shield. I heard the bone in his arm crunch as he fell. He groaned and tried to rise, the weight of the shield hanging from his broken arm.

I took a quick step and kicked him in the side of the head. The barbarian rolled onto his back. Springing forward, I snatched the sword from his hand, spun back to his mount, seized the reins, and slid into the saddle as the horse climbed back onto its legs.

Once in the saddle I rode straight for the legion huddled in its fortress of fallen timber. I cut down three attackers from behind, then a fourth who shouted something to me as he turned to meet the blade that caught him at the base of the neck. I realized then that mounted—filthy with mud as I was and without a Roman shield to distinguish me—the Gothi took me for another barbarian.

I forced my way through the crush, killing at will. Most of those I struck down did not even look back to see who it was that attacked them, and the few who did could not understand why one of their own should turn against them. With careless ease I carved through the mass of warriors, opening a path behind me.

Upon reaching the shield wall, I shouted, "This way! Follow me!"

Wheeling the horse, I started back into the crush that was rapidly filling in behind me. I urged the horse forward, slashing this way and that with my sword, not caring where I struck. Weapons, helmets, shield rims, the shafts of spears—all met my blade, but I hacked away, striking again and again.

Seeing an opening before them, the legion was not slow to follow. With a mighty shout they surged into the gap, forcing it wider, pressing in behind me, and rushing on.

I reached the outer edge of the encircling ranks and saw the forest trail leading to the river. I urged my mount forward, galloped across the gap, and paused at the trailhead to mark the place while the legion followed as swiftly as they could on foot.

General Septimus and Vicarius Columella, surrounded by a bodyguard of soldiers, were among the last to come. "This way to the river, General," I said as they hurried past.

"The vicarius is wounded," the commander told me. "Take him with you."

Columella made to protest. "I can still fight."

"Then fight for us in Rome," replied Septimus. Turning to me, he said, "Cross the river and ride for Banna. Have them send messengers to Agrippina and Novaesium to muster the legions there. We will push on to the river and cross if we can. They are to meet us there."

He motioned to the legionaries with him, and they lifted the protesting vicarius and heaved him onto the back of my horse. "Go with all speed, and do not stop until you have reached Banna safely." He looked at me hard. "Do you understand, soldier?"

"I understand, General," I said; clenching my fist, I struck my chest in salute.

"Hie!" shouted General Septimus, slapping the flanks of my horse.

The animal bounded away. "We will send help!" called the vicarius, tightening his grip on my waist. I gave my mount his head and let him run.

43

 HERE WERE NOW a great many legionaries flee-
ing down the trail, with clots of pursuing Gothi and
Huns. Rather than plowing through the turmoil, I
reined off the track and headed into the forest. I
pushed a fair pace through the wood, listening to the sounds of the battle
receding behind us. When I reckoned we had outrun any pursuit, I slowed
somewhat and worked back to the trail, where I halted.

"What—why are you stopping?" demanded the vicarius. "Are we safe
now?"

"Silence!" I hissed.

The wood was quiet. The tumult reached us as a muffled din, far off and
indistinct. Satisfied that there were no barbarians lurking anywhere nearby,
I urged the horse onto the trail and dismounted. Regarding the vicarius, I
said, "We are safe now, but we must keep moving. The horse is growing
tired, so I will walk."

"Then I will walk, too."

I glanced over my charge. He was covered in mud and blood, as I was,
but seemed no worse for his ordeal. "What about your wound?"

"It is nothing—a lump on the head. Nothing." He slid off the back of the
horse and joined me on the trail. He took but two steps, however, when his
eyes rolled up into his head, and he went down on one knee. I caught him
and bore him up.

"Perhaps we should rest a little," I suggested. The color had drained from
his face, and he appeared about to swoon.

Closing his eyes, he shook his head. "No," he said, his voice tight in his throat, "the men are waiting. We will go on."

"As you say. But I think you should ride."

"I think you are right."

I helped him back onto the horse. "The river is this way," I said, sliding the sword beneath the saddle. Then, handing the vicarius the reins, I started off at a quick pace.

We continued for a time in silence, myself on foot, the vicarius riding slowly beside me. After a while he seemed to improve. Looking down from the saddle, he said, "What is your name, Centurion?"

"I am not a centurion," I told him.

"No?"

I shook my head.

"Well," he said, "you are now. Your name?"

"I am called Succat," I replied simply.

"Stand still," he ordered. I stopped and turned to look up at him.

He raised his hand over me. "I, Aulus Columella, by appointment of Emperor Honorius, Consul and Vicarius of Gaul and Germania, do herewith promote you, Succat, to the rank of centurion in the Imperial Army of Rome."

I thanked him and resumed walking. He rode up beside me, asked what my former rank had been and how long I had been in the army.

"I had no rank."

"But you can ride," he objected. "You have a horse."

"I took the mount from a Goth I unhorsed in battle. Before that I was on foot like everyone else. I had no rank."

"None at all?"

"I was in one of the numera," I told him. "I have been in Germania only a few weeks."

"You have done well to save me, Succat. I can do good things for you." He smiled expansively. "I am not one to forget a favor—as you shall see."

He made it sound as if saving his life were little more eventful than rescuing a pup fallen in a well. To me, certainly, it was nothing more than that. Even so, I thanked him again and continued walking, content to let the matter rest. But, feeling better, and heady with his experience of battle, the vicarius wanted to talk. "Your family will be very proud to hear of your promotion. No doubt they will hold a banquet in your honor."

"No doubt they would," I agreed, "if any of them were still alive."

"There is no one? No one at all?"

I shook my head.

"A pity." After a moment he asked, "Who were your parents, and what happened to them?"

"My father was a nobleman in Britain. We had an estate near the coast. There was a raid, and my parents were killed."

"A nobleman, eh?"

"My father was, yes."

"So be it! Henceforth you shall be recognized as a knight of the empire." He nodded to himself, as if, having nailed down another loose tile, he was trying to decide what to hammer next. "Could you not have taken over the estate?"

"I flatter myself to think so," I granted. "Unfortunately, I was taken captive during the raid and sold as a slave in Hibernia. I lived there for seven years. By the time I returned, the estate had been declared abandoned and sold by the governor to someone else."

Vicarius Columella professed to find this tale fascinating, so I gave him a much-reduced version of the events which had led me to enroll as a mercenary in the Gaulish auxiliary. I finished, saying, "I had heard that a friend of mine, a Briton from near my home, was stationed at Augusta Treverorum. I decided to try to find him."

"And did you find him?"

"No." I shrugged. "He must have been sent elsewhere."

"Most probably he is not far away. I will find him for you."

The vicarius, despite his superior ways, was not a disagreeable companion. The sun burned through the low-hanging clouds, and the day cleared. We reached the river, where I paused to see if any barbarians were patrolling the shores. I saw no one, so I proceeded to water the horse. Columella dismounted and knelt to drink his fill. I drank, too, and when I finished, I started down the bank, leading the horse into the water. The vicarius hesitated. I looked back to see him still standing at the water's edge.

"I cannot swim," he said.

"Then mount up," I said, bringing the horse to him. "Keep your saddle and let Boreas here carry you."

"Boreas?" he wondered. "Why do you call him that?"

"No reason."

I waded into the water once more. The river was deep and the current strong, but not, in this part of the channel, too fast. I was able to keep my head up while holding to the reins, and soon my feet touched the river bottom on the far side some little distance from where we had entered.

"Now," I said, "to find the way to Banna."

"Do you know the place?"

"I know that it lies to the west."

"That way," Columella pointed out the direction.

"The road follows the river," I told him, "so if we continue straight ahead, we should strike it a little farther to the south."

"Lead on," said the vicarius. "I submit to your wise counsel."

Thus we proceeded—Columella mounted and myself afoot. Keeping the river to my back, I soon gained the road and turned toward the west. We had not gone far when we reached a mile marker. "What does it say?" asked the vicarius as I hurried to read the inscription.

"Eight miles," I replied.

"Come." He put down a hand to help me up. "Walking is too slow. If we ride, we can still reach the fortress before the sun goes down."

"We can reach it even more quickly," I suggested, "if only one rides. You ride on ahead and alert the garrison. I will follow on foot. If you hurry, the troops can be across the river before dark."

The vicarius agreed. "I will send a horse for you." With a slap of the reins, he was gone.

I resumed my journey. The sun was moving past midday, and the air grew warmer. As my clothes slowly dried, an immense exhaustion settled over me. My body began to ache, and my muscles stiffened. I walked on, but my steps soon dragged. Bone weary, I wanted nothing more than to close my eyes for a while. When I came to the third milestone, I stopped and sat down on the base of the plinth. The moment I closed my eyes, however, my mind filled with the frenzied, chaotic images of battle: the carnage . . . the killing . . . the terrible, furious excitement.

Strange to say, I felt nothing for my part in it—neither fear, nor relief, nor remorse, nor exultation, nor anything else. Had I been hollowed out and stuffed with dry straw, the events of the last two days would no doubt have roused more passion in me.

Although they had tried to kill me, I did not hate the enemy. I hated the futility more—the needless waste. I thought of poor Quintus, lying there with an arrow through his throat: dead, having given his life for no particular purpose—the acquisition of a few barbarian baubles, nothing more; and he did not even get any good plunder before his life was taken from him. I thought of the others in our numerus, of Varro and Pallio, and wondered if I would ever see them again. It did not seem likely. The legion, I reckoned, would most likely have been overwhelmed soon after we left them. It would be a miracle if any survived, and, as I had long ago discovered, such things as miracles did not exist.

When I stirred myself from this dismal reverie, I saw that the sun was now dropping close to the horizon. I would not reach the garrison until well after dark. As tired as I was, the thought of spending the night alone in the ditch beside the road held no appeal. I rose onto stiff legs and stumped off once more.

I passed another milestone and had a fifth in sight when I heard the sound of horses on the road ahead. Only then did I realize I had sent my only weapon away with Columella. Darting off the road, I hid myself in a clump of bracken beneath two tall pine trees.

The horses came nearer. Soon I could hear the voices of the men as they rode along; though I could not make out the words, I caught the familiar cadence of their speech. I could not imagine any Goth or Hun speaking Latin, so as they passed, I peered out from my hiding place to see who they might be.

I saw five armed soldiers on horseback, their weapons red in the lowering light. One of them held the reins of a riderless horse. They halted at the mile marker, and the foremost among them dismounted to examine the tracks in the road. "He came this way," he called to the others, then looked into the surrounding wood. "He was here."

The others began looking around, too, and the mounted leader of the group abruptly shouted: "Succat!"

Startled to hear my name, it took a moment before I understood they were looking for me.

"Succat, if you can hear me, come out!"

At this I rose from the bracken and stepped out upon the road behind them. "I am Succat. Who calls?"

All five turned to look at me. The leader wheeled his horse and trotted to where I stood. "Succat?"

"Yes."

"Do you not recognize an old friend when you see one?"

I confess I did not. He was large and dark, his face leaner, harder, his body thicker than when I had last seen him. He sat his horse with the superiority of a general, looking down at me with vague curiosity. Then he smiled, and the expression was his own.

"Rufus?"

"Licinius Severus Rufus and none other," he said, the smile spreading into a wide, handsome grin. Sliding down from his horse, he stepped before me, gazed into my eyes, and then gathered me in a rough embrace. "By the gods' own balls, Succat, I never thought to see you again," he said, clapping me on the back. Then, holding me away again, he said, "But look at you now, my friend, you look like you've been wallowing with pigs all day."

"I have been fighting barbarians," I replied, beaming with complete and absolute delight. Tears came to my eyes as relief and happiness flooded through me in rippling waves.

"You're meant to spear them," suggested one of the soldiers, "not wrestle them into submission."

"We were ambushed," I explained, pushing the tears away with the back of my hand. "The legion was slaughtered."

"I know," Rufus replied, growing serious again. "Vicarius Columella raised the alarm. Messengers have gone out, and the ala is hastening to rescue any survivors. The vicarius requested volunteers to come find you. When I heard your name, I had to come and see if it was my old friend."

He hugged me again, then put his arm around my shoulder and walked me to my horse. Rufus motioned to the soldier who had dismounted, and they both helped me into the saddle. Tired as I was, I accepted this small service gratefully. Once I was mounted, Rufus passed me his waterskin. "It is water only, but drink your fill. There is good beer waiting at the garrison—and a hot meal," he said, climbing back onto his mount. "If you are ready to ride, we'll soon be raising our cups to one another over the board."

"Like old times," I echoed, grinning so wide my cheeks ached.

I was conducted to the Banna garrison—slightly larger than the one at Augusta Treverorum but surrounded with the same attendant clutter of mean houses, inns, bathhouses, fields, and cattle pens. We dismounted in a near-deserted yard inside the walls; Rufus sent one of his subordinates to report the successful completion of his mission. Meanwhile I was conducted to the legion's bathhouse, where after a scrub and soak in the hot room and an issue of clean clothes, Rufus took me off to the taverna where the soldiers of Legio XXII Pia Fidelis spent a considerable amount of time. It was a small inn, with low ceilings and cramped rooms, but the tables were big and friendly, as was the master, a wily veteran of twenty-eight years' service to the empire.

"Cassius!" cried Rufus, leading me into a room already filled with soldiers. "Cassius, this is my friend, Succat. I have not seen him for fifty years! So bring the cups and keep the jars overflowing. Tonight we mean to drink our fill."

"I hear you, Centurion!" replied the owner, hurrying away to fetch the jars. "To hear is to obey."

A group of soldiers stood beside the hearth watching a haunch of meat roast on a spit. At Rufus' declaration one of them turned and regarded me casually. "Are *you* Succat?"

"I am."

He smiled suddenly. "Let me be the first to pour your beer."

He thrust his own cup into my hands and hastily replenished it from a jar, calling to his companions as he poured. "Here, now! This is Succat— survivor of the massacre. He has just—"

Before he could finish, the others began hailing me and slapping me on the back, sloshing beer over the rim of the cup. "Drink!" they called. "Drink!" Others gathered around and began clamoring, "What news of the battle? Tell us! What happened?"

That they should know my name astonished me. That they should hail me so amazed me even more.

"Stand aside," said Rufus, stepping in quickly. "Drink up, Succat," he said, "and follow me. I have commandeered some of Cassius' excellent roast pork." To the others he said, "You'll hear all about it, never fear. Just give the man a chance to draw breath."

I drank the offered beer; Rufus pushed through the crowd to a table in the center of the room. The others gathered around, jostling for places on the benches and around the board. "Get back," Rufus said, trying to fend off the encroaching throng. "Give him room."

Bowls and cups appeared, and the beer flowed dark and frothy from numerous jars. "They're saying you're to be awarded the laurel for valor," said the man who had given me his cup. "How many barbarians in the attack?" asked another. Before I could reply to either of them, a third soldier asked, "How many kills did you get?"

Cassius pushed through the crowd bearing plates of bread and chunks of meat, which he banged down on the board before me and, fists on hips, commanded, "Eat up, soldier, and tell me that isn't the best you've ever had."

I took up a fat, dripping gobbet, bit into it, and, truth to tell, had never tasted anything half so good in all my life. Now, it might have been merely the fact that I had eaten nothing for several days and was on the point of swooning from hunger, but at that moment I do believe that roast pork was the finest thing I had ever tasted. "Magnificent," I declared.

"You heard him, men: magnificent!" crowed Cassius. He tapped the bowl with a greasy finger. "Caesar himself never ate pig to compare. Finish that, and I'll bring more." To the men gathered around he shouted, "Clear off! Let a man eat in peace."

No one moved away, of course; if anything, they only crowded in closer. In between bites of meat and bowls of beer, I began to relate the disastrous events of the last three days—the fighting, the hiding, the marching though the night, the falling-tree ambush—all of it. Incidents and details came thick and fast; the words tumbling out in a rush. The soldiers called questions, and I answered as I could; those at the front relayed what I said to those behind. Discussions ensued, arguments broke out; men coming late to the inn clamored to know what had happened; others, having heard, repeated the tale I had told for the benefit of their companions. More plates

of meat were served, more beer drunk, and the evening sped by in a garrulous tumult.

When Rufus, the last few soldiers standing, and myself finally tumbled
out of the inn, a cockerel in Cassius' yard crowed to proclaim the coming
dawn. We staggered back to the garrison; once inside the gates, Rufus led
me to one of the barracks—now mostly empty—where I was given a bed. I
collapsed gratefully and closed my eyes. Sleep gathered me in and folded
me under.

I slept long and could have slept far longer—but for Rufus shaking me
awake with the news that Vicarius Columella demanded to see me at once.

 UFUS LED ME to the cohorts' small bathhouse so I could wash and revive myself. To make me look more like a soldier, he gave me the red *pallium*, or short cloak, of a legionary, and showed me how to fold it over my shoulder. He fastened a spatha to my belt and then, satisfied with my appearance, marched me to the legion commander's house, where the vicarius was waiting.

"Rufus," I asked as we walked across the parade ground, "why weren't you in the battle?"

"I would have been," he replied, "but I had just led a patrol of six cohorts the day before the legion marched. My division was left behind to guard the garrison."

"What will happen now?"

"Here?" He shrugged. "Nothing much. Troops will be pulled from surrounding garrisons to make up the rosters on the border. There will be recruitment in Gaul and elsewhere. And the barbarians will try to kill as many of us as we kill of them."

"Is that all?"

Rufus shrugged again and looked at me. "But you," he said, "things will change for you—and very quickly."

"Me?"

"You're famous, Succat."

"Famous!" I scoffed.

"Truly. Everyone is talking about your triumph and deeds of high valor."

"What triumph? It was a disaster."

"Ah, but you rescued the vicarius, and you survived. Soldiers like that. We shall all have to call you Magonus from now on and bow when we speak your name."

"You make far too much of it," I told him. "It is over and best forgotten."

"It is just beginning. You'll see."

A servant was waiting outside the commander's house. The moment we arrived, he conducted us inside, calling my name loudly as we went. The vicarius, two of his assistants, the garrison second-in-command, and several servants were waiting for us in the commander's dining room.

"Welcome! Hail and welcome!" cried Vicarius Columella, leaping to his feet as we appeared in the doorway. "Come! Come! Join us, my friends. Wine?" He clicked his fingers at a servant standing behind a table spread with dishes of food and jars of drink. "Wake up, Opidus! Bring wine!"

The vicarius, bathed and shaved and immaculate in his purple-edged white toga and red legionary's tunic, took me by the arm and steered me to a chair beside his own. "Sit with us, friends. We have much to discuss. Here, Succat, I want you to meet Tribune Tullius, garrison commander in Duces Faustio's absence."

At this the gnarled soldier before me extended a callused hand. "Welcome, Centurion Succat. Columella has informed me of your courageous deeds." Dressed in a legionary's red tunic and leather breastplate, he spoke with the voice of a croaking crow. "I am happy to meet a hero of the legion."

"High praise, Tribune Tullius. I did what was before me, nothing more." Glancing at the vicarius, I added, "I am only glad I could be of service."

"Glad to be alive, I should think," suggested the vicarius. "I have told the tribune of everything. Your quick thinking and bravery saved my life. It will be written up in my report, which will be read out in the senate and presented to the emperor."

"There was more luck in it than valor, I assure you," I replied, growing uncomfortable with the adulation heaped on me. "Anyone would have done the same."

"Of course," agreed the vicarius, dismissing my modesty with an airy wave of his hand, "of course. Sit now. Here is your wine. I drink to you, Succat."

They all drank to me, and I drank, too, growing more and more uneasy as the moments passed.

"You and Centurion Rufus are friends, I understand," said Tullius. "Both Britons, both noblemen—born in the same town. Extraordinary coincidence."

"Not at all, tribune," countered Rufus. "Succat learned I was at Treverorum and came north looking for me."

"I did not know he had been assigned here," I added.

"Ah!" said Columella. "I told you I would find him for you. But I must agree with Tribune Tullius. It is extraordinary nonetheless." He stood abruptly. "Now, then, friends, the food is prepared. Let us dine together, and I will tell you of my plans." He raised me to my feet and put his arm around my shoulders. "I have great plans for you, Succat, my friend. There is much to tell."

We dined sumptuously and well on wild duck and peppered venison, quails' eggs, trout, wine, thick barley bread, and sweet butter—the best food, I am sure, the garrison could offer. While I ate, I listened as Columella explained his plans.

"Since the hiatus the senate has become increasingly concerned with the defense of Rome. I have long argued that the best way to defend Rome—indeed, the whole of the southern empire—is to build up the border garrisons, restore them to total fighting capacity." He frowned. "The senators resist, of course."

"Why?" I wondered. From the little I had seen, it seemed an eminently sensible strategy to me.

"It costs too much. To pay for it they would have to divert tax revenue from domestic projects—which they are loath to do."

"Until the Vandals come beating down the gates," said Tullius.

"Precisely," affirmed Columella. "But now we have a chance to make them see sense at last. This most recent attack has provided me with just the lever I need to move a very stubborn senate."

"Attack?" I said. "But it was a massacre."

"Unfortunately, yes. And again unfortunately, the senate responds to catastrophe where they will not respond to triumph."

I glanced at Rufus, who was chewing his food thoughtfully. "I am not sure I understand," I said.

"It is perverse, I agree," replied the vicarius blithely, "but true nonetheless."

"Give them a victory," Tullius said, "and they cut the levy, disband legions, make commanders into senators and swiftly force them to retire."

"Ah, but give them a ripe disaster, an insufferable catastrophe—a massacre," declared Columella, "and the senate will loosen the purse strings wonderfully."

His merry, almost gleeful analysis produced a rotten taste in my mouth. I had seen good men slaughtered on the battlefield, and he made a low political game of their unfortunate sacrifice.

"The greater the disaster," offered the tribune in a wry croak, "the more money flowing from the treasury."

"I see."

Vicarius Columella eyed me over the rim of his cup. "You disapprove."

"I suppose the memory of the slaughter is still too fresh in my mind to allow me to credit it as anything but an utter tragedy for the men who paid for the blunder with their lives."

Columella's smile narrowed, becoming sly. "You will most definitely do, Centurion," he breathed softly.

Before I could ask what he meant, he turned to Tullius and said, "You see? I told you he was unimpressed with the trappings of rank and authority." To me he said, "You will be a most excellent advocate for the beleaguered legions."

I glanced at Rufus, whose vacant expression confirmed that he knew less about this than I did. "How is that?" I asked.

"Succat," said the vicarius, leaning over to pour more wine into my cup, "I want you to come to Rome with me. I want you to stand before the senate and tell them what happened here. I want you to speak up for the men who gave their lives on the battlefield."

I stared at him. "You want me to convince the senate in Rome to give you money."

"For the garrisons, yes. I want you to help me convince a selfish and skeptical senate of the very real need and of the cost their dithering extorts in the lives of soldiers, the continuous weakening of the army, and the defense of the empire."

"Forgive me. I have not been a soldier very long, and there is much I do not understand," I began, "but it seems to me the massacre was due not to lack of money but a mistake of the scouts—a dreadful, appalling mistake, but a mistake nonetheless. No amount of money would have made a difference."

"That is a point," conceded Columella, setting it aside even as he granted it. "But we must not lose sight of the greater purpose and the good that can be achieved. We have been given the opportunity to turn a terrible disaster into a long-term benefit for the very men to whom you demonstrate such admirable loyalty."

"Listen to him, soldier," croaked Tullius.

"I am listening," I replied. "Why do you want me?"

"Because you, Succat, have experienced the horrors which the lack of adequate defense can bring: first as a patrician youth carried off into slavery by the Irish and now as a soldier on the battlefield." Columella nodded sagely. "Oh, they will listen to you," he declared. "They will listen, and they will act. I have gone before them to argue this matter on so many occasions that they no longer hear a word I say. Yet"—he held up a hand to prevent any objection I might make—"let a young man of your obvious character come before them to tell what it was like to live as a slave among barbarians, and how it feels to face screaming Goth and Saecsen warriors in battle, to fight for your life and survive—"

"Survivor of a massacre," added Tullius, "savior of the vicarius. They will listen to you, son."

"Let you stand before them and relate the fearful cost of keeping the barbarians at bay and they *will* listen. They will listen, and the money will flow." Columella smiled, bending the full force of his persuasive powers upon me. "You see, my friend? I am placing in your hands the chance to help your fellow soldiers more than you can imagine. What do you say?"

"I am flattered that you think so highly of me, Vicarius," I replied. "Even so, I cannot see what difference it makes what I think. I am a soldier, and yours to command."

"Then it is done," concluded Tullius bluntly.

We finished our meal, and as we prepared to leave, the tribune called Rufus to him and the two exchanged a brief word. "Well, it looks like I am going to Rome whether I like it or not," I muttered as we stepped into the yard once more.

"What is so bad about going to Rome? We used to talk about it all the time! 'One day we'll go and plunder the sights of Rome,' we said—remember? Well, here is our chance."

"We?" I said. "You would come with me?"

"Try to keep me away."

"Was that what the tribune told you before we left just now?"

"He said the vicarius would require a cohort to travel with him and asked if I would care to undertake that duty."

"Well," I replied tartly, "far be it from me to prevent you from realizing your great ambition to plunder the sights of Rome."

"The vicarius honors you highly," Rufus insisted. "Why this reluctance? Is it stubbornness, or pride? What's wrong with you, Succat?"

"Call me stubborn and proud if you will," I snapped, "but the thought of using the sacrifice of those dead men to further the political aims of an overambitious gadfly turns my stomach."

"Is that what you think? Let me tell you something: Whether you go to Rome or not, those soldiers will still be dead. Nothing can change what happened in that forest. But, as Vicarius Columella has said, you have the power to make something good come of it."

"So, it comes down to money."

"Yes, Succat, sooner or later everything comes down to money. And yes, the vicarius is a crass, self-serving opportunist whose political ambition

raises a stench you can smell a mile away. But he is also the principal benefactor and protector of the northern army. He has fought long and hard to
secure the money we need—money for supplies and arms, money to pay
the legions and recruit new soldiers, money to pay tribute to the tribes who
can be bought off so we can spend important resources elsewhere. The
army is a beast that thrives on money, Succat. Never forget it."

He paused, glaring at me with exasperation, then added. "Besides, if we
had had more money to pay the bribes, the scouts might have been better
informed and the massacre might have been avoided."

So this, I thought, must be what General Septimus meant when he told
the vicarius to "fight for us in Rome." Even as he stood facing annihilation
by the barbarians, he appealed to the need. If the general recognized the
supreme importance of the Vicarius Columella's mission, could I, who had
sworn to obey my commander with my life, do less than give it my complete and unqualified support?

The realization shamed me. "Very well," I said, "let us carry the battle to
Rome and see if we can win a flood of wealth for the northern army."

As we were to leave for Turonum the next day, Rufus set about assem-
bling a suitable bodyguard of soldiers to travel with us. Meanwhile, Tribune
Tullius ordered the procurement horses and provisions, and I was given
leave to see to my affairs. This occupied me for as long as it took to walk
back to the barracks. I lay down for a nap and it was late in the day when I
emerged once more. I was standing outside the door of the barracks when
two legionaries approached and hailed me. "We heard you last night," one
of them said. "We would be honored if you would share a jar with us."

As I had nothing else to do, I consented. Cassius was opening the door
of the inn when we arrived. "Here now! Magonus Succat, hail and welcome! Come in, my friends. Sit down, and I will bring the wine." We followed him in and sat at one of the tables.

"The first jar of the day," called Cassius, reappearing a few moments
later. "A good omen, I think, that the hero of the legion should be my first
guest. Therefore, my friends, I shall bear the cost of this jar myself." He
filled the cups and handed one to me, saying, "Drink! Drink, and may the
gods favor him who favors you!"

We drank and talked, and I recited again what I knew of the battle; after
a while more soldiers came, we drank, and I told it all again. I was on the
point of yet another recital when Rufus came looking for me. "We have a
long journey ahead of us tomorrow," he said, pulling me away from the
table. "You should get some rest."

"Whatever you say, wise counselor!" I cried. To those gathered around
the table, I declared, "See here! This is Licinius Severus Rufus, Centurion

of the Northern Army and dearest friend of my youth! I drink to you, Rufus, my friend. We all drink to you! Here, have some wine."

"Thank you, but I think you've had enough. It is time to leave." The others raised a protest at my departure, but Rufus remained adamant. He apologized to them for taking me away even as he pulled me from the table.

He led me out into the cool air of a clear, fresh night. "Why the hurry?" I demanded. "Is Rome on fire?"

I laughed at my own jest, but Rufus remained unmoved. "You are drunk," he said.

"I suppose I am," I reflected. "But I like it."

"Well, you will not like it so much tomorrow when the sun beats down on your aching head and your dry mouth feels like the bottom of your boot."

"Come, Rufus, let us have a drink together. Like old times."

"No more drinking tonight," he replied firmly. "You should eat something instead—it will settle your stomach. And then you are going to get some sleep. We depart at dawn."

"I hear and obey, my commander!" I laughed again and thought how many times I had pulled him from the table after a night's drinking with Scipio and Julian. We passed through the gate and made our way to the barracks.

"Scipio is in Rome, you know," I told him as he led me to my bare room.

"I know. Take off your belt and boots."

"We can see him when we get to Rome."

"Very likely." He helped me unbuckle my belt, rolled it up, and put it on the floor beside my bed.

"And Julian is in Turonum," I said. "We can see him, too."

"It is possible—although we will not be there very long."

"He—you know Julian?"

"Yes, of course I know him." He stooped and began untying my boots. "Lift your foot."

"Julian is a priest—a very priest of the very church."

"So I have heard." He removed my boot. "Now lift your other foot."

"A priest is Julian," I declared loudly, "and a finer priest you never will see. Amen."

"Stay here and be quiet," he instructed, sitting me down on the bed. "I'll go find you something to eat."

I was asleep when he returned, but I awoke the next morning to find a wooden bowl containing fish and bread on the floor next to my bed. Still stiff from the battle, I forced my aching body to rise, and took up the bowl of food. Rufus appeared as I was finishing the last morsel of fish. He carried a basin of water in which I could wash. "Good," he said, seeing that I was awake. "Are you ready to ride?"

"I am as you find me," I said. The sound of my voice made my head throb. I groaned and lay back on the bed once more.

"Up with you now. Put on your belt and boots and come to the parade ground. The vicarius is anxious for an early start, but I will wait to summon him until you have joined us."

He left me to wash my face and lace up my boots. I then took up my pallium, folded it carefully, and draped it over my shoulder, then buckled my belt, drawing the wide leather band around the two ends of the cloak as well, securing it for the long ride ahead. Then I went out and joined Rufus and the other soldiers waiting for the vicarius.

The sun was barely risen. There was no one about. The traveling party was assembled and ready to depart—Rufus and ten soldiers: eight mounted and two driving a covered wagon loaded with provisions. The horse I had named Boreas was saddled and waiting for me. As I joined the company, Rufus sent one of the men to notify the vicarius that all was ready.

Columella and Tribune Tullius emerged from the commander's house a few moments later. The vicarius' horse was led to the mounting block and held there while the vicarius eased himself into the saddle. "Farewell, Tullius," he said, taking up the reins. "Give Commander Faustio my best regards when he returns. Tell him I would like to have stayed longer, but time was pressing and my errand could not wait."

"I will tell him," the tribune replied. "Farewell, Vicarius—until next time."

"Until next time." The vicarius raised his hand and gestured to Rufus, who called the order.

"Be mounted!" he cried, his voice ringing over the empty parade ground. We swung into our saddles, took up our reins, and rode in a double column from the yard, through the garrison gates, and out onto the road.

We were still in sight of Banna when we met two legionaries galloping for the fortress. The vicarius hailed them, and they reined up when they saw who it was that addressed them. "We come from Duces Faustio," one of the riders said.

"What news?" asked Columella.

"The rescue was not successful," replied the rider. "The fighting was over by the time we reached the battlefield. The enemy left no survivors, and the vexillum of the legion has been lost."

Columella thanked the messengers and sent them on their way to inform the garrison. We journeyed on, secure in the knowledge that the catastrophe was utter and complete. The vicarius would have a genuine, unmitigated disaster to lay before the senators' feet.

45

AESARODUNUM TURONUM SEEMED A world away from the vile butchery of the dark northern forests. A lazy, quiet contentment hung over the city and the sun-soaked fields of the farmers along the riverbank. As we rode through the streets of the town, I regarded the complacency of the locals with disgust.

I saw two women standing before a merchant arguing over a bit of cloth one insisted had been sold to her. "He took my money!" she shrilled. "I want my cloth." The other countered, "Not so! It is mine. Let go!"

A few steps away a man remonstrated with a neighbor for trading in rancid meal. The accused loudly denied the charge and called upon passersby to verify the undeniable quality of his goods.

I almost laughed out loud at the absurdity of it. Ten days' march from where these squabbling citizens stood, a maelstrom of death and devastation gathered force. There was no safety, no protection, nothing to prevent the horror from crashing down on their unthinking heads. Even so, they conducted their daily business with the usual dull malfeasance: lying, gossiping, cheating one another, squabbling over bits and scraps like rats on a dung heap.

"Look at them," I muttered, "the imbeciles."

Rufus eyed me dubiously but said nothing.

"Do they not know what awaits them?"

"How should they know?" he asked. "Do you?"

When I refused to acknowledge his gibe, he said, "What ails you, Succat? You grow more sullen and pigheaded by the day."

"I would not expect *you* to understand," I replied darkly.

"No?" he challenged. "I have fought barbarians before. I have seen men slain in battle. I have marched out with good friends who never came back." He blew air through his nose derisively. "I think I can understand whatever it is that has *you* twisting in its grip."

It was no use talking to him when he became contentious—he, I remembered, had always been this way—so I made no further comment.

As we soon learned, the vicarius' entourage was waiting for him in a large villa the vicarius had rented just outside the city. While Columella rode on to the villa, the soldiers of his bodyguard were lodged in the garrison, thus news of the massacre quickly spread through the ranks and into the marketplace and beyond.

As soon as we had seen our horses properly stabled, Rufus and I went in search of Julian. I had no great wish to see him, but Rufus insisted it would be a fine thing to have three of the old band of four together again. As I had nothing else to do and no wish to be thought awkward, I agreed.

We found the plump priest at his evening prayers and waited until he finished. "Here!" called Rufus as the clerics filed out of the chapel. "Is that Julian I see hiding in that robe?"

"Rufus!" exclaimed Julian happily. "It is good to see you again." To me he said, "It seems as if your search was successful then. Look at the both of you—soldiers of the empire! Who would have thought such a thing possible, eh?"

"Come," said Rufus, taking Julian by the arm, "we're on our way to wash the dust of the road from our throats, and you're coming with us."

We marched directly to the inn nearest the garrison.

"Well, I can see you're no better a judge of taverns than you ever were," complained Julian, regarding the filthy yard with distaste. The Sly Ox was a low place, even by our much-compromised standards, but it was prized by the soldiers, so, taking a deep breath, we held our noses and went inside.

The only light came from an ill-vented fire on the stone hearth beside the door. At the other end of the low-beamed room was a board, behind which stood a tall, thin man with a sour face, who frowned when he saw us. Julian took one look and refused to stay. "I will not be seen in here," he said. "I am a priest of the church, for God's sake."

"Too good for you?" inquired Rufus mildly.

Julian rolled his eyes and grunted, and I said, "It is a fine evening. We can sit outside."

As Rufus hurried off to bespeak the necessaries, Julian and I went out to drag together some of the stumps in the yard. We settled in a corner beside a low stone wall separating the inn from the lane by which the farmers drove their livestock to market.

"I heard about the battle," Julian said. "They are saying you are a hero for saving the vicarius. Is that true?"

"If that is what they are saying," I replied, "it must be true."

"You know me better than that, I hope," he said with a sniff. "So tell me, what really happened?"

"That *is* what happened," I allowed, "but I am no hero. I had a horse when a horse was needed, that's all."

Julian accepted this. "I suppose heroism is little more than that anyway."

"You would know, Julian."

"And what do you mean by that?"

"Pay no attention to Succat," said Rufus, arriving just then. He carried a basket of black bread and salt and three leather cups. Behind him came two rangy hounds and the innkeeper's woman bearing two dripping jars in her hands. "He has had a bee in his boot for the last few days."

"I see." Julian shrugged. "You might have warned me."

The woman poured the cups and left us to ourselves. We drank a little, and the hounds, hoping for morsels, settled close by to wait for us to notice them. Save for the stench of the urine-soaked yard, it was a pleasant enough evening—until more soldiers arrived and wanted to hear from the "sole survivor" himself about what had happened and how I had escaped alive.

"I was not the only one to survive," I told them bluntly. "Vicarius Columella survived, too."

"But only because you rode into the battle to rescue him," they insisted.

"The battle was over. We were fleeing for our lives. I had a horse and gave the vicarius a ride. If that makes me a hero, then every soldier is a hero who has a horse."

They stood and gazed at me, uncertain what to make of what I had told them. Rufus saw the disappointment forming in a cloud above their heads. "Forgive my friend," he said. "He came fresh from the fight, and we have been on the move ever since."

This they understood, and they were happy to ascribe my sour reticence to the rigors of the road. Generously they hailed me, poured beer into my cup, and drank my health. They slowly moved off to another part of the yard then, but others came, and the discussion began all over again. It went much like the first, and when the soldiers had gone, Julian said, "Is it going to be like this all night?"

"I cannot see why tonight should be different from any other," I replied.

"It is like this wherever he goes," agreed Rufus. "You cannot prevent soldiers from talking."

"Well, I have better things to do," Julian said. He drained his cup and laid it on the ground. One of the hounds began licking out the little that remained. "I must go. The bishop will be looking for me."

"We might as well go, too," said Rufus. "We'll get no peace here tonight."

Leaving the inn, we moved off into the darkened lane toward the garrison, which lay near the center of the city. "How long will you stay in Turonum?" asked Julian as we arrived at the bishop's lodgings.

"Another day or two at least," answered Rufus. "Maybe more. It depends on how long it takes the vicarius to conclude his affairs."

"Ah, yes," said Julian, "his family is here, I believe. And then — where will you go?"

"To Rome," said Rufus. "The vicarius is making a report of the massacre to the senate. He hopes to be in the city before September."

"I see." Julian paused thoughtfully. "Well, let me see you again before you go."

We left him there and returned to the garrison. Next day it was Julian who came looking for us. "I told the bishop about your departure for Rome. It is most providential, truly. He respectfully requests that we be allowed to travel with you."

Rufus ran a hand over his close-cropped scalp. "I don't see any difficulty myself," he replied. "But it is not for me to say. It's Vicarius Columella's decision. You will have to ask him."

"It shall be done," said Julian.

"Why do you want to go to Rome?" I asked.

"I do not wish to go at all," Julian informed me, "but Bishop Cornelius has requested the honor of taking the documents which have been prepared both here and in Britain to the patriarch of Rome." He delivered himself of small sigh. "Unfortunately, it seems this honor has been granted." Bidding us farewell, he turned and strode away, his robes dragging in the dust behind him.

We did not see him again until we were preparing to depart two days later. The horses and wagons were assembled, and we were waiting in the garrison yard for Vicarius Columella to appear with his family when Julian, the bishop, and two other priests arrived, leading their mounts and mules. Rufus welcomed them and told them where they should ride in the train.

Next, a servant of the vicarius appeared to say that Columella and his family would meet us on the way. "The road passes by the estate where the family lives," the servant explained. "They will be ready by the time you arrive."

The day was fine, the sky high and bright and fair. We rode out in a long double rank, followed by our wagons and pack animals. Two soldiers rode behind to guard the rear and keep the mules together. The road from Turonum was in good repair, and we soon left the town behind, moving through fields green with beans and corn.

Two miles from the city, we came to another road leading off to a nearby estate. Here the vicarius waited with his family and various retainers—a group of nine people altogether, including his wife, son and daughter, their tutor, a secretary, and three menial servants. The family and tutor were conveyed in a covered carriage driven by one of the servants; another drove the provision wagon, and the third rode one of the pack mules, leading three others. The secretary was mounted and followed the carriage.

Columella hailed us and cantered out to join us on the road. "Splendid!" he said. "The weather augurs fair for the next month. We will make good time. I will introduce you to my family later." He wheeled his horse to return to his retinue. "Lead on, my friends. We will fall in behind the soldiers."

As the day was good and the vicarius anxious to make as much of it as he could, it was not until we had stopped for the night that we met the rest of our fellow travelers.

The vicarius' wife was a tall, handsome woman named Helena Constantia. She was part of Rome's ancient and venerable aristocracy—a fact that could be seen in her countenance and bearing. She looked like a larger rendering of the votive statues dedicated to justice or victory. She was grave without seeming dour, and she was delighted to see that we had been joined by a churchman of some distinction.

Columella's son was a boy of eight or nine, who suffered from an acute fascination with the soldiers' weapons and equipment. He adopted Rufus as his personal bodyguard and pestered the long-suffering centurion to allow him to wear his sword, his dagger, or one of the helmets or some other piece of armor. His name was Gaius and, whenever set free by his tutor, he made for Rufus like a whippet on scent. In camp Rufus could not move without tripping over his diminutive shadow.

Once Rufus tried to foist him off on me. "You know," he told the boy as we sat by the campfire one night, "Succat here was the one who saved your father, not me. I did not even fight in the battle. Succat is a real hero."

"I know," replied little Gaius indifferently.

"You should give Succat some of your attention."

"My father said I was not to bother Centurion Magonus Succat."

"So you bother me instead?"

"I like you," Gaius confided happily.

"Cheer up, Rufus," I said. "He likes you."

The boy's tutor was a prissy old Greek called Pylades. He dressed in a long gray tunic which he wore unbelted and sported a long wispy beard that constantly wafted around his chin. He was given to complaints, which he couched as reminiscences of travels with his former employer, the Consul of Epirus, such as "We always had hot water to wash. Know you, the consul would never allow one day to follow another without a bath." Or "Consul Grabbus absolutely refused to eat anything boiled. Anyone who boiled meat, he often said, committed a crime comparable to treason."

Sometimes these observations, aired for his audience's edification, roused the listening soldiers to ire, and they undertook to educate him in rude Latin; mostly he was roundly ignored. This treatment did not dissuade him in the least; he still muttered and spluttered away, but over time we ceased hearing him at all.

Besides the servants and secretary—functionaries with few distinguishing characteristics—the only other member of the vicarius' company worthy of mention was his daughter. I did not see her that first night; complaining of a headache, she remained in the carriage.

The next morning, however, a voice disturbed my rest; I awoke to see a young woman with long brown hair standing over me. "Are you the one they call Magonus?" she asked, her voice shrill in my sleep-filled ears. "You don't look very famous."

"Do I look asleep?"

"Papa says you saved his life, so I suppose I should be nice to you." She seemed to consider the various implications of this course, rejecting them one by one. "But you look like a tiresome pleb to me."

"My name is Succat," I said.

"I am Oriana," she replied, turning away abruptly. "You may call me Lady Columella."

"Your *mother* is Lady Columella," I pointed out.

"Well," she sniffed, "so am I."

This was my first glimpse of Oriana. Like her mother, she was tall and thin—too thin, it could be said—with a prominent jaw and a high, smooth forehead. Her eyes were dark and fringed with thick, dark lashes. At first glance she appeared severe, proud, and willful—and older than her twenty years; her mouth, however, was wide and generous like her father's. If allowed to form anything but the petulant pout with which she habitually greeted the world and everything in it, then her features shone with a light to rival the radiance of the sun. It was, unfortunately, a secret she guarded close and kept well hidden.

She made of the carriage her dwelling, emerging only infrequently. Nevertheless over the next few days I learned a fair number of her manifold dislikes—most of which clustered around her keen aversion to travel and its attendant discomforts: The road was too lumpy, the carriage too cramped and stifling, the weather too hot or too cold, the sun too bright, the clouds too dark, the food fit only for making swill for swine. The soldiers were dull, coarse, and contentious minions. Gaius was a very plague and Pylades a tiresome bore. Soldiering was the most tedious and uninteresting occupation ever imagined. The dust would certainly kill her if the monotony failed to do so . . . and on and on.

"Do you think Gaius is especially intelligent?" she asked me one evening. The sun had gone down, and the heat of the day was beginning to abate; this had drawn her from her stuffy carriage. She strolled around like a queen reviewing her troops as they made camp. She stopped to watch me preparing the picket for the horses.

"Gaius?" I wondered. "You brother seems clever enough to me."

"He is not my brother. He is my cousin."

"Indeed?" I turned to observe her; trying to read her expression so that I might guess what lay behind her question. "Then your mother must—"

"Helena is not my mother," she corrected airily. "My mother was Lucina; she died when I was six. Helena is my aunt; I call her 'mother' because it pleases me."

"Your father married your mother's sister?"

"It is a common enough practice among Roman aristocracy," Oriana informed me, "which, if you knew anything at all, you would recognize."

"As you say."

She frowned with impatience. "Well?"

"Forgive my lack of prescience, Lady Columella, but what has any of this to do with young Gaius' intelligence?"

She rolled her eyes. "I should have thought that was obvious," she replied, strolling off.

I turned to see Julian watching me. He had the reins of his mount and another, and he was waiting for me to take them from him. "She's a conceited one." He grinned, holding out the reins. "High tempered."

"Yes?"

"I brought the bishop's horse, too."

"So I see." I finished securing the picket line and proceeded to tie my own mount to it.

When I made no move to help him, he said, "I thought you would take care of it for him."

"Oh." I stroked Boreas' head. "Is that because I took care of it last night, and the night before that, and the night before that?"

Perplexity squirmed across Julian's fleshy features. "Are you implying something?"

"Not at all." I gave Boreas a pat on the neck and walked away.

Taking the hint, Julian quickly tied the bishop's mount to the picket line and hurried after me. "Have I done something to offend you?"

"Why would you think that?"

"You have hardly spoken to me since we left Turonum," he said.

"What is there to say, Julian? You are a busy priest, and I am a soldier. We each have our duties."

He halted and watched me as I walked on. That night, as the priests and the Columella family sat at one campfire and the soldiers sat at another, I thought I saw Julian staring at me from the shadows. I know he felt my displeasure, and I know I should have been more grateful for all he had done for me.

In truth I no longer felt anything at all. I rose each day and went about my chores, I ate and slept and awoke to another day exactly like the one that went before—all without thinking much or feeling anything. I was an empty, hollow vessel; my life had been poured out in the forest. Since the massacre I had been little more than a ghost, even to myself.

What of that? It was not as if I had held any great prospects or ambitions before that day. I was lucky, to be alive. Beyond that? Nothing. I saw only emptiness stretching before me, endless and complete.

The days passed. We moved into southern Gaul, and the mountains in the distance grew imperceptibly larger day by day. We passed through scores of nameless hamlets, holdings, settlements, and market towns; sometimes we were joined by other travelers—merchants and itinerant traders mostly—who wished to take advantage of the soldiers to journey with protection. But the only hardships were heat, dust, and the occasional thunderstorm that filled the half-dry streams through the dry uplands of southern Gaul.

As the road rose to meet the mountains, our journey slowed and stops became more frequent. I had ample time to observe my fellow travelers and overhear their conversations. Thus I eventually learned why Bishop Cornelius was so anxious to reach Rome before winter: the British heretic, Pelagius, had been found and was living on an island off the coast of Tuscia. Cornelius and his fellow bishops were eager that the documents—so painstakingly prepared—should be delivered to the pope while the priest remained within easy reach of the ecclesiastical authorities.

46

ESPITE ORIANA'S ABHORRENCE of soldiers, on those rare occasions she ventured from the carriage it was to the soldiers she was drawn. She watched them at their chores or engaged them in discussions of questions she had thought up during the day. All treated her respectfully, of course, since to do otherwise with the vicarius' daughter would have brought swift, long-lasting, and painful retribution.

"You are not at all like the others," she informed me one evening. We had stopped for the night in the middle of a high mountain pass, and I was filling the horse trough with buckets of water from a nearby spring while she strolled the hillside above. The air was clean and crisp, the shadows deepening to blue even as the sky glowed like burnished copper.

"They are real soldiers, but I think you are more . . ." Oriana paused, biting her lip as her brow wrinkled in thought.

"More what?"

"I don't know," she said. "Maybe it is less."

"That would be me," I replied. "People often say I am more or less one thing or another."

"Less soldierly," she decided firmly.

"You know a lot of soldiers, I suppose."

"Enough to know that you are *not* like any of them."

"Perhaps not," I conceded. "I try, of course, but conformity often eludes me."

"Real soldiers do not speak the way you do. You speak like . . ." Again she paused, frowning, and then brightened. "Like a *magistrate*."

"Your estimation overwhelms me."

"You see!" she cried. "You just proved it."

"Maybe magistrates talk like soldiers," I suggested.

"Oh, no," she countered knowingly. "They do not. Soldiers are coarse and vulgar. All the fighting makes them callous and indifferent. They think of nothing but drinking and gambling."

"That's true."

"They are but a short throw from the very barbarians they fight," she declared. "It is not their fault."

"No?"

"They have no time for pleasantries," she continued, pacing back and forth on the hillside, hands clasped behind her. "And they possess none of the finer things, for the life of a soldier is cruel and harsh."

"We may not have Greek tutors and carriages," I allowed, "but we have a bathhouse."

"That is why it is the duty of every noble citizen to offer aid and comfort to the soldiers who protect us from the brutal savagery of the wild barbarians."

"And the soldiers respect you for it, too. I know I do."

"There. You see? A real soldier would not have had the least idea what I was talking about."

"Well, I am not at all certain I understand either."

"Oh yes you do," she proclaimed triumphantly. "You're more like a magistrate." The delight she took in having correctly defined me was a pleasure to behold. Her long slender body seemed to tremble from head to toe, and her countenance lit with a sudden and winsome splendor. "You understand me perfectly."

"That I truly doubt."

"You do!" Oriana insisted. She flitted down the hillside and perched on the edge of the stone trough. "Now, let me see . . ." Chin on fist, she narrowed her dark eyes as she studied me. "Your father was a legate or a procurator or something, and he was killed in battle leading the militia against the invaders who attacked your city. You were just a small child but grew up swearing vengeance against those who killed him. When you grew old enough to enlist, you joined the legion, and you've been fighting barbarians on the frontier ever since. One day," she confided in a low voice, "you will return to your estate to take control of your lands and raise a family of sons who will also become great soldiers."

I regarded her closely. She had struck nearer the truth than she could possibly have guessed.

"Well?" she demanded.

"You are right, of course," I answered. "But then you knew that already."

She regarded me skeptically. "Truly?"

"You are indeed a wonderful soothsayer."

"You don't really think so," she said, growing petulant. "You think I'm just a foolish girl."

"Well, since you know what I think, is there any reason to deny it?"

Instantly angry, she jumped up from the edge of the trough. "Hmph!" she snorted as she flounced away. "You're just like all the others!"

I watched her go, vastly enjoying the sight and wondering: How did she know about me? Her speculation was extremely close to the mark. I pondered this as I resumed filling the trough—until I remembered that the family often took meals with the priests. She had probably got most of what she had guessed about me from Julian.

This was the first of a lengthy series of sparring matches between Oriana and myself. Why she picked on me, I cannot say. Perhaps, as she had suggested, she found me different from the other soldiers and determined to make of me a pet she might groom and primp. I found her curiously amusing: charming and flattering one moment, outraged the next—there was no possibility of predicting what she might say or do. Pampered from infancy and indulged by a blindly doting father who obliged every whim, her life a daily round of privilege, comfort, and ease—she knew nothing of want, adversity, or distress. Oriana was a flower raised in a walled garden, protected from every errant wind, grown to grace the palace of some rich and powerful Roman aristocrat.

As the long journey proceeded, the stringent barriers between the soldier escort and the rest of the traveling party gradually broke down. I often rode with the vicarius, the bishop, or one of the priests. With nothing else to do, we talked—often about nothing in particular. Occasionally, however, something of larger import surfaced.

One day I found myself riding behind Bishop Cornelius and Lady Helena, who had exchanged her place in the carriage for Julian's saddle; they were deep into a discussion which I overheard in snips and snatches—nothing that interested me, but apparently it exercised them greatly. All at once the bishop turned in the saddle, saw me, and said, "Look, here is Succat. Let us see what he thinks."

"Very well," replied Helena, glancing over her shoulder, "ask him."

"Succat," called the bishop, "come up and join us. I want to talk to you."

I obeyed, reining in beside him. "I am at your service, Bishop."

"The question is this: Do you think it advisable for priests to marry?"

"Why ask me?"

"Your grandfather was a priest."

"He was, yes."

"So you must have an opinion on the matter."

"It is my opinion that if priests were not allowed to marry, I would not be here. Therefore I am inclined to regard priestly marriage in a favorable light."

"Well said," replied Helena with a nod. "I have been telling this puffed-up priest much the same thing myself. It is not for priests to play God when they know so little about being men."

" 'Puffed-up?' " wondered Cornelius. "I hope you don't mean that. I simply put forward the observation that unmarried priests may devote the greater portion of their earthly allotted time to the pursuit of higher things."

"Come now, dear Cornelius," protested Helena lightly. "Priests are mortal men, are they not? Without the abiding presence of a good woman to help and guide, men quickly descend to the unfettered indulgence of their baser ambitions." Her lips curved in a sweet smile as she delivered her killing stroke. "The only things I see pursued by priests are wealth and power. I strongly suspect that the reason for the church's present aversion to marriage is so that you priests are free to do as you please without having to explain yourselves to anyone."

Turning to me, she said, "Tell me, Magonus, what sort of priest was your grandfather?"

"I honestly have no idea," I told her. "I remember him as a stern man much given to clouting people with his stick when they transgressed."

"Good!" She laughed. "I would have liked to have seen that. It makes a change from the usual sanctimony and simpering."

Cornelius grimaced but held his tongue.

"My grandfather thought his flock weak-willed and largely unworthy of the honor God had paid them in dying for their sins. He always said that men loved sinning more than they loved virtue; otherwise we would have seen the Heavenly Kingdom established long since."

"He sounds like a man who knew a thing or two."

"He sounds, my dear friends," huffed the bishop, "like a true Pelagian."

"Oh, Pelagius again!" scoffed Helena. "You think everyone who disagrees with you is a Pelagian. Tell me, if you can, what you find so repugnant about this poor man that you should persecute him so."

"No," replied Cornelius crisply. "No, I will not be drawn into *that* discussion with you. These are weighty matters and not to be bandied about for the sake of idle amusement."

Helena refused to be put off. "You don't like Pelagius," she declared, "because he dares to question the practices of a priesthood grown too fat and lazy for its own good."

The bishop frowned. "Lady Columella," he said, "one would almost think you a follower of the noxious monk yourself."

"And what if I were?"

"I would pray for you, of course—that you would soon realize the error of your ways and renounce his infernal teaching."

"It is true I have heard him speak," confessed Helena. "His greatest concern was that the high and mighty who came to him should daily practice the faith they professed in their assemblies, lest the name of Christ become an emblem of shame and derision. I found him refreshing—inspiring. A more intelligent and humble priest I am certain I have never met."

"The devil himself has the power to beguile, Lady Columella."

"You condemn him, Bishop. Yet you have not elucidated what you find so offensive in his teaching."

"I do condemn him. For a start he advocates preaching the Gospel of Christ to barbarians—an enterprise fraught with danger to all concerned. As we know—and as our Holy Father the pope has decreed—to enlighten barbarians to salvation merely makes them ripe for damnation."

"Indeed, Bishop?" I countered. "How so?"

"My son, it is obvious, is it not? The barbarian mind is not sufficiently developed to appreciate, much less understand, the loftier concepts that faith naturally entails. Lacking the humanizing influences of civilization, barbarians are foredoomed to remain savages. Introducing them to a faith they can neither comprehend nor honor is cruelty itself, for once the Gospel has been heard, men come under its judgment. The judgment for all who fall short is eternal damnation."

"Suppose they heard and understood," I said, "repented and went away rejoicing. What then?"

"No better," sniffed the bishop. "They have no cities, no government, and thus no way of ensuring a dependable propagation of correct doctrine." He shook his head gravely. "Even if it were somehow possible that they might be persuaded of the truth of the faith, they would soon be floundering in error of every kind and wholly unable to extricate themselves."

"Better they should die in ignorance," I replied, taking up the thread of his argument, "than grasp at a salvation they can never possess."

"Precisely!" said the churchman. "Some vessels, as we know, are made for destruction."

"I beg your pardon, Bishop," I said, "but you know precisely nothing about the barbarian mind. You have no idea what they may be capable of comprehending."

"I can see where you might hold such beliefs," he said, taking on an air of superiority. To Helena he said, "Our friend Succat spent some time among barbarians. Such close familiarity has addled his perceptions."

"If you mean I know how they think and what they might be able to understand, I do freely confess it. You will find among them men as intelligent and discerning as any to be found in the more civilized nations."

"You hold a most passionate view," remarked Lady Columella. "How long did you live among the barbarians?"

"Seven years," I told her, "I was taken captive in a raid and made a slave to an Irish king."

"Seven years is a long time, Bishop. It would seem our friend had ample opportunity to observe them in all their ways. Have *you* ever lived among barbarians, Bishop Cornelius?"

"Indeed no. I did, however, serve for many years in the north of Britain, where barbarians were not unknown."

"I see," replied Helena. "So it would seem that Centurion Succat's convictions have a sound basis in experience, while yours are mere conjecture."

"I protest," the bishop spluttered. "I do think your assessment harsh and simplistic."

"Be that as it may," continued Lady Columella, blithely impervious to his objection, "it seems to me that you would do well to listen to this man and heed him."

"I am happy to consider your views, of course, but you must admit—" began the bishop.

"Further, from what I have seen, the Christian priests of Rome are interested in nothing so much as protecting their lofty and influential position and fomenting nonsensical feuds with anyone bold enough to oppose them. I think they would be far better employed preaching the good news to the barbarians. They might even learn a useful thing or two."

"You are entitled to your opinion," declared the bishop stiffly, adding, "an opinion shaped by the rebellious Pelagius himself, no doubt."

"You see?" crowed Helena. "I offer a contrary opinion and you instantly condemn the same as heretical simply because it differs from your own. That is hardly fair, I must say." She turned to smile at me before directing a last blow to the bishop. "Perhaps you might cultivate some of the tolerance shown by our dear friend Succat. Of any of us, he alone would have ample justification and knowledge to judge the barbarians, yet he does not. I think that indicates an admirable fortitude of character."

Her lavish praise embarrassed me. Regardless, I knew I had made a powerful new ally and friend. From that moment, I entered an exalted position within that family, one I could never have foreseen. In the Columellas' eyes I could do no wrong.

Thereafter I noticed a distinct improvement in my rank within the traveling party. The Columellas invited me to join them at meals, and the vicarius sought my views on diverse matters pertaining to the provinces, especially Britain. In short, my star rose in the heavens of their good opinion.

By the time we reached Rome, I was almost a member of the family. Two months later I was.

47

HERE IT IS, Succat," said Vicarius Columella, indicating the gleaming bowl of the valley with a wide sweep of his arm. "The greatest city in the world."

Leaning forward in the saddle, as if to bring the sight that much closer, I gazed upon the dazzling, sun-drenched sprawl—the deep, ruddy glow of tile and brick; the sparkling glint of whitewashed walls; the dull gleam of the Tiber snaking through. . . . All my life I had heard the word "Roma"—it had passed my lips a thousand times—but never once had I imagined that such a simple word could signify anything so staggeringly, prodigiously, gloriously vast.

"It is dazzling," I said. "Truly dazzling."

"Mother of Nations," intoned Bishop Cornelius tartly. "Whore Queen, Bitch Goddess."

"Come now, Bishop," chided Columella. "Its glory may be somewhat tarnished, but it is never so terrible as all that."

The vicarius pointed to the foremost prominence. "That is Capitoline Hill, and rising behind it is Palatine Hill; next to that is the Aventine Hill, with the Caelian just behind." He shifted his hand slightly to indicate a broad plateau to the east with three projections like stubby fingers. "There is the Quirinal, the Viminal, and the Esquiline. You see? The famed Seven Hills of Rome."

"It is wonderful," I said, staring intently at the staggering immensity of the city spreading before me. A silvery haze of smoke and dust hung over the entire valley, causing the city to shimmer softly in the hard midday sunlight.

"Succat," said Columella, "you are going to enjoy Rome, and I am going to enjoy showing it to you."

He lifted his hand to signal those behind, and we started down the long, sloping road into the shallow Tiber valley and the sprawling city itself—so various, so grand, so impossibly opulent as to make every other place I had ever seen seem like a mud wallow.

The city had long ago grown beyond its protecting walls, and soon we were passing through a district of low houses and hovels: the dwellings of craftsmen, servants, and day laborers. Men, women, and children came running when they saw our company, offering us bundles of ripe figs, olives, and jars of wine. Vicarius Columella, out of the generosity of his rank, purchased figs, dried beans, and olives as we rode along, dispersing coins to the merchants and their ragged children.

Ignoring the cries of the street vendors, we pushed on through the clamor to the high, gated walls, joining the steady stream of carts, barrows, donkeys, mules, and foot traffic pouring through the Flaminia Gate and into the city. The noise was tremendous and the sights overwhelming. Everywhere I looked, some new wonder met my astonished gaze: theaters, palaces, villas, and houses without number.

"It is not what it was, of course," said Lord Columella sadly. "The Vandali destroyed whatever they could not carry away. Much has been restored, but there is a very great deal of rebuilding to be done even now. One day, however, Rome will regain her former grandeur."

The bishop overheard this and delivered himself of a hearty snort of derision.

"Oh, it is easy enough to scoff," the vicarius continued. "But I believe that Rome has yet to reach her pinnacle."

We rode for what seemed half a day before finally reaching the wide, rising street which climbed the slope of Palatine Hill, where the vicarius maintained his city residence: a grand *domus*, or town house, not far from the Curia Julia, where the senate met. The street was lined with princely houses of the principal families of Rome—all white stone and red tile, with ironwork at the windows, carved columns, and statuary in the pediments.

Domus Columella presented a plain, almost drab, buff-colored exterior to the street; inside, it was a palace with mosaics in the vestibule and corridors of dark brown marble, walls painted red or blue or yellow or decorated with frescoes of country scenes: grapes ripening on the vine with Mount Aetna looming in the background, workers harvesting a golden field of grain, oxen pulling a cart down through an olive grove.

A rider had gone ahead to warn the household servants, so we were met at the door with welcome cups of cool, sweet wine and small parcels of

ground meat wrapped in honey-glazed pastry. After eating a few of these, I
was led by a servant to my room in a remote part of the house. Apart from
the size, which was more than bountiful, the room was remarkably like the
one I had known in my father's house. The walls were dark blue below and
pale yellow above, and the floor was covered with red-brown tiles over
which were placed rugs of woven wool. The wall across from the bed was
occupied by a single large window that was closed by sturdy, ironbound
shutters. When I opened them, I found myself looking down into a tidy
square courtyard containing a single tall pine tree in the center, numerous
flowering plants in long stone troughs, and in one corner a large marble box
into which water splashed from the mouth of a white alabaster swan spreading its wings from a blue-flowered niche above.

The day was hot, but my room was cool, and I instantly felt myself at
home. *I was born to this*, I thought. *I belong here.*

Bishop Cornelius and his retinue did not remain with us; after refreshing
themselves, they were conducted to the Church of St. John Lateran, where
they were given lodgings in the extensive clutch of dwellings surrounding
the great basilica. The soldiers were afforded quarters in the Praetorian garrison. I would have been happy enough to go with them—I was still a soldier under command, after all—but the vicarius wished me to remain with
him. "I need you, Succat," he told me, "and I will not have you out of my
sight."

"You are too kind, Vicarius," I replied. "But it is my duty to report to the
commander of the garrison."

"Of course," he agreed. "Yet since I, as Vicarius of Gaul and Germania,
am your commanding officer, you may consider yourself under my authority during your stay in Rome."

My commander's rule was light, however, and I was given free rein to
wander about the city as I would—an opportunity I eagerly grasped. In
those first heady days, I walked the streets of Rome in a continual state of
wonder, gazing upon one extravagance of human endeavor after another:
the Forum Romanum and the Forum Augustum—with their basilicas,
markets, shops, stalls, and magisterial buildings—either of which could
have served as capital city for any nation the world over; temples without
number and monuments to gods whose names I had never heard before:
Temple of Vesta, Temple of Concord, Temple of Saturn, Temple of Venus
Genetrix, Temple of Mars Ultor, Temple of Caesar, Temple of Claudius,
and many another I could not name.

Everywhere I went, I was met by a continual throng of people—most of
them selling something: roast fowl on skewers, boiled eggs, cakes freshly
baked on a griddle; live ducks, piglets, goats, puppies; shoes, belts, hats

made of straw; bowls, cups, and plates made of olive wood, pottery, brass, copper; bracelets of leather, ivory, or silver; tiny bronze votive figures and candles in the shapes of arms, legs, eyes, heads, or entire human figures. These last were meant to be offered in the temples for the healing of particular ailments—a degenerate practice, according to Grandfather Potitus.

One day the vicarius took me to see the Colosseum and, near it, the Baths of Trajan. "There are no games just now," he explained as we strolled in the cool shadow of the enormous curving wall, "and the last gladiator display was over twenty years ago—although, if you are lucky, we might be able to see a wild animal combat while you are here. We could go to one if you like."

I thanked him but declined, saying I had seen enough of combat to last me the rest of my life.

He accepted this genially and asked, "Do you feel the same way about baths?"

"Indeed I do not. My father considered a good bath the very apex of civilization, and I agree."

"Splendid! Then follow me, and I will show you the best bath in the entire world."

For a nominal fee—a few small coins—we were treated to a most luxuriant and refreshing afternoon in the extraordinary baths constructed in honor of Emperor Trajan. The intricately connected domes, halls, and basilicas were covered floor to ceiling with so many murals that I could not take them in. There were shops and exercise halls, spectator galleries where men could relax and discuss business or the events of the day, and rooms where bathers could receive the ministrations of Greek slaves trained in the art of massage. In addition to the usual cold and hot pools, there were plunge pools, swimming pools, and numerous fountains with dolphin-riding nymphs sculpted in gold.

Mosaics adorned every floor and quavered beneath the surface of the enormous swimming pool, too. There was even a library where patrons could select books to read while they rested or refreshed themselves in one of the dining rooms.

"The senate will meet in three weeks' time," Columella told me as we basked in the warm water of the caldarium. "We must prepare what we will say to them."

"My Lord Vicarius—"

"Aulus—always, please—for the man who saved my life."

"I will be more than happy to tell the senate anything—whatever you desire, tell me, and I will say it."

"Your reply is most gratifying," he answered, then paused for a long moment to ponder. "First, I think I would have you speak of your life in Britain before the raid in which you lost your parents, then the raid itself, of course, and your time as a slave in Hibernia."

"Very well," I agreed, "if you believe that it will help."

"Oh, it will. It will," he assured me. "Once you have pricked the senators' interest, then I would like you to tell of the battle." He fell silent, considering how to proceed. "Yes," he said at last. "I would have you tell them what it was like to fight as a soldier on that dire day—what it is like to stand on the line with sword in hand as shrieking barbarians thunder down upon you, to fight and kill, to see friends and comrades slaughtered by your side, and to escape with your life. I would have them hear from the lips of a soldier what unnecessary distress their perpetual vacillation and miserly ways have brought to our fighting men."

"Then that is what they will hear," I told him.

Lady Columella decided that I should take meals at the family table; my initial reluctance melted before her insistence. She also saw to it that my clothes were appropriate for the higher society in which I found myself. Indeed she seemed determined that my sojourn in Rome should be as a member of the ruling aristocracy. She took me under her wing to polish my long-corroded speech and manners so that I might blend more easily among the refined Roman populace. "It is very important," she told me, "not to be thought a rustic from the provinces."

"I *am* a rustic from the provinces," I pointed out.

"Of course, but you need not publish the fact in word and deed to everyone you meet. Let them find out *after* they have had a chance to meet you and assess your character and abilities."

To please her I undertook my tutelage in all seriousness—with the result that very soon I not only looked like a genuine Roman, but I could act like one, too. I moved more easily among the city's elite, and my confidence soared accordingly. This in turn produced a curious change in Oriana. She grew less flighty and capricious and, so it seemed, more charitable in her opinion of me.

She often sought me out either just before or immediately after the evening meal. We would talk, and she would ask my opinions of inconsequential things: whether I preferred a town house or a villa, what was the best time of the year, the way my father governed our estate, how my mother used to make bread, whether I considered soldiering a noble profession . . . and many other such topics. Trivial they might have been, but Oriana took them seriously and listened carefully to all I said—though of course she argued with most of it on principle.

"What possible difference can it make to you how my mother made bread?"

Oriana shrugged. "None at all. I only want to know."

"Why? Are you going to make bread for me?"

"Would that be so terrible?"

I paused, sensing a change in her voice. "Well, I can think of worse things, perhaps."

"You think me a poor cook?" she challenged.

"Lady, I have no opinion whatever on the matter," I declared.

"No?" She regarded me from under arched brows.

"How could I? You know I have never eaten anything you prepared. Anyway, why is it so important what I think?"

She made no reply.

"Well?"

"I know," she said brightly. "I shall prepare a meal for you, and then you can judge."

"If you like," I allowed cautiously. "But I still do not see why it matters even the smallest scrap what I think about y—"

"Tomorrow evening," she decided. "I will make Numidian chicken."

"If it pleases you to make it," I acquiesced, "I will eat it."

The next day I did not see Oriana before I left the house on yet one more excursion into the city. I walked the meandering streets of the older section below the Palatine Hill, an area of small dwellings for people of more humble means. Around midday I found a shady spot under a tree in the extremely modest Forum of Nerva. There was a small fountain, which no longer worked, but I whiled away the day watching children frolic in the dry basin and listening to a boy play a lyre. On my way back to the house, I strolled through a *cuppedinis,* or dainties market, where all sorts of trifles and sweetmeats were sold. On a whimsy I bought Oriana a length of blue silk ribbon from an old woman who wove the stuff herself.

Upon returning to the house, I discovered the place deserted save for one elderly servant and, in the kitchen, Oriana herself. She forbade me entrance, pushing me from the room before I entered, saying, "You're too early. Go wash yourself and change your clothes."

"And then?"

"Find someplace to wait. Just go!" she cried, rushing back to the raised hearth, where a pot was splattering its contents into the fire, creating a black smoke pall which gathered on the ceiling.

I went to my room, poured water into the basin, undressed, and washed away the dust of the city. Then I put on a fresh tunic, covering it with a clean white linen pallium. My shoes were dusty, so I went out into the courtyard to rinse them in the water splashing from the swan's head. As I finished tying up the laces, I heard a light step on the stones and raised my head to see Oriana coming toward me with a fully laden tray in her hands.

Her face was flushed with the heat of the kitchen; there was a fine mist of sweat on her brow, and her tunic was stained with oil spatters and splotches of dark sauce, but she smiled triumphantly as she laid the tray on a low table beneath the pine tree. "Here," she said, summoning me, "I thought you might be thirsty from your day in the city."

"Lady, I could drink the Tiber in a gulp."

She poured pale yellow liquid into one of the bowls. "This will quench your thirst," she said, passing me the bowl, "and taste better, too."

I drank and tasted anise and honey on my tongue. "It is very good," I said. "Did you make it?"

She merely smiled and reached for another of the bowls instead. "Here are roasted pinenuts," she said, offering me the bowl. "And there are olives stuffed with almonds, and rolled anchovies as well. That should keep you busy for a while."

Replacing the bowl, she turned on her heel.

"Where are you going?" I asked. "Stay. Eat with me."

"Dinner is nearly ready," she called, hurrying away. "I must change."

I settled beside the table and dutifully tasted morsels from each of the bowls. The anchovies were soft and salty, the olives firm and dry, and the pinenuts crunchy. Without meaning to, I had nearly emptied the bowls by the time Oriana returned. Her hair was brushed and clasped in tiny golden combs, and her light green linen mantle was spotless. Her long arms and shoulders were bare, and she wore golden bracelets on her upper arms and wrists. Her slender waist was bound in a beaded girdle that glistened like water as she walked.

"You look beautiful," I said, offering her a bowl of the anise drink.

"Thank you," she said knowingly. She accepted the bowl and we drank. For the first time I saw her not as the spoiled, fickle daughter of the vicarius but as Oriana, herself, as she wished to be.

"Where is your family?" I asked. "Will they join us?"

"No," she said casually. "They have gone to the villa. Tonight it is just us."

The villa, I had learned, was the Columella ancestral home; it was a farming estate located on the island of Aenaria in the Tyrrhenian Sea off the coast.

"I see."

An awkward silence descended as I began to grasp the implications of the situation. It was more than a meal she had in mind, then. How much more?

"I hope you are hungry," Oriana said at last.

"I am always hungry, as you well know."

"The evening will be warm. We could eat here in the courtyard if you like." Before I could reply, she jumped up. "I will have Opidus lay the table out here."

This was done, and soon we were reclining on couches before a low table beneath leafy laurel branches. We began with small sardines fried in olive oil and salted; these we ate whole. Next came a clear fish soup with chunks of white fish, tiny whole clams, shredded carrots, fennel, and other herbs.

After that it was time for the Numidian chicken. "This was the favorite of one of the emperors," she informed me as Opidus placed the platter on the table. "I cannot remember which emperor. But everyone likes it."

The piquant aroma rising from the heavily sauced fowl brought the water to my mouth. "I am certain I will like it, too."

Taking up a knife, she carved a juicy slice from the roast chicken and put it on a plate, adding a healthy dollop of mashed chestnuts along with some white beans boiled with coriander and buttered. She passed the plate to me, her expression grave and solemn; I took the plate and set it on the table before me. "It smells superb," I told her. Taking a bit of it between thumb and forefinger, I pulled off a morsel and put it in my mouth, rolling the succulent flesh on my tongue. "Oh, yes, it is a dish fit for the emperor himself," I told her. "But tonight he must weep with envy into his thin gruel."

She laughed, her voice soft and low. "If he were here, you would not speak with such impudence."

"Let him get his own chicken—and his own Numidian to prepare it."

Oriana laughed again, and the sound so delighted me that I tried to think of something else I might say just to hear it once more. I poured more wine into the bowls, and we drank.

The roast chicken was sumptuous in every way, and the other dishes as fine as any I had ever tasted—overlooking the black flecks of charred herbs floating in the pungent sauce, which Oriana had left on the boil too long. Still, in all it was a triumph; Oriana had every right to be justly proud. I ate everything that was given me, and more besides.

After the chicken, Opidus brought new plates containing bowls of fresh greens smothered in oil and vinegar, into which the green tops of onions had been chopped very fine. The sharp vinegar cut the taste of the roast and restored vigor to the appetite wonderfully well.

Next came ripe figs boiled in sweet almond milk and doused in spiced wine. The luscious figs had a creamy texture, and the wine filled the mouth with the delectable sweetness of a kiss. Oriana, eager for my approval, watched me, eyes wide and luminous with anticipation, her breath caught and held between curved lips. In the soft, rose-colored light of the courtyard, she took on a warm glow of expectation. I filled my gaze with her radiant features and wondered what it would be like to dine with her this way always.

As daylight dwindled, Opidus brought out several candelabra, each containing a dozen or more tiny lamps, which he lit, casting the table and surrounding courtyard in a gently shimmering glow. With the deepening of the twilight shadows, the sounds of the busy city faded away and crickets began to chirp in unseen corners of the courtyard. I poured more wine, and we ate and drank and talked, and the warm night gathered close around.

"Tell me about Hibernia," she said.

"Why do you want to know about Hibernia?"

"I want to know all about the places you've been. So tell me."

"What can I tell you that you do not already know? Hibernia—or Éire, as it is known—is a cold, rocky lump of land surrounded by a freezing sea on the edge of the world. It rains without ceasing, and you never see the sun from one day to the next. It is a dark land full of barbarians so fierce even the wolves fear them. The women plait their hair with firebrands, and the men paint themselves blue; they drink rough beer until they are drunk, and then they throw off their clothes and everyone dances naked beneath the light of the moon."

Oriana arched a smooth eyebrow. "Now you are making fun of me. I know it is not like that at all—in fact, it is not so different from the place where you were born. Pylades told me."

"Then he lied," I said bluntly. "Hibernia is nothing like Britain."

She held her head to one side. "Now you are angry."

"I'm not angry."

"You sound angry."

"I am *not* angry." I shoved my plate from me. "I find this constant raking up the past tedious beyond words, that's all."

"Then we will talk of something else." Her smile was hopeful, and her eyes pleaded with me not to ruin the splendid evening we had enjoyed to now.

I felt chastened, so I relented. "Yes. Let us talk of something else. Tell me about the villa."

Glad for a chance to restore the mood, she told me about the estate and the island it occupied. "The villa has been in our family for a very long time," she confided. "It was built by a wealthy nobleman in the time of Nero—a dangerous time to be found with money, I'm told. He was accused of treason, and the property was confiscated."

"Was he executed?"

"No, he was lucky. Nero died, and the nobleman was released from prison. He was destitute, so he sold the villa to my grandfather's great-great-great-grandfather." She shrugged. "We have had it ever since." She looked at me. "I know you lost your estate in the barbarian raid. Julian told me."

"Julian talks entirely too much."

"There is no shame in it," she said, lowering her head. "Such things happen. It cannot be helped. I don't see wh—"

Reaching out, I lifted her chin, put my hand to her cheek, and turned her head toward me. I leaned forward and kissed her. Oriana's response was quick and ardent. She seized my head between her hands and grasped me tight, as if she feared I might flee.

Emboldened, I put my arm around her shoulders and drew her close. She came willingly to my embrace, and we shared a long, searching kiss. Instantly the image of Sionan arose in my mind; it was she who had first kissed me like that, and I could not help but think of her now. I pushed the thought firmly away. It was Oriana, not Sionan, before me, and it had been a long time since I had been with anyone so loving and beautiful. All my pent-up yearning flowed into that moment. Oriana took it all and returned it with undiminished force.

When we broke off to catch our breath, I rose from the couch and stood. "Oriana, forgive me," I said, my heart in my throat.

She looked up at me with wide, dark eyes and shook her head gently. "No," she whispered, patting the place beside her.

As much as I wanted her just then, all I could think of was what Vicarius Columella would say. "I am sorry." I made a clumsy excuse, thanked her for the meal, and retreated to my room.

It was there she found me a short time later. "Lady—" I began as she slipped in, closing the door softly behind her. "I cannot. I am a guest in your father's house."

"It is my house, too," she said. Although her gaze was direct, I thought I could sense a slight hesitation in her manner—as if, having come this far, she did not trust herself to go any further. Or perhaps now that she was here, she was just a little frightened of what was to come.

I think if I had sent her away, she would have gone. No doubt that is what I should have done. Oh, but sending her away was the last thing either of us wanted just then.

So I rose and, taking her hand, drew her close. We stood for a moment, gazing at one another, savoring the delicious thrill of anticipation. Then, placing my hands on her hips, I pulled her body to me. I felt the heat of her flesh through the thin stuff of her dress. I kissed her again.

The large window was open, allowing a little light from the night sky to spill into the room. She unclasped the brooch at her shoulder, then reached around behind her back and untied the laces of her girdle, unwinding it carefully, before tossing it lightly aside. Her mantle slid down over her waist and hips to the floor. The sight of her long, elegant legs stepping from the ring of crumpled cloth at her feet took my breath away.

She moved to embrace me, but I put out a hand. "Wait," I whispered. "Let me look at you."

I let my gaze fall slowly down the long, supple length of her body, from the column of her graceful throat over her ripe, luscious breasts and down along the shallow, sloping curves of her waist and hips, taking in the gently rounded mound of her stomach and the tapering fullness of her thighs.

Slender she was, true, with little enough flesh to cover her bones. Oh, but that flesh possessed a potent charm nonetheless, and I felt myself quicken at the sight.

In the dim light she seemed a creature carved of the same fine white alabaster as the swan in the garden—until she shivered. "I'm cold," she said, her voice trembling. Her eyes glistened; her lips quivered. "I'm not sure I know what to do."

"Then come to bed," I said. "I'll show you."

I gathered her into my arms and drew her down into the sweet, warm darkness.

48

RIANA AND I made love that night and every night from then on, and often in the day, too. Any reluctance I might have felt in ravishing the vicarius' virginal daughter melted away in the white heat of our combined passion. There was no stopping us. At first awkward and uncertain, she quickly became an accomplished and enthusiastic lover, and her ardor awakened in me a genuine desire so long dormant I thought it had deserted me forever. There was much I loved *about* Oriana, but I did not love *her*—at least not the same way I had loved Sionan. Still, I did like her, and I would have crossed a lake of fire to avoid hurting her. I imagined that, in time, I could grow to love her with something of the same intensity I had once held for Sionan.

"My family returns the day after tomorrow," she sighed one afternoon. We were sitting together in the courtyard, drinking cool lemon water from the same cup. Despite the warmth of the day, Oriana had curled herself onto the couch and wrapped me around her. "What shall we do then?"

"Well," I said absently, "I suppose we shall just have to get married."

She turned around so fast that I spilled most of the drink down the front of her mantle. "Do you mean it?"

I thought for a moment. "Yes," I decided at last. "Why not?"

"Do not tease me, Succat. Did you mean what you said just now?"

"Every word."

In truth it was not so much that I was eager to marry her but rather that I had no other prospects whatsoever. I suppose I had grown accustomed to the Columellas and thought to keep myself within the circle of their influence by whatever means possible. Marriage seemed as good a tool as any.

"My love!" She kissed me full and hard.

"Anyway," I suggested, "if I did not, your father would likely gut me and parade my worthless skin through the streets of Rome."

"You would marry me just to save your skin?"

"Of course," I confessed. To be sure, I did not relish the idea of returning to the murderous forests of Germania. "I have grown fond of this hide of mine. Almost," I added, "as fond as I am of yours."

"Well, it *is* a handsome skin after all," she conceded, drawing her fingertips lightly over my chest. "It would be a shame to see it bruised. I suppose I could marry you."

"Thank you," I said.

We kissed again, and she sighed, "Oh, Succat, just think. We shall have the grandest, most dazzling wedding you have ever seen."

"That would not be difficult," I said, "as I have never been to a Roman wedding—or any other wedding, come to that."

Even as I spoke these words, a strange sensation of dread flooded my soul. The face of Sionan floated into my mind, she whom I had used and forsaken—much as I was using Oriana to get what I wanted now. I thrust the image angrily aside. That was my old life, I told myself, a different life. That life was over. I was not the same man.

"What is wrong, my love?" asked Oriana, sensing the sudden change in my mood. "You look so disgusted."

"Do I?" I forced a smile. "If I do, it is only because I did not think to ask you properly."

"Then ask me now."

I took her hand. "Oriana, dearest heart of my heart, will you marry me?"

"Am I really your dearest heart?"

"There is no one else." Again, even as I spoke, my thoughts turned to Sionan, changing the words in my mouth to a lie.

"Then, yes, my love, I will marry you."

Oriana spent the rest of the day planning how she would tell her parents. I left her humming to herself with delight as she concocted her scheme, and I went to the garrison to search out Rufus.

Although lacking any formal duties, he had not been entirely idle during his stay. To my surprise—and mild embarrassment—he had found Scipio. I had intended to search out our old friend first thing on my arrival in the city. But that, like so much else, I had let slip away.

"Good," Rufus said when he saw me. I was sitting in the guardroom, where I had been told to wait while one of the Praetorian servants went to bring him. "I found Scipio—did Julian tell you?"

"I have not seen Julian since we passed the gates on our way into Rome."

He shrugged. "Well, it doesn't matter. I am meeting Scipio tonight at a tavern in the city. You're to come, too. We are all going to be there."

"The four of us together again," I remarked, wondering how that would be. "It will seem like old times."

That evening I met Rufus outside the garrison gate, and we went along to the tavern, a place much frequented by Praetorian officers and ambitious young functionaries—men, as Rufus said, to whom a nodding acquaintance with the upper ranks of the imperial guard could be useful. The place was small and low-roofed like a cow bier, yet clean and well maintained. The owner served good wine for a tidy price, Rufus told me, and cooked chops of pork, lamb, and whole spitted fowls over iron braziers in the stone-paved courtyard.

Julian and Scipio were already there waiting for us. Julian had taken a table in a dim corner of one of the smaller rooms, where we could talk more easily. I saw Julian at once and then looked for Scipio, recognizing him at last as the balding, stooped fellow sitting opposite in a toga.

"Rufus! Succat!" cried Julian, waving us over as we came in. "Come. Sit. The wine is on its way."

"Scipio, is it you?" I said, standing over him.

"By God's holy name," said Scipio, jumping to his feet. "Is that Succat? I never would have known you."

We embraced somewhat awkwardly, patting one another on the back. He was shorter than I remembered and thick around the middle where the beginning of a paunch was starting to spread beneath his fresh, white garment. "God's teeth, man, it is good to see you! Look at you now! Rufus says you are a centurion. I always knew you'd make a good soldier. Didn't I often say it?"

Of course he had never said anything of the kind. "It is one of the few genuine talents I possess," he continued, tapping his nose knowingly. "I can tell a man's character simply by looking at him." He winked. "Why, I would not be at all surprised to see you a tribune one day—and you as well, Rufus, yes, you as well. I am certain of it."

Every inch the smooth Roman official, a small, well-greased cog in the machinery of imperial government, Scipio smiled with oily false sincerity and talked nonsense to flatter his listeners.

"A very prophet," I told him.

"It is, as you can imagine, a great asset in the senate."

The tavern keeper arrived just then and placed two jars and a stack of cups on the table. He paused to exchange a few words with Scipio, who, I gathered, was a regular patron of the establishment.

"Come, pour the wine," cried Julian impatiently, "before we die of thirst!"

"Good old Succat," Scipio chuckled, shaking his head in merry disbelief. "Yours is a face I never thought to see again." He took my arm and pulled me to the bench. "Well, now that we're all here, we can begin properly." He splashed wine into the cups and handed them around.

Rufus stood and lofted his drink, saying, "I raise a cup to friendship. May we never grow too old to remember the green years of our youth."

Julian made a wry face. "Rufus the poet. Sit down, you sentimental sop."

"To friends!" Scipio and I replied, and we drank a long draught.

"What do you think of Rome?" asked Scipio when we had drained the first cup.

"It is magnificent," I replied.

"If you like gaudy spectacle and the continual reek of garlic," muttered Julian, tilting the contents of his cup down his throat.

"Yes, I suppose it does give an impression of magnificence at first," allowed Scipio indifferently. He turned to Rufus. "You have seen something of the world, my friend. What do you think?"

Rufus had never been to Rome either, but he shrugged, affected to be unimpressed with anything he saw, and declared himself bored with its vaunted attractions. "You find them tedious?" I challenged. "How is that possible? Have you seen Trajan's Column? It is over a hundred feet tall! How can you call that tedious?"

"Rufus is right," observed Julian. "One column is very like another."

"And we have no end of columns here," put in Scipio. "You cannot move without bumping into one triumphal something or another."

"You all feign indifference," I said, "but you are just as delighted by this marvel of a city as I am."

"Marvel of a city?" hooted Julian. "You can have it, then, and with my blessing. It is crowded, noisy, stinking, and hot. More sewer than city, if you ask me."

"An expensive sewer," added Scipio. "Since the last invasion the city has become a pit for the empire's refuse. I am moving to Constantinople as soon as I find a buyer for my house. Trouble is, all the best Romans are selling up, too; it drives the property prices down. If I'm not careful, I'll realize only a fraction of what the place is worth."

I could not believe the way they talked; their world-weariness made me feel stupid for enjoying the splendors of the still-splendid city. I drank from my cup and said no more. A prickly silence settled over us.

"This reminds me of the last time we were together," observed Scipio. "It was at the Old Black Wolf, as I recall. I wonder whatever became of the place."

"A blacksmith owns it. He keeps a forge there now," I said.

"Does he indeed?" wondered Scipio, shaking his head as if such a thing were unimaginable. "Well, much has changed."

His bland observation angered me. "It was also the night of the Great Raid," I replied sharply. "We were at the Old Wolf, and the soldiers told us to go home. By the time we got back, Bannavem was in flames. Over a thousand of our kinsmen disappeared on that night, and hundreds more were killed. Estates were burned and whole towns destroyed." I paused, gazing at him with disgust. "Yes, you could say much has changed since that night."

Rufus sat looking into his cup, his expression vacant; he said nothing.

"Are you going to drag up all that again?" said Julian. "That was a long time ago. It is over. Finished. For your own good, let it go."

"Finished? Ha!" I slammed down my cup. "I wore a slave collar for seven years, and I carry the weight of it always."

Julian regarded me icily as he set his cup on the table. "You hold us somehow to blame for your misfortune?" A smirk slid across his fat face as he appealed to the others. "No doubt Succat's captivity has confused his memory somewhat. We cannot be held to blame for what happened that night."

Rufus and Scipio looked on, mute, uneasy.

"I *do* hold you to blame," I answered tersely. "Now that you say it, I do blame you."

"How, in the name of Christ, do you imagine we are to blame?" wondered Scipio, adopting an air of shocked innocence. "It was an unlucky accident. It could have happened to anyone."

"We were friends," I said, the heat of anger rising to my face. "We were friends—all of us together—and you abandoned me."

"We did *not* abandon you," Julian asserted blandly. "You rode off all in a lather on a fool's errand." He regarded me with barely concealed scorn. "Did you really expect anyone to follow you?"

Scipio, uneasy with the acrimony swirling around him, raised his hands in a gesture of appeasement and uttered a thin laugh. "We would have followed you, of course—if we had known."

"No," Rufus said, breaking his stony silence, "we would not have joined him. We were boys. We were frightened. We had our own lives to think about." Hunched over the cup between his hands, he regarded me from under his brows. "I am sorry, Succat, but that is how it is. Nothing we can say will change it now."

His blunt confession did little to salve the raw, aching wound of their betrayal.

"How could we know what would happen?" asked Scipio. "Anyway, it was all a long time ago. Forgive and forget, I say."

"Forgive? Gladly, if you ask it. Forget? Never!" I spat, tasting bitter bile on my tongue as a long-denied rage surged through me. "Seven years I spent as a slave in Ireland. Seven years!"

"Life goes on," offered Scipio blithely.

"Not for me. I remember it as if it were yesterday, and I will bear the scars forever."

"We all have our hardships," Julian snarled, his voice an ugly sneer. "It is over and done and best forgotten. You haven't done so badly for yourself."

"Easy for you to say, Julian," countered Rufus, tossing back the dregs. "Your father made a fair bit out of Succat's estate. I don't suppose you offered him anything from the sale, did you?"

I stared in shocked amazement. "What did you say?"

"Didn't you know?" said Rufus, pouring more wine into his cup. "Julian didn't tell you?"

"He told me nothing." I said, staring at Julian, who sat with averted eyes, gazing off into the room.

"After Calpurnius died, Julian's father had your estate confiscated for nonpayment of taxes. He packed your mother off to a small house in Lycanum and sold off everything. Since he was magistrate, the greater part of the proceeds went into his own pocket."

I turned to Julian. "You thieving bastard! I could kill you for that!"

Julian put out a hand to me. "It wasn't like that, Succat, believe me. Your mother was sick. She couldn't manage the estate anymore. She needed help. . . ."

"You lying filth," I snarled. " 'Forget the past, Succat, look to the future. A man can find himself in Gaul, Succat.' Little wonder you were so anxious for me to leave Britain."

"The circumstances at the time—" blustered Julian, trying to defend himself. "You have to remember how it was—"

I had heard enough. I stood and turned from the table. "The devil take you, my friends. The devil take you all!"

Striding from the room, I heard Scipio call after me, but I did not turn. I never wanted to see any of them again.

It was dark, and the streets were all but deserted, so I walked awhile, thinking about what had happened. Try as I might, I could not make myself feel sorry for anything I had said. In fact, I kept thinking of things I might have added to make them truly feel the lash of my rage.

After a time I found myself in a street where prostitutes prowled for drunken carousers—a wretched, dark, unsavory place that more than matched my mood. However, as I listened to their moans and sighs and deceitful pledges of love, I decided I had a better place to go and something better to do. I returned to Domus Columella, where Oriana was waiting.

The anger and frustration, so long suppressed, surfaced in our lovemaking that night. Oriana took it all, absorbed it, transmuted it, and returned it as tenderness, solace, and warmth. Her willingness to spend herself in this way both awed and shamed me. If I did not love her before, that single, selfless act turned my heart. Our true marriage began in that moment.

Afterward she lay in my arms and I stroked her hair. "I hope," she said, her voice quivering from the violence of our exertion, "whatever demons you brought to bed with you have been banished."

"They are gone, my love," I told her, thinking of my false friends. "We will never see them again."

49

 ADY COLUMELLA COULD not abide the thought of her daughter marrying a soldier. Her refusal sent a tearful Oriana running to her father, who came storming into my room. "My daughter says she wishes to marry you. Is this true?"

"It is."

"You're a soldier!"

"I am that."

He turned his back to me and stalked to the other end of the room, turned, and came back. "How dare you!" He thrust an accusing finger into my face. "I take you in, feed you, clothe you, treat you like my own son . . ." He faltered, lost for words. "And this is how you repay my kindness! You seduce my only daughter!"

Of all the things I might have said just then, none seemed particularly apt, so I kept my mouth shut.

"How dare you!" he shouted again. "I turn my back for a moment and you take advantage of my generosity, my house and home. You take my only daughter."

"I took nothing that was not offered me, my lord Vicarius," I replied firmly. "I am sorry if it displeases you. But Oriana and I are determined to be married."

"Impossible!" he cried. "Her mother will not hear of it. *I* will not hear of it!"

All in all, his rage was not as bad as I feared. He ranted and raved, threatening various ingenious punishments, but I stood up to his anger, and eventually he began to calm himself somewhat.

"Is Oriana to have nothing to say?" I asked.

"I know only too well what she will say," he countered. "All her life she has had whatever she wants."

"And now she wants me," I suggested. "And I want her."

"Bah!"

He strode the length of the room, frowning and pulling on his chin. "Lady Columella will never allow her to marry a soldier. She is quite determined, and that is that."

"So I am given to understand." I did not see any way beyond this impasse; soldiering was all I had. This I told him, and then, remembering who I addressed, I added, "Of course, I would not have to remain a soldier forever."

His frown turned into a scowl, and his eyes narrowed suspiciously. "What did you say?"

"I merely point out that I have no great ambition to remain a soldier. I am certain a man of your experience and wisdom could suggest something more suitable for your daughter's future husband."

"You would marry my daughter for selfish gain?" he cried. "I knew it! I knew it!"

"Oriana told me you married her mother to get the money to advance your career in the senate," I said.

"That was different," he snapped. "That was an arrangement between her father and myself."

"Well," I offered lightly, "perhaps you and I might come to a similar arrangement."

His stare grew baleful. "That was different," he repeated between clenched teeth. "Her mother and I grew to love one another."

"Perhaps," I said, "the only difference is that Oriana and I love each other already."

To his credit, angry as he was, Aulus Columella knew when to be gracious and accept defeat. He gave a final, frustrated bark, then sighed, shaking his head with weary reluctance. "I suppose," he said, "we shall just have to find something for you, then." Clasping his hands behind his back, he strode a few paces away, then looked back at me. "You are of noble blood—a patrician, I believe."

"That is true."

He nodded thoughtfully. "Have you ever considered becoming a senator?"

"It has long been a family ambition."

He nodded again, then smiled suddenly. "By the god who made you,

Succat, you are a man after my own heart." He laughed out loud. "A senator! Well, we will see what we can do."

He strode to me, opening his arms wide in welcome. I moved to meet him, and he drew me into his embrace, then put his arm around my shoulder, saying, "Come, my son, let us go and tell the ladies the good news."

Lady Columella declared herself pleased and happy with the plan. She welcomed me like a son, kissing me on both cheeks and beaming with satisfaction. Indeed, any reluctance she might have displayed melted away so quickly that I suspected her initial refusal was simply a ruse to get her husband to find a more suitable occupation for me. Oriana was delighted, of course, and instantly began planning the wedding celebration. "We shall have the ceremonies here in the hall."

"It will never be big enough," countered her mother. "We will have them in the courtyard."

"Under a canopy!" said Oriana.

"The Archbishop of Rome will hear the vows. . . ." And with that the wedding was well on its way. Nothing short of a three-day feast would suffice for the aristocracy of Rome. The two women purred and twittered for days over who should be invited and what foods should be served to the guests. The vicarius allowed them to get on with it; his mind returned to a more urgent preoccupation: the senate and the appearance we were to make together. He groomed me for the part I was to play in what he considered the most important speech of his life.

"The future of the empire could well be determined by how we perform," he confided. "We must secure enough money to raise new armies and replenish the frontier garrisons. Anything less is a failure I cannot countenance."

"I will do my best."

"I know you will, Succat. Think! You have it in your power to do with your words far more than you ever could with a sword. They call you Magonus now, soon they will call you Beatus."

On the day we were to speak, the vicarius took me to the Praetorian garrison, where I was given the ceremonial uniform of a centurion: a silver breastplate embossed with rearing stallions; a burnished silver helmet adorned with white plumes; the bloodred *lacerna,* or short cape; high-topped sandals of white leather; a wide leather sword belt with a broad silver buckle; and a short, gold-hilted sword.

Satisfied with my appearance, the vicarius conducted me to the Curia Julia, where the senators were already gathering. We stood in the forum outside and watched them enter in groups of two and three—and all of them dressed in the distinctive senatorial toga: white with the purple stripe along the edge.

"They can be intimidating," Columella warned, "but remember, they are men like us. Speak with boldness and do not swallow your words." He paused, offering me a smile of encouragement. "Do as we agreed and they will not fail to be moved."

The curia is a curved marble hall ringed with stepped ranks of wooden benches. We found places on the lowest row in the center and sat down to wait as more and still more senators streamed through the wide open doors to take their places along the stepped rows. After a time a bell sounded; in a few moments it sounded again, and two armed soldiers entered, leading an elderly official, who proceeded to a chair in the center of the low platform between the doors.

As soon as the old man was seated, a senator sitting near us stood up. Great of bulk and terrible of mien, he advanced a few paces into the center of the room and declared, "Senators! Friends! It pleases me to see that so many of you have taken the grave import of this summons to heart. I need not tell you that the decisions we make today will have the greatest consequence for the future of our glorious empire, perhaps for many generations to come."

To my surprise this assertion was met with catcalls and shouted challenges of disagreement. Clearly the senate was not all of one mind regarding the probable future of the empire. The speaking senator did not appear to mind the disruption. He paused until the worst of the commotion was over, then plowed ahead. "I see that some of you remain unconvinced. Therefore I bring before you the esteemed and honorable Aulus Columella, Vicarius of Gaul and Germania, who has come to offer us a timely word." Turning to the vicarius, the senator put out his hand and welcomed Columella beside him.

The two shook hands, and the speaker sat down heavily, like a building settling onto its foundations.

"Thank you, Senator Graccus," said the vicarius. "You are right to remind this noble assembly of the importance of the contemplations before us." Lifting his head to look around the curia, Columella, his voice taking on the timbre of a skilled orator, began. "As some of you will know, I have lived for the last three years in Gaul, looking after the affairs of the Roman state there and in the province of Germania. Early last summer word came to the frontier garrisons that the barbarians were amassing along the border in numbers sufficient to raise the alarm of the generals.

"When notified of this, I rode to meet General Septimus, commander of Legio XX Valeria Victrix at Augusta Treverorum. Together with the commanders of the nearest garrisons, we held close council to decide our course of action. Following on three years of savage predation by the northern barbarian tribes, it was decided to mass the legions to meet the impending attack and vanquish the perpetrators—not merely to defeat them but to destroy both the will to fight and the ability to make war against the citizens of Rome for many years to come.

"The battle plan was drawn up accordingly: We would meet the enemy with sufficient force to crush them utterly. This campaign would be conducted on the far side of the river, to take them in the forest before they had a chance to wreak havoc on imperial soil. Scouts were sent to spy out the barbarian position and ascertain enemy numbers. Upon their return I gave the order to march. The next day the soldiers of Valeria Victrix crossed the Rhenus and proceeded into the forest, where the enemy forces were already gathering.

"The first skirmish was fought that day. The barbarians were unready and were easily routed."

Here the senators, who had sat in silence while the vicarius spoke, gave out a shout of acclaim. "A victory is always gladly received," Columella continued. "Moreover, the ease with which we vanquished the enemy exposed the weakness of their position and leadership. In order to put down the invasion before the enemy had time to regroup, we pursued them deeper into the forest. This was but the first of several calamitous blunders."

The enormous chamber grew silent. Here the vicarius turned and summoned me. I took my place beside him. "Fellow senators, I present to you the sole surviving legionary of that brutal conflict." He placed his arm around my shoulders, saying, "If it had not been for this man, I would not be alive to bring you this woeful report today."

To me he said, "Centurion, tell them what happened. Tell them what you bore witness to in the days that followed our first victory."

As Vicarius Columella stepped away, I looked out on the crowd of faces, all of them interested, observant. My mouth went dry. I swallowed, and then, drawing myself up, I straightened my shoulders and began to tell what I had seen during those last dreadful days.

"General Septimus gave the order to pursue the barbarians . . . ," I began.

Instantly this was met by a voice shouting, "We already know that! Get on with it!"

I had not expected to be shouted down, and it threw me off my stride. The words of my prepared speech left me, and I stared out at the impatient crowd. "Get on!" shouted another.

Any hope of recovering my speech vanished. I swallowed and began once more, speaking simply as the words came to me. "I was an auxiliary. The garrison commander cannot afford to pay full wages to an entire legion of regular soldiers, so he makes up the numbers by hiring mercenaries who will fight for the plunder they can get on the battlefield. I joined a numerus under the command of a veteran named Quintus.

"During the first skirmish we formed a protecting wing to guard the legion's flank. General Septimus' troops were to pose as the main attacking force, to offer a feint to the enemy and thereby draw them from their encampment and allow Legio Gemina and Legio Pia Fidelis to close in behind and seal off any retreat or escape.

"This feint was offered, and it was successful. We fell back to the river, which was the signal for the waiting legions to attack the enemy encampment from the rear. When the counterattack failed to commence, we endured the brunt of the barbarian assault as long as we could. In the end, however, we were forced to regroup and push away from the river. Despite fierce opposition, we opened a way through the enemy ranks. When the barbarians ran, we followed the pursuit into the forest, sealing off any escape and pushing them into the waiting spears of Legio Gemina, which had taken a position well behind the enemy. All that first day we marched, engaging the barbarians as and when we came upon them—until we reached the enemy camp, which we destroyed."

This brought a rousing cheer from the assembled senators, which eased my trepidation somewhat. "Unfortunately, the enemy which had fled before us quickly circled around and was now behind us. General Septimus decided to push on and unite with the Gemina. All through the day we fought a running battle with the barbarians and finally succeeded in reaching the Gemina, which was surrounded by a host of barbarians greater in number than we had yet encountered.

"General Septimus, showing outstanding courage and determination, forced a way through the massed enemy to rescue Legio Gemina. Through dint of strength and discipline, we cut a path through Goth and Hun and Saecsen flesh—"

The senators liked this; they hooted in jubilation.

"—and achieved our purpose. The two legions were united. But then so was the enemy—and their numbers were far the greater. Our commanders formed the shield wall, and we stood as wave after wave of barbarians broke themselves upon our blades.

"Day's end found us deep in the forest. With darkness upon us we moved out, heading west in the direction of the Fidelis. We marched through the night. We met no resistance; neither did we meet the missing legion."

My voice fell as the images of that dire morning came once more before my mind's eye.

"As the sun rose, I saw that the ground where I stood was covered with the corpses of slaughtered legionaries. Everywhere I gazed . . . dead and still more dead. As I looked, I saw that the heads of the soldiers had been cut off and nailed to the trees. Each and every tree bore the bloody skull of a soldier.

"We followed the trail, and came to the place where the main body of the legion had made its last stand. Here the dead were heaped on one another, and all were stripped of their armor and weapons. None survived the ambush. An entire legion had been slaughtered.

"Lest we join them, General Septimus commanded the troops to move on. Alas, the command came too late. No sooner had we turned from the sight than arrows began raining down on us. We ran for the cover of the trees—only to see the forest rise up against us.

"Using horses taken from our own auxiliaries, the enemy rode over us, scattering the cohorts and cutting us down. General Septimus rallied the men to the vexillum.

"I ran to join them but was cut off by a barbarian horseman. In my desperation I succeeded in unhorsing the rider. I took the horse and cut a path to General Septimus, trying to open a way to retreat. The general would not hear of it. He bade me to take Vicarius Columella onto my horse and ride for the river instead.

"Once across the river the vicarius and I made our way to the nearest garrison, where we raised the alarm. The troops went out at once, but it was too late. By the time they reached the battleground, the fighting was over. Not one Roman soldier remained alive." I looked out at the anguished faces of the senators. "Three legions . . . nine thousand soldiers, and not one of them survived."

I finished to silence.

The vicarius allowed the silence to hang in the air. Then, rising slowly, he came to stand beside me. "Centurion Magonus," he said, "were the standards of the legions recovered?"

"No, my lord, the standards were lost."

Turning sad eyes to the assembly, Columella said, "Three legions have been destroyed and the standards lost." Stepping into the center of the chamber, he raised his voice. "Why? Why, you ask yourselves, has this catastrophe come about?" He took another step. "Perhaps they were merely unlucky. The barbarians were more cunning than they knew. Ambushed and outnumbered—the outcome was inevitable.

"Perhaps the generals were inexperienced and the troops—untrained, untried, and unready—were simply overpowered by a superior force. Or perhaps the choice of battleground favored the enemy and hindered the legions; this, combined with foul weather, produced a series of calamities which, piled one atop another, could not be overcome.

"Which of these explanations will you present when called upon to answer for this tragic failure?" He spread his hands as if seeking an answer to the questions he had posed. "For you *will* be called to account for it, my esteemed friends."

This assertion was answered at once. "You seek to lay the blame for this catastrophe at our feet?" said an aging senator, rising from his place across the room.

The vicarius was ready with his response. "I place the blame where it must lie if a remedy is to be effected. The failure is ours, esteemed friends, and ours alone."

"That I sincerely doubt," replied the old man, who promptly sat down.

Lifting his gaze to the rest of the chamber, the vicarius paused to consider his reply. "I sense that many of you yet cling to doubts over who should bear the brunt of the blame for this disaster. So let us consider the possibilities: Were the legions unlucky?

"No. We must reject this suggestion out of hand. An individual soldier may be unlucky. A cohort, or even a division, may in the confusion of battle make a blunder that leads to destruction. But three legions of Roman soldiers are proof against any eventuality in the field; three legions are more than enough to overbalance the vicissitudes of chance.

"Were the generals inexperienced and the troops untried? Again I say no. General Sentius Septimus was the most experienced commander in Gaul, with fifteen years of service on the northern frontier alone and countless victories to his credit. His skill was unquestioned. General Paulus and General Flavia were equally seasoned combat veterans. Flavia served for ten years under Septimus before taking command of the Pia Fidelis. Each of these generals, like all the commanders of the border garrisons, knew their men and knew the enemy. Thus we must look elsewhere for the fault.

"Lastly, was the battleground ill chosen? Were the elements against them? It is true that the forests of Germania have long been a bane to the legions. But the northern troops are well used to woodland combat, and the commanders know how to turn it to their advantage. The weather, too, posed no undue difficulties. There was some rain, yes, but not on the day of battle and not enough to overpower the combined might of three entire legions."

He paused to pace slowly along the rows of seated senators. Then, shaking his head, he said, "You can see that the cause of the disaster lies not with the commanders and the brave dead but with us."

This assertion did not go unchallenged. "Why implicate this august body in what by any account is simply a most lamentable tragedy?"

Murmurs of support rippled through the assembly.

The vicarius drew himself up. " 'Lamentable tragedy,' you say, and so it is. 'Simply,' did you say?" He glared at the speaker. "Senator, there is nothing simple about it—unless you suggest that the failure of this assembly to authorize the necessary payments from the treasury to enable the legions to man and maintain northern garrisons is in some way a *simple* matter."

"Vicarius Columella, you put words in my mouth. I think our esteemed peers will agree that I suggest no such thing."

"You do, Senator. You most certainly do suggest it when you imply that the cause of this disaster can be found in some source other than our own culpability." He turned to address those looking on, "Noble Senators, I do agree with our esteemed friend in this: There is a simple solution to our present difficulty—to vote an immediate increase in the military allowance to be used for the recruitment and training of the northern legions. Needless to say, those garrisons are all that stand between the barbarians and Rome."

"Hear him!" shouted a senator from the back bench. "Hear him!" Others quickly took up the chant.

Senator Graccus rose to his feet. Holding up his hands, he waited until order reclaimed the curia. "I want to thank Vicarius Columella for bringing this matter to our attention. Woeful though it undoubtedly is, our duty is clear. As guardians of the public safety, we must move to vote that the treasury release the necessary funds to restore the northern garrisons to full fighting strength."

This view was instantly ratified by shouts of acclaim, as one senator after another leaped to his feet to add his voice to the call for a vote. Vicarius Columella moved to where I was standing and whispered, "We have carried the day. Your reward is secure."

"I did not do it for a reward," I replied.

"I know." He gripped my shoulder. "That makes the settlement all the more satisfying."

The discussion over the funding for the legions lasted three days. I did not attend the other sessions, and I was content. To have to listen to the senators wrangling over the price of soldiers' lives—for that is what it amounted to—was not to my liking. I would have done it for the sake of Quintus and my friends if it would have helped, but the vicarius did not think it necessary. He came home on the evening of the third day singing to himself. "We have done it!" he crowed loudly. "We have won a mighty victory. The senate has approved the disbursement and has drawn up a petition to present to the emperor. All that remains is for the emperor to give his assent, and the money will begin flowing."

"That is good to hear."

"And you, my friend, have secured your place in the senate."

"I'm to be a senator?"

"Eventually," he said. "All in good time. There is much to be done first, of course. The proper groundwork must be laid. I will introduce you to those who can advance your career. We will start there."

"*After* the wedding," put in Oriana, entering the room with her mother just then.

"There is plenty of time for all that later," intoned Lady Columella, "as your father well knows."

"What did I say? Of course after the wedding, my dear," he added quickly. "I was just saying that we have entered the race and the prize is within sight."

"Senator Succat," said Oriana airily. "I like the sound of that."

She stepped close to kiss me, but her father pulled her from my grasp, saying, "Now, there is plenty of time for *that* later as well. Come," he said, taking each woman by the arm and leading them away, "we are all invited to dine with Senator Graccus tonight at his villa. We will celebrate the glorious victory we have won today and discuss Succat's future."

PART IV

patricius

50

ORIANA AND I were married according to the traditions of Roman aristocracy. On the day of the wedding, I rose in the house where we would live; I washed, ate a small meal of bread and wine, and dressed in new clothes—a white tunic, belt of fine red cloth, and a pallium of light gray. I was aided in these preparations by Columella's son, Gaius, who helpfully neglected to do anything I asked of him and refused to wash or comb his hair until I threatened heaving him bodily over the wall into the kennel of the house down the street.

We then made our way to the bride's family residence, where the wedding ceremonies would take place. Ordinarily I would have been accompanied by crowds of friends and well-wishers, but of these I had none, so I made do with moody little Gaius and two musicians—a piper and a lute player—hired for the occasion.

Upon our arrival I was seized by the hands and conducted through the house to the courtyard by four of Oriana's female friends, who then stood around me to prevent my escape. The courtyard was decorated with garlands of pink and yellow flowers; a long table bearing wine and sweetmeats stood in one corner, and around this was gathered a small crowd of wedding guests, none of whom I recognized. "Am I allowed to have some wine?" I asked one of my winsome guards.

"Shh," came the reply. "Later."

"What are we doing?" I asked.

"Waiting for the bride."

We waited for a considerable time, as it happened. And then, all at once, there came a trill of trumpets from somewhere inside the house, and Oriana appeared between the columns on the courtyard steps. She was dazzling. Dressed in a long tunic of white, with a jeweled girdle around her slender waist, she glittered in the sunlight. On her shoulder was folded the saffron-colored palla, and affixed to a jeweled crown she wore the *flammeum*, or traditional orange veil, which covered her face.

She seemed a very goddess, descended into our midst from on high. The courtyard fell silent as she stood and gazed upon the gathering she favored with her presence. The trumpets sounded again, and Vicarius and Lady Columella appeared, followed by more guests and relatives, and everyone swept down the steps and into the courtyard.

While the guests took their places around us, two of Oriana's maids ran to greet her and brought her to stand beside me. One of them took Oriana's hand and placed it in mine, whereupon the venerable, elderly Archbishop of Rome shuffled out from the crowd; attended by two younger priests—one to carry a cross on a pole, the other to carry his crosier—he smiled and nodded and offered up a small speech in formal Latin. He called upon all present, and God above, to witness the marriage and then blessed the union with a lengthy prayer which ended with the solemn reminder that marriage was meant chiefly for the procreation of children.

And that was that. Senator Graccus approached bearing a parchment scroll which both Oriana and I signed; it was a legal contract stating our intent to form a lasting union. This concluded the formal rites, and then the celebration began: music, dancing, and a prodigious feast. The vicarius had arranged for roving teams of musicians to play and three lambs and a whole pig to be roasted in the hall. Oriana and I spent the rest of the day wandering among the guests receiving their good wishes and small gifts of food and coins with which to begin our household.

The celebration lasted long into the night, but as soon as the sun went down, we departed the bride's home and led a procession down the street to our own modest, unassuming house at the foot of Palatine Hill, within hailing distance of her parents' palatial residence. A young boy held Oriana's left hand, another her right, and, going before her, Gaius carried a torch that had been lit from her mother's hearth. At the door of our dwelling, the procession stopped. Gaius turned and lofted the torch into the crowd; it was caught by a friend of Oriana's, who thus obtained the promise of a long life.

Meanwhile Oriana took tufts of combed wool and placed them over the door; she then smeared a little olive oil and lamb fat on each doorpost. This ritual completed, all that remained was for me to carry her across the threshold and into the house, where she placed her hand on the hearth and on the water basin. I set her on her feet then, and the procession swarmed into the house and carried her into the bedchamber. I waited outside while Oriana was prepared for bed by her female friends. When all was ready, the door opened, and I was pushed inside.

"Now what?" I asked as the last of her departing friends closed the door.

"What do you think?" said Oriana, wrapping her arms around me.

I thought for a moment. "With everyone out there?"

She kissed me on the mouth. "Does it matter?" Oriana whispered, her breath hot on my neck.

"Well . . ."

She kissed me again. "If you're too timid . . ." she said, taking a small vial of blood she had got from the kitchen before leaving the feast. She emptied the vial on a corner of the clean, new bedcovering, rubbed it in a little, gave the covering to me, and pushed me toward the door, saying, "Here, wave it outside."

This I did, to a tremendous shout of raucous acclaim mixed with hooting, whistles, and catcalls. The musicians began playing again, and everyone sang as the procession returned to the feast, leaving the exhausted wedding couple alone at last.

Thus began our life together.

The first two years I worked hard at earning my senatorial seat. It was, I knew, my best—no doubt my *only*—chance to make a life for myself and now, of course, Oriana. Armed with Vicarius Columella's generous recommendation, I entered the swarming ranks of ambitious young noblemen anxious for a prestigious appointment. Thanks to Senator Graccus—a word here and there, dropped into the appropriate ear—I sped to the top of the heap; within a year I gained my quaestorship and proceeded on my way to becoming a praetor, the first rungs on the long ladder.

The wily senator wangled me a position on the directorate which was overseeing the restoration of those parts of Rome that had suffered the worst of the Vandal destruction. Even after five years there were still ruins to be demolished and rubble to be removed; architects to cajole, flatter, and threaten; building plans to be approved; and continual site inspections to be made. Builders were notorious for using inferior substitutes in place of the more expensive materials specified. They also hired fewer laborers than appeared on their salary rolls.

The directorate was employed to keep the building work running smoothly, with as few setbacks, delays, and bribes as possible. Under the tutelage of a seasoned official, a *curator*, charged with the task of making certain that all the various costs were kept to a minimum and that the money designated arrived at its proper destination, I roamed the precinct inspecting the various sites and keeping a tight rein on the builders. I enjoyed the work, and my duties were far from demanding; I had plenty of time to cultivate a deeper acquaintance with the great city and its life. I also had time to spend at home developing a more intimate appreciation of the complex delights of Oriana. She was a perplexing array of contradictions—bewildering, mystifying, baffling, paradoxical, and astonishing by turns.

Ardent and passionate one moment, Oriana could be coolly indifferent the next; expressing both zeal and lethargy in the space of a single sentence; content and happy as we sat down to eat, then seething with frustration and disappointment by meal's end. I rarely knew where or when the next outburst of either joy, sorrow, rage, or exuberance would erupt, or what would set it off. Life with Oriana was exhilarating and never less than surprising. The gods are fickle and inconstant, the poets say, but Oriana could have taught even flighty Venus herself a lesson or two in caprice and whimsy.

"You shivered, my love," I'd say. "Are you cold? Shall I get you a palla?"

"Cold? Why should I be cold? It is a very oven in this house."

"Then let us go out into the courtyard and cool off," I would suggest in all pleasance.

Out we'd go and no more than sit down on the stone bench when up Oriana would leap. "Now, look," she would complain, rubbing her bare arms, "I've caught a chill. Let's go in, and you make a nice fire in the hearth."

One day, a few months after we had settled into our home, I discovered the reason for Oriana's chimerical behavior. I was at Domus Columella, talking to her mother, who had asked me how we were getting on with the task of finding a suitable cook and housekeeper. "Not well at all," I confessed. "The servants we attract are either too old and decrepit, or too haughty, or they do not speak enough Latin to make themselves understood."

Lady Columella smiled knowingly. "They are always like that. But keep looking—you will find someone."

"It would be easier, I suppose, if we could ever agree."

"On what you wanted in a servant? That should be obvious."

"On *anything* at all," I told her. "If I say the sky is blue, Oriana says pink. If I say the soup is hot, she says far too cold. Black is white, and day is night. And if I so much as mention her contrary attitude, she dissolves in a heap of tears and vows never to speak to me again so long as she lives."

Helena pursed her lips and regarded me curiously. "Is she better in the morning? No stomach trouble?"

"A little," I allowed. "But it is only because she has developed a taste for green figs soaked in vinegar. I told her she would make herself sick on such a dish, but she eats them anyway and pays the price next day."

"I see," she said, nodding to herself. "Well, I will go and see her today."

"She would be cross to learn I confided in you," I said quickly.

"A mother has a right to visit her daughter, no?" She smiled and patted me on the arm. "I will be discreet."

I went about my business for the day and arrived home in the evening to find Oriana up to her elbows in flour, humming to herself as she kneaded a heap of dough on the board. Seeing that she was in a receptive mood, I went to her and embraced her from behind. "Oh," she said brightly, "it's you." She let her weight sag against me, and I stood for a moment holding her with my arms around her waist, feeling her splendid warmth seep into me.

"Expecting someone else?" I kissed her neck.

"There have been people in and out all day."

"People?"

"Two servants—both formidable crones and neither one suitable in the least—then my mother and her midwife, and the man selling lemons and pomegranates—"

"What was that?"

"A little man selling pomegranates. You know, the one who—"

"Not him, the one before that. Your mother . . . and her midwife?"

"Yes. They came to see me."

"Why would your mother and her midwife wish to see you?"

Oriana turned in my arms. Taking my face between her sticky, flour-covered hands, she said, "Because when someone is going to have a baby, it is best to engage the services of a good midwife as soon as possible. And my mother's midwife is the best in Rome."

"Your mother's midwife," I repeated as the truth broke on my dull head. "You mean *your* midwife."

"Yes, I suppose so."

"Oriana, you are going to have a baby!"

"I am," she said. "I mean, I think so. Probably."

I threw my arms around her and pulled her close. "My dear, sweet, beautiful girl. I love you." I kissed her and then held her at arm's length. "This is tremendous!" I cried. "Does your father know?"

"Not unless mother has told him. She promised not to."

"We must tell him." I took her hands and pulled her with me. "Come! We will go at once and give him the news."

Oriana held back. "Could it be our secret for a little while? Just for a few days—until I'm certain."

"Well," I replied, feeling the excitement leak away, "if that is what you want. But why not tell everyone?"

"We will," she said. "Soon. But not now."

The moment the vicarius found out, he became a fountain of largesse. He brought presents for Oriana and the child and gave gifts of money—little stacks of coins he left lying around without telling anyone—and took it upon himself to engage a servant for us. Within a few days a tidy, competent, quiet, unassuming Greek woman of tiny stature and limited speech appeared in our doorway. Her name was Agatha, and she instantly folded herself into the rough fabric of our lives and smoothed it effortlessly. She knew that Oriana was with child without being told, and she determined to make the months before the birth as easy for Oriana as possible.

There followed the happiest time I could recall since leaving Ireland. Thanks to Vicarius Columella, my life had taken a turn I could never have imagined. I found myself looking forward to the birth of our first child with almost feverish anticipation. "I am going to have a son," I told everyone who would listen. "He will be called Potitus, after my grandfather."

"No, my sweet," Oriana would correct, "he will be called Quintillus, after *my* grandfather."

"Have you forgotten, light of my life, you promised I could name him? And I think Potitus a fine name."

"I made no such promise, my dear confused man. If you were not so selfish and forgetful, you would know this. Quintillus it is."

"I might sooner have forgotten my own name, my pumpkin. He shall be Potitus Quintillus then, and that is that. I have spoken."

In the end we need not have argued. The babe was born in due course: as plump and healthy a baby girl as ever drew breath to wail. And wail she did: every waking moment, it seemed to me. To all appearances she had inherited her mother's quick, uncompromising temper, but I loved her for it. The first time I held her, a pang of longing pierced my heart, and I wished my mother were alive to see her wonderful, beautiful granddaughter. "Concessa," I murmured.

"What did you say, my love?" asked Oriana.

"It was my mother's name—Concessa Lavinia," I replied.

"A fine name," she agreed sleepily. "Let her be Concessa Helena."

"Concessa Helena Oriana," I amended, placing the infant on her mother's breast. "Grow into those names, little one, and let the world beware."

During the first month or so, Agatha and Helena contrived to keep the house, allowing Oriana and myself to get what rest we could and spend any spare moments with the child. We grew close, and I reveled in creating for my daughter the kind of home my parents had created for me. I wondered what they would have thought of their Succat now—so far away from stormy Britain, living in Rome with a wife and child, a house on Palatine Hill, and, one day, a seat in the senate? I wished they could have seen me.

Duty called the vicarius away to Gaul once more, and this time he left his family behind. Helena remained in Rome to help her daughter with the baby and oversee young Gaius' education, which apparently had reached a critical stage. On the day Aulus departed, I went to see him off.

As he prepared to step onto the mounting block, I embraced him as I would my own father. "Thank you, my lord," I said. "You have given me a new life, and I owe you more than I can repay."

"Not at all." He shook his head, smiling. "If not for you, my son, I would have perished in the German forest. I do but repay in part the debt I owe." He took my arms in a soldier's grip. "Take care of your family, Succat," he said softly. "Whatever happens, look first to their welfare and safety."

"On my life, lord."

He turned, stepped up onto the block, and swung into the saddle. "I hope to return in the spring," he said, taking the reins from the hand of the groom. "If all goes well with the recruiting, we will soon have a real army on the frontier again. And then we can sleep peacefully in Rome."

We made our farewells, and he rode from the courtyard to take his place at the head of the cohort waiting for him in the street. I followed and saw him raise his hand before he passed out of sight down the hill.

I returned to my directorate duties with renewed zeal. Senator Graccus noticed my resolve and began talking about advancing me another rung to a praetorship. "How old are you?"

I thought for a moment. "Twenty-six," I calculated.

"A little young, to be sure," he told me, "but it is not unknown—especially these days. You have shown yourself diligent and conscientious. I would be surprised if anyone in the senate objected."

"What if they did object?"

"I would hoot them down, my boy. I would send them running for cover with their ears on fire." He chuckled. "Oh, I would like that. It has been a long time since we had a good brawl in the senate. Leave it with me; I will let you know when the time is right."

I thanked him and, as I turned to go, asked, "Forgive me for asking, Senator Graccus, but why are you doing all this for me?"

He cocked his head to one side as if he could not understand the question. "For you?" he said, looking away. "My boy, I am doing it for *me*."

"I do not believe you, Senator."

He turned to face me, his jowls arranged in a solemn frown. "Then let us say I am doing it for a soldier who marched off to Germania and never returned. I had hoped one day to help him as I now help you."

"This soldier was someone close to you."

"Yes," Senator Graccus agreed, his voice falling quiet. "He was my son."

"Then I hope I can live up to his memory."

A pensive smile passed his lips as he said, "You already have."

Upon leaving the senator, I proceeded to one of the nearby building sites to meet the *curatores publicorum,* one of the many officials who was to make an inspection of the work to date. I was meant to be familiarizing myself with the site plan and schedule, but all I could think about was how, in such a short space of time, so many people had come to depend on me. I resolved to acquit myself in a way that was worthy of their trust. No matter what it cost, I vowed, I would repay their confidence a thousand times over.

The curatores was less than impressed with his tour of the site, but he found nothing seriously amiss and promised to attach his seal to the pertinent documents. Later that evening, as I walked home through the still-busy streets, I encountered two funeral processions before reaching my front door. The candlelit cortege of the second, attended by pipers playing a dirge and mourners wailing as the black-veiled widow shuffled woodenly behind the shrouded body cast me into a melancholy mood. It took all of little Concessa's bright antics to draw me from my gloomy thoughts.

The next day I saw three more funeral processions and wondered if it was more than mere coincidence. I determined next day to seek the cause. By then it was already too late. The invader had breached the walls.

ARLY THE NEXT morning a knock came on my door. I answered to find a boy with a stick on which was bound a small parchment scroll. "Quaestor Magonus?" he asked, extending the stick. "For you."

"What is it?" called Oriana from inside.

"I am summoned to the senate at once," I answered, glancing quickly at the parchment.

"Oh," she said. "Why?"

"I cannot say." I turned to ask the boy, but he was already gone, taking the scroll with him.

Snatching a bit of seed cake, I hurried off, arriving at the forum with a great number of city officials—various magisters and curatores who had likewise been summoned. Within moments of our entering, the reason was made dreadfully clear. "Citizens of Rome," began an elderly senator, "plague is upon us."

This blunt announcement caused a furor that took a few moments to die down so the senator could be understood. My own heart fell to my feet like a leaden weight. "We have called you here," continued the senator, "at the emperor's request to discuss how best to combat the pestilence and keep it from spreading further."

To this there were cries of "Vacate the city!" and "Get everyone out!"

The elderly senator held up his hands. "Please! Calm yourselves," he said. "Panic is also a potent enemy here." He said that he had seen plague before and knew how it bred and moved through a city population. "In the last outbreak," he warned, "more citizens died from the fires used to contain the pestilence than were killed by the disease itself."

In the simple, decisive speech of authority, he described how the disaster had begun with a rumor to the effect that burning the clothes and bedding of those known to have the plague would keep it from spreading. Frightened and desperate, people had begun setting fire to the belongings of victims, torching the contaminated goods in the streets. Sparks set the roofs of nearby houses on fire, and the wind did the rest. "The fires spread through the city more quickly than did the disease," the old senator explained. "The flames raced out of control. Whole sections of the city burned, killing hundreds who might otherwise have been spared. This must not happen again."

That much was easily agreed; far more difficult, however, was to know what should be done to fight not only the plague but the panic even now mounting throughout the city. The issue was debated well into the day; in the end the assembly adjourned without reaching a final agreement. The simple truth was that no one knew what to do.

"The Vandals were deadly," muttered a disgruntled curatore as we left the Curia, "and *them* we *knew* how to fight."

The next day riots broke out in three markets when a frightened baker, watching his stocks disappear at an alarming rate, suddenly doubled the price of bread. This caused other merchants to raise their prices, too, and their customers, fearing a shortage, began buying up all they could carry. When the bread ran out, they bought grain, and when the day's supplies were exhausted, the mob stormed the granaries. There was fighting in the streets by this time, and bystanders were trampled. The Praetorian Guard was called in to quell the riot, and when the dust had cleared, fourteen people were dead and more than thirty injured.

Plague moved through the city like a stealthy and determined marauder. Within days the fever had spread through the lower city and the reeking slums across the Tiber where the poor sheltered in their hovels of sticks and mud. A few days after that, there was not a house in Rome that was safe from the reach of plague.

I spent the next days working with the curatore—a bald, energetic man named Marius—trying to prevent worried citizens from burning the houses of the afflicted—more easily said than done, for the moment we turned our backs, the flames were kindled. We obtained bread from the imperial bakery and took it to the various quarters, exchanging loaves for promises not to set anything on fire. We secured the services of four cohorts of soldiers to patrol the narrow streets, keeping the way clear and transport moving. We labored from early morning to well past dark to bring a measure of calm to the areas along the river hardest hit by the disease.

The third night, as I walked home, I heard an eerie sound rising from the lowlands along the riverside. At first I thought someone was playing music, soft and sad. I paused a moment to listen and realized that it was not musicians I heard playing—it was an ululation: the voices of the grief-stricken lifted in lament. There must have been hundreds of them wailing, crying, pouring out their sorrow into the night. The sound snaked along the streets, echoing in the empty colonnades and doorways, drifting like a funereal haze over the city.

Sometime during the night someone torched an abandoned wagon bearing a load of corpses covered in straw. The flames spread unchecked, and by morning the smoke was so thick in the streets it looked as though an unseasonal fog had claimed the city. I bade Oriana and Agatha not to go out, not to answer the door, and not to let anyone into the house. Then I went to see if anything could be done.

The streets were full of people rushing here and there, most with rags tied over nose and mouth to keep the bitter smoke and foul air from their lungs. Everywhere could be heard the sound of rushing feet, like the patter of a steady rain on the cobbled streets. Occasionally a scream or shout would overtake the curious rustling sound, but for the most part it remained quiet.

Peering through the haze up ahead, I saw two men bending over the body of a third. He had fallen, I thought, and they were trying to help him to his feet. "Is your friend sick?" I asked as I came up. The two had not heard my approach. They leapt aside. I caught a glimpse of teeth and eyes as they fled. "Here, friend," I said to the man on the ground, "are you sick?"

When he made no reply, I nudged him with the toe of my shoe. His limbs were stiff and unmoving. I had disturbed a couple of thieves in the act of robbing a corpse. I straightened quickly, looked around, and, not knowing what else to do, moved on.

I saw five more bodies in the street before reaching the Via Sacra, the principal street running through the heart of the city. The road was jammed with people, many of whom pushed handcarts heaped with belongings; others carried bundles on their backs or on their heads. The same could be seen in every quarter: people hurrying along the lanes and pathways, making for the wider streets and roads leading to the outer gates—men bustling their families along, women carrying children, the old leading the young. Those who could were leaving the city while they still had strength and life to do so.

I reached the square where the curatore maintained a small office and waited for Marius to arrive. From the doorstep I watched the streams of people build to a river, then a flood. After a time the curatore arrived, harried and disheveled. We had exchanged but two words, however, when a runner appeared to summon us to the Curia; the senate was meeting again in special session to decide what to advise the people of Rome.

As we joined the session, it was being explained how the senate, despairing of the situation and fearing the worst, sought guidance from the emperor. A message had been sent to Honorius in Ravenna; unfortunately, the reply had not yet come back. So, after announcing various possible strategies, the senators lapsed into protracted disagreement: Some called for immediate evacuation of the city, others wanted teams of men organized into a militia of firefighters, and still others thought that special sacrifices might be offered to the gods, who might yet turn the plague away. Needless to say, after half a day's argument the council was no nearer to a unified resolution. The curatore saw which way the wind was blowing and decided to save himself—and me—an aching head by leaving the meeting early.

We pushed through the crowd of onlookers at the door and out across the teeming forum. "What do you think we should do now?"

He stopped and turned to me. "Pray to whatever gods will hear you. There is nothing else."

"There must be *something* we can do."

"If you have anywhere to go," Marius said, "then go. Flee the city as fast as you can." He hurried on, then flung this last over his shoulder: "Do not look for me tomorrow. I am leaving tonight."

I returned home to find Oriana sitting alone with her head in her hands.

"Oriana?" I said, kneeling down beside her. "Are you well?"

"It is nothing. Just a headache."

"Where is Agatha?"

"With the baby." She turned her face to me; her eyes were red from crying. "Mother is sick."

"Have you called the physician?"

She nodded. "He has seen her." She looked at me, and her features dissolved once more in tears. "He was here a little while ago. He said there is no hope."

"But she was fine yesterday. He must be mistaken," I said firmly. "I will go see her." She caught my hand as I turned away.

"No," Oriana said, "she has forbidden anyone to come near her."

"You stay here. I won't be gone long."

"Succat, no! For the sake of the baby," she pleaded. "Mother said we are not to come up to the house."

I hesitated, then decided. "We cannot let her lie in that house alone. She needs help."

"The servants will take care of her. They will do what they can."

"Very well, I will go and speak to the servants at least."

"And you'll come right back?"

"As soon as I've seen that everything's in order."

I hurried up the hill and arrived at Domus Columella to find the court-yard dark and the gate standing open. I entered and called for the porter. When he did not appear, I approached the house. I called for the house-keeper, and when no one answered, I moved to the door. It was closed but not locked; I lifted the latch and went in. The house was dark and quiet.

"Helena?" I called, and then I announced myself. There was no answer, so I called again more loudly as I moved through the silent house.

A weak voice came from her bedroom. "Succat, is that you?"

"It is."

"Go away," she said angrily. "I do not want anyone here—least of all you or Oriana."

I went into the room. A single candle burned in a holder on the table. I took up the candle and went to the bed where Lady Columella was lying, soaked in sweat and shivering. "Go away, Succat. Leave me."

"Where are the servants?"

"I sent them away."

"And Gaius?"

"With Pylades. They have gone to the country."

"But—" I stared at her, as at a stranger. Her eyes were hard, bright cin-ders sunk deep into their sockets, and her flesh was pale yellow and waxy. She had drenched the bedclothes where she lay. "You must have someone to care for you. I will go and—"

"Succat!" she said, struggling up in bed. "Leave me. Think of your wife and child." Exhausted by this feeble outburst, she slumped back. "There is nothing anyone can do. Go away and let me die in peace."

"I will bring you some water to ease your thirst," I said, going to fetch a jar and cup. When I returned, I thought her already dead; she lay without movement, her breath scarcely lifting her chest.

"Helena?" I said, setting the cup on the table beside the bed. Her eyes flickered open. "Drink a little, and then I will go."

She shook her head, the slightest of movements. "Leave the city," she whispered. "Take my daughter and grandchild and go to the villa. You will be safe there."

"Rest now. I will find the physician and bring him to tend you."

"Go!" she screamed, starting up suddenly. "Promise me you will go to the villa."

"I will go. . . . I promise."

She fell back once more. "God bless you, my son. Take care of Oriana and the little one."

"On my life."

"Good . . . good." She offered me a weary, pain-twisted smile. "Farewell, Succat."

I left the house, closing the door behind me. I had no key to secure the gate, so I ran to the garrison to commandeer the services of two soldiers to stand guard on the house lest thieves take it into their heads to plunder the vicarius' palace in the absence of any servants. The physician was not at his home, so I left word for him to look in on Helena as soon as he returned. I then hurried home, where Agatha, having put an extremely distraught Oriana to bed, was preparing my supper.

"That can wait," I told her. "I want you to pack some things for Concessa and Oriana. We are leaving the city tonight."

Then I went in to Oriana. She lay in the dark, sobbing softly to herself. "Is she . . . ?"

"Not yet," I said, "but soon. She made me promise to take you to the villa. I told Agatha to pack some things for you and the baby. We will leave when I come back."

She nodded.

"The curatore is leaving the city tonight. He told me to do the same. We will be safe on the island." I stood and stepped to the door. "I must go out again."

Oriana, worried, rose and followed me out. "No, stay with me."

"I am going to your father's stables to prepare a carriage. Bolt the door after me and don't let anyone in."

Pausing to light a lamp from the kitchen fire, I went out again. The smoke was thicker now, driven on a low, gusting wind. Hot ash and sparks rained out of the air, singeing my hair and clothing as I ran along. Away to the north and east, the sky held an angry orange glow. I passed a group of looters ransacking a house; they were throwing furniture and utensils out into the street from an upper window. The guard was nowhere to be seen, and I did not care to risk my life over a few pots and chairs and a stick of silver or two, so I ran on.

The soldiers I had left at the gate of the vicarius' palace were at their posts. I told them why I had come and asked, "Do you have families here?"

"Yes, Quaestor," replied the older of the two. "A wife and child."

"Then go home to them," I told him. "Gather a few things and flee the city. By tomorrow only the thieves and dying will remain behind. Go now."

As he ran off, I turned to the other one. "What is your name, soldier?"

"Titus, my lord."

"Where is your family, Titus?"

"They live in Lucania," he said.

"Guard the gate while I am inside, and when I am finished, you will come with me. As soon as we are away from the city, you can go home to Lucania."

He looked at me. "What will I tell the centurion?"

"He placed you under my command," I replied. "And I command you to go home and stay there until this plague has run its course. The army will need you then."

He gave me a salute and resumed his place by the door. Holding the lamp, I made my way across the courtyard to the low stable where the vicarius kept several of the horses he used while in the city. He had taken two with him but, as I thought, had left two behind—and they were glad to see me. They were hungry and thirsty, so I watered and fed them and left them to their food while I readied the carriage. It was only a small city carriage—large enough for two but with a small board behind the rear axle which might be used to carry a few things. I filled two jars with water and tied them to the backboard, then led one of the horses to the traces, strapped him in, and tied the other to the rear of the carriage, which I then led into the courtyard.

I paused to look once more at the house. It was dark and silent as I had left it earlier. I did not know whether Helena lived yet or had succumbed, but I knew I would never see her again.

Together Titus and I led the carriage down the hill. I told him to guard the horses while I went inside to get the others. Agatha was ready with a bundle of provisions for us and for the child. "Get some cloth to cover your faces," I told her.

Oriana was sitting in our bedroom holding little Concessa, who was sleeping peacefully in her arms. "I've brought a carriage," I said. "Come, we're leaving."

She nodded, rose, and followed me from the room. Agatha was waiting by the door with a handful of cloth strips. I took these from her, put them in a basin, and poured water over them. "Tie them over your nose and mouth," I instructed, "then Oriana and the child likewise."

Taking one piece of cloth for myself and one for the soldier, I led the women out into the yard. The smoke filled the air like a sour fog; the sky glowed with a filthy, lurid glow. I helped Oriana into the carriage and then turned for Agatha—only to find that she had gone back inside. I ran to fetch her back, saying, "Come, we are all going together."

"I stay here," she said.

"No," I told her firmly. "You must come with us."

Agatha shook her head furiously. "I stay here," she insisted. "Chase robbers away."

"I need you," I told her. "Oriana needs you to help her with the baby." I held out my hand. "Come. It is time to go." She hesitated, but I took her hand in mine, led her out to the carriage, and lifted her bodily into it.

I hurried to where Titus was waiting. "Draw your sword and give me your spear. You lead the carriage, and I will guard the rear."

"Which gate?"

I paused. "Via Appia," I decided. "Make for the Porta Capena."

Putting his hand to the bridle, Titus started off. The street was empty, and the sound of the iron-rimmed wheels on the stone-paved streets echoed back from the houses and courtyards we passed. We soon entered a district of humbler dwellings; there was more activity here: people flitting furtively from house to house, some carrying torches, others darting from one doorway to the next. Some of these were thieves, I was certain, but they could have whatever they could find to steal — much it would profit them when the fever laid them low.

We made good speed through the city and came in sight of the Circus Maximus. The street made a sharp bend and, upon turning the corner, Titus halted. Just ahead of him stood a gang of ruffians with clubs and torches. I hung back in the shadows and heard Titus call out. "We want no trouble here," he shouted firmly. "Stand aside and let us pass."

52

ou can pass," growled the leader of the gang. "But you have to pay the toll." Holding a torch above his head, he advanced slowly. "Those horses will do for a start. And then you can show us what you've got in the carriage."

"Stay back," said Titus. "This is your last warning."

Moving in quickly behind the horse, I stepped to the rear of the carriage, keeping the vehicle between myself and the thugs. "Oriana!" I whispered. "Remain in the carriage and stay down. Whatever happens, stay down."

The chief thug laughed. "Keep your warning. We'll take the horses."

I crouched low, knelt, and untied the horse. Then, taking up the reins, I sprang onto his back and rode out from behind the carriage. "This soldier is under my command," I said, taking my place beside Titus. "Stand aside"—I lowered the spear—"or die."

The chief thug glared at me. "So you say," he growled, hefting his club. "I say you are dead men." Turning to his band of rogues, he called, "There are only two of them. Spread out, all of you. Get in behind and give them the sharp end of your blades!"

As the gang moved warily, fanning out around us, I said to Titus, "When the leader goes down, the rest will scatter. I will take him now. Protect my back."

He nodded to show he understood, whereupon I cried, "Hie! Up!" and slashed the reins across my mount's flanks. The horse leapt forward. I drove right for the bandit chieftain, leveling my spear as I came. A few running strides carried me to him; he flung the torch at me and dived to the side.

It was a clumsy move, easily anticipated, and I swerved the horse into him even as he raised the club to strike. I saw his mouth open in a curse as he tumbled backward. Before he could gain his feet, I wheeled my mount and came at him again. He scrambled to avoid the horse's hooves. I dipped the spear and gave him a sharp poke in the meaty part of his shoulder. I could have killed him without any trouble at all but thought that a painful flesh wound would suffice.

The blade slashed through his tunic and into his skin; the force sent him sprawling facedown in the street. I stopped the horse and stood over him, placing the spear point in the small of his back as he lay bawling and writhing on the ground. Half the gang, seeing how easily I had defeated their strongman, turned and legged it down the street. "Give up," I told him, "and I might let you live."

He went limp. "Now, then, tell your fellow thieves to back off." He made no move to follow my instruction, so I gave him a sharp nip between the shoulder blades. "Now! While you still have breath to do so."

He raised his head. "Get back! All of you get back!" he screamed. "He'll kill me." The thieves, glad to remove themselves from any confrontation with my spear, edged away.

Turning to Titus, I said, "Walk on. I will meet you at the gate."

When the carriage had gone, the bandit chief, somehow imagining he had gained the upper hand, craned his neck around and sneered, "You won't walk away from here. Your soldier friend is gone. We have you surrounded. As soon as your back is turned, I'll have you."

"I thought you might come to that," I told him. "That is why you are going to accompany me to the gate." I prodded him with the spear. "Get up and turn around." He rose slowly and put his back to me. I kept the spear point between shoulder blades. "Now, pick up the torch and start moving," I ordered, "and if I see so much as the glimmer of a knife blade behind us, I will run you through without a second thought."

He lurched forward, shouting, "Stay back! All of you stay back!"

"Hurry!" I said, jabbing him again. "I've wasted enough time on you already." We moved off together—he at a lumbering trot, I on horseback right behind. We rejoined the carriage just before it reached the gate, which was open to allow the unimpeded flow of citizens from the city.

I sent Titus and the carriage through the portal and then said to my hostage, "Get out of my sight!" He stood there blinking, unable to believe that I would not kill him the moment his back was turned. "Go on. Move!" I shouted.

He shuffled backward a couple steps, then, judging he was out of my reach, turned and fled into the darkened street. I watched him go, then rode to where the others were waiting for me on the road. Oriana gave a cry of relief as I rode up. I comforted her and saw that little Concessa slept on, blissfully unaware of the commotion swirling around her.

"You let him go," said Titus. "I would have gutted him."

"He is not worth blunting the edge of your blade," I replied. "Anyway, I did him no favor. If the plague does not catch him, the Praetorians will. Either way he is as good as dead."

With that we joined the desperate flight from the city.

The road was wide and good, but the procession was far from orderly; it jiddered along slowly, like a wounded snake, with many halts and shivering starts. As dawn gathered in the east, shedding a thin gray light on the trail, the awful extent of the flight became apparent. Tangled lines of people stretched to the far hilltop horizon—a turgid black river seeping along pale white banks. As far as the eye could see, people toiled ahead in knots and clumps, many carrying their belongings on their backs or piled high in handcarts—and not people only: horses, mules, donkeys, and even cows, goats, and dogs were hitched to carts.

Daylight strengthened, and I saw, in the ditches and fields 'round about, hundreds of impromptu camps. Too tired to go on, people had simply wandered off the road and slept where they dropped. With daylight came the low, murmuring sound of soft moaning. By this I knew that many of those who had fallen beside the road would not be getting up again.

All through the morning we rolled on. The day grew hot beneath a wide-open sky. When I became tired of riding, I gave my mount to Titus and took his place leading the horse that pulled the wagon. As the sun crept toward midday, the line halted; from someplace up ahead I heard shouting, and, leaving Titus to guard the carriage, I went to determine the cause of the commotion.

A cart was lying on its side in the middle of the road. Under a high and heavy burden, its slender axle had snapped, spilling the contents into the road. The donkey pulling the cart had fallen, and from the way the poor beast was thrashing around, trying to regain its feet, I suspected that it had broken a leg. A desperate man was pushing people away from the wreck in a vain effort to keep them from plundering his belongings.

"Step aside! Step aside!" I said, shoving in to where he stood panting and dripping with sweat. "Here, let me help you." A quick look at his cart and donkey confirmed my suspicions. "The cart is ruined," I told him, "and the animal is injured. If you like, I will help you get them off the road."

"My things," he said, indicating the heap of furniture and utensils. "I cannot leave my property behind."

"I'm sorry," I said. "But you cannot stay here. You are blocking the way."

"Please," he said, snatching at me, "it's all I own! I cannot leave it behind."

"Maybe the cart can be mended," I offered. "Here," I said, turning to the onlookers, "you, you, and you"—I pulled them in—"help me move this out of the way."

"And who are *you*?" demanded one of the men, "the emperor?"

I turned to meet him face-to-face. "I am a quaestor of the city and a centurion of the Roman army, and I am conscripting you to help me. Now, do as I say."

Grumbling, the men stepped forward, and together we unhitched the donkey and dragged the suffering creature away. Next we began shifting the bulk of the man's belongings to the side of the road. One of the men bent to pick up a long, bulky bundle. I heard him curse; he dropped the parcel and jumped back. "There's someone in there!" he said.

"My wife! My wife!" said the owner, rushing forward. He fell upon the bundle as if to protect it from us.

Stooping down beside him, I glimpsed through a fold of the cloth the waxy, bloated flesh of a woman's face: slack-jawed, staring up with dry, clouded eyes, an angry, bulging, blue-black carbuncle distorting the tender flesh below her jaw. The stench emanating from the wrappings banished any lingering doubt that the woman might yet live.

"My wife—" said the man, pushing at me as he tried to rearrange the covering.

"She must be buried at once." I gestured to the men to help me remove her from the road, but they drew away.

"Plague!" someone shouted, and all at once the crowd surged back. "Plague! Plague!" they shouted, stumbling over themselves in their haste to flee.

Instantly angry, some of them picked up stones from the road and began pelting the man. He cried out and fell upon the corpse of his wife. I was struck several times as I tried to get him to help me drag the body from the road. The man refused; he clung to the corpse, shouting and crying. "She is sleeping!" he cried. "She is only sleeping!"

One of the bystanders grabbed a piece of wood from the broken wagon. A whiffling sound filled the air, and I was knocked to my knees. "Stop!" I shouted. "Wait!" I took another blow in the small of my back and rolled onto my side. The improvised club rose high and hung suspended over me.

I covered my head with my arms and braced myself for the blow. Instead, however, my assailant gave out a shout and spun sideways to the ground. Titus appeared above me, took my arm, and pulled me to my feet; he then turned, sword drawn, and shouted, "Stand aside, all of you!"

I strode to the man who had assaulted me. "You there! On your feet. You can help me move the wagon." I chose three more from the crowd, and together we dragged the wagon to the ditch while Titus got the crowd moving again. We carried the corpse of the man's wife to a hollow beside the road, and I made my grumbling volunteers dig a grave for her. The bereft and frantic widower insisted all the while that his wife would wake soon and they would go on, but when the first clods of dirt struck the shroud, he slumped to the ground and wept. He would not be consoled, so we left him there, prostrate on his wife's grave.

By the time I returned to the carriage where Oriana and the others waited, the long, slow migration was moving again. We ate a little bread and drank some water and then resumed the journey, not stopping again until sundown. We camped in a field beside the road, and while Titus grazed the horses, Agatha prepared a simple meal which we ate as the last light of day dimmed in the west.

We were on the road again before dawn, and this time we did not stop. The towns along the way were shut to any fleeing the plague; no one would sell food or anything else to any travelers passing through. I saw people collapse in the road, but we did not stop. I saw an old man, bent double by the weight of the bundle on his back, stagger and fall to his knees; I removed the pack from his back, threw it aside, and gave him water—but I did not stop. The relentless sun beat down on our uncovered heads, Concessa cried through the day, and hungry people begged for food and water as we passed, but I did not stop.

The next day there were fewer on the road, and the next day fewer still. We moved on at better speed and reached the port at Neapolis. It took the remains of that day and most of the next to find a boat and captain who would agree to take us across the narrow stretch of water to Aenaria.

I dismissed Titus, thanking him for his good service, and gave him a handful of coins—as much as I could spare from the little I had with me. I gave him the horses, too, and sent him on his way to his home in the south. Then, taking Concessa in my arms, I led Oriana and Agatha down to the boatyard to wait for the boat to arrive. We sat through the day, watching and waiting.

"Where is he?" I said, growing impatient at last. "He said he would be here. What can be keeping him?"

"Sit down, Succat," Oriana said. "You can rest now. We are almost there." With that she laid her head on her arm and closed her eyes. "I am so thirsty."

I walked back to the carriage and fetched the last of the bread and wine. I drank the wine and refilled the jar with water from a well in the square above the harbor. Upon my return I woke Oriana so she could drink. She rose with difficulty, rubbing her upper arm. I gave her the jar, and she drank, wincing slightly as she swallowed.

"Are you feeling well?" I asked.

"I am just tired," she said, and I noticed a rawness in her voice I had not heard before. "The journey has exhausted me." Unwilling to accept this vague assurance, I pulled aside her mantle, examined the skin of her throat, and felt the sides of her neck but found nothing unusual. "It is just the heat," she insisted.

Concessa woke and began crying then, and while Oriana saw to feeding her, the boat's master appeared. I jumped up and ran to meet him. Slump-shouldered with exhaustion, he removed his wide-brimmed hat and said, "We're losing light. If you want to go, it must be now."

We gathered our few things and followed him down to the wharf, where three of his men were busy keeping a crowd of would-be passengers at bay with the blade ends of their oars. "Everyone wants to leave," said the captain. "I've made four trips to the island today a'ready. This here'll be my last."

"I am in your debt," I told him.

Aenaria lay no great distance off the coast, the last and largest of a string of small islands rimming the great bowl of the bay. Nevertheless the winds were contrary, and the sailors had to row through a rough chop; passage was slow. It was almost dark by the time we reached the tiny harbor of Ischia. After paying the boatman and sending him on his weary way, I turned to Oriana. "How far is the villa?"

She looked at me curiously and opened her mouth to speak. "Ah, it . . . it is—" Her eyelids fluttered, her eyes rolled up into her head, and she collapsed. I caught her and the baby as she fell and eased both of them to the ground.

"Oriana!" I cried. "Agatha, quick! Help me! She has fainted." The older woman was beside me in an instant. Handing her the baby, I said, "Bring some water. Hurry!"

Oriana awoke almost at once and made to get up. "Lie back. Rest a little," I said. "Agatha has gone to fetch some water."

"Let me up," she said, pushing at my hands. "I can stand. I am all right."

"You fainted," I said. "Just lie here a little and wait until Agatha comes back."

"I don't want to lie here," she snapped. "Everyone can see me. Let me up."

I reluctantly helped her to her feet. "Where is the baby?"

"Agatha has her." I saw a low wall nearby. "Here," I said, leading her aside, "sit down here for a moment and regain your strength."

"Nothing is wrong with me," Oriana insisted. "I am weak from the sun—nothing more."

Even as she spoke, I felt a dread coldness creeping into my belly. I sat beside my wife and waited with her until Agatha returned with a bowl of water. "Drink this," I said, placing the bowl in her hands. She sipped a little and then tried to put it aside. "No," I insisted, "all of it."

She made a sour face but did as I commanded. "There," she said, swallowing the last of it. "Happy?"

"Yes. Now, then, how far is the villa?"

"A few miles," she said. "Too far to walk in the dark."

"Wait here," I told her, "I will go and find a carriage."

But the little island port was already closed for the night. There was only one small tavern serving the boatmen of the harbor, but the boatmen were gone and the owner of the tavern did not know anyone with a carriage to hire. "How about a horse?" I asked.

"Old Claudius has a donkey," he volunteered.

"Where can I find old Claudius?"

"Oh, he lives on the other side of the island—near the Columella estate. Do you know it?"

"That is where I am trying to go," I replied, then explained that I had two women and an infant with me and that we were in need of lodging for the night. "Do you have rooms?"

"I am sorry, my lord. I have but two—and they are both taken. There are no other rooms in all Ischia." He spread his hands helplessly. "It is a very insignificant village, and a great many people have come here."

"Do you have a stable?"

"Indeed, sir."

"Then I will have that."

"Never!" he cried in horror. "I could not allow a nobleman and his family to lodge in my stable. What would people say?"

"And what will they say when they learn you let the daughter of Vicarius Columella sleep in the street outside your door?"

Seeing no way out of this dilemma, the tavern owner relented. "It is only a very small stable," he warned. "Ischia is an insig—"

"Yes, yes, it is all very insignificant," I agreed quickly. "Come, show me this insignificant stable of yours."

He led me around behind the tavern to a building that was little more than three wattle walls and a slanted roof. "An excellent stable," I declared. "Satisfactory in every way. Tie those goats to the fence, and I will bring my family."

"Lodging in a stable," said Oriana when she saw it. The rancid straw stank of goat and sour manure "What will my mother say when she hears about this?"

The words were out of her mouth before she knew what she had said. The realization struck her with the force of her pent-up grief, and she crumpled into my arms and wept. I held her and felt the sobs convulse her slender body. Agatha made a place for her in the corner of the stable, where she fell asleep with her face covered in her cloak, soaked in tears.

5 3

**A**T LAST." ORIANA sighed wearily as the carriage turned and started down through the long double rank of tall cypress trees. Their deep green foliage wore a thick coat of powdery white dust from the trail leading to the house.

The carriage rolled to a stop at the rear entrance to the villa, and as I passed the last of my coins to the driver, two aged servants came tumbling out the door, shouting, "Lady Oriana! Lady Oriana! Oh, bless God, here you are!"

They hugged her and stroked her face and hands as if she had been a prodigal daughter whose return had been long awaited. Then they saw the baby. "Oh! Oh! May all the angels bear witness! What is this? A child— such a sweet, darling, tiny thing. It cannot be yours. Is it yours? It is! It must be! Oh!"

The elderly couple took turns holding Concessa, and it was some time before Oriana could break into their prattling and cooing to introduce me to them. "Dea," she said, presenting the little old woman, "and Decimus"—she nudged the old man forward—"this is my husband, Succat."

The two turned their eyes to me, nodding and muttering to one another. "I am glad to meet you," I told them.

"And you, master," said Dea, returning her gaze to the baby. "And you." Then, handing Consessa back to her mother, she bundled us into the house.

Dark-skinned from lives lived in the sun, Dea and Decimus were small,

spry, rustic folk of the kind who had inhabited the island for generations beyond reckoning. Like pagani everywhere, they were wary of strangers and
fiercely protective of anyone they considered kin. They had served on the
estate since before Lord Columella was born. The two of them rushed
around preparing drinks and food for us, stealing glances at little Concessa
all the while.

After refreshing herself, Oriana went to lie down. Leaving Agatha, the
baby, and the two caretakers all to become better acquainted, I went out to
examine the grounds of the estate.

Called Dulcis Patria, it was a most pleasant home: a low, spacious villa of
the old style, with deep eaves to shade a courtyard lined with sturdy
columns supporting a roof of thick red tiles. The stone was old and pale and
pitted where yellow lichen had begun eating into the soft rock. Surrounded
by olive groves, fields of vegetables, and a pond, the house perched on a low
rise overlooking the sea, which shone like molten glass in the hot midday
sun.

Quiet, drowsy with the heat, I walked through a small pear orchard and
stood at the end of the green expanse which ran from the open, horseshoe-
shaped courtyard all the way down to the sea. Fishing boats rocked in the
gentle swell, and the sound of waves lapping the pebbled shore made me
sleepy. I closed my eyes and felt the sun on my face. The wind blew hot off
the water, raising a stink of fish and rotting seaweed.

As I stood there, I felt the tight coil of tension I had carried inside me
since Rome unwind and relax. A dry, enervating fatigue stole upon me.
Eyes closed, face to the sun, I swayed on my feet. My head hurt, and a mild
burning sensation tingled in my throat. I told myself that it was the sun and
heat and exhaustion of the journey—our passage had been a long, tedious
slog after all.

Suddenly tired beyond words, I turned and started back to the house. As
I approached the steps at the bottom of the courtyard, I heard a scream
from deep inside the house.

"Oriana!" I flew up the steps and raced through the courtyard and into
the house. In the bedroom Dea and Agatha were bending over a frantic Oriana, who was thrashing on the bed.

"No!" screamed Oriana, thrusting a hand at me. "Stay back! Stay away!"

Ignoring her protests, I moved to the bedside. Agatha turned and put her
hands on me to push me away. "Go!" she said. "Leave us!"

I brushed her aside. "Oriana, calm yourself. I am—"

"Get him away from me!" she cried.

"Please," I said, sick dread spreading through me, "let me help you." I
reached out to her, but she rolled away screaming.

"No! No! No!" As she raised her hands to prevent me, the loose sleeve of her mantle slid high up her arm.

I saw the red bulge beneath her armpit, and my stomach turned. My hands fell away. I stared at the wicked thing—the undeniable sign of plague. I gazed upon my poor, doomed wife and my strength evaporated like water poured onto a hot stone.

Oriana curled herself into a ball on the bed and lay there wailing and sobbing. Dea hunkered down beside her, speaking softly and low. Agatha took my unresisting arm and led me from the room. I reached the door and looked back. "Oriana . . ."

Shaking off my torpor, I pulled away and went back to the bed. Agatha followed, begging me to leave. "Bring some water," I told her. "And bring a basin and some rags."

I sat down on the bed and gathered Oriana to me. "I am afraid, Succat," she sobbed. "So afraid."

"It is all right," I told her, stroking her hair. "We will take care of you."

I raised the palm of my hand to her forehead; the skin was damp but cool to the touch. There was no fever, which I took to be a good sign. When Agatha returned, I took the cup and made Oriana drink it down. She grew quiet then, and I sat for a long time holding her, reassuring her with soothing words and promises of health restored. At last she drifted off to sleep, and only then did I leave her side.

"We must do all we can for her," I told the women.

"The fever," choked Agatha. "God is punishing us."

"God has nothing to do with this!" I snapped angrily.

"I know a potion," offered Dea. "It could help."

"Go and make it up," I said. "I will stay here with her. Agatha, you take care of Concessa. And keep the baby away from here. No matter what Oriana says, I do not want the baby anywhere near this room, understand?"

The woman nodded grimly.

I sat with Oriana through the night, sleeping in fits and snatches. By morning she was no better but no worse. I examined the red bulge in her armpit, and though the egg-size lump was hot to the touch, the swelling was not so bad, I thought. When she rose, I made her drink some of Dea's remedy, then bathed her head and neck with cool water from the basin and tried to get her to eat some porridge Dea had made.

"Enough," Oriana said, pushing away the spoon. "I must get up."

"Here." I set aside the bowl. "Let me help you."

I lifted her to her feet and supported her as she walked to the corridor. Concessa was crying in another room. "Must she wail like that all the time?" Oriana said, pressing a hand to her head. "Go see to her."

"Are you sure?"

"I can walk," she said. "Go on."

Leaving her in the corridor, I went to see to the baby. Agatha had swaddled Concessa in a cloth and was walking her back and forth across the floor. At my appearance the woman turned toward me, and I saw that her cheeks were wet with tears.

Without a word she turned the child in her arms and, cradling the infant against her bosom, unwrapped the cloth to bare little Concessa's tiny chest. I looked where she was pointing and saw a faint rosy blotch on the pale white skin. On closer inspection I saw that the blotch was a slightly raised, ringlike rash.

I touched the rash gently with a finger, and Concessa wailed all the more.

"It is the mark of death," Agatha whispered darkly.

Angry at her for speaking so, I glared but held my temper. "Say nothing to Oriana about this," I warned her sternly. "I do not want to worry her."

All at once there came a shout from the corridor. "Stay here," I ordered Agatha, and I dashed from the room to find Oriana on her knees, leaning against the wall. Dea stood over her, clutching her by the shoulders. A dark stain of muddy red splashed down the front of Oriana's mantle. Even as I hurried to her, she doubled over and vomited again. The vile stuff spewed onto the floor—blood and bile mixed together.

I ran to Orian's side. Dea and I lifted her to her feet and between us brought her back to the bed. Her chin and lips were stained with black, foul-smelling, clotted blood, and I washed it off with a rag and gave her a drink to rinse the vomitus from her mouth.

"I'm sorry," she said, her voice trembling with the tremors that shook her. "I thought I was better."

"And so you are," I replied. "Dea's remedy has upset your stomach, that's all. I should not have given you so much."

She closed her eyes and lay back. "I'm cold, Succat."

In a chest beside the door, I found a linen palla and covered her with it. She lay in bed shivering for a time, and I sat with her. She did not wake again, but slept through the day. As evening approached, I left her side and went to the kitchen to get something to eat. Decimus jumped up from the small table beside the hearth as I came in and offered me his chair. He poured me some wine and gave it to me, then stood by with the jar as I drank, filling the cup again when it was empty.

Dea brought me some soup she had made, and I sat for a time holding it in my hands, staring into the steaming liquid as at my own beclouded future, and I felt myself sinking beneath a weight I could no longer carry.

Why, oh why, I thought, *did I stay in Rome so long?* I knew the answer: pride, arrogance, ambition—as always. *We should have fled the city the moment I heard the word "plague."* But I had thought more of my position than of my family, and now they would pay the price for my overweening ambition. I cursed myself for the insufferable fool I was.

At Dea's insistence I drank some of the soup, and then returned to Oriana's side. She was still shivering, but her skin was hot and she had sweated through her bedclothes. She roused herself when I dipped a clean rag in water and placed it on her feverish forehead. "Succat . . . ," she moaned, her voice raw as a wound. "I'm . . . , so cold."

"I will warm you," I said, and, stretching myself beside her, I gathered my dear dying wife in my arms and held her close. With this action I knew I most likely joined her in her fate, but I no longer cared. Wretch that I was, I deserved to die with those I had failed to protect.

We remained like this through all the next day and night. The crisis came a little before sunrise of the third day.

Oriana began trembling and coughing and shaking, her jaw so tightly clenched I feared her teeth would shatter. Her eyelids fluttered, but her eyes were vacant, and she seized one ragged, wheezing breath after another, her long body rigid in the bed. I tightened my arms around her as if by strength alone I might keep her from slipping beneath that dark and silent gate.

She gave a last rattling moan, which ended in a gasping sigh. Her fingers straightened as if reaching for the fleeting touch of life, and the fight went out of her. She trembled one final time and lay still. I waited for a moment, and when it became clear that the battle was over, I kissed her lips and forehead and folded her hands upon her breast.

I lay holding her still-warm body until it was light, and then I went to rouse Agatha and Dea to tell them that Oriana was dead. I stumbled through the quiet house, my head pounding with a fierce and fiery ache. At Agatha's door I paused, drew a deep breath, and went in. She was asleep in a chair beside Concessa's bed but woke the moment I stepped into the room.

Her dark eyes met mine, and tears started down her cheeks. "Just a short while ago," I told her. Looking at the sleeping baby, I said, "How is the she?"

Without a word Agatha leaned forward and pulled back the light covering over the small body. I saw the ugly red-black bulge beneath the infant's jaw, and my throat tightened so that I could not speak. I lowered a shaking hand onto the tiny head and stroked the downy-soft hair as the tears fell from my eyes.

Little Concessa died later that same day. Her struggle was mercifully short; the sickness took her in her sleep, and she never woke again. Oriana and her daughter were buried together in the grave I dug with my own hands.

I might have dug another beside that first one, for later that night the sickness came upon me, too. Down and down into the burning fevered depths I sank, until I neither knew nor cared whether I lived or died.

54

OW LONG I lay teetering between life and death, I do not know. Someone came to sit with me from time to time—Dea was there, I know, and also a physician.

Once I awoke and, thinking I was in the German forest, tried to get up and run away to escape the barbarians I imagined chasing me. I did not get far before my legs gave out and I fell sprawling on the floor. Sometime later I found myself back in bed.

Then one evening, just as the sun was sinking, I awoke to footsteps in the corridor beyond the room. "Agatha?" I called out in a voice dry and hollow as the tomb.

Decimus' face appeared in the doorway. He took one look at me and disappeared. I heard him calling for his wife outside, and the good woman arrived a short while later, bearing a jar of wine and some bread soaked in milk, which she fed to me a morsel at a time until I begged her to stop. I sipped some wine then and found I could speak. "Where is Agatha?"

The old woman looked at me with sad, sorrowful eyes and said, "She has died, Master Succat."

"No."

Dea nodded sadly. "The fever took her two days ago. She was not strong." Kindly Decimus added, "I put her beside Lady Oriana."

It was several days before I had strength enough to get up—and then it was only to shuffle from the bed to relieve myself in a pot before falling back into bed panting with exhaustion.

Little by little, however, the disease abated—it happens this way sometimes—and the day came when I could stand and walk without collapsing. I asked Decimus to take me out to see the graves. Summer was beginning to fade; I could feel it in the air and see it in the lowering slant of the sun. Still, the sky was bright and the breeze warm on my skin. With his hand under my arm, the old man led me down the path through the small stand of olive trees to the low bluff above the sea where I had dug that first grave.

We stood for a while in silence, and I could feel Decimus growing uncomfortable, so I said, "You can go." He started to protest, but I reassured him. "I'll be all right. Come back for me later."

The old man nodded and hurried away, and I returned to my contemplation of the graves. The dirt was still fresh on the second, smaller of the two, but on Oriana's grave the mounded earth had already begun to settle. Soon the grass would cover the place, and there would be nothing left to tell that it was there.

I stood staring at the bare mound and thought, _Is this all there is?_

A heap of dirt that would not outlast next year's harvest—was that what life was all about? Was there nothing else? For if all the laughter, hope, passion, and dreams, all the love and life ended in a dank hole in the ground, what was the use? It all came to nothing. In the end the grave loomed over everything—and even that did not last.

The grave swallowed everything. Greedy and insatiable, the grave devoured young and old alike. No one escaped. Death was the answer, the last argument, brutal in its irrefutable finality. Death conquered all, and it would take me as it took everyone else. There was no escape, and nothing I did would ever make the slightest difference.

Even as I stood contemplating this desolate prospect, I heard someone coming down the path. Thinking it was Decimus come to fetch me before time, I turned to wave him off and saw that it was not Decimus but a stranger. Dressed in a simple gray robe, like that of a provincial priest, he came ducking the olive branches and humming a curious tune.

A tall and very plump, round-shouldered man, white-haired but sprightly still, he walked lightly on the balls of his feet. His substantial girth was gathered in a plain leather belt, and though his clothing might have been that of a cleric, the sandals on his feet were those of a Roman soldier.

The happy stranger glanced up as he drew near, smiled cheerfully, and raised his hand in greeting. "So!" he exclaimed in a deep, resonant voice. "Back in the land of the living. Good." He nodded with evident satisfaction. "Not that I had any doubt at all."

He came to stand beside me and looked down at the graves. "Ah, well," he said softly. He folded his hands before him and stood for a moment, bobbing his head. "Ah, yes, well." He sighed and turned to regard me with eyes the same color as the sea. "How are you feeling?"

"You are the physician," I said. "The one who attended me."

"I suppose I am. Although, just between you and me and God, I have been accused of worse." Nodding to himself, he said, "But I am no true physician. I know a little, and I am happy to do what I can. Sometimes it helps."

"If you are not a physician," I said, "who are you?"

"I am called Pelagius," he said. "And, yes, I did look in on you a few times. I am leaving Aenaria in a few days, and I wanted to see you up and around before I left."

"Pelagius," I said. "I have heard about you."

"Ah, yes, well." He sighed again. "I suppose most everyone has by now. Still, I make no secret of it." He peered at me amiably. "Do you have views?"

"None whatsoever," I replied. "I have heard your name, that's all—from a former friend of mine, a priest. *He* had views."

The kindly man rolled his eyes. "Priests! They all have views."

"Are you not a priest?"

"A monk of a sort, but not a priest. Never a priest." He shook his head and looked at me. "Decimus told me you are British born."

"Indeed."

"I am a Briton, too," he confided. He looked out across the sea. "We are both a long way from home, I think. But I at least will not see Britain again."

"Why not?"

"I am bound for Jerusalem," he said. "I have long wanted to go, and now the opportunity has come. I do not imagine I will make any more journeys after that."

As he spoke, a fleeting melancholy tinged his voice. He paused, then said, "I only wanted to see if you were better." He smiled again, recovering something of his former gladness. "And now that I have seen, I will bid you good day."

"Why do they hate you so much?" I asked. The words were out of my mouth before I thought to curb my tongue.

He stared at me, his blue eyes narrowing with the quick intensity of his stare.

"I do beg your pardon," I said quickly. "Please, I meant no disrespect, but as you are leaving soon and I may not see you again, I merely wanted to know. You see, I've heard the way they talk about you, but you are so unlike the person I imagined, and . . ."

"You wanted to know if what they said about me was true?"

I nodded.

"Ah, yes, well, it is not an easy thing to say," he replied, scratching his white-bristled chin. "Am I a fomenter of spurious teaching? A snake in the garden of paradise? A heretic?"

"Are you?"

"Never anything so grand as all that," he confided. "Still, I have made some powerful enemies, and your question is apt. Why do they hate me so very much?" He spread his hands. "That I cannot say. Truly, I find it incomprehensible.

"As to the charge of heresy, I have stood before the pope himself in Rome to receive his judgment. I defended my teaching, and I was acquitted." Pelagius was no longer the jolly monk, his voice taking on the fire of conviction. "*Their* charges, *their* court, *their* council—and I alone, by myself without a friend in the room. The pope heard me out. The pope ruled: 'I find no fault in this man!' "

Pelagius shook his head. "That should have been the end of it. But, alas, it was only the beginning."

"That is the way of the world," I said.

"The way of the world, yes," he agreed, "but not God's way. Truth against the world—ah, now, *that* is God's way."

At his use of the term, I heard the echo of a time so far removed from me it seemed as if it had happened to someone else. "Truth against the world," I replied, unable to keep the sneer out of my voice. "You speak like the Ceile De."

His white eyebrows rose in merry amazement. "You know the Ceile De?"

"I do—in fact, I once considered myself one of their number. At least I wanted to be."

"Once? What happened?"

"I grew up," I replied bitterly. "I got true wisdom. I learned how little it matters what a man believes. Whether a man prays to Zeus or Mithra, Christ or Apollo—no god is ever going to come to his aid; there is no help in trouble, and in the end nothing is going to save him."

Pointing to the graves at our feet, I said, "God's way? I can tell you that from here it looks like God's way is death and corruption in a never-ending parade of brutal and senseless destruction."

"You are bereft," Pelagius told me gently. "It is natural to feel this way in times of grief."

"Grief only sharpens a man's vision," I snapped. "But, no, I have felt this way for a very long time." Indicating the graves once more, I said, "And this—this is merely the final confirmation of a long-held belief. Nothing I have ever seen argues otherwise."

Pelagius was silent for a moment, contemplating the graves at his feet. He nodded to himself, then said, "It is true that we live in a world that does not love us. Our great mother has a voracious appetite for her own off-spring, and she will kill us if she can. And, yes, I suppose she will kill us any-way in the end. Our bodies may be dust, but"—he raised a finger to point skyward—"our spirits were made for heaven."

I complimented him on this well-spoken sentiment and said, "Yet if that is the end, why not just lie down and die and save ourselves all the heartache and trouble?"

"Ah!" He brightened, "It is the trouble that makes it all worthwhile."

"Spoken like a true son of the church," I scoffed.

"Do you doubt it?"

"I do."

He regarded me with kindly indulgence and said, "Give me your hands."

I stared back, uncertain that I had heard him correctly.

"Your hands," he said, reaching out, "let me see them."

Thinking only to humor him and so cut short this increasingly irritating interview, I did as he asked. He held my hands and gazed at them for a mo-ment, as if judging the worth of a pair of gloves. He turned them over and examined the backs, then peered into the palms.

I stood there, awkward in this posture, and wondered how long I must endure his peculiar inquisition.

"They are good hands, strong hands," Pelagius declared at last. "I can see that from a young age you have had to seize whatever has been given you in order to survive. You have done well; you have succeeded where others would have failed, and you have done it by the strength of your hands alone."

My throat tightened with the knowledge that, inexplicably, he spoke the truth.

"Ah, yes, but now"—he continued gazing at my hands as if at a map or chart of an unknown island—"you have reached the limit of what human strength can achieve. You look upon the work of your hands and see how worthless it is. For unless it is allied to something greater than itself, your achievement will not outlast the hands that framed it."

He raised his eyes to mine and saw the confirmation there. "I see that this is so."

Unable to dispute his conclusion, I merely nodded.

"Ah, but see! Your labors have not been in vain," he assured me. "It is a great and wonderful gift you have been granted: Now you know a truth that it takes some men a lifetime to understand—and many never learn at all."

He released my hands, and the spell was broken. "A dubious gift, it seems to me," I muttered, finding my voice again.

"Never say it," he retorted gently. "Truth against the world, remember. In truth is freedom itself. Dwell in truth and the things of this world can no longer enslave you." He smiled suddenly, "And you know something of being a slave, I think, yes?"

Again I merely nodded.

"Wealth, power, fame—all those prizes for which other men strive so ardently—none of them can ever hold dominion over you again. You are free to pursue the things that last."

"What things are those?"

"The things of God."

He genuinely meant it, but I stiffened at this prosaic pronouncement. How little he knew if he imagined I would find any comfort in that quarter.

Before I could protest, he touched my hand again and said, "You have learned what a man can do in his own strength, yes? Perhaps now it is time to learn what God can do with a man who knows the limits of his strength."

He smiled and held his head to one side, as if considering a view he found mildly amusing. "Do you mind if I pray for you in the days to come?"

"Not at all. But why not use your breath for whistling? It will do as much good."

He looked around at the olive grove and the flat, motionless sea glittering beneath the sun. Finally he said, "Ah, yes, well, I have inflicted myself upon you long enough. I must go. I will say farewell, Patricius."

It is an ordinary word, *patricius*; it means nobleman. And I thought nothing of it at the time. I wished him well on his journey and bade him go in peace. He lifted a hand in parting and walked back up the path, humming as he went. In a little while I was alone again, and more bereft than ever.

I visited the graves every day from then on. Each day the despair in me grew. Morose, heartsick, I sank down and down into a black, airless abyss: trapped. There was no consolation, no way out. Dea fussed and worried over me, and Decimus tried to interest me in running the estate. It was a gesture of kindness only; he needed no help from me.

Instead I sat in the olive grove and watched the days pass, sinking deeper and deeper still into a grim and solitary hopelessness.

Then one evening I returned to the house to find a courier waiting for me—a young soldier wearing the blue belt of the *scholae*, or imperial bodyguard.

"Greetings, my lord," he said courteously. "I bring a message from Rome."

He opened the dispatch box at his belt and drew out a small scroll. Thanking him, I accepted it and set it aside. "You must be tired from your journey. Stay here tonight if you like; I will have the housekeeper prepare a meal for you."

I dismissed him then, but he did not move.

"Was there something else?"

"Sir, if you please, I am to watch you read the message and return at once with your answer."

"Of course," I said. "Then we had both better sit down. Dea, bring us some wine and give this hungry soldier some of your good cakes."

Taking up the scroll again, I looked at the seal. It was a senatorial insignia, but I did not recognize the emblem. I broke the seal and unwrapped the tightly rolled parchment. "This is from Senator Graccus," I said. "Did you know that?"

"Yes, my lord. The senator himself gave it to me."

While the housekeeper scurried around preparing supper, I read the message from my friend and guide. His salutation was warm but subdued, and the reason became quickly evident: Word had come from Gaul that Vicarius Columella had been slain in an attack on Augusta Treverorum; the garrison itself had been lost. The senator apologized for having to break the news this way, but inasmuch as he had been reliably informed that Lady Columella and her son, Gaius, had died in the plague it was his duty to inform me that Oriana had inherited the family property. He was certain we would want to make arrangements to return to the city in due course to register our legal claim. Further, owing to the severity of the plague and the concomitant loss of seats in the Curia, he had been empowered to offer me a praetorship—the next office higher than a quaestor—effective immediately.

So there it was. Heir to a fortune and an eventual senatorship as good as secured. A glorious future beckoned, and all it had cost me was everything.

I read the words again, and they turned to ashes in my mouth. The futility! The insane futility of it all struck me as ludicrous and obscene. What was the use of striving, of trying to make a life, when death rendered every circumstance meaningless? Whether success or failure, happiness or sorrow—all was swallowed in the grave. In light of that, nothing mattered. Death claimed everything, the world moved on, and in time, whether good or ill, all was forgotten.

I sat staring at the scroll and felt the soldier's eyes on me. I glanced up at him. "My lord?" he said. "What answer will you give?"

"Tell the good senator that Lady Oriana and her infant child have succumbed to the plague. Inform him that I also was taken ill but am now much recovered. Tell him that I am grateful for all he has done on my be-half, but that I am better occupied here, and therefore I regret to say that I will not be returning to Rome to take up the praetorship so kindly and thoughtfully offered."

He rose at once. "I will tell him, my lord."

"Sit down, friend. You will eat something before you go. The fate of Rome can wait until you've finished your supper."

The soldier thanked me and resumed his place. Dea brought out bowls of fish stew and placed them before us. There was bread and goat cheese, along with some green onions fresh from her garden. I let the young man eat a moment, then asked, "Where is your home?"

"My family is from Lusitania, my lord."

"How long have you been in Rome?"

"Two years."

"Before that?"

"I was at Aeminium, not far from where I grew up."

"Have you served long?"

"Four years," he replied, adding quickly, "It will be five in three months."

I shook my head. Less than five years and already a member of the scholae. But what of that? I myself had become both centurion and a quaestor in less than half the time he had served. The empire rested on such young and inexperienced shoulders. I wondered how long it could last.

We talked a little more, and when he finished, he rose and took his leave. "Stay here tonight," I offered. "It is no trouble. The house is nearly empty. You can be on your way first thing in the morning. Senator Graccus will not mind, I assure you."

"I thank you, sir, but I must return to the port. There is a boat waiting."

"I commend you, soldier," I said. "May your sense of duty serve you well."

He departed then. I walked with him a short way down the path to see him off, then stood for a time looking at the evening sky and listening to the crickets in the tall grass. Rust-tinted clouds sailed low across the dusky horizon. The dark branches of the cypress trees above me were alive with the twitter of tiny birds fidgeting and fussing as they settled for the night. The peace of the place was a balm to me, and I needed it. Let the world go its way, I wanted nothing more to do with it. Let it go—the rank, the wealth, the much-vaunted glory, and all the vain striving that went with it . . . let it all go. I wanted none of it.

Until I read Graccus' message, I had not known what I would do. His question forced a decision, and as I read those efficient and well-ordered words, I knew that there was nothing for me in Rome that I desired. I did not want to be a senator. I did not want property and position. I did not want wealth, or power, or anything else that death would steal in a few years' time.

What, then, *did* I want?

55

UTUMN CAME EARLY to the island. I watched as the harvest proceeded. Grain was reaped, threshed, and stored; fish and vegetables were dried and livestock fattened for butchering. The days drew in slowly, and more often than not, cold winds brought rain off the sea. Most days I sat in a chair beside the brazier in my room feeding twigs to the fire—much to the consternation of Dea, who brought meals only to take them away again cold and uneaten.

Graccus did not let his offer end with a single refusal. He sent two more couriers, each with slightly more urgent messages imploring me to return to Rome and take up my praetorship at once. Plague had devastated much of the city, the senator wrote, and there was a great deal to be done. A good man could advance himself with unprecedented swiftness. Come to Rome, he said, and on my return we would talk about my future, in which, apparently, the rank of vicarius was a juicy plum ripe for the plucking.

This last message was delivered in person. Senator Graccus, on his way to the emperor's winter palace on the island of Capri, stopped by to persuade me to heed the voice of reason.

"I do not wish to be a vicarius," I told him. "I do not wish to be anything—save, perhaps, left alone."

"But you cannot remain here forever."

"Why not?" I countered. "I have all I need—and more besides."

"A very great deal more besides," he declared. "Aulus left everything to you. What about the house in Rome?"

"What about it? Sell it. Give it away. I don't care."

"It is worth a fortune."

"Then it will make some undeserving dog very rich."

"And Columella's fortune—you'd give that away, too, I suppose?"

I shrugged. "Why not? I have more than I can spend now."

"But you don't spend anything at all that I can see," argued the senator. "You live here like a ghost, haunting the groves and shore. It is not healthy. You need to get back to work. Great things are happening in the city; opportunities abound. Now is the time to make something of yourself, and unless you seize the day, it will pass you by."

"Good."

"Come back to Rome," he said, his voice and manner softening. "If you don't want to live in Domus Columella, I understand. You can stay with me until you find a place you like better."

"I like living here, Graccus," I told him.

"But you are *not* living here," he said, "you are wasting away. You are dying."

"Then why can't you just let me die in peace?"

"You cannot mean that. You are distraught." He frowned, puffing out his cheeks in exasperation. "Well, who can blame you? It has been a dreadful ordeal, after all. Perhaps you need a little time to get over it." He seemed to be talking to himself; he sighed, regrouped, and started again. "I am sorry. You are right. Winter here, gather your strength, and we'll talk again in the spring. There is no hurry. No hurry at all." He rose and prepared to leave.

"No hurry for you, but quite the opposite for me. I must go."

"So soon?"

"The emperor is expecting me. We are to sail to Crete for some reason. I will call on you again in the spring."

I saw no one else that winter and received no further communications from Graccus. The rain lashed the old tile roof, and the wind drove the pigeons to hide up under the eaves, but in all it was a mild and fairly short season, and it was not long before the days began to lengthen once more. When it grew warm enough, I went to the graves to sit and watch the grass grow on the bare mounds. Dea gave me some wildflower seeds to plant, which I did—not because I cared one way or the other about dressing the graves but because it was the kind of thing Oriana would have done, and I wanted to please her.

For the rest, Graccus was right. I haunted the villa like a wraith: aimless, wandering, drifting here and there without purpose, without volition, stalking the grounds in a gloom of my own making and slowly succumbing to a sick and debilitating melancholy.

I saw this myself but did nothing about it. I spent whole days strolling along the seaside, listening to the waves, watching the tides sweep endlessly back and forth across the strand. What, I asked myself, was the use? Life was without meaning, and a meaningless life was mere existence—no better than that enjoyed by the snails and mussels in the tide pools, creatures that lived and died by the whims of wind and wave.

All was meaningless. Rank futility wrapped me in its bleak embrace and fed my ever-increasing pessimism on hopelessness. Despair, dark and potent, found in me a fertile field and spread its noxious spores. They festered and grew. As spring drew on, there ripened a black, cankerous fruit in my heart.

Soul-sick and inconsolable, I roamed the grounds, indifferent to all that happened around me. Whether I rose in the morning or failed to rise, bathed or did not bathe, dressed or went about in filthy rags—it was all one to me. I ceased shaving, and my beard and hair became long, tangled, and unkempt—which made Dea cluck and fret like a mother hen over a worrisome chick. She strove with me to eat and drink, but to no avail. Food had lost its savor, and the smell of it turned my stomach. I consumed enough to keep myself alive, but little more, and I watched the bones sharpen beneath my pallid skin.

Sometimes I lay in my room for whole days without stirring, only to emerge at sundown to wander the grove and shoreline the entire evening and far into the night—sometimes failing to come in at all and sleeping under the olive trees or in the grass above the strand.

On one such night I lay awake watching the stars spin slowly, slowly in the heavens until the rising sun leached the starlight from the sky. I stared into that fiery golden disk and felt the warmth on my face as it began to pour heat and light onto the waking world. The brilliant light scorched my eyes, yet still I gazed into the burning whiteness, and into my mind floated the memory of a vow I had made in my former life.

"Three kinds of light obtain," declared Datho on the night I stood before him: "that of the sun and, hence, fire; that of the knowledge obtained from the instruction of wise teachers; and that which is possessed in the understanding of God, which illuminates the heart, and is the true light of the soul.

"Therefore, my son, seek the True Light in all your ways; search diligently and with tireless perseverance. Take the Light as your law, your love, and your guide, now and henceforth, forever. If you would do this, answer now upon your life."

I had stood before him and answered, "Upon my life I make this vow."

It was a lie then, and I felt its wicked sting now. I had gone my own way, and that way had led me to this barren place: alone, miserable, heartsick, and grief-stricken, death hovering at my shoulder. It occurred to me as I lay with the sun searing into my eyes that the lie had triumphed and it was killing me.

"If there is a God in heaven," I muttered, my voice raw with thirst and exhaustion, "hear me now: I am finished. If you want this life, you can have it. Otherwise today I die."

I waited awhile to see if anything would happen. There came no answer—but then, I did not expect one. So it was death for me, too.

Still I endured the fiery light a little longer. At the moment when I knew I must look away or be forever blind, I turned my eyes toward the sea and, in my sun-dazzled sight, saw a tall man walking along the strand: a shadow shape only, a quavering dullness in the radiance.

I blinked and looked away. When I looked back, he was still there, and nearer. As he came closer, his form took on solidity and substance. He was dressed in a green-and-blue-striped cloak, with a red mantle and trousers of black and yellow. Around his neck he wore a torc of red gold as thick as a ship's chain; silver bracelets gleamed on his arms, and rings adorned every finger.

Under his arm he carried a leather bag, and as he strode swiftly nearer, I saw that the bag was full of parchment scrolls—innumerable letters, tightly wound and sealed. He came to where I lay and stood over me, looking down, his face lost in the radiance of the sun. I shielded my eyes from his blazing countenance.

"Who are you, lord?" I asked.

"I am Victoricus," he answered, and, withdrawing one of the letters, he placed it in my hand. Receiving the scroll from him, I unrolled it and read out the heading of the letter. The words shimmered as if made of fire. They said: THE VOICE OF THE IRISH.

Even as I read out those words, I heard a cry falling from the clear, empty sky—a voice I recognized, but who? Before I could discern who it might be, the voice was suddenly joined by others, all of them calling out as one, saying, "Noble boy, noble boy! Come walk among us again!"

It was the folk of Sliabh Mis and Focluit Wood—it was Miliucc's people—calling out to me, begging me to come to them once more. That they should beseech me so pierced me to the quick.

In that instant something broke inside me. It was as if somewhere deep within, a wall that had stood strong and tall and straight for so long suddenly cracked, and great chunks began falling from it, allowing the pent-up waters of a raging flood to surge through and into the void that was my soul.

Overcome by this flood tide of strong emotion swirling through me, I struggled to my feet. I swayed for a moment but, unable to stand, sank to my knees once more, gasping and gulping as my stony heart rent in two. Great tears welled up in my eyes; I lowered my face to my hands and wept—how long, I cannot say, but when I finally raised my head to look around, the man was gone, nor could I find any sign of the scroll—but the sound of the voices still echoed in my ears.

"*Noble boy, come walk among us again!*"

The tears flowed down my cheeks and neck, and I raised my face to the sun and let them flow. I wept for my poor dead Oriana and little Concessa, and for the sad ruined waste of my life. In my shame and contrition, I wept for all those I had deceived and betrayed—all the empty promises and the vows so blithely ignored. I wept for the easy deceits I used and the love I had thrown away and for the stubborn, willful blindness that forever kept me from seeing the truth.

"Truth against the world," Pelagius had said—the axiom of the Ceile De—and I, who had never sought the truth in any way, sought it now with a broken and contrite heart. "Lord and God," I cried, "be my Vision and my True Word. Let me walk in the Land of the Living again."

As if in answer to my plea, the voices echoed once more in my heart: "*Come noble boy, walk among us again.*" And, oh! The sound of those Irish voices, at once so plaintive and appealing, so full of yearning, resonated deep within me. That selfsame longing struck down into my hollow, empty heart, took hold and filled it. I lay on the strand and felt it grow in me until it inhabited all my being and there was room for nothing else.

Inert, unmoving, I felt the sun soaking into my flesh, into my very soul, restoring me with its warmth and light. I lay on the beach clinging to the slender hope that perhaps I might actually do as the voices suggested. As the sun mounted higher, this hope grew into a fragile desire. Still I held to it, refusing to let it go, and desire broadened and deepened into a swiftly solidifying determination: I *would* return to Ireland.

This is what the voices were calling me to do, and this I would do.

Up I rose, turned my back on the sea, and walked toward the house, volition returning, gaining strength with every step. By the time I reached the house, I was all purpose and conviction.

Hungry, thirsty, and full of sorrow at how I had allowed myself to sink so far, I washed myself and then bade Decimus to cut my hair and shave me; he happily obliged, while Dea flitted around the kitchen preparing a meal which she laid before me with manifest pleasure. While I ate, I thought about my decision and wondered if the Irish would truly receive me.

But, I thought, even if they did welcome me, what would I do there?

The question had only to be asked, when like a resounding echo the answer came winging back: become a filidh again.

Mystified by the obvious simplicity of the solution, I could not quite take it in. I walked around the rest of the day turning the thought over in my mind—tenderly, gingerly, like a beggar holding a rare and extremely delicate treasure he has found—unwilling to entrust much hope or confidence in it, lest I deceive myself. Even so, I could not resist fingering it, touching it, examining it from every direction. Could I? Could I really return to the life I had begun there?

Was there anything to prevent me? Nothing that I could discover. Money? I was heir to the Columella fortune. Distance? Danger? With my fortune I could travel the world in comfort and security, if not absolute safety.

Over the next few days, the determination hardened in me to return to Ireland. I would go back and take up my long-vacant place as filidh and complete my training to become a bard.

**AIL AND WELCOME!**" cried Graccus, bounding into the reception room of his fine, palatial house. "This is a pleasant and long-awaited surprise." Taking my arm in his, he walked me through the house and into the palm-shaded courtyard. Water splashed from a marble fountain shaped like a dolphin leaping from a pool. Nearby a small table and chairs were set up beneath a striped canopy.

"I am glad you have finally returned to your senses." The elderly senator was so happy to see me that I could feel my resolve melting away. To disappoint him was the last thing I wanted but the very thing I had come to do.

"I have returned, yes," I replied, bracing myself for his disapproval. "But I cannot stay."

"And why not? We have much to discuss, you and I. A very great deal has happened in Rome since you left, and I have not been idle."

"I'm on my way to Hibernia. There is a ship waiting for me at Neapolis even now. I've only come back to Rome to settle my affairs, and then I am away."

"I see." Senator Graccus gazed at me, the smile slowly fading from his face. "Which affairs," he said stiffly, "do you mean?"

"The property left to me by Vicarius Columella."

"Yes, what about it?"

"I want to sell it."

His good-natured features arranged themselves into an expression of petulant disapproval. "Do you have any idea what that entails?"

"Only that a buyer must be found and a price agreed. Beyond that, I had hoped you would guide me. I will trust your judgment entirely."

"Come along, then. We will talk." Graccus led the way to the canopied table; he took one chair and waved me to the other. Seeing a glimmer of a chance to influence my decision, the astute senator swooped at once. "You have been traveling. You are tired. Here, now, sit with me. Let us have a drink and discuss this."

I sat down, and he took his place across the table, gazing at me with fatherly concern. "It will not be easy," he said after a moment. He picked up a jug of wine and poured the dark red liquid into two glass cups. "With the plague, most of the best people have fled to the country." He handed me a cup. "Buyers for a property of that quality are scarce. It could take"—he puffed out his cheeks—"oh, months at least, perhaps years before you could find a suitable party."

"Would it take that long?"

"You will stay here, of course," Graccus said, moving on swiftly. "What about the island villa?"

"That is settled already. I have given it to Dea and Decimus."

"You just *gave* it to them?"

"I did that."

"Have you any idea what this *gift* cost you?"

"Not in the slightest."

"Well . . ." He shook his head in mild incredulity. "I commend your generosity, if not your sagacity. That estate was worth"—he tapped his teeth in thought—"let us say you could have named your price. I can think of any number of noblemen who would sell their firstborn for a chance to own it."

"Maybe some of them would feel the same about the town house."

"I would not count on it," he warned. "No, that will be a far different matter. There are properties aplenty in the city now."

The mere thought of waiting chafed me raw. I could see my newfound determination ground down and down to a fine powder to be blown away by the first contrary wind. Reckless in the grip of my decision, I pressed ahead. "Graccus," I said, "tell me the truth. What do you think the house is worth?"

He swirled the wine in his cup. "In excess of seven hundred thousand solidi," he answered at last, "more or less."

"I will sell the house to you for half that amount. What do you say?"

He laughed. "I say you are being very foolish. Even if I had that much money ready at hand, friendship would prevent me from taking advantage of you."

"Two hundred thousand, then," I said.

"Succat, please." He held up his hands. "I cannot."

"One hundred thousand," I said firmly. At this the senator's eyes grew round.

"I begin to believe you are serious."

"One hundred thousand gold solidi—and Domus Columella is yours."

He hesitated, licking his lips. I could see him weakening.

"Come, Graccus, I know you want it as much as I want to give it to you. Take it and let us part as friends."

"You are insane," he declared, shaking his head firmly. "No. I will not do it."

"Please, Graccus. I cannot stay here any longer. The ship will not wait forever. When it sails, I mean to be aboard."

He gazed at me, a paternal sadness stealing into his eyes. "Why must you go away?" he asked. "And why, of all places, to Hibernia?"

"There is nothing for me here," I began.

"Not true," protested the old statesman quickly. "The way is open for you to become a senator and then surely a vicarius. Beyond that who knows? One day you might even become a consul. A man of your integrity and intelligence—why, anything is possible."

I smiled in gentle reproof at his shameless flattery. "Please, Graccus, we both know better."

"It could happen," he insisted.

"Then let it happen to someone else."

"But why, of all places on the civilized earth, choose Hibernia?"

"I want—" I began, my voice tightening as emotions seized the words. "I left something of myself there, and now I must find it."

He frowned. "You were a slave in that barbaric land, were you not?"

"I was a slave, yes. But I was alive there, too—in a way I have not been alive since."

"Nonsense!" he snorted, dismissing the idea.

"No, it is true," I insisted. "I tried to live as a Roman. I loved Oriana, and for her sake more than for my own I tried to make a life here in Rome. But this was never my home."

"And Hibernia, I presume," he said, "is where you now belong?"

"I cannot say," I replied. "But I know that my time here is at an end." I could see he did not believe me. "Listen, Graccus," I said, and then I began to tell him of my life in Ireland. I told him of Sliabh Mis and King Miliucc's holding, the people there and their simple, forthright ways. I spoke of Sionan—the first time I had mentioned her name aloud to anyone since the day I left—and Cormac and Datho. I described the wooded hills and green valleys, the mountains and plains, and the all-encircling sea; I told him of the druid house, the study there and the daily chores; I described the Comoradh as Filidh, the Gathering of Bards, and the initiation I had undergone to join the ranks of the druids.

I told him of sitting on the hillside watching the blue winter shadows creep across the valley and listening to the sheep bleat as the shepherd led them to the enclosure for the night. I described the taste of honey mead in the cup, the smell of peat smoke on the evening air, and the soul-stirring sound of a bard's voice lifted in song. I told of watching the summer stars wheel slowly through the heavens, trailing a deep, fathomless peace in their wake.

As I spoke, other memories crowded in, too. The savage beatings, the aching hunger, the filth. I remembered picking lice from my tangled hair, walking barefoot in the snow, and eating maggoty meat because there was nothing else. No, all was not harmony and bliss in Éire—and yet . . . there was something more, something I could not name. Against all reason I was being drawn back to the place I had suffered my greatest humiliation, endured the cruelest hardship, and which I had striven so mightily to leave. But the force drawing me back was greater than myself and more powerful than my own volition; it had placed within me an urge so enormous that it dwarfed all reason and reduced all argument to silence. I was compelled to go.

This I explained to Graccus, too. The aged senator listened without comment or interruption. When I finished at last, he sat quietly for a time, his kindly eyes searching my face. Finally he drew a long, reluctant breath and said, "Anyone so desperate to part with his inheritance will certainly fall afoul of someone less scrupulous than I."

"You'll help me?"

"Mind, you may not find it all as you remember it, but I see now why you must go. Yes, I suppose I will have to help you."

I thanked him and praised his kindness and liberality. "Not at all," he said. "I do not do it for you. I do it for myself, and I am not so generous as you think. I mean to extract a vow from you."

"Anything," I agreed. "What is it?"

"Only this: that if you do not find what you seek in Ireland, you will come back to Rome and allow me to establish you here."

"You have my solemn promise," I said. "Thank you, Graccus. You are a true friend." In a fit of exuberance, I leaped to my feet, seized him by the shoulders, and hugged him.

"That will suffice, Succat," he said, pushing himself away. "Now, sit down, and I'll tell you what I intend." He waved me back to my seat and poured more wine, saying, "What if I were to advance you the hundred thousand against the eventual sale of the property—would that be agree-able to you? When the house sold, I would naturally deduct the advance from the total and send you the rest." He raised the cup to his lips and sipped, watching me over the rim. "Well? What do you say to that?"

"Agreed!" I shouted, jumping to my feet again. "But you must be paid for your efforts. You say the house is worth seven hundred thousand, yes?"

He nodded. "If not far more."

"Then anything over five hundred thousand is yours to keep. That is my final offer, Graccus. Take it or leave it."

"I accept."

The documents were drawn up and signed that very night. At Graccus' insistence we celebrated with roast suckling pig, and the next day he took me down into the storeroom beneath his house, opened his strongbox, and brought out the required amount. The gold coins were counted into leather bags, and these in turn were placed in a small, ironbound chest. "Take an old man's advice," he said, "and keep enough money with you to satisfy any thieves, but under no circumstances let on that you have more in the chest. It would be more than your life was worth if anyone guessed how much you carried."

"Thank you, my friend," I said. "You have helped me far more than you know."

I tried to say farewell then and there, but he insisted on accompanying me to Neapolis to see me safely aboard the ship. Thus we traveled the next day to the seaport with a guard of two Praetorian soldiers. It was a pleasant ride, and when we arrived at the wharf, I was sorry to see it end. We dismounted, and as the strongbox—safely hidden among my other belongings—was carried aboard, I turned to take my leave of the old senator.

"I will miss you, Graccus," I said, and thanked him once again for all he had done on my behalf.

He waved aside my thanks. "It is nothing. I stand to make a considerable amount out of our arrangement. Anyway, you will see me again—perhaps before another year is out."

"How so?"

"Five hundred thousand in gold is too great a temptation to place before anyone, not least a ship's greedy crew."

"Then just keep it," I offered.

"I will do no such thing," he sniffed. "I will bring it to you myself."

"Hibernia is a long way from Rome," I warned.

"I have often wondered what it would be like to travel beyond the frontier. This will give me a chance to find out at last."

He embraced me then and said, "Farewell, Succat, my son. I hope you find the happiness you seek."

"When you come, ask someone to lead you to Lord Miliucc in the Vale of Braghad," I said. "I will not be far from there, I think."

I made my way onto the deck then, and in a little while the master threw a line to one the smaller rowboats and the crewmen began towing the ship out into the bay. I stood at the rail and watched until the encircling arm of the coast took Graccus from view. I then turned my face to the west and to the journey ahead.

That night I slept on deck beneath the star-clouded heavens and dreamed of Ireland. In my dream I held the parchment letter and heard the voices calling me once more. "*Come, noble boy,*" they said, "*walk among us again.*"

Only this time the word they used was *Patricius*—the name given me by the monk Pelagius. This so surprised me that I came awake with a start—as if someone had called my name. But there was no one about, and all was quiet save for the softly lapping waves against the hull of the ship.

Patricius . . . I heard in the name a sound like thunder a long way off. It filled me with a strange and wonderful anticipation. I lay on deck beneath the stars, watching the inscrutable heavens and wondering what it meant.

57

HE VOYAGE TO Éire was not as smooth or tranquil
as I had hoped. Three days out from Neapolis, the
ship's steering oar snapped; repairs were attempted,
each as useless as the last, and after drifting with the
wind for several days, we were rescued by a passing fishing boat and towed
to the port at Marsalla. I waited four days while the ship's master tried to
find a suitable replacement; when he informed me it would have to be
made anew and that this could likely take a month or more, I decided to
search for another ship. Within the week I found a vessel bound for Britain
and induced the ship's master to convey me to Hibernia, promising an
abundance of trade among the Irish, of whom he knew nothing.

We departed two weeks later and made good time until passing the
Straits of Hercules, where, once beyond the famed pillars, we encountered
a storm that hurled rain upon us in a seemingly never-ending deluge. The
pilot could find no safe harbor and did not care to chance an unknown cove
or bay, so we had no choice but to ride it out. Tossed to and fro from prow
to stern, I retreated to my small quarters belowdecks, where I became instantly and violently sick. All that night and all the next day, I lay on my
sweat-soaked bed: stomach heaving, mind spinning, body trembling in
agony with every shuddering rise and heart-stopping plunge of the hull. In
truth it was worse than the plague.

For six days and nights, I lay in stifling darkness, unable to raise my head.
The crewmen regularly brought me water and dry bread to eat, but even
that would not stay down. I swallowed a few bites, only to have them come

surging up a few moments later. In my fevered sleep I dreamed of scaling impossible cliffs and falling, then woke to a room that pitched and lurched like a box on the back of a wild horse. Once I gathered my fast-fading strength and climbed on deck to escape the stench of my quarters and take in some fresh air; I staggered the few steps to the rail, vomited over the side, and promptly fainted.

When I woke the next day, I was lying on my bed, my clothes fouled and reeking. But the ship had stopped spinning and dancing, and the wind had dropped to a stiff, whining gale. More dead than alive, I dragged myself up onto the deck.

The sun was shining, and the sails were full, the waves were running by the hull with satisfactory speed. I clung to the mast and drew the fresh, cool air deep into my lungs until my head began to clear. The crew, much amused by my infirmity, inquired with insincere compassion after my health and suggested ludicrous remedies I might try. I accepted their taunts as a form of rough affection and bore it all with good grace. The master ordered one of the crewmen to bring me a bowl of sweet wine and some bread; I sat holding the bowl with one hand and dipping the bread with the other. The food went down and stayed down, and, for the first time in what seemed an eternity, I felt much better.

I endured no more sickness, and after two stops along the coast for fresh water—fifteen days apart—we finally came in view of Britain's renowned white cliffs. Try as I might, I could not persuade the master to continue to Ireland. Despite our agreement not to stop until reaching our destination, he insisted on making landfall at Londinium—a rank and weedy market town surrounded by a stinking marsh. We remained there ten days before the paltry charms of the place withered and the master could be convinced to move on.

So it was that, after nearly two months, we sailed into Mare Hibernium and that same day glimpsed the far-off hills of Éire. Over the next few days we moved slowly up the coast; I pointed out the best trading places along the way but would not permit the master to stop just yet—I knew only too well what would happen. Instead we crawled northward, hugging the coast, with me at the prow searching the shoreline for the high headlands that protected Miliucc's realm in the Vale of Braghad.

From time to time the ship was seen by those in settlements near the shore; sometimes we were followed and hailed from the strand in hopes that we would turn aside to trade. The master was desperate to oblige them, but I remained firm in my purpose, and with a ready supply of promises and threats kept the ship headed north until at long last we came to a bay I recognized. "Here!" I cried. "This is the place! We have found it!"

I was over the rail the moment the keel scraped the bottom of the bay, plunging into the cold, blue-black water. In my eagerness I began swimming to shore. Bracing myself against the churning wash, I stood as soon as I felt the pebbled strand beneath my feet. After so many days aboard ship, walking was more of a challenge than I could meet; I staggered, fell back, and went under. Pummeled and dragged by the rolling surf, I swallowed a fair amount of water before scrambling from the waves.

Tottering onto the beach, my heart high and lifted up, riding the crest of a great wave of anticipation, I raised my eyes to the mist-wrapped, gray-green bulk of Sliabh Mis looming in the distance. The top of the mountain was lost to view, but the lower slopes glowed in the westering sun with a warmly welcoming light. If I hurried, I could still make it to the ráth before dark.

Yes, this is where I belong.

Never before had I experienced a feeling like it. A true homecoming! For the first time in my life, I knew that delicious, all-consuming, dizzying jubilation the wanderer feels when arriving at the ardently sought destination. The blood quickened in my veins, and I gulped air to calm myself—but to no avail. I had been too long asea, too long banking my anticipation for this moment.

I called a hasty command to the ship's crew and started off at once, reaching the huts of the fishermen, now empty, and moving quickly on toward the gap in the headland leading to the Vale of Braghad and Miliucc's fortress beyond. I walked for a good while, shaking seawater from my clothes and hailing each familiar hill and stone and tree as a fondly remembered friend. The sight of the ráth, when it came, stopped me in my tracks. Never had that simple wooden fortress seemed so pleasant and welcoming as it did just then: peaceful in the deepening dusk, the wispy smoke of the king's hearth fire threading into the air as twilight claimed the wide valley.

The first stars were beginning to glow in the pale heavens. I hurried on once more but had walked only a few paces when I heard a sound in the distance and glanced up to see a movement on the path leading out from the fortress: The ship had been seen, and Miliucc had sent riders to meet us.

Moving on quickly, I soon came within hailing distance of the riders. "Greetings, Forgall!" I cried as the warriors reined to a halt on the trail before me.

From their reaction I could tell they did not recognize me, and indeed, of the five, Forgall was the only one I knew; he regarded me closely, his frown gradually turning to an expression of amazement as recognition broke upon him. "You!" He did not remember my name.

"It is myself, Succat," I told him. "I have returned."

He stared at me in wonder. "So you have," he said, shaking his head slowly. "Why?"

"I have returned to redeem myself."

"This I do not understand," he said. One of the others with him pointed to the sailors toiling up the path some distance behind me. Forgall observed the crewmen for a moment, then said, "Ah, you have come to trade!"

"I have that," I told him.

He smoothed his mustache with the flat of his hand. "Lord Miliucc vowed your death if he ever caught you again," he warned.

"I know, but let us go and see if I can persuade him to a better course."

Forgall shrugged, consigning me to my fate. Turning in the saddle, he motioned to three of the warriors to dismount, and I was given one of the horses. "Wait here for the others," he said, indicating the sailors, "and bring them to the ráth." To me he said, "You always were a bold one." He smiled with sudden warmth. "Did I not often say this?"

"You did that, Forgall." I climbed into the saddle. "Well, let us see if Miliucc is in a mood to welcome me."

We rode in silence through the valley, watching as the sun disappeared behind the hills, flaming the swiftly scattering clouds and briefly illuminating the solitary track that ran through the vale to the foot of the hill upon which perched Miliucc's fortress.

As we turned onto the path leading up to the ráth, I paused to gaze up at the straight timber walls, dark against the deepening blue of the sky, and a quiver of dread snaked through me. I had contemplated this moment countless times, but the uncertainty of my reception had always failed to reveal itself—until now. Would Miliucc even listen to me? There was no reason he should. He was a proud lord, and I had defied him. The penalty for this I knew only too well.

Little had changed in the ráth. Outwardly, at least, everything appeared just as it had the day I left—even if a little more worn and ragged. Behind the timber walls the huts still clustered close around the bare expanse of yard before Miliucc's hall. Dirty-legged children still ran after barking dogs, and the twilight air still smelled of pine smoke.

And then we were up the path and through the gates, riding into the ráth. Upon our arrival before the king's hall, we were met by the greater portion of the settlement; the tuath formed a respectfully curious ring around us— keeping their distance, I decided, until they could see how Lord Miliucc would receive me. Though I saw many familiar faces in the crowd, I did not see the one I longed—and feared—most.

Forgall gave shout to summon those within, and we waited. In a moment the door to the hall opened, and out stepped a big man in a dark robe. "Suc-cat!" he cried. "Succat, is it you?"

"Cormac!" I shouted, flinging myself from the saddle. "It is myself! Succat!"

The big druid crossed the distance between us in a bound, swept me up, and crushed me hard. "Cormac . . . ," I said, gasping for breath. "I did not know if you would be here."

"It *is* you, Succat. You have returned at last."

"I have that," I replied.

He wrapped his arm around my shoulders and held me tight. "On my life," he declared, "it is good to see you, brother. You left a stripling youth, and you have returned a man full grown. It looks good on you."

"And you, Cormac, have not changed at all."

"A little fatter perhaps." He smiled. "And a little wiser, I hope. But now the king is waiting, I will tell him you are here — if," he added, growing sud-denly serious, "you are ready. Are you?"

I nodded my assent, and he hurried inside. I stood waiting, surrounded by the silent, watching tuath and felt the dread I had so long held at arm's length fall upon me in a rush. Even so, as the door opened once more and Lord Miliucc appeared, tall and stern, followed by his principal warriors and advisors, I squared my shoulders, straightened my back, and prepared to accept his justice.

"So!" said the king, folding his arms over his chest. He glanced at me, then called to his serving boys. "Bring torches. I want to see him better."

The torches were fetched, and while they were placed in their sconces, the king stared at me across the distance between us. I could not tell what he was thinking, and I knew better than to speak before I was addressed. He appeared exactly as I remembered him. His long dark hair was gathered and tied in a single braid and bound in a ring of bronze at the side of his head. A gold torc gleamed at his throat. Queen Grania, solemn and silent, assumed her place beside him, her gaze quick with interest and I took heart that she at least did not scowl when she regarded me.

"How is this?" he asked.

"Lord Miliucc," called Cormac, "see here! A wandering sheep has re-turned to the fold. This is a cause for rejoicing."

"A runaway *slave*," corrected the king firmly.

"I am that, my lord," I replied, trying to calm my rapidly beating heart.

"How is this?" he asked again, and I heard in his voice a cautious note. In that moment I realized that he was genuinely mystified and more than a little fearful. Never once had I imagined that my reappearance could have frightened anyone, let alone a king with fearsome warriors at his back. Yet for all that he seemed less surprised than alarmed.

"Lord Miliucc, I know well the punishment for a slave who escapes. Even so, I do return to face your judgment."

A genuine expression of awe came into the king's face. He looked to Cormac, who stood off to one side, his eyes lowered, frowning at the ground.

"You know it is death to return here," said Miliucc slowly, "yet you deliver yourself into my hands." I could see even as he spoke that his displeasure was at odds with his fear and amazement. "Why is that?"

"I return in the hope that I may be forgiven, O King," I answered. "Nor do I come empty-handed." Reaching for the leather bag at my belt, I drew it out and held it before me. "I ask you to accept this gold in payment for the slave you lost and, in accepting, grant your slave his freedom."

The king regarded the leather bag, and his eyes swung back to mine, but he made no move to accept the offered payment. Did he imagine some trick or treachery?

Untying the bag, I shook out a handful of gold solidi and offered these to the king. "This," I said, holding out the small heap of coins, "is for the purchase of my freedom."

He eyed the gold but still made no move to take it.

Holding the coins before him, I poured the rest of the bag—more than fifty coins in all—into my hand until they spilled onto the ground. "And this," I declared aloud, "is the honor price."

The gathered crowd murmured approval behind me.

"My Lord Miliucc, I ask that you accept this in payment for the debt I owe you."

The king raised his eyes from the gleaming coins at his feet; I suspected he was on the point of refusing my offer when Cormac clapped his hands and declared, "Here is a wonder! Has anyone ever heard of such a thing? An escaped slave returning to buy his freedom! Tell me, Lord Miliucc, in all of Éire has such a thing ever been known?"

Miliucc frowned. "The lords of Éire will laugh at me when they learn I am mocked by a slave," he complained. "They will hold me a king of low account, whose slaves command their master."

"The lords of Éire will grind their teeth in envy," I countered, "that *they* do not own slaves willing to buy their freedom with good gold."

Still the king hesitated. "I could kill you now and take the gold anyway," he said.

This brought a swift response from the queen. "Stay your hand, my lord," she whispered. "Is not your honor worth more than the price of a slave?"

"Heed your queen," Cormac advised. "There is glory to be won here, but you must act wisely. If you accept his money and free him, it will show you a man of honor and fairness second to none. Your name will be lauded throughout this island as one who earned such great respect that even run-away slaves cannot rest until they have redeemed themselves."

For the first time Miliucc allowed himself to bend a little. I could see he liked the sound of Cormac's suggestion; it gave him a reason to be gener-ous and allowed him to keep his dignity. He turned to Forgall, his battle chief. "Do you think I should accept this gold?"

"At once, my King," replied the warrior, "and without hesitation."

Looking at the glittering coins in my hand and on the ground, Miliucc said, "How much gold is there?"

"An amount double the price you paid for me," I answered, "and as much again."

"Why?" Lord Miliucc could not believe what he heard. "Is it to shame me with your wealth?"

"By no means," I said quickly. "The first amount is to redeem myself from slavery, and the second is to repay you for the loss of my services while I have been away."

"Hear, now!" cried Cormac. "Lord King, this is a just and honorable offer. Show yourself its equal and accept it in the spirit in which it has been made."

The warriors, led by Forgall, acclaimed this plan, and Miliucc, unwilling to show himself mean and grudging in the eyes of his people, raised his hand and said aloud, "Because this man, who was my slave, has honored me by acting justly, I forsake the death I vowed for him." To me he said, "I accept this gold in payment for your services."

"And free him, my lord," added Cormac.

Miliucc hesitated—still distrusting his good fortune, I think—then al-lowed himself a final grimace before acceding. "And I give this slave his freedom."

Cormac stepped forward and, raising his hands in declamation, cried, "May all bear witness! This day Succat has redeemed himself from slav-ery. Henceforth he is a free man. Let no one seek to hinder or constrain him."

He turned and embraced me, and the people, who had waited to see how the thing would go, suddenly surged forward, and with much jostling and good-natured buffeting, I was welcomed back into the tuath. I thanked the king and was escorted into his hall, where I was received with all courtesy. The king brought me to sit at his table with his warriors and poured me a cup of beer with his own hand. "Sit and be welcome," he said, then fell silent, uncertain what to say.

Cormac made up for the awkwardness. He settled beside me on the bench. "I knew you would come," he said, clapping me on the back again. "Although I didn't know it would be today."

"I went to find you," I said. "Oh, Cormac, I wish I *had* found you." I gazed at him, the memories of the last years instantly arising and washing over me in a flood. A lump formed in my throat. It took a moment to pass; when I could speak again, I said, "I meant to come back. I truly did. But when I failed to find you, everything changed." I told him of my experience wandering injured, freezing, and dying, and my rescue by the Saecsen farmers. "After that, something hardened in me. I lost my way."

"And have you found it again?" he asked, watching me for my answer.

"I believe I have," I replied.

Cormac put his arm on my shoulder. "Welcome home, brother. I have missed you."

"And I you," I replied. I looked quickly around the room. Cormac saw my glance and read it. "You have not asked me about Sionan."

I nodded. My mouth went dry. "Is she well?"

"She is that."

He waited for me to say more, but I could not. My heart was in my throat, and my tongue would not move.

"She is not here," he said. My expression must have given away my sudden and acute disappointment, for he quickly added, "She no longer serves in the queen's house."

"No?"

"Not for three years."

"I see."

"I know she would like to see you," Cormac said. "You should go to her."

"Oh, I will," I replied. "I want to."

The ship's master and crew arrived just then, entering the hall in a timorous clump. They glanced around the hall, visibly unsettled by the strangeness of their surroundings as much as by the size of the warriors. I rose and went to reassure them. "All is well," I told the master. "We are welcome here. Come, I will present you to Lord Miliucc. He will want to hear what you have brought to trade."

"I will take care of them," said Cormac, intervening. Turning me, he gently pushed me toward the door. "Go and see her," he said.

"And you will see to the sailors?" I said, edging hesitantly toward the door.

"Go, Succat. She will know you are here by now."

The next thing I knew, I was running through the narrow lane to the house where I had last seen Sionan. I forced myself to slow down and walk the last few paces. When I had calmed myself, I stood before the door and knocked.

In a moment there came the soft tread of a step, the door opened, and there stood Sionan: slender and erect, her head high, a strange and uncertain light in her eyes.

I took half a step toward her and found that my voice had abandoned me. All the things I had imagined saying—all I meant to tell her at this long-anticipated moment—flew from my mind. "Sionan . . . ," I began, forcing lips and tongue to move at last.

She stiffened at the utterance of her name and closed the door in my face.

I stood for a time, feeling foolish for having presumed she would receive me after all. "I have come to speak to you," I called through the rough wood.

There came no reply.

"Sionan?"

Again there was no reply.

"Sionan, if we cannot talk now, I will come back later. Maybe that would be better. Is that what you want?"

At this the door opened slowly once more. She stood there as if frozen, gazing at me without expression.

"Sionan, I have come back," I told her. "I've come back to stay. I know I have no right to ask this of you, but I would like to explain." She made no move or sign that she had heard me at all.

"Will you not hear me at least?" I blundered on. "I've come a very long way."

I looked at her face in the gloomy half-light of the doorway. She had changed but little that I could see; her hair was slightly shorter, and her form, still slender, had gained a pleasant fullness, but that was all.

"Please?"

Still she stared, mute and unmoving. Then, with a slow shake of her head, she said, "Why?" Her voice was soft and low, and the sound of it sent a pang of remorse through my heart. How could I have deceived this woman? How could I have abandoned her and caused her such pain?

Now, seeing her face-to-face, all the reasons, all the explanations and excuses, turned to dust in my mouth. I sank to my knees on the threshold and bowed my head before her. "Lady, I do not blame you for being angry," I said, pouring out my heart, "and if you should send me away, I will go. Even so, I want you to know that I am sorry for deserting you, and I do most heartily and contritely beg your forgiveness."

"What are you doing?" she said. "Get up."

"I cannot," I said, "until I know what is in your mind."

Again a great and awful silence stretched between us. When she did not speak, I glanced up to see tears glistening in her eyes.

"Please," I said, "for the sake of the memory of our former life—if for nothing else—I beg you to forgive me."

She stood unmoving over me, and then, reaching down, she placed her hand on my head. "But I have forgiven you a thousand times already, if you only knew it."

"Thank you," I whispered. My throat closed over the words, and I was unable to say more.

Taking her hands in mine, I kissed them. She grasped my hands and raised me to my feet. Hardly daring to meet her gaze, I rose and stood before her. "Will you come in?" she said, stepping back into the hut.

Without waiting for an answer, Sionan took my hands and drew me inside. We stood in the dim light of the single room. Newly kindled flames smoldered on the hearth, sending thin tendrils of smoke coiling into the air and lending the room a pungent smell. The pallet bed lay on the bare earth floor in one corner, and the small table and two low chairs sat in the other. In all, it was as far away from the splendor of Domus Columella in Rome as the earth is from the moon, yet my heart soared: It was exactly as it had been the day I left.

"Welcome home," said Sionan. "I knew this day would come, and yet now that it is here, I am not ready." Her voice trembled as she spoke, and the tears she had held back until now began to fall. "I have missed you so much."

Overwhelmed by the grace of Sionan's loving forgiveness, I lowered my head and wept. "I am sorry, Sionan," I said, "I am so very, very sorry."

"Oh, *mo croi*," she whispered, gathering me in her arms, "my heart, my heart. Nothing matters, save that you are here and we are all together now and always."

It took a moment for her meaning to come clear. "Together—" I said. "All?"

Her eyes played over my face, her expression at once proud and a little uncertain. "Succat," she said, "would you like to meet your son?"

58

STOOD FOR A long time just gazing upon the small, dark-haired boy as he played with sticks from the woodpile stacked behind the hut. Engrossed in his game—pulling twigs from the pile to form a neat little heap of his own—he remained oblivious to our presence. Then Sionan took my hand and drew me toward him, saying, "Here, now, it is time he met his father."

We moved closer. "Ultán," she called gently, "your father has come to see you."

At the sound of his mother's voice, the boy looked up and, oh!—the light of love that shone in that child's face shamed the sun with its brilliance. "Mam!" he shouted.

Scrambling to his feet, he ran to her arms. She swooped him up and held him close. He clung to her, his head pressed against her cheek, regarding me with shy, almost apprehensive interest. Slender and long-limbed like his mother, he also had her large brown eyes. Then he turned his gaze to me, and I realized that the face observing me with such serious curiosity was my own.

I reached a hand to him. "Ultán, I am glad to meet you."

The sound of my voice inspired him to bury his face in the hollow of his mother's neck. "It is your father," she told him. "He has greeted you nicely. What do you say?"

After a little coaxing the youngster was finally persuaded to part with a murmured greeting. Then, in a gesture that warmed me to the soul, he reached out a hand. "Papa!" he said, squirming toward me.

I took him into my arms and clasped him to my breast, exulting in the bundled warmth of his small body as he put his arms around my neck and snuggled close. I carried him back into the house, where, after a simple meal, little Ultán was put to bed, and then Sionan and I sat down by the fire, and I began to tell her all that had happened since the day I left.

Dawn found us that way, drowsy before the glowing coals of a spent fire, having talked through the night. Pale pink light stole through the chinks in the door as I told of the plague and all those close to me who had been swept away. I described Oriana's death and my debilitating despair. I told of meeting Pelagius and, shortly thereafter, receiving the vision that set my feet on the homeward path.

"But tell me," I said, "were you never angry with me?"

"Angry?" she replied. "I was furious! When the months passed and you didn't return, I raged at you. I cursed you and swore bloody vengeance. When Cormac returned to say he had no word of you, I began to fear the worst. I thought you shipwrecked and drowned or made captive again and carried off somewhere else, and I hated you all the more for leaving and taking such a risk. But by then the baby had begun to grow in me, and Cormac said I must forgive you—that whatever had happened, it would not be helped by hating the father of my child."

She paused, glancing down at her hands. "That was a hard, hard time, to be sure. But it passed. And when the child was born, I did not hate you anymore. Who could look upon Ultán and harbor hatred in her heart for the man who gave him to her? Maybe some can, but I could not." She raised her head and smiled at me sadly. "Oh, but I so often wished you could have been here to see him grow. Oh, how I wished it.

"And often is the time I thought about what I would say if you ever came home. I would be noble and kind. I practiced in my mind until I had it all just right. But tonight, when I saw you standing there, all my fine words deserted me. The old rage came back instead, and I thought to punish you." She shook her head slowly. "Oh, my heart, I could not. Seeing you on your knees in the mud, your eyes so full of hope and love . . . I knew it was you I wanted, not the spite." She smiled pensively. "I chose you. I have always chosen you."

Sionan sat in silence for a moment. "I am sorry about the woman's suffering," she said at last. "But, God help me, I cannot feel sorry that she died, since it was her death that released you to come back to me."

"Oh, Sionan." I sighed. Clearly there were mysteries here too deep for me to comprehend. "I do wonder—might there have been another way? Then Oriana would not have had to die for me to return."

"Perhaps," Sionan suggested, "it took something as strong as death to save you."

EPILOGUE

HUS BEGAN THE long pilgrimage to this time, this place, and the bonfire that flares high and bright on this Beltaine night. Curious how fire has always marked the more significant events of my life. As I look back over the years, I see that the path has been illumined by the shimmering glow of fire.

Like the apostles of old, I have been kissed by the flame, and my soul burns within me. I am alight with God's holy power; his ineluctable strength flows from my hands. I live and move at his command. My master is the Lord of Light, and I am his slave.

Tonight we have ignited a beacon that will awaken a land too long aslumber. Tonight we defied a king and kindled a blaze in Ireland that will never be quenched.

"Why antagonize him?" said Cormac when I told him what I had in mind. "Let him have his fire; it means nothing to us. We will go to him tomorrow and hold council with him. If we tell him our grievances, he will listen. He is not unreasonable."

"Loegair must be made to understand that a new power is at work in the land—a power he cannot stifle with his puny decrees and self-important displays of arrogance." I saw the way clearly before me and was surprised Cormac did not see it, too. My teacher and *anam cara*, my soul's true friend—it was Cormac who smoothed my return to the druid house and Cormac who stood by me when the storm broke over my joining the Ceile De priesthood—he most often grasped the nature of things far more quickly than I ever did.

"Hear me, Cormac," I declared, "we have worked long and hard with the people of this region and have accomplished much—no thanks to Loegair and his piddling interference."

"In truth," agreed Cormac. "Which is why it makes no sense to risk throwing it all away."

"He is doing this only to intimidate us, brother," I insisted. "It is time our king learned the limits of what human strength can achieve. He thinks himself a king of kings? Well, I propose to give him a taste of true sovereignty."

A deep frown creased Cormac's broad face. "It is dangerous. Buinne will be there. He is sure to make trouble, and someone could get hurt."

"Do you think I will fail?" I regarded him closely. "For if that is what you think, tell me now. Do you think I will fail?"

He hesitated, then puffed out his cheeks and shook his head. "No, I do not see that."

"Then be of good cheer," I told him.

"Do you want me to go with you?"

"Let the brothers attend me," I suggested. "You stay here with the others and uphold us in prayer."

So now I stand waiting for the confrontation to begin. The king arrives as I knew he would, with his chariots and warriors, bristling with weapons and stewing for a fight. It took him long enough. Well, he will have his fight, but the streams of regret flowing from this contest will not be mine.

King Loegair lurks there, hovering just beyond the circle of light thrown out by my bonfire. The king's druids know better than to allow him to come within the radiance of my presence. They think to make me come to them and thus demonstrate their king's superiority over me and mine. I will go. It makes no difference—homage is a hollow gesture unless both heart and will are broken, and poor Loegair will take some breaking before he bends his stiff neck.

Listen! They summon me. I rise and take up my staff.

"Do not go out there," cautions Forgall. Firstborn of my little flock, the former battlechief steps into my path to prevent me. "They mean to attack and kill you."

"Fear for nothing, brother," I tell him, placing my hand on his shoulder to move him aside. "Remember your Psalms: Some take pride in chariots, and some in horses, but we shall walk in the Light of the Living One."

"We will go with you," says Brón, stalwart friend.

"No, it will be better if I go alone."

"Then we will pray for you."

"Pray rather for Loegair and his warband," I tell him, turning to meet my visitors. "A proud and haughty king is about to be humbled. Let the world beware!"

So saying, I step to the edge of the light, where the king and his retinue can see me. Thus we meet, face-to-face across the battle line: Loegair with his warhost, his company of druids, his splendid weapons, his many gated fortresses—and I with my small, trusted band of believers. I feel sorry for Loegair, I do. The sides are so uneven.

"Greetings, Lord Loegair," I call. "May the peace of Esu be yours tonight."

The haughty king draws himself up. In his chariot he looks nine feet tall. "Did you think to defy me and escape my judgment?"

"The only judgment I fear is not yours to perform, O King."

"You revere another king over me?" he roars. "I am king here, and my kingdom extends as far as a man can walk in seven days."

"The king I serve holds all powers and dominions in his grasp, and his kingdom extends forever."

Loegair's features twist in a snarl of rage. "See now!" he cries to his wise advisors. "Out of his own mouth he has confessed his crime. My decree stands! Death to him who defies the sovereign lord on this night."

The high king takes up his spear and levels it at me. He shouts a command to his waiting warriors. "Seize him!" They dismount from their horses and move to lay hold of me.

"Peace, Loegair," I counsel, raising my staff. "You tread on holy ground. Show some respect, or the consequences will be on your head."

The warriors hesitate. They waver between their king's command and my own.

"Take him!" shouts the king.

They come at me in a rush. Lofting the staff, I turn my eyes to the night sky. "High King of Heaven, we enthrone you this night. Shield your servants from the harm of evil, and reveal, O Power of my power, the glory of your everlasting kingdom!"

As my prayer resounds in the hall of heaven, a cloud of dark mist falls between me and the attackers. Taken unawares, they cry out in confusion. Their weapons clash to no purpose. I hear them shouting; the horses rear and bolt; the chariots crash into one another, and men are thrown to the ground. An instant is all it takes for the fearsome attack to dissolve into chaos.

I know I should stop it before it comes to blows, but it cheers my soul to hear the king whining like a strap-beaten whelp. Well, I warned him. He should have listened.

As the chaos thickens around me, I turn to regard the brothers praying behind me. They are anxious. They stand in a hesitant huddle, wishing they were somewhere else. Away in the east the light of a new day is playing on the far horizon. Perhaps it is time to end this confusion before Cormac's prediction of harm comes to pass.

"We have done what we came to do, brothers," I tell them. "We will go home now. Follow me. I will lead you down. Look neither left nor right and do not linger. No harm shall befall us."

Raising my staff, I move a little closer to the veil of darkness separating the king and his warband from the blazing light of the fire. I draw the figure in the air and speak the words of the *caim*, the protecting charm surrounding us. Slowly the darkness thins, and the light of the bonfire blazes in the eyes of our attackers once more.

"There!" shouts the king. "I see them! There they are!"

Turning to the brothers, I say, "Ready? We go." With the fire at our backs, I lead my faithful band down the hill the way we came, as behind us the king strives to gather the shreds of his dignity, which has been torn and trampled in the chaos."

"Keep walking," I call to the others behind me. "Do not stop or look around."

"After them!" cries Loegair, growing desperate. "Ride them down!"

A horse neighs, and the dogs begin barking and whimpering. At once the pursuit falters. The warriors, still confounded by the darkness, pull up short.

"Hie! After them!" cries Loegair.

"Where?" comes the answer. "We cannot see them!"

"There! There!" screams the king. He is frantic now, shouting like a man bereft of reason. He cannot understand why his warriors will not see what is before their eyes.

We pass from view behind the broad shoulder of the hill, and I hear the king berating the stupidity of his men. He rages at their incompetence and breaks dire oaths upon their unthinking heads. "Lord, we do see them," his battlechief protests, "but it is only a herd of deer."

"A stag, six deer, and a fawn," adds Dubthach helpfully. He is the king's bard, but I think his days in the king's service are drawing to an end. He will join the Ceile De yet.

"Deer!" shouts the king. He rages at his battlehost; he calls them fools and idiots. He implores his wise counselors to do something, anything, to prevent us from getting away. But it is already too late. We fade from sight in the early-morning mist, leaving only the impression of deer in the minds of our would-be pursuers.

We move down into the deep-shadowed valley. Our hearts sing with the triumph we have won. I lead the brothers in a song that is at once a lorica of protection and a psalm of praise to the All-Encompassing.

With my face to the rising sun, I sing, "I arise today through a mighty strength! Christ my shield and my defender!"

The brothers take up the well-known verses. Timidly, yes, but it is good to hear them all the same. They are learning. "Sing, everyone!" I cry, and they sing:

I arise today
In Heaven's great might,
In Sun's fair brightness,
In Moon's splendid radiance,
In fire's dancing glory,
In Lightning's excellent swiftness,
In wind's matchless dominion,
In Sea's majestic depth,
In Earth's steadfast stability,
In Sky's dazzling splendor. . . .

They sing, and my mind flies ahead to the battle to come. One day soon I will stalk Loegair in his chamber. He will rage, and he will roar. He will call upon his druids to test me and try me, as he must. I welcome the test. Buinne will do all he can to destroy me, but he will fail, and in the end he will fall. That is as it should be. Buinne has evaded justice for his crimes long enough, and the king must see him bested and bettered—and not only the king: The people, too, must behold the power of a bard of the Ceile De. Only then will they truly believe.

Later, when Loegair has regained his temper, I will go to him, and we will sit down together and speak to one another like grown men. I will ask him for that piece of land I need for the church we will build. And he will give it.

In his eagerness to align himself with the new authority in the land, he will give me whatever I ask. He will seek to possess the power, and, failing that, he will try to possess the one who wields it. But I will not be swayed. In time Loegair will learn, as all must, where true power and wisdom can be found. And then he will be called upon to make a choice.

I will pray he chooses the way of truth and love.

Truth and love—the twin pillars of our faith. But for me they will forever be embodied in the flesh and bone, heart and soul, of my dear wife. It is to Sionan that I owe my salvation; it is Sionan who befriended me, and loved me, and has remained these many years steadfast and faithful beside me.

Sionan spoke the truth in love. It took a power stronger than death to save me. It is Sionan now I think about as I lead my little band home. Night still lingers in the west; in the east darkness flies before the light of a new and glorious day—a day to be cherished and forever remembered as the day Ireland received her True King.